Red Right Returning

A Novel

Charles B. McLane

TILBURY HOUSE · ISLAND INSTITUTE
Gardiner, Maine   Rockland, Maine

Tilbury House
2 Mechanic Street
Gardiner, Maine 04345
800-582-1899
www.tilburyhouse.com

Island Institute
386 Main Street
Rockland, Maine 04841
207-594-9209
www.islandinstitute.org

First printing: June 2004

10 9 8 7 6 5 4 3 2 1

Published 2004 by the Island Institute
Distributed by Tilbury House
Editing and proofreading by Ravin Gustafson,
    Melissa L. Hayes, and David D. Platt
Design and production by Charles G. Oldham
Cover photograph by Christopher Ayres
Back cover photograph courtesy of the author
Printed in Canada by Friesens / Four Colour Imports, Ltd.

For Carol

Great Ram Island

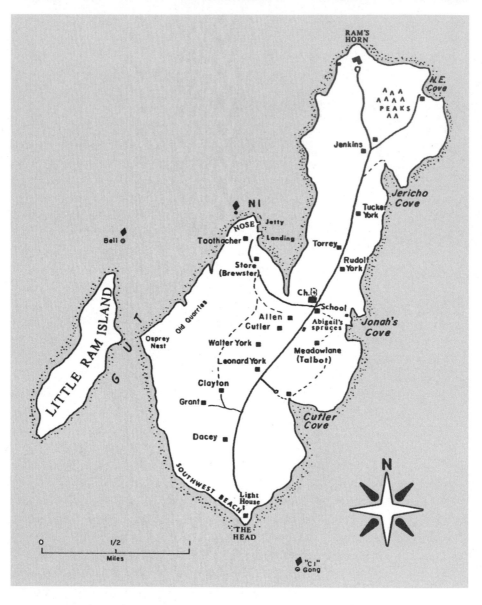

*"Seaward bound vessels should keep
red markers to port, black to starboard.
Inbound vessels do the reverse."*

—*Ancient maritime manual*

Or, in the seaman's vernacular:

"Red Right Returning"

Ram Islanders • 1945

(Age in parentheses as of September 1945)

Talbot
  Frank (1875–1943)
  m. Lucy Dacey (64)
    - Stanley (1919–1939)
    - Belle (17)

Dacey
  Jethroe (1890–1948)
  m. Belle (1850–1926)
  Arthur (67) m. (1) _____
  (2) Winifred Holbrook (60)
    - Jennifer ("Jingle") (24)

Brewster
  Caleb (54)
  m. Jenny _____ (52)
    - Elmer (26)
    - Sharon (23)
    m. "Turk" Jenkins (*see below*)

Jenkins
  Charles (1885–1935)
  m. Claudia _____ (67)
    - Turk (25)
    m. Sharon Brewster (23)
    - Chucky (5)
    - Barbara (2)

Grant
  Clarissa (80)
    - Clyde (54) m. Clara (49)
    - Mary Lou (22)
    - Willy (20)
    - Joel (15)
    - Susan (12)
    - Ames (50, removed)
    - John (44)
    - Ginny (47)
    m. Zip Clayton (*see below*)

Clayton
  Zip (45) m. Ginny Grant (47)
    - Cotton (22)
    - Sam (21)
    - Mickey (15)
    - Bets (12)

Cutler
  Lloyd (49) m. Jesse (47)
    - Bobby (19)
    - Lucille (16)
    - Mark (14)
    - Tony (12)

Allen
  Cecil (50) m. Constance Cutler (46)
    - Jack (26)
    - Betsy (21)
    - Janie (14)
    - Cindy (11)

York
  Lydia (87, widowed)
    - Rudolf (65, widowed)
    - Leonard (40) m. Jessica (37)
    - Johnny (14)
    - Bubber (12)
    - Daphne (8)
    - Walton (36) m. Marian (35)
    - Penny (10)
    - Rudy (7)
    - Tucker (60) m. Joanne (57)
    - Bill (27)
    - Rodney (1923–1944)
    - Mimi (20)
    - Silas (17)
    - Jeff (15)

Torrey
  Alfred (44) m. Janice (45)
    - Peter (16)
    - Pat (15)
    - Paul (13)
    - Matthew (12)
    - Judy (9)

Miscellaneous
  Gertrude Bakeman
  (67, schoolteacher)
  Horatio Leadbetter (67)
  Widow Barnaby (85)
  Harold Toothacher (65)

Book 1 *Jingle*

1

The *Laura Lee* resumed service between Rockland and the mid-Penobscot islands on the second Saturday in September 1945, a month after the end of the war. The old mailboat was freshly painted and her trim varnished, after wartime duty farther down the coast, but she was the same creaking sixty-five-foot steamer that had ferried the islanders back and forth from the mainland since 1922. Horace Snow was still in command.

I went aboard a half hour before departure time at eight o'clock. It was a clear, still morning. Fog patches obscured parts of low-lying islands to the east so that it was impossible to tell where one left off and another began. Beyond these islands the long domed profile of higher land pushed into the September sky, sky the color of a robin's egg. In the foreground, past the mouth of the harbor, a dozen or so lobster boats circled slowly, followed by clusters of herring gulls.

A prewar Studebaker—what car was not prewar in those days?—came onto the wharf and parked facing the mailboat fifty yards away. Sun striking the windshield obscured the face of the driver, but his companion was visible: a brunette who looked to be in her mid-twenties. Both were in naval uniform. They appeared to converse idly for several minutes before she leaned toward him abruptly to peck him on the cheek, then got out of the car and came aboard. The Studebaker drove off. The girl—she was a WAVE petty officer— glanced briefly at me and exchanged greetings with Horace Snow, leaning out of an open window in the wheelhouse above the deck. A nonregulation musette bag hung loosely on one shoulder and her regulation hat sat high on her wavy hair; a gust of wind would have scaled it off. A button of her jacket was undone. She wore no makeup. I was aware of her studying me for several minutes before she moved toward the after-rail, where I was standing with my luggage. She saluted casually.

"Morning, Commander." She flicked away a dried gull dropping and balanced her musette bag on the rail. "You'll be going to Thorn or Blueberry," she said in a clipped provincial accent. It was a statement, not a question.

I told her I was going to Great Ram Island and she studied me again.

"This'll be your first visit," she pronounced. "We're not used to seeing such rank."

I shrugged and mumbled something about my rank disappearing as soon as I had something else to wear. She asked what brought me to Ram Island and I said a legacy: a friend had left me his bungalow there.

"Robert Bartlett," she pronounced after reflecting a moment. "He died in the Pacific early in the war."

On Guadalcanal, I told her, but I stopped there. Robert Bartlett had been my closest friend during the first year of the war, perhaps ever. We had been lieutenants, j.g., together on the same aircraft carrier after Pearl Harbor, and I was with him when he died after a Japanese shell exploded on his battle station. Some whim caused him in his last hours to execute a will—his only living relation was a sister settled in California—leaving me his bungalow on a Maine island; I didn't even know where the island was until I located it on a map a year or more later.

I was conscious of having been rather cursory with my self-assured companion at the stern rail in order to discourage more probing questions than I cared to answer, but I did feel, if she was a neighbor, I'd better be civil. I asked her—in light of her prompt identification of my legator—whether all legacies were known to everyone on Ram Island. They could be, she said, if anyone took the trouble to figure them out. In my case, there were only five "bungalows," as I would call them, on the island; four had proper heirs. "Not that you're improper," she added, and this time she smiled. A quick compulsive smile, brown eyes dancing. I felt better about her.

Was *bungalow* the wrong word to use? I asked. She said *cottage* was what they were usually called—that is, by the summer people. Even though one cottage had about twenty rooms. The islanders, she said, generally spoke of them by the name of the place where they were built. "Like yours is just Cutler's Cove. . . . But Cutler's Cove really is a bungalow."

A yellow school bus pulled up at the end of the wharf and a dozen teenagers crowded noisily out. The Camden High contingent, my companion explained, returning home after the first week of school. When they were aboard, several of them came forward eagerly to greet her.

"Hey, Jingle! Another stripe! Are you an ensign yet?"

"Another war," said Jingle.

"Are you back for good? You oughta be, all you've done."

"Three more months. Day after tomorrow."

"You got it figured."

"Say, Jingle, did you see the Sox play last week . . . when they shut out the Yankees, the lousy rats?" This from a shaggy lad of sixteen or so who must have weighed close to two hundred pounds.

"Joey," Jingle said, "I didn't have to go. I could hear the shouting all over Boston."

More teenagers were now boarding—the Rockland High echelon, I was told—and added their bit to the general uproar. "The GIs are still to come," Jingle said between greetings to the newcomers.

At ten to eight a train whistle sounded at the far edge of town, and five minutes later there were approaching shouts from the direction of the station.

"Brace yourself!" said Jingle.

Half a dozen servicemen charged presently around the corner of a McLoon company shed, duffel bags on their shoulders, and jostled each other aboard.

"Hey, what d'ye know, she floats!"

"She shoulda been sunk by U-boats . . . where's that diesel we was supposed to git?"

"That's the Vinalhaven run, pinhead."

"Quicker t'go there an' swim!"

Horace Snow, in reply, blew two short blasts on the horn.

"How 'bout that, it works!"

A sandy-haired army sergeant, spotting us in our blue uniforms at the stern rail, said with good humor, "Watch it, guys! The navy's takin' over here. Now we're sunk for sure."

A lanky Marine private halfway up the gangplank shouted in jest over the heads of those in front of him, "Hey, don't you dumb GIs know your manners? Permission to come aboard, *sir?*" In jest I gave it. On deck, the Marine went straight to a group of high school girls and demanded a kiss from each of them in honor of his safe return.

"Knock it off, Willy," a seaman taunted him. "You ain't been away yet six months."

"But look what I done," Willy said. "The bastards quit, di'n't they?"

The army sergeant, who was older than the other servicemen, said sourly, "Battle of Parris Island."

Willy paused in his pursuit of a skittish redhead and drew himself up in mock dignity before the sergeant. "Why, if you wasn't a sergeant and if I didn't have a natur'l respect for author'ty, I'd show you right now who's better, GIs or

Marines. Anyways, the captain give me permission, didn't ya, sir?"

"Commander, Willy, commander," Jingle said.

"Well, I promoted him, didn't I? . . . Besides, who ever heard of disobeying a commander's VOCO? That's the army for you! You guys prob'ly ain't even got VOCOs in the goddam army." And he went on exacting tribute where he could, assisted by his brother Joey.

"Now the war's really over," Jingle said, and she went off to greet several of the new arrivals.

The last to board was an air force lieutenant with two rows of ribbons, including the Distinguished Flying Cross and a Purple Heart, on his flying jacket; he walked with a cane. He moved slowly through the passengers on the afterdeck, greeting several of them by name and exchanging a word or two—but I could see he wasn't one of them. He was tall, though his height was minimized by a stoop that seemed unrelated to his injury. His right ear stood out from under his soft air force cap and this gave his face a comic lopsided appearance. At the same time it was a face with gentility written unmistakably across it: long thin nose, high cheekbones, and deep-set brooding eyes. He moved on through the enclosed cabin amidships to the forward deck, and I didn't see him again until we docked.

A few minutes after eight a deckhand on the wharf freed the hawsers and Horace Snow headed the *Laura Lee* out of the harbor and into the bay.

"Gabriel's Hole," an elderly gentleman said as we stood near each other at the port rail an hour or so later. We were passing a heavily wooded island, and I had been studying a narrow opening that cut into the rocky shore and led into a tidal basin beyond. "They've hidden contraband there for over a century, most recently during Prohibition."

We watched the water surging over a sunken ledge in the center of the channel, awash at half-tide. I said I shouldn't like to run in there during fog or in a heavy sea.

"Nor did the rumrunners," the gentleman said. "But they did it nonetheless." He explained that this was Thorn Island, nearest neighbor to Ram. The harbor and buildings were on the western shore, away from us. The *Laura Lee* stopped there on the return run from Blueberry Isle, a small island farther up the bay where he lived—or summered, for there were no year-round residents on Blueberry.

We left Thorn Island behind us and moved into an open stretch of water toward a larger island to the east. I knew from studying a map the day before that it was Ram. Midway across we passed a low rocky outcropping, no more than fifty yards of it showing above water. It was hardly an island at all, but it did have a small beach and a clump of spruce trees at one end, stripped by nest-ing birds. The outcropping was surrounded by breaking ledges. At the end near-est to us a lobster boat circled slowly, its staysail flapping in the light westerly, as a lone lobsterman hauled in a trap. The sergeant studied the boat a moment from the rail, then said—to no one in particular—"Hey, that's Rod Allen." He gave a shrill whistle with two fingers. "Ho there, Rod baby!"

Everyone turned to look at the lobsterman off the ledges, who of course heard nothing over the roar of his own engine and the *Laura Lee*'s. But he waved a hand when it was free.

"Pullin' Ram Island traps, no doubt," Willy said. He said it in a stage voice, more in jest, I thought, than accusation. But the sergeant heard him and instant-ly stiffened.

"*Your* trap, leatherneck," he said sharply, turning on the Marine. "I hope he is. Fish on your own shore."

Willy reddened. "Yeah? Tell it to the warden, wise guy."

Horace Snow, who had been looking down from the wheelhouse, said, "Pipe down, you two, you hear?"

But the exchange broke the mood of conviviality that had prevailed on the mailboat since we left Rockland. Willy and the sergeant sulked off to opposite sides of the deck and the others grew silent, separating into smaller groups. A curly-haired Camden student who had been in the cluster surrounding the ser-geant when he came aboard—they were apparently brothers—had gradually moved close enough to another group to exchange a word with a pale shy girl with blue eyes; now he moved away again.

"What's that about?" I asked the gentleman from Blueberry Isle when the high school students near us had moved out of hearing. "Service rivalry?"

"Would that it were, my friend. Then it would pass. . . . No, that's an ancient feud between the two islands. So old no one around any longer remembers how it started. Some ancient injury, real or imagined. Some slur of each other's sov-ereignty. . . . It could even be one island was loyalist in Revolutionary times, the other republican."

I said I was surprised to hear that the islands were inhabited so long ago, and he said there were more inhabitants on some of the islands at the end of the eighteenth century than now. "But in modern times," he went on, "the feud's been kept alive by lesser grievances. Disputes over shares of the contraband in Prohibition, for instance. Back there in Gabriel's Hole. Why Ram Island got a telephone in the 1930s and not Thorn. And, of course, fishing rights. Who's to put traps off these ledges, for instance. . . . But mind you, their rivalry's not a constant thing. They intermarry. They depend on each other in many ways. Only, every now and again they erupt . . . like Sergeant Orcutt and Clyde Grant's

boy did a moment ago." I nodded, but before I could question him further a fellow passenger from Blueberry Isle claimed his attention and soon bore him
away.

Twenty minutes later we came to Ram Island, and even if you were blind
you would have known it from the swell of voices on the deck. My WAVE (*my*
WAVE, already!) had rejoined me and now pointed out various landmarks as we
moved up a narrowing passage between the larger island and a smaller one off
its western shore. The Gut, it was called, and the current was strong in the channel as low tide approached. The smaller island was uninhabited but well
groomed by sheep. A dozen of them grazing near the shore scrambled to higher
ground as we passed.

The dominant feature on Ram Island itself, as one approached from this
angle, was a bold headland at the southernmost tip of the island rising seventy-
five to a hundred feet above a sandy beach that curved away from us. A lighthouse stood on the head facing seaward—glistening white but apparently abandoned. The keeper's cottage was boarded up and the great light in the tower
long extinguished; a triangular structure below the tower housed a fog signal
that we could hear intermittently even a half mile offshore.

From the head a long ridge ran along the center of the island, parallel to us.
The rooflines of half a dozen farmhouses—one of them was hers, Jingle said—
were visible above the orchards and overgrown fields sloping down to the passage between the islands. I wouldn't, in fact, have known they were fields if she
hadn't said so, for they had long since been abandoned to alder. I looked for
evergreens, but there were few visible in this quadrant of the island—in contrast
to the thick matting of softwoods we had passed on Thorn. The shore north of
the sandy beach was . . . well, to put it bluntly, inhospitable: straight and strong,
with a few neglected and rotting fish shacks tilting over eroding banks. Slimy
green rocks covered with seaweed were exposed fifty to seventy-five yards away
from the shore, with scattered treacherous boulders.

I made no comment, of course, on the desolate aspect of Ram Island from
the Gut, but my companion must have guessed my reaction, for she laughed at
me and said I didn't have to worry: Cutler's Cove was on the eastern shore,
where it was all spruce. But then she berated me for want of imagination. This
was a wonderful part of the island, she said. It was where the early settlers had
lived and farmed. There were a dozen or more cellar holes in those alder groves,
there were family plots with stones going back a century and a half, there were
bits and pieces of ancient plows and household utensils, there were lush swamps
that had been watering holes, and there was an ice pond where they skated
(three at a time, because that's all the skates there were on the island). And there

were the red deer, a dozen of them at last count. There might still be foxes, from a pair brought out twenty years before, though no one had seen them since before the war. And the birds . . . and so on and so forth.

"Don't hole up in that snug little bungalow of yours at Cutler's Cove," she admonished me. "Get out and find these things."

I said I counted on her to show me how, and I think she liked that.

After we'd passed the narrowest part of the Gut, weaving our way through rows of colored lobster pots pulled seaward by the tide, the shoreline changed abruptly. It was as though the Gut itself marked some ancient geologic gateway with the osprey in their high nest by the shore serving as sentinels. Now sharp cliffs and ledges plunged steeply into the sea. Behind them, through the thick growth of fir and pine, one could occasionally make out the escarpments and fault lines of abandoned quarries. At several points the shoreline was broken by narrow inlets slicing into the island at the foot of these quarries. At the head of one of these slips, hardly wider than the *Laura Lee*, the remnants of a granite landing lay exposed in the mudflats. To port, meanwhile, Little Ram gave way in a series of broad flat slabs to a string of half-tide ledges stretching parallel to us five hundred yards to a gong. The Graves, Jingle said it was called.

Ahead of us, past a neck of low-lying land that jutted out from one lip of the harbor, a large multilevel structure came into view at the northernmost tip of the island. Its walls were masonry and stone; large sections of the exterior were glass. A wide porch that ran around as much of the water side of the house as we could see was cantilevered over boulders above the shore. I whistled gently.

"Ram's Horn," Jingle said. "That's the cottage I was telling you about—with twenty rooms. The Bannisters. Kevin Bannister is the air force pilot up forward."

Horace Snow blew two short blasts as we rounded a red nun off the neck of low-lying land—the Nose, it was called—and we moved into the harbor. A battered jetty of granite blocks stretched a third of the way across the mouth of the harbor from the Nose. On it, close to land and anchored down by cables, a weathered fishing shack perched precariously. Wearing a gray woolen shawl, an aged woman, possibly in her eighties, stepped out of the open door and peered at the *Laura Lee* as it passed. Several of the high school girls waved, but she gave no sign of recognition.

"She sees us," Jingle said, "but she won't wave. Against her principles . . . That's Widow Barnaby. She's lived in that shack, if you can believe it, fifty years. Waiting for her husband to come in, she says. He was lost in a storm and last seen from this point. Oh, she's cuckoo, all right, but she's a dear soul."

Horace cut speed, winding among dories and double-ended peapods at mooring. There were a few larger boats in the harbor, but most of the lobstermen, Jingle explained, were still out. We kept close to the western shore, where the water was deepest. The harbor angled back sharply so that while its mouth was near the northern tip, its head was close to the geographic center of the island. The inner harbor emptied at low tide, leaving long stretches of mudflats where abandoned boats of all types lay moldering. Around the shores of the harbor there were aged sheds and fish shacks, but no larger buildings other than the store, which stood on high ground beyond the landing. A few houses were visible along the ridge, several of them with swaths cut through the spruce to the harbor. The spire of a church rose above the cut at the head of the harbor beyond the mudflats.

Twenty or thirty people gathered at the harbor were watching our approach.

"That's more than a reception committee," Jingle said. "That's most of the island. . . . Want to know your neighbors?"

I said I did, and she identified a number of them as Horace Snow slowly eased the *Laura Lee* alongside the pier. I have looked up too often at the same faces on that pier, arriving and leaving, to be certain which were there that morning. I know that Caleb Brewster was, in his straw hat and apron. Also Sharon Jenkins with her two children. And Clyde Grant and Clara, down to greet Willy, the marine, home on his first furlough. The Cutlers were there to meet their son Bobby, an army corporal. I believe Rudolf York and Harold Toothacher were leaning against Harold's battered truck. Jingle's mother was a matronly, white-haired islander standing beside a tall, severe woman dressed in black, Aunt Lucy. Jingle pointed out her father, standing in knee-high boots on a float across the harbor, and waved to him. "He keeps the car," she said, and when I looked blank, she added, "He's the buyer—he buys the lobsters and takes them to Rockland."

She punctuated her identifications with asides, irreverent but trenchant, then asked me just before we tied up whether I wanted the summer people as well. I said I'd better have it all. So she started on the Bannisters. Sally and George were by an oil drum, looking clean and prosperous. "The pretty one in blue is Karen."

"In blue?"

She followed my eye. "You're looking at Belle, my cousin. She is pretty, isn't she? She's . . ." But Jingle didn't finish her thought, and instead went on to the Thatchers, the only other summer people on the island at that date. Wylie and— what was her name?—Louise, and Gloria. "Gloria is Kevin's intended . . . or so they say. But twixt thee and me, I think the intending's more on her side than his. Anyway, they'd all be gone by now in a normal year. They stayed on to welcome Kevin. He's just home from a POW camp in Germany . . . wanted to set down here first. Now, that's not so dumb."

We were now docked, and the shouts back and forth from deck to pier drowned out further conversation. Even Willy's shrill voice, raised since we first came into harbor, blended in with the others. I managed, before the surge toward the gangplank carried her away, to remind my friend she'd identified nearly everyone in sight except herself; there must be more to her name than Jingle.

"Ha!" said Jingle, eyes twinkling. "I'll make that our first secret. . . . What's yours, by the by?"

"That," I said, "will be our second."

I was the last to leave the *Laura Lee*, after saying my good-byes to the gentleman from Blueberry Isle. As I climbed the gangplank with my luggage, the sandy-haired sergeant called after me from the far rail, where the Thorn Islanders had retreated: "Come see a real island sometime, Commander!"

I waved a free hand in reply and moved into the milling throng above.

Caleb Brewster drove me out to Cutler's Cove in his antique Ford pickup after I had bought enough provisions at the store to see me through the weekend. We climbed to the ridge, maneuvering around craters, and turned south at the crossroads. Past white frame farmhouses whose surrounding fields were better tended than they had appeared from the Gut. Half a mile up the ridge, Caleb turned onto a narrow track that twisted down through thick spruce to a small turnaround in a clearing. We continued on foot another two hundred yards down a rocky, overgrown path to the shore. The bungalow was perched on a grassy bank overlooking a horseshoe-shaped cove. Rough wooden steps, most of them rotted away, led down to a pebbly beach. The sides of the cove were granite slabs and boulders. Spruce woods, interspersed with birch, came down to high water level in a tangle of blowdowns on all sides. Two dories tied together were moored in the middle of the cove.

"They'll be Clyde Grant's," Caleb said, eyeing them. "Clyde's been seinin' the eastern shore."

Caleb worked a key in the rusty lock for a few moments before the door yielded, long enough to warn anything inside that we were taking possession. A red squirrel was leaving through a broken window as we stepped into a large L-shaped room bent around a massive stone fireplace. The kitchen area, including a wood stove, a sink, and a rusty kerosene refrigerator, was in the short end of the L. An enclosed bedroom, with windows facing south and east, opened off the front of the room beyond the fireplace. There was a thick layer of dust everywhere and a strong musty odor characteristic of houses long empty. But apart from this, and some damage the squirrels had done to the upholstery of the long low sofa, the bungalow appeared to be as Robert Bartlett had left it five years before.

"Not too bad, considerin'," Caleb said as we made a quick inspection. "If we'd known when you was comin', Jenny'd been down to clean up."

We continued our rounds, making a list of immediate necessities that Caleb was to run over for me later in the day. The water flow from a spring up the trail was uncertain at first, and rusty, but it was adequate for the moment. Caleb managed to light the kerosene unit in the refrigerator after several tries. And there was wood in a shed outside.

As he was about to leave me, he remarked, "I see you struck up 'quaintance with Jingle Dacey on the mailboat."

"Dacey, is it?" I said, and told him of our last exchange on the *Laura Lee*.

"That's Jingle for you. Always clownin' . . . but she's a corker," he went on. "Ain't nobody on the island better'n Jingle Dacey to fill you in on what's goin' on."

Caleb started for the door, then turned back. "How long you fixin' to stay with us, you figure?"

I stood at the large window at the end of the room, looking out across the bay to the high domed profile of what I now knew to be Isle au Haut. And I told him I hadn't a clue.

2

As things turned out, I stayed on the island until after Christmas that first year. There was plenty to keep me busy. Robert Bartlett's papers and possessions needed sorting out before I shipped them on to his sister in California, as I had promised. The bungalow required more attention than Caleb and I had suspected in our brief initial inspection. The foundation under the bedroom had been crushed by ice during a winter storm two years before and needed shoring up. The floorboards had rotted away under the broken window. The roof leaked in half a dozen places. The chimney was in urgent need of repair. And the outhouse, for all its virtues of location and panoramic view, tilted so precariously that it was only a matter of time before it would pitch me into the cove. Meanwhile, I had reading and writing of my own to catch up on after four and a half years of active duty. . . . But I digress, for this is not a record of my affairs but of those of my island neighbors, as well as I could understand them.

I came to know all the islanders during those first months. Indeed, thanks to Jingle Dacey, I knew most of them by sight and name before the end of her week's leave. I never knew—and here I digress again—why she took over the management of my life on the island as she did. She might easily have ignored me, in which case it is unlikely, as I look back on it, that I would have stayed through the fall. I might, of course, have become a transient summer resident, like the Bannisters and the Thatchers. But it's more probable I would have quit my legacy altogether and moved elsewhere. For I came out of the war, after wandering about the world for more than a decade, with a strong urge to put down roots. I didn't really expect I could put them down on a remote Maine island, but my purpose in coming out that September was to find out. Well, Jingle didn't ignore me. On the contrary, she deliberately sought me out, and, as Caleb Brewster said, there was none better to ease a stranger into this proud, self-contained community. The stars were with me that morning I met Jingle Dacey on the mailboat—though there was a time some months later when I couldn't bring myself to think so.

The Tuesday after my arrival she came down to Cutler's Cove and found me dozing on the sofa after lunch.

"On your feet," she said, walking in after a perfunctory knock. "You've been seen only once at Caleb's and people are beginning to gossip. They say you're a recluse. Or an alcoholic. Time you paid your respects around."

She was wearing a shapeless gray turtleneck sweater and knee-high boots over corduroy slacks. She eyed me across the room as I tucked in my shirttails and pulled on a plaid lumberman's jacket that had arrived in a footlocker on the *Laura Lee* the day before.

"You look less imposing out of uniform," she said.

I said she looked more so. But then I wasn't sure she'd care much for that, so I added that I liked her better in uniform because I couldn't study her legs through slacks; that was an era when you could say such things without giving offense. Jingle let the remark pass.

She glanced about the room, at the books stacked on the floor, at the unwashed dishes in the sink from the day before, at my clothes from the footlocker draped over the furniture.

"You'll need a housekeeper," she said. "Or a wife."

"Or a wife."

We walked up through the spruces and turned down the ridge toward the crossroads. It was another soft September day, the fourth in a row, but rain was forecast before nightfall. High clouds were already moving in from the west. We passed the first farmhouse on the left, since Jessica York had gone to Rockland, Jingle explained, and Leonard was still out. She seemed to know by some instinct, I noticed, where the islanders were likely to be at any time of day. We went on to the next farm down the ridge, a trim white house with green lawns and well-kept sheds and barn beyond. The Cutlers.

"Lloyd and Jesse," Jingle prompted me as she knocked at the back door and stepped ahead of me into the kitchen.

"Bless me! Jingle!" Jesse said from the stove. She was an ample woman who looked to be in her forties and, to judge from the appearance of her kitchen, was an immaculate housekeeper. The room was antiseptically clean, bare of all but utter necessities. A tinted print of the Crucifixion hung on the wall over the kitchen table.

"A social call, Jesse," Jingle said. "I've brought a neighbor." She introduced me without my rank, I was pleased to note; (she had, of course, learned my name as easily as I learned hers—from Jenny Brewster at the post office). Jesse wiped a clean hand on her spotless apron and shook mine.

"I'm pleased to meet ya, I'm sure," she said. "We were beginnin' to wonder whether you'd ever get up from your cove."

"Rather yours," I said. "Cutler's?"

"Oh mercy! Cutler's Cove's no part of us. Lloyd's grandfather used to keep his dories there. That's how it got named. But I don't think there was ever a Cutler lived down there. Was there, Jingle? You and Lucy're the island historians."

"If there was, Granny Belle chased 'em out," Jingle said. "Like everyone else that side of the island."

"Now don't be running down your grandma. Least of all, 'fore strangers."

Jesse called out through the shed to Lloyd, who was chopping wood behind the barn. Then she brought in chairs from the parlor and poured us scalding coffee from the back of the stove.

"Bobby's at the harbor," she said. "He's makin' up for his three years in the service. The boys'll be home from school pretty quick."

The girl with the pale blue eyes I'd noticed on the mailboat came into the kitchen from the front of the house and leaned on the back of Jesse's chair.

"Not at school this week?" I asked.

"Lucille's home sick," her mother answered for her, and Lucille blushed.

Lloyd Cutler came in through the shed, buttoning his jacket, and we were introduced.

"Pleased t'meet ya, I'm sure," he said, as Jesse had. He gave me a strong callused hand, then took his mug of coffee and stood by the stove staring at the floor. He was of medium height and unambiguous in his movements. His face—like the faces of all the senior lobstermen—was creased and weathered. Unlike most of the other men, however, he was cleanly shaven. The impression of austerity he gave was relieved only by the impish blue of his eyes (it was clear where Lucille and her brother got theirs). To make conversation, I asked him whether he'd been out that day.

"We leave at daybreak, as a rule," Lloyd said.

"And don't ask him why," Jesse put in. " 'Cause his granddad did."

Lloyd made a slight movement of his shoulders but said nothing. I asked what a good day's catch would be, and he said two hundred to two hundred fifty pounds. "Dependin.'"

"Dependin' on a miracle!" said Jesse. "When d'you ever catch two hundred fifty pounds, Lloyd Cutler?"

"Clyde weighed in two sixty-five last Friday," Lloyd said. He spoke deliberately and precisely. Humor, I could see, was not one of his strong points.

Jesse said, "Well, good for Clyde," then poured us more coffee.

There were shouts in the yard a few moments later, and the two younger Cutler boys tumbled into the kitchen from school. Mark, the eldest, was dark and lean, like his father. Tony was fair and full, like Jesse. Neither had blue eyes. They wanted to know where Bobby was, but not finding him home as they'd hoped, they made do with me. Though they were clearly put off by my being out of uniform.

Was I a paratrooper? Tony wanted to know—but Mark reproved him. "How can he be a paratrooper, stupid? I told ya, he's in the navy."

"He *could* be if he wanted to, I bet. Couldn't ya?" Tony appealed to me.

I equivocated and said it might be hard to be in two places at once, in the air and on the sea.

"Well, are you a pilot anyways?" Tony was determined somehow to put me in the air.

I confessed I wasn't, but appeased him a little by explaining that I'd served on an aircraft carrier. Did it have diesels? Mark had to know—diesel engines were then the talk amongst the lobstermen (though it was still some years before the first ones were installed in the Ram Island fleet)—and we were off for a quarter of an hour into the mysteries of locomotion on modern warships, something I knew a little bit about in those days. I hadn't begun to satiate Mark's curiosity, Lloyd listening gravely in while the women talked apart, when Jingle reminded me we had other calls to make. Jesse promised me a blueberry pie for the next day, and I turned at the door to order a lobster from Lloyd to go with it—but Lloyd had already slipped out through the shed to his chopping. Mark and Tony insisted on keeping us company down the ridge.

"Home sick!" Jingle said after the two boys had run on ahead to alert the Allens of our approach. She seemed almost to be speaking to herself. "I bet she's pregnant. That'll add fuel . . ." But she thought better of whatever she was about to say and changed the subject.

I pass over the details of the calls we made along the ridge during the next hour and a half. I met two dozen or more of my neighbors that afternoon, including the children. *Including the children!* That's an understatement. They were the most neighborly of all. By the time we reached the Torreys, our last call before the Peaks, our escort party had grown to ten or a dozen—the two Cutlers, two Allens, and assorted Yorks and Grants who joined us along the way. Not without design, be it said, for there was reasonable assurance of handouts in most kitchens. A doughnut, cookies, a piece of pie preempted from some lobsterman's supper.

I have to admit I had a pretty hazy impression of young people in those days. I'd spent most of my adult years out of their company, and quite candidly, I preferred it that way. But that afternoon I learned something about island children—I have never found the quality so prominent in children elsewhere—they know only a peer relationship. Maybe existence on an island strips one of inhibitions at an early age. Maybe the special limitations of an island community cause everyone to attach importance to every human tie. Whatever the reason, the fact is they accepted me from the start as an equal. They addressed me by my given name. They were not in the least put off by my being what must have seemed to them middle-aged (or worse). They discussed their affairs with me, boys and girls alike, with as much insouciance as if I had been a contemporary. And they relentlessly explored mine—not excluding my intentions with regard to Jingle. Jingle, hearing me stumble through some evasive reply, thought this a huge joke and made no effort to help me out.

Jingle didn't let our entourage of children interfere with her chief aim of introducing me to the adult islanders. They played in the yard as a rule, after receiving what portion was their due at the kitchen door, and waited until we were ready to move on. The island women greeted us cordially. Forewarned or not, they dropped whatever they were doing to pour us black coffee and sit with us a quarter of an hour in their kitchens or parlors. Their homes were different, in style and taste. Constance Allen's fine eighteenth-century farmhouse across from the empty parsonage, for instance—a house she'd inherited from her mother—was a far cry from the Torreys' unfinished story-and-a-half house above the mudflats, still in tar paper after five years. The cluttered corner parlor where Lydia York, at eighty-seven the island's most aged resident, spent most of her days was quite unlike the barren sitting room with the horsehair furniture her daughter-in-law Joanne York led us into to escape the unwashed dishes in her kitchen. But the reception given us was everywhere as warm as Jesse Cutler's. An introduction by Jingle Dacey was a guarantee of acceptance by the island women.

The men were more reserved, those of them we found at home. Rudolf

York, to be sure, was hospitable—limping in from the barn when he saw us arrive, then bringing the coffee himself into the corner parlor where we sat with Lydia and their boarder, Gertrude Bakeman; Gertrude had taught school on the island for forty years. Was it his years a widower and virtual housekeeper for the two aged ladies which had softened him? Or was he naturally sociable, like the children? In any case, Rudolf was the exception. Tucker, his son, sat with us for a few moments, then excused himself on some pretext and left us with Jeanne. Cecil and Jack Allen, finishing an early supper before going out seining at dusk, ate stolidly and silently, taking little notice of us. Alfred Torrey, caulking a dinghy in his yard, merely waved us on to Janice inside.

Jingle asked me my impressions of my neighbors as we walked along the final stretch of ridge road toward the Peaks. A light drizzle had begun to fall. Our escort had disbanded at the Torreys' and returned severally home. It was after five. She asked me again, since I didn't immediately reply. I said, after some further deliberation, that I found the children most accessible, the women next, and the lobstermen—to put a fine point on it—barely civil.

Jingle laughed and asked what I had expected, arriving with a convoy of children in tow. Like the Pied Piper.

"A lobsterman spends too much time alone to worry about being civil to strangers. That's women's work. . . . But they've nothing against you personally," she said, touching my arm briefly. "They're reserved, not . . . not resentful."

I said I'd have to see it to believe it, and we walked on in silence, the rain occasionally gusting in our faces. As we approached the Peaks, Jingle slowed her pace and said she wanted to tell me about Turk and Sharon Jenkins. Because if I didn't understand about Turk and Sharon, I'd never understand anything about the island. "There were five of us," she said. "Sharon and Elmer Brewster. Turk. My cousin Stanley Talbot . . . that's Belle's brother. And me. I don't mean there was nobody else our age around. After all, there was Billy York and Jack Allen. And Mary Lou and Cotton Clayton were only a year or two younger. But we were . . . we were . . ."

"A tight little clique?" I suggested.

"Yeah, why not? A clique. The boys were in it first. The three Musketeers, Caleb called them. Then I got big enough to want to do everything they did . . . well, *almost* everything. And pretty soon Sharon was the baby of the group, the clique. Stanley was the leader, and the crazy things he put us up to . . . Someday I'll tell you."

We had come to the Peaks, where the ridge road forked, one branch winding down to Ram's Horn, the other to Northeast Cove, where the Thatchers had their cottage. We stopped before turning into the Jenkinses' yard, on the harbor side of the fork. His mother's small gray cottage stood inside the fork, underneath several rock outcropping that gave this sector of the island its name.

"To make a long story short," Jingle went on, "Stanley was drowned in an accident before the war. Elmo was already settled on the main by then, and he's going back to his old job in Bangor when he's discharged next month. I'm half ashore . . . maybe more, who knows? So only Turk and Sharon are left—"

She stopped abruptly, apparently feeling she wasn't getting her point across about Turk and Sharon. "Oh, shit," she said. "You're probably saying, so what?" Since I hadn't said anything, I made a gesture to this effect—but there wasn't time for further exchange because Sharon came to the kitchen door just then and stared out at us. "I'll tell you later," Jingle murmured.

"Whatever're you two talking 'bout out there in the rain?" Sharon called. She had a checked apron over her maternity dress, and her long brown hair was tied in a ponytail.

"Goblins, baby. Just goblins," said Jingle, moving toward the house. She introduced us.

"Jingle said she'd bring you 'round," Sharon said, giving me a soft hand and leaving it a moment in mine. She studied me, her pink face crinkled in a shy smile. She still had the downy softness of an adolescent, though I knew she was almost twenty-five and carrying her third child.

"Turk went down to the shore with Chucky," she said, leading us into a large warm kitchen overlooking the harbor. "He'll be right back."

I asked where Turk got his name. It didn't sound like Maine.

"Horatio Leadbetter's s'posed to have named him that when he was four or five," Sharon said. "Waddlin' bow-legged 'round the harbor."

Jingle said, "How Horatio's supposed to know what a Turk looks like isn't in the legend."

"Anyways, it suits him. He's short and dark . . . and sometimes he looks pretty fierce." Sharon giggled and made what was meant to be a fierce face, failing hopelessly.

"That's the Portuguese blood in him," Jingle said. "Some dago seaman . . . They're from Lubec, about fifty years back. Comparative newcomers."

I said if a lobsterman was still considered a newcomer after fifty years, I could never expect to meld.

"That's right, chum," said Jingle.

"She exaggerates. It's nowhere near as bad as that," Sharon said mildly. "How long *are* you staying?"

I told Sharon her father had asked me the same question and I had no answer. I didn't know.

"Till the first nor'easter," Jingle said. "But he'll be back."

Sharon said, "I guess we ask that 'cause everyone counts out here. In the middle of the war we were down one winter to thirty-seven. . . . Soon be like old times again, eh, Jingle? Everyone back from the service."

"Sure, sure. Babies underfoot. More in the pot. Just like old times."

"Same old Jingle," Sharon said. "What about those four you were goin' to have? Two girls, two boys?"

" 'I ain't quite fixed the order,' " they quoted together, laughing at an old joke between them.

A child woke crying in the next room. Sharon disappeared and returned with a yawning two-year-old girl, black curly hair matted over her forehead. This was Barbara, she said, and Barbara buried her face in her mother's shoulder.

Jingle summoned me to the large window facing the harbor, and we watched Turk and his towheaded son wind up to the house through the pasture. Turk was not only dark and squat, as I knew, but massive through the shoulders. His arms hung nearly to his knees. They came in through a back door, peeling off their sou'westers and boots before entering the kitchen. Turk shook hands with me silently and roughed up Barbara's hair.

"You been workin' the ridge?" he asked Jingle. "Then you'll have java comin' outa your ears."

He went down into the cellar and came back in a few moments with a dusty bottle of loganberry wine.

"Celebration," he said briefly. "Woman, fetch the mugs."

"He's puttin' on his act," said Jingle. "Old tar."

"Next he'll be callin' me 'deah,' " Sharon said, standing from the stool where she was feeding Barbara. "The Tiffany or the five-and-dime?"

"Whichever's handy," Turk said, searching for a corkscrew.

Jingle picked up the tall dusty bottle, which once held a Moselle. "Prewar vintage?" she asked Turk. He nodded. "I remember it," she said. "The Blueberry Isle lot."

Turk shook his head. "You and Stanley and Elmo finished that lot off 'fore we ever got it into bottles."

"While you and Sharon sat quietly watching."

Turk worked the cork out in pieces and poured the dark red liquid into the orange juice glasses Sharon had placed on the counter. He sniffed his.

"Here's nothin'," he said, and drained his glass in a single gulp.

"God A'mighty!" said Jingle, choking on her first sip. "That's gone to pure alcohol, Turk."

"Better'n back to berry juice."

Sharon brought chairs, and we gathered around her wood stove, nursing down Turk's fiery concoction. We could hear the rain now falling steadily outside, occasional gusts pelting the western windows. Chucky lay his head on Turk's lap, thumb in mouth and a finger in one eye while with the other he gravely contemplated me. Barbara, her meal finished, squeezed next to Chucky between Turk's stubby knees and played with the zipper on his fly until he distracted her with a ball of marlin.

"Can't keep nothin' private 'round here," he grumbled, and Sharon said, "What manners!"

We talked—or they talked—about the island during the war. The islanders hadn't made out badly on the whole. The market price of lobsters had tripled from before the war, since lobsters were counted a luxury product and so were exempted from price control. Gas rationing was liberal for lobstermen, though the gas itself was sometimes in short supply. Spare parts were in even shorter supply, and repairs were difficult. For this reason the lobstermen put out their traps closer to the island than usual, but since lobsters were plentiful, this was no handicap. It also meant they could haul from dories if their engines temporarily broke down. Even with half a dozen younger lobstermen in the service, family incomes were higher than in the prewar years. All in all, the current boom in the lobster industry was directly attributable to these favorable conditions during the war.

The isolation of the islanders was the greatest hardship. Suspension of regular ferry service by the *Laura Lee* meant that established habits had to be given up—like the monthly shopping expeditions to Rockland or Camden. The Islesboro ferry was supposed to call twice a week, on Tuesdays and Thursdays, but the call was often canceled due to fog or high seas. The captain, according to Jingle, had a "paranoia" about the Gut.

"I don't know nothin' 'bout that," Turk said, "but I seen him turn back on a clear day in a two-foot swell."

Even when the Islesboro ferry did arrive, the schedule was awkward. The Tuesday shoppers were put off far up the bay in an area they didn't know and had to lay over two nights before catching the next boat back—if it made it. The winter Frank Talbot died, the island was without mail and fresh supplies from early February to mid-March. The only contact with the mainland after the cable broke was by radio telephone. The high school students, meanwhile, couldn't come home for weekends unless someone fetched them and returned them on Monday morning. Jingle and other men and women in the armed services didn't dare risk coming home on short furloughs for fear of not returning to duty on time.

"You'd think we wouldn't be livin' out here if we minded bein' lonely," Sharon said.

Turk refilled our glasses, and we conversed for another thirty minutes before

Jingle rose and said it was time to stagger homeward.

"Stagger home for good," Sharon said.

"I just might," said Jingle.

I asked Turk, as he stood in the door with Chucky on his shoulders and Barbara between his legs, if I could go out with him someday.

"The *Sunrise* is no aircraft carrier," Jingle said, teasing me. "You might get sick."

"It's not the sea as gets me," Sharon said. "It's the bait."

Turk, who'd said nothing, gave me a laconic smile. "I don't know's I want a navy commander seein' how we find our way around out here . . . 'by guess and by golly,' as my old man used t' say."

"Try me," I said.

Turk said, "I will."

As we walked back up the ridge, heads bowed against the rain, Jingle finished up the point she'd been trying to make earlier about Turk and Sharon. And I think she was pleased she'd waited.

"It's just this," she said, "they're what keeps this island held together. The Cutlers, you've noticed, are strong on virtue . . . virtue and respectability. The Grants—you'll see more of them another day—are big on laughs. Vitality. Passion. They're really great fun, the Grants. The Yorks bring in more lobsters than everyone else together . . . which isn't surprising, being as how every other person on the island is a York. But I'll tell you something. This place couldn't get along without Turk and Sharon. I mean, it just wouldn't last . . . well, I don't expect you to see this now. But someday you will."

And eventually I did.

3

Jingle's next step in my arranged introduction to the islanders was supper with her parents. Her aunt and cousin, Lucy and Belle Talbot, were to be there, too.

"Six sharp," she'd told me the day before, as we parted company on the high road. And she'd advised me to have that little sip, if I needed it, before I came, because I'd get no loganberry wine at the Daceys'.

I came in at the end of the afternoon from a long walk in the fog along the eastern shore and did as she had advised, reading again a note I found pinned on my door when I returned. It was written in a long cursive hand on Ram's Horn stationery, and read as follows:

We would be most happy of the opportunity to meet you before we leave for the season on Saturday. There are secrets we can tell you about this island! Shall we say tomorrow? Cocktails and dinner. If I do not hear from you to the contrary, my son Kevin will pick you up at seven.
Sally Bannister

I put the note in the pocket of my jacket, and when it was time walked up through the spruces and along the ridge to the Daceys', the last house toward the Head. It was an ample white farmhouse with a fine westerly view of the Camden Hills over intervening islands. Well-built sheds and a barn stretched out behind the house, as at other farms along the ridge.

Jingle was waiting for me at the front door—the only front door on the island, I later discovered, that was used regularly, because, as Jingle explained to me one day, Winifred Dacey considered her kitchen her "fortress" and wouldn't have "just anybody traipsing through." I nodded approvingly at Jingle's flaring skirt and ruffled blouse.

"First clothes I've had on since Pearl Harbor," she said, and whirled the skirt out in a pirouette.

"Must have been a long, cold war," I said as she led me into the parlor to meet her father. Arthur Dacey rose from his leather rocker where he'd been reading a two-day-old issue of the *Courier-Gazette*. He was a tall spare man in his late sixties or so, slightly stooped. He moved deliberately as he talked. He had the distinctive island accent, but he spoke grammatically, unlike the other lobstermen. He had, of course, like all male islanders except Caleb Brewster and Harold Toothacher, lobstered all his life. But now he gave most of his time to running the car, which meant providing bait and fuel for the lobstermen, stocking lathes and warp for their traps, extending credit when times were bad, and above all, buying the lobsters and running them over once or twice a week to Rockland in his forty-five-foot lobster boat, the *Sarah Lou*. He even kept a modest supply of "emergency" spirits on hand for the lobstermen, though he was a teetotaler himself.

Arthur ran the car for Frank Talbot when Frank was stricken with arthritis a few years before the war, and after Frank's death he took over the business in his own right. I had no clear impression of Arthur Dacey before we met that evening. I knew, of course, that he was the eldest son of the almost legendary Granny Belle—of whom I shall have more to say in due course—and that he and his sister, Lucy Talbot, had inherited between them Granny Belle's extensive holdings on the island. But I hadn't gathered, from what I'd heard so far, that Arthur Dacey was ever a force on the island comparable to his mother or to Lucy's husband, Frank. Quickness of mind, I could see, wasn't Arthur's principal strength. Rather, dignity and honesty and an absolutely unflagging sense of fairness. He would have been a superb judge.

Winifred Dacey, who joined us presently from her "fortress," was Arthur's second wife—his first died in childbirth, with their child. She was in her mid-thirties when she married Arthur, then in his mid-forties. Jingle was their only child. Winifred was a Holbrook from Belfast, daughter of a sea captain, and in her childhood had made several voyages to the Caribbean and the Mediterranean, and two around the world. It was hard to tell what impression these voyages left with her, for she never spoke of them; even Jingle could tell me nothing of these romantic adventures. Winifred gave one an unmistakable sense of breeding with her silver hair and erect carriage; indeed, in appearance she stood apart from the other islanders. Earlier in the week I'd seen her from a distance on the high road and for a moment mistook her for some summer visitor I hadn't yet identified. But she was so effacing in her manner, so subdued and reserved, that it was an act of self-deception to imagine her as Jingle's mother.

Lucy Talbot and Belle arrived five minutes after I did, while we were still conversing in the parlor. Lucy was again in black, as she'd been the day I arrived, but it didn't seem to be a mourning black. She didn't strike me as the type of person who'd carry mourning two and a half years after the death of her husband. She was tall and spare, like Arthur. She seemed severe at first impression, her wispy hair drawn back tightly from her forehead, her features sharply chiseled and stern. But her smile was warm and her eyes compassionate. I could see she was a woman with reserves. And she had need of them, for she'd lost not only a son at sea but her father as well, as I knew from Jingle, and she'd watched her strong-willed husband waste away before her eyes, victim of a painful and crippling arthritis.

Belle was seventeen and, as I'd already gathered the day before whenever her name came up, an object of special affection to the islanders. She was fair and gentle, less downy perhaps than Sharon Jerkins—at least than Sharon must have been at that age, to judge from Sharon today—but she still had the softness of a prolonged adolescence. She wore a blue cotton dress with a simple print, a dress that succeeded in obscuring rather than accenting the contours of her body. It was a serene face, perhaps less decisively pretty than I had thought when I first saw her from the deck of the *Laura Lee*—mistaking her momentarily for Karen Bannister. Her complexion was pale and she showed faint traces of acne, as though she was recuperating from a long illness. In any case, she exercised a very strong attraction over me, and I found it hard to keep my eyes off her those first few minutes—until Jingle caught my attention from across the room, making a droll face and shaking her head.

Winifred summoned us to the dining room, and we gathered around the oak table, where Arthur said grace. As we took our seats, I happened to feel Sally Bannister's note in my pocket and passed it quietly to Jingle, who was sitting beside me. She read it, smiled, and without asking whether I minded, passed it across the table to Belle.

"Dig those cocktails!" she said to me under her breath. Aloud, she said, "Isn't that typical of Sally Bannister, telling 'secrets' about the island!"

"What secrets?" Arthur said, taking his place at the head of the table.

"Secrets Sally's made up about the natives and wants to tell . . . she's awsked the Commandah for dinnah tomorrow evening, I'll have you know," she mimicked Sally.

Belle passed the note on to her mother, and I gave up hope of getting it back before it had been the rounds. I asked the company at large—in a jocular way, I suppose you'd call it—whether I should take up the invitation, realizing as I asked that I hadn't considered the question myself.

"I would," Belle promptly said.

"Of course you would," Arthur said, patting her wrist. "I would in your place, a good-lookin' war hero to gawk at."

Belle blushed—but of course she blushed at almost anything in those days. "I wouldn't go because of Kevin," she said. "I'd go for the house."

"Why for the house?" I asked her. I'd taken it for granted the islanders must find Ram's Horn offensive, with its angular planes and reckless expanses of glass, not to mention its extraordinary cost, which surely mocked their meager budgets.

"It's a wonderful house," Belle said. "I can't think of anybody not wanting to live there."

"Well, I can't say's I'd care to *live* at Ram's Horn," Arthur said judiciously. "Be a mite cool in a nor'easter, come November. But I'll agree with Belle—it's a mighty interestin' place."

Lucy Talbot had folded Sally's note while we were talking and now passed it back across the table to me. "I doubt this was meant to be shown about," she said, a hint of reproval in her voice.

I said I hadn't intended it should be, and passed on the reproof to Jingle in a sidewise glance.

"Sorry," she said, "*sir*." And when I reproached her again, for we'd tacitly agreed from the outset to make nothing of our different ranks, she said, "Sorry again. That was mean."

"Jingle's afraid she'll lose her position as escort," Lucy remarked, then she added, referring again to Sally's note, "Of course you should go."

Jingle said, "Well, there's your answer, chum."

Winifred Dacey brought in a steaming tureen of fish chowder and ladled it into Cantonese soup bowls. As we ate we talked of the eastern shore I had explored that day. In 1942, Arthur said, there'd been a three-day submarine watch in Jonah's Cove, the one next to mine, following rumors the Nazis planned to put spies ashore there.

"Logical place from which to subvert the republic," Jingle said.

"I 'spect they wanted to give us something to do," said Arthur. "Make us think we were being helpful. Only one landing was ever reported, so far's I know. Somewhere east of Schoodic."

I asked Belle if she felt cheated having to stay at home through the war when others only a few years older went off to serve. I knew from my sister this had been a constant complaint of *her* daughter, who was Belle's age.

"You've no idea!" Belle said with a burst of intensity. "We felt so useless."

"But dear, you rolled bandages last summer in Rockland," Winifred said mildly.

"Bandages!" Belle exclaimed.

"What did you miss, Belle?" Arthur said after studying her a moment. It was clear to see he stood to her as a father. "What duty could you have had that'd have made all that much difference to you?"

"She could have filed my papers," Jingle said, "while I filed the lieutenant's, who filed the commander's, who filed the captain's."

"I'd have filed anything or anybody," Belle said, "just to be doing something."

"Belle's afraid there'll never be another war," her mother said.

"I'm not that . . . morbid," Belle said, groping for her word. "I just wanted to be part of it . . . since it was happening anyways. But never mind."

"The lost generation," Jingle said. "Well, cheer up, Belle. Now we've fixed the world all up for you, you can go mess it up again."

"Just whose generation are you, Petty Officer Dacey?" her father asked. "You fixing to retire?"

Jingle said, "I lay down the sword."

Conversation flowed on agreeably and inconsequentially in this fashion as we ate our way through Winifred Dacey's roast lamb and pumpkin pie. Jingle more than anyone gave focus to what we talked about, but I have a hazier recollection of the focus than of her good-natured bantering with Arthur. Winifred occasionally reproved her with a cautionary "Jingle!" if her tongue grew too free, or with "Jennifer!" (her given name) if what she said seemed particularly outrageous to that proper matron. I asked during a pause how Jingle got her nickname, and Arthur explained it was Caleb who gave it to her: "She scrambled about so much when she was little, Winnie tied a bell around her neck so's we'd know where she was. Well, one day she scrambled into the store, and Caleb says,

'I do declare, here comes Jingle Dacey' . . . and the name just stuck with her all these years."

"And I'm scrambling still," Jingle said, giving her father a good-natured poke in the ribs. But Jingle had lived too long among the island elders to let her wisecracking go too far or to say anything that gave lasting offense.

Lucy Talbot, meanwhile, entered the conversation from time to time, her remarks usually brief and shrewd. Belle was alternately animated and withdrawn. She would gaze for minutes at a time into empty space, distracted by her private thoughts. She was a maiden in suspension, awaiting the proper knight errant—or other catalyst—for her release.

Arthur Dacey and I sat in the parlor while the women cleared up in the kitchen, under some protest from Winifred, who preferred to do it alone. I asked Arthur about the summer residents on Ram Island, since Jingle had overlooked this element in her escort duties. Arthur said he wasn't at all surprised and identified several I hadn't heard of: a pair of retired schoolteachers, for instance, in a cottage opposite the jetty; and a Boston dentist and his family at Jericho Cove. They'd left the island some weeks before. It was the Bannisters, Arthur said, who'd been longest on the island and who owned the most land. He paused to light his pipe.

"Rufus Bannister—that's George's father—bought the northeast end of the island from my mother before the war. The other war, that is. Well, he was a millionaire, all right. Used to stop in once or twice every season in a thundering big schooner he couldn't bring in much past the jetty. *Albatross,* he called her, sixty-five feet long. She carried a crew of half a dozen, let alone the passengers. She was a beauty. Well, Rufus's idea was to build himself a cottage on top of the Peaks. I guess he wanted to see every which ways. But the war came along 'fore he got more'n a rough plan laid out, and that was the end of it. Flu took him in 1919. I often thought what good was all that money if it couldn't keep him from a little thing like the flu."

Arthur relit his pipe, slowly shaking his head. George inherited the property, he went on, but not being a sailor like Rufus, he gave little thought to it for half a dozen years. Until he married Sally. "Well, that same year they came out on the mailboat for about ten days. They put up at Caleb's, and they went back and forth all over that end of the island like they were looking for buried treasure. It was Sally decided to build at Ram's Horn, and that settled George. Sally," Arthur remarked between puffs, "was a model . . . whatever that's s'posed to mean."

Once the decision was made, Arthur continued, construction on Ram's Horn got under way immediately. They hired an architect from Boston, carpenters from Rockland, and stonemasons from Deer Isle. Decorators were imported from New York City. "They were all ready to move in the next summer . . . that was the year Kevin was born. And I hand it to 'em, they've had a pile o' pleasure out of Ram's Horn. Not something they put up and forgot about, which I guess George's rich enough to've done. They've been out every year since it was built, even a week or two each year during the war."

"What does George Bannister do?" I asked.

"*Do?* Well, he doesn't do much of anything for a living, if that's what you mean. He's no need to. He's s'posed to be some kind of a writer, but there's no great profit there. During this war he had a civilian job up in Washington, but that's ended."

I said, after a pause, that George Bannister sounded like a drifter; he seemed to have no will of his own.

"Well, t'would seem so, wouldn't it?" Arthur said thoughtfully. "That's what Jingle and some others say. . . . But there's no kinder man, I'll warrant, than George Bannister."

He went on, more perfunctorily, to describe the Thatchers, to whom George Bannister had sold Northeast Cove a dozen years before. Wylie Thatcher, who owned a ball bearing plant in Pennsylvania, was a friend of George's from preparatory school. The Thatchers had built a less-imposing—but still spacious—"cottage" to which they returned for a month each summer until war broke out. They were back only once during the war before their current visit.

The others came in from the kitchen as Arthur was finishing his account of the Thatchers. Jingle leaned over the back of Arthur's chair and wound her arms around his neck.

"Giving him the dirt on the summer folk, Pops?"

"Facts," Arthur said equitably. "Simple facts. Dirt's your department, my high-flying friend."

When they were settled, I asked Arthur—carrying on our conversation, but meaning to include the others as well—whether there was a mix between the summer people and the islanders.

"Our 'rusticators,'" Arthur remarked, but he went no further.

No one else volunteered an answer immediately, and after a moment Jingle spoke up—and I was glad to see she was serious for once, not trying to bury my question under a string of wisecracks.

"Yes and no," she said, "if you want a straight answer. On the surface, we get along fine. Why shouldn't we? We meet at Caleb's, around the harbor. We come and go together on the *Laura Loo* . . . like the other day. Kevin used to play in the Little League. Karen had a big birthday party every August, and all the kids on the island were invited. . . . The parents came later to pick us up and got cocktails on the porch. Very—"

"I loved those parties," Belle interrupted, curling her feet under her on the sofa. "Blindman's bluff and kick the can—"

"Sure, sure. And cigarettes and post office in the treehouse. Kevin delivering all the mail."

"Jingle!" her mother said.

"Anyways, that's one side of it," Jingle went on, turning back to me. "The other is . . . was . . . we didn't have anything to say to each other. Too much came between us. Like ten months of every year when they weren't around. Oh, we never took them seriously enough, I'll agree. We laughed at them a good deal more than they deserved."

"Well, that's the most sensible thing you've said," Lucy Talbot remarked.

Jingle said—more to reaffirm her reputation as enfant terrible than with any other design, "Wait till I catch him alone."

"Jennifer!" her mother said. "How you talk!"

Our conversation drifted on to other topics for a half hour or so before Lucy and Belle rose to leave. I followed them, and Jingle accompanied us down the ridge to visit awhile with Belle at Meadowlane. The fog had cleared, and the stars were bright and cold. The moon hadn't yet come up. Jingle lingered a moment with me at my turn-off as the other two moved slowly on.

"Well, tomorrow—" she began.

"Say the word and I'll chuck it," I interrupted, half in jest. But I could see she was piqued at my invitation to Ram's Horn.

"I bet!" said Jingle. "Anyway, it'll do you good. Just beware of Sally Bannister."

"Hm," I said, still teasing her. "A siren?"

She thought a moment and shook her head. "Shoal water, rather." She moved on down the road after Belle and Lucy.

4

I was shaving at my kitchen sink the next afternoon, after another long exploration of the eastern shore, when Kevin Bannister came for me. I saw him from the window, swinging his way down through the spruces, his cane slung over one arm, and called to him to come in. He was still in khaki but without insignia.

"I'm early," he said as I greeted him at the door. "I was going to pick up lobsters at the harbor and thought you'd like to come along. The local color."

Kevin looked about the bungalow while I finished shaving and dressed. This was the first time he'd been at Cutler's Cove, and he whistled appreciatively at the layout. He spent some time studying my library, which, with the addition of

two more crates that had arrived the day before, had now swelled to eighty or
ninety volumes jumbled together on makeshift shelves. Economics periodicals
and Southeast Asian pamphlets lay cheek by jowl with contemporary fiction.

"I can't catch the drift of your taste," he said after a few minutes. I said I
wasn't surprised and asked him to tell me if he ever caught it.

When I was ready, we walked back up to the clearing. Kevin was surprisingly
agile, despite a recent operation in Europe to remove pieces of shrapnel from his
left knee; a shell had exploded in the cockpit of his fighter plane over Germany,
and he hadn't had proper surgery until after his release from prison camp. His
leg was temporarily in a brace that immobilized his knee. At the turnaround we
climbed into an early Model A Ford station wagon that started after several tries.
Kevin rested his bad leg on the running board with the door open and used his
right foot for clutch and brake; he manipulated the hand throttle on the wheel
when he needed it.

"My contribution to the cause of progress in 1945," Kevin said with a touch
of irony, "has been to put this buggy in motion again."

I said it was a worthy achievement. Who was to say there was a better one?
He maneuvered the vehicle skillfully through the spruces and onto the high
road. As we dodged the craters on our way to the harbor, I asked what the future
held for him.

"Back to Princeton," he said. "Junior year . . . a week from tomorrow, no
less."

I asked what he was majoring in, and he said comparative literature, but he
was debating a shift to political science; he would do graduate work in politics in
any case.

Joel Grant—the large, shaggy, high school student on the *Laura Lee* called
Joey—was waiting for us at the landing and rowed us out to his father's lobster
boat, the *Clarissa B.*

"Remember how they used to call you 'Half-pint' at Thorn Island, Joey?"
Kevin asked. "When you were batboy for the Little League? They'd eat their
words now."

"They et 'em then," Joel said. "Stanley Talbot made 'em."

"What's happened to the Little League?"

"All growed up." He spit inexpertly over the side and hit the gunwale. "Turk
says we'll have a new ball club nex' year."

The sun, which had been hidden all afternoon behind a thick overcast, now
dropped below the lower edge of the clouds and flooded the harbor with a
translucent orange.

"Playing hookey this week?" Kevin asked.

"Well, 'twixt us and the lamppost, I took sick Monday mornin' and dang'dest thing, it lasted through boat time Wednesday. I commenced to feel a mite perkier the end of the mornin'—"

"Say, about the time the mailboat cleared the jetty?"

" 'Bout then," Joel said, grinning broadly. "Well, my pop said no use goin' all the way to Camden for a couple days' schoolin' . . . so I figured I better get me in a little fishin'."

We came to Clyde's boat, and Joel netted out a dozen lobsters from a crate tied astern. Back at the pier, Kevin paid for the lobsters with a five-dollar bill and told Joey to keep the change. We climbed back to the high road as the sun dropped below the horizon, leaving the sky aflame behind us. At the crossroads we passed Lucy and Belle Talbot walking home from the Peaks. I waved a greeting, and Lucy waved back. Belle smiled.

"You've met the Talbots, I see," said Kevin, and I told him I'd had supper with them the day before at the Daceys'.

"Supper! You've made fast time. In twenty-one years I've never had a sit-down meal in an islander's home." I had nothing to say to this, and he asked after a moment if I knew about Stanley Talbot. I said I knew he'd drowned in an accident before the war. "Caught in his own lines pulling traps in the Gut," Kevin said, shaking his head. "That nearly folded this island up. . . . I barely remember the war breaking out a month later. It was like a small footnote to that episode."

When we reached Ram's Horn, the colors from the sunset had diffused in varying shades throughout the entire sky over us, even in the east. Sally Bannister, who had been on the lookout for us, was at my door before Kevin brought the wagon to a halt on the gravel circle.

"I'm not letting anyone speak to you, Commander, until you come look at this sunset."

She took my arm and led me quickly off through the kitchen and onto a wide-open verandah facing the sea. Kevin, trailing behind us with the lobsters, told his mother not to be fatuous; the sunset was the same all over the island. Sally paid no attention to him. We stood at the rail taking in the colors—which were, in fact, dramatic, the more so because the sunset had come on so unexpectedly at the end of a gray afternoon. The horizon arced almost two hundred and seventy degrees from the Camden Hills to Isle au Haut. Ledges and a few small islands broke the near foreground. Several larger islands, including Thorn and Blueberry, melded in the middle distance. In the western sky the pinks had begun to go to purple.

"How can anyone bear to leave this divine place?" Sally Bannister said, her arm linked through mine. I couldn't quite place her accent, but it seemed genuine; only the words were affected—for my benefit, I gathered. In a few minutes she guided me along the verandah to meet the rest of the company, who were also watching the sunset from under a striped awning where the house angled. I told her I hoped she'd let me revert inconspicuously to civilian status and told her my given name.

She pouted. "No more glamour. I'd set my heart on knowing a commander." And she proceeded to introduce me around as "ex-commander—he won't tolerate his rank another day" until I regretted my warning. Kevin, joining us finally from the kitchen, said, "Come on, Mother. Can't you see he means what he says?" Sally made a face at Kevin and went on introducing me in her own way.

We went through sliding glass doors into a high-ceilinged living room that joined the center angle of the house and dominated the seaward side. The angle itself was filled by a massive stone fireplace that burned logs tilted on end under a copper hood. Kevin put on another log, stirring up the embers underneath. Wide window seats with cushions stretched along the sides of the room facing the sea, and low sofas and chairs, expensively upholstered and separated by glass-top tables, were drawn in a loose semicircle around the hearth. The walls, which were white, were hung with Oriental tapestries and sea paintings, including one large Winslow Homer under a long balcony. It was a showplace room, beyond any doubt, in which the architect had indulged a sense of space and planes in an unusual setting. But it was not a gallery. That is, it was not a room where only space and glass and expensive furnishings and objects mattered. People gave it personality as well— as the two girls, Karen Bannister and Gloria Thatcher, presently demonstrated by stretching out in a tête-à-tête on a crimson couch. It was a room that could have books, though there were few in evidence.

George Bannister brought me a drink as I admired the fireplace with its raised hearth.

"A m-m-mason from Stonington did that," he said. "From granite out at Crotch Island. That's the b-best there is." He said it to flatter Crotch Island, I could tell, not Ram's Horn.

George Bannister was six feet or more and heavily framed. He was not athletic. His thick hair, cut short, was already white, though I suspected he was only in his mid-fifties. His eyes were gray. Jingle had told me that he stammered; still, I was unprepared for it. I discovered later that his stammering was erratic. He often stammered out of shyness, when he met people he didn't know or hadn't seen for a long time, but once engaged in conversation he got over it. On the other hand, in the presence of certain people—usually people he liked—he stammered almost continuously.

"You were in the P-P-Pacific, I believe?" he said. I nodded. He mentioned several naval engagements, including one or two that were not well-known, and asked if I had been there. I said I had and remarked that he must have been in

Naval Operations to know of those obscure battles.

"Oh, not at all," he said. "I had a very lowly assignment . . . in OSS. But I'm interested in n- naval history. Sometime I'd like to hear about your experiences."

I said, not to be rude but to discourage any probing of a life I was trying to put behind me, that I was doing my best to forget them.

"It's a pity," George said after a moment. "The ones who were in combat try to forget. The ones who stayed home try to remem-member."

He seemed about to go on, but Wylie Thatcher joined us at this point and broke into our conversation. Wylie's handsome, slightly ravaged face was flushed from numerous martinis, the last of which he held unsteadily in one hand while trying to light a cigarette with the other. He affected an English accent, which I couldn't explain—since his native Main Line accent was already distinctive enough—until I discovered later he'd been a liaison officer with a British regiment early in the war.

"Can't tell you how delighted we are, old man, to have you on the island," he said when he had his cigarette going. "Bloody shame about that chap Bartlett. We only saw him once or twice, of course, but he seemed a decent sort, didn't he, George?" George nodded.

I made no reply. Robert Bartlett was too rich a personality to be slighted by this trifling tribute to his memory by someone whose existence he probably would long since have forgotten, were he alive.

Wylie Thatcher asked how long I'd be staying that season, and I said I might not leave at all.

"Oh, you'll bugger off by November," he said. "No one can stand the winter out here."

I said the islanders seemed to manage it.

"The islanders," Wylie said, "are built into the landscape."

He asked me presently, as I knew he would, what college I had attended, and I mentioned a small one in the Midwest he'd obviously never heard of.

"We're Ivy, I'm afraid," said Wylie, draining his glass. "George is Princeton. I'm Yale."

Finding no suitable reply to this revelation, I watched Sally coming toward us from the kitchen, her pink slacks clinging to long, supple legs and still-slender hips. Mary Lou would have the lobsters ready in ten minutes, she said. There was time for another round, and she gave George her empty glass. George took mine as well, and Wylie minced after him to an oak cabinet in the corner that served as a bar.

Sally was studying me with an enigmatic smile, which I dutifully returned. She was still a handsome woman at forty and had obviously been a beauty in her day, as I already knew. An image came to me, as she faced me in her tight slacks and low-cut sweater fringed with gold brocade, of another Sally in the mid-1920s (what was her name? something Irish, I remembered): bobbed hair, short satin dress above the knees belted low, champagne glass in one hand and a long cigarette holder in the other. That was Sally Bannister's era, the jazz era. She seemed out of place on this remote island—yet if Arthur Dacey had it right, it had been her decision to build this house at Ram's Horn and to spend two months of each year in it.

"Your reputation precedes you," she said, still smirking.

I asked how this was possible, since I knew no one on the island before I arrived.

"But you have arrived. Now you belong to Ram Island." She took a cigarette from a silver case and waited for me to light it. "One, you're rather bookish. Two, you're not overly tidy. Three—"

"You peeked in my bungalow when I wasn't there," I interrupted.

"Three," she went on, ignoring my interruption, "you dined last night at the Daceys'—and I certainly didn't peek there." Kevin, conversing with Lou Thatcher near us, overheard but shrugged when I caught his eye, disclaiming any communication with his mother.

I said she seemed to have a talent for ferreting out secrets, and asked what they amounted to in my case. Sally replied, with mock provocation suitable to the occasion, "A very unsettling neighbor."

George returned with our drinks, Wylie in his wake, and conversation remained general until we moved into the oval dining room overlooking the tip of the Horn. Mary Lou Grant, who had worked intermittently for the Bannisters since she was fifteen, was placing a platter of steaming red lobsters at one end of the table. She glanced at the company filing through the paneled doorway, then tossed her curls as she took a tray back to the kitchen, opening the swinging door of the pantry with one even motion of well-rounded hips.

"Local Victory girl," Wylie Thatcher, who was walking next to me, whispered in my ear. "Nice piece of tail for the chaps, what?"

I moved away from Wylie to the other end of the table, where Sally beckoned me, and found a seat between her and Gloria Thatcher. As we sat down, I asked Gloria, to make conversation, where she was at school.

"Miss Godwin's," she said, making a long face. "I've got another year, worst luck."

It would pass, I assured her. Where then?

"Then I'm supposed to go to a junior college in New Hampshire. Mummy's college . . . that's even worse. It's about a thousand miles from Princeton." She glanced at Kevin, who was watching Mary Lou bring in another platter of lobsters for George's end of the table.

I told Gloria gravely that her future looked bleak indeed and perhaps she should take it in hand. She stared at me with wide eyes as though I'd pinched her under the table.

"How?" she said. "What can one do?"

"*Faut revolter,*" I said recklessly. "Run away. Take a job as a waitress at the Nassau Inn."

Sally, catching the last of this, said, "Are you subverting the young already?" She fixed me with her Mona Lisa smile and added in a husky voice, "Try me." Gloria looked mildly shocked and turned away.

George came up from the cellar carrying three dirt-encrusted bottles of pre-war Moselle. Wylie led a one-man cheer. Lou Thatcher called George Santa Claus and asked how he'd managed to keep such a treasure. "Buried under two feet of f-fertilizer," George said, opening the first of the bottles.

Kevin said, "Against Nazi invaders, no doubt."

"Against Maine w-winters."

"Or natives?" said Lou Thatcher.

George poured the wine and we fell to the lobsters. Conversation was muted for a time, limited to the circulation of various instruments essential to our business and desultory discussion on the merits and demerits of eating the green tomalley. Later, when the meal was well advanced and after George had refilled our glasses with what wine Wylie had left in the third bottle, Sally said we should have a toast to mark the occasion.

"Bully! A victory cel'bration!" Wylie said, his speech thickening as the Moselle on top of the martinis reached his tongue.

"That was August, sweetie-pie," his wife said. "Remember? This is September."

"Whoever heard of a single cel'bration for so grand a war?"

"The last victory celebration went on for three weeks," Lou Thatcher remarked to the company at large.

Sally said, "Come, George. A toast. Then we'll hear from our boys."

"That's the spirit, Sally. Speeches from the returning heroes." Wylie was growing maudlin, and I doubted he would see the evening out.

We looked at George, who was fingering his glass uneasily and staring at a plate of ravished lobster shells in front of him. "Well, yes, this is an occasion," he said finally. "The war over at l-l-last and our soldiers and sailors coming home. I don't seem to find quite the right w-words for it. So I'll just propose a little toast. First, to Kevin and our guest tonight and their safe return. Second, to those who didn't return. And third to our gallant allies, the English and Free French."

Kevin said into the pause that followed George's toast, "And to the

Russians."

"The ruddy Russians!" Wylie said. Kevin flushed but said nothing. We drank the toast in silence.

"Kevin feels he owes a special debt to the Russians," Sally said to me, as though in apology. "They liberated his stalag."

Kevin, overhearing her, said down the table, "Come off it, Mother! Why is everyone so self-conscious about the Russians? Didn't they win the war as much as we did?"

"They'd never have crossed the Elbe without American help on the western front," Wylie said, finding his tongue again and losing his fake English accent at the same time.

"And we'd never have landed in Normandy without theirs at Stalingrad."

"That's debatable, my friend. Ver-y debatable."

"Oh, let's not fight the war all over again," Gloria Thatcher said, looking unhappily from Kevin to her father.

George Bannister remarked, trying to be fair, that when he was in London on a short mission in 1943 the English had seemed very grateful to the Russians for Stalingrad. Londoners would hear no evil said of their Soviet allies.

"They're singing a different tune now, I bet," Wylie said, "watching Stalin grab off Poland . . . damned Attlee government probably in on the plot."

"Let's leave Poland to the United Nations," Karen said.

"The United Nations!" Wylie sputtered. "Bolshevism dignified by Stalingrad and now the United Nations! What's come over you young people? You've taken leave of your senses. . . . George, can't you find another bottle of that Moselle? I'm parched."

"Let's have coffee," Sally said, rising from the table. She asked Kevin to make a fire in the library and led me back onto the verandah for a breath of air. The last afterglow of the sunset had long since disappeared. The night was cool and starless except on the western horizon. Pinpricks of light stabbed the darkness along the shores of distant islands. Half a dozen flashing buoys marked channels and navigational hazards, most of them still unknown to me by name at this time. A faint conical glow hung in the sky over Camden and another over Belfast. Below us, the sea surged onto the ledges of Ram's Horn and made deep sucking noises as it retreated.

"I can't abide politics," Sally remarked, and when I asked why, she said, "Inane remarks about things no one knows anything about . . . or if one person does, no one else is supposed to. Besides, nobody ever convinces anyone, do they? It's mostly ego building."

I laughed and said she should run for office.

"Wouldn't I just be the queen bee?"

"What's better than politics—as you call it—for general conversation?" I asked her.

"People. I could talk about people forever."

I said talk about people usually came down to gossip, and where was the gain in that.

"So gossip about people. It's more amusing than gossiping about politics."

A few minutes later she pressed my arm and said we should go in, George would be wondering. Again, the mystifying suggestion of some imagined liaison between us—or was it an invitation to one? She seemed to feel a need to assert it in any case, and I was mellowed enough by dinner to humor her. I squeezed her hand in response, and we joined the others in the library.

The library, Sally explained as we moved along an interior corridor with illuminated recesses for her pewter and China collection, was George's domain. It was a medium-size room paneled in cedar and lined with books and Currier and Ives prints. Most of the books were bound in sets, but one entire wall was filled with volumes grouped alphabetically by subject with appropriate shelf labels: ANTHROPOLOGY, BIRDS, FOREIGN RELATIONS, HERALDRY, ISLANDS, NAVAL HISTORY, and so forth. Current issues of a dozen or more contemporary magazines and journals, including several obscure ones, were lying about on various tables and settees. I was on the verge of asking George about his collection when Wylie, miraculously sobered and spoiling for further discussion, broke in.

"You're going to have to tell us where you come out on the Russians, old man. Are they bastards, or am I a liar? Did we win the war, or didn't we? Are things to go on as they were, or are we all to become Bolsheviks?"

I didn't try to answer Wylie right away. Mary Lou had followed us into the library with the coffee tray, and I was distracted momentarily by her arranging the cups, managing in the process to show a generous stretch of thigh to Kevin and me as she leaned over the low table. After she had left, hips again in motion, Gloria gave a passable imitation of her as she passed Kevin his coffee, but Kevin gave Gloria only a small smile. Finally, when we had settled ourselves, Wylie put his question to me again.

"You're about halfway between, us, age-wise. How do we put sense in these kids' heads?"

Well, I had, in fact been aware all evening of a generational confrontation going on. You couldn't miss it. I guessed it had been building up in both families since Kevin returned. George, I could feel, was watching me expectantly from the fireplace, and the others were silent, waiting for me to speak. Sally rolled her eyes upward in mock resignation and sank deeper into the sofa beside Kevin. I chose my words carefully, feeling very professorial. I said I couldn't presume to serve as arbiter between their generations without betraying my own, but a reasonable way to proceed might be to lay differences openly on the table. For instance, what did each of them expect from the war? That is, beyond defeating Germany and Japan. What were their hopes for the future? As, for instance, during the First World War many had argued it was to "make the world safe for democracy." War was necessarily destructive, intended to correct abuses, eliminate grievances, satiate vengeance. War could not of itself create anything lasting. But now that the war was over, what was to be created or re-created? In a word, what were their *values?* (Oh, I was ponderous enough for twenty Ph.D.s!)

"Values for what?" Kevin wanted to know. "Nations? Classes? . . . Individuals?"

"Say, start with people," I said, glancing at Sally.

"P-Plato would have started with people," George remarked.

"Whichever way, it's a capital idea," said Wylie. "It'll take all night, and George'll have to go down in his ruddy cellar and dig up *something.*"

"It won't take all night for me," Sally said. "About thirty seconds."

I said in that case we'd better start with her.

"Why not?" she said, sitting forward abruptly and clutching her knees. She thought a moment before speaking. "Well . . . security, first of all. You *have* to have security. That means an income. It doesn't matter where it comes from, so long as it's . . . well, honest. Not crooked, I mean. And a comfortable home—"

"Or two," said Kevin.

"Or two. Oh, I'm not worried like you young people about having too much money. I had much too little when I was your age. But I don't mean only material security. There should be security of one's privacy, too. I don't like people nosing around too much . . . though, I admit, I don't mind nosing around a little myself. And emotional security. A person shouldn't be torn apart by . . . by fears, worries, jealousies." She stopped. "That's about it. Isn't that thirty seconds?"

"What about other people's security while you enjoy yours?" Kevin asked.

"Oh, I want everyone to have security," Sally said. "I'm utterly generous on that score. Only . . . only how everyone gets it is their business. I just assume there's enough to go around."

Kevin was going to make some rejoinder, but I restrained him, acting as self-appointed moderator, and told Sally her statement seemed honest—if brief.

"Brief? Well, maybe I should have mentioned sex," she said, pulling her legs under her. "But I thought it would shock the young."

"I doubt it," said Kevin.

"It might shock George," Wylie said, leering.

"Nothing Sally does sh-shocks me," George said, and he gave her a kindly smile. It *was* a kindly smile—it was not perfunctory—and she returned it. I hadn't remarked any special communication between them before this, but the way they looked at each other told me that despite appearances—on Sally's part, that is—and despite the obvious differences in their tastes and personalities, there was empathy between them.

"Anyway, sex is important," Sally was saying. "In the proper setting . . . and quantity."

"Isn't it just another facet of your benighted security?" Kevin asked. "Security of the bedchamber?"

"Well, I hadn't thought of it quite—"

"Security of the bedchamber?" Lou Thatcher broke in. "That means security from being found out. That's not what Sally meant, is it, dear?"

"Kevin so often tells me what I mean," Sally said, not greatly caring one way or the other.

"Now, wait a minute," Kevin said, trying to do battle with both of them at once. "I didn't say anything about being found out. We're not talking about partners . . . or morals. It's been suggested that sexual gratification is an important aspect of a person's makeup. And I agree with this. I'm only arguing that the gratification is part of one's personal sense of security . . . well-being. Like having food and shelter and material things."

Lou, who had been frowning through this, said, "Kevin, how can you separate . . . well, sex and morals?"

"How *can* I?" Kevin said. "I don't have to, Lou. In most societies sex and morals are already separated."

"Not in most, Kevin," his father said.

"Well, in sophisticated societies like ours, they are."

I said into the silence that followed it was time we heard from a Thatcher, and proposed Gloria.

"Me?" she said, suddenly flustered and inadequate. "What should I say? . . . What's the question again?"

"What are your objectives, priorities?" I prompted her. "What do you want in life?"

"Golly! This is like a quiz. How am I supposed to know? . . . I mean, I haven't begun to live yet." She looked at Kevin for inspiration, then blushed and turned quickly toward Karen. Karen looked at her sympathetically but offered no help. I suggested she might try it the other way: What did she want *least*?

"That's even worse," Gloria said. "I'll try the other." She bit her lip and haltingly began. "Well, I guess I want children . . . I mean, a husband *then* children. That's obvious, isn't it? I mean, who doesn't want a family? . . . Then I want to travel. Somewhere beyond Pittsburg, Baltimore, and Maine. Jeepers, I haven't even been to Vermont!" She paused and bit her lip again. "Well, apart from all that, I guess I agree with Sally. . . . I mean, I'd like money enough to keep from starving."

I said I thought Sally meant more than that.

"Well, you know what I mean. Enough to be comfortable on, the way we are now."

"We're rich, Gloria," Kevin said. "Not just comfortable."

Wylie said, "Speak for yourself, m'boy. Another New Deal and we'll all be on relief."

"Is that it, Gloria?" I asked. "You want the same things, more or less, that Sally wants?"

"Well, just about. Except . . . well, I mean the last part."

"Sex?" Sally said. "You don't want it? Or you don't think it's important?"

"That's it." Gloria blushed again. "I don't think it's worth making a big fuss about. That's natural, isn't it? . . . I mean, at my age?"

"It's natural," Karen said—and the words, coming from this eighteen-year-old beauty, carried a certain authority. Karen had said little all evening. She sat now on a low Moroccan hassock by the fire, her long tanned legs alternately pulled up under her chin or stretched out in front of her. She had kicked off her sandals. Her dress, an elegantly simple white frock, was belted tightly at the waist and sleeveless. Karen had removed her cashmere sweater by the fire, baring arms as brown as her shapely legs. All in all, it was an act of discipline to keep your eyes off her.

I cast my eye about the room to see who might be next. "Shall we have all the ladies first?"

"That lets me out," Lou Thatcher said. Lou was given to hyperbole.

"Boasting again," said Wylie.

I glanced at Karen, and she said, "I pass. Honestly. I just like to listen." She actually smiled.

So Wylie said, "I'll go next . . . only George has to fix me a drink or I'll die of thirst."

George poured two Scotches from a cabinet in the corner and gave one to Wylie and the other, without asking her, to Sally. Kevin went to the kitchen for beer for himself and me. When he returned, Wylie was settled in his chair—cigar in one hand, drink in the other—and began.

"Well, everyone's been talking about people so far, and I mean to talk about the whole shebang. I'm a live-and-let-live type so far as individuals are concerned. Every man's sins are his own. But when it comes down to general principles for society as a whole, I'm a fundamentalist . . . and I'm not ashamed to admit it. Church, family, property, class, free enterprise . . . all the old-fashioned principles right down the line, that's what I stand for. Now, I'm not saying everything that comes out of this mix is going to look shiny and pretty. There are people, like some of the poor people on this island, who are poor beggars, and they'll probably stay that way. But as soon as you start messing around with the economy—say, with subsidies and handouts—you're headed for trouble. You can't balance a delicate economy like ours by robbing Peter to pay Paul."

Wylie went on to develop a conservative's standard justification of the capitalist system, with emphasis on the risks to healthy sectors of the economy if they were persistently called upon to help the weaker sectors—not to mention the alleged risk of demoralization of those who had to be helped. He persisted in using subsidies to the lobstering industry to illustrate his argument, even after I reminded him—as anyone might have—that lobstering was then entering a boom era and wasn't in the least in need of federal aid. This didn't affect the validity of his central argument, Wylie said, concerning the iniquities of handouts in general.

When Wylie had developed his ideas about as far as I thought he could and was beginning to repeat himself, Kevin said—calmly enough, but mincing no words, "These ideas are as old as the Industrial Revolution, Wylie. Isn't there some *social* philosophy that goes with your economic theory?"

"Social philosophy be damned!" Wylie answered sharply. "You wouldn't need social philosophy if you tended to your economics."

"That's almost neo-Marxian," Kevin said mildly.

"Is it now? Well, you'd be the authority on that." He took a long drink from his glass. "Anyway, let me get on. You'll have your turn, my young revolutionary." And he went on to extol the virtues of incentives—income differentials to guarantee initiative, the dynamic force of the free enterprise system. "Maybe God made men equal. I wouldn't know about that. But it hasn't worked out for 'em to stay that way." He acknowledged class and privilege, founded on wealth, to be necessary phenomena under capitalism. "You could call them the price of our prosperity and stability."

"Nice price if you're in the right class," Kevin remarked.

"Hush, Kevin," Sally said, laying a hand on his.

"Now, I admit," Wylie went on, ignoring Kevin, "that these privileges would be immoral if they were a right of birth, as they used to be—and still are in some parts of the world. But privileges in America are based on work. You earn them. George and I leave you young people something to get started on, but you've got to replenish it. Otherwise your inheritance runs out and you sink down on the economic and social scale. The Talbots and Grants and Lloyds overtake you, and that's exactly—"

"Cutlers, not Lloyds," Kevin corrected him tonelessly.

"Call 'em what you please," said Wylie, and he relit his cigar. George, who'd never earned a nickel in his life except his small wartime salary, stared fixedly at a shelf of books across the room.

"Well, to come back to the war, which is where all this started," Wylie went on, "the Allies won the war because the Americans were in it, and no number of Stalingrads and Molotov cocktails will persuade me otherwise. Stalin's as much our enemy as Hitler ever was. Even more, he's opposed to *every* one of those basic principles I mentioned: family, property, church, and so forth. Why mince words? If we don't move first, Stalin will. In ten years we'll all be cracking mussels for a living—like what's-his-name Leadbetter on the west shore."

Wylie stopped abruptly, and we sat in silence for several moments before Kevin spoke.

"So we move the Third Army to Moscow, I suppose?"

"Well, that's very generous of you, m'boy," Wylie said. "Myself, I'd go one step at a time. Say, first to the Elbe . . . where Georgie Patton should've gone anyway if he'd had any sense." He reached for the glass on the table beside him and inadvertently knocked it over. "Damn! George, look what I've done like an ass!"

"It's nothing," Sally said. "Leave it."

George took the glass and refilled it.

"Wylie doesn't believe *everything* he says," Lou Thatcher said apologetically while George was at the cupboard.

"Oh, yes, I do," Wylie contradicted her. "Every dam' word. 'N then some." He was getting that glazed look he'd had earlier.

When we'd settled down again, I turned to Kevin.

"This isn't a bad exercise," he said to me, running his hand through his hair. "But it takes a certain tact to carry it off. I expect if we were all completely candid, we'd hurt each other."

"Don't weasel out, boy," Wylie said. "We wanna know where you stand."

"Well, you might not. . . . For instance, those fundamentals of yours, Wylie, do you know I stand in opposition to every one of them? Except family, if family means no more than gut loyalty to nearest of kin. You know, it's interesting that the one fundamental I thought you'd mention and with which I could easily have agreed, you overlooked: free elections, free speech, free press—the whole business of democracy."

"Count me for it," Wylie said, waving his glass expressively.

"But it didn't occur to you to bring it up. Why? Presumably because you thought it less important than church and class and laissez-faire. Well, to me that's incredible. Czarist Russia had church and class and laissez-faire. How does your model differ from that?"

"You're the specialist on Russia, it 'pears. You tell me. . . . "

But that was as far as we got with our discussion that evening. Mary Lou came to the door of the library and said she was ready. Kevin rose to drive her home. Sally, anxious to keep her guests together, tried to put Mary Lou off a quarter of an hour, but George wouldn't hear of her waiting, and in the course of deciding who would drive her back it became apparent the party was breaking up. Wylie hastily drained his glass in the chair by the fire.

"Don't everyone go," Sally said. "It's the shank of the evening."

"Time for this *shank* to be rolling home," Lou Thatcher said, helping Wylie unsteadily to his feet.

I said I'd catch a ride downisland with Kevin. I had to be up early.

"Fine thing!" Sally said to me as we left the library. "Bare our innermost secrets, then leave everyone in the air. You were supposed to tie things up."

I said I'd work on the tie-up over the winter.

"I bet," she said. She went on to speak to Lou and Wylie, and I turned to Gloria, who was standing near me—a wary eye on Kevin as he disappeared toward the kitchen after Mary Lou.

"Come along," I said to her. "I'll show you my bungalow. . . . Bring Karen."

She looked at me uneasily, then a smile of comprehension slowly spread across her face. "You're really sweet," she said, and went back to the library to find Karen.

Outside, on the gravel driveway, I took Kevin aside and told him there'd been a change in plans; Gloria and Karen were coming along to inspect the bungalow. He stared at me with a slightly peevish look, and I stared back. Neither of us spoke, but we understood each other. Then he gave me a wry grin, tugged at his ear, and went around to open the door for Mary Lou. I turned back to say goodnight to the others.

"Wha's that college in Ohio again, old man?" Wylie asked, easing himself, with Lou's help, into the front seat of their 1938 Oldsmobile.

Indiana, not Ohio, I said, and told him again.

Lou said, as she closed his door and went around to the driver's side, "Put it on a postcard. It's the safest way."

The two girls came out of the house, and after a word with their parents, climbed into the backseat of the station wagon. Sally, sizing up the situation, said to me, "The little manipulator, aren't you? Someday try your hand on the rest of us."

I squeezed in beside the girls and we followed the Thatchers out of the drive. Mary Lou sat primly—and I thought a little sullenly—beside Kevin in front.

5

I apologized for the state of the bungalow as we felt our way down the path from the turnaround after dropping off Mary Lou. I had managed to stow most of my clothes, I said, but couldn't seem to make such headway on the dishes. And to confirm this, a mouse scampered away from the sink when I opened the door. I lit a kerosene lamp and stirred up the coals on the hearth, still warm from the afternoon. The girls studied the lights in the outer bay, orienting themselves, then sank into the sofa flanking Kevin. They watched the shadows dance on the exposed beams as I piled logs on the fresh blaze.

"I could live here," Karen said.

"Except that he does," said Gloria.

"I mean it's so . . . far away."

When I was satisfied with the fire, I asked if they'd have a glass of Calvados. It was all I had until I could get to Rockland the following week.

"What's Calvados?" Gloria asked.

I told her it was a liqueur fermented from apples, and Gloria said it sounded lethal.

Karen said, "In that case, we should try some."

"To be savoring one's first Calvados!" Kevin said.

I remarked that Kevin couldn't have savored it very often in a prison camp in Germany. He said his squadron had been based outside Cherbourg after D day.

Gloria said, "I hope we're not going to talk about the war again."

Well, that's how the conversation went, nice and easy. I brought out what was left of my Calvados, the gift of a friend recently returned from France, and found four jelly glasses to serve it in.

"It looks like water, doesn't it?" said Gloria.

"Just don't drink it as though it were," Kevin warned her.

Karen took a sip of hers. "Wow! It's pure fire, isn't it?" She took another sip, her eyes watering. "That's super!"

Kevin took out a pack of cigarettes, and Karen wanted one, though I'd noticed earlier she didn't smoke. Then Gloria asked for one.

"Might as well try everything," she said, choking on her first puff and spilling some of her Calvados.

"One sin at a time, Glowworm," said Kevin; it was apparently an old nickname between them, derived from her given name.

I settled into the leather chair next to the hearth and during the silence that followed, as they coped with their smokes and drinks, studied my young guests in a bemused way. They sat close together on the sofa, faces aglow from the reflection of the fire and eyes held by the flames enveloping a birch log, so they were unconscious for some minutes of my inspection.

They were an arresting trio by any measure, especially the brother and sister. Kevin, as I have said, was tall—like George—and he sat now, as he usually stood, with his shoulders thrust forward. His hair, still short from prison camp, was dark and thick. His deep-set dark eyes were alternately playful—like Sally's— and brooding. And that right ear! It stood straight out from his head like a wing, exaggerated by his other ear's lying flat against his skull from a mastoid opera- tion in childhood. His comical appearance was further emphasized as he now crossed his bad leg over his good so that it rose rigid into the air in front of him—as though he were punting a football into my rafters. But Kevin was no intentional comedian. I knew from the way he'd grappled with Wylie Thatcher's antiquated theories and from his quick, ironic smile that this was no idle dilet- tante. And I knew from the good-natured way he'd abandoned, for the moment, whatever designs he had on Mary Lou, in order to pour balm on Gloria's ache, that he wasn't heartless or merely frivolous. The evening, I guessed, didn't begin to give scope to the full breadth of his personality.

Karen, in contrast to Kevin, was predominantly somber. In this she took more after George than Sally, though in physical appearance she resembled her mother—only doing Sally one better. She had Sally's high cheekbones and finely molded features, but her coloring was fresher. She had Sally's wavy blond hair, but without the tinting, and her eyebrows were naturally darker. She had Sally's sensuous lips, even down to the same shade of ruby lipstick, but hers were the lips of an eighteen-year-old; Sally was over forty. Karen, meanwhile, had the firm high bust, the rounded hips and supple legs of a fully matured young woman.

But beauty is a difficult commodity to measure. It exists in the eyes of the beholder. I doubt whether judges at a beauty competition, if they threw away their measuring tapes, would be able to agree on what it was they were looking for. When I say Karen was beautiful, it will simply have to be accepted on faith. Sally's beauty was easy to take in because it was so much an extension of her personality. Belle's, I appreciated even then, was a reflection of her character. But Karen's beauty seemed something apart from her, the combination of features and form that made up her physical person and over which she had no con- trol—any more than a scarlet tanager controls its plumage. I think Karen would have worn a mask of plainness if she could—to achieve anonymity. I wondered idly, watching her, how she had coped with the mawkishness of transient GIs in bus stations and railway depots she must have passed through during the war. I knew from experience how a roomful of bored and lonely servicemen could suddenly become electrified by the passing of a pretty girl, who in a single instant could whet their appetites for a quick (and improbable) sexual adventure, at the same time managing to remind them of younger sisters and the girl next door in hometowns across the country. In all likelihood, Karen remained indifferent to any stir she caused—if, indeed, she noticed it—for her beauty was not a thing she cultivated or thought about.

But I found Karen's beauty even that first evening less remarkable than her inscrutability. She'd hardly spoken at Ram's Horn. And the few times she'd smiled, it was to herself, never with the rest of us. A private inner smile. Her reserve intrigued me. I might have thought her stupid if it wasn't so obvious she wasn't. She took everything in. She simply kept it to herself. She sat now, as she had all evening, motionless, expressionless, neutral, but wary. *Wary* was the word for Karen. I came suddenly on a red deer one day in a clearing above Jonah's Cove and thought of Karen. It had heard me approaching and stood frozen in position watching me. I stopped, and it stayed as it was for at least three minutes—until I breathed too deeply and broke the spell, and in a single bound it disappeared into a thicket, white tail bobbing. Karen was as inscrutable as that red deer.

Gloria was less interesting than the other two. Less interesting to me, anyway. She was more conventional, less given to doubts. The only child of parents a good deal less contrasting in personality and outlook than George and Sally Bannister, she tended to accept what Wylie and Lou prescribed as a natural, logical order. Oh, I'm sure she was shaken by Kevin since his return, with his nonconformist views on politics and foreign affairs. But instead of trying to understand these views and acknowledging them, right or wrong, as genuine, she seemed bent on retrieving Kevin from his nonconformity. It was the only way she could imagine him.

Fundamentally, she was insecure. You could see this in the way she watched Karen, which she did a great deal (mine weren't the only eyes, after all, drawn to Karen). It wasn't simply the look of intimacy exchanged between girls of a certain age, nor merely of adoration—though there was that, too, I suppose. It was the look of dependency. She looked the same way at Kevin. Their romance, I knew from various things said in passing during dinner, had blossomed midway through the war, before Kevin went overseas. Now, it was clear to anyone, the relationship had begun to weary Kevin. But Gloria had staked too much on this romance to let him go, and she was as possessive about him as a fishwife—as she demonstrated now, for instance, locking her fingers in his as soon as he put out his cigarette and had a hand free. Kevin absentmindedly thrust his hand into his pants pocket, taking her hand with it.

Kevin, aware at last that I'd been studying the three of them for some time, gave me another of his wry smiles and asked for my verdict.

Verdict on what? I asked.

"Now you've dined at both ends of the island, which end wins?"

"Does someone have to win?" I said he'd been playing at war too long.

"You're ratting," Kevin said. "Come on, give out. It'll strengthen our characters to hear the truth."

I asked if I was expected to compare Arthur Dacey with Kevin's father and Winifred with his mother; Lucy Talbot, say, with Lou Thatcher.

"That's the general idea. . . . Or Belle and Jingle with Karen and Gloria."

"Oh, don't compare me with Jingle," Gloria said. "She's much too smart."

I asked Kevin with whom I should compare *him,* and he said, still smirking, he was incomparable. In that case, I said, he should do the comparing, not I.

"And you'll correct me if I'm wrong, agreed?" Kevin was going to have his game one way or the other, so I nodded. He disengaged his hand from Gloria's to light another cigarette.

"Well, for one," he began, "we're more sophisticated, and they're wiser." I said nothing, and after a moment he went on. "We're more educated, and they know more. . . . We e-nun-ci-ate more clear-ly, and they make more sense." He paused again to study my reaction. "In a word, we're a bunch of crap, and they're the real McCoy."

"Oh, Kevin!" Gloria said, less in shock than disbelief.

"What are you trying to say, Kevin?" Karen asked.

"More or less what I just said," he went on, still smiling but persistent. "We're mainly ornamental. They—"

"Crap isn't ornamental," Karen said tonelessly.

"Okay. Vestigial, peripheral. *They* play a role. Their lives have a point."

I said, reaching for some balance, that he compared unfairly. Vacationers on a Maine island couldn't be expected to play the same role played by native islanders.

"It's the same wherever we are," Kevin replied. "In what way are our lives less ornamental in Bucks County? What do we contribute to . . . well, to anything?"

I asked how one measured contribution. Did a third-rate lobsterman contribute more or less to the course of progress than, say, a third-rate scholar? "Like me," I added quickly, lest he think I had George in mind, which I didn't.

"Kevin would say there's no such thing as a third-rate lobsterman," Gloria said.

"That's right, I might," Kevin agreed, lowering his left leg gently to the floor again. "At least it's irrelevant whether he's third-rate or not, because he's coping with a real world. He's facing real problems."

Karen said, again in her flat, dry voice, "The rest of us have no problems."

"Wise guy, eh?" Kevin said, and mussed up her hair; Karen left it as it was.

"Sure, we've got problems. Nearly everything we do, we make ourselves problems. I'm talking about problems that are already there, not made up. The real world."

I said I thought his distinctions were muddy.

"Say, is everyone being dense?" Kevin said, his good-natured banter now yielding to a note of irritation. "Or just picky?"

"Level with us once again," I said equitably, and poured out the last of the Calvados. "We'll try harder."

Kevin went on, now more deliberately, to develop his argument that the Ram Islanders lived a more fully integrated life than the rest of us as a result of their closer interaction with each other, with the environment, with the seasons, and with the weather. Even the least of the islanders left a mark on the life of the island in a way that Bannisters and Thatchers could never expect to on the life of their communities. I asked about Wylie Thatcher. Didn't his ball bearings leave some mark on the national economy?

"Don't bring Daddy into it," Gloria said. "Kevin sees red whenever Daddy's name comes up."

But Kevin conceded that Wylie Thatcher played a role. Not a critical one, perhaps—he didn't know what technological advances Wylie had made in his business—but a role nonetheless. Anyway, Kevin went on, he wasn't thinking of individuals but of their class as a whole. It was the *class* that was superfluous. He compared it to the Russian aristocracy in the nineteenth century—which lingered on, long after it had ceased to have any power of its own, to provide a convenient backdrop for czars who did have power.

"That's what we do, provide a backdrop for a modern army of entrepreneurs who run things. Now and then we put forth one of our brighties, like Wylie, to become a captain of industry in his own right, but for the most part we're happy being what we are—ornamental drones."

He had laid it on a bit thick—more, I think, to generate a response from the other two than because he attached much importance to his simple formula. It wasn't a time for heavy conversation, we seemed tacitly to agree.

Gloria said, "It's crazy, Kevin. To hear you, you'd think we all looked alike and acted alike and never had a different idea. . . . How did you get the way *you* are if we're all the same?"

"Good point," I said.

But Kevin wouldn't yield his belief that it was their class as a whole he was speaking of, not individuals in it.

"Classes exist in textbooks," Karen said. "There are only people. . . . Take Mummy."

I asked her what she meant, and she explained. Her grandfather—Sally's father—was an Irish policeman in Newark. Her grandmother ran a Swedish laundry. Sally, because she was beautiful (Karen said it as she would have noted the color of someone's bathing suit or the condition of one's teeth), went to New York to become a fashion model and married George. Her Aunt Hilda didn't, and she ran the laundry. "Where's the class there?"

Kevin had no better answer for Karen than he'd had for Gloria, but they kept up the desultory argument anyway for another quarter of an hour—until the two girls stifled yawns simultaneously and Kevin said it was time sleepy teenagers went to bed. They got up without protest and prepared to leave.

"Come again, ornaments," I said as they started up the path.

Kevin lingered a moment at the door, balancing on his cane.

"And now, *sir,* have I permission to—"

"Carry on," I said, returning his mock salute. I believe it was the last I ever gave.

6

Whken I returned from the store with groceries the next afternoon, I found Jingle Dacey washing two days of dishes in my sink.

"Don't get any ideas," she said. "Just my inherited sense of tidiness."

"Develop mine."

I put away the groceries and tried to help, but she sent me away to gather my laundry, which she *told* me—she didn't ask—she was taking home that afternoon.

"Thereafter every Tuesday, which is also bath day, Mum'll be expecting you for supper."

"I'm almost thirty-five," I reminded her.

"I've seen slobs at eighty. Go do's you're told."

She had already made my bed and cleared the bedroom. When I returned with a pillowcase full of dirty clothes, she was sweeping the kitchen.

"My char," I said, trying to catch her from behind. But she moved to the other side of the table and swung the broom over my head.

"I see you've had company," Jingle said a few moments later, emptying an ashtray that held the girls' lipstick-tinted cigarette butts from the night before. "Ruby gold, I'd say."

I said nothing, waiting for her to go on. "Aren't you curious?" I asked finally.

"You'll tell me in your own sweet time," Jingle said, and went on with her sweeping.

"Mary Lou Grant?" I proposed.

"Not her shade . . . also not your dish. Try me again."

I suggested Lou Thatcher.

"She'd never come unchaperoned."

"But there were *two* shades; didn't you see? Ruby and vermilion something-or-other."

"That lets out Sally Bannister. She'd never come chaperoned."

She swept a pile of dirt into the dustpan and started silently on the living room, playing the game her own way. I said at last if everyone else was eliminated, it must have been Karen and Gloria.

"Robbing the cradle," Jingle remarked.

"Some cradle!" I said. "I wonder where Kevin could have been . . ."

"Ah, Kevin," said Jingle, and she nodded approvingly.

I finally took the broom from her, saying enough was enough, and we walked out to the end of the cove over the granite slabs. She let me take her hand from time to time as we maneuvered around deep cuts in the shore. But she always let my hand go when the maneuver was over. She wasn't the hand-holding type . . . so what type was she? She certainly defied all categories of women I then knew. She had on the same oversized fisherman's sweater, baggy corduroy trousers, and knee-high boots she'd worn all week, items so shapeless that they perfectly obliterated any contours of her body. Wisps of dark hair protruded from a faded bandanna she'd tied over her head against the weather. As usual, she wore no makeup. In short, she made minimal concessions to femininity. And yet, despite this—or just possibly because of it—I found her captivating. And desirable.

Jingle's eyes were the controlling feature of her face. They were dark gray and alert, set in a spray of freckles across her cheeks. They missed nothing.

"Look at the turnstones," she said suddenly in the middle of a sentence, pointing ahead of us. "No, not on the rocks, numskull, on the mussel bed." I looked and saw nothing, until a wave rolled in and about fifty barnacle-encrusted mussels—or so it seemed—rose in unison and wheeled away across the cove, pink undersides flashing. But by then she was talking about something else.

Jingle was an uninhibited talker: I suppose some people might have thought she talked *too* much in those days, but her speech was too terse for anyone to call her garrulous. Short, usually pungent comments, that was her style. She meant to be funny, of course, and as a rule she succeeded. She certainly had a reputation on the island for her wit and already, at twenty-five, was the one most quoted when current anecdotes made the rounds. "D'ya hear what Jingle said when the slats rotted outa Zip Clayton's car and all his lobsters swam away? . . . 'If he'd fed 'em proper, they'd've fixed those slats 'emselves, kept any others

from comin' in.' " "Know what Jingle told Clara Grant th' day her panties got
blowed off the back line into the crow's nest in the old oak? . . . 'Clara, you
puttin' on a minstrel show up there, you gotta dress 'em better'n that.' " It was
too brisk a wit to have been nurtured on the island. It drew more from the
provincial main, I knew even then, than from offcoast folklore—the kind quoted
in well-meaning appreciations of Downeast by dilettantes who spent a season or
two compiling stories. But it mingled both. The vernacular, let's say, was pure
Rockland, or Portland, but the sense was of the islands.

The life of Ram Island moved in some measure around Jingle Dacey in that
period. Her comings and goings were marked, like the tides. When she used to
come regularly home from secretarial school in Portland before the war, or during the war somewhat less regularly from the Boston Navy Yard, the islanders
were seized by a certain buoyancy. When she left, there was a hesitation in the
island's pace, a momentary disorientation. She registered the pulse of the island
like a barometer. She knew everyone's troubles, from Widow Barnaby to the
youngest York. She was the natural confidante of every islander. During the first
week she was so open with me about my new neighbors that it was some time
before I appreciated how well she could keep a trust when she needed to,

As I say, many of these aspects of Jingle's character and personality I learned
later. For the moment, the afternoon we scrambled out across the granite slabs
to the end of Cutler's Cove, she was still my somewhat puzzling and often disquieting WAVE on her last home leave.

A damp fog that had stood off to the east all afternoon rolled in from the
open sea as we stood at the tip of the cove. When we were thoroughly chilled, we
returned to the bungalow, stirred up the fire and made tea. I said I'd have
offered her a drink if my guests hadn't finished off my supply the night before.

She shrugged her shoulders, pulling off her boots and stretching out on the
bearskin in front of the fire. "We need it less than you," she said. "Besides, it was
too scarce to count on during the war."

I asked where the logic lay in *their* needing it less than *we*. "And who's 'you'
and who's 'we'?"

"We're islanders. 'You' is everyone else. . . . That's a state you'll stay in forever." This wasn't the first time Jingle had made me aware of it, nor was it the last;
I think there was more defiance in her remark than prescription, for she
presently added, "Well, almost forever. A dozen winters might turn the trick. . . .
As to *logic*," she went on, "there isn't any. Logic would probably say we need
liquor more. Drown our troubles in booze."

I said she hadn't much faith in logic.

"Hmm," she said. "Maybe you're right . . . but don't drag me into a deep discussion. I draw a blank on philosophy." She rolled on the bearskin so she could

see me better in the leather chair. "How was Ram's Horn?" she said abruptly. "You haven't said much about it."

"You haven't asked."

"Oh, I'm supposed to ask, am I?" she said, eyes wide.

I told her I agreed with Belle that the house was superb, and I liked the people in it more than I had anticipated. The young especially. Jingle nodded.

"Did Sally make passes at you?"

"Let's say she showed affection appropriate to the occasion."

"Whatever that means . . . And how about Wylie? He drank himself silly, I suppose."

Silly, I said, part of the time, but he talked sense when he wanted to. I gave Jingle a brief account of our discussion in the library.

"George tried to keep the peace, I bet. Keep anyone from being upset."

I said, yes, he had been measured and restrained.

"And Sally only wanted to gossip."

"How do you know these things, Jingle?" I asked her. "You've never given them the time of day."

"Stanley," she said. "He knew them pretty well . . . and I was close to Stanley." She stared at me from the bearskin with so blank an expression I couldn't tell whether she was trying to let me know she'd had an early romance with her cousin—worse things had surely occurred on Ram Island—or was merely trying to impress upon me that Stanley had been no ordinary islander, which I already knew. It could have been both. "Anyway," she went on presently, rolling back onto her stomach and digging her toes into the soft fur, "it sounds like a lively debate. You won't have many like it out here. Talk like that takes a different sort of learning than ours."

I said I doubted whether discussions at dinner parties amounted to much, but Jingle seemed uninterested in pursuing our conversation about my evening at Ram's Horn and changed the subject. I made more tea, and we talked for another half hour or so before Jingle pulled on her boots and rose to leave.

"Will I find you here Thanksgiving?" she asked.

I said she would if I could keep the bungalow warm and dry.

"If not, move in with my folks. They'd welcome you."

We stood at the door looking at each other. I held her hand loosely in mine.

"Kiss me," I said on an impulse.

"Okay," she said in a matter-of-fact tone. "But it won't do us any good." She put her arm around my neck and kissed me squarely on the lips, eyes open. I slipped one arm around her waist under the gray sweater and pressed her close to me.

After a moment she tilted her head back to look at me. She said, "A week ago you could have been court-martialed for this."

"I'd have risked it," I said. "What do you mean, it won't do us any good?"

For answer she kissed me again, eyes still wide. When I felt her lips go soft, I began to work my tongue between her teeth—but she pushed me abruptly away and stepped back.

"That's enough," she said, but she was flushed and smiling. "I hadn't even planned that much."

"Plans, plans, plans."

"Disgusting, isn't it? See you Thanksgiving." She tossed the pillowcase of laundry over her shoulder and strode up the path through the spruces.

7

J ingle left on the mailboat Saturday morning, at the same time as the Bannisters and Thatchers. Clyde Grant ran Willy and the other servicemen over to Rockland early Sunday, in time for various trains and buses that would return them to duty before their furloughs ran out. Arthur Dacey took the high school children over on Monday morning with the week's catch. These multiple departures made the island seem comparatively deserted the following week. To mark the change, the mild weather ended and for three days a stubborn easterly storm pounded the seaward shore, keeping most people indoors. Gale warnings flew one day and small-craft warnings the other two. Only a few lobstermen ventured outside the harbor, and they soon returned. The *Laura Lee* canceled its midweek call because of high seas, which meant I had to put off my shopping trip to Rockland. During this period, you could walk the length of the island on the high road at almost any hour of the day, except the half hour after school let out, and meet no one. There was always some activity in the harbor, to be sure. A few lobstermen sculled back and forth from boat to shore between rain squalls, tending their gear. Half a dozen islanders could usually be found around the pickle barrels at Caleb's. But the normal pace of the island in most respects came to a halt.

I hadn't been cast so much on my own resources for some years and found the experience frankly sobering. The days were tolerable, walking high along the outer shore to watch the breakers and then returning drenched through to my fire and my books. But the evenings after an early smoldering dusk were long. The groaning of the horn at Ram's Head, at thirty-second intervals night and day, began to mesmerize my brain—though in clear weather I hardly noticed it. The last night of the storm, as I cleared the bungalow of smoke for the fifteenth time that day and tried to staunch a fresh leak over the bookshelves, I decided that island life out of season was not for me. Wylie Thatcher, much as I hated to admit it, was right after all. Only a native islander could put up with so much discomfort. But next morning, as I first stirred from a deep sleep, I was conscious of a strange brightness in the room and slowly realized it was the sun, rising clear and yellow over Isle au Haut, oblivious of any inconvenience its three-day holiday might have caused. The wind had backed to the north and the bay was already dotted with lobster boats bobbing on the whitecapped sea as the fishermen pulled their neglected traps. So my crisis passed. An extensive shopping trip in Rockland that same day made my decision to stay irrevocable. At least through the fall.

Belle Talbot and I were the only passengers on the *Laura Lee* that Saturday morning. I pause to describe Belle's departure because it was, in a certain way, an historic and emotion-charged moment in the life of the island and revealed the extraordinary affection the islanders had for this seventeen-year-old girl. She was on her way to Orono to begin her freshman year, and it had been her idea to leave alone rather than with her mother. Lucy was to visit her in a few weeks, when she was settled in.

Half the island came down to see Belle off. Caleb and Arthur Dacey wrestled the creaking wardrobe trunk down the narrow gangplank onto the deck. Jenny Brewster presented Belle with a basket of fruit and hard-rock candy tied with a huge red bow.

Belle, looking incredibly like a girl of fifty years before in a two-piece woolen traveling suit that fell three inches below her knees and a matching pancake hat, was wreathed in smiles. Her absurd hat, as she embraced each in turn, kept tilting back, held on only by the ribbon under her chin. The older women would gaze at her, then turn away to daub their eyes.

"Was there ever *anythin'* so pretty?" Jenny Brewster said, her arm around Winifred Dacey, and Winifred in turn had to dig into her pocketbook for a handkerchief.

Lucy stood erect and somber, watching her daughter go from neighbor to neighbor saying her good-byes. At the end, Belle came back to her mother, who was holding her coat and handbag.

"Oh, Mummy!" Belle said, and suddenly overcome, buried her head in Lucy's shoulder.

"There, there," said Lucy, rocking her child gently from side to side. After a moment she disengaged her arms and gently propelled Belle toward the *Laura Lee*.

Belle stood beside me on the afterdeck blinking away her tears and smiling again as we eased away from the pier. Horace Snow blew six blasts on the ship's whistle, and the children set up a cheer on shore. Horatio Leadbetter, who almost never noticed what was going on in the harbor, stood in his dory and shouted a farewell. Turk, back in the harbor for the occasion, had rigged two pumps on the stern of the *Sunrise* from which jets of seawater arced ten feet into the air in imitation of a New York fireboat. He circled at full throttle around and around the *Laura Lee*, blowing short blasts on his electric foghorn. When we passed the jetty, Widow Barnaby came forth from her shack as always. Belle stepped forward to the rail to wave, and the eccentric old lady, after a moment of hesitation, described a vague half circle with one arm, which could only be interpreted as a greeting.

"Golly!" said Horace Snow, who had been watching from the wheelhouse. "I ain't never seen her do that before."

A few minutes later, as we passed the red nun, Turk let out one long blast before going back to his traps on the northeast shore, and the *Laura Lee* headed up the bay toward Blueberry Isle.

That's all there was to it. In later years, as I saw Belle in many moods and many settings around the world, I thought often of her departure from Ram Island that September morning after the first storm of the season. She'd been away before, of course—not merely four years of high school in Rockland, but visits to Jingle in Boston and several to an aunt in New Hampshire. But this was a different sort of parting. She was the first islander in more than a decade, apart from her brother, to go off to college, and the first island girl ever. Obscure hopes were placed in her. She was the fulfillment of expectations the islanders couldn't articulate. If Jingle Dacey inspired the islanders' confidence, Belle was still their darling. Lucy had named her well. She was truly the island belle that day, leaving home to seek her fortune in the world. Belle herself seemed to sense, watching the island disappear behind us as we chatted inconsequentially, that this leaving was a landmark.

My shopping trip in Rockland produced a qualitative change in my style of life, for I brought back not only household goods in short supply on the island and building materials with which to repair the bungalow, but a wide assortment of items to indulge secondary needs: a shortwave receiver, for instance, over which I could pick up foreign broadcasts; a battery phonograph on which to play my record collection, en route from storage in my sister's attic; two powerful Aladdin lamps so that I could read at night without risking my eyesight; and, surely not least of my purchases, several cases of bonded bourbon, assorted liqueurs, and the first wines imported from France since the war. Caleb Brewster, helping me unload these last items from the *Laura Lee*, asked if I was "fixin' to set up a casino at Cutler's Cove." He drove me down with my stores, and after we had the better part of them under cover, we opened a bottle of

Kentucky mash to mark the occasion. Caleb mellowed over the second tumbler-
ful, and as he left, he said, as one storekeeper to another, "Mind you keep 'em
stowed well."

My days now fell into a pattern. I usually rose at daybreak, laid a fire, and
made breakfast while the bungalow was heating up, then read or wrote until
noon. I did my housework after lunch, and in the afternoon took long leisurely
walks about the island, usually stopping at Caleb's for groceries or my mail—or
for a half hour's conversation with whomever I found there. I was home by six
to prepare my dinner, which I did in leisurely fashion—over my bourbon and
using recipes selected from half a dozen foreign cookbooks. I was something of
a gourmet in those postwar years. The evenings passed quickly with distractions
adjusted to my mood (except, of course, the distraction of female society). If
menacing weather outside threatened the atmosphere within, there were potions
in my larder strong enough to dispel any gloom. I was regularly in bed by ten, in
time for the last news roundup, a habit from the war.

Tuesdays, as Jingle had ordered, I dutifully bathed at the Daceys' and stayed
on for supper. Occasionally I dined with Lucy Talbot, and now and then, after
dropping in at the Peaks, I stayed to supper with Turk and Sharon. I had trouble,
however, persuading my friends to reciprocate. They refused my invitations to
dinner so many times, on one pretext or another, that I finally appealed to
Jingle, with whom I was, of course, in correspondence, for the reason. "You
knucklehead," she wrote back with her usual reserve. "You try to take a Maine
island like you used to take a Japanese naval fortification in the Pacific—by
direct assault. Don't you know we've never been liberated? We still live in the age
of the common man. Roughly translated, that means no one accepts a stranger's
hospitality unless we *all* accept it. You're the stranger, bub. Ask the whole island,
and I'll guarantee you a party you'll remember for years—and you won't have to
worry anymore about hiding that bourbon. But ask Daceys, Talbots, and
Jenkinses without Grants, Cutlers, and Yorks, and you'll have a small civil war on
your hands." She ended the letter by suggesting that when she and Belle were
back at Christmas, if I still wanted my "exclusive little dinner party," they might
be able to do something about it, which indicated to me she thought better of
the idea than she let on.

It was a different matter, of course, for my neighbors to drop in informally
at Cutler's Cove, and I had half a dozen callers a week—not counting the children, who were likely to show up any time they weren't in school. In fact, all my
callers came at such unpredictable times of day that after being surprised once
or twice in my underwear, my normal attire in the forenoon, I took to dressing
fully when I arose and making the bungalow presentable. Like any good island
housekeeper, I kept a pot of coffee on the back of the stove against all contin-

gencies.

Jesse Cutler continued to bring me a pie every week or ten days, sometimes coming with Lucille—who, as Jingle had predicted, was being kept home "sick" that fall. Winifred Dacey brought back my laundry on Thursday, and I made special efforts that day to tidy up. If I hadn't passed by the store for a day or so, Jenny Brewster, when her arthritis wasn't troubling her, walked the mile and a quarter from the harbor to bring me my mail and see how I was making out. Lucy Talbot was my most regular caller, dropping in once or twice a week. She was also my easiest guest. Sometimes we would talk over our coffee for half a morning, usually about the history of Ram Island. She knew the genealogy of every family and the history of every building, past and present. She showed a fine precision of detail, combined with a vivid imagination, about how life had been. She brought along early photographs and prints showing the harbor crowded with pinkies and coastal schooners seventy-five or eighty years before. Other days, once she was assured I welcomed her company, she would sit quietly with her needlepoint while I worked, occasionally glancing at me over the top of her gold spectacles. Then as silently as she had sat, she would roll up her work and rise to leave. She was always solemn, always reserved, always just. I never heard Lucy Talbot say an unkind word about any islander.

My daily routine was interrupted for a week in late October when Harold Toothacher was finally free to do the long-delayed work I had planned on the bungalow. He was once a ship's carpenter but over the years had acquired skill in all the arts and spells that keep island homes intact. Inevitably he was in great demand, the Bannisters and Thatchers naturally claiming the greater portion of his time—and providing by far the largest share of his income—for projects at Ram's Horn and Northeast Cove. Harold was a lifelong bachelor. He lived in a cabin beyond the pier, his yard piled high with odd pieces of lumber and discarded engines, plumbing systems, and other scraps he hoped someday to put back to use. Wylie Thatcher, Caleb told me, had once offered to pay for having Harold's junk pile moved behind his shack, where it would be less of an eyesore from the harbor, but Harold, far from taking up Wylie's offer, managed to accumulate even more useless bits and pieces in his yard by the following season. He moved himself and his equipment from job to job in an antiquated Model A truck, which had years ago lost its muffler and could be heard over a good part of the island. Harold addressed male and female impartially as "deah," a habit of many older Downeasters.

"Well, deah," he said the morning he arrived, as we walked about the bungalow studying its faults. "Where'd we best begin? . . . I'd say the chimbley, so's we won't git smoked out when we move inside." I agreed.

We climbed onto the roof, and the day being unseasonably warm, we made good progress. Harold stripped down the loose stones above the ridgeline and fixed a new flashing before remortaring the stones back in place. He added six inches for better draft with stones I found along the shore. Meanwhile, I replaced rotted-out shingles under his supervision. By the end of the afternoon, as the sun dropped over the Head, we had finished the roof and "chimbley" and surveyed our work with satisfaction.

"She's stood up purty good, all considered," Harold said. "Twenty-one years since we put 'er up. She'll last that agin . . . and that'll beat me."

The following morning there was a cold drizzle, and for the next two days we worked inside on cabinets, bookcases, and other small improvements I had designed. By the end of the week we were able to get outside again to rebuild and seal the fallen foundation. On Saturday we rebuilt the outhouse, after a brief debate on where it should be located: Harold wanted it in a clump of new spruce on the north side of the bungalow; I insisted on it remaining where it was—with its magnificent view of Isle au Haut. And there was bitter irony in my insistence, as I was later to discover.

My neighbors were presented to me in a harsher light through the eyes of Harold Toothacher. I doubt if Harold thought as badly as he let on about so many of them, but he had a gossip's instinct and a malicious tongue, and the combination was libelous. I gave him small encouragement, after an innocent question or two the first day, but this made no difference to Harold. He managed to give full rein to his venom whether I encouraged him or not—or whether I even listened.

His estimate of the Bannisters and Thatchers was predictable. Most of what he had to say about them I had heard before. Sally's alleged availability to all men, with the usual absence of detail. George's ineffectiveness as a man and husband, and his unproductive life. Wylie Thatcher's arrogance and drinking habits, exaggerated out of all proportion to their reality. Lou's airs. Harold thought better of Kevin and the two girls but expected them to take after their parents in due course. "Give 'em time to show their stripes, deah," he said.

But it was Harold's view of his fellow islanders that jolted me most. Reputations I thought firmly established everywhere were vulnerable before Harold Toothacher. Caleb Brewster, for instance. I mentioned at one point that Caleb had trucked out most of my gear, and Harold remarked, "Bet that cost ya a pretty penny." I said I hadn't noticed it on the accounts, and he said, "That's the last place I'd look for it. It'll show up on yer taters 'n onions come winter. You'll see. . . . Ain't a tighter man with a dollar 'n Caleb Brewster."

Harold unearthed for me an ancient family feud I hadn't yet heard about—between Grants and Cutlers. It dated back to a boundary dispute fifty years ear-

lier over the pasture lands above the Gut. The boundary issue itself had been
settled in court years before, but the rivalry, according to Harold, had lingered
on. I said I doubted a little dispute over a pasture would keep two families apart
for half a century.

"Don't you b'lieve it," Harold contradicted me, and he lowered his voice,
though no one was within a quarter of a mile of us. "When Willy Grant was
home last month, know what I see'd 'im do? I seed Willy pull six traps in a row
off Ram's Horn. . . . Now who d'you s'pose's got traps off Ram's Horn? Ain't
been nobody but Lloyd Cutler's had traps there for ten years."

Harold himself professed to be neutral in the feud—and I suppose he *was*
neutral in the sense that he had no good word for the members of either family.

"Now Clyde's a very soci'ble fellar to meet at the store. I'm fit to die laughin'
listenin' to Clyde Grant's jokes. But I tell ya, he's just 'bout the meanest lobsterman there is. He don't think nothin' of snarlin' up any traps he finds within fifty
feet of his'n. . . . As to Lloyd Cutler, hear him talk, you'd think he was Preacher
Hargrave hisself. But where was Lloyd, deah, when his own daughter was gittin'
herself fetched up over to Rockland?"

I had expected Harold to come around eventually to Lucille's condition—
which by now was altogether obvious to all of us—and not caring to hear his
homilies on teenage morals, on and off the island, I took myself out of earshot.

The Talbots and Daceys, I had imagined, might escape Harold's grim perspective, since they were surely above family feuds and restrained in their relations with other islanders. But Harold found other failings for them. Their
wealth, in particular—or, as he would have it, their greed.

"How d'ya think Frank Talbot made his fortune, rest his soul?" Harold asked
one day, poking his head out from the plumbing under the sink. "Some of it,
sure 'nough, runnin' the blockade in Pro'bition. Nobody ever's goin' to hold that
'gainst him. But there war'n't enough in that to keep two boats and six dories, all
the while he was plantin' ten acres o' corn, grazin' fifty sheep on Little Ram, and
milkin' twenty cows. Till he took to bed with rheum'tism."

I pointed out that some of these activities must have been profitable, or
Frank Talbot wouldn't have engaged in them.

"Don't you b'lieve it, deah," Harold went on, eschewing logic. "What he put
into his sheep 'n cows 'n corn 'n everythin' else come straight out of the lobstermen's pockets. Frank Talbot never pulled a trap after he was fifty-five, but he
made more'n the rest of 'em put together sellin' their lobsters in Rockland. . . .
Now Arthur Dacey's runnin' the car, and he's doin' the same thing. He'll be as
rich as Frank Talbot ever was, if he ain't already."

I had already learned enough about the lobstering industry to know that no
buyer could stay in business if he didn't give the lobstermen going prices for

their catch, but arguing with Harold was a futile exercise. I would have changed the subject—since silence was impossible with Harold once he'd started talking—but he was already on to Stanley Talbot. And even that sacred reputation was not immune from Harold Toothacher's acid tongue.

"I'll own he was an awful sweet ballplayer," Harold judiciously observed. "We never had a better club 'n when Stanley Talbot played. . . . But that boy was a woman chaser from the time he stopped peein' in his britches. If he hadn't drownded hisself when he did, he'd 'a fetched up every girl on the island."

I remarked sarcastically that I hadn't realized there were so many girls his age to fall victim.

"What's age to do with it, deah? I guess he had Sally Bannister 's often 's he wanted her, didn't he?" I professed ignorance of it, and making a quick calculation of the difference in their ages, thought it unlikely. But I didn't press the point.

Jingle and Belle, at least, were above reproach in Harold's eyes. "Talks a mite too much for my taste," he said of Jingle—and coming from Harold, this was ironic. "But she's a good heart." As for Belle, tears welled up in the old man's eyes when he spoke of her. "Ain't she the darlin' though? . . . She's got even prettier 'n her grandma." Beauty must have had a benign effect on Harold, for I remembered now that in his catalog of greedy islanders he had omitted Belle's notorious grandmother, who managed in the years immediately after her husband's death to acquire half the island's shores and three quarters of the island's wealth—in her relentless drive for independence, Lucy told me.

But I was glad to be rid of Harold's company when the week was up. If there were skeletons in the island closets, I preferred to learn of them in my own way, rather than through the jaundiced eyes of Harold Toothacher.

8

Turk took me out with him one morning early in November, as he had promised. In fact, I had been reminding him about this promise for some weeks. ever since Harold Toothacher and I had finished the repairs on the bungalow. I knew the sea well enough from the decks of carriers and battleships, but I'd never had the intimate experience of it in a small boat. Moreover, I considered this part of my education with respect to the islanders. I had them placed in my mind now as *islanders,* but still had little feel for the profession that provided their livelihood. So I went out with Turk to learn.

I was up before daybreak, and after a quick breakfast walked to the harbor carrying my oilskins. There was a light frost, the first of the year. The weather

vane on the church showed the wind in the west, and from the feel of it in my
face as I dropped down to the harbor, I guessed it to be about twenty knots. The
seas were still moderately high from an easterly blow two days before.

Turk was already aboard the *Sunrise,* engine running. He cast off from his
mooring when he saw me and picked me up at the pier. I pulled on my oilskins
as we headed into the chop at the mouth of the harbor. A few lobstermen had
already gone out, but most of the fleet was still behind us. We kept close to the
shore around Ram's Horn and out to a five-fathom shoal off the northeast tip.
The Bannisters' "cottage" rose imposingly above us as we passed, its cantilevered
verandah bare of furniture and awnings, the two large windows flanking the
chimney boarded up against winter gales. Turk studied the east wing of the
house for a moment through binoculars. "Shutter loose," he said briefly.

I asked if he were caretaker as well as lobsterman, and he shrugged. "I keep
an eye out for George."

Five minutes later we came to several rows of brightly colored floats strain-
ing against the tide above the shoal. Turk's were blue and yellow, and he went
straight to work. He cut speed as he gaffed the line between the first float and its
toggle, hooking the warp over the davit that swung out from the open side of his
wheelhouse and simultaneously putting the *Sunrise* in starboard helm to keep
the warp away from the propeller. He wound the line twice around a hoist driv-
en off the engine—the niggerhead, he said it was called. Why, I wanted to know,
was it called a niggerhead? He said he guessed it was because it was supposed to
look like one. I said I'd never seen a Negro's head that shape, an elongated shaft
with a lip on the end to keep the warp from sliding off.

"Come to think on't, I ain't neither," Turk said, watching the line come in
cleanly and fall in coils at his feet. "Guess if we was niggers, we'd call it somethin'
else—like dagohead. . . . But we ain't," he concluded cryptically as he turned to
his trap, now angling into view beneath the surface festooned with kelp. He disengaged the niggerhead before the crate reached the davit, then swung it neatly
onto the washrail, where he balanced it with one gloved hand while clearing
away the kelp and clinging sea urchins with the other. Inside the trap, after he'd
uncleated the soggy twine that held the door shut, there were more sea urchins,
half a dozen crabs, three or four starfish, and a spiny unappetizing fish that
looked as though it had never left the muck of the ocean floor. And, to be sure, a
few lobsters. Three were shorts and went immediately back into the sea along
with the crabs and starfish. One, which Turk tossed into a barrel behind him,
was clearly legal size, and another, which was questionable, he measured from
the eye socket to the end of the shell with a gauge hanging above his head. Three
and one eighth inches. It passed and joined its companion in the barrel. Turk
shook the remaining crustaceans free by banging the crate several times sharply

on the washrail, rebaited the trap with a prepared bait bag from a keg next to him, and heaved the trap into the sea, standing clear of the hissing warp as it uncoiled. The *Sunrise* had meanwhile completed its circle and was headed toward the next float in his string.

Well, I watched Turk pull a hundred and fifty traps that morning, and the anticipation of what he'd find inside, as he swung the trap onto the washrail, was as great with the last as with the first. Except that he showed no emotion. His expression was the same after he'd pulled his eighth pot in succession without finding a single legal lobster as it was when he found four two-pounders in the ninth. He averaged, on the whole, one per trap. Once he found a good-size cunner, which he cleaned and set aside for lunch. Turk worked steadily and methodically. He was constantly busy as he moved down a line of traps, tying a fresh bait bag to keep ahead or pegging the claws of the lobsters in his barrel during the short run between pots. But he gave the impression of being unhurried. Unlike Willy Grant, for instance.

Willy had the reputation of being able to clear a trap faster than anyone else on the island, and I saw him give a demonstration of it in the harbor one Saturday morning in September before his furlough was up. He was pulling his half dozen pots inside the jetty—from his open skiff with its reconditioned outboard—and chose a time when he had an appreciative audience, mainly the high school students just arriving on the mailboat. Willy would race up to a float, feet planted wide in the bottom of his skiff, oilskins flapping, and seize the line even before cutting speed. Then he'd haul in his trap over a makeshift davit like you'd haul in a buddy going down for the third time. He'd rest the trap on the gunwale and, arms flapping like a windmill, spew forth the contents in all directions. He'd rebait in a single motion, arc the trap into the harbor, and would be racing on to the next pot before the warp had cleared. He was clocked at fifty-two seconds for one of the traps. It was a bizarre ballet to behold—but was it lobstering? Arthur Dacey, with whom I was watching the spectacle from the pier, said laconically, "Seems from here Willy's throwing out as many good lobsters 's he's taking in."

Turk's style, in any case, was the reverse of Willy's. Deliberate and unrushed. Why hurry? He spoke little as he worked. He answered my questions, but tersely. He volunteered nothing. Silence was Turk's milieu—at least what silence he could find above the idling motor. There was little enough when the *Sunrise* moved between pots at full throttle. There was a radio in Turk's cuddy, but unlike the other lobstermen—who kept their radios at peak volume while they worked—he turned his on only once that morning, for a weather report. This was Turk's element, it was easy to see. He and the *Sunrise* were one with the sea and the rocky shores and reefs around us. Ashore, his silence could be mistaken for uncertainty, indecision. Here it was authority. Ashore, his lumbering gait seemed hesitant, ungainly. Here his movements were natural to a heaving deck. And another thing. Where most of us compensate for a rolling sea by shifting our position to keep upright, Turk, braced against the jam of his wheelhouse, rolled with his boat.

When Turk had finished pulling the traps at the five-fathom shoal, we headed westerly toward Seal Ledge, and the wind and seas increased as we came out from under the island. Waves broke occasionally over the bow and froze into slush on the wheelhouse window. Turk flicked on the electric wiper. We stood close in under the overhang out of the spray, peering ahead through the streaked window. The heat from the engine gave off a feeble warmth we could feel through our oilskins. Sky and sea met in an even slate gray, the only horizon marked by a few distant islands and breaking reefs.

Turk had out several experimental traps at a fifteen-fathom shoal halfway between Ram Island and the ledges and was pulling them when Clyde Grant passed near us. Clyde came over to talk, pulling the *Clarissa B* alongside. He cut his engine, and Turk did the same. The two boats rose and fell together on the swells, occasionally nudging each other.

"Coffee, Clyde?"

"Don't mind 'f I do."

Turk poured the coffee, already sweetened, from a thermos in the cuddy and passed around a bag of fresh doughnuts.

"Sharon's treatin' you right, boy." Clyde relit his cigar. He was an ox of a lobsterman, six feet tall and weighing two hundred and fifty pounds or more. He was reputedly the strongest man on the island and had once lifted a loaded dory off a reef where it had stuck on a falling tide. His face, always pink, was now crimson against his yellow oilskins. Like Turk, he was hatless despite the cold, his mat of red hair giving all the head cover he needed.

"Turk," Clyde said, "you been gettin' anythin' at the ledges?"

"Dozen or so," Turk replied. "We ain't been there yet today."

"I'm goddamned 'f I've had a dozen in the last two weeks. I ain't never seen so few lobsters out there."

"They're startin' to crawl, Clyde. The weather's changin'."

Clyde said nothing immediately, and I asked *where* they crawled.

"Off'n the ledges anyway," Turk said. "Into the mud. Out to sea. . . . Ask Clyde. He knows all the secrets about where lobsters go in the winter."

"If you asks me, they go straight into the crates of those bastard Orcutts 'n Hopewells. And they don't go without a little help." Turk said nothing to this, and Clyde went on after a moment, his face redder than ever. "No, Turk, I've had 'bout all I'm gonna take from those sons o' bitches. Another season like this out there . . ."

We didn't hear the end of his sentence, for a large swell bumped the two boats together, and the force of it drifted us apart. Clyde tossed his coffee mug across the gap between the two boats and went on his way. Turk turned back to the last of his pots over the shoal.

As we crossed the last stretch of water to the ledges, I told Turk about Harold Toothacher's account of the feud between the Grants and the Cutlers and asked if there was any truth in it.

"Harold's stories're a mile wide," he said for reply, and took down the binoculars to study a line of lobster pots near two black cans to starboard. Then he added, as an afterthought, "Yeah, there's some bad blood left there, but th' less said about it, th' better. Clyde's got somethin' else to worry 'bout now. . . ." He swung the *Sunrise* closer to the nearest black can and took another look at the lobster pots. "Clyde's more comf'table when he's mad at somethin'," Turk said with a grin as he put the binoculars back on the shelf.

Ten minutes later we came up to Seal Ledge, a more desolate outcropping in November than I had imagined when I first saw it from the *Laura Lee* in September. It was about an acre in size at high water and surrounded on all sides by reefs and boulders stretching one to two hundred yards from its shores. You could land a small boat, I suppose, on the popplestone beach on the side facing us—but who would bother? The island was completely bare except for clumps of withered grass in crevices and three skeletonlike spruce trees denuded of their greenery by nesting seabirds. Cormorants were perched in rows along a shelf of gray rock, wings spread to the wind to dry. At the far end of the island gulls circled over a solitary lobster boat, swooping down on the discard when a trap was cleared.

I remarked that it seemed a useless island, and Turk said promptly that they hadn't thought so when they were thirteen. "We used to come huntin' gulls' eggs. Me and Stanley and Elmer Brewster . . . when we could get Elmer into a boat." He swung the *Sunrise* toward the first blue-and-yellow float. After he had cleared it, and as we headed toward the next trap, he said, "We was goin' to build a dance hall here."

"A dance hall!"

"Only island we could think of nobody owned," Turk said. He broke into a broad grin. "Also . . . it seemed the easiest way to get us some women."

I said he'd had pretty advanced ideas at thirteen.

"We grow'd up early," Turk said. He hauled and cleared another trap, taking in two full-size lobsters. "Once we brought Jingle 'n Sharon out here," he went on. "Only we caught hell for it 'cause we didn't tell anybody where we was, and it come up foggy."

I recognized the episode from a more detailed account of it Jingle had given me: five hours wandering about in a rising sea until Turk recognized a string of his father's pots off the Graves and brought them into harbor just before dark.

Halfway down Turk's string of pots we passed the other lobsterman, a Thorn Islander who looked familiar. Turk waved, but the Thorn Islander made no response except to stir up a large wake as Turk was clearing his next trap. Turk said nothing until he heaved the trap back into the sea.

"Dander up, I guess," he said placidly.

After Turk had added thirty lobsters to his catch from half as many traps, I said I had to think Clyde Grant wasn't as good a fisherman as he was. Clyde must have his string on the wrong side of the ledges, I guessed.

Turk merely said, "Clyde's the best there is," and went on stuffing a fresh bait bag with his spudger.

As we approached the end of the string of pots off the ledges, a gray power-boat with a tall aerial came around the south end of Seal Island and pulled abreast of us. A man in a fur-lined jacket and matching hat stepped out of the enclosed wheelhouse and signaled to Turk. Turk finished clearing the trap he had on the rail and switched off his engine.

"Morning, Turk," the man called across to us through a megaphone. "Who've you got aboard?"

Turk introduced me and told me this was the warden, Cliff Dawson, from Belfast. The warden waved a greeting

"How's things, Turk? . . . No troubles?"

"None worth botherin' with."

"Who was that out here half an hour ago?"

"Barney Orcutt. Sam's boy." Suddenly I remembered why he had looked familiar—he was the sergeant on the *Laura Lee* the day I arrived.

"He's out of th' service, is he?" the warden asked.

" 'Bout ten days now."

"What's he usin' for a boat?" He spoke with short vowels, like a true Downeaster.

"Clarence Darling's, just now," Turk said. "He's ordered a new one in Camden."

The warden nodded and looked around him at the thickening weather and leaden sky. They were silent a moment as the two boats slowly rose and fell on the shoaling sea. Voices cackled indistinctly from the shortwave receiver in the warden's cabin.

"Well . . . everything all right, Turk?" Cliff Dawson called across, using his megaphone again.

"There's a tangle at Three Fathom Ledge," Turk said, waving a hand toward the two black cans. "I didn't go close enough to make it out."

"Three Fathom? Clyde Grant has traps there, don't he?"

" 'Less he moved 'em this week. He was fixin' to."

"Who else fishes Three Fathom?"

"Well . . . Will Hopewell sometimes."

"He's yellow on white, ain't he?"

"Yellow and gray," Turk said.

"Much obliged, Turk. I'll have a look." The warden considered a moment, then waved his hand before stepping back into his wheelhouse. The patrol craft circled off at fifteen knots toward Three Fathom Ledge, leaving a long sleek wake behind it.

Turk pulled his last traps off the ledges, and we headed back across the bay toward Ram's Head. The sea was calmer on the return trip, but the overcast had lowered, and it was growing colder.

"It'll snow some," said Turk, looking up at the dense sky.

By the time we reached Great Popplestone Ledge, a quarter of a mile off the Head inside the gong, the islands to the west were disappearing from view one by one. Turk pulled his traps quickly, glancing occasionally at the advancing snow squalls. The first one enveloped us before Turk reached the end of his string. Rudolf York was near us in the *Annabelle* when it struck. Turk hailed him, and they both switched off their engines.

"How many more you got, Rudolf?" Turk asked.

"Seven or eight," said Rudolf.

Turk nodded and turned his engine on again.

"Rudolf sometimes loses his bearin's," Turk said when we were out of earshot. And indeed, I remembered hearing that Rudolf York had lost himself twice that season in fog and had to spend the night anchored off some lee shore waiting for the weather to lift. I asked why Rudolf didn't have a chart, then remembered I hadn't seen one aboard the *Sunrise.*

"What about you? Don't you carry a chart?"

"We got charts," Turk said—and he grinned again, like a boy might when his maiden aunt pesters him about forgetting his galoshes. "Mine're in the cuddy somewheres, under the bench. Rudolf'll have some charts too . . . but that don't say he'll use 'em to plot a course. We don't none of us pay much notice of charts."

I asked how they found their way in fog without charts.

"Tide rips. Surf on a ledge or a rocky shore. Sometimes the sheep on Little Ram . . . that's when we're close in. If it's a run, like in from the ledges, we got the compass."

"But what bearings if you don't use a chart?"

"Well, we just learn 'em, I guess. It's five degrees off north from the bell out here to the middle of the Gut. So from where we are now, it'd be 'bout ten degrees off, give or take a few points for tide. The tide's goin', so we take a few. . . . Like I said, it's not like running a battleship."

Turk had pulled his last trap and was circling slowly, keeping the *Annabelle* in sight.

"Trouble with Rudolf," he said, "he's as likely to go west as north. . . . He's gettin' on."

Rudolf waved as he heaved his last trap overboard, and Turk swung the *Sunrise* onto a 352-degree course, the *Annabelle* trailing behind. Another squall hit us, thicker than the first, and Turk cut his speed. In ten minutes we picked up a string of lobster pots. Turk shifted his course slightly, and five minutes later the osprey nest at the head of the Gut came into view off our starboard bow. We eased our way around the Nose in another squall and into harbor.

Turk brought the *Sunrise* alongside the lobster car and left his catch with Arthur Dacey. One hundred and ninety-three pounds, Arthur weighed it on his scales before emptying the crate into one of the compartments under the platform.

"Not bad," Arthur said, "for November. . . . Cash or credit?"

Turk said credit, and Arthur calculated in his ledger. "That's two seventy-seven and a quarter owin' you, Turk. You're a rich man, and I must be a poor one."

Turk said, "Tell it to th' tax collector."

They passed the time of day before Turk started to cast off. It was not yet one o'clock. The snow in the harbor was falling straight down now, melting everywhere as it landed.

"Mailboat make it?" Turk asked.

"Horace got 's far as Thorn, then radioed it was thickenin'."

"Anyone aboard?"

"Jessica York. Leonard went over to fetch her. He got in about a half hour ago."

They were silent for a few moments. "Clyde's still out," Turk said, letting the line go.

Arthur nodded and glanced at his watch. "He'd be at the Shoals, I reckon."

"Or Three Fathom Ledge."

Turk started his engine, and we circled slowly to his mooring. He cleaned up his gear, unhurried. When the decks and washrail were swabbed down and the lines coiled, he sat on a crate and fixed bait bags, occasionally glancing toward the mouth of the harbor. The snow continued to fall. At one-thirty Clyde Grant came in and went straight to his mooring. A few minutes later Turk stood and pulled off his oilskins.

"Let's get Sharon to fry up that cunner," he said.

The early November snow squalls did not mark the beginning of winter, but a northeaster during Thanksgiving week did. The mailboat made it to the island on Wednesday—with the turkeys and a few of the high school students who could get away early—but that was the last ferry until the following Monday. Jingle and Belle, planning to come over on a special run of the *Laura Lee* for off-islanders on Thanksgiving morning, were stranded in Rockland. Turk toyed with the idea of running over to pick them up in the *Sunrise* but thought better of it when gale warnings were displayed along the entire coast from Eastport to Cape Hatteras. Besides, Winifred Dacey wouldn't hear of the girls coming out in that kind of weather. They eventually went back to Orono for the weekend, and we spent the holiday as best we could without them.

There were apparently two storm systems, for after blowing hard all Thanksgiving day, the wind hauled to the northwest, and Friday broke clear and fiercely cold. Gale winds were forecast again for Friday night, and the tides were expected to be two to three feet above normal. Every able-bodied person on the island fell to the task of securing gear and boats against the storm. The lobstermen spent the better part of the day bringing in their traps, returning repeatedly to the harbor raw with frostbite, their overloaded boats glistening with ice. They left the traps helter-skelter on the pier to sort out later and went straight out for another load. They worked close together for the most part, moving as a fleet from ledge to ledge and keeping each other in sight, for an engine failure in those conditions was no light matter. Will Hopewell's fuel line clogged off the ledges at noon, and Clyde Grant towed him back to Thorn Island, Turk standing by. It was not a time to stand on old rivalries.

By high tide, which was delayed an hour or more that day because of the seas, the lobstermen had finished their work "outside" and turned to the boats and gear in the harbor. The traps had to be stacked and secured against any blow. The children separated the floats and stowed them away in sheds, while the women struggled with frozen coils of warp. I spent most of the afternoon, together with other land-borne residents like Caleb and Harold Toothacher, lining up the dories and smaller boats for the high tides, and when the lobstermen came in, we hauled these one by one into the tall eel grass at the head of the cove. We left the larger boats to the last. Several were coming out for the winter, and these we guided onto cradles and secured, to be hauled off at low tide to their winter quarters in barnyards along the ridge. Others we careened at the high-water mark on the mudflats opposite the store. Only three boats were left at mooring when we were through our work: Arthur Dacey's *Sarah Lou,* whose thousand-pound mushroom anchor was believed capable of withstanding any gale; the *Sunrise,* which with extra cables and a strong stern anchor Turk considered quite safe under the lee of the old warehouse pier; and the *Clarissa B,* which Clyde Grant insisted on leaving in the water, not because his mooring was as secure as Turk's or Arthur's, but simply because he doubted the northeaster would be as severe as forecast.

"I ain't never heard of a nor'easter come on hard after a cold snap like this," Clyde said, his knuckles as red as his face as he shoved at Cecil Allen's boat to nudge it higher up the shore. "Goddam if I'll be without my boat a month waitin' out the next spring tide to haul 'er off." It was his same sense of northeasters that led him, in contrast to the rest of the lobstermen, to leave all his deepwater traps where they were.

"I hope he's doin' the right thing," Turk said, cautious but impressed.

As early darkness settled over the island, hastened by a denser cloudbank that moved in from the east at sundown, the islanders drifted gradually homeward, stopping to warm themselves at Caleb's on the way. The store was so jammed at times it was hardly possible to open the door for new arrivals.

"Well, come in or stay out, Arthur Dacey!" Jenny Brewster shouted across the room. "Don't stand there in the door freezin' all of us."

"Jenny, I never knew you to take chill so quick," Arthur replied, squeezing his way into the throng.

Bottles circulated freely, something Jenny rarely allowed in the store but forbore now in deference to the cold; the thermometer outside the door stood at ten degrees at four-thirty. I wondered how so much whiskey had suddenly materialized until Turk explained these were the bottles the lobstermen kept on their boats for "emergencies" and were now returning home for safekeeping—if there was anything left to return.

"Leonard, keep your clumsy feet outa my cookie jars, if you'd be so kind," Jenny bellowed above the noise. "And Clyde Grant, git your backsides off'n the stove. I can smell it all the way over here."

"Why, Jenny, I was just cookin' up a piece o' raw meat for your supper."

"I'd like mine better done if it's all the same to you. . . . Why, thank you kindly, Rudolf. Don't mind if I do. Just a drop, right in that tumbler there."

Spirits rose as the bottles went the rounds—isn't it always so? One found its way into teenage hands, and there was considerable horseplay in what Jenny called the "children's corner" before it was retrieved. Mary Lou Grant, home for Thanksgiving from Rockland, where she was a waitress at the Thorndike, made off at one point with Tucker York's bottle, and there was a small scrimmage around the pickle barrel as he sought to recover it. Mary Lou, shielded by partisans, waved the bottle over her head and stuck her tongue out provocatively at

the sixty-year-old Tucker; provocation, with her fine figure and saucy face, came
naturally to Mary Lou.

"Why, you little polecat!" Tucker leered at her. "If my old lady warn't
watchin', I'd trundle you straight off to th' quarries for stealin' my whiskey."

"Listen to the man boast!" said Joanne York—indulgently.

At about this point several of the mothers saw fit to take the younger children home—Jesse Cutler had herded hers out of the store as soon as the first
bottle made its appearance—and the rest soon followed. By six o'clock, as a fine
sleet began to fall over the island, driven by rising winds, the last of the islanders
had found their way home to wait out the storm.

But Clyde was right. It was not a great northeaster, as northeasters go. It
blew itself out by noon the next day, and the damage was negligible. No gear was
lost. The boats at mooring rode out the storm with ease. Fewer than half a
dozen old trees along the ridge were upended.

"That's the way it goes," Arthur Dacey said at our delayed Thanksgiving dinner on Sunday. "The times you get ready, nothin' happens. Then one comes
along you're not looking for and makes matchsticks out of everything you've
got."

The cold weather, however, stayed with us and was followed a week or so
later by sizable snowfalls, which left the island covered until March. When the
careened boats were eased off the mudflats at the next spring tide, winter fishing
had begun. The lobsters had crawled into deeper waters and were scarce, which
was the signal for most of the lobstermen to turn to clamming and dragging for
scallops.

9

Jingle and Belle coordinated their return at Christmas and arrived together
on the mailboat the Wednesday before. I would have met the *Laura Lee*, of
course—for I won't conceal my impatience to see those two again—but I
was nursing a torn ligament from a fall at Ram's Head the day before and feeling
in consequence somewhat dejected and superfluous. During the course of the
afternoon, immobilized on my couch, I worked myself into an even gloomier
frame of mind wondering if they would come down that day, alternately charging them with black ingratitude if they didn't and reproaching myself for allow-
ing my peace of mind to depend so much on their society. But of course they
came, at the end of the afternoon as it was growing dark, and the sound of their
voices coming down through the spruces was all it took to revive me.

Jingle had been discharged five days before, but nothing in her appearance or manner signified her changed status. She still wore the oversized gray sweater, now with a heavy woolen scarf against the winter winds, and the baggy corduroy slacks. And the knee-high rubber boots, which she kicked off as she came in. She greeted me on the sofa, bending to kiss me on the forehead while Belle demurely looked on, then went off to inspect Harold's improvements in detail. She was some time rummaging about in my bedroom, and when she returned, she pronounced herself satisfied.

"This is more civilized," she said, dropping into the leather chair by the fire opposite me. "You were on your way to becoming an eccentric when I left. . . . Now even your laundry's in order."

"Was that what you were doing in there?"

"One judges from little things." She studied me with her piercing gray eyes. "You just might make it. What do you think, Belle?"

Belle, sitting on the hearthstone, knees pulled under her chin, said, "I think he already has."

Belle had imperceptibly changed in three months. To be sure, she *looked* the same. She blushed as quickly as she used to. She still had the same shy smile. She still reminded one more of a *Saturday Evening Post* cover than flesh and blood. But at the same time, she was taking on individuality. She was less remote, less distracted. When she spoke now, she looked you squarely in the eye. She had more self-assurance.

"Belle's in love," Jingle said, following my gaze. "A tycoon of a senior. BMOC." Belle lowered her eyes but said nothing. "She's even been crazy enough to ask him out over New Year's."

I said I hated to see any island girl fall in love unless it was with me.

"I don't know about *love*," Belle said. Oh, she was serious! She was too much a novice at falling in love to think it a joking matter. "But we . . . well, we seem to get along."

"Just don't get pregnant," Jingle said.

"You don't have to worry about *that* anyway."

"I don't. You do."

I gave Jingle a stern look (which she ignored) and asked Belle her friend's name. It was Harvey Brown, she said. She was even willing to provide a few biographical details—like, he was from Portland, he had three brothers and two sisters, and he majored in business administration. "His father's . . . in lumber."

"In lumber!" Jingle exclaimed, and she burst out laughing. "You'd think he was a lumberjack! He owns most of the woodlands in the state of Maine."

"A slight exaggeration," Belle said. "As usual."

"*Very* slight," Jingle insisted. "Anyway, baby, you're giving the guy some test . . . bringing him halfway across the Atlantic Ocean in midwinter to be given the once-over."

I said I thought it was a good test. Anyone deserving Belle should pass it . . . but Belle wasn't enjoying the conversation, and I changed the subject. I asked her about her courses at Orono. Except for one, they were the usual freshman distributives of that era: a science course, which she found tiresome; beginning French, which she liked; a course in English composition; and a required course in home economics. The exception was a seminar in political theory taught by her advisor, which he had suggested she take after exempting her from the regular social science requirement.

"Be careful of that creep," was Jingle's comment. "He's collecting all the pretty freshmen."

I asked Belle what she was reading in the seminar, and she said the textbook mostly, and named one currently in use. "But we read a few things in the original—I mean, in translation. Niccolo Machiavelli's *The Prince*, for instance. *The Social Contract* by Jean-Jacques Rousseau . . ." She was very precise about the titles and authors. "Now we're reading *The Communist Manifesto* by Karl Marx."

I asked her how she liked Marx.

"Well, I wouldn't say I *like* him, exactly . . . but he makes you think about things. I guess I don't really understand him yet. He seems to base his ideas more on theories than facts."

"Most worthwhile ideas start off with theory."

"But what good are they if the facts don't fit?"

I said a Harvard professor I once heard lecture had the answer to that, and put on my best Teutonic accent: " 'If ze facts don't zuit ze zeries, zo much ze vorse for ze facts.' "

But Belle was only mildly amused. Learning hadn't yet become a game for her. "Take this island," she went on. "Where's the class struggle here? The summer people don't exploit us. In fact, we'd be a lot poorer if they didn't come."

I said Marx wasn't talking about summer people.

"Well, certainly we don't exploit each other," Belle said.

"Are you so sure?" I thought of telling her Harold Toothacher's idea that her father had exploited the lobstermen by acting as middleman, and now Jingle's father was doing the same thing. But I decided against it. Instead I suggested that Marx never meant to imply capitalists had to be mean to exploit workers. Exploitation was simply in the nature of certain economic systems.

Belle said, "It still seems farfetched to me. You must know if you're hurting someone. Then . . . well, I guess you'd stop."

I remarked it would be a tender world if this were so, then went on to ask her how her advisor treated Marx in the seminar. Was he sympathetic?

"Oh, he's very anti-Communist," Belle said—and added, by way of explanation, "He was in Russia before the war."

"So was I," I said.

Both girls looked at me in some surprise. And, in fact, I was surprised myself it hadn't come up before. But it hadn't. "Are you anti-Communist?" Belle asked.

Neither pro nor anti, I answered her after a moment's deliberation. Just neutral. They continued to study me gravely—trying to decide, I suppose, whether I were guilty of some obscure deceit.

"Well, I can't see how one would decide to be a Communist from reading Karl Marx," Belle said at last. "At least from what I've read so far."

I told her if she found Marx inscrutable, she should sample some of the later Marxists. They were less rigid, less arrogant. She asked which ones, and I mentioned Rosa Luxemburg.

"Rosa Luxemburg?" said Belle. "She's . . . she's Jewish, isn't she?"

I looked at her sharply. "So?" I said.

Belle blushed and seemed confused. "I didn't mean . . . I mean, I don't know what I meant. I was just identifying her as a Jewish person . . . that's all," she ended unhappily. But she recovered her composure quickly, and in a moment asked what she should read by Rosa Luxemburg. I pointed out a volume on the bookshelf by the door and told her to take it home with her.

Jingle had been silent through this conversation, but she listened carefully, her eyes mainly on Belle.

"Jingle's bored," Belle said, coming back from the bookcase. "She can't stand philosophy."

"Baby," Jingle said, and for once there was no trace of irony in her voice, "I could listen to you talk forever."

Well, the remark was a bit thick, I thought, almost pagan—and it surprised me, coming from Jingle—but Belle had heard too many of these veiled and not-so-veiled allusions to her bright prospects to be troubled by them. She paid no attention and sat down again on the hearth, thumbing through the book she'd taken down. I turned to Jingle.

"What's it like to be a civvy, mate?" I asked.

"Same as it was being a sailor," said Jingle. "Except no more regulation underwear."

Now she could spend that winter on the island she'd been denied the last ten years, I said. Jingle shook her head slowly and looked at me a moment before speaking. She was staying in Boston, she said, and I asked why Boston.

"You mean, why not stay here? Well, figure it out, pal. Gertrude Bakeman's good for another few seasons at the school. Jenny Brewster doesn't need help. And I'm not much good at dragging for scallops."

I said I thought she was hiding a man in Back Bay.

She ignored this and went on to describe her job in Boston: essentially the same duty as a lab technician at the naval hospital the last year and a half, but now as a civilian employee. She was very serious, and I thought she seemed defensive about her decision, as though she felt she was somehow deserting me. I thought of reassuring her by telling her I too might be going away for a time. But I've always had a block about discussing my plans before they are definite, so I said nothing. Still, Jingle's news put something of a damper on our conversation for a few moments. We looked at each other without speaking while Belle remained absorbed in her book. Whether we could have found anything particular to communicate to each other had Belle not been there, I couldn't say. Jingle's look was enigmatic, as though she might have something else she wanted to tell me—but then again, she might not. I'm sure I had nothing more precise on my mind at that point than the pleasure of seeing her again, of knowing that for the next few weeks at least she could never be more than a mile or so away. Which is one of the comforting things about an island, knowing people you want to see can't be far off.

I said, to break our silence, that Jingle must now feel she was really leaving Ram Island, not simply going away for education or national emergency. "That's why you're so solemn," I said.

"Solemn, my foot!" she cracked. "I was just waiting for you to break down and cry." Then she made an observation about islanders I've always remembered: "No, seriously, if you're born out here, you never stop being an islander. This is always home. Take Elmer Brewster, for instance. He hasn't been back a dozen times since he got out of high school, but if Elmo's here for three days, you forget he ever left. Clyde's brother Amos Grant has lived in Castine twenty-four years, and he's still as much a Ram Islander as the day he went."

"Which you wouldn't recall too well at the age of one," Belle put in from her book.

Jingle threw a pillow at her and turned back to me.

"Cheeky l'il critter, i'n she?"

I said there wasn't much doubt how she got that way, and caught a second pillow in the face for my pains.

Jingle and Belle left me shortly thereafter, and I spent a meditative hour on the sofa calculating how I could fill my life more with one or both of them.

By Christmas I was enough recovered from my injury to resume normal activity. I had Christmas dinner with Lucy and Belle at Meadowlane, and the Daceys joined us in mid-afternoon for an exchange of presents. Theirs to me were mainly items for my larder: choice preserves, rock candies, rare herbs and spices—and winter apparel, including scarlet flannel underwear, which Jingle presented to me with some ostentation.

"Well, really, Jennifer!" was Winifred's comment on that.

My presents to them were for the most part books, which I'd had the forethought to order from New York, and a small watercolor by Andrew Wyeth I'd found in Rockland. It was a fragment, really, no more than that. It was a glimpse over a stark kitchen table through a section of open window into an orchard. Only part of it was painted in, the rest merely suggested in clean, thin strokes. I gave it to Winifred—and hardly knew myself *why* I did, since she was the one with whom I had the least communication. Perhaps that was why. She didn't know quite what to make of the painting and sat for some minutes studying it in silence. I think at first she felt obscurely offended, wondering whether it was meant to represent *her* kitchen, which was just as immaculate but much more gracious than Wyeth's. None of them had heard of Andrew Wyeth at that time, but Belle and Lucy at least recognized his talent.

"It's unbelievable!" Belle said. "You can *feel* the splinters on that sash."

Lucy, sitting beside me across the room, said in a low voice, "You shame us. It's altogether too much of a present." But there was no reproof in her tone.

The end of the afternoon I walked out to the jetty with Jingle and Belle to leave a large basket of food for Widow Barnaby. This was my first visit to the eccentric old woman, the island's second-oldest inhabitant—after Lydia York, who was almost senile. The weathered gray shanty, pieced together originally from driftwood, looked more than ever as if it would topple into the harbor on the first good blow. But it was firmly moored, I knew. Harold Toothacher had doubled the anchor cables around the shack during the Thanksgiving storms. Two generations of islanders, meanwhile, had replaced broken panes in her two windows and filled the chinks with moss. The Yorks, to whom she was distantly related, kept her woodbin filled and emptied her pail. There was hardly a day in the year when one islander or another didn't drop by to see that she had food. She was a corporate responsibility, without benefit of any formal engagement beyond the small sum voted annually at Town Meeting toward her standing account at Caleb's.

Widow Barnaby was dozing in her rocker when Jingle knocked and opened the creaking door.

"Merry Christmas!" Jingle said, raising her voice so the old woman would hear. "We've brought a basket for you."

"Another Christmas already," she said, starting to rise. "Fancy."

"Sit where you are. We'll only stay a minute." Jingle introduced me and sent me out for more wood while she revived the dying fire in the stove.

"You'll have a cup of tea, won't you, dears?" Widow Barnaby said when the fire was crackling again.

"I'll make it," Jingle said, and put the kettle on to boil.

The old woman took Belle's hand and looked long at her. "You're little Belle, aren't you? You're so like your grandmother when she was your age." Granny Belle, I calculated quickly, had been eighteen in 1876—almost seventy years before.

Turning her attention to me, she said, "I haven't seen you before, have I? You're a newcomer."

I said I was.

She took my hand in turn and held it in a dry bony clasp. "Have you come to marry one of these girls?"

I said I'd like to but couldn't decide which.

"Which?" she echoed me.

"That's the trouble," I spoke out. "Which?"

"Let them decide," the old woman said, squeezing my hand before she let it go. "That's the best way."

"Swords or pistols, Belle?" Jingle said, pouring the tea.

"How's that, dear?" said Widow Barnaby.

"I asked Belle whether we should fight for him with swords or pistols."

"Oh, you mustn't fight."

Jingle handed us our tea, and we sipped it a few moments in silence, listening to the surge of the tide rising on the jetty.

"I've lived here so many years," the old woman said, peering at me. "I don't remember how many."

"Nearly fifty," Jingle said.

"Is it so long?" She sipped her tea again, then looked up at the darkening light in the window. "John comes in at dusk," she said, turning to me again. "That's my husband. He'll be in straightaway."

A whistle sounded three times around the Nose, muffled by an offshore breeze. I wouldn't have thought the old woman's ears good enough to hear, but she heard. She raised her head.

"That's the *Sunbeam*," she said. She rose slowly and peered through the frosted window facing the bay. The rest of us stood behind her, looking over her shoulder. Presently a high-prowed steam vessel, painted black with a white cross on its hull, came into view and swung around the red nun into the harbor.

"It *is* the *Sunbeam*," Jingle said, then added in a low voice, "Now, how the hell did she know that? They weren't expected until the end of the week."

As though she'd heard, Widow Barnaby said, "They always blow three times . . . three times." She wrapped a heavy gray shawl over her shoulders and shuffled toward the door. "I'll just see them in."

We followed her around the lee side of the shack and out onto the jetty. The sturdy little mission boat, encrusted with ice from the freezing spray, was passing slowly abreast of us. Two crewmen on the forward deck waved a greeting; three of us waved back. We watched the *Sunbeam* maneuver into the landing before we left.

"I'll stay on awhile and wait for John," Widow Barnaby said, pulling the shawl more tightly around her. "He won't be long now."

Jingle tried to persuade her to wait inside, by the warmth of her stove, but that was not the widow's way. So we left her to her solitary vigil and walked slowly back along the shore, keeping her in sight.

"She's almost rational, isn't she?" Jingle said. "Except for that one detail about John coming in at dusk. . . ." Jingle glanced back at the lonely figure silhouetted against the flat December sky. "What is she now? Eighty-six. . . . I wouldn't mind having a single obsession at eighty-six."

We paused at a bend in the shore trail until we saw the widow turn slowly back along the jetty, then we went on to join the islanders arriving at the pier to greet the *Sunbeam* crew.

I saw Jingle daily during the week between Christmas and New Year's. We were usually with other islanders, and then she was her normal self, gregarious and self-assured. But we were also by ourselves enough times for me to sense some uneasiness on her part—uneasiness about the current stage of our relationship. She came down to Cutler's Cove one morning when I was working and said she wouldn't disturb me. She just wanted to sit with me in the bungalow for an hour or so. And she did just that. After washing my dishes and making my bed, she sat and crocheted in the leather chair by the fire. If I said something to her, she answered monosyllabically or not at all. She wouldn't stay for lunch.

Another day she came at noon to take me out to see her sheep on Little Ram. We rowed Arthur's double-ender out past the Graves in a brisk northerly and beached it opposite the osprey nest. After we'd found the sheep and counted them, we roamed over the island for an hour or more. Much of the time we were silent, but when we came to the indian shell heap on the southwest shore, she talked for twenty minutes about the artifacts dug up there and what they suggested as to the date and duration of the island's use by Tarantine Indians, a band of the Penobscot. Rowing back against the wind and tide—since I had rowed out, the easy run, she insisted on rowing back—she hardly spoke a word.

These occasions might have lacked manifestation of a growing ardor between us, but they were in no way irksome to Jingle. Sometimes within hours of our most uncommunicative meetings, she would seek me out again for some fresh enterprise. The weather held clear and cold all week so that the snow on the trails was firm, and walking anywhere on the island was no chore by day. Nor by night, for that matter, with the rising moon. I fell in, needless to say, with all that she proposed. I placed no obstacles to her management of my life—the more easily since she left my mornings free. And one other thing. She had taken to kissing me when we separated, whatever time of day it might be and whether or not we were to meet again within a few hours. I thought at first it was some perfunctory kiss she meant, a grazing buss on the cheek after the fashion of old friends. But this was not it at all. Rather, it was a full honest kiss square on the lips, not caring where we were or who might be watching. Harold Toothacher, bouncing down the high road in his pickup one afternoon, very nearly bounced into a culvert watching Jingle bid me good-bye at my turnoff.

I was frankly at a loss to comprehend Jingle's changeable moods that week. If I had already mentioned the possibility of my going away for a time, I might have suspected this as a reason for her moodiness—for she had been at some pains to settle me properly for the winter, even though she herself would be away. But I received the confirming letter on my plans only the last day of the year, and when I told her, that same afternoon, I was going on an assignment to the Far East, she seemed neither surprised nor disappointed. Apart from her natural curiosity as to why I was going and where, she merely wanted to know when was the earliest I would return.

Jingle talked little about herself during those days. She said nothing, for instance, of friends in Boston—and I remembered wondering why, if she knew so few people there, she bothered to go back. On the other hand, she told me a good deal about my neighbors that week. More than I suspected I had to learn. It was then she told me the drama of Turk and Sharon's wedding—and if I doubted how intimate we had become, in our fashion, her telling me dispelled it. For this was a tale only a few islanders could ever know.

We had stopped one afternoon at the Peaks on our way home from a long walk around the northeast tip of the island. As we were leaving, Turk stood in the door with Chucky, as usual, perched on his shoulders, and I was struck again by the extraordinary contrast in coloring between the two of them: Chucky's nearly bleached-out locks against Turk's kinky jet-black hair. I remarked on the contrast as we moved down the high road in a light snow shower. Jingle made no reply, and I suspected she hadn't heard me or had her thoughts elsewhere.

"I guess I better tell you about that," she said finally. "Before some garbled version of it comes to you through gossip. There'll be talk someday . . . when Chucky's a few years older."

She slipped her arm through mine—a thing she rarely did—and we walked a moment in silence.

"Chucky is Stanley's son," she said, and waited for me to take in this revela-

tion. "Sharon got pregnant, if you can believe it, the *day* before Stanley's accident." I must have whistled through my teeth, for Jingle promptly scolded me
for sounding so shocked and said island teenagers, after all, were no different
than teenagers anywhere. She went on to spell out the relevant teenage relationships on the island that summer—a more-or-less classic triangle involving
Sharon, who was in love with Stanley; Turk, who was in love with Sharon; and
Stanley, who was in love with no one but was quite willing to go to bed with any
girl who was willing. I said I'd heard something to this effect.

"From old lady Toothacher, no doubt."

I said she must have a low opinion of ladies. Jingle let that pass but said in
the case of Stanley, Harold Toothacher hadn't been far off.

"Including a fling with Sally Bannister?" I asked slyly.

"You two did get pretty chummy rebuilding the bungalow, didn't you? . . .
'Course, any island gossip would pass on the rumor about Stanley and Sally
Bannister. It does us proud, don't you see? Local boy makes good. But you'll get
no satisfaction out of me on that particular rumor. Figure it out for yourself,
chum."

I told her to go on with the story.

After the accident, Jingle continued, everyone on the island was so numbed
by the tragedy that no one paid particular attention to Sharon. She herself didn't
suspect she was pregnant until after she'd returned to nursing school in
Rockland in September. And then she was paralyzed by the shock of the discovery. She kept making excuses all fall for not coming home weekends, as she
always used to. Even Thanksgiving found her in Rockland. Jingle, who was in
Portland that fall, also hadn't been home since September and learned about
Sharon's absence only when her mother mentioned it in a letter early in
December.

"It was only then, nut that I am, that I suspected anything was wrong.
Because I knew Stanley had been with Sharon that last afternoon. . . . Now, don't
put on that pained expression again. We didn't go around *telling* each other
everything we'd done as soon as we did it. And I didn't *watch* them, if that's
what's eating you. But Stanley and I happened to have a long, serious conversation that night, and it came up. . . . Okay, okay, I wormed it out of him, if you
want it that way. Anyway, I took the next train to Rockland, and there was
Sharon, five months gone. Was she in a state, poor kid! She hadn't been to her
classes in three weeks. She'd hardly even left her room, she was so embarrassed.
Of course, she hadn't dared tell anyone. She'd thought of abortion, but how
would an eighteen-year-old island girl go about having an abortion? I wouldn't
even know now. She'd thought about suicide, too, and I wouldn't have put it
past her if things had gone on much longer. But what mainly was the matter was

she was in a state of shock. She couldn't bring herself to do *anything*. . . . I came busting into her room straight from the station with some dumb remark like 'Prithee, pretty maiden,' trying the laugh cure, I guess—and she burst into tears. And she cried and she cried. It was three quarters of an hour before she calmed down enough so I could persuade her the world wouldn't end because a girl was going to have a baby."

Gertrude Bakeman came out from the schoolhouse as we passed the cross-roads, and we exchanged a word with her before moving on. Jingle continued with her story. She moved Sharon to Mrs. Broadstreet's, a house owned by a fine and discreet elderly widow with whom island girls often boarded. Then she caught the school ferry out to the island—Horace Snow made a special run on Fridays in those days, bringing the high school students home for the weekend. Turk was still in the harbor when they arrived, and Jingle rowed straight out to the *Sunrise* and told him about Sharon. It hadn't taken long.

"Well, let's get a move on, Jingle," was all Turk said.

Jingle asked what his idea was, and Turk said, "Idea? Why, I'm gonna marry 'er, ya nitwit. We ain't gonna let Stanley 'n Sharon down, are we?"

"So that was the idea, all right," Jingle went on. "I had a hard time persuading him to wait till morning, but he finally agreed. I also convinced him to bring Aunt Lucy in on it, and she was the one really with all the sensible ideas. Like Sharon's staying in Rockland until Chucky was born, and our putting out the story that Turk and Sharon had been secretly married in the summer. . . . That was a brilliant idea, actually, since everyone was behaving in a screwy way after the accident and no one would wonder at Turk and Sharon's running off like that without telling anyone. But Aunt Lucy wasn't suggesting they were supposed to have got married *because* of Stanley. I mean, she wasn't trying to cover up for Stanley . . . even if he was her son. The first thing she asked when we came in to tell her on our way up from the harbor was if Turk *wanted* to marry Sharon. She had to be sure he wasn't just doing it for Stanley. And the same with Sharon. She wanted us to wait a couple of days so she could go ask Sharon herself. But Turk wouldn't wait . . . and we thought it would look funny if we all left together the next day. So she gave us a letter to take to Sharon and made us promise we wouldn't rush her into it."

Jingle went home—making up some story for her mother as to why she'd come all the way up from Portland just for one night—then returned to Rockland on the mailboat the next morning. Turk went over later in the *Sunrise*. He and Sharon were married that afternoon by a justice of the peace, with Mrs. Broadstreet and Jingle as witnesses.

"And they lived happily ever after," she wound up.

"Sharon made no objection to the plan?"

"She cried again when I told her what we were up to and read Aunt Lucy's letter, but it was more out of tenderness for Turk than for her own shame. . . . She was still quivering a bit when we got to the justice of the peace, but Turk put a big hairy arm around her and said, 'Now, there ain't nothin' to it, tiger. If when he asks th' words you don't wanta go ahead, you just say *I don't* 'stead of *I do.* And I'll do likewise.' When it was over, Turk had to scoot back because there was an easterly coming in. The poor guy hadn't even thought about spending the night in Rockland. Which he could have done, of course, since, according to the story we put out, they'd been married since August. But maybe he didn't want to press Sharon too fast. Anyway, he made up for it later by spending one or two nights a week in Rockland all through the winter. . . . Everything else went as planned. Chucky was born in April—a mite premature, the gossips were quick to point out. But, of course, that was just what we wanted them to say."

We walked on a few moments in silence. It was a marriage, I said, with no regrets from any quarter I could see.

"Absolutely none," Jingle said. "We should all back into our marriages." She gave me a brief sidewise glance before letting go of my arm.

After a moment I said, "Still . . . you took a chance."

"Me? Or they?"

I said that depended on whose idea it had been in the first place. "I'd like to have heard that conversation in the harbor between you and Turk."

Jingle lowered her head against the snow, which was turning to a fine sleet. "It *was* Turk's idea," she said. "But I know what you mean. If he hadn't thought of it, I would have."

I asked Jingle what she'd have done in Sharon's place.

"You mean if I found out I was going to have Stanley's child? . . . You must think we spent our lives going around screwing each other."

I assured her I had no such idea. I merely wondered whether she would have married someone to save Stanley Talbot's reputation.

"Well, I wouldn't have had to. I'd just have gone off somewhere and had the baby, then given it up for adoption. . . . But you're right about one thing. I *was* thinking about Stanley more than anyone else. I didn't like the idea of people criticizing him for the way he left Sharon. It didn't seem right after the life he'd had. It was too . . . too untidy." She went on in a softer tone than I'd ever heard her use. "Everything he did, he did with flair. The way he handled a boat. The way he fished. The way he played baseball. Even that business with Sally Bannister—in case you ever find out it was true. Really, damn it, it was too much to have everyone saying he'd pegged out leaving Sharon knocked up—like any pimply soda jerk on the main."

We were coming to the Daceys' yard, and she slowed her steps, pressing close to me again.

"Just one more thing . . ."

"Don't tell me," I said. "I'm not to mention this to anyone, including Turk and Sharon."

"And Aunt Lucy. . . . I'm sure you think there's already more secrecy about this business than there should be. But there has to be, believe me. People won't be able to help suspecting in another few years, when Chucky begins to look more like Stanley. I've caught some resemblance already. But suspecting's one thing; *knowing* is another. Caleb and Jenny Brewster would be absolutely crushed, even now, if they knew the truth. You've no idea how old-fashioned they are. Not to mention Ma Jenkins. She's insecure enough as it is. If she ever knew Chucky was not Turk's son, she'd wilt, she really would. As for Uncle Frank, he'd roll over in his grave if he knew a son of his had 'ruint' Caleb Brewster's daughter. . . . You understand, don't you? I can tell you these things because you're not really one of us."

I said—a little stiffly, I suppose—that I thought her telling me meant I was making progress in that direction. We had stopped on the road outside the house. Winifred Dacey, spotting us from the parlor window, had come to the door to greet us.

"I offended you," Jingle said, squeezing my arm. "I'm sorry." She stood on her toes and kissed me, her mother looking on.

"Well, really, Jennifer, of all things!" Winifred exclaimed as Jingle went toward her and I turned back down the ridge. "And right out there on the high road."

10

While I was preoccupied with Jingle during that week between Christmas and New Year's, Belle was preoccupied with her friend Harvey Brown—and I must say something about that episode, for it was not without significance in the shaping of her character.

Harvey Brown arrived on the mailboat the day after Christmas, two days earlier than originally planned, and he was an instant success with the islanders gathered at the time in the harbor. He strode down the gangplank in his faded trench coat and fur hat, embraced Belle in a great bear hug, and greeted every one around him with a wide smile as Belle introduced them. Belle led the cortege up to Caleb's, and it was there he met his first real test.

"Well, where's your axe, young man?" Jenny Brewster greeted him after Belle had presented him to her. "When I heard Belle Talbot was bringin' out a fella whose old man'd chopped down all the trees on the Androscoggin, I thought the least he'd bring was his axe."

"And I would have if I'd known there were so many trees left out here. But my old man said not to bother. He said *his* old man had cut over the islands seventy years ago. That's why he went looking for more timber up the Androscoggin."

"Why, the woods on this island grew so tough there warn't an axe blade in the state o' Maine could cut through 'em. They all blew down in northeast storms."

"Is that so? . . . Well, now I see why they had such an easy time of it. They just found the timber floating around in the bay and towed it off."

A few exchanges like this were enough to establish Harvey Brown's reputation as a man who could hold his own with the island pundits and who was not in the least embarrassed about being as rich as he was supposed to be. An heir, if he is also unpretentious and unencumbered by his wealth, is of all men the easiest to get along with. And this was the case with Harvey Brown. Before he had hoisted his duffel bag onto his broad shoulders and started up the ridge beside Belle, he had won a fair number of supporters to his suit.

"Well, that's the sort of young man, I don't mind sayin', I like to see come courtin'," Clara Grant said to Mary Lou, watching from the store window. "Don't they make a nice-lookin' couple?"

Mary Lou, who had come out on the mailboat with Harvey Brown, made no reply.

Harvey's reception, to be sure, was not everywhere as smooth as at the harbor. Later in the day, after Belle had taken her friend home to Meadowlane for lunch, Jingle collected the two of them for a walk out to the Head before dusk. They stopped to pick me up on the way. Belle and Harvey walked ahead of us along the high road, hand in hand.

"Teach me how to get along with your mum," he said, intending us to hear. "I don't get the feeling she goes for me in a big way."

"She's . . . reserved," Belle said.

"All the more reason I need help. Tell me if I'm doing something wrong, okay?"

Belle said nothing immediately, and Jingle put in, "For a starter, I'd call her 'Mrs. Talbot' if I were you. Not 'Mother.'"

"Is that right, Belle?" he said, looking down at her. Belle wasn't short, but he was a good head taller than she was.

"I . . . I guess so," Belle answered. Her heart wasn't much in this conversation.

"Not 'Aunt Lucy' or 'Mrs. T.' or something like that?"

" 'Mrs. Talbot,' " Jingle said.

"Okay, okay, that's what I want to know. . . . What else?"

Again, Belle was silent. After a moment, Jingle—perhaps more severely than she intended—said, "A word of advice, Harvey."

"What's that?"

"I wouldn't draw Belle into schemes against her mother."

"Brr!" Harvey said, pulling up the collar of his trench coat in mock defense against Jingle—at the same time glancing back at her in good humor.

"I feel the north wind blowing down my neck. I better go back to the harbor and start all over again."

"You did all right down there," Jingle said.

"Up here things are different?"

No one answered him, and after a moment I said, "Speaking as an old hand, up here things are different."

But the shafts Jingle occasionally dealt him those first days didn't mean she was displeased with Harvey Brown. Any more than Lucy's reserve indicated *her* displeasure. Harvey might have mistaken Lucy's habitual gravity for disapproval of his easy and open manners, but I knew that in reality she admired his buoyancy. She was entertained by his bantering way of dealing with the islanders, young and old. She watched the comings and goings of the pair with a certain amused detachment.

"Now, Mrs. Talbot, don't wait up for us," he said one evening after we had all dined at Meadowlane. "Belle and I are going to drop in on Turk and Sharon, then we're going to prowl around that big place out at the Horn in the moonlight. . . . But if you want Belle in by ten, just say the word."

"Belle will bring you back when she's ready," Lucy said with a distant smile.

It was hard not to feel sympathetically toward Harvey Brown the three or four days he was with us. He had quite obviously fallen in love with the whole island. The romantic idea of this freshman beauty from a remote island community in the Penobscot had seized him in Orono, and now that he was on the island, he wouldn't rest until he had captivated the entire community. He quite unashamedly sought to ingratiate himself with everyone he met. But they were flesh and blood to him, not stereotypes. They were Maine men and women, like himself, and he instinctively accorded them that respect. I had to admit—and the admission must have cost me something—that he came closer to many of the islanders during those few days than I could ever expect to.

Harvey viewed me differently from the others. Belle had told him about my being on the island, but he still seemed surprised to find me there. Occasionally he would engage me in discussion about world affairs, then break off abruptly with a look that implied he thought we were talking over the heads of others around us, including Belle. His father had held a reserve commission in the navy during the war, also as commander, and perhaps because of this he persisted in calling me "sir" the first few days—until Belle apparently discouraged it. Anyway, he seemed to consider me an ally in his pursuit of Belle and sometimes asked me, when no one was near us, how I thought he was progressing. My replies were noncommittal.

One bright morning, after working their way around the shore from Jonah's Cove, Belle and Harvey dropped in on me and sat for an hour over coffee. Harvey told me of his plans to work for a few years after college with one of the large lumber companies in Oregon before returning to Maine to enter the family business. He might do two years at the Harvard Business School in between—if he was admitted. The last he offered to affect modesty, I thought, rather than because he thought there was any doubt about the admission. But on the whole he talked sensibly and realistically. And his concern about conservation and reforestation, two activities not usually associated with his family's business, seemed genuine. Indeed, he held quite advanced views for that era.

"We've plundered this state," he said, "from the king's foresters down to the present. It makes you want to scream when you think how the coast used to look. . . . Somehow, we've got to make it up."

I asked if planting more trees was the answer.

"And legislation. I'd like to try my hand at politics someday." He implied, with more self-consciousness than vanity, that here too he would meet success. I asked what party he was, knowing as soon as I asked which party—in Maine—it had to be. He said his mother was on the Republican State Committee. When I remarked that Democrats were more likely than Republicans to press for conservation, he said, "If I can't persuade Republicans, I'll become a Democrat." And he gave the appearance of meaning it.

Later he took Belle's hand (he'd had it and lost it half a dozen times since they came in) and said in a confiding tone, "I'm trying to persuade this cute little monkey"—Belle winced at that—"life doesn't end on the shores of Great Ram Island. I can see after three or four days here why she thinks so. But I want her to see more of the world. . . . How do I get her to do that, tell me?"

You could see the world from anywhere, I said. It depended how you looked.

"Oh, sure, anybody knows that," he said, brushing aside my wisdom—then went on to his pet theme. "Want to know what I think she should do?" He gave the impression of having weighed all other options. "Transfer next year out to Oregon."

I didn't quite laugh in his face, and, in fact, I couldn't be sure whether he was being serious or facetious. "Orono seems to have been good enough for you," I said. "Why not for Belle?"

"I went to UM because my dad wanted me educated in the state of Maine . . . and he had a beef at the time against Bowdoin. Besides, forestry's good at Orono. It's different with Belle. The kind of things she's interested in, she's not going to get at UM. Heck, she's already taking about the deepest courses they've got there, like that seminar in political philosophy. . . . She should transfer." I had to admit there was some validity in his argument—though not necessarily in the self-serving solution he proposed, which he now reiterated: "The only place for Belle next year is Eugene, Oregon."

"Really, Harvey!" Belle said.

He smiled at me, man to man. "See what I mean? She's giving me a hard time."

Harvey, meanwhile, was not giving Belle an easy time of it. About the fourth or fifth day he was on the island, he seemed to confuse his priorities, and his troubles, I think, stemmed from this. He was really in love with Belle; none of us had any doubt of it. But he was also a romantic, and he was impulsive. He apparently formed an idea in his mind of a young Lochinvar—himself—come to the rescue of a maiden who was in distress without knowing it: locked in the insularity of her native environment, her potential unrealized, her unique promise insufficiently appreciated. His mission was to liberate her, and this meant not only shaping her mind but also possessing her person. The two were evidently inseparable in his imagination. The seduction was to be followed by a reconciliation (tearful, no doubt), which would pave the way for a vigorous new relationship based on mutual trust.

This, in any case, was the way Harvey's scheme appeared to Jingle and me as we watched the affair unfold. "The guy is an incurable romantic," Jingle pronounced.

Belle, it goes without saying, was hardly an agreeable partner in this enterprise. She was surely still a virgin at that time—just as surely as Harvey, four years her senior, was not. This was also Belle's first mature love affair—the only other I had heard of was a brief romance with Rodney York midway through the war when he was home on his last furlough before he was killed in the Pacific. Harvey, by contrast, openly hinted at his reputation as a ladies' man, even while pretending to disparage it. The situation, in short, called for a certain delicacy. A delicacy Harvey, for all his good sense in dealing with the other islanders, couldn't seem to summon in his behavior with Belle.

It would be hard to imagine a less-congenial setting for seduction than a Maine island in winter. The weather, it is true, was considered superior the week after Christmas, for that time of year, but this meant only persistent high pressure and prevailing northerlies. If the wind swung into the south, the snow cover usually thawed in the afternoon to slush. Nowhere outdoors could one escape the rawness and dampness that are the hallmarks of a coastal winter. Indoors, where there was always warmth, there was never privacy.

But Belle was unresponsive, and this, not the weather or season, was the controlling factor in Harvey's suit. She put up with the hand-holding as the accepted thing, though it was new to her, but she had no appetite for the rest of Harvey's lovemaking. By the end of the week, Jingle and I gathered, their walks around the island were punctuated by awkward and unresolved physical struggles. We came upon them unexpectedly the last day of the year in a remote clearing near the osprey nest where there had once been a cutting shed. Jingle, who was in front, stopped when she heard voices ahead and put a finger to her lips, listening. Then—incorrigible as she was—she took my hand and led the way up a steep escarpment before I knew what she was up to. We came to the rim of an old quarry from which, kneeling behind a boulder, we could see down through the trees to a clearing. Belle was on the ground and Harvey half on top of her. We couldn't hear what they were saying, but it wasn't difficult to guess the topic of conversation. Harvey kissed her from time to time, and this she appeared to endure.

"He's making progress," Jingle whispered, and inched forward to see better. I tugged at her sweater, feeling our spying on Belle like this was somehow disloyal, but I might as well have tried to dislodge an eagle from its aerie. Jingle wouldn't be denied her satisfaction. So in the end I lingered on after wrestling inconclusively with my conscience.

Well, there wasn't much to see. They were fully dressed, of course, and Harvey's maneuvers—so far as we could make out—consisted chiefly of trying, while distracting her with his kisses, to slip a hand stealthily inside her blouse. Belle regularly and resolutely removed it. This pantomime continued for ten minutes or more, interrupted occasionally by scraps of conversation we couldn't hear. Finally we saw Harvey's hand slide down in a bold motion and seize her crotch. Then we heard Belle say distinctly, "That does it, Harvey! We're going home." She jumped up, pulled him to his feet, and led him off at a brisk pace toward the ridge.

Jingle and I waited until they were out of earshot, then moved away—a little sheepishly—in the opposite direction.

"Jesus!" Jingle said. "I don't know whether to feel sorrier for Belle or him."

11

The islanders celebrated New Year's Eve, as they had for many years, with a movie and a dance at the church. The plantation had appropriated funds for the entertainment at Town Meeting the previous March, and a three-piece band, a current Western film and rented projector, together with a man from Rockland to run it, arrived on the *Laura Lee* in the forenoon. A crew of men kept the fires going in the four church stoves through the day. A crew of ladies decorated the hall with spruce boughs and a box of mistletoe sent by a cousin of Winifred Dacey who lived in Seattle. Most of the wives brought pies and cakes for the intermission.

The church bell, silent through the war because of a broken hammer, had been repaired ten days before—in time for the tolling at eight o'clock for the movie. The islanders assembled from all directions. A light snow had begun falling early in the evening, but the night was mild. There was much stomping and coughing as outer garments were hung in the entry and each person found his or her company inside the church. The younger children raced back and forth in some nameless game between the rows of folding chairs set up for the movie. Teenagers clustered in groups along one wall, boys separate as a rule from the girls. A cordon of island wives guarded cakes and pies along the opposite wall. The men gathered in knots at the rear. A collapsible screen was already set up on the dais, flanked by two portable speakers. In the choir balcony at the rear, the operator from Rockland worked over his projector and its mysterious wiring, which dropped over the railing behind the men and passed out through a window to a gasoline generator coughing rhythmically outside. The three musicians, in their fixed bow ties and matching double-breasted jackets, were crowded in a corner up front until the dais was free. Their instruments were an accordion, a violin, and drums. When the hall was half full, they played contemporary tunes, poker-faced and remote, not yet in the spirit of their engagement.

By eight-thirty all who planned to watch the Western had found seats, and Horatio Leadbetter, who doubled as gravedigger and verger, turned down the kerosene lamps on the walls. The film started with a deafening roar, then ground immediately to a halt, one frame flickering over and over again.

"Lights!" the man from Rockland called from the balcony. But before Horatio could turn up enough lamps to oblige, the beams of a dozen flashlights arced through the semidarkness, and one rested long enough on the projector for the operator to resolve the problem.

"Now, Rudolf York!" Jenny Brewster meanwhile shouted into the confusion. "If you'll be kind enough to keep yer rubber boots outa th' wiring, we can get on with the entertainment."

"Why, Jenny, I'm in my stockin' feet. I never come to church in my boots."

The projector started up again, synchronized to within a quarter of a second of the soundtrack, and the flashlights were turned off. It was a film titled *The Gambler from Cripple Creek,* with two actors in the leading roles I'd never heard of—and I doubt if anyone else had, either—but whose names on the screen nonetheless prompted as great an outburst of enthusiasm from the audience as if they had been Clark Gable and Hedy Lamarr. Gradually the rustle of excitement subsided and an awed hush fell even over the front rows as the story unfolded.

The film was not far advanced when I felt a tug at my elbow—I was sitting in the back row next to Jingle—and Clyde Grant summoned me outside with a conspiratorial wink.

"Go join the boys," Jingle said, patting my arm. I slid past her and followed Clyde. A dozen or more of the men were gathered outside the church, standing under the wide eaves away from the falling snow. A kerosene lantern outside the entry lit up the faces enough to distinguish one from another. Tucker York was just finishing up a story about a great storm on New Year's Eve in 1913, when the end of the jetty broke apart and they had to take Widow Barnaby out of her shack for fear it would fall into the harbor.

"But she crawled straight back into it nex' day," he wound up. "The old crow—I say so even if she is my . . . what's the widow to us, Rudolf?"

"Well, she was married to Great-uncle John, on Mother's side. Him that was lost in 'ninety-two."

"She's a spunky old woman," Caleb said, speaking for everyone.

Someone handed me a bottle, and I helped myself before passing it on. I noted it was one of my Christmas presents the week before to neighbors who had befriended me in the fall. Another bottle from the same supply circulated in the opposite direction a few minutes later. As my eyes grew accustomed to the light, I could see that nearly all of the lobstermen were there—all but Lloyd Cutler, who disapproved of liquor, and his son-in-law Cecil Allen. I puzzled for a moment over a tall form in the shadows next to Willy Grant, home again on furlough, then realized it was Harvey Brown; he had been summoned forth the same way I had been.

We made an irregular circle, the outer edge of it beyond the protection of the eaves. If no one felt inclined to command the general attention with a story, we stood in silence or conversed in low tones with our neighbors waiting for a bottle to pass again. When someone was moved to recount a tale—most of them were about the sea—the rest were immediately attentive. Harvey Brown, to my surprise, told a story of the Maine woods, and a mildly spicy one at that. I thought as he began it that it was in dubious taste, coming from a stranger and very nearly the youngest amongst us. But I was wrong. He sensed his audience better than I, and he told his story well. It concerned a laconic lumberjack, a Maine stereotype, who had married one of the Jewell girls, the one widely regarded as the "good looker." A leisurely dialogue, punctuated by pauses that grew in length, progressed between the lumberjack and a companion who was inquiring about the wife's particulars. Having found them to be satisfactory in all respects, the companion at length observed, "Seems like she must be pretty good humpin'." To which the lumberjack replied, after a pause that Harvey drew out plausibly for nearly thirty seconds, "Well . . . she ain't." There were appreciative chuckles around the circle as others, the whiskey now loosening their tongues, cleared their throats to tell their own off-color stories.

Before the next one was under way, Clyde Grant leaned toward me and said, "He's a good feller, i'n he? Think he'll take 'er?"

Not knowing just what he meant by the expression, I said I thought Belle was still a little young to be "taken," and Clyde said he wasn't sure about that. We gave our attention to Zip Clayton's tale of a lighthouse keeper's wayward daughter, a stock-in-trade among the lobstermen at such times.

The bottles were pretty well empty when the scraping of chairs inside signaled the end of the Western. We drifted back into the church in twos and threes, faces flushed, and mingled with the others.

"Whew!" said Joanne York, catching a whiff of Tucker as he came up behind her. "It smells like a saloon 'round here. I can't b'lieve where it comes from."

"Turk Jenkins!" Jenny bellowed across the hall. "Don't you know 'nough to come in outa th' weather? You look like a snowman!"

Everyone turned to look at Turk. He had been standing hatless at the outer edge of our circle, and a layer of snow covered his black hair and shoulders. Turk grinned broadly and winked at Sharon, but said nothing.

The musicians took their places on the dais after the screen was rolled up, and started a fast fox-trot. When the chairs had been pushed back against the walls, some of the young people began to dance, Willy taking the lead. The older citizens, however, demanded a square dance, and Caleb resolved the problem by having the band play first a modern piece—"modern," for the most part, meaning anything after the First World War—then a traditional jig. He called the squares in a stentorian voice and with a good deal of individualized encouragement to keep the sets from becoming entangled.

"*Bow to your partners . . . Bow to your corner lady . . .* No, Lloyd, your corner ain't Lucy, it's Joanne . . . *Four hands 'round . . . Swing your opposite . . .* Your opposite's in *front* of you, Rudolf, not behind! Where've you been all these years? . . . *Swing your own . . . Ladies change . . .* well, what d'you know, everybody done it right! . . . . *Allemande left to the corners all . . . Left,* Gertrude, what're things comin' to even the schoolteacher don't know her left from right! . . . *Forward and back* . . . *Pass through* . . . Whoa there, Turk, I said *through,* not outside. Come back in here! . . ." And so on.

Order eventually came to the sets, and we performed several very intricate squares without grave mishaps. But Caleb ran out of calls, and square dancing yielded entirely to fox-trots, waltzes, an occasional polka, and a mid-Penobscot version of the tango. A wide variety of dance styles were in evidence, some dating back to the 1920s and a few defying any identification. The prevailing style among the young was cheek-to-cheek, with some wartime refinements I was surprised to see—notably what Jingle called the "bear hug": arms clasped firmly behind your partner's back, a style (if it may be so dignified) that precluded much dancing as such but gave license to a degree of public intimacy. Mary Lou was chief practitioner of the "bear hug" and not surprisingly had many partners—including, quite regularly, Harvey Brown. Cutting was endemic and followed no known rules or patterns. Arthur and Winifred Dacey were as likely to be cut by Joel Grant, aged fifteen, as Mark Cutler and little Betsy Clayton by Harold Toothacher, aged sixty-seven. Nor was cutting confined to a single sex, and Harvey Brown, a vigorous and accomplished dancer, was cut almost as often as Mary Lou. Girls even cut girls, for there was no barrier, of course, as in more inhibited modern societies, to girls dancing with each other. The line, however, stopped there.

At intermission, after the rush on the food tables had subsided, there were some impromptu solos and duets. Rudolf and Tucker York did a sailor's jig they did together as boys, Walter accompanying them uncertainly on the harmonica. Betsy Allen did a Highland Fling, for which she'd won a prize in Camden the year before. Willy, resplendent for the last time in his dress uniform (for he was to be discharged in the spring), played a fast Marine march on the drums—the drummer from Rockland looking nervously on. I did a creaking Russian mazurka, which lasted until my knees gave out and landed me on the floor; volunteers picked up where I had left off and did about as well. There was also singing. John Grant, Clyde's youngest brother, gave us a sad and toneless sea chantey. Turk, weaving like a lord, sang a Portuguese love song his grandmother had taught him. But the most sensational performance, it was generally agreed—and certainly the noisiest—was a series of Alpine yodels by Harvey Brown, fruit of a winter holiday in Switzerland before the war; it brought the crispness of high mountains to the island church, and for the next quarter of an hour the vaulted hall reverberated with the mispitched imitations that inevitably followed.

Spirits rose even higher as midnight approached. The few bottles still left with anything in them circulated more openly. Old Clarissa Grant, catching sight of one of them as she sat beside Gertrude Bakeman, said, "Mercy on us! In

God's own house!"

Harold Toothacher, standing behind them, slyly poured whiskey into a glass of punch and handed it to Clarissa.

"Try this, Clarissa," he said. "It'll ease your soul."

She took the drink and sipped it gingerly. "Now that's a nice clear punch," she said. "What's in it, Harold?"

"Barley water and lemon juice," Harold lied. "Same's usual."

Clarissa took another sip, then drained the glass in one long swallow. "That's what I call a good clear punch," she said again. "Now, why don't the boys drink that instead of spirits?"

Gertrude, catching a whiff of the spiked punch, looked around at Harold and frowned but said nothing.

Only Belle among us grew more subdued as the evening wore on. She danced, of course, since no one would hear of her sitting out, but she entered little into the general gaiety. I charged her during a waltz with being too withdrawn.

"Is it too obvious?" she asked, giving me a quick look.

I told her it was obvious; whether *too* much so, I couldn't say.

"Well, I *feel* withdrawn."

"Everyone's privilege," I said, and added lightly that it was ironic she should be withdrawn when everyone else felt so drawn together.

"With some help from your whiskey, I see."

I said in that case, she should have some too.

"Ask me another time," Belle said. "When I feel—"

But Caleb Brewster cut in at this point and ended our conversation. I didn't see Belle again that evening to speak to privately.

At midnight horns and clackers, hidden away from previous New Year's celebrations, were brought forth and supplemented with washtubs and other makeshift noisemakers. The din they produced must have made the gulls and cormorants fly off their ledges on the north shore. Skittish girls were now dragged under the mistletoe to be pecked at by lads too shy the rest of the year to glance in their direction, or too preoccupied to care. More mature citizens, like Willy and Mimi York, needed no prompting of mistletoe to exchange the season's greetings in appropriate fashion. The elders, seized by the contagion, embraced each other in their separate ways. At one instant, as I stood with Jingle, there came into our line of vision Mark Cutler embracing Susan Grant under the mistletoe in the foreground, Clyde with his arms around Jesse in the middle distance, and in the rear, Lloyd solemnly bussing Clarissa Grant—a three-way kissing spree between the island's oldest rival families.

"That," said Jingle, "is a moment to record."

The band soon struck up "Goodnight, Sweetheart," and all who were able found their proper partners for the last dance. Harvey danced with Belle, and the eyes of nearly everyone, I noticed, eventually rested on them.

Good night, sweetheart,
Sleep will banish sorrow . . .

They danced silently, her head resting lightly on his shoulder. Once or twice, when he bent to whisper something in her ear, she smiled distantly but made no reply.

. . . but with the dawn
a new day is born . . .

Joel Grant, making for them at one point to cut in, was shooed away by his mother.

Dreams enfold you
In each one I'll hold you.
Good night, sweetheart, good night . . .

At the end of the dance, we locked arms in a large circle extending around the hall, and Arthur led us in "Auld Lang Syne," the traditional close of the New Year's celebration.

A snowball fight developed outside the church as we prepared to leave. Harvey was quickly in the middle of it, and since he was the tallest, became everyone's target. Mary Lou, after several near misses, caught him finally on the chest, and though it was not the worst damage done him, he promptly chased her into a snowbank to . . . well, to administer appropriate justice, I suppose. Others piled on top of the two, and it was some minutes before the pile disentangled itself. Jingle and I, Belle between us, had already started down the ridge when Harvey came panting after us, a hail of snowballs following him. One broke on the back of Belle's neck and fell inside her collar, but she brushed the snow away without turning around. We left them at the turnoff to Meadowlane, Belle walking briskly in front, Harvey behind her—still flushed from his wrestling bout in the snowbank.

I saw Harvey again that night. He came down to Cutler's Cove three quarters of an hour later, as I was preparing for bed. I had made a small fire and opened a beer to unwind from the evening's festivities.

"I dropped by to see if you were still up," he said.

I could have told him it was damned inconsiderate of him. He couldn't have known Jingle wouldn't be with me. At the present stage of our relationship, she might well have been. In fact, when she kissed me good night on the high road, I thought she hesitated. She knew I wanted her. But then she said good night abruptly and strode on down the ridge. Even then I thought she might come later, after putting in an appearance at home. But by one o'clock I knew she wouldn't.

As I say, I could have told Harvey he was damned thoughtless, but he looked so disconsolate as he dropped onto the sofa that I hadn't the heart. The whiskey had worn off and his eyes were listless. He stared for some minutes into the fire without speaking. Since I had no inclination at that hour to engage in lengthy conversation, I too was silent. I went to the icebox to get him a beer.

"I fudged it," he said as I returned. "I won all the time trials, but I lost the prize." I still said nothing, and he went on. "The goddam frustrating thing is I really wanted her. I still want her."

I said Belle was probably too young for what he wanted.

"How do you know what I wanted?" he asked sharply—and I realized they were the only abrasive words I'd heard him use since he arrived. "Goddam it, I didn't want her *body* . . . I mean, who wouldn't? I wanted more than that. I wanted to give her form. Jesus, I dreamt about it. This terrific island girl! I was going to show her places beyond Orono . . . and out here, great as this place is." He sipped his beer and lit a cigarette. "You know, for a while I thought it was me who was doing *her* the favor. . . . Boy, was I misguided!"

There wasn't much I could say to Harvey's lament, so I held my peace. But when he too fell silent, I muttered something about having found the islanders generally impervious to the influence of outsiders; you had to take them as they were—and that included Belle.

"You can say that again," Harvey said. "Still, I managed things badly. . . . Tonight, for instance, I thought if I didn't hang around her too much, she'd want me more. You know what I mean . . . play up a bit to Mary Lou, make her jealous. It sure as heck didn't work out that way."

I said, to make him feel better, that I doubted whether his caper with Mary Lou had had anything to do with Belle's mood. Belle simply wasn't ready for love.

"I hope that's it," Harvey said. " 'Cause then maybe there's still a chance when we get back to school. . . . Only you'll admit this has been one piss-poor beginning."

I said nothing, wondering whether it wasn't a beginning and an end. A few minutes later Harvey drained his beer and stood up. He'd come to a decision, he said. He would catch the ferry in the morning rather than wait until Friday.

"It'll be easier for both of us," he said.

"Sleep on it."

We shook hands solemnly at the door, and he stepped out into the snow, still falling silently, stealthily.

The snow stopped before dawn, and the day broke still and gray. A fresh cover of six or seven inches blanketed the island. Snow had followed the ebb down to low water and by midmorning was being washed away as the tide came in again.

I awoke late, made myself a large breakfast after building up the fires, and was still in my bathrobe reading when Belle came by just before noon. She came, she said, to return the Rosa Luxemburg volume, but I suspected she had another matter on her mind. Nonetheless we conversed on various topics for a good half hour before she mentioned Harvey Brown. In the middle of some involved explanation I was giving her—I forget about what—she became distracted, lost the thread of my discourse, and presently told me, as though it were a natural sequel to what I had been saying, that Harvey had left on the morning mailboat.

I said I knew. She looked up at me quickly, and I explained he'd come down the night before.

"Did he really?" Belle said, surprised and shocked. "Wasn't Jingle with you?"

It was my turn to look up quickly at her. "I wish it were so," I said.

Belle flushed deeply and apologized for asking; she hadn't meant to pry. I waved it off and poked the logs in the fireplace until they blazed again. Belle watched the flames for some moments without speaking. I waited until her blush subsided before asking whether, all things considered, she wasn't relieved at Harvey's going.

"More . . . more dissatisfied than relieved," Belle said, choosing her words. "With myself, that is. Not him."

I asked why, and she raised her shoulders slightly. "I asked him out here, and he didn't have so good a time."

I said I wasn't sure I agreed, but even if it were so, was she to blame?

"Everyone else got along with him. Why didn't I?"

Belle was in a self-critical mood, and it didn't seem worth pointing out to her that she stood in a very different relationship to Harvey Brown than other islanders. I said instead I thought perhaps she'd been more afraid of him than she let on.

"Afraid of what he wanted to do, you mean?" she asked, turning large innocent eyes on me. "Yes, that *is* the problem, isn't it? . . . I must be a freak or something?"

I said I could never believe that.

"Is it normal," she went on after a moment, "to want someone you like not to touch you? I don't mean not *want* to touch you, but want *not* to touch you."

I disclaimed any special knowledge of how eighteen-year-old girls were supposed to behave in these matters, but told her I couldn't believe a little reticence was unnatural.

"A little reticence!" Belle exclaimed. "You should see me. . . . If I'm normal, Mary Lou must be a monster."

I reminded her Mary Lou was half a dozen years older. "Would you want to be like Mary Lou?" I asked.

Belle gave me a slow, sly smile—the first since she'd come in, I reflected. "I wouldn't mind," she said.

In that case, I told her, she was one hundred percent normal.

"Only some girls are more normal than others," she said—paraphrasing Orwell, whom I had quoted to her a few days before.

A quarter of an hour later Jingle came down with my laundry from the week before. "What's this?" she asked, surveying me in my bathrobe and Belle on the sofa. "The island love nest? . . . Belle, you're not stealing my man! Where's your own?"

I signaled a caution to Jingle and said he'd left on the morning mailboat.

"Oh, baby!" she said to Belle, changing her tone instantly. "I *am* sorry . . . or should I be?"

I said we'd just been talking about it.

"I'm not surprised. The whole island'll be talking about it."

"Well, why the heck should they?" Belle said with spirit. "It doesn't concern anybody but me."

"What concerns you concerns everyone," Jingle said, sitting on the sofa and putting an arm around Belle. "Especially you, baby." Jingle looked as though she were settling in for a good heart-to-heart chat about the whole affair. "There'll be talk, all right, whether you want it or not, and some'll be mad at—"

"Let's skip it, do you mind?" Belle broke in, shaking off Jingle's arm. "And don't call me 'baby' anymore."

Jingle looked more startled than put out by Belle's sudden show of independence, but she recovered quickly. She hadn't lived twenty-five years on the island without learning to respect another islander's assertion of independence. "Roger," she said. "Let's skip it."

I poured coffee for Jingle and refilled the other two cups. The girls were silent for some minutes, staring into the fire while I stepped out to bring in more wood. Then Jingle said—in a wholly altered tone—"Seriously, Belle, we have a problem, you and me. . . . Stanley would have had the same problem. We can't bring our lovers or whatever you want to call 'em out here for inspection. Either everyone here likes them and we don't, or the other way around. . . . Don't ask me why it's that way, but I know it is. Marry 'em ashore, *then* bring them out, and everything will work out all right."

"Or marry on the island," I said.

Jingle looked me squarely in the face. "There's that too," she said without expression.

Soon thereafter I went into my bedroom and dressed, and the three of us took a long walk along the southwest shore.

12

The dinner party for the Daceys and Lucy Talbot that I'd tried to bring off in the fall was finally arranged for the Saturday after New Year's, with Jingle's help. By then I had been long enough on the island, I suppose, for them to set aside their scruples about dining with "strangers," or perhaps I was beginning to qualify as "family." Jingle also persuaded Turk and Sharon to come, and Ma Jenkins was only too glad to sit with the children.

We made it a festive occasion. Jingle proposed that we dress up—not in costume, of course, but in best clothes—and said that, for me, meant my blues, which hadn't been out of the footlocker since the end of the war. Meanwhile, I bravely undertook, in honor of the occasion, a Provençal recipe given me by a friend in Marseilles before the war. Arthur Dacey was able to procure the proper fish for me, including bass and halibut in addition to lobster, and a bakery in Camden sent out French bread. I still had some Chablis left over from my Rockland expedition in September. I started preparing the stock at four and had the garlic aioli under control by six, after my mayonnaise had curdled twice. My guests were invited for seven.

Lucy and Belle arrived first, Lucy in a long velvet gown and embroidered shawl of her mother's, Belle in a wide flowered skirt and a blouse that for once accented rather than hid her firm, high breasts. Turk and Sharon followed. Sharon wore a blue maternity dress and a string of Mexican beads. Turk had on a checked jacket with tight-fitting pants he'd hardly been able to squeeze into, also an antique derby he'd found in his mother's attic. He arrived smoking a large cigar and was in a puckish frame of mind.

"Hey, this mus' be the doorman," he said, eyeing my row of miniature dress medals and tugging at my fourragère as I greeted them at the door. "When d'we git t' meet the boss?" When I asked for his hat, playing my role, he said, "What'll it set me back?"

The Daceys arrived last, Arthur in a striped double-breasted suit and bow tie, Winifred in a satin gown and pearls. Jingle wore a knee-length Spanish dress with high neck and long sleeves, topped by a homemade tiara of seashells and sand dollars. She carried a fan which she opened as she curtsied into the bunga-low. "It *was* tonight, wasn't it, Commandah?" she asked, holding a gloved hand out for me to kiss . . . they'd been so "fra'fully engaged." She swept across the room to greet the others by the fireplace.

"Ah, the Talbots of Meadowlane! Deah Aunt Lucy . . . and Belle! How she's grown. . . . Would you imagine I eveh called her anything as vulgah as 'baby.' . . . And of all things, the Brewster-Jenkinses down from their lovely Peaks! . . . Darling Sharon and—"

"Just call me Popeye," said Turk, doing her one better. He flicked his cigar ashes on the hearth.

I mixed old-fashioneds for Turk and myself—Arthur declined—and brought sherry for the ladies. And gradually we reverted to our normal dialects.

My Marseilles dish was a success, if I do say so. I doubt if it was a recipe, with its strong garlic base, calibrated to the pristine tastes of coastal Maine, but my neighbors took to it like native Provençals. The two bottles of Chablis I put outside to chill were not enough. A third bottle, pulled out from under my bed, we drank tepid, and when that was gone, Turk and I finished off what was left of the Graves I'd cooked the fish in that afternoon. I turned the lamps low when we sat down, and we ate by candlelight and light from the well-stacked fire reflected off the walls and ceiling. The candles periodically flickered in unison as gusts of wind from a restless southerly found their way through cracks in the bungalow.

"I'm glad it's only wind comin' through," Turk said. "Not water."

"Still, a snug haven," Arthur commented.

Turk agreed. "So long's we don't try 'n sail it."

Our conversation was parochial. We touched on national and world affairs only once or twice in passing. Even though they knew I was leaving momentarily for the Far East, there was little reference to it. Not because they were indifferent to my leaving—Lucy, I know for a certainty, deeply regretted my departure—but because they knew too little about the Far East even to question me. Yet there was probably not one of them, I reflected, whose forebears hadn't put in at Shanghai or Hong Kong or Singapore; Winifred, I knew, had been in all three as a child. So we confined our conversation to the affairs of the island, and as usual there was no end of topics to discuss—even without reference to Harvey Brown, out of deference to Belle (although, as Jingle had foreseen, the islanders had talked about little else the past three days). We considered who should replace Arthur as Moderator when he retired in March, at the next meeting of the plantation. We raised the question of how long Gertrude Bakeman could continue to manage the school and who should replace her when she left. We debated the costs of restoring the telephone cable, originally installed when the lighthouse was in use and now lying parted on the bottom of the bay, casualty of a winter storm during the war. We touched on the perennial problem of relations with the Thorn Islanders over fishing rights at Seal Ledge, though the issue was muted now that the lobsters had left for deeper water. We mulled over

Elmer Brewster's stock car accident in Bangor the week before, which landed him in the hospital with a broken leg.

"If Elmo'd ever learned to row that peapod in a straight line," Turk said, "he'd 'a saved himself a pile o' trouble."

"He'll be back yet," said Jingle. "Won't he, Sharon?"

"We keep tryin'."

But the best talk that evening was, as usual, about the old days on the island. Arthur and Lucy swapped stories for more than an hour about the escapades of their mother, who had herself been a fine storyteller and left her children a fund of tales about the past. Granny Belle survived several reputations in her long and eventful life, the most persistent of which was her reputation as a beauty. She had a number of romances in her youth, one of which took her away from Ram Island for three years with a French sea captain, whom, however, she never married. When she returned, she married Jethroe Dacey, a handsome and easygoing fisherman, and was for some years a tyrannical wife to him, trying to turn him into what he was not—an island entrepreneur. She herself acquired several properties and enterprises, not always as scrupulously as one might have hoped. The greater part of Little Ram, for instance, was said to have passed into her hands during a brief extramarital relationship with Bartholomew Cutler, great-uncle to Clyde, during the early years of her marriage. She also owned the quarries and for a dozen years conducted a flourishing business in paving blocks. She built a warehouse in the harbor, now moldering in the mudflats by the abandoned pier near which we had careened the lobster boats during the Thanksgiving storm. She ventured briefly into the fishing industry itself by financing a small fleet of seiners. Jethroe Dacey good-naturedly refused to have anything to do with these activities and continued to pull his traps from an open dory—from which he unaccountably fell into a mild sea on a mild day in December 1892. He was forty-five years old. His widow mellowed in the following years, gradually divesting herself of much of her property to meet family expenses and engaging her energies more explicitly in community affairs, including the church. She never married again, though she had many offers from widowers and bachelors both on the island and from the main. Belle Dacey was over fifty when she took up nursing, and for the last twenty-five years of her life she was the island's only nurse and midwife. This was the Granny Belle the islanders remembered most vividly, the still-handsome white-haired woman in ankle-long dresses and knee-high boots who trudged over the island in all seasons with her black bag of medicines and her wonderful stories of the past.

"She was no angel of mercy," Lucy said to me. "She was *not* pure gold."

Jingle said, "Just an alchemist's idea of it."

Belle, who could listen for hours to these tales of her grandmother, told us one herself which she said Stanley used to tell her when she was little. It was about a young orphan fisherman who lived, unknown to anyone but Granny Belle herself, in the eaves behind her bedroom in the old house at Meadowlane before it burned . . . but it's too long a story to retell here. Curiously, neither Arthur nor Lucy had ever heard it.

"Stanley must have made it up," Lucy speculated.

"He *said* Granny Belle told him," Belle replied.

We were silent a moment as Arthur and Lucy considered whether their mother might have held back so tender a story to pass on to her grandson.

"It's just possible," Arthur said. "Stanley was six or seven when she died."

Belle helped me clear the table and prepare coffee. In the kitchen, out of hearing of the others, I asked how our "cute little monkey" was making out. She made a face and dug an elbow into my ribs—which suggested to me her recovery was proceeding normally. I asked if she'd heard from Harvey.

"Mummy had a letter yesterday," she said, "thanking her for the visit. . . . Actually, it was a good letter. He apologized for running off unexpectedly. He said he'd have to come back someday to split that wood he promised to. . . . He sent me his love."

"So where does that leave you?"

"Well, about nowhere," Belle said. "Or anywhere. I mean, we have to start all over again . . . if we do."

I offered no comment on this, and we returned to the others with the coffee.

I had cognac and liqueurs on the after-dinner menu in the back of my mind, but watching Turk stand unsteadily from the table with that Cheshire cat grin I recognized from the New Year's Eve party, I thought better of it. It was, in any case, after ten, and Winifred had already stifled several yawns. We drank our coffee slowly around the fire before Arthur rose and said all things must end. Lucy and Sharon followed.

"Jus' as I was gittin' myself settled," Turk said, sprawled out at one end of the sofa. " 'Sides, the commander was 'bout to dig out another bottle of that Shablis, wasn't you . . . sir?"

I said I would if I could.

"You mean the saloon's run dry? Wal, in that case . . ." And he lumbered slowly to his feet with some help from Sharon. "Go buy back me derby hat."

As they gathered their coats from the bedroom and buttoned them against the wind, Jingle announced she would stay to help me clean up.

"Don't be long, dear," her mother said at the door.

"If you mean don't try and take his cabin from him the way Granny Belle took Little Ram from Bartholomew Cutler—"

"Really, Jennifer, what a tongue you have!"

Jingle and I stood at the door shining a light ahead of them into the spruces.

"What d'ya know?" Turk said, bumping into a low-hanging branch at the side of the trail. "It's all growed over here since we come down."

I told Jingle, as we returned to the fire, that I welcomed any excuse for her staying, but absolutely refused to let her help with the dishes. It was my party. To my surprise she agreed without fuss and dropped into the middle of the sofa, tucking her legs under her. I started to sit beside her, but she pointed to the chair by the fire and told me to sit there.

"No, get us some coffee first," she said. "And take off that jacket. It intimidates me."

I did as she asked, puzzled by her manner. When I came back with the coffee, I was even more puzzled to find her smoking, a thing she never did. I gave her the coffee and sat facing her on the leather chair. I waited for her to say something, but for several minutes she remained silent, puffing at her cigarette and drinking her coffee in short gulps. A sharp gust of wind drove an eddy of smoke from the fireplace. I moved a log to start the blaze again. Finally, Jingle crushed out her cigarette and put down her coffee cup.

"I'm having trouble finding my tongue," she said in a low voice.

I said that was a novelty; I said it lightly, but I was now growing uneasy.

"Just when I need it most." She put her hands over her face and sat silently a few moments longer before she lowered them abruptly. "Look . . . there's no percentage beating about the bush. I've made one God-awful mess of this. But I've got to tell you something, and it won't wait." She was looking me squarely in the face, and a cold, clammy sensation seized me. "I'm getting married," she said.

I caught my breath. "It's not possible," I said. "I won't believe it."

She flushed more deeply than I'd ever seen her—I'll say that. "How could I have been so dumb as to think you wouldn't mind?"

"Mind!" I practically shouted at her, and flung my unlighted cigarette into the fire. "For Christ's sweet sake, Jingle, what the hell d'you think I am? A . . . goddam robot?" Well, I went on like that awhile. Then I stopped. She looked at me so sadly, so hurt by my reaction, I thought she'd cry. "Tell me," I said finally, "is this . . . irrevocable?"

She nodded her head slowly, still flushed, and I knew it was. I got up to pour myself a brandy from the pine cupboard.

"Me too," she said. When I brought her the brandy, she made room for me on the sofa beside her, but I took my seat again in the leather chair.

"Then I'll come to you," she said, and sat on a cushion by the hearth, her back against my knees. She sat for some moments looking into the fire, stirring the embers idly with a poker. "I made one holy mess of this, I'll admit," she said, shaking her head slowly. "But what I'm doing is right. Right for you, right for me, for everyone. . . . Can we talk about it?"

I shrugged my shoulders, still stunned and uncommunicative.

"I *have* to talk about it," she went on. "I wouldn't feel right if you didn't understand why I'm doing this." She shifted her position on the cushion so she could see me. "Well, I've always had this idea of what kind of marriage I wanted . . . since I was fifteen or sixteen, anyway. Stanley used to kid me about it. He'd say I was taking all the odds out of life. But he didn't change my mind. What I wanted was to raise a family on the main and come out here summers, that was the idea. My house was going to be one of those story-and-a-half Cape Cod cottages, white with dark green shutters and a picket fence in front and a big yard out back. . . . Oh, I'll admit, I had a better idea of my house than my husband. I never gave him much thought. I didn't even much care what he did, so long as he made enough money to take care of us. I knew I could make him happy. We would have four children—"

"Two boys, two girls," I interrupted. "I've heard—"

"That's right. Everything even, no odds. . . . Oh, my idea's easy to poke fun at, I know. It's not very courageous. But it's what I've always wanted—it's what I want still."

Jingle went on to develop her ideas on matrimony, and I had to admit—despite myself—she'd given the matter more thought than I had supposed. She was hardly consistent on all points, but she did have an original and unconventional view of marriage. Marriage was not to her the principal relationship in a person's life. It served rather as a backdrop to multiple relationships outside the marriage. (I asked her facetiously if she was planning to keep a bordello, but she ignored the question—I think she didn't know what a bordello was.)

The object of marriage, she said, was to provide one security. And identity. Oh, it had to be harmonious, she acknowledged. Otherwise it defeated its purpose by creating problems and distractions of its own. As an example of the extramarital relationships she had in mind, she mentioned her ties to the island—including our relationship. These ties were closer than she could ever expect to have with her husband, she said. She didn't pretend to know how it was elsewhere, but island relationships were too demanding (*pesky* was the word she used) to accommodate relationships established on the main, and the two were best kept separate. Harvey Brown's visit had only reinforced her views in this respect.

When she'd finished, I acknowledged a certain willful logic in her ideas (she let the irony pass), but said I agreed with Stanley Talbot: Her scheme left no room for odds. "You don't take into account things that actually happen," I told her. "Suppose you should fall in love?"

"But you still don't see what I mean. Love and marriage don't have to go together."

I said the burden of her argument seemed to be that they *shouldn't*. She pondered this and conceded that for some the natural sequel to falling in love was marriage. "I wouldn't expect Belle, for instance, to marry without being in love, very consciously in love . . . but this doesn't necessarily hold for me. Don't you see?"

She wanted my concurrence, but I had none to give her. "Well, go on," I said after a pause. "Who is he?"

Jingle was silent a moment—wondering, I suspect, whether I was still in too hostile a frame of mind to hear the rest of her story—then she went ahead anyway. "Probably you won't like the sound of him at first . . . but you'll see he's consistent with my idea of a husband. He's a dentist, a dental surgeon, actually. I met him once or twice in Portland before the war. Then he turned up last year at the naval hospital in Boston. . . . He gets his discharge in June and starts practice in Portland in the fall."

She stopped, and I said, "Surely he has a name."

"Of course he has a name," she said testily. "I didn't think you seemed interested."

Interested or not, I went on—oh, I was really being a bastard at that point—I had to know what she was going to be called.

"Emil Zukin," she said briefly. "He's Polish . . . a goddam Polack, if you want t'know." She'd come to the end of her patience with me, I could see. So I shut up. I didn't trust myself to say anything. . . . Well, to Jingle's credit, she recovered quickly from her irritation—her well-justified irritation—at my boorishness. I think she realized that however badly I might be carrying on, I was, after all, the aggrieved party and entitled to my moment of bile. She wasn't going to make matters worse by confronting me. Within five minutes, simply by talking of matter-of-fact details about the projected wedding in the spring and other domestic trivia, all the time leaning against me with one arm draped over my knee, she managed to bring me back to a civil state of mind. The antagonism subsided between us.

She'd had doubts, she said. She was even glad the storm over Thanksgiving had kept her from coming out; it gave her more time to think. "At one point I nearly wrote you to come to Boston . . . so we could talk things over."

"Why didn't you?"

"Because I knew it wouldn't make any difference in the end. I had to make the decision. In fact, I'd already made it before you arrived . . . the night before, actually, when Emil drove me up from Boston. You understand . . . I made a promise to Emil." I remembered the prewar Studebaker at the wharf in Rockland in September, and Jingle, after sitting for some moments, leaning toward the figure at the wheel before she boarded the *Laura* Lee. "I was going to tell Mom and Pop during that leave, but I put it off to Thanksgiving . . . I've kept putting it off."

"You mean they still don't know?"

She looked at me in some surprise. "How could they?" she said. "I certainly wouldn't tell them before I told you. . . . I haven't screwed things up that badly." She rested her head on my knee, gently caressing the calf of my leg while I ran my fingers through her hair. "You'll see," she said dreamily. "This is going to work out for the best. . . . And admit it, you hadn't seriously gotten around to thinking about marrying me anyway. You wanted to keep me on ice a little longer, just in case."

I started to protest, then held my peace, knowing she was right.

"Oh, we could have had an affair," Jingle went on. "You'll never know how damned easy that would have been. But where would it have led us? Exactly nowhere. Eventually we'd have gotten bored with sex. . . . No, we're better off as we are, not messed up by affairs. And marriage."

So we sat a little longer in this friendly, reconciled fashion. I'd never seen Jingle more serene, a great weight off her mind. Finally she looked at her watch and stood up. She wanted to catch her parents, she said, before they fell asleep.

At the door, after she'd buttoned up her jacket over the Spanish dress, she said, "Kiss me." Just the way I'd said it to her in September.

And I said, "Even though it won't do us any good?" She smiled, remembering.

"It always does good to lovers," Jingle said. And we kissed on the mouth, as usual, before she went up through the spruces with her flashlight, never looking back.

Two days later, as scheduled, I took the ferry to Rockland on my way to Washington and Manila.

I should ask myself in all honesty, at the end of this initial four months of narrative, what the thrust of my story is. It started off—sensibly enough, I supposed—to recount the lives of the islanders during the span of time I lived with them. (Part of the span, be it said, for I still live with them in my way.) I was to be anonymous, as faceless as the narrator in nineteenth-century Russian novels whose intrusion into the plot was confined to periodic reminders to the readers that the action was taking place "in our gubernia." I didn't even give myself a name—and wasn't that a clever subterfuge? How anonymous can one be! Yet before the action was half developed, it was apparent I was intruding recklessly into my story by pretending to fall in love with one of my own heroines. By Christmas (in my narrative), any reader could be pardoned for wondering whether the story wasn't after all about me, the islanders playing merely complementary roles.

Perhaps it's easier to be faceless in a sprawling Russian gubernia *than on a two-and-a-quarter-mile-long island in Penobscot Bay. I'm not familiar enough with the vastness of* gubernias *(or their successor* oblasts *and* uezds*) to be sure. But I suspect the problem lies with authors, not geography. Authors are egoists, whatever stratagems they use. Turk is the love of animal competence in me, Jingle of uncut vitality, Belle of sweet sanity. When my thirteen-year-old stepson read an early version of what I've written, and—recognizing a number of my characters, asked if they were real—I could only reply they were real to me. More so than many people I met every day. In that case, he was kind enough to say, they must be real. But the question of reality in fiction is a nagging one—and I suspect the last person to give an honest answer is an author.*

In any event, I proceed as I must. My narrative truly is about the Great Ram Islanders, but I make no false promises. I'll intrude as little as I can, fully aware that this may be a good deal more than most readers want.

Book 2 *Turk*

13

I returned to Ram Island during a sultry spell in the latter half of July, when the temperatures inland had risen into the nineties for three days running and even towns along the coast were paralyzed by the intense humidity. The night train from Boston, barely tolerable in the best of seasons, was a waking agony. The heat, for incomprehensible reasons, had been on in the smoking car half the night, and those of us there were too prostrate to move. We emerged at Rockland bleary-eyed and numb, the stale taste of tobacco thick in our mouths, our shirts clinging to our backs. A middle-aged woman in a starched maroon dress had circles of perspiration that nearly intersected over her bosom. The train arrived a half hour late, so there was barely time for coffee at the station before the *Laura Lee*'s warning whistle sounded across town.

Once we were in the bay, the movement of the *Laura Lee* stirred enough air to give the impression of a breeze, though the sea was glassy. Mirages had already begun to form by mid-morning, making conical islands into fortresses and distant lobster boats into towering derricks. Isle au Haut hung several hundred feet in the air above where Isle au Haut was supposed to be.

Of the half dozen passengers aboard I knew only two—Joanne York, Tucker's wife, and the elderly gentleman from Blueberry Isle who had been on the mailboat the day I first arrived. I greeted Joanne and asked her for news of the island since late spring, when I'd last heard from Lucy Talbot in Singapore. Lucy had been my most faithful correspondent while I was away, although I had heard once from Belle and several times from Jingle. Jingle had given me essential vital statistics, such as Sharon Jenkins's son born in February and Lucille Cutler's daughter born in March—in Massachusetts, where she had been visiting an aunt since just after Christmas. Lucille's baby was given up to adoption in

April, and she returned home immediately thereafter. Jingle never mentioned her own approaching marriage. She wrote as though it were an event apart from us.

"I guess things're 'bout as they've always been," Joanne said in her reserved way. "Now let's see, the summer folk are all back, 'cept Wylie Thatcher. He'll be comin' on for the month of August. The Peabody cottage is open this season at Jericho Cove. The Delaney girls are back. . . . I should guess that's about it."

I said that was it for rusticators, but reminded her jokingly I was now a native; I wanted to know about my neighbors.

"Why, you didn't 'spect a big change in us islanders, I hope?"

"I hope not," I said. "I just wanted to be sure."

"Well . . . Sharon Jenkins's boy—Stanley, he's called—is doin' just fine," Joanne began, as glad as any island wife for an excuse to gossip. "He's the spittin' image of Turk." (I tried to guess whether she said this because Chucky *wasn't*— but it didn't appear so.) "Grandma York is poorly. She's eighty-eight, you know. She won't see another spring. Horatio Leadbetter's got the lumbago again . . ." And so forth. She worked her way through the island's ailments, which were neither better nor worse than might be expected.

I asked after Tucker, and she said Tucker had bought himself a new boat, like Clyde Grant—"So's the boys'll have something to fish now they're back from the service. That is, Willy and our Bill . . . they're all home from service now, praise the Lord. Bill, Willy, Sammy Clayton, Bobby Cutler . . ."

All but one, I reflected as she paused—her own son Rodney, Belle's contemporary, who was killed at Midway.

"Well . . . then the weddin'," Joanne went on, recovering her composure. "That was a big event for us. We don't have so many island weddin's. . . . Jingle was out a week or so before, visitin' around and keepin' everyone in stitches. The doctor—what's his name?—came out with some of his people on the mailboat. All but his mother, I guess. She took sick last minute, poor soul, an' couldn't come. They were married straightaway at noon. Jingle . . . well, she looked pretty as a picture in her mother's weddin' gown. " 'Course, she was crackin' jokes right up to the last minute. She told Mr. Hargrave who'd come over from Rockland to marry them that if it didn't turn out to be a good marriage they'd ask for their money back. . . . We were sorry to see her go. Though the doctor seemed a good sort. Serious, you know, but kindly." Joanne looked sidewise at me. "Some of us were sort of hopin' you'd fetch her," she said.

I could think of no adequate reply to this, so I simply smiled and said nothing. A few minutes later Joanne climbed up to the wheelhouse to talk with Horace Snow, a second cousin. Half the islanders, I had noticed, were second cousin to Horace Snow.

Later, as we skirted the western shore of Thorn Island, I fell into conversation with the gentleman from Blueberry Isle. He was a retired lawyer, I now knew, who divided his time between his summer cottage and a house in Augusta. He introduced me to a friend who was traveling with him, a professor of social anthropology at Bowdoin.

We passed a cluster of lobster boats off the tip of the island, and recalling our conversation the year before about disputed fishing rights, I asked how relations between the islanders were progressing this season. The lawyer glanced discreetly over his shoulder before he answered—to be sure we were out of hearing of two Thorn Island wives standing near us. "They're considerably worse," he said. "If you've been away, you won't have heard."

I said that when I left in January the rivalry seemed to have quieted down.

"It always does in winter. But it freshens in the spring . . . now it's a serious thing." The troubles, as he understood them, were not confined to the old dispute between Thorn Island and Ram Island lobstermen over rights to Seal Ledge, but had spilled over to relations among the Ram Islanders themselves—centering principally on Cecil Allen, Lloyd Cutler's brother-in-law, who was a Thorn Islander by birth but a Ram Island lobsterman for the past decade, since he'd moved over with Constance into the old homestead she inherited from her mother.

"So Cecil's caught in the middle, you see. He's still a Thorn Islander at heart, and this aggravates the old feud you've possibly heard about Grants and Cutlers . . . for Clyde Grant is the one who's most outspoken about fishing rights at Seal Ledge, and Lloyd Cutler is loyal to his brother-in-law, who sides with the Thorn Islanders on this issue. Both sides, of course, have an equal right to fish those ledges—in *law*."

The anthropologist, his eyes sparkling, said it sounded like a Penobscot version of the Hatfields and the McCoys and asked what they did to each other to vent their spleen.

"Snarl traps, cut lines, poach . . . pretty much the whole gamut of petty violations."

"Still, no one's been shot yet, I take it," the professor remarked meditatively—then, having no stake in the quarrel, since he knew neither the islands nor their inhabitants, he went on to generalize on the lobstermen's dilemma in the language of his discipline. "Why isn't this like any neighborhood rivalry? A man wedges me in too closely when he parks on Main Street, and I nudge him lightly when I pull out. He'll pass the compliment one day to someone else. It's a small thing. . . . My neighbor's dog defecates every morning on my lawn, so in the fall, in reprisal, I rake my leaves into a great pile where they will blow over *his* lawn the first windy day. He understands why. If it weren't for these little outlets for our exasperation, we'd repress our antagonisms to the point where they might indeed become serious."

"I call it already serious," the gentleman from Blueberry Isle said, "when forty or fifty traps a day are cut and as many more snarled. It's their livelihood that's at stake."

The professor acknowledged that this sounded more menacing than scratched bumpers and blowing leaves. He asked who was to blame.

"Who's to blame?" my friend echoed him. "I've lived on these islands off and on for thirty years, and no lobsterman has ever complained to me explicitly about another. Some things they keep to themselves."

I respected his twenty-nine years' advantage in experience too much to challenge him in this. I asked instead what the people on Thorn Island were like, since he seemed to know them as well as he knew my neighbors on Ram Island.

"They're much the same," he said. "Orcutts, Darlings, Hopewells. Very comparable to Grants, Cutlers, and Yorks. Large, close families, many of them interrelated. . . . There are also a number of summer lobstermen who move out from the mainland for the season. Some with their families, others not. They're a different breed . . . and I've little doubt that some of the trouble starts there."

"Why is that?" the anthropologist asked.

"Well . . . they work on a narrower margin—a shorter season, that is—and generally with worse equipment. Since they're not around to suffer the long-term consequences, they're not above pulling someone else's traps from time to time."

"Is that worse than cutting them?" the other asked. "After all, more lobsters crawl back in if the traps are still there."

"Is poaching worse than molesting, you ask? From the perspective of the victim, perhaps not. But there's a big difference in the doing. Sam Orcutt, for instance, or Lloyd Cutler would never empty each other's traps, though they might be provoked into snarling them."

I said I couldn't see Turk Jenkins doing even that. And the gentleman from Blueberry Isle agreed.

The *Laura Lee* had by now cleared the Gut, and I moved to the starboard rail to pick out familiar landmarks along the shore as we rounded the red nun and worked our way into harbor.

The hot, humid weather gave way the day after I returned to cooling northerlies, and within another day or two to the normal midsummer pattern of still mornings, sometimes with fog, and southwesterlies after noon. These stretches would be followed after a few more days by a new thickening of the atmosphere until another cold front passed over us, letting loose a series of

thunderstorms and clearing the air again. In this way we passed imperceptibly
into the dog days of August.

I settled gradually into my old routine, working mornings and retracing my
steps about the island in the afternoon. I had thought the island itself had few
secrets to yield to me, yet in the first week I discovered three old cellar holes I
hadn't found before, one Indian shell heap on the southwest shore, and two
grave plots of families I hadn't even heard of. These discoveries humbled me. It
was not only the spruce forests and stands of birch that flourished briefly and
returned to earth, but also man and his most intimate constructions. So little
trace was left of what our predecessors on the island had created that even the
slightest evidence of it came to light inadvertently. Only at the quarries, could it
be said, was the island altered permanently—and even this hypothesis became
doubtful when, on the fourth day after my return, I came upon an old granite
cut behind the Allens' I hadn't known existed, now choked with sumac and surrounded by a dense barrier of alder. I was never so conscious as during that
summer of the transience of life on Great Ram Island, man's and nature's.

I resumed some old friendships easily. Turk, for instance, coming into harbor as the mailboat docked, recognized me at the stern rail and swung the
Sunrise close enough to ask, with a wry grin, whether I'd remembered to bring
more "Shablis." Jenny Brewster hailed me loudly from her grille when I stopped
to pick up six weeks of accumulated mail. And Lucy embraced me as a long-lost
neighbor when I stopped by Meadowlane on my way to Cutler's Cove. (Belle
had left the day before to spend a few weeks helping Jingle settle into her new
house in Portland.) But my position with most of the islanders remained . . .
well, anomalous, at least so long as the summer vacationers were around. I was
inevitably identified with them—the more readily, I suppose, when I resumed
acquaintance with the Bannisters. Sally took this acquaintance altogether for
granted. She had written me a long rambling letter in March about Bannister
comings and goings as though I were a longtime family intimate; Jenny forwarded the letter to Singapore, but it reached me on the eve of my return, and I had-
n't replied.

I met Sally at the crossroads the same day I arrived. I was on my way to the
store to lay in supplies and she to meet Kevin and Karen, who were out sailing
along with Gloria Thatcher. Sally greeted me effusively, then daubed at my cheek
with her handkerchief to remove a smudge of lipstick.

"You lost your girl, I hear," she said with her characteristic directness, especially when relations between the sexes were concerned. "Then went out to the
Far East to forget."

"Is that what they're saying?"

"That's what I say."

We started down the hill toward the harbor. "Anyway, I'm sorry," she went on, not much sounding as though she were. "Jingle Dacey should have married you. Whether you wanted her or not. Bachelors have to be taken into hand at a certain age . . . otherwise they grow dangerous."

She looked at me archly, but I gave her little encouragement, and presently she shifted to Kevin and Gloria.

"I wrote that they'd solved their little dilemma, didn't I?"

I said she'd written they were working on it.

"Well, they solved it. Rather, Kevin solved it. He told her . . . when was it? sometime last spring, I should guess . . . anyway, he told Gloria he'd no idea of marrying for some years, and he didn't think they should tie themselves up now. He'd probably have a lot of different girls between now and then, and he told her she should too. Boys, I mean."

I wasn't greatly interested in all this, but to be polite, I asked how Gloria had responded.

"Like an old trouper," Sally went on. "They're happy as clams now. Inseparable. Off climbing in the quarries, picking blueberries, out sailing nearly every afternoon. If Karen wasn't with them all the time, I'd begin to have suspicions. . . . But Kevin makes out all right in that department, in case you want to know. Guess who he runs after up here?"

I might have guessed, but didn't, for Sally provided the answer: "Mary Lou Grant."

I said—still to make conversation—that required quite a sleight of hand, since Mary Lou, if I understood correctly, was working in Rockland.

"Don't I know it, sweetie pie. At the Thorndike. That's where Kevin discovered her . . . when he came up with us to open the house in June. We stopped over for the night, and after dinner Kevin did his disappearing act: 'Have to catch up on a little reading, Mom, night-night.' But when I stopped by his room just before midnight, he wasn't in. Now, what does one do in Rockland after midnight?" The question was rhetorical, so I didn't answer. "Then when he came back after the Fourth, he arrived two days late. Said he missed the ferry because his car broke down. Ha!"

Sally was prevented from further speculation on her son's peccadillos by our coming into view of the harbor, into which a small sloop was reaching smartly past the jetty.

"There they are," she said.

We stopped to watch them maneuver between the lobster boats toward their mooring. Kevin, shirtless, was at the tiller. Karen, in yellow shorts and a dark blue jersey, hair blowing across her face, was forward with the gaff ready to catch the mooring float. Gloria, in shorts and a striped polo shirt, sat by the halyards, ready to lower the sails at Kevin's command.

"Aren't they beautiful" Sally murmured. And they were indeed a striking trio in their sleek blue boat with its unnaturally white sails. Everyone at the harbor paused to watch. There was confusion at the mooring—a misjudgment of distance, a sudden jibe as the wind came off the opposite shore, and Karen in a flash was overboard, gaff and all. Kevin hauled her over the transom, pulling her jersey nearly over her head in the process so that she was exposed for a moment from the waist up except for her pink bra. Kevin fetched the mooring on his second pass, and a cheer went up around the harbor—as much, I thought, for Karen's exposure as for Kevin's success in ending the brief crisis. Then Gloria began to giggle—uncontrollably, as only a teenage girl can. Karen, usually as grave as a church warden, presently joined in, and their laughter, rippling across the water, infected all who watched—from Horatio Leadbetter, standing in hip boots in his dory, to Bubber York, rowing in a peapod off the pier.

"Hey, Karen, crab git your toe?"

"Kevin, you should'a joined the navy!"

"Glad it warn't me. I'd be fish bait for sure!" This last from Joey Grant, racing about the harbor in his new ten-horsepower Evinrude and not paying much attention to where he was going, just before his propeller fouled one of the harbor traps and pitched him headlong into the bottom of his scow. This led to a fresh round of good-natured commentary at Joey's expense as he dragged himself to his feet and, grinning foolishly, disentangled the line.

The excitement in the harbor over these episodes still had not died down a quarter of an hour later, when I emerged from Caleb's with my order and joined the hapless mariners at the landing.

I saw a fair amount of Kevin and Karen during the next week or ten days, before Kevin went off to an air base in Massachusetts to do his required flying time. He had recovered from his war injury and walked without a cane, though he still had a slight limp, and I gathered always would. It gave him a certain dignity, I thought. His hair was longer and partially hid his comic right ear. An undisciplined black lock persistently fell over one eye. Kevin was more serious than the summer before—despite his idyllic distractions on the island with Gloria and Karen, not to mention his amorous adventures. Sally, I had to admit, was probably right in her analysis there. He managed to slip off once again for a night in Rockland before he left, on the pretext of seeing a movie he had missed but that proved, when Sally compulsively checked up on it, to have played the week before.

"I ask you!" was her comment when she told me—gleefully, I thought—of this latest escapade.

But Kevin had matured. He took the world more to heart. He belabored the administration for our domestic ills and was caustic about the direction of our foreign policy. It was insane, he said, to jettison wartime collaboration with the Russians, which alone could make a stable world. Kevin was also passing beyond mere words now. He planned to do something about his beliefs. For instance, when I chided him lightly for talking almost subversively—he was still an officer in the air force reserve, after all—he said he knew it and planned to look into the matter of resigning his commission during the coming duty. Meanwhile, he was active in several left-wing groups at Princeton and in one or two national organizations.

Well, I respected the way Kevin grappled with these problems. Not his views, necessarily, but the forthright approach he took. He might have been wrong, but there was nothing namby-pamby about Kevin. I also respected him for not forcing his views on anyone and everyone—Sally and George, for instance, and Wylie Thatcher after he arrived. What Kevin believed in, he believed. But he wasn't seeking converts or arguing for the sake of arguing. We therefore struck an easy relationship, unencumbered by past association, though I could see Kevin was often perplexed on where I stood on many issues of concern to him.

As for Karen, my impressions remained much as they had been the year before. Her beauty—let me confess it—continued to haunt me. It distracted me more than I cared to admit, so that I was not a particularly acute observer of her development. At the same time, Karen really was an enigmatic personality, in those days without explicit form. I learned her interests quickly enough—United World Federalism (UWF) and minority rights; her commitment to both, I believe, was genuine, not simply lip service to two currently popular causes. But when she talked about these issues, it was without passion. Or imagination. The idea kept creeping back that perhaps Karen was, after all, stupid; realization of it was simply deflected by her good looks. But you no sooner reached this conclusion than you knew it wasn't so. She perceived too much, she understood too promptly for anyone observing her carefully to imagine she was slow of mind. Reserved, yes. And solemn—except for moments like the incident at the mooring. She was capable of laughter. What she seemed *incapable* of was warmth toward people. Including herself, I might add. I don't believe I've ever known anyone as indifferent to *self* as Karen Bannister.

But I find I confuse my impressions of Karen that summer, after her first year in college, with those of some time later, when I knew her better.

I want to talk about the islanders now, not the young Bannisters. There was a deceptive atmosphere of tranquility on the island when I arrived. If I hadn't had that conversation on the mailboat with the gentleman from Blueberry Isle, I might have thought all was normal. The lobstermen went out in the morning and came back in one by one during the course of the late afternoon. They gathered in clusters around the harbor or at Caleb's, as they always had. But if one looked carefully, one detected tension. Especially among the senior citizens. If any adult Grants or Claytons were at the store, adult Cutlers and Allens were apt to walk on by. And vice versa. If a summer vacationer joined a group of islanders, the islanders would break off what they were saying and conversation would become desultory. They kept their thoughts to themselves. They weren't inclined to discuss lobster piracy and sabotage with summer people. And I was summer people.

I made the mistake of telling Caleb, finding him alone at the store a day or two after I returned, what the gentleman from Blueberry Isle had told me aboard the *Laura Lee.*

"That so?" Caleb blandly commented. "Well, he must know more'n I do."

After that I probed no further, even with Turk. Even with Lucy.

It was only ten days after I returned that I first learned from Arthur Dacey the magnitude of the lobster war. We were walking home from the harbor early one evening, having just returned together from Rockland, where I had picked up a few supplies while Arthur was selling a week's accumulation of lobsters. We had been struck by heavy thunder squalls on the way and were drawn together by the exhilaration of battling steep seas and driving rain in the *Sarah Lou.* The squalls had now passed, and the air was fresh. I had asked Arthur earlier—quite routinely—how the lobsters were behaving this season, and he had replied, "The lobsters are behaving fair enough. . . . It's the lobstermen." Following my rule of not prying into the lobstermen's affairs, I had said nothing. Now, on the high road, Arthur came back to the subject of his own accord.

"You ask how the lobstering's going this season, and I'll tell you. We'll all be out of business if things go on as they are. . . . This week alone Clyde Grant's lost sixty traps according to his calculations, including Willy. Zip Clayton's lost seventy-five, and Lloyd Cutler says he's lost thirty-eight. This isn't counting the traps snarled up every day around the Ledges and elsewhere. The catch this week was less'n half what's normal this time of year."

I asked why the warden couldn't get on top of the trouble and put a stop to it.

"Cliff Dawson means well," Arthur said, "but he's a coaster. He comes around every few days and takes notes. He's got a book full of complaints. But that's as far as it goes. Complaints!"

"If Cliff Dawson can't do it, who can?"

"That's just our problem. . . . At some point, when there's enough suspicion on who's to blame, the lobstermen're going to take the law into their own hands. And that's where more troubles start." Arthur slowed his pace, apparently weighing something in his mind. When he spoke again, it was in a different voice. "Now, you keep this under your hat, 'cause you're outside this, remember. But I suspect Willy Grant's behind some of this business. You most likely didn't notice him, but Willy was over in Rockland today . . . and that's the second time I've seen him there the last month. Now I can't for the life o' me think what Willy Grant'd be doing in Rockland if not dropping off lobsters he'd come by illegally. He can sell 'em anywhere on the coast he's a mind to, of course. I don't run a monopoly on buying lobsters. But I know he can't pull his traps and take the time to run 'em over to Rockland as profitably as he can sell 'em in the harbor to me. Besides, he already sold me three hundred dollars' worth this week . . . and that's a fair catch for the traps he has out. Then the crazy hours he keeps. Some days he'll be out 'fore daybreak. Other days he's not in till after dark. And he's got his traps scattered so far apart—'testin,' he calls it—no one knows where he'll turn up next."

We had stopped at my turnoff, and Arthur stood in the middle of the road digging his toe into a rut.

"Now I don't know whether the Thorn Islanders have their suspicions of Willy, but they know something's fishy over here, and that's why we get so many snarled-up traps—and cut ones. . . . 'Course, our folks do the same back to them. That's the way it goes."

I asked if anyone had complained to the warden about Willy.

"I shouldn't be surprised," Arthur said. "But Willy's smart. He's always on his best behavior when anyone's around. And he's always the first one to run up to Cliff and tell him 'bout a tangle of pots he's just noticed . . . Then he likes to play the clown, you know. He'll get everyone laughing, and they want to think he's a good fella. I don't think Clyde himself suspects Willy would do anything."

Since Arthur had taken me so far into his confidence, I thought I could ask him how the lines were drawn on the island—that is, apart from the Grants and the Cutlers, about whose rivalry, I told Arthur, I was aware.

Arthur pondered the question a moment before replying, debating *whether* to reply, I think, not how. "Well," he said finally, "the Yorks are divided on this one. Rudolf and Leonard 're friendly to Clyde Grant; Leonard's wife and Clyde's are sisters, I guess you know. Tucker and Walter York tend to side with Lloyd Cutler, and Lloyd o' course is loyal to his brother-in-law, Cecil Allen. Bill York's pro-Bill, and he goes whichever way the wind blows. Alfred Torrey goes back and forth, dependin'. . . . I tell this so's you won't blunder more'n you have to with your neighbors. Turk's neutral, of course."

Arthur cautioned me again to keep what he'd told me to myself, and I did.

But I was grateful for his having filled me in on the background of the lobstermen's dilemma. It helped to put into perspective the events of the following
weeks.

Two days later I came across Willy in Clyde's old boat, the *Clarissa B,* outside Little Ram. We were returning—Karen, Gloria, and I—from an afternoon
sail. The other lobstermen had gone in, and Willy was alone among a string of
buoys behind the island. The stern of his boat was piled high with traps he was
apparently moving from one location to another. We waved, and he drew close
to us as we ran slowly before a light southwesterly.

"Pretty-lookin' sight," he called, switching off his engine. "Don't jump overboard, Karen."

"No danger," Karen said.

I asked where he was taking the traps.

"Off the Head. No future here."

"What color are your traps, Willy?" Gloria asked. "So we won't run over
them."

"Green 'n' white . . . and go right ahead. You couldn't snarl 'em up any
worse'n they are already. Someone's been messin' around again."

"Who?" said Gloria.

"You tell me, sugar. Most likely them bums over to Thorn."

I asked how many lobsters he'd caught that day. Willy looked into the barrel
behind him.

" 'Bout sixty-seventy pounds," he said.

"Where do you sell them?" I asked—I hoped not too archly.

"Sell 'em? Why, with Arthur, of course. Where else would I sell lobster?"

I suggested he might sell them in Stonington. Or Rockland.

"'Twouldn't pay," Willy said. "No one'd go so far."

"You could see Mary Lou in Rockland," Gloria remarked.

The breeze had moved us away from the *Clarissa B.* Willy waved and circled
off toward the Head.

"Willy's my favorite lobsterman," Gloria said. I made no reply.

As we passed the string of pots where he'd been, I saw none that were green
and white—but then, I reflected, that proved nothing, absolutely nothing, for he
could have just taken his out. Cliff Dawson's task, I decided, was more difficult
than it seemed.

14

T he infection on the island hadn't yet spread to the Little Leaguers, at least not to such an extent that Turk couldn't fashion them into an imposing baseball team, the best since the days of Stanley Talbot. Turk was the force behind the team, assisted by Willy Grant. Three afternoons a week they practiced behind the school, and there was normally a game on Sunday. They'd beaten Stonington once at home and lost an extra-inning game there the Sunday before I arrived. They'd also won a game at Vinalhaven as well as the first game at home with Thorn Island. That was the end of June, before the troubles began. The second game with Thorn Island, away, was set for early August.

A large number of islanders went over for the game, a larger number than usual—not only because of the traditional prewar rivalry between the two clubs, but also to provide safety in numbers. Just in case. Rudolf York, who hadn't watched a game in fifteen years, went along "to protect his own on furrin' soil," as he put it. There was a light fog in the morning, but it had burned off by noon when the islanders gathered at the harbor for the expedition. Turk and Willy carried the players, all in uniform, together with their equipment. The rest of us making the trip distributed ourselves in one boat or another in the flotilla. I went with Arthur, along with George Bannister and the two girls.

"Looks like a danged Armada, don't it?" Caleb said, surveying the harbor from the pier. "The invasion of Thorn Island."

Arthur said to me privately, as he swung the *Sarah Lou* into the procession, "Nothing like a ball game to pull an island together."

We went off in convoy when the last passengers were berthed. Willy Grant, with his new stepped-up engine, cut in and out among the other boats, egged on by his youthful crew.

At Thorn Island's harbor, after discharging their passengers, the lobstermen found moorings or anchored in the cove among the other boats. Turk tied up the *Sunrise,* which carried all the equipment, at the dock. A number of Thorn Islanders were on hand to greet us, led by Clarence Darling, a portly ex-lobsterman in his seventies and the island's acknowledged patriarch.

"Welcome to the queen of the Penobscot, Arthur," he said as we climbed up from the float. "What're all them clubs and masks I see? I hope you're not comin' in a warlike spirit."

"Just enough of it to beat the britches off your ball club, Clarence," Arthur said.

"Well, if that's all, there's no danger. The Thorn Island team, I'm told, can't be beat."

The greeting wasn't everywhere so courtly. The islanders we met on our way to the baseball field, located on a saddle in the middle of the island, were for the most part sullen. A few Thorn Island wives nodded to our women as they passed, but the men avoided each other—except for Cecil Allen, who went off with a group of Thorn Island lobstermen soon after we arrived and reappeared only at the end of the game.

The Thorn Island players were having infield practice when we arrived, and they presently yielded the field to our lads, then stood along the first base line to watch. And comment. These young players knew each other well. They attended high school together in Rockland or Camden. They shared the *Laura Lee* on trips to and fro. They, accordingly, had fewer inhibitions than their elders.

"Ya brung along your cheerleaders, I see," a towheaded boy called out— referring, of course, to Karen and Gloria, whom most of the Thorn Islanders hadn't seen since before the war and who naturally aroused a lively curiosity.

"You'll need 'em, I tell ya," another added.

"Better 'n' bringin' your whole team over here from Camden, anyways," Silas York shouted back, referring to two seventeen-year-olds in the Thorn Island lineup who lived on the mainland. But Turk had already checked this out with the umpire from Stonington and found they were eligible; the two were spending the month of August with their uncle, a lobsterman who was summering on the island.

"They're okay, Si," Turk said, hitting him a bouncing grounder that he bobbled. "Keep your mind on what you're doin'."

As the game was about to start, a swelling rumble rose from the west end of the island, and a few seconds later a silver-winged Lightning streaked a few hundred feet above the field, banked, and climbed steeply seaward, leaving a deafening roar behind.

"Kevin! Kevin!"

"Hey, we're bein' bombed! They've brung out the air force!"

We watched the twin-fuselaged plane travel over Ram Island, then slowly turn and come back. It passed again over the field, in two right rolls, before it disappeared over the western bay. The entire exercise lasted less than three minutes.

"I don't th-think Kevin should be doing that," George said, beside me.

"Oh, Uncle George! Why shouldn't he?" said Gloria. "I mean, it's a tribute to the team. He remembered the day."

"A tribute to himself," Karen said, but there was a glint of satisfaction in her eyes. And George himself didn't seem too unhappy, seeing the pleasure Kevin's caper gave the islanders.

One reason George Bannister had come over to Thorn Island that day was to visit Gabriel's Hole, the legendary cove the gentleman from Blueberry Isle had pointed out to me from the *Laura Lee* the year before. When the game was under way, I accompanied George to the famous smugglers' lair. We followed a winding road up the ridge, past several abandoned farms and orchards choked with alder. Thorn Island had a more neglected look than Ram, yet appeared to have had a larger population earlier in its history. Now the western end of the island was deserted, the present inhabitants concentrated in a cluster of houses on the northeast tip beyond the saddle. No one lived any longer on the harbor.

When the road gave out, we continued on a footpath over a shoulder of the high ground that dominated the island's southeast flank and then descended steeply to the rim of the Hole. It was not more than seventy-five yards across and seemed at first inspection to be totally enclosed by heavily wooded slopes rising sharply on all sides. In short, it was an island pond, fed by a thin stream that found its way between ledges at one end. Five dories loaded with seining gear, at anchor in the center of the cove, however, dispelled this idea, and as we moved along the shore, we could make out a narrow winding channel to the sea past the Sentinel, a massive rock in mid-channel that covered at half-tide. It was half-tide now, and the sea coming in sucked greedily at the seaweed clinging to the rock.

"What a nasty w-w-welcome to anyone not knowing it was there!" George said.

We climbed onto a boulder below some caves and watched until the Sentinel was covered and the sea rolled smoothly over it. George, who knew the legends, told me several of them—including one about a colonial privateer that hid for a week from a British war sloop patrolling offshore, its masts cut down and its hull covered with spruce boughs. As we rose to leave, a figure appeared on a high ledge at the head of the cove. He stood for a moment surveying the Hole before he saw us. George waved, but the figure drew back into the woods as abruptly as he had appeared.

"Wasn't that T-Tucker York's boy?" George asked. I said I thought it was, and George remarked, "I wonder how he got up there." But George was presently into another legend, and I think he forgot about the episode entirely. Indeed, I very nearly did—until some days later, when it seemed to have some relevance. I didn't notice whether Bill York was back at the baseball field when we returned.

The game was entering a critical stage when George and I rejoined Karen and Gloria. The Thorn Islanders were coming to bat in the sixth, and there was still no score. Harassment of the batters by both sides had grown as the game proceeded, the girls told me, and the umpire was beginning to show his irritation. The first batter drew a base on balls, as Peter Torrey's control began to flag. The second batter was Danny Orcutt (Jesse Cutler had, of course, kept Lucille at home), and since he was the Thorn Islanders' longest hitter, the catcalls rose immediately from our benches, Willy Grant leading the chorus. I could see that Danny's brother Barney, who coached the Thorn Island team—this time, without his oilskins, I recognized him right away as the sergeant on the *Laura Lee* the previous September—was livid with anger. The umpire let two pitches pass, then he stopped the game and strode deliberately over to the Ram Island side.

"You shut your mouth, young fella," he said, shaking a finger at Willy, "or you'll forfeit the game."

Gloria, as play was about to resume, whispered to George that it wasn't fair. "I mean, anyone ought to be able to say what they want."

George said equitably, "It seems f-fair enough to me."

Fair or not, Danny Orcutt hit the next pitch into the bushes in left field, and that started the Thorn Islanders' big inning. By the time Peter Torry had retired the last batter half an hour later, they had amassed six runs. The Ram Islanders came back with three runs in the next two innings, holding the Thorn Islanders hitless, but their first two batters struck out in the ninth. Mark Cutler got a single, and Mickey Clayton drew a walk. Jamie Allen hit an easy grounder to third, but the third baseman dropped it, and the bases were loaded. One of the twins, Paul Torrey, was up next, but since he was a weak hitter, Turk sent Joey Grant in to bat. Joey, at two hundred pounds, was too clumsy in the field to play a regular position, but he was a good batter, and Turk often used him as a pinch hitter to keep up his enthusiasm. Joey swung at the first pitch and lifted it into center field, not a long fly, but the center fielder was blinded momentarily by the sun, and the ball fell behind him. By the time he'd recovered it and threw it back in, three runs had crossed and the score was tied. It stayed that way the rest of the inning, and the game proceeded into the tenth. In the last of the tenth, with two out, Danny Orcutt hit a high fly to right field, where Turk had put Joey—on the theory, I suppose, that he was less of a liability there than anywhere else. Well, Joey tripped and fell running for the ball, and Danny made it easily around the bases before Joey could get the ball back into the infield. So the game ended.

A great cheer went up from the Thorn Island side as the players swarmed around Danny Orcutt, slapping him on the back and pumping his hand.

"If it'd been anybody but that bugger," Willy said.

Danny, impassive, walked away from the group around him and shook hands with Peter Torrey.

"Good game, Pete," he said.

Joey was still standing disconsolately in the outfield. He'd hardly moved from where he'd finally picked up Danny's fly. Turk walked slowly out to him.

"What's eatin' you, boy? You saved the game, didn't you? Guess that gives you leave to do what you want with it."

He put a hairy arm around Joey's shoulder, and they walked back together to the infield as the Ram Islanders were preparing for the return home. The Thorn Islanders dispersed quickly, except for a few who accompanied us down to the harbor. Danny Orcutt was one of these. He walked with his second cousin, Jamie Allen, just behind George and me.

"How's Lucille?" he asked after some moments.

"She's okay."

More silence. "Is she goin' back to high school in September?"

"Yup. She's goin' to Rockland now."

Then another long moment of silence.

"Say hi to her, okay?"

At the dock as we were embarking again in the lobster boats, Clarence Darling stood solemnly beside Arthur Dacey, looking out over the breakwater to the open bay.

"I don't get out there so often as I used to, Arthur. . . . I hope our people ain't goin' to do each other harm."

"Clarence, there's nothin' I wish more than that, believe me."

I went back with Turk in the *Sunrise*, since most of the Little Leaguers had joined their families for the return trip. Halfway home his engine coughed once and died. Turk checked the engine, looked puzzled, and peered into the gas tank. It was empty.

"Well, I'm a son of a bitch!" he said softly.

He hailed Arthur, abeam of us in the *Sarah Lou* with a boatload of passengers, and Arthur swung around to our help.

"What's your trouble, Turk?"

"Plumb out of gas. What d'ya know about that?"

Arthur looked at him curiously, but Turk merely shrugged his shoulders. Arthur threw him a line and towed us into harbor.

"Well, if it gets no worse'n a practical joke like that now and then," Turk said, "maybe we'll still make it through the season."

But it did get worse. That Sunday early in August was the last time the inhabitants of the two islands met in anything resembling civility until late in the fall.

15

The first more-or-less declaration of war came three days after the baseball game when Willy Grant, pulling traps off Seal Ledge late in the afternoon, was chased off by Barney Orcutt and Wilfred Hopewell. According to Willy's story, which spread rapidly over the island as soon as he came in, he

had been pulling his half dozen traps there in a light fog when the two Thorn
Islanders came up on each side of him and told him to clear off and not come
back.

" 'We catch ya 'round these ledges again, Leatherneck,' " Barney Orcutt had
said, as Willy told the story, " 'we're gonna sink your fuckin' boat.' " Willy quoted
the words relentlessly to male and female alike. "How d'ya like that? My 'fuckin'
boat,' he said."

"Well, clean it up, Willy," Jenny Brewster told him after hearing the story for
the fifth time. "We don't have t' hear it 'xactly like he said it."

The senior lobstermen—except for Clyde, of course—reacted cautiously to
Willy's story. Rudolf and Tucker York and Lloyd Cutler heard him out patiently
and shook their heads, whether in astonishment or disbelief it was hard to say.
Cecil Allen heard the story once and left the harbor. The younger fishermen
wanted to do something immediately—they weren't sure just what—but by the
time they'd come together at the landing the fog had thickened and there was
only a half hour of daylight left.

Arthur and Turk came in late from Rockland on the *Sarah Lou* and were the
last to hear Willy's story. Arthur listened gravely, asked Willy a few questions,
and after conferring briefly with several of the lobstermen, he put in a call to
Cliff Dawson in Belfast. Caleb's phone, still the only one on the island, was in a
storeroom behind the counter, and Arthur left the door open. The group in the
store fell silent when the call went through. It was a poor connection, as usual,
but Arthur could make himself understood.

"Cliff . . . Arthur Dacey here. Can you hear? . . . We've had some trouble at
the Ledges, one of our lobstermen chased off. . . . Yes, Clyde Grant's boy Willy. . .
. By Sam Orcutt's son and Wilfred Hopewell. . . . Now, listen, Cliff, we plan to
pull our traps out of there tomorrow morning. Can you stand by? . . . How's
that? . . . Be about seven o'clock if the fog's lifted. . . . All right, make it eight."

Arthur rang off presently and turned to the lobstermen.

"Eight o'clock. Anyone has traps there oughta be on hand."

He left Caleb's with Turk and started up to the crossroads. The other lobstermen soon followed.

"What the hell's Cliff Dawson suppos'd to do?" Willy said to Bill York as
they stepped out into the fog. "Anchor himself at the Ledges ever' mornin' at
eight o'clock?"

The fog was thick in the harbor the next morning but seemed thinner away
from the island. It was light overhead and promised to be clear by ten. I had
already planned to spend the day out with Turk, and he saw no reason why I
shouldn't. Arthur Dacey joined us.

We reached the Ledges shortly before eight, along with the other lobstermen. Turk pulled his traps and found them all intact and the catch normal. Clyde found most of his traps snarled, and the half dozen Willy said he had at the Ledges were missing. One or two of the other lobstermen reported some molesting; others found their gear intact. About nine, as the fog lifted, we saw Cliff Dawson hovering by, a quarter of a mile away. A few Thorn Islanders were visible along their own shore, but none of them came near Seal Ledge. Cliff came in to us and made notes on reported sabotage.

"Arthur," he said, throttling his engine as he pulled alongside the *Sunrise,* "Sam Orcutt says Willy Grant's been pullin' everybody's traps out here but his own for the past month. Sam's boys seen him do it."

Arthur said nothing, and Turk asked who else besides Sam's boys had seen Willy pulling traps illegally.

"Well, I guess there's plenty who'll *say* they seen him. Anyway, they're that sure he's doin' it . . . and . . . well, I don't want to stir up no trouble, but I'm leanin' that way myself."

"Have you talked to Willy, Cliff?" Turk asked.

"Ever tried to outtalk Bob Hope? Same difference. He's got fifty funny things happened to him that mornin' he's got to tell you 'bout and a hundred reasons he couldn't 'a been where you asked him if he was. He puts on those big brown eyes . . . 'Oh, no, Cliff . . . Mr. Warden, sir . . . I was on the other side of the bay untangling a few o' my traps got mixed up somehow.' . . . Arthur, I was wonderin' if you'd have a go at Willy. I think he might listen to you."

Arthur was still silent, staring up at the gulls circling over our stern.

"What d'ya say, Arthur?"

"Well, I'll talk to him," Arthur said at last. "But if Willy tells me he's doing nothing wrong, I'm going to believe him, Cliff . . . Least till we have better evidence than what Sam Orcutt's boys say."

"Do what you can," Cliff said, and pulled away.

We crossed to the northeast shore and worked the eastern side of the island, but came in soon after noon when the marine forecaster reported line squalls moving down the coast. Willy was just behind us. We dropped Arthur off at his float, and ten minutes later, there being no one around, Arthur hailed Willy as he rowed from his mooring to the pier. They had their talk all right, but as Arthur told us about it later, it proved fruitless. Willy denied touching any traps but his own and said Cliff Dawson had been listening to "a bunch of crap from that no-good bastard Barney Orcutt and his gang. He'd call his grandma a poacher if it'd do him any good."

"So Cliff's got no grounds for his suspicions?" Arthur asked.

"Uncle Arthur, what would I be pullin' other traps for when I got more out 'n I can handle myself?"

Arthur asked how many traps he had out, and Willy told him ninety-five; he was putting out fifty more the next day.

Then Arthur had shifted to generalities, trying to explain how everyone suffered if two or three lobstermen started their own private vendetta. There'd been the same kind of trouble fifteen years earlier, and incomes were halved for that season. Already this season, he told Willy, they were running a quarter to a third behind the take last year at this time.

"I was beginning to sound like Preacher Hargrave," Arthur told us, a rare twinkle in his eye that reminded me of Jingle. "But I might as well have saved my breath . . . as Willy said to me straight out. 'I know everythin' you're sayin', Uncle Arthur,' he said. 'I heard it a million times. If those sons o' bitches'll leave me alone, I'll leave them. Okay? And don't be forgettin' *I* was the one lost six traps today, not that bugger of a sergeant over to Thorn Island.' About that time Zip Clayton came along, and that ended our little talk."

Arthur was silent for a few moments as we came to the crossroads. Then he said, "Still . . . where does he get the ready cash for fifty new traps?"

That night the dories were cut adrift in Gabriel's Hole and the seines mutilated. Three of the dories were smashed beyond repair by heavy seas breaking on the Sentinel. Cliff Dawson called Caleb at seven in the morning, soon after the vandalism was reported, and asked for Arthur Dacey to call back when he came down. Arthur reached the harbor a half hour later and returned the warden's call. Cliff was grim.

"Arthur, I don't need to tell you this is a damn big loss; I can't reckon now how many thousands of dollars in net and boats. As you gotta know, they own the seines in common over there. . . . What I gotta know, Arthur, is who of your people were out last night."

"Cliff, I can't do that for you. I live out here."

"Arthur, you got to. Otherwise, we're goin' to ask the commissioner to suspend your licenses till this is cleared up. . . . There's got to be a way o' findin' out who went out last night."

Arthur was silent at his end of the line. "D'ya hear me, Arthur?" Cliff asked.

"I hear you, Cliff," Arthur said.

"If you can't find this out for me"—Cliff raised his voice above the static—"I'll have to ask for help from the Sheriff's Department. There's no other way."

"I know," said Arthur gloomily. "We'll see what we can find out."

"I'll drop by toward the end of the afternoon," the warden said, and rang off.

Caleb had been listening from the counter and said to Arthur when he returned from the storeroom, his solemn features more lugubrious than ever,

"We didn't hear a sound last night, Arthur. I thought o' this soon's Cliff called, and Jenny and I talked it over. I'll swear no lobster boat left the harbor after dark."

Harold Toothacher, the only other islander except Widow Barnaby who lived at the harbor, swore the same. He said he slept so light he'd have "heard a pollock jump; it was that still."

It might have been still in the harbor, but it was a restless night in the bay. The seas had been building for two days from a storm blown out over the Maritimes and were churned up still more by the line squalls that afternoon. The breakers were five or six feet high off the Head at dusk, and the wind was from the south at twenty knots.

So Arthur set about his thankless task of trying to discover how any islander could have gone across to Gabriel's Hole in those seas, if not in one of the larger boats. There were half a dozen smaller boats in the harbor sturdy enough to make the trip, especially with a powerful outboard motor. One of these could have been rowed out past the jetty, so as not to disturb even Harold's light sleep. One could have been left outside the harbor earlier, to be picked up after dark. But after as careful a check as he was able to make, Arthur concluded that no lobsterman could have gone over to Thorn Island that night from the harbor and returned before Horatio Leadbetter came down at four-thirty. He was at the harbor for the rest of the morning.

I think I was able to give Arthur almost the only clue he could find any-where that day, and this amounted to no more than a shaky hypothesis. I remembered noting only one of the two dories Clyde kept moored in my cove when I stepped out to the outhouse about midnight and thought to myself he must have towed the other away without my noticing. Both were there when I woke up at seven. I mentioned this to Arthur later in the day, and he speculated that a pair of strong oarsmen might have rowed around the Head and across to Gabriel's Hole, then back again, under cover of darkness. The visibility was good, and though the surf was heavy on the shore, the swells were long and even. The wind had dropped shortly after midnight. It was a possibility, Arthur felt—but he seemed almost relieved when I emphasized that I couldn't be cer-tain a dory was gone, for I hadn't checked carefully. Clyde, meanwhile, said he knew nothing about a dory missing from Cutler's Cove . . . but, of course, there were other dories moored in secluded coves around the island, ready on short notice for seining if there was a run of herring. Any of them could have served the same purpose. Some were on pulley lines attached to shore. And if there was no other way to reach a dory, several of the younger lobstermen, unlike their elders, had learned to swim.

I also told Arthur about seeing Bill York at Gabriel's Hole the Sunday before, and he brooded about this for some moments before going on with his inquiries.

Arthur—and I say this to his credit—was not cut out for the work the warden had charged him with. It was repugnant to him to be seeking evidence from some islanders that might inculpate others. He was almost resentful, I felt, when I told him about Clyde's dory and about seeing Bill York at the Hole. Meanwhile, he had to keep everything he learned to himself, for the least indiscretion in present circumstances could throw the whole delicate balance of island relationships into jeopardy. There was literally no lobsterman other than Turk with whom he could discuss the new developments—and Turk had left early that day to set out new traps on the far side of the bay and wouldn't be in, Sharon said, until late in the afternoon. This was still before any of the lobstermen in our fleet had installed shortwave receivers. Some of the lobstermen were distinctly unhelpful, even hostile, when Arthur approached them. Zip Clayton, for instance.

"Arthur, why're you troublin' yourself over this? The Thorn Islanders lost their nets an' got a couple o' dories staved up. But you know 's well 's I do they deserved it. . . . I don't care shit who done it," Zip opined.

After Zip had left the shore, Caleb said, "Arthur, I wouldn't be in your boots if you gave me a thousand dollars."

"It'll cost us a sight more'n that before we're clear of this one," Arthur said.

When Cliff Dawson dropped by at four, Arthur told him that no boat had been out of the harbor the night before, so far as anyone knew.

"Now, someone could've rowed a dory across," he said, "but I don't know who, and I don't think I can find out."

Cliff was skeptical about the dory thesis, but he thanked Arthur anyway, and after jotting down more notes in his book, he went off again.

"About Bill York," Arthur said to me privately as we walked away from the landing after the warden left. "I decided against saying anything about that. It seemed a mean thing to do to throw suspicion on a man 'cause he happened to be in a place where something happens five days later, a place anybody might go to look at . . . the way you did." We walked on in silence. "That doesn't mean I don't have my ideas on the matter. . . . I just don't want to point a finger at Bill York, anymore'n I did at Willy Grant, till I'm surer than I am now."

16

The next episode in the lobster war seemed a deliberate piece of provocation, not mere reprisal. On a foggy Sunday, a day when the Thorn Islanders did not go out as a rule, Turk Jenkins lost every trap off Seal Ledge, half his string outside Little Ram, and most of the new traps he had out across the bay. Ninety-three altogether, or nearly two thirds of his total gear. His buoys from the cut lines were drifting around the bay for the next week. No other lobsterman from Ram Island lost a single trap that day.

The islanders were incredulous as the news of Turk's loss spread on Monday morning. Turk had long since been recognized as a restraining influence in the rivalry between the lobstermen of the two islands, just as he was neutral in the intrafamily feuds on our island. If there was anyone with whom the Thorn Islanders might be expected to sit down and talk out their differences, it was Turk. To single out Turk as their victim, therefore, meant that the Thorn Islanders—and there wasn't any doubt that Thorn Islanders were behind this act of vandalism—were declaring total war. It was no longer a tooth for a tooth. Most of the Thorn Island lobstermen, it was calculated, must have had a hand in the raid, for it would have taken that many to piece together where Turk had his traps and then to find them in the fog.

Turk himself came in early and went straight home after filling his tanks at the landing and telling Arthur the extent of his losses. The other lobstermen, as they came in, stood about in clusters on the pier or at Caleb's waiting for Turk to reappear. But Turk didn't go down to the harbor again that afternoon. I stopped by at the Peaks later in the day, and Sharon said he was still off in the woods, chopping. He'd been out there since he came home. He wouldn't even come in to eat, she said. Sharon was drawn and tense, her eyes moist with anguish for her strong-willed husband.

"I'm afraid what he'll do," she said. "He can be so . . . so headstrong."

I asked whether Turk had spoken with anyone, and Sharon said he wouldn't talk about it, even with her. She hadn't known herself what had happened until she went to the store after lunch.

"We'll buy new traps," I said, trying to be helpful. "Turk shouldn't worry about replacing his equipment."

"It's not the traps," Sharon said, and I knew as well as she it wasn't. "He's just hurt it was him. He's like a . . . well, you know, a little bird mindin' its own business after it's been attacked by a big bird. Like a sparrow hawk."

I said I'd come by later. Maybe he'd feel more like talking after supper.

"Bring Arthur," Sharon said. "He always likes to talk to you and Arthur."

When Arthur and I returned, about nine in the evening, Turk had already left.

"I stepped out to his ma's for a few minutes after I put the kids to bed," Sharon told us, "and when I came back, he'd gone. . . . He left this." She handed Arthur a note that read, "Tiger—I am going out tonite. Don't worry about me. I will be back before daybreak. Your loving husband."

Arthur passed the note to me, and I stared at it in silence, listening to the wind rising in the spruce trees outside.

"I followed him down to the shore and saw him go aboard," Sharon said. "But I didn't try to stop him." Now that Turk had made his decision—what it was none of us dared guess—Sharon was more in control of herself. She was almost serene. "Does he have enough gas, Arthur?"

"He's got enough to get to Portland and back," Arthur assured her.

Sharon insisted we have a glass of wine, and we sat with her for half an hour, talking about one thing or another but staying clear of the war between the islands. It began to rain, at first in spasmodic bursts against the windows, then more regularly. The wind continued to rise from the east.

At the door, as we were leaving, Arthur asked Sharon if she'd like her mother to spend the night with her. Or Lucy or—

"No one, Uncle Arthur. Really. I'm not afraid."

"Well, like Turk says, don't worry, Sharon. I feel worse about what he'll do to the Thorn Islanders than what the weather'll do to him."

Still, it was impossible not to be concerned for Turk that night. The wind rose steadily until the early hours of the morning, reaching twenty-five to thirty knots and lashing the eastern shore with six-foot breakers. Visibility was nearly zero at times, thanks to the scudding, the driving rain, and the fog blown in with the easterly. Arthur spent most of the night, he told me later, walking back and forth between the harbor and the Peaks, keeping a watch out for Turk and over Sharon. Other lobstermen were up, too, since several islanders had seen Turk go out after dark, and the word spread. During a lull in the storm, Clyde Grant and Leonard York actually set out to look for the *Sunrise,* but turned back when they realized how high the seas were beyond the lee of the island. Not a few islanders that night were sleepless in their beds, listening to the rain whip on window-panes and imagining Turk somewhere out on the bay alone.

I was up at dawn. The wind had dropped somewhat, and the visibility was improved, but the seas still ran high. As I drank my coffee by the rain-streaked window looking out over the cove, preparing to go down to the harbor for news of Turk, a lobster boat came into view through the mist and rode in toward the two dories on the shoaling sea. I knew even before I could make out its lines it was the *Sunrise.* Turk swung neatly around the stern of the nearest dory and grabbed its painter with his gaff. In a few moments he had secured the *Sunrise* to the mooring and cast off in the dory for the beach. I was there to help him land. The tide was still going out, so we left the waterlogged dory where it grounded and walked up to the bungalow.

"I put in here to duck questions," Turk said. "And to git some advice. . . . Sharon all right?"

I said she had been at ten o'clock the evening before. And not too worried, considering. Turk stripped off his dripping oilskins and pulled of his boots while I poured coffee for him, topping it up with rum. I put on bacon.

"I had a change o' heart," Turk said. "I didn't go through with it."

"With what, Turk?" I was feeling cold in the pit of my stomach.

"I was gonna scatter their fleet. . . . I figured if I couldn't fish in peace, they oughtn't to neither."

"So what did you do all night?"

"Well, I started out with my plan. I had 'em in tow, all right—"

"You had *all* their boats in tow?" I asked incredulously.

"The lobster boats, that is. I had nine of 'em. Couldn't git the other three. I hauled 'em out past the light, figurin' to drop 'em off one by one and let 'em fetch by where they would. I actually let two of 'em loose. Then I had my change o' heart and picked 'em up again. Barney Orcutt's and Will Hopewell's . . . I got to thinkin' I oughtn't to be punishing the whole island just 'cause I lost a mess o' pots. How'd they feed their kids?" He stopped to sip his coffee, then went on meditatively. "You know, I b'lieve if I'd had the whole fleet in tow, I wouldn't've changed my mind. I'd 'a been that dumb. . . . Anyways, that's what I came in to ask you about. We need a lawyer."

"But where are the boats now? Did you tow them all back to harbor?"

"I couldn't do that with the sea runnin' like it was. I hung 'em on the Old Woman."

"The red gong?"

Turk nodded and sipped his coffee again. "That's illegal, of course. The Coast Guard'll be after me for that. . . . But the boats 're safe there. I stuck around till the wind let up some to be sure they was ridin' easy. They was."

In my mood of relief at Turk's safe return, the irrelevance somehow of the Coast Guard's concern over a gong—or of Turk's concern over theirs, after battling all night through a thirty-knot easterly with a string of lobster boats in tow—suddenly struck me, and I laughed in his face. Turk glanced at his watch, then he too broke into a grin—for the first time since he'd come ashore. "They'll just be comin' down over there to go fishin'."

I took the bacon off the stove, poured more coffee, and we made our plans. I thought the gentleman from Blueberry Isle could help us find a lawyer, and we decided to go over that morning to ask him. Then we'd go on to Camden and make arrangements. Turk still had enough gas. I went up to tell Arthur our plan—Turk didn't want to see the other lobstermen yet—and to get word to Sharon that Turk was safe. Arthur also thought it wise to call Cliff Dawson to tell him where the Thorn Island boats were, since it was still too thick in the bay to see as far out as the Old Woman. He planned to tell Cliff that Turk's escapade was by way of a practical joke he'd thought better of; Turk would have brought the boats back if he could have managed it.

When I returned to Cutler's Cove, Turk was stretched out on the sofa asleep, and I let him sleep an hour before we set off on our expedition.

We found my friend on Blueberry Isle, and he promptly identified the lawyer we needed, an attorney in Portland who specialized in marine law. His name was Otis Lieberman, and he had graduated from Harvard Law School before the war. My friend strongly approved of the Ram Islanders' retaining a lawyer. The situation could only go from bad to worse if things continued as they were. As for Turk's adventure the night before, he was more amused by it than worried about the consequences.

"I'll bet you kicked yourself for letting those two boats go," he said to Turk, "once you decided to pick them up again."

Turk conceded that had been the toughest half hour.

As we left Blueberry Isle for Camden, the fog cleared enough for us to make out the string of lobster boats at the Old Woman, far across the bay against Deer Isle. Turk eyed them impassively, then took down his binoculars and counted.

"All nine," he said.

Before we lost them from view, half a dozen other lobster boats had begun to gather at the scene.

Halfway to Camden I made some remark about the motives of the Thorn Islanders in singling out Turk's traps for vandalizing. He was the last one, I would have thought, they would pick out for revenge.

"I wouldn't bet on that," Turk said, and he told me for the first time about his father's part in the old feud between the two islands during Prohibition.

"Pa never talked much 'bout rum-runnin'," Turk said. "That was 'cause he spent six months in jail for it, and he wasn't too proud about that. But some o' the others talked, like Rudolf and Clyde, and I pieced the story together from them. . . . Well, there was a big shipment from France one September, I guess the biggest they ever had. Nineteen twenty-five, I b'lieve it was. The Coast Guard knew somethin' was up, but they didn't know where. They still hadn't found out about the Hole then, but they know'd there was a hidin' place somewhere on one o' the two islands. They had a watch on both of 'em for better'n a year. . . . What they used to do, the runners, was to meet up with the freighters outside the three-mile limit off Isle au Haut. Usually at night. Then they'd run into the Hole, dodging the cutters. They used lobster boats rather'n seiners or draggers 'cause they was shiftier and could duck in behind the islands if they was chased. Anyways, the big boats couldn't make it into the Hole. . . . So that's how the lobstermen got into it. Also, the fishin' was bad for a few years there. Pa and Frank Talbot were the main runners from Ram. They had the fastest boats. Rudolf and Tucker and Clyde run the blockade if the weather was good. Arthur did for a spell, but Winifred didn't like it, so he quit."

"What about Lucy?" I asked.

"Well, Lucy never mixed up much in what Frank was doin'. They was too separate people. They got along good, you know, but they didn't git in each other's way."

I asked what happened to the contraband after it was dropped off at Gabriel's Hole, and Turk explained that they hid it in the caves until it could be picked up from Rockport. Sometimes it would go right away; other times it might stay at the Hole for months. Clarence Darling, who owned the shores around the Hole, was in charge of operations there.

Turk checked our position off a mussel shoal stretching out from a small island to port, then went on.

"Well, the night of this big shipment, the cutters were all around the islands. They must'a had a tip. Rudolf and Tucker was turned back off Mark Island. They was goin' seinin' out there, they said, but the Coast Guard told 'em there was no seinin' out there and to git their asses back to harbor. Then they came 'round to see who else'd gone out. And, o' course, Pa and Frank Talbot had. At Thorn, Sam Orcutt, the two Hopewells, and half a dozen others were out, They had more boats over there than we did. . . . Well, the sea was runnin' high that night, and they had quite a ride comin' back in. The Thorn Island boats stuck together and almost made it through a foggy patch off the Thoroughfare, but then they come on two cutters and had to dump their sacks in a hurry—they packed the stuff in gunny sacks. The Coast Guard took in their boats but let 'em go next day when they couldn't find nothin' on 'em.

"Frank Talbot had the biggest load that night 'cause o' the size 'n' speed of his boat. A cutter spotted him outside Isle au Haut and chased him a couple o' miles, then lost him. Frank ducked into a cove on the south side o' the island and beached the *Lucy Belle*. He scratched out the name and covered 'er over with seaweed, makin' it look like she'd been there a long time, so they missed him when they came out lookin' next day. But he'd driven 'er up the beach so far he couldn't git 'er off with his big load. He had to wait till the next spring tide 'fore he could git home. Everybody'd given him up for gone when he finally made it back and dropped off his stuff—less a couple o' sacks. He'd been livin' off it out there for ten days. He told the Coast Guard he'd had a spot of engine trouble, an' they couldn't prove he didn't."

We passed over a bar south of Islesboro and headed for Camden.

"Well, Pa wasn't so lucky. He'd gone east of Isle au Haut on his way in, thinkin' he'd find fewer cutters in Merchants Row. The passages are tighter there, and there's comfort in the islands. He was 'bout halfway home when the moon broke through the clouds, and there was a cutter blockin' his way. Pa tried to sneak in behind one o' the islands, dumping his sacks overboard as he went, but he might've saved hisself the trouble. When they caught up with him, he still had half a load aboard. . . . Well, I guess there was a little scuffle when they took him in. One of 'em—a young feller, new at it—was tryin' to put handcuffs on Pa, and Pa could be pretty ornery if anyone touched him. So in the shovin' and pushin', the young feller fell overboard. 'Course, they pulled him out right away, but Pa got charged with resistin' arrest, 'long with runnin' the blockade. . . . He pleaded guilty and went off to jail in Thomaston for six months. He didn't even bother to hire a lawyer."

Turk paused to wave at a lobsterman pulling traps off a shoal we were passing. I waited for him to explain the connection between his father's arrest and the feud with the Thorn Islanders.

"The raid at Gabriel's Hole was 'bout two weeks later," Turk continued, "couple o' days after Frank Talbot dropped his load. They took almost half a million in contraband from the caves and off the bottom and impounded all the fishin' boats on the island for a year. The Thorn Islanders was wiped out after that raid. They all claimed, o' course, they didn't know nothin' 'bout what was goin' on at the Hole. Clarence Darling was a respect'd man—his dad had been in the legislature—and they didn't want to take him to court. He didn't even git a fine . . . but they was wiped out all the same. They could fish the next season, but that was the end of the smugglin' business. They had some bad years. . . . They always thought Pa made a deal, took a shorter sentence than he'd oughta had for bein' caught red-handed in return for tellin' where the contraband was hid."

Turk stopped to blow his nose over the washrail. "Well, I don't think he did. I guess Frank Talbot thought at first he might've, 'cause he turned back his share of the last haul to Clarence after the raid. But later Frank changed his mind. He and Pa were always good friends. Frank made sure Ma had enough while Pa was in jail, and after he came back, Frank loaned him enough to git started again. . . . But the Thorn Islanders never changed their minds about Pa. Maybe that's why they're takin' it out on me."

Twenty years seemed to me a long time to bear a grudge against the family, and I said so.

"They held it 'gainst all the Ram Islanders that they stood behind Pa," Turk said. "They held everything against us. We got our telephone cable 'bout that time. We got a bell off the Horn. They got nothin'. They didn't get their break-water for 'bout ten years."

I asked Turk what happened to his father after he came back from Thomaston.

"Well, he'd lost his license for a year, and they took his boat for the fine, so he spent the time buildin' this one. Took him fifteen months. After he started fishin' again, he kep' to himself. He'd put his traps away from anybody else, and the only one he'd talk to much was Frank Talbot. I used to fish summers with him from the time I was twelve. He was just getting' himself fixed and talkin' about buildin' a sunporch for Ma when he died. Had a heart attack out in the bay. Made it back to harbor and walked home, but he was dead by mornin'."

It must have been the exhilaration of his night at sea that made Turk talk so much—certainly longer at a stretch than I'd ever heard from him. Now he seemed to sense he'd talked too much and abruptly stopped. He answered my questions, of which I still had many, so pointedly in monosyllables that I soon stopped asking them, and we approached Camden in silence.

I went ashore to call Otis Lieberman's office in Portland while Turk took on gas, and found that by a lucky coincidence he was in court in Rockland that morning. I reached him there and made an appointment at the courthouse for mid-afternoon. Turk and I went down aboard *Sunrise* after lunch.

I liked Otis Lieberman instantly, and I think Turk did, too, though he'd certainly never met anyone like Otis. He was a large hulking man, about my age, with a gruff manner and an acid sense of humor, but with such personal warmth that he gave the impression of having put up with life's mediocrities thus far just to be around when you came by. He had on a dark baggy suit, shiny at the elbows, and the top button of his shirt was undone under his tie. He wore thick glasses with dark frames which he pushed up periodically into his thick black hair—though he couldn't see much without them. His shoes were worn and spattered with mud.

Contrary to my expectations, based on what the gentleman from Blueberry Isle had said about his reputation as a specialist in Maine marine law, Otis wasn't a Maine man at all, but a Jew from Brooklyn. He hadn't even been in Maine before graduating from law school, but once he came, he stayed. He was kept out of military service during the war by a chronic heart condition, so he settled in Portland and practiced there. He was unmarried. Otis and I had a number of common acquaintances, it turned out, and we spent a few minutes discussing them while Turk listened—taking Otis's measure, I could see. We were meeting in the library of the courthouse.

"Let's cut this crap of who knows who and get to business." He turned to Turk. "What the hell's going on out there? You're getting into the newspapers."

He handed Turk a Boston paper from the day before, folded to an inside page where he had marked a short item headed LOBSTER WAR GROWS IN MAINE. Turk read the story, which reported merely that the rivalry between the lobstermen of two Penobscot islands had intensified in recent weeks and that reported losses had reached epidemic proportions. He passed the paper to me. I said the item missed the latest episode and gave Otis a brief account of Turk's sortie the night before. Otis whistled when I was through and looked at Turk with a new respect.

"Too bad you didn't hang them on Matinicus Rock while you were at it," Otis said, and added that someday he wanted to hear all the details of Turk's adventure. "Seriously, though, you're sure about that gong? It didn't slip its mooring? Or drag?"

"I'm sure o' that," Turk said.

"What was the tide doing? Falling, wasn't it?"

Turk nodded. "It turned just after midnight."

"How long did you stay around?"

"More 'n an hour."

Otis nodded, apparently satisfied. "You'll be all right on that. Maybe a small fine. . . . Well, what do you people want me to do for you? Help cut traps?"

Turk explained that all they wanted was assurance of their rights to fish at Seal Ledge. Or anywhere else, for that matter.

"You've got the *right*, you know," Otis said. "You can fish anywhere you want to on the whole damned coast."

"But what good's it do us if they mess up our traps 'n' chase us off?"

"You've got a point there, boy," Otis conceded. "Have you actually had someone chased off?"

"Willy Grant. They told him to fish somewhere else or they'd sink his boat," Turk said—without the expletive.

"I expect they'd deny they said it," Otis remarked thoughtfully, pushing up his glasses. "Why'd they pick on this Willy Grant? Was he messing with their pots?"

"Not so far 's anyone knows for sure."

"You don't sound too damned convinced." Turk said nothing, and after a moment Otis went on, his glasses back in place. "We might get the Superior Court to give us an injunction against their interfering with the fishing at Seal Ledge . . . on the basis of their having chased one man off. That would slow 'em down—unless they could show Willy Grant *was* messing around with their gear." Turk still said nothing, and after a moment Otis continued. "Let me ask you this, Turk. How well can you lobstermen on Ram Island control yourselves? Can you keep away from their traps long enough for the injunction to take effect? Because if you people go out and rip up their pots the day after the judge gives you an injunction against them for doing the same thing, then the injunction isn't worth the paper it's written on. In fact, it would hurt you."

Turk said, "What's an . . . an . . ."

"Injunction? It's a court order, given by a judge, which says you can't do something, usually something you're not supposed to be doing anyway, like fouling lobster pots. Then if you go ahead and do it, you're directly in contempt of court. . . . Actually, what we'd get is a temporary restraining order, but it comes to the same thing."

Turk took this in slowly. "You mean it's like spittin' in the judge's face, 'stead of the warden's?"

"That's the idea," Otis said, watching Turk intently. "You see the situation, don't you? If you're appealing to law for help, then you've got to play the law game all the way. No more poaching. No more snarling traps. . . . No more capers around the bay at night."

"I got ya," Turk said.

"Can you people keep yourselves in check, Turk?"

"We can try."

Otis wanted to come out to explain the situation to the lobstermen—I think he wanted to see for himself what sort of people they were—and we set this up for the end of the week, when he had to be in Rockland again. He would come over on the mailboat Saturday morning, and Turk would take him back in the afternoon in time for the Portland train. As we left the courthouse, I stayed back for a moment with Otis while Turk walked on ahead. I told him not to worry about his fee; we'd put it together somehow.

He waved the question aside. "My best clients never pay me," he said. "But how'd they think of getting a lawyer? Was it your idea?"

"Turk's," I said. "After he hung the boats on the Old Woman."

"You mean the other lobstermen don't know about it yet?"

I said they knew by now Turk had gone to Camden to look for a lawyer, but no one had been consulted about the idea.

"Well, let's hope it takes. It'll be the first ray of light in some years in that murky business if it does. . . . Still, they'd better keep a watch on their own fleet the next few nights."

There must have been a lookout for us at the Head, for by the time we rounded the red nun at the Nose, nearly everyone on the island had come down to give Turk a hero's welcome. A cheer went up from the landing as Turk swung the *Sunrise* into its mooring. The flat-bottomed punts with outboards raced wildly around the harbor, and a flotilla of skiffs surrounded us.

"Hey, Turk, why'dn't you cut 'em loose after all that trouble?"

"You got radar 'tween your ears, find your way around like that?"

I don't think Turk expected such a reception, though he might have. Anyway, you could tell from his sudden gruffness he didn't mind it.

"Pinch a few boats 'n' everybody loves ya," he muttered as we put off in his peapod.

Chucky was the first to greet him, climbing down the ladder and jumping into his father's arms. Turk swung Chucky onto his shoulders and slowly climbed up to the assembled islanders. His fatigue was beginning to show now, after thirty-six hours without sleep except the hour or so on my sofa. The pouches were dark under his eyes, and his three-day stubble seemed gray against his weathered skin. He grinned at Sharon, standing at the top of the ladder with Barbara.

"Crazy Turk," she said mistily.

Wylie Thatcher, who had arrived two days before and was still fiercely celebrating the start of his annual vacation, insisted on presenting Turk with a mock trophy for his exploit. He had spent the afternoon burning an inscription into one of Turk's lobster buoys that had drifted ashore near Northeast Cove: "For valor beyond the call of a lobsterman's duty. August 14, 1946." Lou Thatcher had tied a gold loop onto it, and Wylie, with a certain flourish, hung it around Turk's neck amid cries of "Speech! Speech!"

But Turk was as likely to give a speech at that moment as Widow Barnaby, peering from her jetty up the harbor and wondering what all the commotion was about. He was even grudging with details of his adventure, at least enough of them to satisfy the islanders' appetites. But they were extracted from him in time—and where he seemed too reticent, I supplemented his story from what I had heard during the course of the day: how he had waited outside the Thorn Island breakwater for an hour until two lobstermen down at the harbor with flashlights had disappeared up toward the saddle; how he had then slipped the boats from their moorings, one by one, and tied them in a line behind Clarence Darling's dragger; how, after he had given up on the last three moored close to shore, he had hooked onto the dragger and towed the entire string out past the breakwater, hoping the last boats wouldn't fetch on the ledges outside—then not caring if they did; how an hour or two into the bay, in six-foot seas, he had circled inside the string and cut the last boat loose, then ten minutes later the next; how, as he was proceeding with the third, wondering how many he could cut loose separately like this before the circle grew too small, he suddenly had his "change o' heart" and went after the two already gone; how he had found the first easily enough and taken it alongside (not without some bruising), then spent three quarters of an hour searching for the second—Barney Orcutt's—before he found it drifting toward Mackerel Shoals; how he had taken this one on his other flank and headed into deeper water as a fresh squall struck the convoy; how, deciding to tie up to the Old Woman, he had found the gong in the storm, secured Clarence's dragger to it, and returned the two castoffs to the end of the string; how, finally, he had circled the area until the seas began to subside, checking the position of the gong against some lobster pots nearby, before returning to the island as dawn was breaking.

"*Sunrise* must'a felt like a speedboat once you unloaded," Rudolf remarked, shaking his head.

Turk said, "She was never meant for a tug."

The crowd slowly thinned out at the pier, leaving Turk with a number of the lobstermen. He still had Chucky on his shoulders.

"The Coast Guard came by," Arthur Dacey said. "They didn't seem too het up. They wanted to know the time you got to the Old Woman, how long you were there . . . stuff for their report. They'll be back tomorrow."

Turk nodded but made no reply. "Well, we got ourselves a lawyer," he said presently. "Fella from Portland. . . . He's comin' out to see us Sat'day."

Several of the lobstermen looked skeptical.

"What good'll we git from a lawyer, Turk?" Clyde Grant asked.

"He'll tell us how we can keep Willy from gettin' chased off the Ledges," Turk said.

"I hope he's fixin' to camp out there with a gun."

"He's goin' to git us a . . . What's it called again?" he asked me.

"An injunction," I said, and explained what it was.

"What'll it cost us?" Lloyd Cutler asked.

I said the restraining order itself wouldn't cost anything. We could take up a collection for the lawyer's fee. I caught George Bannister's eye, listening at the edge of the circle, and he nodded.

"Well, if Cliff Dawson can't stop 'em," Rudolf said, "it beats me what a lawyer from Portland can do."

The lobstermen gradually dispersed and joined other islanders drifting homeward in small groups, still talking about Turk's escapade. Later, embellished with each retelling, it was to take on the proportions of a Penobscot legend. The number of boats in tow crept from nine to several dozen, the winds climbed to gale force, and in one version I heard some years later, the boats were hung up on so many gongs and buoys around the bay that the Thorn Islanders were a week recovering the entire fleet. But the day after Turk's adventure, most of us were still numbed by its nearness, too gratified the nightmare was over, to take in the heroic details of what he actually did.

"Chucky," Turk said, swinging him off his shoulders and handing him Wylie's trophy, "take this danged thing, boy; it's stranglin' me."

17

Life continued on Ram Island despite our preoccupation with the grim milestones of the lobster war. The corn tassled and grew long and firm. The cabbage headed. The young ospreys grew strong enough to leave their nest above the Gut. The lambs grew nimble and the ewes were sheared late on Little Ram. The mailboat arrived on Mondays, Wednesdays, and Saturdays between ten and ten-thirty, bringing new arrivals and bearing others away— thus creating new patterns of relationships on the island. It brought Kevin back, for instance, in the third week of August, home from his two weeks of flight duty. Two days later it bore Gloria Thatcher away; Gloria was leaving for the rest of the summer to visit school friends on the Cape. Belle arrived on the *Laura Lee* at the end of that same week, after a longer stay in Portland than she'd originally planned. She had extended it, I knew from Lucy, by a short visit with Harvey Brown at his family's summer home on Sebago Lake.

Belle came down to see me at Cutler's Cove the afternoon of the day she arrived, a wet and windy afternoon. She was radiant, I thought. She seemed to have grown several inches since Christmas—until I realized it was not height but redistribution of weight that made the difference. She was leaner through the middle, fuller in the bosom, and more erect. This meant that her clothes hung on her differently. She dressed conservatively, as usual—wide cotton skirt below the knees, loose-fitting white blouse under her blue slicker—but she had flair. She even had on a trace of pale lipstick, which I'd never seen before, though this was an integral feature of a young lady's getup in that era; one was supposed to look unhealthy without it. Well, in a word, Belle had quietly acquired sex appeal. Not that it hadn't always been there, lurking beneath the surface for those who troubled to look for it, but now it stared you in the face.

Belle, when she'd taken off her blue slicker and settled down, was full of news of Jingle. "You'd be amazed," she said.

"At what? The change in her?"

"Just the opposite. She's exactly the same—except that she's married. And has number one 'in the pot,' as she puts it."

"Already!" My tone must have suggested to Belle I thought that was going too far. She laughed at me.

"It doesn't take so long, you know." And when I had no reply, staring blankly out the window, she said, "Well, that's what she got married for, isn't it? To have four children."

I changed the subject and asked Belle about Harvey Brown, but Belle ignored the question. "She talks about you all the time, you know."

I said, "Dandy for her husband."

Belle looked at me for several moments in silence. "Don't be peevish about Jingle," she said quietly. "Take her as she is. I'm just telling you she hasn't changed . . . even though she married another man. That's all."

Properly chastened by my young friend, not yet half my age, I apologized for my surliness and asked for more details of Jingle's new life: the house she lived in, the people she saw, the things she did, and so forth.

Later, Belle returned unprompted to my question about Harvey Brown. "We're still stalled," she said. "I guess he's still pitying himself for . . . well, last Christmas. So now he won't touch me, won't let anyone leave us alone together. I feel like some rare flower."

"He's overcompensating," I said.

"It may be just as well," Belle said presently, speaking of their relations in general. "His folks are pretty snazzy people. They live differently. . . . I feel like the fisherman's daughter when I'm with them."

I made a gesture to suggest that was natural enough, since that's what she was, after all.

"I mean, they *make* me feel it. It's different when I feel it myself because I want to. . . . It's the same with the Thatchers and the Bannisters."

"Do the Bannisters really make you feel like a fisherman's daughter?" I asked pointedly.

Belle thought about this. "I doubt if they mean—"

I interrupted her. "Or is it *you* who keeps insisting on it to emphasize the difference between you and them?" I added that Kevin and Karen, if they had the choice, would probably prefer to be the children of a Ram Island lobsterman than what they were—particularly if the lobsterman were a Talbot.

Belle reflected on this, too, biting her lip. "You may be right. I don't know them as well as you do. . . . But there is a difference anyways. I feel it in both Harvey's family and in the Bannisters. And I can't forget it easily, fisherman's daughter or not."

I conceded the difference, but accused her of being an island aristocrat, as intractable in her setting as she perceived them to be in theirs. We went on to other matters. Belle had brought back books she'd borrowed while I was away, as I had urged her to, and we talked awhile about these and her courses during the second semester at Orono. The seminar in political theory was disappointing in the end, she said. From Marx they had passed on to anti-Marxist writers, many of them Jesuits, and finally to ultraconservatives and even neo-Fascists. The instructor said he wanted them to see all sides of the "social revolution," but Belle suspected it was chiefly right-wing attitudes he wanted to leave in their minds.

Her English course, by contrast, flourished in the second semester, especially in the spring when they came to the Russian novels: *Anna Karenina* and *Crime and Punishment.* She had been reading more Tolstoy and Dostoevsky, she said, since June. I said this was heady fare for a mere "fisherman's daughter," and she stuck out her tongue at me. Belle said she had also been reading Sholokhov's *Silent Don,* the first volume of which had recently appeared in English and was attracting comment. She loved the story, she said, but she couldn't fathom the Cossacks. Whose side were they on? I gave her some background on the Don Cossacks and told her if she wanted another view of Cossacks in the Russian civil war, she should read Isaac Babel. I took down my copy of *Red Cavalry* to loan to her.

"Is Russian hard to learn?" Belle asked presently.

I told her it was not much more difficult than any new language and brought out a dog-eared Russian grammar I'd carried around with me for years. We sat on the sofa together to look at it, Belle with her feet tucked under her, leaning toward me. I caught a whiff of her aroma, distinctive, personal. We went over the alphabet together, and I explained the sounds—or I gave the best approximation of them I could after some years without practice.

We were enough absorbed in this exercise ten minutes later to miss hearing Kevin and Karen approach from Meadowlane until they were at the door. They entered without knocking, as they often did, oilskins dripping.

"Oh, are we intruding?" Karen asked, stopping at the door as she saw us huddled on the sofa. I rose quickly, dropping the grammar. (Was I blushing? I think I must have been.)

"Not at all," I rallied. "Come in, come in." I explained we were doing lesson number one in Russian—and picked up the grammar in proof of it.

"You looked so cozy there," Karen said, peeling off her oilskin.

I was, if the truth be known, a little irritated at their bursting in on us, though there was no need to be. Both Kevin and Karen were in the habit of dropping in at Cutler's Cove from time to time, together or separately, and indeed, I had encouraged them to. Today, after waiting at the harbor for an hour in the hope it would clear so they could sail, they had decided to look in on me. Very natural. So it was unnatural for me to resent their coming. I set aside any idea of growing possessive of Belle and played my role as proper host.

Kevin, I knew, had been at the harbor when the *Laura Lee* came in that morning, so he'd already seen Belle that day. Indeed, watching his appreciative gaze at Belle as he moved to the bear rug in front of the fire, it occurred to me that it was his having seen her at the harbor—apparently for the first time this summer—that brought him down so promptly to our end of the island. This would also explain their coming from Meadowlane, instead of directly down my trail from the ridge as they normally did: Kevin hoped to catch another glimpse of Belle along the way. Well, these were a few thoughts that passed through my mind as we settled ourselves around the fire.

"So you're taking up Russian?" Kevin asked with just a trace of his sardonic smile. "Why?"

"Why?" Belle repeated. "Well, inasmuch as the idea first came up ten minutes ago—"

"Kevin," I said, "you must have learned some Russian at your stalag."

"Oh, I did. I acquired great fluency . . . *Zdravstvyite, tovarish . . . ya amerikanskii pilot . . . daite mne stakan chaiu, pazhalyista . . . spasibo . . . do svidaniia.*"

"It's beautiful!" Belle said. "What does it mean?"

"This is a very chintzy passage," Kevin went on, enjoying himself. "Early Pushkin. It's never been adequately rendered in English. But translated roughly—very roughly, you understand—it runs like this: 'Hello, comrade . . . I am an American pilot . . . give me a cup of tea, please . . . thank you . . . good day.'"

Belle laughed. "There must be a hidden meaning."

"Speaking of tea . . ." I said, and went off to put on the kettle.

"Belle, what's your college like?" Karen asked, tucking up her feet beside her on the sofa.

"Orono? It's not very grand. Old brick buildings, high ceilings. And trees. It looks like any state institution, I guess. . . ."

"I mean the people," Karen said.

"They're like people anywhere. Boys and girls."

"Are they mostly from Maine?" Kevin asked.

"Mostly. But they come from other places, too—New Hampshire, Massachusetts, some from New York."

"Do you have sororities and fraternities and things like that?" asked Karen.

"You mean do we sit around and sing the 'Stein Song'? I've done it once or twice."

"How . . . how are the teachers?" Kevin wanted to know.

"Some are good, some not so good . . ."

And so on. They questioned her relentlessly, but hardly took in her answers because they were both so absorbed in Belle herself—her mannerisms, her way of speaking, her accent. They'd known her as long as they could remember, but it was as though they'd never focused on her before. Suddenly she seemed more like themselves than a native islander, and they were tongue-tied by the discovery.

Kevin, sitting cross-legged on the bear rug, couldn't take his eyes off Belle—until Karen poked him with her foot and said, "Don't stare so. It's rude." Belle flushed, and Kevin grinned foolishly, but he shifted his position so he wasn't directly in front of her.

I called in from the stove to ask who wanted milk in their tea—if they didn't mind my interrupting their elevated conversation.

"The master disapproves of small talk," Belle said, making a face. "Let's go ahead anyways. . . . Karen, how's Bennington?"

"Oh, Bennington . . ."

"Don't you like it there?"

"Well, actually, it's not so bad. I'd rather be there than boarding school. The art is fantastic."

"Are you going to major in art?"

"Most probably . . . What about you?"

"I can't decide. Most of the girls at Orono do home ec or secretarial. The boys take agriculture or forestry or business administration. I know I don't want any of those. I've got to work something out. . . . What are you doing after next year, Kevin?"

It was the first time Belle had addressed him directly, and he seemed startled. "Me? I've got another year at—"

"I know. I mean after that."

"How did you know, may I ask?"

Belle opened her eyes wide. "It's not a secret, is it? I mean, everyone knows you're at Princeton . . . Aren't we s'posed to?"

I said, as I brought the tea in, that Kevin was leading a double life as a revolutionary. And now, if the children were through with their chitchat, we could have a serious discussion. Besides, no one was getting milk with their tea because no one asked.

"I hate structured conversations," Belle said. "And I *do* like milk." She went out to get it. Oh, she was cool that day, Belle was. Not put off by anyone or anything. Where was the demure island beauty who went off to college in her pancake hat and ribbons a year before?

We sipped our tea and let the conversation flow "unstructured" until it eventually came down on politics—the forthcoming midterm elections. Kevin would be voting for the first time, and Belle asked whether he would vote Republican or Democrat.

"What's the difference?" Kevin asked. "Tell me the difference between a

Republican and a Democrat."

"Well, one's 'fat and mean,' " I said, quoting from Pogo. "And—"

"And the other's 'lean and mean,' " Kevin broke in. "Don't kid me."

Belle said, "I'm not sure I know which is which."

"The fat one has dollar signs tattooed on his chest," said Karen.

"Now I see."

Karen asked how people usually voted on Ram Island, and Belle, hesitating a moment, said, "In the polling booths at the school." We laughed, Kevin especially. I think he didn't want her to be too serious that day.

"I guess we vote 'bout like anyone else," Belle went on. "Daddy was Republican. Mummy's a Democrat. Gertrude Bakeman was a Prohibitionist. Jingle voted once for Norman Thomas. Jesse Cutler wanted to vote Baptist, but they didn't have any candidates."

"You mean there's no good Communist lobsterman?" Kevin asked, back with his sardonic smile.

"That'd be something, wouldn't it?" Belle said, keeping right up with him. "I'm afraid he'd be lynched by the other lobstermen."

I said there'd be no Soviets on Ram Island.

"Mightn't be the worst thing if there were," Kevin remarked. "It might end this crazy lobster war they're having."

I asked myself whether Kevin should bring up the lobstermen's troubles in front of Belle, but she wasn't in the least fazed.

"I doubt if it would make any difference," she said in a matter-of-fact way. "They'd still be islanders long after there were Soviets." She looked Kevin squarely in the face. "Are you a Marxist?"

"Am I a Marxist?" Kevin repeated.

I cautioned Kevin not to fiddle-faddle with Belle; she'd been reading Rosa Luxemburg and Karl Kautsky.

"How did you know I'd been reading Kautsky?" Belle asked me, surprised.

I said I'd found an open volume under the sofa, and Belle said, "How untidy of me! I must have kicked it there by mistake last spring."

Kevin was studying Belle with fresh interest—if that was possible. "What did you do? Come down here to read Marxism on the sly?"

"Why on the sly? Mummy came too sometimes."

Kevin said, "Well, I don't read Marxism with my 'mummy,' that's for sure."

"Isn't there something on the love affairs of the early Marxists?" Karen said. "Mom could read that."

Kevin was still looking intently at Belle. "And you? Are *you* a Marxist?"

Belle laughed and said, "I'm too much of a lobsterman's daughter to be a good Marxist." I caught her eye and winked at her. Belle went right on. "Besides, there's something about reading Marxist literature in this room that doesn't rouse you to . . . to violent deeds—the way reading it in a city slum might."

I said I hoped the atmosphere in my bungalow wasn't *too* soporific.

"I don't know what that means," Belle said simply, and without waiting to find out, she went on again. "I only know that after being down here a few hours, I don't feel like going out to do battle. I feel like Lenin said he felt when he listened to . . . to Beethoven, wasn't it?"

"The Appassionata," I said. We sat, the three of us, absorbed in Belle. I'd never seen her so animated. Her eyes sparkled as she moved them back and forth restlessly from one of us to another. She was witty, good-humored, self-confident. She seemed to be blossoming before our eyes, like an orchid we'd surprised at the instant of its bloom. Kevin and Karen might have felt the transformation less than I, since they hadn't known her so well. Besides, Kevin was so obviously smitten by this unsuspected beauty right under his nose, as it were, that if he wondered anything, it was how he could have overlooked her so long. As for Karen, I think she had herself been idolized for so many years—by Gloria Thatcher and how many others I could only guess—that she took pleasure in idolizing someone else. In any case, she was hardly less smitten than Kevin.

Kevin presently proposed a walk out to the Head, rain or no, and the girls instantly agreed. I had work to do, so saw them off at the door. Belle and Kevin started up the trail—and I could almost feel his hand itching to seize hers on any pretext, or none at all. Was hers as anxious to be seized? I thought it likely.

"Your book, Belle," I called from the door—like some neglected school-marm. I held out the Babel volume.

She came running back, eyes bright, put the book under her slicker, and for the first time in her life kissed me.

"Now, why did I do that?" she murmured, as surprised as I. But she wasn't in the least embarrassed.

"Hey, can I loan you a book sometime?" Kevin joshed her from the foot of the trail.

As the two of them started up through the spruces, Karen stood by me buttoning her oilskins. "She's so wonderful," Karen said. "You should keep her for yourself."

I said, looking after the other two, it was perhaps already too late for that.

So romance came to Belle Talbot on the second try. It came swiftly and surely and with few misgivings from any quarter. Within forty-eight hours everyone on the island who cared knew about Belle and Kevin, since they made no effort to conceal their fondness. It was one of the few episodes that grim summer that gave genuine pleasure to nearly everybody. No island boy—except

Rodney York—had seriously made up to Belle, so none felt jilted in her choice. A few, it is true, remembering the lively New Year's party eight months before, expressed regrets that Harvey Brown hadn't been able to carry things off, but this was a low-keyed partisanship. Kevin, after all, was well liked by the islanders and, of all the summer people, was closest to them. He knew all of them by name (something, incidentally, Karen was hopeless at), and he was on cordial terms with most of the younger lobstermen with whom he had played in the Little League before the war. His war record, needless to say, added only luster in the islanders' eyes. It was therefore gratifying to them to see Kevin fall so head-over-heels in love with an island girl. To be sure, one or two perennial cynics, like Harold Toothacher, doubted the affair would last.

"Why, there'll be naught left of it long before the first frost," he told Rudolf York. "If there is, deah, I'll eat one of your lobsters live."

"I'll hold you to that, Harold, if I may."

Lucy was perhaps a trifle uneasy, behind her composure, but she raised no obstacle. She put up with Belle's frenzied schedule of walks with Kevin about the island, day and night and in all kinds of weather, and listened patiently when Belle returned, flushed and excited, to recount their conversations—at least, the portions of them that could be recounted. George Bannister, an enthusiastic admirer of Belle Talbot since she was a child, was overjoyed by his son's good sense. He was, to be sure, also sensitive about Gloria Thatcher's possibly hurt feelings and thankful she'd left before Belle returned, but this didn't diminish his warmest endorsement of the new romance. I hadn't seen George in so expansive a mood since I'd known him.

"If I c-c-could only do something for that child," he said to me one afternoon as we watched Belle and Kevin sail out of the harbor with Karen and Joey Grant—for something in Belle's sense of proprieties kept her from sailing in the blue sloop with Kevin and Karen unless another islander were with them. "Buy her clothes or b-books? Send her to Europe? Tell me w-what she needs."

I said there would be ways to help Belle Talbot at the proper time, but advised against gifts of any sort at the present stage. Belle, after all, still had that "difference" to surmount—and I knew she had to do it in her own way—though I didn't mention this, of course, to George.

Sally Bannister was nervous, as I was, about Mary Lou Grant, who had unexpectedly thrown up her job at the Thorndike and planned to spend the last several weeks of the summer on the island. Sally, rather uncharacteristically, had not discussed Kevin's probable relations with Mary Lou in Rockland with anyone but me, and no one else on the island, so far as I was aware, had any suspicion of them. George certainly didn't. And if Karen did, she kept it to herself.

Well, we underestimated Mary Lou. That remarkable young woman arrived

home on a Saturday, heard the gossip immediately, and without further thought
of Kevin set her cap for a tall, shy nephew of Janice Torrey visiting from Bangor,
whom she had fully tamed by Monday. When Kevin, meeting her at Caleb's a
few days later, tried to soothe matters with a little small talk, she cut him dead.

"I like her spunk," Sally said as she told me about the episode. "Maybe she's
a tramp, but she's more to my taste than Belle Talbot. . . . Mary Lou and I have
something in common."

Kevin and Belle dropped in at Cutler's Cove from time to time—less for the
need of my company, I was sure, than to revisit the setting where they had discovered each other. One gray afternoon, at low tide, they rounded the far edge of
the cove and were a quarter of an hour making their way along the shore, oblivious that Clyde Grant was watching them as he set his seines across the cove or
that I might be watching from my window. They walked slowly over the cracked
granite slabs at the edge of the sea, hand in hand, occasionally picking up some
crustacean to inspect. Once, Kevin waded into the seaweed to catch a crab.
Farther on, they sat on a broken lobster trap washed ashore and shared a cigarette. It was the first time I saw Belle smoke.

When they reached the bungalow, they were bright and shiny—and so
enrapt in each other there was no driving between them. I said if they continued
to explore the island at the pace they explored the northern shore, the summer
would run out on them.

"So we'll finish up another year," Belle dreamily said, summers like this one
stretching out endlessly before her.

I asked if I could offer them something against the gray afternoon. A
Pernod, for instance, which I had just received.

"Is it strong enough?" Belle asked.

"For what?"

"For my mood."

As I passed her going to the cupboard, I said softly, "Easy, baby, easy," but a
private aside to Belle at this stage was about as manageable as a confidentiality
to Drew Pearson.

"You're afraid he'll seduce me, aren't you?" she said. I started to make some
vague disclaimer, but she ignored it. "We're not having sex for a year. That's what
we decided. . . . Didn't we, Kevin?"

I glanced at Kevin from the cupboard. He looked uncomfortable, but
shrugged his shoulders and said nothing.

So the youngsters of the postwar generation, self-confident in all things,
arranged their sexual relations the way they tried to arrange everything else—by
frontal assault and in the open, overlooking the fact that generations before
theirs had foundered on this same dilemma. We drank our Pernod with a gravi-

ty befitting the occasion, and after a half hour's conversation (on topics other than sex, I'm glad to report), they went on their way. But they left me, perhaps because of the other business hovering over all of us, with the uncomfortable feeling their lives were too good to be true. The secret of happiness could not be discovered so quickly or so easily.

18

Otis Lieberman came out to the island, as planned, the Saturday after Turk and I met him in Rockland. He minced no words with the lobstermen. He'd dealt with island lobstermen before and wasn't disposed to coddle the Ram Islanders because they were his clients. I always thought he gave a virtuoso performance on that visit.

He sent word out to Turk the day before that he wanted to meet with the lobstermen at noon, and only the lobstermen. He left it to Turk to work out the details. Turk met Otis at the pier when the *Laura Lee* came in, and they spent an hour and a half together at the Peaks before the meeting. The rest of us—Turk had asked Caleb and me to be present as well, Caleb as one of the plantation's assessors and me as a party to the initial arrangements—gathered at the church just before noon. We unfolded enough chairs to go around and waited. Caleb and I sat in the rear.

It was a sparkling day on the Penobscot, and I thought it a good omen that the lobstermen had come in early for the meeting. There had been some grumbling the day before. Why should they quit hauling at midday just to please some "lawyer fella" from Portland? If he had sumpin' to tell 'em, why din't he come on Sunday when they wasn't workin'? But they all showed up—all but Cecil Allen and his son Jack. Jack Allen had told Turk he'd be in Camden, and Cecil had said, "I'll see." Cecil, in fact, came in early on Saturday, but he went straight home, and there he stayed. From where I sat I could see him through one of the windows, splitting wood alone in his backyard.

It was a sad time for Cecil Allen. All his relatives were on Thorn Island, and he himself was a Thorn Islander by birth and instinct. Yet his adopted home was on Ram Island, and his younger children were as much Ram Islanders as the Grants and Yorks. Constance tried to preserve a strict neutrality in the interisland feud and forbade discussion of it around the house. Only Jack, brought up on Thorn Island until he was sixteen, shared his father's sympathies. They fished close to each other and usually went out before daybreak to avoid the other lobstermen. They bypassed the store when they came in—Constance did all the buying for the family—and rarely used the road, preferring a path that ran straight from the harbor up through the fields to the back of their house.

Cecil and Lloyd Cutler, the two brothers-in-law, had respected each other over the years, and Lloyd had done all he could to make Cecil's transplant on Ram Island a successful one. But this summer he had sometimes been irritated by Cecil's partisanship.

"Dang it, Cecil," Lloyd would say. "I don't like havin' my traps snarled any better'n you like havin' Sam Orcutt's. . . . Whyn't you cry for me for a change?"

So Cecil and Jack withdrew more and more from the Ram Island community while compelled to live moodily and uneasily in it.

As Turk and Otis came in from the rear, the lobstermen turned to take stock of their "lawyer fella," with his thick glasses, baggy suit, and shirt unbuttoned at the neck. He stopped by Caleb and me; he'd met Caleb at the pier that morning.

"You two want to be a part of this?" he asked us gruffly.

Caleb said Turk thought it was a good idea, and he agreed. Otis nodded and walked on to the low dais in front.

"Pass me that chair, young fella," he said to Rudolf York, dean of the working lobstermen at sixty-six.

Otis sat down, shuffled a few papers in his briefcase, then peered out at the lobstermen, now silent in front of him.

"My name's Otis," he said. "Otis Lieberman." He went on in a matter-of-fact way to say how he'd met Turk in Rockland four days before, as he guessed they all knew, and now had been talking with Turk the last hour or so since the mail-boat came in. He paused and pushed his glasses up on his forehead. "You people got a problem, and I'm not going to minimize it. Go on the way you're going, and one of two things'll happen. Either the commissioner will suspend your licenses so there won't be any traps out to frig around with. Or the Superior Court will order a special warden or a sheriff sent out here to keep order. Take your pick." He looked at Clyde Grant, sitting in front of him. "Know what it would cost you to keep a warden or sheriff out here?"

"T'ain't gonna cost me a penny," Clyde said, " 'cause I ain't gonna pay him." A few of the lobstermen snickered.

"That's where you're wrong, my friend," Otis went on. "You're Clyde Grant, aren't you?" Turk had done his briefing well. "Well, Clyde, I did a little figuring on my way out here, and it came out like this. You'd be lucky on the salary, 'cause that would be paid by the state if you had a warden or by the county if you had a deputy sheriff. But you'd have to put him up . . . and the way things are out here, he wouldn't want to compromise himself by living with any family. I guess there's no place quite ready for him, is there? So you'd have to fix up the parish house. Say, two thousand bucks. Then there'd be his groceries. And fuel. He might get lonely if he had to stay a long spell, so he'd bring out his family;

then you'd have the cost of educating his kids. . . . Add it all up, and we're talking about something like half a grand a year for each working household on the island. That's the price you'd have to pay to keep fishing if the Superior Court judge decides you couldn't be left without supervision . . . that's *if* the commissioner lets you keep your licenses in the first place."

Otis paused, and there were murmurs of protest from the lobstermen.

"Now, why d'we git the sheriff and not the Thorn Islanders?" Lloyd Cutler said. "We ain't to blame for—"

"Who said the Thorn Islanders don't get the same thing?" Otis broke in, lowering his glasses and staring at Lloyd. "I didn't say the judge would charge you people and not them. Judge Peabody's a fair-minded man. I'm assuming he can't tell who's to blame, so he gives equal treatment. . . . Maybe if he's in a good mood, he'll say one warden's enough for both islands and you share the costs. Two hundred and fifty bucks per family. Now that's a bargain, a warden or a sheriff at half price."

I wondered, listening to a fresh groundswell of mumbled protests, whether Otis wasn't going too far with his heavy-handed sarcasm. I also wondered whether he was fairly representing to the lobstermen the cost to them of supporting a court-appointed law enforcement officer. But Otis knew what he was doing.

"I'm giving you the good news first," he continued, his voice less truculent. "The worst is the commissioner suspends your licenses. The next worse is the Superior Court orders a warden or . . . No, I take that back. The *really* worst thing is one of you takin' a shot at a Thorn Islander you think is poaching and is unlucky enough to hit him. That's a jail sentence for sure, ten to fifteen years, depending on circumstances. . . . How many of you carry rifles in your boats?" Otis asked abruptly.

No one answered.

"Come on! Don't kid me. I saw one slung in the *Virginia D*. That's Zip Clayton's boat, isn't it? . . . Turk, didn't you tell me you carry a rifle?"

"For target practice," Turk said, and everyone laughed.

"Target practice, my ass!" Otis said. "You've been hunting mermaids on the sly. . . . Wait'll I tell Sharon."

He was beginning to get them on his side now. "I'd check those rifles with Caleb till deer season, if I were you. Then no one'll be tempted to use 'em. Because murder's a crime I can't help you on. . . . By deer season we shouldn't have too big a problem, 'cause no one to my knowledge ever mistook an Orcutt for a deer."

This time there were appreciative guffaws from nearly all the lobstermen, and several shouted-out remarks to improve on his joke.

"Well, let's get down to business," Otis said when the laughter subsided. "And remember this—I'm on *your* side. I wouldn't be out here on a Saturday afternoon if I wasn't."

"What can we do, Otis?" Arthur Dacey asked.

Otis then outlined his plan: to seek a temporary restraining order from Judge Peabody against the Thorn Island lobstermen in the use of any form of harassment, obstruction, or intimidation directed against the lobstermen of Great Ram Island in the exercise of their lawful rights to fish anywhere in the Penobscot, especially in the vicinity of Seal Ledge. The lobstermen listened with blank expressions to Otis's legal terminology, slowly taking in the import of his strategy.

"Why'll this . . . this restrainin' order keep 'em off us any quicker'n anything else?" Rudolf asked.

"Because if they ignore it, they'll be in contempt of court. . . . Turk put it just about right the other day. It's like spitting straight in the judge's face, where before it was the warden's. What's his name? . . . Cliff Dobson?"

"Dawson," Turk corrected him.

"It's a much more serious offense, let me tell you, to spit in Judge Peabody's face than in Cliff Dawson's." Otis waited a moment to be sure they were with him, then went on. "Now, let's look at what the Thorn Islanders are going to say when the temporary restraining order is issued and the judge asks them why he shouldn't make it permanent. Oh, they'll look innocent and say it was us who were messing with their traps first, not the other way around. And the judge'll come back to me and ask what I have to say to *that*. 'Well, Judge,' I'll tell him, 'you know how these things are. There's been some bad blood between those two islands for a long time.' And so on and so forth. But the important thing, I'll tell him, is we're being chased off the Ledges. It's bad enough to mess around with someone else's lobster traps. That's what Cliff Dawson's out there to stop. But when a Maine lobsterman can't even put his traps out in free fishing grounds, that's a deprivation of his rights. . . . I think Judge Peabody'll give us an injunction on that argument."

"What'll happen if they keep chasin' us off anyways?" Clyde asked.

"The judge'll call 'em into court, and if they don't desist, he'll order the commissioner to suspend their licenses."

Clyde said, "I ain't never heard of a judge doin' that."

"You've never heard of it, Clyde, because it's never happened . . . to my knowledge. But it can. A judge can do that and a lot more if there's a need. . . . Don't forget, you've got more than a skirmish out here. You've got a full-fledged lobster war."

Willy said, "I wish to hell I was a judge right now." The younger lobstermen laughed, but Otis was stern. He looked at Willy some moments in silence.

"If you're Willy Grant," he said, "let's get one thing straight. I'm not saying you didn't deserve to be chased off Seal Ledge . . . I—"

"Now, wait a minute!" Willy broke in, flushing with sudden anger. "What d'ya mean by that?"

"I'll tell you just what I mean," Otis came back at him quickly. "We're not asking for this injunction to protect you, boy. It's to protect everyone. I don't know why they chased you off the Ledges, Willy, and at this point I don't give a damn. I just want to be sure they don't do it again—to you or anyone else. . . . And when we get our restraining order, let me tell you something: Everybody better be on his best behavior out there. Because if Judge Peabody hears there's any monkey business after he's gone to the trouble of issuing the order, he's going to be hopping mad. It won't be the Thorn Islanders who'll lose their licenses. It'll be some of you."

Otis stared solemnly at the young lobstermen sitting in a row at his left. In addition to Willy Grant, still scowling and looking at the floor, there were Bill York, Sam Clayton, and at the far end, a little removed from the other three, Bobby Cutler. All ex-servicemen.

"Let me tell you young fellas something," Otis said slowly. "Maybe you won't like to hear it, but it'll be good for you. This isn't the only place where there's been trouble this summer over lobstering. All down the coast, traps have been raided and snarled and cut. And when you look to see who's behind it, likely as not you find a few men back from the service. Not the older lobstermen like Rudolf York and Clyde Grant. Or like Sam Orcutt and What's-His-Name Hopewell over at Thorn. But young people like yourself, just home from the wars. Or Barney Orcutt. . . . Now, here's what I think happens. In the service you learn some pretty fancy ways to make a buck. You buy cigarettes at the PX in Frankfurt for a dollar and a quarter a carton, and they sell on the black market for . . . what d'they sell for, Bill? A hundred bucks?"

" 'Bout that," Bill York mumbled, keeping Otis in focus first with one eye, then the other.

"Everyone gets a chance to think he's a crackerjack businessman, right? . . . Well, over there, it doesn't make a pile o' difference. The money's unreal— Occupation marks. Everyone's doing it. . . . You bring those habits home, I tell you, you got a problem."

Otis stopped. The older lobstermen had listened to him intently, several of them nodding their heads from time to time. The younger men were sullen, their feet stretched out in front of them. Willy yawned at one point and whispered something to Sam Clayton.

"What'll we owe you for this, Otis?" Turk asked.

Otis thought a moment, his glasses back again on his forehead. "I've got fishermen all down the coast owe me something. . . . One of 'em in Casco Bay owed me fifty bucks for about three years, so when I came on him once out hauling traps, I said, 'Jethro, I think I'll just take that fifty dollars in live lobsters.' He was so embarrassed at putting me off so long he dumped his whole catch into a basket for me, but I insisted he weigh it so neither of us would feel cheated. It came to two dollars and twenty cents more'n he owed, so I tossed him back three good-sized lobsters and told him I didn't take tips. Well, I was eating boiled lobster and lobster salad and lobster bisque for the rest of the season. . . . No, Turk, I ought to get paid for whatever I can do for you. Let's wait till we get the restraining order, then we'll see."

Otis closed his briefcase and stood up. "Well, do you want me to see the judge?" The older lobstermen all nodded. "How about you young fellas? Willy, are you with us?"

Willy shrugged his shoulders. "Why not?" he said.

"I'll see what I can do," Otis said. "Now get back to your pots. I'm sorry I had to bring you in on a day like this."

After the meeting broke up, I walked with Otis back to the harbor, where he was to meet Turk for the run back to Rockland. After complimenting Otis on the way he had managed to get his point through to the lobstermen, I asked him—for my own information—whether it was true the islanders would be so much out of pocket for the services of a deputy sheriff or warden.

"That was a bit thick, I admit," Otis said. "But I always think they see things better if it's put in dollars and cents. . . . Anyway, they're losing that much already the way things are. And they'll be losing a hell of a lot more if this continues."

Turk came down a quarter of an hour later, and I waved them off at the landing.

19

The next trouble came from an unexpected quarter. For some days after Otis's visit, there were no reports of tangled buoys, pilfered pots, or cut lines. Willy Grant set new traps at Seal Ledge, with Turk and Lloyd Cutler standing by, and pulled them for a week without incident. Cliff Dawson came into the harbor one afternoon and asked Arthur Dacey what had come over the two islands.

"Why, Arthur, there ain't been a complaint out here since the middle o' the month."

"Cliff," Arthur said, "everybody's scared to death of you."

The threat of a Superior Court injunction was apparently having its effect. Otis called Caleb to pass the word that Judge Peabody had agreed in principle to an injunction and would issue a temporary restraining order on further complaint of interference. The Thorn Islanders had been notified of this, and Otis thought they were looking for a lawyer to protect their interests as well. Rudolf and Lloyd, after a good deal of talking, persuaded most of the lobstermen to bring their rifles ashore, as Otis had suggested.

Still, tension persisted. The lobstermen fished close to each other and kept an eye on the Thorn Islanders. If they saw any in the vicinity of their pots, they converged quickly on the area. They took turns, since Turk's raid on the Thorn Island fleet, standing watch in the harbor after dark. On foggy nights one or two of them wandered over the island checking dories in the coves and listening for the sound of a motor or of oars offshore.

Cecil and Jack Allen, meanwhile, became even more distant from the other islanders. They moved their traps away from the island, and they sold their lobsters and bought bait in Stonington—not because they had anything against Arthur Dacey, but to minimize the likelihood of encountering the other lobstermen. Cecil, who had always been a placid man, grew edgy. When his son Jamie came into the yard one afternoon with Joel Grant and Mickey Clayton after baseball practice, Cecil, for no good reason, ran out of the shed, arms flailing, and drove Joel and Mickey away.

"Land's sake, Cecil!" Constance called from the kitchen door. "They're just boys." Cecil went back into the shed without a word. Jamie flung his mitt onto the ground and went up to his room, where he locked the door and stayed through supper.

The fire was two nights after this episode. I had worked late and stepped outside before going to bed sometime after midnight. The night was clear and moonless. The tops of the trees stirred around the cove, which meant the wind was in the north. There was a slight smell of smoke in the air, which I thought must be from the island dump. A faint glow hung over the center of the island, and at first I associated it with the northern lights I'd noted earlier in the evening. Then I heard a few muffled shouts on the high road and at the same time recognized the distinctive crackling of burning timber.

When I reached the ridge, the Allen home was half enveloped in flames. Leonard and Walter York had just arrived with the fire cart from behind the schoolhouse, and we pumped furiously in pairs to bring forth water from Cecil's well. It was a futile effort, and we soon shifted the pump across the road to wet down the front of the empty parish house and play the hose on burning debris blown over by the wind. Others, meanwhile, were carrying furniture and anything they could lay hands on through the front door, still in the lee of the blaze.

The fire, which started in the barn, had been driven quickly by steady northerlies through the connecting sheds and into the house itself. It was soon impossible to get into or out of the house anywhere except through the front door. A quarter of an hour after I arrived, even this was impossible. The timbers of the old house, the oldest on the island, were bone-dry after a relatively hot summer, and the flames consumed them greedily, creating an intense heat.

The family stood together in the yard after all hope of saving anything further had vanished. Constance occasionally sobbed and dabbed at her eyes. This handsome century-and-a-half-old homestead, with its classic lines and meticulous detailing, was not only her present home but the house in which she'd grown up—not to mention three generations of Cutlers before her. Several of the island women sought to console her, but Jesse Cutler waved them off. Cecil stood grimly next to Lloyd but said nothing, not even answering questions put to him. Jack, from time to time, moved a piece of furniture farther from the blaze.

The rest of us watched in a state of helpless fascination as the tongues of flame crept through new crevices in the roof or burst from a still-whole window, sending down a fresh cascade of tinkling glass. We kept backing away from the fierce heat until the entire house became enveloped in one wild column of fire reaching several hundred feet into the sky. When it subsided, the roof had fallen in. Five minutes later the walls collapsed, leaving a single shapeless pyre pierced by two brick chimneys in what had been the parlor and the kitchen. The destruction of the house had taken less than an hour. Ironically, most of the barn was still standing.

The islanders were now all solicitude for the Allens' comfort, and offers of beds and food came from every household. But they were well provided for at the Cutlers' next door and soon withdrew, leaving the rest of us to contemplate the desolate scene before drifting homeward in small groups, numbed and saddened. Cecil and Jack, avoiding the high road, walked down to the harbor before dawn and went over to Thorn Island. They returned by eight, having arranged with Sam Orcutt, Cecil's cousin, to move in with his family until a vacant cottage near the saddle could be fixed for the Allens. Cecil intended to leave immediately and sent Jack to collect the family. Word passed quickly of the Allens' departure, and most of the islanders gathered at the landing for the melancholy farewell. None of the lobstermen had yet gone out. Caleb went with his pickup to bring down the few boxes of clothing and personal possessions they had managed to save. Lloyd had the salvaged furniture moved into his barn until they sent for it.

Cecil had brought his boat into the pier for loading, but he didn't come ashore again. The islanders had hastily gathered household articles they thought would be useful to the Allens and had brought them down to the harbor. Clara Grant, for instance, had a set of plates and mugs. Jessica York had a full complement of kitchen utensils and pots. Winifred Dacey had silverware. But Cecil wouldn't let Constance accept anything beyond the loan of blankets from Sally Bannister and a box of groceries from Jenny.

"Now about last month's groceries, Cecil," Jenny called down to him. "Here's the bill, and here's what I'm doin' to it." She tore it in two and threw the pieces into the harbor.

Turk and Arthur, restless on the pier, where they couldn't exchange a private word with Cecil, climbed down into Arthur's peapod and circled the stern of the *Ladybug* until they could make him hear without raising their voices.

"Cecil," Arthur said, "I guess you know how we feel about this."

Cecil was silent.

Turk said, "I wish you wouldn't go, Cecil. I wish you'd . . ."

But Turk's voice was drowned out by Cecil's shifting a bait barrel to make room for another box of salvage. They waited until he'd finished.

"We could build a new house for you," Arthur said. "Everybody pitchin' in, we'd have it done by spring. . . . Will you think about it?"

"I wouldn't set foot back on this goddam island," Cecil said, "if'n you paid me a million dollars."

He turned again, and the peapod drifted away.

Turk said, "Well, remember, you got friends here, Cecil. . . . Remember that."

The Allens were finally aboard with their scant belongings, and Jack pushed off. Constance and Betsy waved bravely from the well of the boat. But Jamie, who'd been manly enough until now, a blackened baseball mitt over one arm, suddenly dissolved against his mother in uncontrollable sobs as his world came crashing down. It was hard to tell whether anguish over the sudden change in his life or the humiliation of not being able to hold back his tears precipitated his collapse. Cecil dropped Jack off at his boat, and together they moved out of the harbor for the last time.

Is anything more drawn out than a departure at sea? Train departures are awkward enough, with the empty thoughts repeated over and over through an open window, but they end quickly enough and are forgotten once the whistle blows and the train moves out. Departures by car can be prolonged or tolerable, depending on the ingenuity of whoever's at the wheel. But a parting at sea has a pace all its own. A boat won't be hurried through water, and there are no overheads or city blocks to hide its progress. So it was with the Allens. It seemed an eternity before the two boats cleared the harbor. Yet no one would leave the landing until they had disappeared from view, past the inscrutable sentinel on the jetty and around the red nun.

The cause of the Allen fire was never discovered. Tucker York, returning from his watch at the harbor after being relieved by Turk, first spotted the fire at the back of the barn and roused the family. He tried vainly, with Cecil and Jack, to beat out the flames with burlap bags, while Constance gathered clothing and got the children out of the house. By the time Tucker went off to get the pump and give the alarm along the ridge, the fire was already beyond control. A fire warden came out the next morning from Rockland but could determine nothing beyond the approximate point where the fire had broken out. It could, of course, have been started by combustion of old hay, or of some other substance. Such things were not unknown. There was no evidence of arson. Yet few of us believed it was *not* arson.

That was as far as it went, however. No one would hazard a guess as to which of the half dozen possible perpetrators of the presumed crime might be responsible. Nor would the warden speculate on this point without some evidence. No islander, needless to say, admitted to being outside at midnight— apart from Turk, at the harbor, and Tucker, on his way home. Neither of these two saw or heard anything to arouse suspicion until Tucker discovered the blaze itself. The warden accordingly reported a fire of unknown origin, and the episode was closed—as far as the official record was concerned.

The fire and the departure of the Allens, on top of the long weeks of tension over the lobstering, cast a pall over all of us as the summer drew to a close. Out in the bay, after the brief respite at the end of August, traps were molested again and lines snarled. Nothing compared to the damage in midsummer, but enough to remind us the lobster war was not yet over. On the island, feelings of guilt and suspicion intermingled. Clannishness intensified to the point where any imputation of guilt made by a member of one family about a member of another sufficed to set the members of both families at loggerheads at all age levels.

Thus, Mary Lou, cavorting carelessly at the end of August with the Torrey cousin from Bangor, took such offense at his imprudent suggestion that her brother Willy was chiefly to blame for our troubles that she broke with him immediately and precipitated a minor feud between the Grants and the Torreys, traditionally neutral in these island rivalries. Clara Grant, who had always been civil toward Janice Torrey, and often friendly, now snapped at her at Caleb's. Alfred and Clyde, who had seined together earlier that summer, now passed each other without a sign of recognition. Joel and his cousin Mickey Clayton quarreled so much with Peter Torrey and the twins at baseball practice the day after Mary Lou's blowup that Turk sent all the Little Leaguers home and said he didn't give a shit whether they beat Vinalhaven or not. Turk was acutely depressed after the Allen fire.

Otis's second visit to the island, over Labor Day, was a welcome distraction—especially for me. He sent word out after the fire that Judge Peabody had changed his mind about the injunction and was no longer considering a temporary restraining order; the situation on the island, the judge said, was too "unsettled" to warrant it. Meanwhile, Judge Peabody, at the request of the Commissioner of Sea and Shire Fisheries, was calling a hearing on September 18 for the lobstermen of both islands. Otis was coming out this time to discuss the position the Ram Islanders would take at the hearing. He planned to come out on the Monday morning mailboat and sent a note to me taking up an earlier invitation to spend the night with me—if I could find him a ride back to Rockland the next day. Arthur, as it turned out, was going over in the morning on Tuesday, so that was settled. Otis wrote that he was bringing the ingredients for dinner.

The lobstermen met at the church, as before, and once again Caleb and I were onlookers. Otis was grim.

"Well, we lost the injunction," he said after a few preliminary remarks. He was striding back and forth on the dais, hands thrust into his baggy pants. "Round one to the Thorn Islanders. Judge Peabody believed, as I did, that a restraining order would be a sensible way to let things simmer down out here. But when he heard about the Allen fire and figured we couldn't keep order even in our own house, he was goddamned if he was going to give us an injunction against the Thorn Islanders . . . who he hadn't any clear proof had done anything wrong in the first place."

He paused, glowering out at the lobstermen through his thick glasses.

Clyde Grant said, "Otis, there's no proof that fire didn't git started by itself . . . is they?"

"There isn't any, and there won't be," Otis said. "But you know 's well as I do, Clyde, that a fire doesn't break out on a clear night in the back of someone's barn without help. Especially when that barn just happens to belong to a lobsterman who's out of tune with the community and whose loyalties are in doubt."

The men stared back at him stonily. Otis was laying it on pretty thick, I thought. He was treading on ground they wouldn't tread themselves. They couldn't have lived with each other if they had.

"Look, my friends," Otis said more equitably, after the glowering match had gone on some moments, "no one is making accusations about that fire. There's not going to be any prosecution. Whoever lit it is going to have to live with it on his conscience. The Allen fire's a thing of the past . . . just like Willy's being chased off the ledges and the seines cut up at the Hole and Turk hanging their boats on the Old Woman. What we're trying to do now is stabilize things out here so you can make a decent living. Are you with me? . . . 'Cause if you're not, I might as well pack up my briefcase and get along back home."

This seemed to bring them around. A sense of accusation still hung in the air, but the lobstermen were now ready—or a majority of them were—to talk about the hearing. Otis outlined to them the position he planned to take. The present difficulties, he would tell Judge Peabody, arose from the widely accepted and generally praiseworthy practice of self-restraint by Maine lobstermen. That is, the lobstermen, while recognizing that there was no basis for it in law, normally refrained from placing their traps close to the shores where other lobstermen lived. It was a form of courtesy. In the case of islands, this common-law practice was especially well established, and no Ram Islander had for years sought to place his traps inside the traps of Thorn Islanders off their shores. And vice versa.

This practice was not as a rule extended to smaller uninhabited islands or outlying ledges and shoals, but some ambiguity on this point had arisen with respect to Seal Ledge—which all Penobscot lobstermen recognized as highly active fishing grounds. The ledges lay closer to Thorn Island than to Ram, by a quarter of a mile, but in years past the lobstermen of both islands had fished them equally. During the past decade, however, and particularly during the war years—because of fuel and equipment shortages—the Ram Islanders had not fished at Seal Ledge, and the Thorn Islanders had in consequence come to feel a proprietary stake in these grounds. The Great Ram Islanders were now seeking to reaffirm their traditional common-law rights—as well, of course, as their legal right—to fish there. In seeking an injunction against the Thorn Islanders, Otis would tell the judge, there had been no thought of depriving them of *their* rights, but simply of guaranteeing the equivalent rights of Ram Islanders.

Otis explained all this in simple and concise language, and when the lobstermen had taken it in, there was no objection to his presenting their case in this way. A few of them, it is true, would have preferred to have the Thorn Islanders portrayed as interlopers in what were traditional Ram Island grounds, but the majority recognized that if they expected any remedy from the Superior Court, Otis's presentation would have to be restrained. There was less agreement on another proposal Otis put to them: a pledge of cooperation with the warden in reporting any interference with the traps and lines, no matter who the offender might be.

"You mean, Otis," Rudolf said, "we tell Cliff Dawson if we happen t'see . . . well, another islander messin' with their pots?"

"I mean you tell him if your own brother's doing it," Otis said.

Tucker said, "I guess he'd do that gladly"—and there was an immediate ripple of laughter, since the two brothers were known to have a fierce loyalty to each other.

"It's like . . . like squealin', ain't it?" Zip Clayton said.

"You can call it what you want, Zip," Otis said, "but if we don't show the judge this much goodwill, and if things go on the way they have been, he might end up asking the commissioner to suspend our licenses."

"If'n he does that, I'm gonna keep on fishin' no how," John Grant put in with a show of stubbornness. John, though closer in age to the older lobstermen, shared the contempt of the younger men for most rules and regulations—and for Cliff Dawson, in particular.

"Yes, you could do that," Otis said slowly. "For about three or four days. Until the judge sent a sheriff out to impound your boat." He swept his eyes again over the group of lobstermen. "I don't mind telling you gentlemen that Judge Peabody's a sight more pissed off with us at the moment than he is with our friends across the bay."

Otis didn't press the lobstermen further in the matter of a commitment to cooperate with the warden, and I think he was wise not to. He couldn't go further on that ticklish issue without jeopardizing the unity among the lobstermen he had already—in fact, almost miraculously—achieved. I hadn't expected to see the lobstermen this much in accord so soon after the Allen fire.

The meeting soon broke up, and Otis went off for lunch as planned with Turk and Sharon, leaving me to carry his overnight bag and a carton of exotic-looking groceries down to Cutler's Cove.

Turk took Otis out in the *Sunrise* in the afternoon to visit Seal Ledge and other grounds where the islanders had traps. Turk dropped him off at Cutler's Cove late in the afternoon. I rowed out in my new skiff to bring him ashore. The squalls that morning had given way to a light westerly and that too had died early. The sea was glassy as far as the eye could see. A few late-summer yachtsmen were moving slowly toward Merchant's Row, sails limp. A few others, motionless against Isle au Haut, were waiting hopefully for a final breeze to ease them into port.

As I pulled alongside the *Sunrise*, I asked how things were in the bay.

"Sweet as a baby's ass," Otis said. "There never was a war out there. It's all made up."

"September days'll fool you," Turk said.

I asked Turk to join us for a drink, but he'd promised Chucky a row in the peapod before dark. Otis climbed into the skiff, still in his city clothes, and we pushed off.

"That's one great lobsterman," Otis said as the *Sunrise* churned out of the cove. "How do they make 'em that way?"

The question was rhetorical, but I answered it anyway. You start off, I said, by sending the old man to jail.

"You must be kidding!" Otis was astounded. "What for?"

As we tied up the skiff on my out-haul and walked slowly along the pebbly beach, I told him the story of Turk's father during Prohibition, not omitting the suspicions the Thorn Islanders had of Charlie Jenkins's having given information about Gabriel's Hole in return for a shorter sentence.

"They're nuts," said Otis. "That's not a short sentence. Usually there wasn't *any* sentence, just a fine. . . . They called it their 'license' to run the blockade. No, to get a sentence like that, he must've really bopped that Coast Guard officer. I'm going to look that case up." We came to the end of the beach and climbed the wobbly steps. "So that's how Turk got put together," he said.

Otis, of course, hadn't been in my bungalow and immediately set forth on a minute inspection of every detail. He poked into cupboards and closets, he studied the driftwood shelving, and he even lowered his large frame through the trapdoor to see how the floor joists were fastened. When he'd finished, he pulled off his shoes, now grimier than ever, and dropped onto the cot I'd prepared for him by the window.

"This is fabulous," he pronounced. "There're only a couple of things wrong with it. You need a spare bunk for me when I come down, in its own alcove, and it's got to have a window low enough for me to see out of lying down."

So while I made drinks, he made a rough sketch of the alcove opening off the northeast corner of the living room, with the low picture window, a wide built-in bunk, and bookshelves underneath. He handed me the sketch with a rough calculation of costs scribbled in the margin. "After your next article, chum, get Horace Bellyacher—or whatever his name is—to knock this up for you." (Some years later I had this alcove added, much as he described it, and the cost came to within a few dollars of what he'd figured.)

We took our drinks outside and sat on slabs of granite, watching the last of the yachtsmen disappear behind the islands and the shade of Isle au Haut change from blue to deep purple. When the light had faded and the chill of the September evening settled over the cove, we went back inside, and Otis began preparing dinner from the special supplies he'd brought.

"Tonight, goy," he said, "you eat Jewish."

We lingered long over dinner, talking for the most part of matters far removed from the business of Otis's visit, and were on our second bottle of hock with coffee when Kevin, Karen, and Belle dropped in—as I had urged them to that afternoon. They were eager to meet Otis, as indeed most of the islanders were, for his reputation after his first visit had spread quickly.

But if Otis had actually met few of the islanders, apart from the lobstermen, he knew most of them by name and even something about them. He had an uncanny memory for detail and retained nearly every scrap of information he learned about people. He would open a conversation with someone he was meeting for the first time as though they were old acquaintances. The way he greeted Belle, for instance. He remembered my having mentioned earlier, when I told him the three young people might stop by, that Belle was dining for the first time at Ram's Horn. (She agreed to this, incidentally, only after extracting a promise from Kevin that it would be a simple family meal and that Pat Torrey, Mary Lou's replacement at the Horn that summer, wouldn't be hovering in the kitchen.)

"Well, tell us," Otis said to Belle as the three came in—he identified her immediately, before I could introduce them—"did you use the right fork?"

"The right fork?" Belle echoed him, but she caught on right away. "Golly! I hope so. . . . Did I?" she appealed to Kevin.

Karen said, "The only thing she did wrong was insist we all do the dishes. Poor Mom!"

"I'm Kevin Bannister," Kevin said, coming forward just when I had decided introductions were superfluous.

"I thought you must be," Otis gravely replied—with just enough sarcasm in his voice to put Kevin off, I could see.

"I'm Karen."

"That, too, I guessed."

"And I'm Belle."

"You're all beautiful," Otis said, and insisted they sit down with us to finish off the hock.

When we'd finished it, a quarter of an hour later, Karen helped me clear the table—on the explicit understanding that in this bungalow no dishes were ever washed until after breakfast. In the kitchen, out of hearing, I asked Karen how Belle and Sally had hit it off.

"Oh, famously," Karen said. "They just made up their minds to get along, and they did. . . . Daddy, of course, was gaga. He could hardly talk he stammered so . . . that's what he does when he likes someone." Karen was in an exhilarated mood, it was plain to see. She rarely talked so spontaneously. "She's so terrific, you know," Karen went on after a moment. "I'm afraid Kevin'll lose her." Then she remembered she'd once consigned Belle to me—about two weeks before, to be precise. "I mean . . . since you wouldn't keep her for yourself."

I took down brandy glasses, and we presently rejoined the others. Kevin and Belle were sitting side by side on the sofa; Otis was slouched in the leather chair, a beefy leg draped over one arm. He still had his shoes off, but otherwise he was dressed as he always was—in his crumpled, shiny suit and shirt unbuttoned at the neck under his tie. They were talking about Jews, the subject having come up when Belle asked about the persistent odor of gefilte fish that lingered from our dinner, and Otis delivered a short, wry lecture on the primacy of Jewish cooking. Kevin had just remarked, more ponderously, I think, than he intended, that Jews were first in everything.

"How many Jews do you know?" Otis broke in.

"It's no great thing to know Jews," said Kevin, set back by the bluntness of Otis's questions. "Most of my college friends—"

"Most?"

"Well, half of them, anyway . . ."

"And how many of your Jewish friends have you brought home?"

"That's no test of friendship," Kevin said. "It's kinder to friends not to."

"That's unfair, Kevin," said Karen.

"I'm always suspicious," Otis remarked, lighting a cigar, "when kids from Far Hills and Katonah boast they have Jewish friends. It usually means they don't but think they should."

"What am I supposed to understand from that?" Kevin asked after a pause. It was easy to see he was put off by Otis.

"No one's locked into his culture—or subculture. Not in our world, anyway . . . At the same time, no one gets altogether away from it either. Take Belle."

"What about Belle?" Kevin said, instantly on the defensive.

"Belle could show up anywhere in the world, but I bet she'd still talk and act like a girl from a Maine island."

"Weep for islanders, too," Belle said. "We're also oppressed—by winters and the sea."

I had poured the brandy, and now passed it around before sitting at the end of the sofa away from Belle and Kevin. Karen sat sidewise on the bear rug, facing Otis, her long brown legs tucked under her.

"What I was leading up to," she said in her usual grave manner, "is our own culture or background. Kevin's and mine, that is. You're proud of being Jewish, I gather. So you remain a . . . I mean, you remain Jewish. Belle is proud of being an islander, so she remains one. But it isn't the same for us. Kevin and I don't feel especially proud of being . . . well, I mean, whatever we are. So isn't it easier for us to break away from our background?"

Kevin, who'd been brooding in silence for some minutes, broke in at this point. "This is a bunch of crap," he said. "Pretending that Jewish culture or island culture or Ivy League culture has anything to do with the way people behave. You're not telling me, I hope, that a Jewish cabdriver in New York has more in common with a Jewish banker than with another cabdriver—say, an

Irishman?"

Otis stared at Kevin for a moment, rolling his cigar in his mouth, before replying. "I wasn't saying that, as a matter of fact. But since you say it for me, pal, let's take it from there. . . . The counterthesis, I presume, is that the cab-drivers, downtrodden and persecuted, ignore their heritage, forswear their religious and other loyalties, and band together against—"

"Let's put it straight," Kevin interrupted him again. "They don't 'forswear' anything. They simply act together where their interests coincide. In matters of wages, for instance, in conditions of work, in guarantees against layoffs, benefits, and so forth. Usually in voting habits, too."

"Straight Marxian diagnosis," Otis said. "And leave Belle's hand alone. It distracts me. You don't own her." He said this last with a smile.

"Marxists never own their women," Kevin replied, as Belle, flushing, withdrew her hand from his and shifted her position on the sofa.

Otis said, "Well, that's a good omen." He waited, looking expectantly at Kevin. But Kevin stared back at Otis and said he didn't suppose anyone wanted him to restate the Marxian thesis of society.

"Why not?" Otis said. "Since I wasn't putting it straight . . . State it at least as it applies to what we've been talking about—Jews from Brooklyn, islanders from Maine, Anglo-Saxons from Duchess County."

"Bucks County, to be precise," said Karen.

"You'd have to tell me if there's a big difference."

"There isn't," she said.

"Then off you go, Vladimir."

Well, Vladimir was by this time too antagonized by Otis's manner to spout Marxism just because Otis asked him to. And, of course, he was past caring what sort of an impression he was making on this prickly transplanted Jew simply because he happened to be a friend of mine. But Kevin went ahead anyway—after a few moments' deliberation—on condition that Otis keep his mouth shut until he was through. I say it to Kevin's credit that in eight or ten minutes he gave a lucid and quite eloquent Marxist analysis of American society, accenting the economic motives behind all crucial decisions and activity of different social groups. What was particularly good in Kevin's analysis, I thought, was his restraint in using sweeping generalizations.

Belle, I could see, was awed by Kevin's facility, especially in the presence of so critical a listener as Otis. She glanced frequently at Otis to see if he, too, was impressed. But Otis listened without interrupting, his gaze resting occasionally on Belle and the rest of the time on the ceiling; he yawned only once, and inconspicuously. Karen stared somberly into the fire.

After Kevin had dealt with general principles, he tried to link some of them

to the things we'd been discussing. He didn't find it difficult, he said, to relate
Marxist ideas to the behavior of most people of middle-class background like
his own. He used Wylie Thatcher as an example: Wylie played a predictable role
in the economic system, expanding his business as rapidly as he could, hiring
more workers in good times, laying them off in a recession. He supported conservative politicians wherever they turned up, including Jews, and he was virtually without social conscience—except where he could conveniently satisfy it
through tax-deductible gifts to charity.

Otis started to say something but thought better of it. "Go on," he said,
relighting his cigar. "What about Jews?"

"Jews are no different when it comes down to fundamentals," Kevin said. "A
Jewish industrialist might have a preference for Jewish workers—I don't know
about that—but when all businessmen join forces to put pressure on the government for a tax easement, or whatever it might be, Jews and non-Jews behave
alike."

"Does it ever occur to you, Kevin," Otis said, staring up at the open beams,
"that this system of yours is static as hell? I suppose next you'll be telling us that
two lobstermen with identical incomes—one on Ram Island, the other on
Thorn—have more in common than two Ram Islanders with a spread of ten
thousand dollars in their earnings?"

"And I suppose you'd like to think it isn't so."

"Let's ask Belle," said Otis. "Belle, is your uncle more likely to identify with
Clarence Darling, who runs the car over at Thorn, or with Horatio Leadbetter,
say, here on Great Ram?"

"Well . . . I'd have to agree," Belle said. "Uncle Arthur thinks a lot of
Clarence Darling. They're old friends. But if it came to a real question of helping, he'd help Horatio."

"It's a loaded question," Kevin said, "with this lobster war going on."

"Even in a normal season, Kevin," Belle said.

We all laughed, and Kevin said he gave up; Maine islanders were beyond the
reach of Marxian logic.

Karen said, "Thank God for that."

I thought, as I poured more brandy for those who wanted it, that the dialogue between Kevin and Otis had ended. And it didn't seem a bad thing, since
the debate threatened to grow acerbic. But I was premature.

Otis was back at Kevin a few minutes later. He was reasonable enough, but
he was relentless. Suppose, he said, for the sake of argument, that we granted
Kevin his thesis: Bankers consorted with bankers, workers with workers, and so
forth. "What then? Do we have to mount a revolution to force them to play
together?"

"You're being cute," Kevin said. "No one has to answer a dumb question like that."

Karen said, "Come on, Kevin! That's rude."

"No, he's right," Otis said with his belly laugh. "Even a smart kike sometimes asks dumb questions. I'll try again. . . . What's wrong with bankers and workers and so forth lining up with their kind? Why aren't they simply competing constituencies? Like rivals anywhere. Government sets up ground rules, and they slug it out. Not to finish each other off, of course—because then they'd have to go out and find new bankers or workers, depending. What each side wants is an advantage. . . . Now, why isn't this natural rivalry between competing groups a healthy thing in any society?"

I think Kevin felt Otis was trying to bait him with these simplistic questions, because he didn't try to answer them directly. "Look," he said, "what magic formula do *you* have up your sleeve for a lil' ol' thing like curbing the power of Wall Street?" I thought Kevin was treading on slippery ground, trying sarcasm on Otis. It was apt to boomerang.

"There's no magic in anything, least of all in revolution. . . . Politics is your weapon, Kevin. Build up more politically minded unions. Study the general strike. Support liberal candidates. Use the political parties. Develop—"

The mention of political parties to Kevin, I knew, was like waving a red flag before a bull, and as soon as Otis had mentioned them, he broke in. "Who're you trying to kid, for Christ's sake? Change the country through those two parties!" Kevin went through a catalog of evils that the two parties shared in common and ended by asking Otis, "Can you tell me one fucking difference between Republicans and Democrats in this country?"

Otis said pointedly, with hardly a moment's hesitation, "The greatest difference imaginable in democratic politics, boy—the difference between one and two."

"And having two is supposed to be a virtue when both are equally bad? Shit, that's twice as bad as having none at all."

Otis looked steadily at Kevin for some moments before he spoke again. I really did think now that the dialogue had gone on long enough—but I doubted whether either of them would pay attention to me if I tried to stop it.

"My friend," Otis finally said, "you've lost all sense of democratic theory, and I can't talk to you. You leave off where I begin." Kevin started to interrupt, but Otis went right on, simply speaking loudly and drowning Kevin out. His voice was like steel. "To analyze American society in a Marxist way is naïve, from my perspective. But it's harmless. However, to risk collapsing an entire delicate system you don't begin to understand, causing untold misery to millions, in the vain hope things will be better when you're through—that's arrogance. Maybe it's the arrogance of youth. I hope it's not the arrogance of your so-called class. But it's arrogance in any case, and it imperils all of us."

"Your view," Kevin said—but without great spirit.

"That's right. My view."

Now I did interrupt them and said that was enough politics for one night. I tried to focus their attention on other subjects, but conversation was desultory. Karen asked Otis how the meeting had gone that afternoon with the lobstermen, and he gave her a brief summary of how things stood—as much, that is, as he would have told anyone who asked. Otis was not one to reveal secrets out of school. Kevin stared moodily into the fire, his shoulders hunched forward more than usual. He intentionally avoided Otis's eyes, which turned frequently toward him. Belle moved back closer to Kevin on the sofa and took his hand. She glanced sidewise at him from time to time, and they exchanged a few remarks privately, but for the most part they were silent. The three young people soon left—without our having regained the spirit of communion we had when they arrived.

Otis stood for some time in silence by the fire after they had disappeared up the path.

"I laid it on too thick," he said. "He doesn't fight back . . . like a kid from Brooklyn."

I said maybe it was because Kevin had listened to what he'd said.

"Fat chance," said Otis. "I'd feel better if he had."

We chatted about other matters for another half hour before turning in.

The next morning, on the way to the harbor to meet Arthur, we stopped for a quarter of an hour at Meadowlane. I wanted Otis to meet Lucy. And Otis wanted to speak to Belle—to apologize for cutting up Kevin the night before. I knew this had been on his mind from hearing him thrash about on his cot half the night.

We found Lucy and Belle over a second cup of coffee in the kitchen and joined them there. Belle managed a wan smile, but she was subdued. She took no part in our miscellaneous conversation about island affairs as Lucy and Otis sized each other up. Belle was meeting Kevin and Karen for one last sail on the blue sloop before it was hauled out for the season, and after we'd been there five minutes or so, she rose to get ready. Otis walked with her into the hall.

"Belle," he said, putting his hand on her shoulder. "I'm sorry I made your friend uncomfortable last night. I can be pretty blunt, I guess."

"You're that, all right," she said.

"I meant it for his good . . . and yours," he added. "I like the idea of you two. Tell him that."

"I will," Belle said.

"And my advice to you, Belle, is go slowly."

Belle nodded and went upstairs.

Well, human emotions are a curious thing, the way they respond to different stimuli. Those few words from Otis transformed Belle. When she stopped in the kitchen a few minutes later on her way out, she was a new person, her radiance and gaiety returned. She kissed her mother and, quite unconsciously, me—simply, I think, because she didn't feel she could kiss the only one present she really wanted to.

20

The accident at Seal Ledge occurred ten days after Labor Day. The summer people had left for the season, and school had reopened. The high school students had returned to Rockland and Camden the week before. A weak low pressure system over Cape Cod had kept the coast in fog for four or five days, but the fog wasn't thick enough in the middle of the day to keep the lobstermen from going out. Most of the Ram Island fleet was out that day.

The first word of the accident was when Turk came in at two bearing with him a shaken and subdued Willy Grant. Willy had gone out in the *Clarissa B* at ten, taking Joel with him. Joey, repeating his stunt of the previous year, had managed the first short week at Camden High, then played sick long enough the second week to make going back to school a waste of time. That was why he was aboard the *Clarissa B* that day.

Willy had reached the ledges shortly after noon to pull his string of traps there, and he was actually pulling them—not some others—when Barney Orcutt came on him. Barney evidently mistook his position in the fog and thought Willy was pulling a string of Thorn Island pots almost the same color farther along the ledges. He was alone, and he thought Willy was alone, since Joey had gone forward in the cuddy to read a comic book. He'd been there a half hour, Willy said, lying on the anchor rode. We never knew whether Joey had fallen asleep or simply didn't hear the sound of Barney's engine at full throttle as he bore down on the *Clarissa B*. Willy, working the pulley on the other side of his boat, neither saw nor heard Barney until he was fifty feet away. Then it was too late to do anything. Willy had time only to shout a warning to Joey and jump clear of the wheelhouse before Barney's boat, a new diesel-powered lobsterman nearly twice the size of Willy's, sliced halfway through the bow of the *Clarissa B*—at the very point where Joey was lying on the rode.

Willy was thrown to the deck by the impact, gashing his head on a bait barrel as he fell, but he was otherwise unhurt. Barney backed away from the wreck, and the *Clarissa B* began to sink immediately. Barney came alongside and shouted roughly to Willy to get aboard, but Willy, staggering to his feet, ignored him and rushed forward to the cuddy, which was rapidly filling with seawater through the hole in the bow. He found Joey motionless in the middle of the cabin, pinned down by a broken plank and his head already submerged. Willy tried frantically to wrench him free, but was unable to move him. When the *Clarissa B* lurched suddenly to port, Willy wallowed out of the cuddy and jumped clear of the boat as it sank beneath the surface. Barney, who had been standing by shouting angrily to Willy to get off his boat, hauled him immediately over the transom.

What followed is unclear. As Turk pieced it together later, largely from Willy's account, the two lobstermen fought each other wildly on the deck of Barney's boat—but for how long and with what weapons other than their hands, it was impossible to say. Turk thought it a miracle one or the other of them wasn't killed. In any event, having exhausted their energies in physical combat, they resorted to verbal abuse . . . and it was this that Turk, happening to switch off his engine a quarter of a mile away to change a fuse, heard through the fog. Happily, it was Turk who heard them and not some other Ram Islander, for there might have been another tragedy that day.

When Turk found them, they were still pointlessly circling the loose boards and other floating debris spewed forth by the *Clarissa B*, too distracted to realize the tide had already carried the debris some distance from where the boat went down. They were in a frenzied state, Turk said. Willy's face was smeared with blood from the gash on his head and a broken nose, and his arms were covered with purple welts. Barney had a lump on his forehead the size of a golf ball and a long slash on his leg where his oilskins had been ripped to shreds. He still held a lethal-looking plumber's wrench in one hand. They both began shouting at once as Turk drew the *Sunrise* alongside, and it was some minutes before he could quiet them down enough to learn what had happened.

"What we gonna do with the sonovabitch, Turk?" Willy said. "We'd oughta tie him up right here and run him over to the Rockland jail."

"My ass, you gonna do that!" Barney said, waving his wrench.

"Lay off it, both of you!" Turk said. "Willy, get aboard."

Barney's face had been livid with anger when Turk first arrived at the scene, Turk said; now it became white, ashen—his fury giving way to mortification as full realization of what he had inadvertently done came over him, and he began to calculate the consequences.

"For one lousy fuckin' poacher . . ." Barney mumbled. "Me? Do time for a bastard like that!"

"You kill't my brother, you sonovabitch!" Willy screamed, still in the well of Barney's boat. "I hope you burn—"

"Shut up, Willy, and git your ass over here," said Turk.

"I'd burn gladly, if it was you I got!" Barney screamed back as Willy climbed over the railing into the *Sunrise*. Barney continued to glower at Willy. "I'm goddamned if I let a two-bit piker mess my life up." The two boats began to drift apart. Barney looked at the wrench in his hand and suddenly threw it with all his force at the stern panel of his boat, where it broke apart. "Goddam if I ain't in a mind to put both you bastards outa your misery! Then no one's gonna be spreadin' stories. Sonovabitch if that ain't what I'm gonna do!"

"Yeah? Just try it, ya mother-fuckin'—"

Turk swung on Willy with the back of his hand, catching him across the mouth. He felt a tooth go. "Inside, Willy!" he said, shoving him toward the cuddy. Willy began to whimper, holding a hand over his bleeding mouth. But he did as Turk said.

Turk explained later he wasn't really worried what Barney might do, but he'd noticed a rifle hanging in Barney's wheelhouse and figured this wasn't the time to take any chances.

"Barney," Turk said, "a sixteen-year-old kid's been drowned. This ain't no time to be fightin'."

"Jesus, I didn't mean no harm to the kid. You know that, Turk." (Turk told us later Barney looked as if he was on the point of bawling, tears already welling up in the corners of his eyes . . . tears of frustration.) "What's José gonna say?"

And then I remembered an announcement in the inside pages of the *Courier-Gazette* a couple of weeks before about the marriage on Thorn Island of former sergeant Bernard L. Orcutt and José Hopewell in a double-ring ceremony.

"Look, Barney," Turk said. "It was an accident. We both know that. . . . Now git along home to José and let me take care of the rest."

Barney moved toward his controls, then turned back. "Turk," he said, "tell Clyde I'm . . ." But he could get no further and returned to the wheel. He moved off into the fog without looking back.

Turk now tended to Willy. He cleaned off his face and bandaged the gash on his head. The break in his nose didn't seem serious once the blood had been cleared away, and only one tooth was broken. He had Willy put on a dry shirt, then wrapped him in a blanket and gave him a shot of whiskey—for Willy was quivering all over, still in a state of shock. When he had somewhat recovered, Willy guided Turk back to where the *Clarissa B* had gone down. But, of course, there was no sign of her except a few oily bubbles rising to the surface over six fathoms of sea.

Clyde Grant wasn't yet in when Turk and Willy returned to harbor. Turk had Arthur Dacey take Willy home to break the news to Clara—they went through the fields to avoid meeting other islanders—then he telephoned the county sheriff from Caleb's. He was some minutes talking to him, with the store-room door closed, before he came out and told folks about the accident. In addition to Caleb and Jenny, there were half a dozen islanders in the store at the time. Turk omitted any mention of the fighting on Barney Orcutt's boat or of Barney's threat after Turk joined them. He speculated that Barney thought Willy was pulling Thorn Island traps—but this wasn't so, Turk emphasized. He'd seen the spot where the *Clarissa B* sank, and all the pots around were Willy's.

News of the accident spread quickly, and when they heard, the islanders came inevitably to the harbor in twos and threes. Turk stayed on at Caleb's, patiently repeating the story of the tragedy over and over as each new cluster of islanders arrived. But he never mentioned the angry scene on Barney's boat. It had been an accident, Turk insisted. Barney had meant to damage the *Clarissa B*, that was plain enough, but he'd never meant to hurt anyone—least of all Joey, whom he hadn't even known was aboard.

Turk's measured account of the accident stayed the passions of some islanders, but not all. When Clyde came in at four and heard the news, he want-ed instant revenge. He wanted all the lobstermen to go off immediately to Thorn Island, in convoy, and demand Barney Orcutt—what our people were then sup-posed to do to him, no one ventured to say. If the Thorn Islanders refused to surrender Barney (as refuse they must), then we were to sink all their boats at mooring. It was a wild idea, but it had support from a surprising number of lobstermen—not only the younger men, which was perhaps to be expected, but Zip Clayton, and even Rudolf York, who had always had a soft spot for Joey Grant—nearly half of them altogether. Several who had brought their rifles ashore earlier actually went after them.

It was a chilling prospect, Clyde's expedition. Arthur Dacey, who had come back from seeing Clara Grant, pointed out the obvious folly of Clyde's plan: It would not only be interfering with justice—for it was now up to the county sheriff to arrest Barney Orcutt and charge him with manslaughter—but it could lead to actions that would put half the Ram Island lobstermen in jail as well.

"But goddam it, Arthur," Clyde shouted at him, his face three shades redder than usual, "are we gonna sit here and do nothin' about Joey? Are we gonna let 'em sink our boats whenever they feel like it . . . just because they *think* we're pulling their traps? You heard what Turk said."

Turk took no part in the debate outside Caleb's. He merely listened, from time to time glancing at his watch or looking out to the mouth of the harbor, where the fog was thickening. As it turned out, Turk's voice of moderation wasn't needed, for before the lobstermen could reach any decision a call came through from the county sheriff ordering all boats of any description on Ram Island impounded until further notice; the order had been issued by the Superior Court, and violators would be fined $3,000 or receive thirty days in jail, or both. A similar order had been given to the Thorn Islanders.

The court order abruptly ended Clyde's vendetta. The islanders gradually dispersed, still stunned by the tragedy—perhaps more than at first, now that their preoccupation with revenge was over.

"It's curious, isn't it," Lucy said, standing beside me outside the store, "that when there's tragedy, people take their minds off it by inviting more. . . . I think Clyde's plan coming to nothing will make everyone braver."

Lucy and Belle went on ahead, and I walked slowly up to the ridge with Turk and Arthur. The fog now blanketed the island, and the early September dusk was already falling. It was then that Turk told us about the scene aboard Barney's boat when he'd found them circling off Seal Ledge. He told the story deliberately, with more detail than he was accustomed to give—not omitting the crunch of Willy's tooth when he struck him. After he'd finished, he was silent a few moments.

"It didn't seem likely to improve matters much," Turk said, "so I didn't tell it down there."

"What about Willy?" Arthur asked. Willy hadn't returned to the harbor after Arthur took him home, and none of the lobstermen had seen him.

"Willy's not gonna talk," Turk said. "I told him Barney's got about all the trouble he can handle, and it ain't all his fault. I said it's gonna be better for all of us if Barney gets off with as little as they gotta give him. . . . Well, after a while, Willy come 'round."

"I hope you're right, Turk," Arthur said. "I hope Willy keeps his mouth shut."

"He will. . . . A lot happened to Willy out there today he ain't gonna forget for a while."

We had come to the crossroads, and stopped before going our different ways.

"I don't think this oughta go beyond the three of us, either," Turk said. "That means Otis, too," he added, looking at me. "Otis is a very honest man an' a very convincin' one. He'd find some way to make me b'lieve it's better we put out all the facts. And I don't wanta b'lieve it. Not this time. . . . Are you with me, Arthur?"

Arthur said, "I'm with you, Turk. And even if I wasn't, I wouldn't breathe a word o' this."

I told Turk, of course, that I wouldn't either. Still, I wondered a little why, if he felt so strongly about not spreading the story of the fight and Barney's threat, he had told us. Later, walking on up the ridge with Arthur, I mentioned this.

"Comfort in numbers, I reckon," Arthur said. "Nobody likes to live alone with a bad secret."

But there was one more piece of information that came out before we separated at the crossroads—and it showed how essentially cautious Turk was, despite his reputation for being stubborn and, as Sharon put it, "headstrong." We were standing in silence when there seemed no more to say, digging our toes into the loose gravel and listening to the cadence of the horn at the Head. Arthur remarked casually that he thought it was a near thing at the harbor before the sheriff called. "I was afraid we were heading for more trouble."

"They'd never 'a come to a decision 'fore it was too dark to git over there," Turk said. "They'd 'a been scattered all over the bay by now in this fog. . . . 'Sides, they didn't really want to go."

"I guess Judge Peabody and the sheriff thought they might," said Arthur.

Turk was silent a moment, then he grinned broadly. "I wouldn't know what th' judge and th' sheriff thought," he said.

Arthur and I both stared at him, not at first understanding. Arthur said, "You mean you . . ."

"I didn't know any more'n you did, Arthur, how Clyde'd behave when he come in . . . times like this. I figured a court order'd slow things down, whichever ways."

Arthur whistled softly through his teeth and turned to me. "Seems like we got ourselves a one-man island here," he said.

Still we lingered, reluctant, I suppose—as people all over the island were at that hour—to quit each other's company with our lonely thoughts of Joey Grant. A deer came around the corner of the schoolhouse and, seeing us, snorted a warning to its mate before bounding across the road.

"Well," Turk finally said, turning toward the Peaks, "we'll never know how he'd 'a growed up. Maybe he'd 'a been the best o' the lot."

Barney Orcutt did not go directly home from the ledges that day. He cruised aimlessly about the bay the rest of the afternoon, avoiding other lobstermen, then dropped anchor off one of the Porcupines when darkness came. A warrant for his arrest had already been issued, but since he couldn't be found when a sheriff's deputy came over from Rockland to fetch him, the deputy left with instructions that he should be notified as soon as there was any knowledge of Barney's whereabouts; the deputy warned the Thorn Islanders that any failure to cooperate would lead to heavy penalties.

By daybreak Barney had made up his mind what he'd do. He found his way back to Thorn Island in the fog, put in at the Hole, and walked over the saddle to the cottage he'd just finished fixing up for himself and José. José's mother had insisted late the evening before, when Barney still hadn't returned, that José come home for the night. But José must have had some premonition that Barney would go straight to the cottage, and at dawn she went back. She was there when he arrived. She cleaned him up and fed him—Barney hadn't eaten since dawn the day before—and at eight o'clock, freshly dressed, he turned himself in to his uncle, Clarence Darling.

Clarence called the sheriff's office on his shortwave radio, and the deputy arrived in the forenoon to take Barney away. Bail was requested but refused on the grounds that a man so heedless of human safety as Barney had been at Seal Ledge, whatever his intent, was a menace to society and didn't deserve to be free pending trial; moreover, he had deliberately avoided arrest for eighteen hours. Otis explained later, after talking with Judge Peabody, that the principal consideration in the judge's mind in upholding the bail commissioner's ruling was not the stated argument but his fear of a possible act of revenge by Ram Islanders if Barney were out on bail.

Two investigators from the county attorney's office and a state trooper came over to Ram Island two days later to take statements from Turk and Willy Grant. Arthur and I had thought it prudent to have Otis on hand in case any legal questions came up, and he came out on the patrol boat with the investigating team. He spent a half hour with Turk and Willy before the hearing in the church. Both then and during the hearing itself, Otis was astounded at the change in Willy. As indeed we all were.

Willy's statement was the longest and most detailed, since he was the only witness of the accident. He described the episode simply and unemotionally. He said he guessed Barney thought he was pulling Thorn Island traps, which he wasn't. They asked Willy if he'd ever done that before, and Otis told him he didn't have to answer, but Willy did anyway. He said he had—sometimes because he was mad at the Thorn Islanders for snarling his lines and other times . . . he didn't know why. Didn't Willy know this was a serious offense? they asked. And Willy said he did, but he hadn't been thinking about that at the time. The chief inspector asked if Willy and Barney had had any previous encounter at the ledges, and Willy described the incident early in August when Barney Orcutt and another Thorn Island lobsterman had come up and asked him not to fish there anymore.

"Get that!" Otis said, describing the hearing to me when we met outside after it was over. " 'Asked him not to fish there anymore'! . . . What's come over this kid?"

Concerning the accident itself, Willy said he hadn't seen Barney until a few seconds before the impact and didn't know whether Barney had been trying to attract his attention. He thought at first Barney was simply trying to scare him by passing close to his bow. (Turk, Otis said, looked at Willy in some surprise when he said this.) If so, Willy went on, he misjudged; the impact was about three or four feet down the port side. The inspector asked if that was about where Joel was lying, and Willy said it was. He'd been there about a half hour and might have fallen asleep.

"I don't b'lieve he knew anythin'," Willy said. "It happened too quick for him to move. . . . Joey was a big kid for his age. He weighed a hundred and ninety-five pounds, you know."

Willy's eyes moistened, Otis said, when he spoke of Joey, and the inspector skipped over the part about the *Clarissa B* going down. They asked what happened after he jumped overboard.

"Well, Barney was right there and hauled me over the stern of his boat."

They pressed him for details of what happened next, but Willy had little to tell them. He made out that he was dazed and couldn't remember clearly.

"We just circled around . . . hopin' somethin'd come up, I guess. I dunno."

"What did you say? Were you mad at each other?"

"Well, we wasn't quite friendly . . . but we didn't say much. We kep' lookin' at where my boat'd gone down."

"Where'd you get all the cuts and bruises on your face?"

"That was when I fell, after Barney banged into us. I got a few more in the cuddy, I guess, tryin' to pull . . . I lost track."

"How did Barney get the lump on his head?"

"Yeah, I noticed that. . . . He must've bashed his head on the windshield when we hit."

"Well . . . how long were you aboard Barney's boat before Turk Jenkins came up?"

"Seemed like 'bout a quarter of an hour. Maybe more."

"And all that time you just circled around looking for signs of the wreck?"

"That's it. . . . We kep' on lookin'."

Turk's testimony was briefer. He described hearing shouts from the direction of the ledges sometime after noon and going straight over. What kind of shouts? he was asked—of anger, for help, or what? Just shouts, Turk said; he didn't wait to distinguish. When he found them, he took Willy aboard and told Barney to go back to harbor; he'd report the accident. Turk described finding a few bubbles at the site of the wreck and noted that all the pots in the vicinity were green and white—that is, Willy's. The chief inspector asked what shape Willy was in when Turk found him, and Turk said he was pretty bruised from his fall on the deck, especially a deep gash on the side of his head.

"But no sign of there having been a fight or anything like that?"

"Not so far 's I could see," said Turk.

Otis stood shaking his head outside the church after he'd given me an account of the hearing. Turk, who'd been talking with the state trooper, joined us. Willy had gone home immediately after the hearing to wait until the statements were ready for signing.

"It beats me," Otis said. "Barney Orcutt sinks his boat and kills his brother after a feud that's been building up all season, and Willy sits there and says Barney didn't mean to do it."

"Isn't that the way it was?" I said.

"As *we* see it, undoubtedly. But that's not the Willy Grant I remember. If I hadn't heard it with my own ears, I wouldn't have believed it. . . . Know what he asked the chief inspector as he was leaving? Was Barney making out all right in jail!"

Neither Turk nor I spoke, and Otis presently went on. "You know, there's something fishy about that silent pantomime on Barney's boat after the accident. Two mercurial types like Barney Orcutt and Willy Grant . . . Willy's hiding something that happened there." Otis glanced at Turk, but Turk was looking down across the cemetery toward the harbor. "Whatever it was," Otis went on, "it makes things easier for Barney, so there's no harm. . . . Maybe a new era of sweet reason began that afternoon on Barney's boat after Joey drowned."

"Then—or a little later," I said for Turk's benefit.

But Turk appeared not to have heard. He left us a few minutes later, and Otis and I went on to Meadowlane for lunch with Lucy and Belle while the inspectors were preparing the statements for signing before they left.

Joey's body was recovered the Monday after the accident. The Coast Guard undertook the operation with the help of two frogmen who were brought up from New London. Turk led them to the area—fortunately, it was a day of calm seas—and in three quarters of an hour Joey's body was raised to the surface and borne off to Camden for autopsy. The examination was complicated by the fact that the body had lain four days at the bottom of the ocean, but it was clear death had come instantaneously. The county medical examiner reported death as a result of severe skull fracture, prior to drowning.

The funeral service for Joey was held on Wednesday, a day of slate-gray overcast. Most of Joey's immediate contemporaries, the high school students in Camden and Rockland, came home the day before. Others arrived on the *Sunbeam*; the mission had been able to arrange a change in schedule, and the *Sunbeam* would bring the body from Camden, together with any off-island mourners who needed transport. There were more of the latter than I might have expected, including several I knew of but hadn't met—such as Caleb Brewster's son Elmer, for instance, who was back for the first time in more than a year. Clyde's brother Amos, now living in Castine, was over with his entire family. There were also a dozen Fawcetts from Camden, Clara Grant's people. Clarence Darling represented the Thorn Islanders—after radioing to Arthur to ask if it would be appropriate for him to come; Cliff Dawson brought him over, since their boats were still impounded. Kevin Bannister returned for the funeral, a gesture the islanders appreciated (though it was a small sacrifice on Kevin's part, of course, since Belle had delayed her departure for college a few days to be at the service). And, finally, Jingle came home.

Belle had been right about Jingle. She was as uninhibited as ever, and as irrepressible. Despite the solemnity of the occasion, and despite her pregnancy, she bounded up the gangplank as soon as it was fixed and greeted each of the islanders in turn, loudly and effusively. Nearly everyone on the island had gathered for the *Sunbeam*'s arrival. She caught my eye on her half a dozen times as she went on her rounds—deliberately saving me for the last, I think. When she finally came over to me, she kissed me squarely on the mouth, as she always had, and continued to hold me by the arms, studying my face.

"You bastard," she said. "Why haven't you written?"

I reminded her she hadn't either, at least since her wedding, but she brushed this aside.

"That's no excuse. I've been busy . . . and don't tell me you have too."

Her words might have been brusque—when were they not?—but her spirits were gay. She hugged me again and turned, one arm still around me, to survey the scene. Her mother, looking uneasy as she habitually did when she observed Jingle in public, came up to us.

"Jingle," Winifred whispered, "don't carry on so. Remember where we are."

But Jingle wasn't to be tamed by appeals to any conventional behavior. "Now, Mother, whispering and tiptoeing around's no way to pay respects to Joey. Why, he'd be insulted! . . . He's brought us all together, and I know he'd want us to behave just as we are. The same way he would."

"Sometimes I despair of you, Jennifer," Winifred said, but she was mollified when Jingle relinquished me and put an arm around her mother. We stood at the edge of the pier looking down on the deck of the *Sunbeam*, where they were preparing to remove Joey's brown oak coffin. Mr. Hargrave said a brief prayer, and half a dozen islanders carried the coffin with some difficulty up the narrow gangplank.

"I bet they wish it was any kid but Joey," Jingle said, but this time she had the delicacy to lower her voice.

We followed Mr. Hargrave and the coffin up to the church. It was slow, heavy work for the bearers, and all the men took turns. A few drops of rain fell out of the leaden sky as we made our way. Horatio began to toll the bell before we arrived. The bearers carried the coffin to the front of the church, in front of the row of seats set aside for the Grants. The rest of us found seats behind, gathering partly by family, partly by age group.

I think every person on the island was there except Widow Barnaby. Stanley Jenkins, the newest member of the community, was in Sharon's arms. Lydia York, the eldest and long since senile, had insisted on coming and was carried into the rear of the church in her rocker after being driven down by Caleb. Jingle stopped to say a word to her as we passed. "She's come to see what it'll be like when she goes," Jingle whispered in my ear when she rejoined me. Including the visitors, I counted seventy-one people gathered in the church. Even the half dozen island dogs were there, twice shooed down the aisle and driven outside. The men were all dressed in their best suits—their only suits, in most cases, taken out of mothballs for the first time since Frank Talbot's funeral midway through the war. Most of the women wore shawls, but several—like Jingle— were bareheaded. We bowed our heads as Mr. Hargrave opened the service with his rich, deep voice:

I am the resurrection and the life, saith the Lord: he that believeth in me, though he were dead, yet shall he live. . . .

Some minutes later, as we opened the hymnals to sing "Eternal Father, Strong to Save," Jingle whispered to me, "It's uncanny how this brings back Stanley's funeral . . . the same sort of day, only a month earlier. The same people, most of them. The same hymns." The organist played the first few bars. "Except that then everyone was bawling," Jingle added.

I glanced sidewise at her, implying a question: If then, why not now?

"Stanley's death was so unnecessary. Joel's has a point. . . . You'll see."

Winifred looked along the row at us and frowned.

The hymn began, and we surprised ourselves, after a modest start, with the power of our singing. Elmer Brewster, two rows in front of us, had a fine tenor and improvised a descant on the mighty refrain where the minor chords shift to major:

. . . hear us when we pray to Thee
For those in peril on the sea.

Elmer's courage prompted others to experiment with harmony, and the rest of us provided enough volume to drown out any discords. By the time we came to the end of the third verse, the last Mr. Hargrave had announced, the rafters reverberated with our voices. The silence was overpowering when the organ stopped. Mr. Hargrave started to go on to the next part of the service, then closed his prayer book and took up the hymnal again.

"No," he said. "I do believe we'd better sing two more verses. That was splendid!" So we sang again—if possible, even more powerfully than before.

I had heard Mr. Hargrave deliver one or two sermons since I'd come to Ram Island and never thought of him as a fire-and-brimstone preacher, but one of his prayers—improvised between the formal prayers prescribed for burial at sea—brought us back sharply to the reality of the struggle we'd been living through.

"Lord, watch over the people of these islands. In their anguish they have plundered each other's livelihood. They have destroyed the tools by which they work. They have driven an innocent family from its home in fire. They have caused, however inadvertently, the death of a mere lad, whose memory we celebrate today, and sent yet another lad to jail for it. . . . These costs are too high for pride and false honor. These are the consequences of suspicion and mistrust. Lord, grant these people forbearance and patience. Grant them the fortitude to withstand the just penalties civil government exacts for their misdeeds. Above all, give them the will to resolve their misunderstandings in a true spirit of Christian love. For Jesus Christ's sake. *Amen.*"

At the end of the service we filed out and gathered around the family plot in the cemetery behind the church, where Horatio Leadbetter had dug a fresh grave. The coffin was borne forth for the last time and placed on ropes over the grave, then slowly lowered into the earth as Mr. Hargrave read the final prayer— the traditional prayer on the island for those lost at sea, regardless of where they were finally laid to rest:

Under Almighty God we commend the soul of our brother departed, and we commit his body to the deep. . . .

The women went up to embrace Clara, red-eyed from crying and leaning on Mary Lou. Lucy was first.

"I kep' thinkin' of you, Lucy," Clara said through her tears, "the times you been through this."

"The pain goes away, Clara. Then the good memories are left."

When Jingle's turn came, Clara said, "Ain't you good, Jingle, to come all the way down for Joey."

"Clara, I hate to admit it, but I'm a sucker for a good funeral. And this one was a beauty."

"It *was* kinda nice, wasn't it?" Clara said, smiling in spite of herself. "Wasn't that hymn somethin' though?"

Mary Lou stayed beside Clara until the last of the mourners had left the cemetery. Black became her, and everyone's eyes were drawn to her at one time or another during the service and around the grave. She had come home from a new job in Rockland the day after the accident and had stayed close to her

mother during the past five days. Throughout the service, I noted, she had taken
care that Clara didn't break down entirely, as Clara seemed once or twice likely
to do. Now, leaving the cemetery, Mary Lou greeted old friends somberly but
dry-eyed. One of these was Elmer Brewster, who'd been waiting for some time to
exchange a word with her.

"Long time, Lou," he said, shaking her hand as Jingle and I passed behind
them.

"Don't you ever come home, Elmer?"

"Next summer, no matter what. . . . You gonna be here?"

"I will if you are. What month?"

"Be August, most likely."

That was apparently all the conversation they had, for Mary Lou moved off
presently to rejoin her family, and Elmer went on to the harbor to rejoin his. But
it was enough to start Jingle thinking.

"Now that's a way to bring Elmo back I never thought of," she said.

At three, having lunched at various places around the island, the visitors
reassembled at the landing to board the *Sunbeam*. The high school students
were also returning to the mainland. Belle was off to college, Kevin having
offered her a ride to Orono before he drove back to Princeton; Lucy had expected her to stay another night, but yielded gracefully when Belle proposed this
new plan. A good number of islanders gathered to bid the off-islanders farewell,
including all the Grants—except Willy. For Willy disappeared behind the church
as soon as Joey's coffin was lowered into his grave, and he didn't appear again
until the end of the day.

Jingle stayed on for several days after the funeral. Her purpose, of course,
was to see something of her parents, whom she hadn't seen since she was married, but she saw as much of me during those days as of them. We quickly recovered our old intimacy, lacking only the suspense of knowing where it was leading us. Or so I thought, at least, but Jingle wouldn't even yield the suspense.

"You know, don't you, we could still become lovers," she said as I was leaving her late one evening after we'd been talking about ourselves.

I asked her—a little stiffly, I suppose, though I have to confess the idea had
occurred to me, too—if that's what she had in mind.

"Well, I don't really," she said. "But if you do, I'd consider it."

"Even while you're bearing your husband's child?"

She peered at me in the faint light of a waning September moon. "Is that so
awful?" When I said nothing, she added, "Remember, I loved you first." I told her
I'd never understand her and went on home.

Well, we didn't in the end become lovers—in the usual sense of the word, that is—though I'm sure there were some who thought we were. Winifred, in particular, seemed very nervous that we might be, until Jingle, in her blunt way, assured her mother we weren't. When Jingle told me about this, the morning before she left, I asked her what she would have told her mother if we *had* become lovers.

"Just that, I suppose. At least it would have put her out of the misery of not knowing."

But we did establish during those days the basis of a lifelong friendship. We had been close before her marriage—at least before she told me about it that terrible night early in January—but there was a new dimension to our relationship by the time Jingle left after Joel Grant's funeral. I think Jingle worked hard to fix this new relationship, because it was what she had promised herself when she decided to marry Emil Zukin. If it meant having extramarital relations, she was ready for that too. Anyway, her working at it made no difference. I mean, our relationship was no less real in the end for having been nurtured first in her mind. There was literally no topic too sensitive for us to discuss in our long hours together. But we were not in need of constant dialogue. We were equally at ease in silence. The fact of the matter was that we found pleasure in each other's company whatever we were doing—or not doing. In that sense we were truer lovers than many who shared a richer physical intimacy than ours.

Oh, there were irritations. But Jingle had a way of turning even these to advantage. For instance, she found me one morning in the outhouse, overlooking the cove, and instead of turning away, as she should have in common delicacy, she sat on a stone and watched me, chattering away as though there was nothing in the least unusual in the situation. Since the door of the outhouse had long since blown off, I was defenseless against her gaze and finally drove her off with harsh words.

"Jesus Christ, Jingle! You should give even your husband that much privacy."

"Oh, but I do," she said mildly, and left to go inside; she seemed vaguely hurt.

I walked out to the end of the cove to calm myself, and when I returned, she was in the leather chair darning my socks.

"I'm sorry," she said without looking up. "I'll never do that again." And that was the end of it.

After she left for Portland, we began a correspondence that lasted, rarely with an interval exceeding two weeks (when we were not together, anyway), for many years. Jingle was the closest friend I had during those years—the years I write of here.

21

The hearing in Rockland, originally scheduled for September 18, several days after the accident at the ledges, was postponed. The real order impounding the boats was lifted after a week, but all fishing licenses of Ram and Thorn Islanders were suspended until after the trial of Barney Orcutt. The grand jury was in session at the time of the accident, and early in October returned an indictment for manslaughter; Barney, represented by a lawyer in Camden, pleaded not guilty. The case was scheduled to come up at the end of November. Once it was decided, Judge Peabody would advise the commissioner whether, in his view, the suspension order should be lifted or extended for a further period of time. The lobstermen, meanwhile, were allowed to use their boats to take in traps, but they were not allowed to keep any accumulated catch. The suspension did not extend to hand fishing or seining by the lobstermen along the shores of their respective islands.

Judge Peabody's suspension order, needless to say, worked financial hardship on the Ram Islanders. With their income virtually stopped, the lobstermen couldn't pay their monthly bills at Caleb's or order special provisions, as they were accustomed to, from the mainland. Arthur extended credit for gasoline and other supplies as far as he could, but by mid-October he had to devise an informal rationing system for the lobstermen or risk going heavily into debt himself. John Grant and Horatio Leadbetter left the island to take jobs at the sardine factory in Rockport, and others were thinking of it. Alfred and Janice Torrey were on the point of bringing their three high school children home from Rockland to save the expense of room and board beyond the plantation's allowance—until Lucy Talbot heard of it and advanced the necessary funds.

The islanders took their hardships philosophically at first. After the traps were in, piled in stacks around the harbor, most of the lobstermen took to the overgrown alder groves crowding in on their fields or to long-neglected repairs to their sheds and barns. The ring of ax and hammer sounded across the island during the last still days of September and the first crisp days of October. The island had never looked tidier in her lifetime, Clarissa Grant said. Orchards were trimmed. The school and church were painted for the first time since before the war. The Allens' cellar hole was cleaned up, and the barn repaired. The roads were raked down from one end of the island to the other so that even Harold Toothacher's truck passed almost noiselessly along them. The island dump opposite Caleb's, an eyesore for many years, was closed out, and a new one, out of sight, opened near the quarries. At the harbor, where the islanders by habit still gathered, conversation turned more often to farming and forestry than to lobstering—though there was longing in the men's eyes when a passing lobsterman came in to buy bait from Arthur and reported that the lobsters were hanging in particularly late that fall with the prolonged mild weather.

Only Willy Grant was despondent. He had recovered from his bruises, but he was rarely seen about the island. Clyde reported that he'd go a whole day without speaking—which, for Willy, seemed a virtual impossibility. He had made no move to find another boat. Turk, clamming late one afternoon at Southwest Beach, came across Willy sitting on a boulder staring toward the Camden Hills. Turk hadn't seen him to speak to since the inspectors were out and told him he'd made a good statement; it was certain to help Barney's defense. Willy shrugged. Turk asked if he'd like to fish with him when the suspension was lifted, and Willy said he'd think about it.

But Willy's thinking, it turned out, was in another direction. Early in October he announced he was giving up lobstering. He planned to return to the Marines, and he wanted to enlist right away. Clyde and Clara were at first startled, then deeply disturbed by Willy's decision, but they knew from the moment he told them, after returning from a long walk in the rain, that they wouldn't dissuade him. To lose two sons in such short order—on top of Mary Lou, who now had a steady job in Rockland as a seamstress and would be spending more time there than at home, and Susan, who would be starting high school next year—was more than Clyde and Clara could contemplate. That large, boisterous house, for years full of laughter, suddenly grew silent. Clyde himself, now approaching fifty-six, wondered whether he too should throw up lobstering and move to the mainland to take up new work while he was still able. He wrote his brother Amos to inquire about jobs in Castine, and Amos promptly replied that the boatyards there were looking everywhere for help. The prospect of Clyde Grant's departure, needless to say, had a profoundly depressing effect on the other lobstermen—and, indeed, on all of us.

"This is how the islands get depopulated," Arthur gloomily remarked. "A few experienced lobstermen go. Then the store can't make a go of it and closes up. The young people stay on the main after high school. More lobstermen leave. . . . And pretty soon there's no one left except a few too old to move away—like me."

Otis came out to spend a weekend on the island about this time, partly to pay a visit to me, partly to see how the lobstermen were making out under the suspension order—although Turk had told me, "You know 's well as I we ain't got a plug nickel to pay him." I assured Turk that if there was ever a bill from Otis, which I doubted, I'd take care of it myself. Otis arrived on the mailboat Saturday morning and spent most of the day with the lobstermen—at their homes, at the harbor, wherever he found them. He was shocked at what he found.

"Three lobstermen already gone out of fifteen," he exclaimed when he returned to Cutler's Cove toward the end of the afternoon, "and maybe a fourth! That's more than a quarter of the island's income. Not just for a few months, but maybe forever . . . That sure as hell wasn't what the judge intended."

The next morning Otis spent two hours at the store going over accounts with Caleb in some detail. He did the same with Arthur at his car in the afternoon. Then on Monday he had Turk run him over to Thorn Island, where he planned to catch the *Laura Lee* on her return trip. He had a long talk there with Clarence Darling and Sam Orcutt, and found the situation of the Thorn Islanders, he later wrote me, similar to ours—or worse. Several of their lobstermen had taken temporary jobs in Camden, and at least two of them were thinking seriously of staying. Clarence managed to keep the store open there—it was a considerably smaller operation than Caleb's—only by relying on existing stocks.

Otis saw Judge Peabody in Rockland that afternoon, and after explaining to him the situation on the islands, secured a hearing for the following Monday— that is, about five weeks before Barney Orcutt's trial was scheduled to open. The lobstermen of both islands were asked to attend, and though it was a wet and blustery day, all but three managed to make it. One was Cecil Allen, still determined to have nothing to do with any Ram Islander. Our people, to save gas, crossed in Arthur's large boat, the *Sarah Lou*. I went with them. The Thorn Islanders came with Clarence Darling. We met Otis outside the courthouse and assembled in a conference room off the judge's chambers, the Thorn Islanders on one side of the long mahogany table, the Ram Islanders on the other. The judge entered presently, without his robes, and motioning us to remain seated, took his place at the head of the table. Otis was opposite him with Barney Orcutt's lawyer, and I sat with several other observers along one wall.

Judge Peabody, even without his robes, was an austere-looking man. He was in his early sixties, gray-haired, and he sported a hairline mustache—except that *sporting* somehow fails to convey anything relevant about the judge's appearance; rather, *fastidious*. His pinstriped suit was severely (though elegantly) cut, his cufflinks were amber, and he wore a subdued bow tie. He sat upright in a high-backed leather chair, occasionally drumming the table lightly with his knuckles. From time to time he penned a note on a small pad in front of him. The table was otherwise bare. Judge Peabody had a reputation for being brusque, even caustic, in hearings like this, but he was also impartial, distributing his reproof equally on petitioners, witnesses, defendants, and attorneys. No one was immune from his sting. He was a stern judge, it was commonly felt, but a fair one.

"Very well, gentlemen," he began after looking deliberately up and down the table. "Mr. Lieberman tells me there are circumstances that warrant reconsideration of my order of September 14, which led to the suspension of your fishing licenses until after the trial of Mr. Bernard Orcutt next month. Since this is an informal hearing, we may conduct it informally, without oaths and other usual court procedure. You may proceed, Mr. Lieberman."

Otis stood and faced the judge. I noticed his shirt was buttoned to the top, the first time I'd seen this since I'd known him.

"Sir," he said, "what brings us here today is the serious situation which has arisen on the two islands as a result of your order. It is, I believe, a simple question of economics and in no way reflects on the wisdom of the order itself. I doubt, sir, that there is a man present here today who thinks your order unreasonable or unfair."

Several of the lobstermen nodded in agreement. Otis went on.

"You see at the table here fewer fishermen than were engaged in the so-called lobster war between the two islands last summer. Eight fewer, to be precise. Three of them were unable, for personal reasons, to be present today, but five are absent for the good reason that they are no longer lobstermen and are otherwise employed. Five lobstermen represents a net loss to the islands of some thirty thousand dollars in income, figured conservatively. At least one other lobsterman, a senior member of that community and the fourth generation of his family to fish there, is thinking of leaving Ram Island."

"Which is he?" the judge asked.

"Mr. Clyde Grant, sir," Otis said, indicating Clyde. The Thorn Islanders who hadn't heard of Clyde's plan stirred, and Clarence Darling shook his head.

"I know the Grants by reputation," Judge Peabody said, his eyes resting on Clyde.

"Mr. Grant's brother and son—the one whose boat was in the accident off Seal Ledge—have both quit Ram Island in the past month."

The judge nodded gravely, made a note on his pad, and asked Otis to go on.

"Sir, I made inquiries on both islands last week and discovered that the total sale of lobsters this season to the buyers who carry them to market in Rockland is under one half of the total sale last season. Is this not correct, Mr. Dacey and Mr. Darling?"

"Fifteen thousand, eight hundred and seventy-five dollars was the value of lobsters received this year before September 14," Arthur said, consulting a paper he took out of his pocket, "as compared to thirty-three thousand, six hundred for the total season last year."

"I do not have the exact figures with me, Judge," Clarence Darling said, "but the percentage is just about the same as Arthur's . . . as Mr. Dacey's."

"These gentlemen recognize, sir," Otis went on, "that much of this loss was caused by their own actions last summer. That part is never going to be recovered. If, however, the suspension order runs its full course—that is, until the end of November at the earliest—there will be so little time left before cold weather sets in that the yearly earnings of these gentlemen will be barely a half of their earnings in a normal year. I need hardly remind you, sir, of the burden this places on the two islands in meeting obligations such as schooling, harbor maintenance, and general services. If more lobstermen were to become discouraged and leave, the burden could become intolerable and the state or federal government would be obliged to help. At the worst, these islands, like many others, could lose their indigenous communities entirely and the properties be sold to out-of-state vacationers. Already, the two general stores, which survive on the earnings of the lobstermen on the islands, are severely strained in their finances. I can give you the figures, if you—"

"No need, Mr. Lieberman," the judge broke in. "You have given me a clear picture of actualities and probabilities." He looked slowly up and down the two lines of silent lobstermen, drumming lightly on the table. A gust of rain beat on the high windows behind him. "And what of you gentlemen? Are you ready to fish again?" He turned to Leonard York, on his left, asked him his name, and said, "Mr. York, if the commissioner were to reinstate your license on my order, where would you put your traps?"

"Wal . . . along our shores, like we always do, and—"

"Would you fish at Seal Ledge?"

Leonard looked startled and glanced around him, but the other men were stony-faced, no better than he at guessing what the judge was leading to.

"Wal, if t'was allowed, I would, Judge. Them's the biggest lobsters by a long sight."

Judge Peabody turned to Wilfred Hopewell, on his right, and after asking him his name, said, "Now, Mr. Hopewell, if you were to come across Mr. York's traps at Seal Ledge next to yours, what would you do with them?"

"Why, I wouldn't touch 'em, Judge," Wilfred said, happy to have such an easy question. "Leonard's got 's much right to fish the ledges as me, don't he?"

The judge turned to Rod Allen, Cecil's younger brother, sitting next to Wilfred. "Suppose, young man, despite what Mr. Hopewell says, you came across him cutting Mr. York's lines. What would you do?"

"I'd tell him straightaway he shouldn't be doin' it," Rod Allen answered.

" 'He shouldn't be doin' it,' " the judge repeated. "And suppose he continued anyway?"

"Well . . . I guess I'd tell Clarence 'n' Sam Orcutt. Then we'd have a meetin', I guess."

"Would it not occur to you to notify the warden?"

"Cliff Dawson?" It was Rod Allen's turn to look startled. "Well . . . I guess if it kep' goin' on, we'd have to tell Cliff, yes."

" 'Have to tell Cliff,' " Judge Peabody repeated. "Mr. Dawson is the chief enforcement officer in the mid-Penobscot for the state fishing laws. You are witness to an infraction of those laws. Mr. Dawson is the one you should tell first."

The lobstermen shifted uneasily in their seats, but it was a few moments before Turk spoke up. "I don't want to be disrespectful, Judge, but we gotta live with each other. I agree with Rod Allen . . . we'd be better to settle this 'mongst ourselves 'fore we go to Cliff Dawson."

"I'm not interested in your opinion, young man," Judge Peabody said coldly. "I'm telling you that if you are witness to a crime, you are under obligation to report it. Otherwise you may be considered an accessory to that crime. . . . I don't say every court would judge you so. I merely say you run that risk."

Turk flushed, but said nothing. The judge turned next to Zip Clayton and, after asking his name, put several questions to him about the placing of his traps—the distance from other traps, the number in a given area, and so forth. Then he asked whether Zip would place traps along the shores of Thorn Island.

"Why, we don't put our traps on their shores, Judge. Leastways never inside theirs. That's the law."

Judge Peabody stared for a long moment. "Mr. Clayton," he finally said, "that is *not* the law. That is your custom. A licensed fisherman in the state of Maine may legally fish anywhere he chooses below mean high tide." He paused again. "I don't say your custom is a bad one. Any device that keeps order is useful. But I find it curious that you honor a custom of your own while you ignore the laws of this state which explicitly forbid the plundering of another man's traps and the fouling of his lines. . . . What have you to say to that, Mr. Clayton?"

Zip looked acutely uncomfortable and slid down farther in his seat, avoiding the judge's eyes. Arthur Dacey spoke for him. "I'd say, Judge, that we should honor both the custom and the law. And we mean to."

Clarence Darling said, "That goes for us, too."

Judge Peabody again looked over the lobstermen deliberately—whether to inspire greater awe in them or to discover in their expressions some further sign of their contrition, it was hard to tell.

"My order of September 14," he said gravely, "was not intended to deprive you of your livelihood, but precisely to prevent you from doing it yourselves. You seemed determined to do so. I thought, and the commissioner agreed, that by restricting your normal activities for some period, we could bring you to a sharper sense of your responsibilities toward your families and toward each other. Today I see the first intimation that this strategy may be succeeding."

He paused, looking once again at the weatherbeaten faces turned towards him. "What has moved me most this morning to reconsider my order is not your financial burden, which is the consequence of your own foolhardiness and which was in any case very heavy even before my order, according to the evidence of Mr. Dacey and Mr. Darling . . . but the very real danger of a migration from your islands. Should this occur, even though you all found gainful employment elsewhere, it would be a grievous blow to the economic stability of this area. I sincerely hope that Mr. Grant and his family will reconsider their intention to quit Great Ram Island. . . . Now, I should like to consider this matter overnight and will give you my decision in the morning. Is there anything further, Mr. Lieberman?"

Otis thought a moment, then leaned forward. "Sir, I'm sure you know how anxious these gentlemen are to learn your decision. They would be very happy to remain in Rockland until midafternoon, if—"

"I will give you my decision tomorrow, Mr. Lieberman," the judge broke in icily, rising from his seat. "Good day, gentlemen."

We all stood as he left the conference room, then filed out ourselves, saving our remarks until we were outside the courthouse.

"Wal, he ain't 'xactly the funniest man alive, is he?" Sam Orcutt said. "He seemed to like you a lot, though, Zip!"

"About as much as he did Rod and me," Turk said. "Right, Rod?"

"Goddam old woman!" said Rod Allen, still smarting.

"I don't care what kind of 'n old woman he be if he lifts that suspension," Rudolf said. "Will he do it, Otis?"

"He'll do it," Otis said, "but not before tomorrow afternoon now . . . if I know him. That was a dumb move, trying to get him to move up his decision. I hoped I could get you guys another day's fishing."

Judge Peabody's severe manner, especially his tendency to embarrass Ram Islanders and Thorn Islanders alike, had the effect of lowering the barriers among the lobstermen. There was not yet intimacy, but for the first time in many months there was an absence of animosity. Otis remarked on it as we fell in behind the lobstermen, making our way through the streets of Rockland to McLoon's Wharf.

"They're like players on rival ball clubs, aren't they? Wary of each other, inherently hostile, but drawn together by the need to razz the umpire. . . . Judge Peabody did them a favor in there."

At the wharf we bade farewell to Otis and made our separate ways back to the islands through mounting seas and driving rain.

Judge Peabody rescinded his suspension order on Tuesday—but not before late afternoon, as Otis had predicted. The lobstermen of both islands were out to reset their traps at daybreak the next day, despite the high seas left from the easterly storm the night of the hearing. The lobsters had already begun their crawl into deeper water, so the catch was less than expected, especially after the grounds had been undisturbed for nearly six weeks. However, the lobstermen were too pleased to be out again to mind the sudden severe weather or to grumble more than usual at the meager take.

John Grant decided not to return from his job in Rockport, but Horatio Leadbetter came back and, most important of all, Clyde gave up his idea of moving to Castine. It was not so much the stirring of life again on the island that convinced him to stay but the stirring of life inside Clara—for after thirteen years she found in late October that she was again pregnant.

"Don't tell me, you incurable Victorian," Jingle wrote me when she heard the news, "that sex doesn't matter." (Since I'd never told her anything of the kind, I charged her in my next letter with having sex on the brain—like Sally Bannister.)

There was one last episode in the lobster war of 1946—at least one last episode I knew about. Turk again was a central figure in it, and I happened by chance to be a witness. I had gone out with Turk on a raw Saturday morning in mid-November, raw less from the temperature of the air than from a fine dense fog driven in from the northeast. It was to be my last time on the bay in many months (apart from departing on the *Laura Lee*), since I was scheduled to leave in two weeks for an extended visit to West Africa and had a heavy load of work to get done before I left.

Turk pulled his traps along the outer shore of Little Ram, then set his course westward across the bay to the string he had off Vinalhaven. We passed close on this course to Drowned Peter, a four-fathom ledge southwest of Thorn Island where the catch was sometimes reported to be good. Ram Island lobstermen rarely fished at Drowned Peter because of the distance from port, but Thorn Islanders did. As we passed on our compass course a quarter of a mile south of the shoal, the fog thinned out for a moment and we saw Bill York circling in the area. He didn't see us, since his wheelhouse opened away from us, and the fog closed in again before he completed his circle. There was no doubt, however, that he was pulling a trap. Turk said nothing, but his jaw hardened.

We went on to the Vinalhaven shore, where Turk pulled his two dozen traps, and returned to Seal Ledge by way of Drowned Peter. Bill had left, and no other lobstermen were in the vicinity. Turk circled for ten minutes but found buoys of only two colors—belonging to Sam Orcutt and Rod Allen.

"I'm a sonovabitch," Turk said. "I know Bill's not so smart . . . but how dumb's he gotta be?"

We went on to the ledges, where Turk pulled his traps in silence, barely grunting at my occasional remarks. As we left, the fog thinned out again and we found Cliff Dawson nearby; the commissioner, we knew, had ordered a close watch over our area since the suspension was lifted. Cliff hailed us, and Turk turned toward him.

"How's she doin', Turk?" Cliff called out as we came abreast of him. Turk idled his engine but kept it running.

"Good, Cliff."

"Any troubles?"

"Not 'nough lobsters."

"That's all anybody's complaining about now. . . ."

When we'd moved on, after exchanging a few more inconsequential remarks with the warden, Turk said, "Well, I guess I'm a . . . what'd the judge call it?—accesserary."

I corrected him, but he wasn't listening. We returned to the harbor in silence. Turk brought the *Sunrise* alongside Arthur's car and waited for Horatio Leadbetter to row out of earshot.

"Arthur," he said with a queer smile, "how many lobsters you got on hand?"

"Should be about four hundred and fifty. Why?"

Turk thought a minute, then said, "That'll do it."

"You planning a clambake for the city of Rockland, Turk?"

"Arthur," Turk said, the smile still there. "I'm gonna try one last experiment—providin' you two keep your traps shut. If this don't work, I'm goin' straight. . . . Load up those lobsters in crates so's nobody sees you. I'll be 'round to pick 'em up later."

"That's a mess of lobsters, Turk," said Arthur. "What're we going to use for legal tender?"

"More lobsters, 's quick as I can catch 'em. Put it on the books, Arthur. I'll pay you back."

"I don't doubt that for a minute," Arthur said. "But what're you up to? That's what I can't figure out."

Turk, however, wouldn't say. He merely told us we'd find out soon enough if we kept our mouths shut, and two days later—when the lobstermen went out again after the weekend—we did.

Bill York came in late on Monday afternoon and went straight to his mooring. Turk, who'd kept Bill in sight all day, followed him in, and after casting off in his double-ender, circled casually past Bill's boat on his way to shore.

"Good catch, Bill?" he called out.

"Well . . . so-so," Bill said tentatively. "How 'bout you, Turk?"

"Usual thing, twenty or thirty . . . Holy cow!" Turk exclaimed, looking over the side of Bill's boat. "You drug up the whole ocean there, boy! I never seen so many lobsters!"

"Jesus, Turk, they was everywhere today!" Bill said, eager to discuss his good luck now that the secret was out. "I didn't have a trap with less'n five."

"If I didn't know you, Bill, I'd'a said you must've pulled all the traps in the bay since Sat'day. Nobody can catch that many lobsters in a day."

"Honest to God, Turk! I didn't pull another trap . . . I mean . . . Jesus, I didn't have to!"

Turk glanced toward Arthur's float and saw no one was there. "Well, git 'em over to Arthur, Bill. Don't heave 'em overboard tonight. They might swim away."

"Yeah, I guess I better do that."

Turk watched him cast off and followed him over to the car.

"Six hundred and eighty pounds of lobsters," Arthur said after he'd weighed them in batches. "That's a mighty fine haul, Bill. I've never seen a bigger one."

Bill stood grinning in the well of his boat, hands thrust into his apron, his crossed eyes moving back and forth from Turk to Arthur.

"How'd you ever do it, Bill?" Turk asked. "Spike your bait?"

"Herrin', same as always . . . No, I figure there must be a special run on. You know, crawlin' out for the season . . . 'cept . . ."

"Except what, Bill?" Arthur asked.

"Well . . . some of 'em was already pegged."

"That so?" said Turk.

"I wasn't gonna say nothin' 'bout it, but . . .and a lot more of 'em looked as though they'd been pegged. . . . How you figure that out?"

"That must mean someone put 'em there, Bill," Turk said gravely.

"Why'd anybody fill my traps with lobsters?"

"I ain't got a clue—you, Arthur?"

"Not an inkling," said Arthur, poker-faced.

"Unless—" Turk began, then stopped. "Hell, no, it couldn't be that."

Bill looked uneasily at Turk but didn't press him to go on, and after a moment Turk said, "I wouldn't spread this too far, Bill. Every lobsterman in the bay'll be into your traps thinkin' they got some kind of magic in 'em."

Bill returned to his mooring after Arthur had given him all the cash he had on hand and credited him with the rest. Shortly thereafter, Turk and Arthur came ashore, where they met me and told me the story of Bill's haul as we walked up to the ridge.

"That was a pretty expensive experiment, Turk," said Arthur as we stood at the crossroads, where the three of us had stood many times previously weighing events on the island before parting. "I hope mightily it works."

"It'll git Bill thinkin' anyway. That's his great weakness—thinkin'."

"Yes, he did seem to get the idea so many lobsters couldn't have got into his traps without some help. . . . How'd you manage it, Turk?"

Turk shrugged and showed that enigmatic grin he reserved for occasions when he was pleased with himself.

Arthur said, "I guess you never got to Rockland at all yesterday, like you said you did?"

"Didn't have time," said Turk.

"I can believe it," Arthur remarked. "I take it you worked so fast you didn't have time to pull all the pegs."

"I left those on purpose . . . 'case Bill didn't notice the lobsters'd already been pegged once."

"Leaving nothing to chance," Arthur said, shaking his head. "Except the chance Cliff Dawson might find you out there pulling Bill's traps . . . or that the fog might lift and everyone could see you hadn't gone to Rockland at all."

The islanders soon learned of Bill York's famous "catch," since Bill himself couldn't resist the temptation to talk about it, despite Turk's warning. Turk had expected this. Bill, of course, made no mention of the fact that some of the lobsters had been pegged, and Turk and Arthur were naturally silent on this point. A number of the lobstermen took it for granted that Bill had made an unprecedented raid on all the traps in the area and wondered why he was dumb enough to boast about it. They were gloomy about possible repercussions—until Turk assured everyone, including Cliff Dawson, that Bill had pulled only his own traps; Turk had fished near him all day and vouched for this. The exact number of lobsters in the catch inevitably escalated in time, as Bill told the story again and again at Caleb's, but he usually scaled the number down to an approximation of the reality if Arthur or Turk were present.

Bill's moment of glory, not to mention the hard cash he received on the catch, sweetened the realization, which gradually came to him, that his poaching had been discovered. Whether he suspected it was Turk who discovered it is uncertain. Clearly, he never reasoned out *why* whoever found him out chose so odd a way to let him know. But Turk's "experiment" seemed to work. Bill York kept to his own traps the rest of that season, and he fished close to the other lobstermen so they could see that he did.

It was Lucy Talbot's idea to invite the Thorn Islanders for an interisland picnic at the end of November. The lobstermen had been on increasingly good terms since the hearing in Rockland, and when they met in the bay, shouted remarks back and forth as they always used to. Or they pulled their boats together for a half hour while passing around a bottle of "emergency" spirits. The high school students in Camden and Rockland, sharing the *Laura Lee* on their trips home on weekends, also were on good terms again. But the women hadn't had an opportunity to mark the truce, and they felt a need to.

Thanksgiving, when the largest number of off-islanders would be home for the holiday, was the day chosen for the picnic. Belle, for instance, was back from Orono, and Mary Lou from Rockland. Even Jingle came up for the day from Portland, after persuading Otis—whom she had, of course, met by now—to drive with her to Rockland in time for the special holiday ferry. Otis had at first demurred, believing his presence an intrusion in a purely island affair. But Jingle told him he was nuts. They wouldn't be having the picnic at all if it wasn't for him, and he'd better come along and enjoy it because it was probably the only fee he'd ever get for his trouble.

"She could persuade the ears off a donkey," Otis said, explaining his arrival to me as he stepped ashore from the *Laura Lee.*

The weather was clear and mild, which added zest to the occasion after another week of fog and squalls. Tables had been set up in the schoolhouse in case of rain, but when it was apparent there wouldn't be any, they were carried outside. The Ram Island wives did the turkeys and vegetables, the Thorn Islanders the pies and puddings. Lucy put me in charge of beverages, and after rejecting the idea of hard liquor—which would be in the background anyway, if I knew the lobstermen—I had on hand a case of California burgundy and another of Moselle, with a keg of beer for the baseball game. My calculations proved accurate, but it was a near thing.

The Thorn Islanders arrived just before noon, the lookouts at the Nose carrying word of their approach as they came into view. We greeted them at the harbor, and there were many warm and some tearful reunions—with Constance Allen, for instance, back for the first time with the children since the fire. Cecil and Jack did not come, but since this had been expected, no one commented on it. The only other Thorn Islanders I can think of who were absent were Barney Orcutt, whose trial was scheduled in Rockland the following week, and José, who had temporarily moved to Rockland to be able to see him during visiting hours at the county jail.

When the boats were secured, we walked in groups to the schoolhouse and began our assault on the enormous spread of food—six stuffed turkeys, a bushel of mashed potatoes, a dozen winter squash, and ten quarts of canned peas, not to mention various side dishes like celery, ripe olives, cranberry sauce, and roasted chestnuts. Then eighteen pies, five steamed puddings with hard sauce, ice cream made in Clyde Grant's hand freezer, along with nuts and raisins and candies. A flaw in the wine distribution, until I was able to correct it, allowed nearly as much to flow unchecked to the teenagers as to the adults—but to good effect, Jingle and I decided, since the teenagers' hilarity proved contagious long before the last pie was broached.

The centerpiece for the afternoon was the baseball game, which Turk decreed was to be generational rather than insular—that is, those over twenty opposing those below. There was a good-natured debate as to who was impartial enough to umpire so delicate a confrontation. The young ruled out any islander over twenty for fear of bias, and the old ruled out any of the younger citizenry for the same reason. For a time it seemed likely that Gertrude Bakeman would win the assignment, until she ruled herself definitively out because of poor eyesight. Then Clarence Darling had the happy idea of Otis, and Otis allowed that inasmuch as he was under option to the Brooklyn Dodgers, he was disqualified anyway from playing sandlot baseball and so might as well umpire. He took his position behind the plate with a certain flourish.

Otis ruled that every male islander over ten must have a turn at bat, and as many female islanders as demanded it; further, no player could remain in the game for more than six innings of the scheduled nine. These requirements called for some advance strategy by the hastily elected team captains—Wilfred Hopewell for the seniors and Bobby Cutler for the juniors, both of whom showed ingenuity in sorting out the advice freely given by teammates. Eventually, Otis got the game under way.

Will's strategy was to pile up a commanding lead in the early innings by throwing in all his strength at the start, then coasting through the last innings when he would be obliged to field indifferent athletes like Horatio Leadbetter . . . and me. Bobby Cutler's strategy was the reverse. The game was accordingly uneven at both ends, but the contrasting strategies made for a dramatic finish as the juniors battled to close a deficit at one time as high as twelve runs. They finally managed to do this in the bottom of the eighth and, all desiring to bat having done so at least once, Otis declared the game ended with a final score of twenty-eight to twenty-seven in favor of the youngsters.

"Why, major league clubs would have to play a week to tally up scores like that," Otis said in justifying his ruling to a group of youngsters who would have played on until dark.

We gathered about in groups on the grass, finishing the last of the keg before the Thorn Islanders had to prepare to leave. The sun was already low over the Head and the first nip of the November evening was in the air, though the thermometer outside the school still stood at sixty-five. Half a dozen younger girls were playing tag in the field across the road. Some of the boys were doggedly going ahead with an impromptu game of scrub. Will Hopewell and two other young lobstermen from Thorn Island were gathered around Mary Lou. Otis was stretched out on the ground after his exertion talking animatedly with Belle. Danny Orcutt, who'd been eyeing Lucille Cutler furtively all afternoon, and she him—they'd met only once or twice on the mailboat since Lucille's pregnancy—at last found his courage to approach her and the two were slowly walking together toward Abigail's Spruces. Bertha Orcutt followed them nervously with her eyes and finally started after them, when Jesse Cutler restrained her.

"Leave 'em alone, Bertha. Glory be. They're not goin' to go at it again for a while."

And that remark, as much as any other that day, typified the new spirit that had come over the islands.

I had already left for Africa when Barney Orcutt was tried in Rockland. Jingle wrote me about the trial and enclosed a detailed account of it by Otis, who had put himself at the disposal of Barney's attorney. Willy Grant and Turk gave their testimony as expected—Willy in his Marine uniform, on a two-day furlough from Quantico—and there was little doubt their evidence blunted the prosecution's contention that Barney had acted deliberately and vindictively and therefore deserved the maximum penalty. Willy's explicit admission of having disturbed Thorn Island traps at the ledges prior to the day of the accident went well beyond his signed statement and further influenced the jury in Barney's favor. The jury was also much impressed by evidence, which the defense skillfully developed, of the wholly changed mood of the islanders following the hearing with Judge Peabody. The Thanksgiving picnic, for instance, was cited as proof of the islanders' wish to live peaceably with each other. In charging the jury, however, Judge Peabody reminded the twelve jurors that their responsibility did not extend beyond a determination of Bernard Orcutt's guilt or innocence with respect to a single charge: manslaughter. They were under no obligation to consider motive, prior grievances, or any other mitigating circumstances.

Judge Peabody's charge, delivered in his dry, forbidding manner, had a chilling effect on jurors and spectators alike. The latter, mostly Thorn Islanders, because they had thought the case was going well for Barney, and expected an acquittal. The former because they had forgotten, after the attention lavished on them by prosecution and defense lawyers for a day and a half, that their role in the ultimate disposition of the case was a limited one and did not extend to clemency. The jurors were in session overnight, and the next morning delivered the only verdict they reasonably could: guilty as charged. Though they had been cautioned to do no more than return a verdict of guilty or not guilty, the jurors recommended leniency and the foreman was on the point of reciting the reasons for their recommendation when Judge Peabody interrupted him. Sentencing, he said coldly, was the prerogative of the court, and the court needed no prompting in the present case. He discharged the jury with cursory thanks, and the trial was over. Sentencing was set for the following Monday, the final day of the current session of the Superior Court.

The Thorn Islanders spent a restless weekend, needless to say, bewailing a judicial system that put Barney Orcutt's fate in the hands of so unbending a figure as Judge Peabody. But they misjudged him, for the sentence he gave was lenient beyond even Otis's expectations: three years, of which two and a half were suspended, and the balance to be counted from the date of his apprehension in September. When reduction of sentence for good behavior was calculated, it meant Barney had only three more weeks to serve.

"So Barney," Jingle wrote, "goes home to his José for Christmas."

My stepson looked over my shoulder while I was at my desk today, and noting I was still working on my "story"—both of us are a year or so older than when I first introduced him—he asked, with the arrogance of a newly revealed teenage critic, whether all my characters were good; one couldn't tell a true story if there were no true villains. I put him off, but I've been considering his point. Why must there be villains? Is there anyone so depraved, so persistently mean, so unremittingly sinister that no redeeming qualities ever show through? Willy, for instance, was sneaky and mischievous, and certainly dishonest, up to the moment of the accident at the ledges, but after that he was contrite. Bill York was covetous and deceitful, but was so addled a brain capable of perpetrating conscious evil? Barney Orcutt smoldered in righteous indignation until he became inadvertently a murderer, but no murderer bore punishment more nobly than he. Nor could Sam Clayton—whose role in that time of troubles was never quite clear—qualify as a villain. The long and short of it is I've never encountered the "true villain" my stepson speaks of. Either that, or the line between good and evil is too fine for me to detect.

So I must write my story without the benefit of villains. And without heroes either—for without villains, heroes would be superfluous. (I must be careful of Turk, incidentally; he verges on the heroic. I'll have to find some meanness there— or invent it.) In any event, next time my stepson looks over my shoulder, I'll have my answer ready.

Book 3 *Karen*

22

My African assignment lasted nearly a year, and I was another month in Washington before I returned to Ram Island in mid-December of 1947. I stopped several days in Portland en route to visit Jingle—also to let Jingle, together with Otis, elevate my spirits after an unsettling year. I won't go into it beyond noting that I had had an inconclusive love affair in Nigeria and on the Ivory Coast had contracted an obscure fever that landed me in a hospital in Dakar for six weeks. In a word, I wanted to be babied back into my habitat, for Ram Island was the only home I had.

Jingle and Otis, as I might have predicted, had become inseparable during the year I was away. They enjoyed each other in a rather raucous and bawdy way—too ostentatiously so to leave any suspicion of an intimacy beyond that.

"Woman, how many times do I have to tell you?" Otis would say. "Will you keep your legs together so I don't have to see up your goddam crotch every time I look at you?" And Jingle, to provoke him, would be likely to open her legs a little wider.

Or he might comment on her recent miscarriage—for Jingle had had her first child, Zbigniew, in March, was pregnant again in June, and aborted in October: "The crazy bitch! She's told everyone she's going to have four kids, and now she thinks she's got to have 'em all at once . . . like a damned machine gun." Then to her: "Give the poor guy a rest, Queenie!"

Emil Zukin, whom I hadn't met before this visit, was forbearing. I don't know what he thought of these two—or the three of us, for that matter—but he seemed not to mind sharing Jingle with us. He was generous to a fault, as I already knew from report (as well as from Jingle's letters), and much preoccupied with his professional work. He and Jingle had established an easy if somewhat formal relationship—without misunderstandings, as far as I could judge. He listened gravely to our meandering and largely irrelevant conversation at dinner the night I arrived, then excused himself after coffee and retired to his den to read the latest dental journals.

"Don't keep her up too late," he admonished us—as a father might admonish the suitors of a sixteen-year-old daughter with wayward tendencies.

When we were settled in Jingle's cluttered living room after Emil left us, I pressed them for scraps of news from Ram Island. Lucy Talbot had, of course, kept me abreast of major developments on the island: the death of Lydia York at eighty-nine the winter before, for instance; the birth of Clara Grant's boy, Chip, in July; and epochal changes like the decommissioning of the *Laura Lee* in favor of a smaller, diesel-powered mailboat bearing the same name. But I thirsted for more details; I wanted to feel the pulse of the island before I went back.

Otis was impatient at my thirst for what he called "rank gossip" and told me so. "You come back from an exotic place like Equatorial Africa anyone'd give his back teeth to see, and all you can talk about is what people have been doing on a fogbound Maine island while you've been away. . . . The same goddam things they've been doing for a hundred and fifty years."

But Jingle had a finer appreciation of "rank gossip" and catered to my appetite. There were changes in the offing, she said, and she mentioned as one of them the possibility that Elmer Brewster might come back for good. He'd been home for a month during the summer while she was there.

"To see Elmo and Turk, heads down, for three days inside the *Sunrise*," Jingle said sentimentally, "that brought back old times."

I said I thought Elmer was allergic to boats.

"Not boats," she said. "The sea. Elmo's big on anything that runs. Or fixing anything that's supposed to. He's thinking of setting up a boat shop in the shed below the store."

I asked if Mary Lou Grant had played a part in Elmer Brewster's thoughts of coming back, as Jingle had speculated she might.

"Caleb's not for it," she said, then added, "And that's an understatement."

"What about Elmer and Mary Lou?"

"Well, Elmer doesn't know anything's going on—yet. . . . As for Mary Lou, she plays him cool."

I said *cool* wasn't a word I associated with Mary Lou.

"That's why something might develop there," Jingle said. "You ask about changes . . . There's one: Mary Lou." When I asked how, Jingle said, "She's more discriminating. She doesn't tease every prick on the island."

Otis guffawed at this and said, "You should have been a sailor, Jingle."

"Don't forget, I was," Jingle said. "Four long years."

Otis himself now succumbed to "rank gossip" and was as informative as Jingle about changing times on the island. Indeed, he was better informed than she on some aspects of island life, for he'd been back several times since the lobster war—usually staying with Turk and Sharon—and knew in detail about new developments in lobstering: the steady rise in the price of lobsters, which was altering the economy of the island; the fathometers and ship-to-shore radios now on the market; the new diesel engines actively under consideration by lobstermen like Clyde Grant, Leonard York, and Turk. Otis also knew about negotiations just begun for an island generator and for the repair of the telephone cable, broken again during a gale in March. So between the two of them, I learned much of what I wanted to know.

"Want some more island romance?" Jingle asked me at one point during the evening.

"Anything," I said. "Everything."

"Well, you'd never guess this one . . . Lucille Cutler and Danny Orcutt."

I said I thought that romance had matured about as fully as it could some years ago.

"This is phase two," Jingle said. "I was at the Cutlers' one afternoon last August when Danny called. Dressed to the nines, clean shirt and tie, freshly shaved. He'd come over in his boat—he's fishing on his own now. Jesse looks out the kitchen window and says, 'I do declare, here comes Sam Orcutt's boy to pay us a visit . . . now, i'n that nice of him? Go put on your jacket, Lloyd.' Lucille blushes and runs to the mirror to comb her hair, and Tony starts whistling 'Here comes the bride' until Jesse shoos him out of the kitchen. When Danny came in, we all went into the front room and sat on the horsehair sofas and talked about Barney and José's new baby and Sam's arthritis and God knows what. Danny would glance at Lucille occasionally, and she'd lower her eyes shyly, as though she'd never spoken to him alone. . . . It was out of the nineteenth century."

"From the bushes to the parlor," Otis said. "That's the route everyone should go."

Later I asked about Kevin and Belle. I knew from Belle's letters, as well as Lucy's, that they were as thick as ever, but I wanted to know how Jingle and Otis viewed this romance. Jingle glanced at Otis and said I'd have to judge for myself. Kevin was coming out after Christmas, she said. I detected some coolness in their attitude toward Kevin and said so.

"Oh, Otis is lukewarm," Jingle said casually, speaking as a wife might who didn't want to disparage too much the views of a slightly cantankerous mate. "I'm still . . . What was the word you once used talking about them? *Sanguine.*"

I reminded Otis he used to look more favorably on the idea of romance between Belle and Kevin —if I had heard correctly from Belle herself. He shrugged his shoulders and tilted his head to one side—the way he did when he wasn't quite sure where he stood on something.

"The *idea's* still good," he said. But he went no further, and Jingle again insisted I judge for myself.

"It's one thing for us to tell you about Elmo and Mary Lou or Lucille and Danny," she said. "With Belle and Kevin, you're on your own."

I mentioned at one point, when I was telling them I expected to remain at Cutler's Cove a full year at least this time, that I doubted I would ever be taken as a bona fide islander. I reminded Jingle she'd once suggested a dozen years might turn the trick. Jingle relented and said I'd made such progress, maybe six would do it. Otis was typically contemptuous of such calculations.

"Does everyone have to *belong*?" he asked. "You've got as good relations with those islanders as any outsider ever had . . . probably better with Jingle's old man and Lucy Talbot. What more do you want, sport? The whole island kissing your ass?"

"Tough talk by a kid named Schmaltz from Brooklyn," Jingle said. "Listen carefully."

Otis wasn't fazed. "Righto, baby," he went on. "I'm a Jew boy from Brooklyn who's got about as much natural right to be on the coast of Maine as an African antelope. And you know what? I'm more comfortable here than I ever was in Brooklyn—despite the fact I don't belong. Let me tell you about my partner. A guy named Cooper, born and reared at Falmouth-Foreside, descendant of Anglo-Saxon shipbuilders from before the Revolution, Bowdoin, short trip to Harvard for his law degree, and now he's back in the mainstream of Portland social life. I couldn't get along without him, and he couldn't get along without me. I trust everything he does as my partner, and vice versa. Every day we're both in town we have lunch together at a little restaurant we found off Canal Street. If he ran short of cash, I'd loan him what I had. He'd do the same for me. Yet I've never been inside Cooper's house, and I've never met his wife. Know why?"

"She's Jewish," Jingle facetiously suggested.

"Pipe down, punk. . . . She hates kikes, that's why. I sat behind her once at a concert and heard her say so. How she knows she does beats me, since she's probably never met one. But she thinks she does, and Cooper's not going to risk his marriage crossing her in this. . . . Now, my point is that it doesn't matter a goddam in my relations with Cooper that I don't belong to their little circle—any more than it matters to him that he doesn't belong to ours."

"Our great circle of immigrant dentists and kikes," said Jingle. Like Otis, she had to have her wisecrack, but she grew more serious right away. "Anyway, it's not a fair comparison. We've got alternate resources here. If we're crowded out of one community, we turn to another. Where are the alternate resources on Ram Island?"

"Where are the resources on Great Ram Island! Didn't you ever look around growing up out there?" He gave up on Jingle and turned back to me, still holding to his basic argument. "If there was hostility out there, that would be something to worry about. But you're not rejected. You're just not accepted by everyone. Name me the islander who's uncivil or would refuse you a favor. In fact, they're *less* likely to refuse you than another islander. So you're better off as you are."

Jingle said, "The power of a lawyer's logic! It used to be calamitous *not* to be an islander. Now it's chancy being one."

Otis looked across at her as he pulled on his shoes to go and said, in perfect good humor, "It must be exasperating, Jingle, being married to you."

"Oh? Emil has a different view on that," she said.

And that was when he made one of his remarks about her goddam crotch.

23

Jingle had said I must judge Belle and Kevin for myself, and there was plenty of opportunity for this between Christmas and New Year's. Kevin came out on the mailboat the day after Christmas, the last trip for five days because of a severe northeast storm. He had written ahead asking to stay with me, and, of course, I welcomed him. This was Belle's idea, I gathered, and it was altogether a prudent one in light of the strains caused by her earlier suitor, Harvey Brown, who had lived at Meadowlane two years before.

Kevin was in all respects a gracious visitor. He was as uncompromising as ever in his politics—I was to discover in due course—but he was modest and considerate in his dealings with people. At Cutler's Cove he was tidy and unobtrusive, cleaning up if there was cleaning to be done, leaving me alone when I worked. He was a model guest. With Lucy, he struck just the right note of easy familiarity without presuming too much or underestimating the instinctive objections Lucy would have to their carrying their romance forward too precipitously. And he was natural and courteous with the islanders. He didn't forget that Belle still belonged more to them than to him.

I took it for granted from the outset that they were lovers. Not from anything they specifically said, nor because the year of probation Belle said they'd agreed to the summer their romance started was over, but because of the way they behaved together. Like a settled couple. They could sit for hours in perfect contentment without speaking. They needed only a look to understand each other. Occasionally they held hands, but rarely, and never for long in Lucy's presence, and if they came upon an islander on the high road, they promptly disengaged their hands until they passed. Their outward manifestations of affection, in short, were never obtrusive—even in my presence, and they seemed less restrained with me than with anyone else. But neither were they furtive in showing their affection. Kevin, for instance, would stand for a moment in the store listening to Caleb with an arm over Belle's shoulder. Or she would unconsciously slip her arm around his waist. When they met each morning or parted at night, no matter who was present, Belle kissed Kevin—not the customary peck on the cheek of genteel society but the full-blown island smacker, square on the lips.

"Nothing mawkish about those two, is there?" Lucy said to me one wet afternoon as we watched them start off on a walk through Abigail's Spruces. "Still . . . they're not quite a match yet, are they?" she went on. "Perhaps they will be one day. . . . Who knows?"

I said nothing.

Belle had transferred to Smith College in September, at the start of her junior year. There was a small subterfuge in the financing of the transfer about which only George Bannister and I knew. It came about in this way. Kevin, from the time he took Belle back to Orono after Joel Grant's funeral, had pressed her to transfer to a more traditionally oriented liberal arts college. Belle was at first defensive about the University of Maine, arguing that you got out of any college what you put into it, but she understood his arguments better after visiting Karen at Bennington on a long weekend in October. She had talked about the transfer idea with Otis and me at the Thanksgiving picnic with the Thorn Islanders later that fall, and we both encouraged her. But there was the question of added costs.

Lucy's income was too slender to cover tuition and board anywhere except at Orono. Indeed, the year before she had sold me some land, including the north shore of Cutler's Cove, to raise even this much. Belle, meanwhile, wouldn't hear of borrowing from the Daceys, and she absolutely refused Kevin's offer of a loan from his own funds. There the matter rested until George wrote me in January. He said I was the only person Belle might accept a loan from, and he proposed putting into a special fund in my name enough for Belle to complete her last two years at Vassar, Smith, or wherever she chose. I could tell her it was a family legacy or whatever I liked, so long as Belle didn't know the true source of the funds; he didn't care whether he was ever paid back. George added that he had not discussed the project with Sally, and certainly not with Kevin, and bound me to secrecy if I agreed to his proposal. I did, and wrote both Lucy and Belle urging them to make use of my "legacy" since it was more than I could spend on my own needs. They could repay me, without interest, when it was convenient. To George I wrote that it would look damned funny if royalties on a forthcoming monograph weren't enough to cover plantation taxes on the new property I had acquired from Lucy, and he wrote promptly back: "In that event we may have to increase the legacy to cover occupational destitution."

Belle therefore went to Northampton in September, and the scope of her education widened perceptibly. She was majoring in art history and taking courses in Byzantine and Renaissance art to meet prerequisites. She and Kevin had met most weekends during the fall—in Northampton; in New York, where Kevin was in his first year of graduate school at Columbia; or off on their own in the country.

"But where do you stay, dear?" Winifred Dacey asked, wide-eyed, when Belle had described to her a long weekend with Kevin on Cape Cod.

"Inns, motels. Sometimes with friends."

"But surely there must be chaperones?"

"Chaperones are old-fashioned, Aunt Winnie," Belle informed her. "They went out . . . gosh, when did they go out? With Prohibition, most likely."

"Why, that's dreadful!" Winifred proclaimed, speeding up her knitting so that she dropped a stitch. Arthur listened gravely, drawing on his pipe. Kevin stared at a neutral point in the middle distance. Lucy smiled noncommittally, watching Belle.

"Well, it's only dreadful if you think it is," Belle said, preparing to do battle with the Philistines. "I don't happen to think it is, so it isn't."

"But, dear child . . . I mean . . ."

"You mean, do we share the same room?" Belle said—more belligerently perhaps than she intended. "Usually we do."

Winifred shook her head in disbelief and went back to her knitting, dropping another stitch in her confusion. Then she added on a postscript to her disquieting discovery: "Well, at least you don't smoke, Belle. Thank the good Lord for that." (But I think if there had been a cigarette at hand, Belle would have exploded that thesis as well.)

As we were leaving the Daceys'—Kevin, Belle, and I—Kevin said, "Just as well you didn't happen to mention we sometimes share the same toothbrush."

"Golly, isn't she dense, though?" Belle said. "Don't you suppose she ever curled up with the first mate on those long voyages around the world?"

I said it was unlikely—at the age of ten or twelve, which was all she was.

"I'm sure Granny Belle did."

"Granny Belle was a woman of a different mettle."

"Well, all respects to Aunt Winnie, I like that mettle better."

Kevin said, "And I wouldn't be here if you didn't."

But this was the only time they made allusion in my presence to their physical relations. Their behavior, as I have said, was in all respects exemplary. If they indulged themselves that week, they did it so unobtrusively that no one, not even Lucy, could take offense.

Kevin and Belle came down to Cutler's Cove the evening before Kevin left. It was a clear, cold night with a full moon. The northeaster had finally blown itself out the day before, leaving high seas and strong westerly winds. We stood outside for a few minutes and watched the breakers of a rising tide crash on the granite slabs across the cove, sending plumes of seawater high into the air against the moonlight. It was an awesome display of power, but we were soon numbed to the bone and sought the warmth of the fire. I poured cognac and gave Kevin a cigar.

We had not, since the day of Kevin's arrival, when I probed him perfunctorily on his politics, discussed his current views on the state of the world, and I felt he wanted to. I therefore obliged. I started by asking him whether knowing Belle had changed his outlook in any way.

"The world's the same," he said. "What's changed because of us?"

"You," I suggested.

"You mean, have I started to purr gently because Belle's . . . well, Belle?"

"Just pretend I'm not here," Belle said, digging her toes into the bear rug. She was lying there facedown in front of the fire, occasionally lifting her head to sip her brandy.

"Anyway, the answer's no," Kevin said from the sofa.

I said I only meant to ask whether his views on his fellow man had mellowed.

"They haven't," Belle remarked, then she added, "Sorry . . . I'm not supposed to be here, am I?"

"Hey, what gives?" Kevin said in some irritation. "You two sound as though *I'm* the one to blame for the state of the world. I merely see things as I must. Am I to blame for that?"

I said it was a question of perception, not blame. A hungry man saw the world with a certain bias, a full man with another. There was no ultimate truth in perception. I was simply trying to discover whether his had changed, and I gathered it hadn't.

"Let's start again," Kevin said, and relit his cigar. "You see the state of the universe in terms of the people who view it. No absolutes. Everything relative. All views are distorted in one degree or another. I see the state of the universe as a fixed reality, our different views of it valid only insofar as our perceptions are valid. Okay?"

I nodded noncommittally, and Kevin went on. "Well, the validity or nonvalidity of one's perception depends upon the tools one uses. If one uses inadequate or inappropriate tools—that is, what you call biases—then the perception is useless—"

"And if you use Marxism, the perception is a true one?"

"That's the general idea. If you use it properly."

"But who decides this? Is my perception of things less valid or useful or accurate than yours if, God help me, I don't consult Marx and Engels?"

"It is to me," Kevin said.

I remarked that in that case we were back where we started: Everyone perceives the universe, as well as other peoples' perceptions of the universe, according to his own lights—Marxist, Christian, Muslim, Jeffersonian, hedonist, and so on.

"If I believed that," Kevin said, "I would believe in no progress from the simple to the complex, no dialectic of ideas, no maturing—"

"I didn't say the sophistication of different systems was always the same. I merely said that, simple or complex, they are different."

Having worked our way inconclusively through this little exercise in semantics, we moved on to certain specifics of the current scene—but not before Belle remarked on our dialogue: "Golly, how you two love to fight over morsels."

She turned to look at him from the bear rug, but he had only a fleeting smile for her before turning back to me.

I asked Kevin whether his judgment of the Russians was as charitable as the year before, now that the thrust of their policies was clearer. I mentioned in particular the tightening of their control over Eastern Europe, their obstructionist tactics in the United Nations, an the apparent revival of international activism through the Cominform.

"Scrap 'charitable,'" Kevin said. "I give nothing in charity." I nodded agreement, and he went on. "Well…what's the model against which we're supposed to compare Soviet policies? The State Department's?"

I said I had no model in mind, least of all the U. S. Department of State, but suggested one might agree to certain standards of international behavior to which one held nations like the USSR accountable.

"I don't make a big thing of the Russians," he said. "If it's necessary to defend them against unfair accusations, I'll do that. But I'm not so much interested in the Soviet Union."

"Then in what?" I asked.

"In what's happening here. This is where the troubles are. The world's not going to pot because of Russia but because of us."

"He's a tiger on American capitalism," Belle said.

"Hey, baby," Kevin said, nudging Belle with his foot. "Keep out of this—

unless you have something constructive to say."

"Don't be intimidated, Belle," I said.

"Intimidate Belle! Have you ever tried?"

"I'll keep quiet. Call me if either of you needs help." She buried her head deeper in the bear rug while we shifted the focus to domestic ills as Kevin saw them: the slow strangulation of the labor unions; the mounting disparity of incomes; the growing ties between the military and big business; the worsening plight of Negroes; and many more. I thought Kevin more controlled and articulate than when he argued with Otis fifteen months earlier, but he was also more doctrinaire. He used expressions like "tools of Wall Street" and "running dogs of imperialism" as though they had a meaning of their own outside the context of editorials in the Leftist press. I charged him with this and asked if he would use these phrases in a seminar at Columbia.

"Are they worse," he said, "than the phrases 'Communist aggression' and 'Soviet imperialism' you read every day in the *Wall Street Journal*?"

I said a graduate student at Columbia shouldn't have to rely on extremist opinions, Left *or* Right.

"But isn't the object of a seminar to communicate ideas? And how does one communicate in a language that's lost all relevance to what's going on today? There have to be new words, new expressions, to express new ideas."

"Change the language, by all means," I said, "but not into the worst gibberish out of Soviet propaganda. You've a whole Marxist literature to draw on."

Kevin looked at me for some moments in silence, so long that Belle raised her head to see why he hadn't responded.

"Know your trouble?" Kevin said at last. "You can't bring yourself to act on your Marxist convictions."

"Know yours? You act before your convictions have fully matured."

"A standoff," Belle said.

I asked Kevin why, assuming I had Marxist convictions (which I didn't for a moment admit that I did), I should be obliged to act on them.

"Because a Marxist is an activist," Kevin replied promptly. "If you are not an activist—"

"But that's circular, Kevin. According to your lights, if I were a Marxist, I *would* be an activist. Since I'm not, I can't have very highly developed 'Marxist convictions.' "

"It's a standoff and it's circular and we've got to go to bed," Belle said, rising from the bear rug.

"Come on, baby," Kevin said. "We're just getting into something."

"Sweetie pie, you've got to get up at six to get ready to leave, and it's going on midnight."

It was true—I had momentarily forgotten—Kevin was going over early with Arthur Dacey and was spending the night at Meadowlane to be ready. We said our farewells, and I remarked that so long as a Marxian activist could call his girl "baby," and she could call him "sweetie pie," capitalists and imperialists could rest safe in their hammocks.

Kevin left for Bucks County as scheduled the next morning, and when we met again, it was under very altered circumstances for all of us.

<h1 style="text-align:center">24</h1>

Gertrude Bakeman, who had taught island children for forty-six years, was obliged to retire during the Christmas holiday. She had complained of recurrent chest pains during the fall and went into the hospital in Rockland just before Christmas for tests. Two days later she sent word to Lucy Talbot, chairman of the school board, that she would be unable to continue teaching after the holiday. She didn't mention it, but we soon learned she had cancer.

It was Belle who suggested Karen Bannister as Gertrude's replacement for the rest of the school year. The two girls had become close friends during the last fifteen months and particularly after Belle's transfer to Smith. Karen had joined Kevin and Belle on several weekends during the fall—twice by herself, once with a Negro friend from Newark, Jerry Lincoln. Karen had spent her winter work period the year before teaching at a predominantly Negro grade school in Newark (where she met Jerry), and she'd returned to Newark for a month in the summer to run a special children's program. She therefore had some teaching experience. Her plans for the coming winter work period were not settled, Belle knew. If she came, Belle was quite certain she could arrange to take a leave of absence from Bennington for the spring in order to finish out the school year on the island. There was no doubt in Belle's mind, as she told her mother, that Karen would be an excellent teacher. Kevin, who was still with us when the idea was first broached, didn't try to pass judgment on how good Karen would be as a teacher, but he agreed with Belle the experience would be very worthwhile for her.

There was some hesitation among the school board members about hiring Karen. Lloyd Cutler felt she was too young and inexperienced. Jessica York thought she would be lonely on the island without family and friends. Ginny Clayton, without exactly saying so, implied that so pretty a schoolteacher might turn the heads of the younger lobstermen. Everyone, I suppose, felt constraint in one degree or another about inviting a summer vacationer into the island community. In the end, however, no objection seemed strong enough to prevent Lucy from writing to Karen to see whether she was interested. Karen telegraphed back immediately that she was, and after another short meeting of the school board, she was hired.

She arrived on the mailboat on a frosty Saturday morning early in January, and a rather larger number of islanders than usual contrived to be at the harbor when the *Laura Lee II* came in. I expressed some surprise at this, as I walked down to the landing with Lucy, but she assured me it was quite natural. Karen had always evoked a sense of mystery among them—from the days when she first used to go forth with her mother, immaculately put out in pastel playsuits or jumpers, her blond curls buried in Sally's groin if they stopped to meet someone. The women stroked her hair if they had a chance. People at the harbor would stop what they were doing and stand distracted for minutes at a time, simply watching her. If she slipped on seaweed or tripped coming down the steep steps outside Caleb's, a dozen hands reached forth to set her on her feet again, as Karen turned startled blue eyes on those who helped her. Karen in a new party dress, gravely cutting her birthday cake, Lucy said, was as much an attraction as George's cocktails at the annual celebration the islanders were invited to at Ram's Horn before the war.

In adolescence, when Karen blossomed into such an extraordinary beauty at the age of thirteen or fourteen, she continued to cast her spell over the islanders. She was still, however, removed from them—Lucy thought from shyness, but I wondered; I wondered, without saying so, whether it was not simply indifference. Karen's reserve—in any case, from shyness or indifference—only heightened the aura of mystery that surrounded her and added to her appeal.

"Karen brought out the guardian instinct in us," Lucy went on. "I suspect the lads her age lying in wait along the high road to catch a glimpse of her used to imagine situations where they could save her from some calamity. The mothers, meanwhile, were wondering how they could avoid any embarrassment to Karen from the behavior of their teenage cavaliers. And grown lobstermen lingering in the harbor when Karen rowed about in the little red dinghy George gave her would keep a weather eye on her—to be sure she came to no harm. . . . There's no doubt about it: Karen made protectors of all of us. That was before the war."

Since the war—and I could see this for myself—it was no longer the same. Karen was still surrounded by mystery, it was true, but she was eighteen when the islanders saw her again after several years' absence. She was no longer anyone's to protect. The island women could admire her good looks, and they did. The men could look covetously at her full bosom and shapely tanned legs— until snug-fitting printed dresses and Bermuda shorts gave way to dungarees and baggy sweaters, hallmarks of the American college girl. But Karen was beyond the reach of the islanders. They could no longer stroke her blond hair or rescue her from calamities.

"The real question, I suppose," Lucy said as we reached the landing, "is whether the new Karen can manage to give us enough consciously to replace what she used to give us unconsciously as she grew up."

The *Laura Lee II* rounded the red nun and churned briskly into the harbor, its decks and rigging glistening with a thin film of ice. We didn't at first recognize Karen among the half dozen passengers outside the cabin, muffled as she was against the cold in a long trench coat, her hair done up in a plaid bandana. Then she waved, and we waved back. The islanders lingering about the harbor slowly gathered on the pier as Horace Snow brought the boat in. Karen stepped onto the gangplank, a monogrammed suitcase in one hand, a duffel bag over her shoulder. She was grave, as always, far graver than the islanders there to greet her.

"Hey, Karen!" Bubber York called up from his double-ender near the pier. "We thought you was gonna jump overboard . . . like that time you flipped off the sailboat, 'member?"

Karen put down her suitcase and waved at Bubber, then turned to the rest of us. Her face was thinner than when I'd last seen her. And paler, I thought. I wondered whether she'd been sick on the trip over until I realized that her pallor was due chiefly to the absence of any makeup. She had never, to be sure, used much, but she did use lipstick, and without it, I thought, her face was severe—until she smiled, greeting Belle—and the islanders had their reward.

"Do we hafta call you 'Miss,' Karen?" Judy Torrey, one of Karen's new pupils, asked.

"You call me Karen, and I'll call *you* 'Miss.'"

"Who'd ever thought we'd see so many Bannisters the first of winter," Clara Grant said. "A few more 'n' you'll have enough to open Ram's Horn."

"Brr!" Karen said.

We moved on up to the store, where more islanders had gathered out of the cold to greet their new schoolteacher.

"Karen, we're openin' up a special branch post office just for you," Jenny said, coming out from behind the grill with a packet of letters for her. "Most of 'em from a fellah calls himself J. Lincoln."

"Now, how'd you find that out, Jenny?" Rudolf York called across the room.

"Why, it's writ all over the outside o' the letters," Jenny shouted back. "You don't think I looked inside, you no-good lobsterman?"

"Jenny, I never know what t'think you do behind them bars."

"You ain't had a letter in eight months. You wouldn't know even if I did peek."

Eventually, after more good-natured pleasantry at whoever's expense it suited the pundits (not excluding Karen's), the islanders departed well satisfied, and we bore Karen off to Meadowlane, where she was to board.

Belle stayed on a few days before going back to college, passing up a long weekend with Kevin in Vermont in order to help Karen settle in. Karen needed no help so far as her job was concerned. Belle had been quite right—and Lloyd Cutler's doubts quite unwarranted—concerning Karen's competence as a teacher, as we were to discover. Nor was Karen in the least anxious about being lonely on the island. She preferred to be alone, and I was struck during the next weeks, as I came to know her better, how few friends she appeared to have. Apart from Belle and Gloria Thatcher (who was now married and living in Wilkes-Barre), and Jerry Lincoln in Newark, she had no intimate friends so far as I could tell—and surely this was not from lack of opportunity. Where she needed Belle's help, and where Belle was ideally suited to provide it, was in becoming better acquainted with her neighbors.

Karen, given the fact that she had spent most of her summers among them, had the islanders hopelessly confused in her mind. She mixed up Yorks and Cutlers. She mistook old Clarissa Grant, whom she met on the high road the first afternoon, for Widow Barnaby, and was surprised to see her off the jetty. She had even forgotten that Sharon Jenkins was Caleb's and Jenny's daughter, though she surely knew that at one time. These lacunae in Karen's familiarity with rudimentary island genealogy, which became apparent almost immediately, troubled me. Karen seemed to have immunized herself from the islanders and their activities, except in the abstract. She had ceased to think of them—apart from the few with whom she had regular contact—as separate and distinctive personalities.

Belle, on the other hand, was not in the least bothered by Karen's confusion. She thought it altogether natural and was even amused by some of Karen's mix-ups, especially among the lobstermen. Belle did, however, set about immediately to put Karen straight on the island families, going over each of them with her, household by household, the night she arrived. And Karen, it should be said in all fairness, learned quickly and eagerly.

The day after Karen arrived, Belle escorted her house by house down the ridge to pay her respects—as Jingle had escorted me the week I arrived. Karen's pilgrimage, from all reports, was marked by more hilarity than mine, for the gaiety two young women as handsome as this pair are capable of arousing has a contagion all its own. Word went ahead of their movement along the ridge, so that before they reached the crossroads, they were expected at each homestead long before they arrived. The men had put on clean shirts, kitchens were freshly swept, and young faces were pressed against frosted windows covering the route of their approach. Snow, the season's first, began to fall by mid-afternoon.

I was at the Peaks when they reached the end of their trek at dusk. Turk and I had been cutting firewood with Sam Clayton in a lot above Jericho Cove. When the snow began to fall too thickly to see what we were doing, we came back to Turk's for coffee. Sharon told us about the pending visit.

"Guess that means 'nother bottle of the old loganberry," Turk said, and went off to get it.

Sam slipped off to the bathroom and returned a few minutes later, freshly washed and hair slicked down.

"Sam," said Turk, "I do b'lieve you got into Sharon's hair lotion."

"Can't take no chances, Turk."

"Chances on what?"

But there was no time to reply, for at this moment Chucky announced excitedly from the window they were turning into the yard, and a moment later they came in, shaking the snow from their fur-hooded parkas.

"Why, if we'd known most of the bachelors on the island were down here, we'd have started off at the Peaks," Belle said. "Wouldn't we, Karen?"

"We sure would have," Karen said, giving Sam a slow smile.

"Well, if'n you started down here," said Sam, eager to say something but never sure what, "we'd . . . we'd'a been in the woods."

"Then we'd have gone looking for you in the woods, Sam," Belle said.

That bit of witticism collapsed Sam into a series of guffaws, after which he stared speechless at Karen.

"Have you got everyone straightened out, Karen?" Sharon asked. "Do you know who's related to who?"

"I should by now," Karen said. "Try me."

"Who's my folks?" Sam asked, finding his tongue again.

"That's easy. Virginia and Zip."

"I ain't never heerd her called Virginia."

"I'll bet she was baptized Virginia."

"Well, maybe you got somethin' there. If'n she was ever . . . what-d'you-call-it."

"Who's Widow Barnaby related to?" Turk asked, opening a dusty bottle.

"Hmm . . . don't tell me," Karen said, furrowing her brow and glancing at Belle for encouragement. "She's a York anyway. Probably an aunt of Rudolf."

"That's closer'n I'd git it," Sam said.

"I guess everyone's related to everyone else if you go back far enough, aren't they?" Karen said. "Except maybe Gertrude Bakeman."

"And Harold Toothacher," Sharon said.

"Harold ain't related to no one," said Sam. "I doubt he even had a mother, the old geezer."

Karen said, "That would be quite a trick, wouldn't it?"

We parried back and forth in this manner, finishing off Turk's prewar loganberry and gaily taking Karen's measure. Sam, it was easy to see, was smitten. Sharon and Turk were sympathetic—more so than I believe they expected to be. Chucky, thumb in mouth against his father's knee, couldn't take his eyes off Karen. Belle, meanwhile, beamed with satisfaction at her protégé. And Karen herself, her reserve already breached farther up the ridge, was as animated and responsive as I'd ever seen her. She matched any of us with her wry rejoinders, her usually impassive face giving an added fillip to what she had to say. Sam, bewitched as much as anything by the way she talked, often missed what she said and asked her several times to repeat herself—which Karen graciously did, favoring him again with her slow, shy smile. But her most incandescent smiles were saved, conspiratorially, for Belle.

Darkness had fallen when the girls rose to leave, Sam rising with them. I followed.

"Come any time, Karen," Sharon said. "Don't wait to be asked."

"I will," said Karen.

We walked up the ridge together, the girls in the center, arm in arm, Sam and I flanking them. Conversation was made difficult by the driving snow. Sam continued on past the crossroads, though he had told me earlier he had to stop at the harbor to secure a dory against the next high tide. We left Belle and Karen at the turnoff to Meadowlane and walked on until we were out of hearing. Then Sam said, with more passion than I'd thought him capable of, "Jeez, she's sure one good looker!"

It was only then he remembered his dory—or, as I suspected, he had remembered all along but couldn't bring himself to part company with Karen until the last possible moment.

25

Belle left the next day for college, and Karen started school two days later. There were six pupils that year, ranging from Chucky Jenkins, who was seven, to Bubber York, who was fourteen: three girls; three boys. Karen was an instant success with all of them. She was disciplinarian enough to cope with Bubber, and at the same time able to channel his energies into something more constructive than teasing his sister Daphne. She was tender enough to transform Rudy York's tantrums into tearful reconciliations. She was adroit enough to bring order to Chucky's wildest fantasies. And she was affectionate enough to satisfy even the adolescent worship of Judy Torrey and Penny York, who would have spent all waking hours of the day with Karen if they could. For several weeks the children could talk of little else at home but "Kairen." And the mothers, occasionally dropping in at the school on one pretext or another, agreed that Karen had started well.

The schoolhouse, meanwhile, was never better heated than it was that winter. Horatio Leadbetter, whose task it was to light the two stoves in the morning and keep the woodboxes full, was regularly assisted, on an entirely voluntary basis, by one or another lobsterman who managed to wander by as school was opening. One morning Karen found six of them stomping in and out of the schoolhouse carrying wood, filling boxes that one of them alone could have filled in five minutes. In the afternoon, when school let out, it seemed half the islanders managed to be passing by the crossroads. Karen, walking home, was never without the company of islanders who "just happened to be goin' her way"—among them, as often as not, Sam Clayton. If she happened to linger on at the school a half hour or so to prepare a lesson for the next day, it was a certainty someone would look in to see if everything was all right.

Karen bore these attentions with equanimity. She neither encouraged nor explicitly discouraged them. Nor did she take them as her due. She expressed gratitude for favors. If a lobsterman, for instance, brought her a fresh harbor pollock or crabmeat to take home to Lucy, she would first try to pay him for it, and when this failed, as of course it did, she would thank him with warmth—indeed, with such a show of warmth that, while she surely didn't intend it, it guaranteed his coming back with fish again as soon as he decently could. Meadowlane had not, since before the war, been so well supplied with fresh fish as it was that winter.

Karen, meanwhile, behaved impartially to all islanders, especially the male islanders, during those early days. She smiled—when she smiled at all, for smiling was not her style—as often at cross-eyed Bill York, lingering openmouthed outside Caleb's, as she did at her "steady," Sam Clayton. If she walked home along the ridge with Sam and Clyde Grant, she minded as little if it were Clyde who shoved her lightly, to accent the punch line of a story, as she would if it had been Sam, who claimed it as a right.

Success did not turn her head. Karen was a dedicated teacher, and the social interludes along the high road or at Caleb's, to the regret of many, were as nothing to the hours she spent at her work. She declined all evening invitations—unless to the homes of her pupils—and usually retired to her room right after supper, often working there as late as midnight. She was most at ease in her large, bright classroom hung with school exercises and visual aids she had ordered in Boston—most of them at her own expense.

In school, her reserve fell away and her natural talents came into play. She was a different person. She succeeded in getting even Bubber to concentrate his attention long enough to complete two sketches of a lobster boat in the harbor—one of which she displayed prominently on the art panel between the stoves; the other she had him take home to his mother. One stormy evening she worked late with wrenches and pliers to bring the ancient upright piano in the schoolhouse into some semblance of pitch so that she could begin singing practice. By the end of January she felt enough encouraged to send word around to the parents that on the second Tuesday in March, following the plantation meeting, there would be an art exhibit and a program of music at the school.

Karen made mistakes in those first weeks, to be sure, but as often as not she turned them to her advantage. Once, for instance, she was invited for supper by Jessica York, and in her absorption over a new math textbook that had arrived in the mail that day, she forgot about it. Daphne asked her next morning where she'd been, and Karen, remembering, went immediately to Jessica, leaving Bubber in charge. She apologized and begged to be asked again, and when, a few days later, she was, she arrived with a string of shell beads, which she'd made herself, for Daphne and a silk scarf from Hong Kong for Jessica. Leonard said he hoped she'd forget again the next time and come with presents for him and Bubber.

Karen did not seek out company among the islanders. She did not, for instance, take up Sharon's offer to drop in at the Peaks—though I often urged her to. Nor did she call at the Grants' when Mary Lou was home for a long weekend at the end of January, although the two had been friendly when Mary Lou worked summers at Ram's Horn; it was Mary Lou who finally sought out Karen at Meadowlane the afternoon before she left. Karen did not, indeed, come often to visit me, though she knew she had a standing welcome at Cutler's Cove.

Her relations with Lucy Talbot were polite but never warm. Actually, that didn't surprise me. Lucy was a formidable figure, not much given to intimacies with young people. My own close relationship with Lucy Talbot (who was surely my closest companion on the island) was based on a communion of interests and common values—interests and values not likely to be shared by Karen Bannister. I had noticed that Lucy was not particularly close to Jingle, though she respected her. Even Turk and Sharon, despite the crucial role Lucy once played in their lives, could not be considered intimate friends. Indeed, I believe Lucy enjoyed true intimacy among the islanders only with her daughter.

But Lucy was scrupulously fair with regard to Karen and would say nothing ill of her. She agreed with the rest of us that Karen had started off well. Lucy adopted a mother-to-daughter attitude toward Karen from the outset, arranging for her laundry, watching over her health and diet. Lucy also made herself judge of Karen's proper appearance. When Karen came down to breakfast in dungarees the day school started, Lucy didn't hesitate to tell Karen her mind.

"Karen, I don't think you should go to school your first day in trousers."

Karen said nothing, but after breakfast returned to her room and came down a few minutes later in skirt and blouse. Thereafter that was her normal attire. Later in the month, during another easterly storm, Lucy suggested it might be wiser if she *did* wear slacks or ski pants, but Karen demurred. She said she preferred a skirt, and anyway, her mother was sending her more of them.

Lucy's sense of responsibility for her ward was not confined to suggesting what she should wear or not wear. An episode occurred at the end of January that involved Lucy and Karen in the first serious impasse in their relationship. The Christmas visit of the *Sunbeam* that year was postponed because of the northeaster at the end of December, and the mission boat arrived unexpectedly, between storms, some five weeks later. A church supper was hastily organized, and following the service and traditional distribution of presents, an impromptu dance was arranged. Karen provided the music—on the upright piano, carried over from the school—until demands for her as a partner exceeded demands for her accompaniment, at which point Winifred Dacey replaced her as best she could, confining herself to airs from bygone days, whether they lent themselves to dancing or not. Lucy left early with a headache, and I accompanied her on my way home.

The dance continued until sometime after eleven, and Karen was one of the last to leave, since she had to supervise the safe return of her piano to the schoolhouse. Sam Clayton escorted her home. Like the rest of the lobstermen, he had partaken liberally of the bottles that passed freely about outside the church and was thus emboldened to press his suit with Karen on their walk back. Karen, I gather, didn't resist. Lucy, already in bed, heard them come down the lane from the high road around midnight, talking rather loudly and gaily.

Then there was silence as they stood under the eaves outside the kitchen door. After what seemed to Lucy an interminable period of silence, with no sign that Karen was coming into the house, she threw open the window and called down.

"Is that you, Karen?"

"Yes, Lucy."

"What are you doing outside so long?"

"I'm with Sam Clayton."

"Well, come on in, child, and go to bed. It's after midnight."

"Aw, Lucy, tha's when things crank up 'round here," Sam said thickly.

"Not in this house they don't. Now, run on home, Sam, and let Karen get some rest."

Lucy lost no time at breakfast the next morning in giving Karen her view of these "goings-on" with Sam Clayton. She told Karen that flirting with a lobster-man, especially after he'd been drinking, could lead to very serious conse-quences. It was not merely a question of morals—if contemporary morals weren't enough to restrain her—but of common prudence.

Karen at first passed off the incident—"Oh, that," she said—but as Lucy bore down on her, she became defensive.

"Well, what's wrong with kissing a lobsterman? If it pleases him—"

"Of course it pleases him. Why should it not? But where does it lead, Karen?"

Karen shrugged and passed her plate for eggs.

"But don't you care, child? What are the other lobstermen to do if they know you give your kisses freely to Sam? Won't they all be along to have their share—first the unmarried ones and finally the husbands and fathers?"

"I wouldn't kiss a married man," Karen said.

"But you'd kiss all the unmarried ones?"

"Not if they had girls of their own. Sam doesn't."

Karen glanced at her watch and turned to her breakfast. Lucy watched her for some moments in silence from the stove.

"Karen, if I thought there could be . . . romance . . . between you and Sam . . ."

"I don't think there's anything more to talk about, Lucy," Karen said coldly. "We just don't see things the same way, that's all."

And that ended the conversation. Later in the day I met Karen at Caleb's, and we walked home together. She told me about the episode the night before and her talk with Lucy in the morning. She expected my sympathy, but I had lit-tle to give her. Like Lucy, I told her I thought she was running a dangerous risk.

"One thing leads to another," I said.

"So what if it does?"

I looked at her somewhat incredulously and said I assumed she wasn't con-templating a full-blown affair with Sam Clayton.

"I'm not 'contemplating' anything," Karen said. "But you and Lucy talk as though it was such a damned awful thing to have sex with a lobsterman. I thought you were supposed to be such a great democrat. Equality of classes and so forth."

I told her equality of classes had nothing to do with the case. Behaving responsibly in matters of sex should be a rule for everyone, regardless of class. (I was beginning to feel very ponderous and out of my element.)

"Look, what's the great mystery about sex?" Karen went on. "After all, it's only a natural function. If two people feel attacted to each other, why shouldn't they…"

"And what about the consequences?" I interrupted her.

"Getting pregnant? That's my problem."

I said it was only one of the problems. What about the feelings of the other person? Sex, I assumed, was more than an expression of mutual passion. It was also an expression of mutual respect. Love, in short. (This was really getting sticky.)

We passed Winifred Dacey and exchanged a word with her, continuing on for a time in silence after she was out of hearing.

"Well, you don't have to worry too much," Karen finally said. "I'm not going to freeze myself in some lobster shack making love to Sam Clayton, and I doubt anyone is going to offer us a bed. . . . But I'll say this. I'd find more pleasure making love with him than with some drunken fraternity bum at Williams on a Saturday night."

I told her she'd been reading too much D. H. Lawrence—rather, not reading him well enough. For in his affairs between upper-class women and their lower-class lovers, there was at least a sentiment that passed for love.

"Love," Karen said, "is for the birds. You're too old-fashioned." (And, indeed, I did feel uncomfortably old-fashioned on that occasion.)

So I made no more impression on Karen than Lucy had in the matter of Sam Clayton. I discussed the situation with Lucy a few days later without telling her the full import of my talk with Karen.

"Something got left out when she became a woman, didn't it?" Lucy said. "A quality of human compassion. . . . I think she'd have stayed out there another hour spooning with Sam if I hadn't called her in, yet I doubt she enjoyed it much. Certainly not the way Mary Lou would." Lucy carried a basket of laundry into the bedroom, and when she returned, she said, "You know, I think Karen despises her physical self . . . probably because people admire it too much. She seems to do everything with her mind. Yet she doesn't show good judgment, poor child. I worry for her."

I had more direct experience of Karen's perverse approach to sex about this time, in a way I dared not communicate to Lucy. Karen came down one evening to talk about a lesson she was preparing in social studies for her three older pupils, and I gave her a scotch and soda. Later, when she wanted another, I poured it for her—perhaps unwisely. I rose at one point to look for a match to light her cigarette, and when I turned she was standing close to me, a strange look in her eye. Without a word, she put her arms around my neck and began to kiss me on the mouth. This was not altogether unusual, since we did embrace each other from time to time, and even kissed each other on the lips—in the island fashion. But it presently became clear that Karen was being deliberately provocative. Eyes closed, she pressed her tongue against my teeth to force them open and moved her hips slowly back and forth against mine. Still, I did not immediately restrain her. I'm only human. The thought even flashed through my confused brain: Why not? This might be better all around than Karen chasing after the lobstermen. But I returned to a clearer sense of reality before matters had progressed much further and pushed her gently, but firmly, away.

"Don't want to play?" she teased me, her arms still around my neck. "Afraid one thing will lead to another?"

I mumbled something about being twice her age, and she said, "I thought middle-aged men loved college girls."

I let the "middle-aged" bit pass and said whether we did or not, it didn't follow that we carried them off to bed on an impulse.

"Well, have it your own way," she said. Then she kissed me again, so hard it left me breathless, and ended by sinking her teeth into my lower lip and drawing blood.

"Karen! What are you doing!" I daubed at my mouth with a handkerchief.

"Oh, I'm sorry," she said, turning away to light her cigarette. "I shouldn't have done that."

When I came back from the kitchen, having staunched the bleeding with cold water, Karen was sitting on the sofa again—the incident, to all intents and purposes, out of her mind. But it was not out of mine. Quite apart from the badly swollen lip I nursed for the next few days (which I explained away as an encounter at night with my closet door), I was haunted for some time by Karen's deliberate cruelty. It was not simply the peevishness of a spoiled child. It was a mature perversion, and therefore all the more disturbing.

A week or so after this episode, I passed Karen one afternoon on the high road, walking home with Sam Clayton, and she told me she was coming to see me that evening to talk over something. I said I would look for her—but in reality I didn't look forward to her visit, since I expected she wanted to apologize for her behavior the last time she was at Cutler's Cove, and I was never strong on scenes of contrition. In Karen's case, however, I had to admit it would do her good. I had inevitably seen her almost daily and had supper with her twice a week at Lucy's, as usual, but she hadn't mentioned that episode again. I doubted in any case that she wanted to talk to me about Sam Clayton. So far as I knew, that relationship had progressed no further, though Sam was as much in attendance on Karen as during the first weeks after her arrival, and a number of the islanders were interested in his suit.

I saw her flashlight through the woods about eight o'clock and called out to her to be careful of the ice on the path. The spray from a heavy sea two days ear-lier had left a sheen of ice high up on the eastern shore and even into the spruces. The night was cold and starless.

Karen came in, kissed me perfunctorily on the cheek, and handed me a let-ter. It was from her friend Jerry Lincoln, addressing her as "Sugar Chick." The letter explained, amid further expressions of endearment and in rather stilted and ungrammatical prose, that he had quit his job in Newark. He proposed, before finding another, to come up and spend a week or so with Karen. She wanted to know what I thought of the idea.

Karen had told me a little about Jerry Lincoln soon after she arrived on the island in January. He was born in Georgia, the son of a sharecropper, but moved north with his family when he was ten. They lived first in Harlem. When his father disappeared, his mother moved the family—there were six children—to Newark, where she had relatives. Jerry finished high school in Newark and after military service, which he spent chiefly at Fort Dix, won a scholarship to Howard University. He spent two years there, then quit to earn money for the rest of the family when an older brother also dropped from sight. He hoped to return to Howard in another year or two, or so Karen said. He was twenty-five.

Although I knew few American Negroes in those days—despite a wide acquaintance with Africans—Jerry Lincoln's history seemed to me fairly typical for a southern Negro moved north. (I use the term Negro, as we did in that era—for this was still some years from the time when we began, at their urging, to call Negroes "Blacks" or "Afro-Americans.") I doubted, judging from Jerry's prose, whether he had promise as a scholar or even the ambition to finish col-lege, but I accepted Karen's opinion that he was a talented administrator. He had a forceful personality, she said, and he had succeeded where others had failed in organizing successful programs in his job in the Department of Social Welfare in Newark. He had been Karen's immediate supervisor in her winter work project from Bennington the year before.

Karen had not intimated to me that there was more than casual friendship between them. She had explained the frequent letters I knew she received from him, when I twitted her about them, by saying, "Jerry's lonely again" or "Jerry's got this crazy new idea for a neighborhood athletic center." Sally, it is true, when she wrote in mid-January to plead with me to stand as foster father to her "obstinate" daughter, had offered as one bit of evidence of Karen's obstinacy her having fallen in love "with a coon." But since Sally's letter was written in a maudlin state (". . . and my son's a Communist and my husband's a bore—God bless him—and I'm a goddam alcoholic . . ."), I had discounted her report. Still, the endearments in Jerry's letter did not quite square with what I understood to be a platonic friendship, and I said so.

Karen shrugged. "That's Jerry," she said. "But let's not go into that all over again."

I should make one thing clear about my view of Karen's relationship with Jerry Lincoln, whatever it was. This was a period when there was a growing sympathy for American Negroes, at least in the circles in which I moved (away from the island, that is). It was still some years before formal desegregation was launched in most areas, but any breaking down of racial barriers through informal social integration was considered a healthy development. I accordingly approved fully of Karen's relationship with Jerry Lincoln from the moment I first learned of it and had no misgivings whatsoever—if, indeed, I gave the matter a thought—on the question of sex between them. It was only in the context of Jerry's projected visit to us, especially in light of events of recent weeks, that this latter aspect of their relationship took on importance.

When I had read the letter through twice, Karen asked me what I thought. "Is it a good idea or not? You know these people better than I."

I said, after a few more moments of deliberation, that it depended on how the two of them behaved themselves.

"If you mean sleeping with each other, we ought to be able to control ourselves in that." She said this with sarcasm, but I wasn't sure how much. "It's the attitude of the islanders that I'm interested in," Karen went on. "Are they biased toward Negroes? Because if there's going to be any nastiness, I'd rather he didn't come."

I said I was sure there was no instinctive bias against Negroes among the islanders. Or *for* them, for that matter. But she should ask Lucy.

"I wanted to ask you first."

"Well, since you ask me, I tell you that I think any awkwardness will come not from Jerry's being a Negro but from his appearing to be your boyfriend just when the men here are beginning to think you belong to them. . . . What will Sam Clayton say?"

"I don't see that it makes any difference what he says . . . since there's nothing between us but a little necking. You can't tell me that binds me to Sam."

I said Sam might not see things in the same light, and Karen said, "Well, tough for poor Sam."

We talked on other aspects of the proposed visit, in the course of which I suggested Jerry shouldn't in any case stay at Meadowlane.

"He could stay with you," Karen proposed, not taking into account any inconvenience to me in having Jerry on my hands for a week or more.

I said this was possible, and Karen said, "Yes, that would be best. I agree."

I told Karen again, before she left, that she should talk this idea over with Lucy, for Lucy sensed far better than I how the islanders might react. And if

Lucy was doubtful, I urged Karen to give up the project.

But Lucy favored Jerry Lincoln's visit. I think she saw in a short visit by Karen's friend the possibility of checking a relationship with Sam Clayton that could become awkward and even dangerous. Karen would perform better in the long run, Lucy felt, if she detached herself from this tie and enjoyed a normal relationship with all islanders. Meanwhile, Jerry's staying with me at Cutler's Cove would minimize any gossip that might arise from Jerry's and Karen's living under the same roof.

Karen accordingly wrote Jerry to come along—and it was this which began our troubles.

26

Jerry Lincoln arrived on a mild sunny day in mid-February. Jessica and Marian York, returning from a two-day shopping expedition in Portland, met Jerry on the mailboat, and it was clear, as Horace Snow nudged the *Laura Lee II* in, that he had already captivated two of the island women. He stood bareheaded on the deck, towering over Jessica and Marian, an arm over the shoulder of each, and scanned the shore for Karen. But Karen wouldn't interrupt school to meet the mailboat and had asked me to greet Jerry instead. I introduced myself, and he came ashore.

"I know all about you," he said, his deep voice booming out in the quiet harbor. "Karen wrote me the whole scoop out here . . . and, say, if everybody's as great as this here Jessica and Mary Ann, I'm gonna like this place a whole lot."

Jessica and Marian, moving toward Caleb's ahead of us, giggled—and I say this to Jerry's credit, for I hadn't heard a full-fledged giggle from either since I'd been on Ram Island. Since no visitor was officially on the island before matching wits with Jenny Brewster, we stopped at the store to complete this formality.

"Now, I seen all them letters comin' from one J. Lincoln," Jenny said as I introduced them, "but I never knew till Karen told me yes'day that J. Lincoln'd be a darky."

"Is that so? Well, Karen never told me for sure either, Jenny, but I suspected all 'long you wouldn't be."

There was appreciative laughter from the dozen or so onlookers at this exchange, and Jerry had passed his first test.

"You're welcome, whoever you be, if you're a friend of Karen," Caleb said.

I picked up my groceries, and we walked up the hill, greeting islanders coming down for their mail.

"Man, this is a friendly place," Jerry said. "It beats me what Karen was worrying her head about."

We stopped in for a moment at the school. Jerry gave Karen a bear hug, but didn't try to kiss her.

"Say, you've put on weight! You look great, baby!"

The children laughed at this, and he turned to them.

"So these are the kiddies. Don't tell me who you are," he said, pointing a finger at Bubber. "I came out on the ferry with your mammy."

"Mine too?" asked Rudy York.

"If your mammy's Mary Ann, yours too."

"Are you r'lated to Abr'ham Lincoln?" Chucky asked. The other children snickered.

"Well, not quite, young fellah. But Abraham was a right good man. He freed us darkies."

Karen said under her breath, "Shove off, Uncle Tom. I've got work."

He patted her once on the shoulder, smiling broadly. "See ya!" he said to the children, and we moved on up the ridge to Cutler's Cove. But an hour later he was back at the harbor with Arthur Dacey, working over a faulty carburetor in the *Sarah Lou* while half a dozen lobstermen looked on. Karen hadn't mentioned it, but Jerry, in addition to his other accomplishments, was an excellent mechanic.

So Jerry Lincoln's reception on Ram Island was no less cordial at the outset than Karen's. As I had foreseen (and Lucy agreed with me), there was no perceptible bias toward Jerry because of his color. A few, like Jenny Brewster, persisted in referring to Jerry as a "darky"—a term I hadn't heard since childhood, but understandable on a Maine island where no Negro had set foot in living memory. The older islanders spoke of him as Karen's "colored gentleman." I heard him called "nigger" only once while he was with us, and I'll come to that.

There must have been a natural affinity between the working islanders and this chance representative of a race long known for its sense of travail and suffering—one buffeted by perverse natural forces; the other exploited by human inequity. The lobstermen immediately accepted Jerry, and they did so with less reserve than they accepted other outsiders—including, I regret to say it, harmless dilettantes like me. Jerry dressed the part better than I, I have to admit. He habitually wore army fatigues and parachute boots, with a gray turtleneck sweater under a leather jacket. He was normally bareheaded, his thick black hair proof against any weather. Later, when it stormed, he wore a yellow sou'wester Arthur Dacey loaned him.

Jerry was enough of an extrovert to breach the defenses of the most taciturn islander. With his booming voice and deep rumbling laugh, he would plunge into topics I had assumed unmentionable. Like income. "What d'ya make a year fishin' lobsters?" he asked Leonard York one afternoon at the harbor. "Can you really make a living at it?" And Leonard, to my astonishment, recited figures that represented, so far as I could make out, his actual annual income. Another day, carrying Winifred Dacey's groceries back from Caleb's, Jerry succeeded in loosening the tongue of that prim islander to the point where she voluntarily recounted to him episodes from a voyage around the Horn fifty years before.

The lobstermen, to be sure, ceased to pay court to Karen after Jerry arrived. Horatio Leadbetter was left alone again to fill the woodboxes in the chill mornings. The cluster of islanders at the crossroads when school let out dwindled. But then it grew again a few days later for a different reason—Jerry's famous touch football games after school. An unusually mild stretch of weather the week Jerry arrived thawed the snow and ice on the baseball field beside the school and left it nearly dry. Islanders were baseball players as a rule, but when Jerry proposed touch football Bubber York found a dog-eared ball in his grandfather's attic, and the game was a fixed thing by the end of the week. There were only a handful of players the first afternoon, but within a day or two half a dozen lobstermen managed regularly to finish up their work in time for the daily game at three o'clock. Over the weekends, when the high school students were back from Rockland and Camden, the teams were nearly at full strength. Jerry was the hero of these contests, and whichever side he was on would win, no matter how strong an opposition was put together. Tall and superbly conditioned, he writhed uncannily away from pursuers until he found a receiver free—as often as not, Bubber York—to whom he lobbed an easy pass for a spectacular gain or score. Nonplaying islanders came out to watch his wizardry. If there was an injury to one of the younger players, like the day Rudy York sprained an ankle, it was worth it for the ride home after the game on Jerry's shoulders.

The islanders—men, women, and children alike—thus accepted Jerry easily. If several of the younger lobstermen were at first resentful of his coming, because he intruded between them and Karen, Jerry won them over quickly with his openness and boisterously high spirits. What was one of Karen's rare smiles to Bill York, for instance, compared to the infectious companionship of Jerry Lincoln?

With Sam Clayton, to be sure, it was different. He had committed himself to the pursuit of Karen and felt, quite reasonably, that he had been encouraged. Moreover, the islanders knew—even if he hadn't boasted openly about it—that he'd been "makin' time" with Karen. He therefore suffered loss of face when Jerry arrived, and he was, in fact, deeply hurt. He sulked about the harbor, bearing in silence the unkind taunts of his peers and avoiding at all costs any encounter with Karen or Jerry. Inevitably they did meet—by chance late one afternoon when Sam came suddenly onto the high road from a spruce grove as we were returning exhilarated from a football game. When he saw us, he started to draw back into the woods, but Karen called to him.

"Sam, don't run away! You haven't met Jerry."

Sam stopped reluctantly and stood waiting while we approached. He looked past us and pretended not to see Jerry's hand stretched toward him.

"Where have you been all week, Sam?" Karen said. "I've been looking for you."

Sam, as a rule never at a loss for words, mumbled something about his traps, still looking to one side of us or the other.

"If I were Sam, I sure know where I'd be," Jerry said. "Out fishin', man! Great weather like this."

Sam gave him a fleeting and venomous look, glanced as briefly at Karen, and flushing deeply, turned back into the spruce without a word.

"Now, there's the first uncivil fella I've met out here," Jerry said as we walked on. "Sugar baby, you know what I think? I think he must be sweet on you."

And he gave forth his big laugh—*too* big, for Sam could hear it. Karen said nothing.

Karen's relations with Jerry, so far as she revealed them, were casual to the point of indifference during those first days. Jerry normally ate at Meadowlane, and sometimes I joined him. Once Lucy and Karen came down to Cutler's Cove to dine with us. If Karen had work to do after supper, she simply said good-night and withdrew to her room. She paid little attention to his comings and goings, leaving him free to roam about the island making friends as he pleased. She seemed to be neither exhilarated nor burdened by his presence on the island. If I hadn't seen Jerry's letter and had that conversation with Karen about his coming, it wouldn't have crossed my mind that their relationship had ever been anything but platonic. Indeed, I wondered whether it wasn't anyway. When he touched her, it was as he touched any of the island women—that is, a great forearm resting on their shoulders or a light thump on the back as he guffawed at some remark—as often as not, his own. Even the occasional pat on the rump he gave Karen was no more than he gave the high school girls when they were back over for the weekend. And as far as the terms he used to address Karen— "baby," "sugar," "chick," or some combination of these—he didn't seem to endow them with any special tenderness; they were simply the form of address he habitually used. Jerry and Karen gave no sign of wishing to be alone. Once or twice when I tried to give them a few minutes by themselves at Cutler's Cove on the pretext of having some errand to do elsewhere, Karen would say, "Don't go away for our sake" or "Go along with him, Jerry. I've got something here I want to read."

Jerry expressed an interest in seeing Ram's Horn, and Sunday afternoon, since Karen had no interest in walking the length of the island, Turk and I took him out there. It was another warm afternoon, the last in that prolonged spell of mild February weather. The temperature stood at sixty-five at four o'clock. The days were already beginning to lengthen perceptibly after the long winter solstice so that it stayed light until nearly six.

We found the key under the arbor in the patio and let ourselves in. The sun, laying in all afternoon through the large glass windows, had left the unheated house as warm as on a day in midsummer. Flies, stirred by the warmth, buzzed in swarms against the windows as we moved from room to room. The furniture, draped with sheets against the dust, was pushed back against the walls, giving the illusion of even greater spaciousness than usual. Jerry, needless to say, was awed.

"My dump would go ten times in here," he said. "Don't anyone ever break in?"

"Well . . . Stanley'n me *got* in once," Turk said. "Through an open window in the kitchen."

"Wha'ja snitch? You must've snitched somethin', man. Come on!"

"One bottle of Johnny Walker." Turk grinned. "Come to think of it, we never paid George back."

"If he got off with one bottle of scotch, he got off damn cheap."

In the large and elegant master bedroom facing Deer Isle, Jerry picked up a photograph of Sally from the mantel. He whistled softly.

"Hey, who's this chick?" he said. "Is she ever stacked!"

I said it was Karen's mother, the photo taken a long time before.

"That's the way she looked when they first came out here," Turk said.

"What a broad! Karen's a good-lookin' kid, but she ain't ever gonna look like this." He put the photograph back on the mantel.

After we'd locked up and were starting back to the Peaks, Jerry glanced again at the house and shook his head slowly. "Karen never told me she had anything like this out here," he said. "Her old man must be loaded."

But if Jerry was learning of the Bannisters' wealth for the first time, he gave no sign to Karen that it disturbed him. When they met again, at supper that evening, he said merely that her father had "a mighty nice summer place" out at the point. "I'd get lost tryin' to find my way around." Karen said nothing, and that was all the mention there was of Ram's Horn.

After supper Karen had to go to the school to set up a model she was using the next morning, and Jerry, who was going on to Turk's to help him repair an old sewing machine he'd bought secondhand in Rockland for his mother, went along with her. Lucy and I walked halfway down the ridge with them for the air. On our way back we inevitably talked about Karen and Jerry, since there hadn't been an occasion to all week.

"What do you make of them?" Lucy asked me.

I said, after a moment's deliberation, I thought they seemed good friends. Not very obviously in love.

"Do you think so?" Lucy said. "Karen might challenge you there. . . . I think she's in love with the *idea* of being in love with Jerry Lincoln, and she doesn't care much whether or not she really loves *him*. It's the same thing we were talking about before, isn't it? She does things with her mind, not her heart."

I said if she had to go through some such exercise, she could have found a worse partner than Jerry to go through it with. He seemed to me as casual and impersonal about Karen as she about him.

Lucy agreed. "He's a big, friendly, easygoing, and . . . not-too-bright Negro, isn't he? I can't pretend to know what his interest is in Karen."

I mentioned that he'd been surprised and impressed that afternoon by the elegance of Ram's Horn.

"I shouldn't wonder," said Lucy. "So would I in his place. But he doesn't impress me as someone interested especially in Karen's wealth . . . or prospects of wealth."

"Or her looks," I said, and told her Jerry's reaction to the old photograph of Sally.

Lucy said, "I can't agree with him there. I think Karen Bannister much more handsome than Sally ever was." She thought a moment, then went on. "I wonder if it was the . . . earthiness in Sally that attracted him. She came from a working-class background too. In fact, right there in that same New Jersey town."

Lucy's image of Newark seemed to be Bangor or Portland writ large, only with a more identifiable proletarian element. I couldn't agree with her implication that Irish-Swedes and Negroes, on the strength of their working-class origins, had any more in common in Newark than elsewhere—but I forbore mentioning this. Lucy was surely right in detecting a quality of earthiness in both Sally Bannister and Jerry Lincoln that Karen lacked.

As we left the ridge and walked slowly down to Meadowlane, we could feel the easterly in our faces, still mild, but laden with moisture. Before we parted, Lucy said, "It was a good idea, wasn't it, Jerry's coming out here? It brought Karen back to reality, and it made our winter a little gayer. . . . A week has been just about right."

27

B ut it wasn't a week, as things turned out. Jerry announced the next morning as I gave him breakfast that the island suited him so well he would stay on a while. At least until Karen's Easter holiday in April, when she planned to return home for a few days. He would see if he could find work fixing the lobstermen's engines and doing other odd jobs to make enough to live on. I concealed my general uneasiness about his plans, but told him unequivocally there was no money on the island to support an outsider. In that case, he said, he'd borrow money from Karen.

He didn't want to impose himself any longer on me. To this I made no objection, since Jerry had, in fact, disrupted the rhythm of my life. It wasn't just his sleeping late—for I was an early riser in those days and normally would have been at my desk for three or four hours by the time he woke up. There were also little irritations—like his sleeping in the nude, for instance. I don't think of myself as particularly fastidious, but I was offended by this in some obscure way. I used to keep an anxious eye on the path those days, afraid someone would come down and surprise Jerry exposed on his cot, bedclothes half on the floor. (But as a matter of fact, the one time someone did come—Lucy, bearing fresh doughnuts about eleven o'clock on Saturday morning—Jerry heard her even before I did and greeted her at the door, fully wrapped in an adobe blanket and looking like an Indian chieftain; Lucy thought nothing of it.)

Then there was Jerry's laundry—it was surprising how much of it there was, since he came with so few clothes—draped here and there about the room or spilling out of his imitation alligator suitcase on the oak table. Oh, I should talk, I suppose. But my own untidiness (I liked to think) had a certain order: laundry stowed in a bottom drawer until it was full, then transferred to a pillowcase in the back of my closet until wash day; dirty dishes in a rack out of sight under the sink until I got around to washing them. In any case, it was my mess, and mine alone. I suppose bachelors of a certain age with a natural tendency to slovenliness develop a strong distaste for anyone else's. . . . Well, I put up cheerfully enough with Jerry's for a week, especially in view of all the compensating benefits of his being with us, but by that Monday morning I confess I was looking forward to his departure in a day or two, as initially scheduled.

I took it for granted that Jerry had discussed his plan with Karen, but when I met her later in the day and made some reference to it, she appeared to have heard nothing about the idea. She was indifferent in any case.

"If he wants to, it's his business," she said. "I guess no one will object . . . except you," she added. "He ought to move somewhere else."

I said he'd gone off to ask Winifred if she would rent him a room. "He has no money," I remarked.

Karen said, "That's no problem."

So Jerry Lincoln moved that afternoon to the Daceys', and we adjusted ourselves to his staying on with us for some considerable stretch of time. Most of
the islanders were pleased.

But things were not as they were before. It's strange how combinations of
circumstances can change an atmosphere, a mood. An ambiance that seems a
fixed thing one day is suddenly shattered the next, beyond hope of recovery. I
would be hard put to place a finger on the precise moment at which Jerry
Lincoln's fortunes changed, when the islanders' attitudes toward him shifted
from benevolence to indifference—and finally to hostility. Certainly it was related to the storm that week which broke our midwinter respite. The easterly we
felt in our faces Sunday evening made up all the next day and by Tuesday had
developed into a full gale. Since the rain was spasmodic, Jerry would have continued the football games between squalls, despite the soggy field, but the lobstermen had no heart for it. Unable to go out to bring in their traps because of
the seas, they spent most of the afternoon at the harbor securing their gear and
doubling the lines at moorings.

The low tide at dusk was several feet below normal, laying bare the inner
sector of the harbor where the small boats were on their pulley lines. Even the
Sarah Lou rested on the bottom of the harbor, tilting at thirty degrees. The
weather report at six o'clock forecast high water of three to four feet above normal due to the coincidence of the storm with the new moon spring tides, and
this meant that the half dozen boats careened on the east side of the harbor had
to be hauled farther up the shore. High tide was due shortly after midnight.

By seven o'clock word had spread of the anticipated high water, and all able-
bodied islanders assembled at the harbor. There was much to be done. In addition to the hauling of the boats on the east shore, several other boats whose
moorings were precarious had to be beached, one or two low-lying sheds needed reinforcement, lobster traps had to be removed from the pier, and all loose
gear had to be secured. Then there was the delicate task of removing Widow
Barnaby from the jetty—delicate not merely because she was a frail old woman,
but also because she hadn't left her shanty in over fifteen years and would resist
the move. The islanders, however, had settled it among themselves after a section
of the jetty washed away in a northeast gale the winter before, leaving her
stranded for two days, that she would have to be moved to safety during the
next major storm, come what may.

Jerry was inevitably left out of much of this activity. He was a willing worker, of course, striding back and forth in his yellow sou'wester and high boots
Clyde Grant loaned him and offering himself for any task. But he bungled

things. He pulled one skiff so impetuously across rocks that he stove a hole in its side. In hauling a dory into the eel grass with Rudolf York, he moved too fast for Rudolf, with his game leg, so that Rudolf fell, gashing his good knee on a half-buried anchor. The gash wasn't serious, but it put Rudolf out of commission for the rest of the evening and left us short a man; any of the lobstermen working with Rudolf would have geared their pace to his. Then Jerry was too noisy for the occasion, his deep voice booming out at regular intervals above the wind and bursts of rain. He probably had more than his fair share of the few bottles circulating among the lobstermen, and this made him even noisier.

Jerry meant well, of course. He wanted to raise the spirits of the lobstermen as they worked, but I could see that his boisterousness in the end grated on them. They were accustomed to meeting the easterly storms that periodically lashed at the island with a certain grimness. They preferred to work in silence, talking only enough to complete what had to be done. There was enough exhila-ration in the storm itself without the need to contrive more—although the resort to whiskey on such occasions was, of course, ritual and the conviviality at Caleb's taken for granted when all was secure.

What Jerry didn't understand—indeed, how could he? I barely understood it myself at that time—was that the lobstermen's concern was not for the boats and gear in the harbor, which no high water could damage irreparably after our attentions (and not very seriously without them), but for the miles of traps and line stretching around the island and far out into the bay. How many of these would be washed ashore in the storm and smashed on granite boulders? How long would it be before they could recover their losses and fish normally again, and at what cost in funds set aside for other purposes—new gas refrigerators, generators, stoves, depth-finders, ship-to-shore radios, and, for a few dreamers, a car on the main that could bear them away to remote vacations as far away as Florida? The energy they expended on the relatively protected harbor, away from the full force of easterly storms, was to distract themselves from their helpless-ness outside. Jerry, ignorant of all this, intruded unwittingly on their vigil. At an appropriate moment, therefore, Turk proposed to him that since matters were under control at the harbor, he go on down to Cutler's Cove to board up my large window facing the sea; we would be along presently to help. Silence descended over the harbor as Jerry's bass voice receded up the road singing "Roll me over . . ." When we had done all we could, we stood in groups along the shore watching the water rise higher with each fresh surge of sea, while Rudolf and Clyde reminded us of how high the water had been at comparable stages of the tide during previous storms.

After midnight Turk and I went down to Cutler's Cove to see how Jerry was making out and found a single board banging harmlessly in the wind against the window frame. Jerry was asleep on the sofa inside.

The gale blew itself out the next day, but it ushered in several weeks of unsettled and unsettling weather. The seas remained so high after the storm that it was not until the end of the week before the lobstermen could go out to ascertain the extent of their losses. They were higher than feared. Sam Clayton lost seventy-five percent of his traps, and there were few lobstermen with traps out that winter who lost less than half of them. No traps survived the pounding of the easterly on the seaward shore. These losses cast a pall over the islanders and cut deeply into savings. Arthur was obliged to extend credit almost beyond his means for the warp and laths needed to replace the smashed traps. Few bills were paid at Caleb's that month, which meant that Caleb had to cut back on his orders for March. To add to our woes, two snowstorms in rapid succession dumped more than a foot of snow, which turned quickly to slush and then froze. Before and after the storm fog enveloped the island almost continuously so that the mailboat came out only three times in two weeks' time.

The islanders withdrew into themselves during this bleak period. If the lobstermen could go out at all, it was rarely for more than a few hours, and they went straight home as soon as they came in. The women stopped at Caleb's only for the barest essentials. When islanders passed each other on the slippery roads and wooded paths, they nodded greetings perfunctorily but rarely spoke.

Jerry grew bored with nothing to do. Islanders who had previously welcomed him in their homes and urged him to return were now preoccupied if he dropped by. Either that or they withdrew into the interior of their houses and stayed out of sight until he'd gone. Jerry made blunders, too, during these days. Bobby Cutler, for instance, asked him one day if he would help him start up his engine, clogged with silt from a leak sprung during the storm, and Jerry imprudently answered that he would—"For a small consideration, man." Bobby walked off without another word. When Jerry described the episode to us at supper that evening, laughing at it as a great joke, Karen told him bluntly that he'd been stupid and said he should go down first thing in the morning to make it up to Bobby. Jerry did this, but Bobby wouldn't let him aboard.

"Come on, Bobby boy. I was only kiddin' around. Lemme fix up that Cadillac engine you got. For nothin'."

But Bobby disappeared into his cuddy and didn't come out until Jerry had left the harbor.

Put off by the islanders, Jerry fell back increasingly on Karen. When he first arrived, absorbed as he was in the life of the island, the lobstermen, and his football games, he had paid as little attention to Karen as she to him. Now he was with her a good part of the day. He would drop in at the schoolhouse three or four times during the course of an afternoon, as he walked aimlessly up and down the ridge looking for activity. Finally, Karen told him he was bothering her and to stay away. After school he would accompany her to the store for the mail and any groceries, then go back with her to Meadowlane to sit in Lucy's parlor while Karen worked. Or they would come down to sit with me for a desultory conversation—or none at all. In the evenings, after supper at Lucy's, they would often go to the schoolhouse, more, I thought, to avoid having to spend the evening in Lucy's parlor, with or without Lucy, than because Karen had urgent work to do. They would stoke up the fires and Karen would busy herself with her lessons for the next day, while Jerry stretched out on the floor reading from a stack of comic books he found cached in Bubber York's desk. I found them like this one evening when I looked in at the school on my way home from Turk and Sharon's.

It was a week or two after Jerry's decision to stay on that Lucy, coming home earlier than she had expected from a visit one snowy afternoon to the jetty, found Karen's schoolbag in the hall but the parlor empty, and assumed the two had gone out again—until she heard sounds in Karen's room upstairs. She listened a moment, then went up and knocked. There was no immediate answer.

"Karen," Lucy said firmly, "is Jerry in there with you?"

"Yes, Lucy, we're here," Karen finally said.

"I want Jerry to go home, and I wish to speak with you downstairs."

Lucy went down to the kitchen and waited. Jerry presently followed her, putting his head in the kitchen door as he went out.

"No harm in a little lovin', I hope, Lucy?" he said with a broad grin. "You know how it is when you're kinda sweet on someone."

"I'll take that up with Karen. You run along till supper."

"If that's the way you feel . . ." He buttoned up Arthur's sou'wester against the snow and left, slamming the door behind him.

Karen came down five minutes later, her face pale and drawn. She sat at the kitchen table without a word.

"Karen," Lucy said, "I thought it was clear how people are to behave in my house. Young people do not meet in bedrooms, but in the kitchen or parlor. Kevin and Belle met this way, and I won't have it otherwise with you and Jerry."

"But it's so absurdly old-fashioned," Karen said. "I'm twenty and—"

"It may seem old-fashioned to you, but it seems very sensible to me. But more than that, Karen, this is my home. This is where I live. I couldn't be comfortable with you and Jerry up in your bedroom with the door closed."

"I could move somewhere else," Karen said.

Lucy turned quickly from the stove and stared for some moments at Karen before speaking.

"Do you want to, Karen?" Karen was silent, and presently Lucy went on, "I sincerely hope not. And besides, it would be the same in any house on the island. You're our schoolteacher, Karen. It's quite unthinkable that you could carry on like this with Jerry while you have your job."

Karen asked suddenly, looking directly at Lucy, "It's because he's a Negro, isn't it?"

"Child, how can you think that matters?"

"Everyone's suddenly turned against him," Karen said.

"I don't see that at all. The men are disconsolate over their losses. It's always been this way after a bad storm. Sometimes Jerry . . . presses too hard for their attention."

Karen said nothing, looking out at the snow swirling about the window. Lucy came up behind her and in a conciliatory way put her hands on Karen's shoulders.

"You're cold, Karen. Go have a bath before supper. I'll put on the hot water."

And Karen, still silent, went back upstairs.

Lucy told me about this episode only some weeks later. "When I touched her, poor thing, she was as tense as a coiled spring," Lucy said. "And so unresponsive to my touch. It was quite frightening."

But Lucy, of course, told no one else about the episode, so that whatever went on in Karen's bedroom that afternoon was never suspected by the other islanders.

Karen and Jerry were less fortunate—indeed, we all were—several days later. It was another wet day over the island, foggy with frequent squalls of mixed snow and sleet. By mid-afternoon it appeared to lighten, and I went off to the Peaks to chop for a few hours with Turk in the lot above Jericho Cove. I met Karen and Jerry on the high road coming from the schoolhouse and exchanged a few words with them before continuing on my way. The squalls resumed, and we gave up chopping after half an hour. On my way home I met Harold Toothacher returning from a job at the Grants' and asked him to look at my privy, which had been damaged during the storm. We walked down the trail from the clearing and took a shortcut through the spruces to the outhouse, bypassing the bungalow. If the outhouse had been on the other side of the cabin (where Harold wanted to build it two years before), we would have warned them of our approach because they would have heard our voices, Harold chattering on as usual about anything that came to mind. But located where it was, they couldn't know of our presence until we came out of the woods. The privy was the only place near the cabin where you could see directly into my bedroom, and there they were—Karen's bare white legs locked over the backsides of Jerry Lincoln as he moved rhythmically on top of her. Their heads were out of view, and of course they had no idea we were near. I saw them first and pulled up abruptly at the edge of the spruces. I motioned to Harold to be quiet and turn back, wishing it were anyone but Harold Toothacher or that his eyesight were poor. But he saw and he understood.

"Well, bless me, ain't that a dandy sight!" he said in a whisper.

I pushed him roughly back into the woods, though he would have lingered, and we made our way back to the high road. When we were out of hearing, Harold said, "Now, I had a mite of suspicion that—"

"Then you had suspicions I never had, Harold," I broke in harshly. "And you keep this to yourself, hear? You could ruin that girl with your damned stories."

"Unless that colored gentleman's ruint her already, deah," Harold said blandly.

But pledging Harold Toothacher to secrecy was as fruitless as persuading Horatio Hornblower to stop stammering, and I knew that word of Karen's indiscretion would soon be all over the island. After I had seen Harold down the ridge, I wandered aimlessly about the dripping woods for a half hour, sick at heart, before returning to the cabin. Since I was still carrying my ax, I took the precaution of limbing a few trees noisily as I approached. I needn't have. They were settled before a roaring fire when I came in, Karen in her usual position, cross-legged on the bear rug, and Jerry sprawled over my leather chair. He was in unnaturally—or perhaps naturally—high spirits. Karen was quiet, a faint glow in her cheeks that only accented her beauty. I puttered needlessly at my desk, hardly listening to Jerry's chatter and wishing they would go. Karen noticed my mood after a time and, catching my eye, gave me a shy smile, to which I made no response. A few moments later she rose to leave. At the door, after Jerry had gone out ahead of her and started up the path, she turned back to me.

"You know something," she said. "Something you're not supposed to know." I nodded.

"Well, we had to," Karen said defiantly. "I mean, there was no other place to go. Jerry was going nuts."

I told her my knowing didn't matter, but Harold Toothacher had been with me.

"Oh, Jesus! That's going to be awful for you, isn't it? Everyone will think you let us."

"I'm not worried about that. I'm worried about you, Karen."

And in an instant the glow was gone from her face, and she was taut again, withdrawn into herself. She would accept no one's sympathy or help. "Don't worry about me. I can cope."

28

Word of Karen's act of love at Cutler's Cove, as I had foreseen, spread quickly over the island, embellished by certain details Harold Toothacher added on his own.

"They didn't neither of 'em have a stitch o' clothing on 'em . . . she'd even taken off her stockin's. Near 's I figure, they'd been at it ever since school let out 'fore we come along."

His salacious details were reserved, of course, for the adult males, but the story, suitably tailored, reached the womenfolk soon enough and even most of the children. If any of them doubted the story, knowing Harold's reputation as a gossipmonger, he had only to refer to the fact that he was with me. I was never explicitly asked to confirm Harold's account, but neither could I come forward to deny it, so the story stood.

The repercussions were not long in making themselves felt. Jenny Brewster, always talkative when Karen came in for her mail, slapped Karen's letters down on the counter without a word the day she heard the story. Jesse Cutler passed Karen on the high road without acknowledging her greeting. Janice Torrey kept Judy out of school a day, on the pretext of chills, but relented after Judy pestered her all day to return and after Karen sent over a note hoping Judy would recover soon, since she had such a big part in the program scheduled for town meeting day.

Karen went about her work as though nothing had happened to change the islanders' attitude toward her, although she could hardly have been oblivious of the change. Indeed, I told her the day after the episode at the cabin that Harold's story was generally known. Karen shrugged and said she wasn't surprised. She did her best to keep the gossip about her from affecting her relations with the schoolchildren, with some success. Relations with Bubber tested her ingenuity more than with the others, for Bubber was now a full-fledged adolescent and was more vulnerable to the gossip. He had heard the full version of Harold's story, standing at the edge of a circle of young lobstermen at the pier.

"Why are you looking at me like that, Bubber?" Karen asked him one afternoon, surprising him in openmouthed stare at her calves as she turned from the blackboard. And when Bubber flushed crimson, she said, "I'm me. Remember? Let's read together."

And she read with Bubber for half an hour, doing most of the reading herself while she let him play with her bracelet. Meanwhile, the two twelve-year-olds, Judy Torrey and Penny York, clung to Karen as closely as ever, their devotion a defense against any scandal. Rudy, with the artlessness of the very young, asked if it was true Jerry was her sweetheart. "You're my sweetheart," Karen said.

"How can I have two?"

Karen's relationship with Lucy—to the surprise of both, I think—took a turn for the better after Lucy heard of the incident at Cutler's Cove. Lucy never mentioned the episode, but she put herself out to win Karen's confidence. She shared Belle's recent letters with Karen, for instance. She brought up for discussion general topics that she knew interested Karen—like the civil rights movement, world federalism, and UNESCO. And they spent many hours discussing the coming program and exhibit at the school. At night, when Karen went up to bed, Lucy would quietly embrace her and kiss her on the forehead. I was not with the two of them enough to know whether Karen's response was as genuine as Lucy's compassion, but Karen did seem more serene. I think Lucy's deliberate display of goodwill fortified Karen in the coming weeks, despite Karen's show of not wanting to rely on any of us.

Jerry's illness the day after the episode at Cutler's Cove made things easier for Karen. He came down with a fever during the night and by noon had symptoms of bronchial pneumonia. Sharon Jenkins came over to nurse him during the afternoon and brought a supply of medicines. Late in the day she spoke with Dr. Merriam in Rockland over Caleb's short-wave radio, but they decided there was no need for him to come out. And in any case there was little chance of it, since another snowstorm was upon us. Several of the island women, even though the story of Karen and Jerry at Cutler's Cove was now generally known, dropped by Winifred's to help if they could—Jesse Cutler, for instance, wondering no doubt if Jerry's illness was some divine retribution. Karen, notified at the school, came by when school was over and sat with Jerry for an hour, always in the presence of Winifred or someone else. Winifred, Sharon, and Lucy kept vigil through the snowy night.

Jerry's fever continued through the next day before it began to drop, but then he was confined to bed for another four days so that it was nearly a week altogether that he was out of circulation. He knew nothing during this time of the gossip going about the island, and this was just as well. In one mood he might have entered fully into the ribaldry around the harbor and even boasted of his prowess, giving offense to those who took his transgression seriously. In another he might have been bitterly resentful of implied criticism of Karen and so heightened passions among the islanders. Whichever way, it was not a bad thing for all of us that one more unpredictable variable was kept out of a situation already charged enough with high feelings.

One immediate awkwardness in Karen's situation was the behavior of the younger unmarried lobstermen. Their appetites aroused by the now much embellished tales of Karen's alleged promiscuity, and with Jerry for the present out of the way, they followed her with lustful eyes. Turk and I, coming up to the

crossroads from Caleb's one evening after working on the budget for the plantation meeting, found Bill York lurking in the shadows opposite the schoolhouse—waiting for Karen to come out after an evening rehearsal with the older
children; the children had already left and Karen was alone.

"That you, Bill?" Turk called out sharply. "Come on out here."

Bill came slowly forward, grinning foolishly.

"What the hell you hangin' 'round here for?" Turk said. "Leave Karen alone,
you hear? She's got work to do."

"I'll tell ya she's got work t'do!" Bill said, his crossed eyes dancing back and
forth. "I'm gonna git me a little piece o' that work. Wha' d'ya think about that
now?"

"You're a goddam fool, Bill," Turk said, and I'd never heard such steel in his
voice, not even during the entire lobster war. "Now git your ass along home."

"Turk, she loves it, an' you know it."

"Look, you dumb bastard, whether she loves it or not don't mean she loves
it with you. You git twenty years for what you're thinkin'. Now, beat it 'fore I tell
Tucker to put the strap to you."

"You're a mean son of a bitch, tha's what you are. I got 's much right to her
's anyone else." But he shuffled off down the ridge, and I marveled at the way
Turk had handled him.

"We gotta put a stop to this," Turk said when Bill was out of hearing. "You
take Karen home and tell her not to parade her ass out at night without somebody's with her. . . . We got troubles enough."

There was no more trouble from that quarter, but a few days later, before
Jerry was on his feet again, I was walking back with Karen from the schoolhouse
late in the afternoon when we met Sam Clayton. Sam, I knew, had been drinking
heavily in recent days. I didn't know whether this was because of the loss of so
much of his gear in the storm or was some delayed reaction to his blighted
"romance" with Karen. He was very drunk in any case this afternoon. I felt
Karen grow tense as we watched him stagger down the road toward us, but she
made no effort to turn aside. Sam didn't recognize her until he was twenty feet
away.

"Wal, 'f t'aint th' lil' bitch herself," he said thickly.

"How are you, Sam?" Karen said in an even tone.

" 'How are you, Sam'!" he mimicked her, dancing about unsteadily on the
road. "How the fuck d'you s'pose I'd be, you lil . . . lil cock teaser?"

"Get a hold on yourself, Sam," I said. "Don't be saying things you'll regret."

"No, he's right," Karen said. "He's got every right to be angry with me."

"Wha'cha know! She says I kin be angry with 'er . . . now she's got the big
nigger's prick t'play 'round with—"

"Say what you want about me, Sam, but leave Jerry out of it. He never did anything to hurt you."

I maneuvered Karen past Sam on the other side of the road, and we left him shouting meaningless obscenities into the dusk, stripped of the last shred of dignity. I could sense Karen on the verge of tears beside me, but when I tried to take her arm, she pulled away.

"That's my work," she said a few minutes later.

I told her whiskey was more responsible than unrequited love for Sam's troubles, aggravated by the loss of his traps.

"But it's me he *feels* is to blame, and that's what counts. . . . Lucy was so right." And that's about as much contrition as Karen allowed herself those days.

We heard later that evening that Sam had staggered down to the harbor and with a sledgehammer staved in three planks of his lobster boat on the mudflats before falling insensible on his face. Arthur Dacey found him there as the tide was coming in.

The forces on the island for and against some disciplining of Karen for her indiscretion were focused initially in the six-member school board. (The total of six, incidentally, rather than the usual three on district boards, dated back to another school crisis years before, when Granny Belle, who was chairman, found herself in a minority of one and so imperiously packed the board with three trusty sycophants to carry the day; the islanders, Lucy told me, had never taken the trouble to reduce the number to three again.)

Lloyd Cutler was the most outspoken of Karen's critics. He couldn't hear the episode at my bungalow mentioned without growing purple at the neck, and thought Karen should be dismissed immediately. Ginny Clayton seconded this view, but not, like Lloyd, on moral grounds; rather, she was reacting to the turmoil Karen had caused in Sam. If it had been Sam and not Jerry we had surprised with Karen at Cutler's Cove, Ginny's position would undoubtedly have been different. Alfred Torrey, never an outspoken advocate of anything, on balance favored some sort of punishment for Karen but was unsure how it should be carried out.

Jessica York, her puritanical pedigree tugging powerfully at her reason, was shocked beyond belief by the gossip, which she found particularly difficult to hear because she had been so sympathetic toward both Karen and Jerry; at the same time, she was so grateful to Karen for what she'd done that winter for Bubber and Daphne that she felt there must be some solution other than letting Karen go. If the two promised never to misbehave again, or if Jerry would leave the island, Jessica favored keeping Karen on. Sharon also thought it best that Jerry leave as soon as he recovered from his pneumonia. Only Lucy then, of the six school board members, was disposed to ignore the episode at Cutler's Cove, with an appropriate reprimand to Karen that she would undertake to deliver.

These positions had crystallized by the Monday following the incident, when Lloyd Cutler insisted on a school board meeting to discuss the matter. It was held in Lloyd's parlor, rather than at Meadowlane as usual, and it was not decisive. Lucy argued the case for Karen with considerable force, I gathered from reports of the meeting that circulated the next day, but she didn't persuade her fellow members to settle for a reprimand.

"Of course, it's a misfortune Karen did what she did," Lucy conceded. "And it's even a greater misfortune she was discovered. But it is, after all, her private business. I'm sure she's not the first pretty schoolteacher who's been found in a compromising position here and elsewhere. Meanwhile, she has been—she *is*— an excellent teacher. The children have never had better instruction than under Karen. Where would we find another teacher to replace her for the rest of the year were she to go? . . . Would you try it, Jessica?"

"Heavens, Lucy! I can barely manage Bubber and Daphne at home, say anything of at school."

"Sharon, I'm sure you couldn't manage it with Barbara and Stanley at home. And I know I'd never try at my age. . . . Who else might we find to finish out the year?"

There were no suggestions, needless to say, and after a moment Lucy went on. "As for her friend's leaving, I agree it would be helpful if he did, but I'm reluctant to press Karen in this. She's very sensitive where Jerry Lincoln is concerned. His being a Negro, that is. We might make matters worse by bringing him into—"

"Lucy," Lloyd broke in, "are we suppos'd to keep this girl from feelin' bad over what she's done? Or are we suppos'd to protect our children from someone who's broke the Commandments? Just tell me that."

"Is she the only one who's broken the Commandments, Lloyd?" Lucy said, looking steadily at him and thinking of Lucille. "If each of us who misbehaved were obliged to humble ourselves before the others, I doubt many of us would be left here. I'm sure my mother wouldn't have stayed on Ram Island if she'd had to humble herself every time she did wrong."

In the end it was decided, despite Lucy's uneasiness on the subject, that an effort would be made to persuade Jerry to leave of his own free will, and Lucy was to ask me to speak to him since I was supposed to know him best.

I undertook my assignment, none too eagerly, two days later. Jerry had by this time recovered enough to go out and was slowly regaining his spirits. Karen had told him the day before that they'd been seen the afternoon in my cabin and that the story was all over the island. Jerry thought this a huge joke.

"Man, that'll give 'em something to talk about!" was his comment.

Karen didn't tell him the episode had caused something of a scandal on the island and that certain people, as Lucy had told her, wanted her dismissed. I told Jerry this as we walked slowly out to Ram's Head on one of the few mild days we'd had since the great storm.

"Fire Karen 'cause of a little thing like that!" Jerry exclaimed in disbelief. "They must be nuts. She's the best goddam teacher they'll ever get out here."

I said it wasn't a question of her teaching but of the moral values of some of the islanders.

"Moral values, shit! There ain't a bastard on the island wouldn't climb onto Karen give him half a chance. . . . They jus' don't like it when a nigger gets there first."

"That's not so, Jerry," I said sharply. I told him it wasn't the identity of Karen's lover that mattered, or even the probability of her having one, but her having been caught at it. But Jerry kept shaking his head. He wouldn't be dissuaded.

"Look, man, don't kid yourself. When a nigger buck gets to a white chick, all the white folks gangs up against him. . . . Maybe you think it's different when a white boy screws a black chick?"

We came to the lighthouse, looked briefly around, and on the way back I moved on to my main point. If Karen were dismissed, there would be much unpleasantness on all sides. Not only would the school be left without a teacher, probably for the rest of the year, but her family's relations with the islanders might be irreparably damaged. This could affect Kevin and Belle's relationship. Karen herself might never want to come back to Ram's Horn. Oh, I laid it on thick! Now I was getting to him—or so I thought.

"Finally," I said, "the humiliation to Karen in being fired from her first job might be more than she could stand."

"Oh, I don't know 'bout that," Jerry said neutrally, hocking his phlegm to the side of the road. "Karen's a tough little cookie."

"I wouldn't want the responsibility of seeing her pushed too far." I told him then what I had in mind: If he were to leave Karen to finish out the rest of the school year, the crisis would pass and the incident at Cutler's Cove would soon be forgotten. He only half listened while I outlined the advantages of this course, then he gave one of his booming laughs and clapped an arm on my shoulders.

"You sure all want this nigger off the island, don't you? So's nice white folks can have it *all-l-l* to themselves. . . . You talked this over with Karen?"

I said, with a sinking feeling that I had mismanaged my assignment, that it was his decision—not Karen's—whether he left or not. No one was trying to force him to. "It's for Karen's good," I said weakly.

"Well, I'll just have a lil talk with her," he said. "You know, my friend, Karen may not see it the same way you all do."

I left him at the Daceys' and went back to Cutler's Cove, depressed at the turn our conversation had taken, yet unable to figure out where things had gone awry.

Karen came down that same evening after supper. She was alone, and grim.

"You've joined the philistines, I hear," she said, dropping onto the sofa rather than the bear rug.

"Be fair, Karen. I did what the school board asked me to do."

"Well, I consider it a violation of Jerry's rights—not to mention gross interference in my personal life."

She'd never spoken to me so severely, and to ease matters I offered her a drink. She declined, so I poured myself one, very deliberately, then stirred the fire and added another log before sitting opposite her on the hearth. I lit my pipe.

"Well?" I said when she still hadn't spoken, staring at me without expression.

"Well what?"

"I thought you wanted to chew me out."

"I came down to find out where *you* stand in all this."

"What difference does it make where I stand, Karen? You've got yourself into a jam, and we're all trying to help you."

"By telling Jerry to run away?"

"Look, no one's *telling* Jerry to do anything. And as for 'running away' . . ." But I might as well have been talking to a wall for all the attention she gave me.

"Negro people have been running away for a thousand years," she said. "Because it was inconvenient for white people to have them around."

I said this was no new revelation, but it was irrelevant.

"What's relevant then, Socrates?"

I ignored her sarcasm and told her bluntly there was only one thing that was relevant as far as I was concerned: for her to get on with her job, which she could do best without the help of Jerry Lincoln.

"It's convenient, that is to say, if Jerry Lincoln shoves off?"

"It's reasonable, it's sensible, it's prudent."

"It's racist," Karen said flatly. "Jerry's being told to take off—or urged, it's the same thing—because he's a Negro, and you damned well know it."

"It isn't true, Karen. If Belle had your job and Kevin came out and they were found in the same compromising position you and Jerry were, Kevin would be expected to leave. And he'd go . . . with no fuss. You damned well know *that*."

But I made no more headway in persuading Karen than I had in persuading Jerry that race was not at issue.

During a pause in our conversation, I remarked in an undertone—half rhetorically, and immediately regretting I had said it—"Is he worth it, Karen?"

It was exactly *not* the thing to say to her.

"What d'you mean by that?" she snapped, eyes blazing.

I fumbled around for words. "Well . . . only that Jerry seems to be causing you a lot of trouble and . . . and . . ."

"And he's not just the company you'd like to have around?" she broke in. "*Now*, if Jerry just happened to be a Ph.D. or a big intellectual, somehow we'd muddle through, is that it? But since he's just an ordinary Negro, not too bright, not too well brought up, a little too noisy, then we've got to get rid of him. . . . You phony liberal!"

I was, in fact, beginning to feel a little stretched out over this matter, but I merely said, "You put words in my mouth, Karen."

"Because you haven't the guts to say them yourself."

"Well, let me try again," I said, getting up to pour myself another drink. "And it's not going to help matters if you pass this back to Jerry."

Karen, more subdued after her outburst, said she wouldn't, and after I had mulled things over a few moments, I told her what was on my mind. Jerry Lincoln wasn't cut out, I said, to be the focus of a cause célèbre. It wasn't that he was too brash or too insensitive. He simply didn't care. It was even perverse of her, I went on, to gratify her own sense of justice by using Jerry in a scheme for which he had no obvious appetite. If she let him alone, I told her, he'd probably leave of his own accord.

She offered no comment until I turned to the probable consequences to her of the course she was taking. I told her, in effect, that I thought it a sad mistake to risk her reputation and the goodwill of the islanders just for Jerry Lincoln.

"I don't give a fig for my reputation or what anyone thinks of me, if you care to know." She spoke with as much conviction as before, but more calmly. "It's much more important to me that Jerry doesn't get pushed around because he's a Negro than that I finish up the school year with a nice clean record."

Well, I respected her for that and told her so. But I got no further in persuading her to change her mind. A few minutes later, she stood up to leave.

"So where does this leave us, Karen?" I said. "Suppose the school board makes it a condition of your staying that Jerry leave the island?"

"He goes, I go," Karen said.

"And if the school board buys that and lets Jerry stay, how about . . . well, your personal—"

"I'm not taking a pledge of chastity for anyone," she said coldly—although sex, I gathered, was the farthest thing from her mind at the moment. "I've already told Lucy we'll be more . . . careful."

I stood watching her at the door. She was firm-jawed and stubborn. "You're a tough cookie—as Jerry says," I told her.

"I'm not as tough as I may sound," Karen said. She zipped up her parka, kissed me quickly—out of habit—and left.

Lucy told the school board members individually the next day that Karen would not ask Jerry Lincoln to leave the island, and he wouldn't go unless she did. It was a matter of principle with Karen, Lucy explained, not defiance. No one, Karen felt, and least of all a Negro like Jerry, should be pressured into leaving a place where he had as much right to be as anyone else. Lucy proposed that under the circumstances the school board let the matter drop. She was sure Karen and Jerry wouldn't misbehave again. A majority of the school board members were disposed to agree with Lucy, not wanting to stir up more trouble than had already been stirred up. But Lloyd Cutler wouldn't let the matter die.

"Are we runnin' this school? Or are we turnin' it over to a snip of a girl who don't even know how to behave herself?"

Two days later Lucy learned that Lloyd had gathered enough signatures to introduce into the warrant for the forthcoming meeting of the plantation a resolution, the effect of which was to ask Karen to send her friend away or herself be dismissed from her post. The affair was now out of the hands of Lucy's school board and had been passed to the islanders themselves to decide, since the annual meeting of the plantation was also the annual school district meeting. The actions of the district, of course, took precedence over any action of the board itself. Lucy was sick at heart over this turn of events and blamed herself for not having dealt with the matter more skillfully within the school board. There was nothing left for her to do but persuade as many islanders as she could to vote against Lloyd's resolution.

Karen, during the days before the plantation meeting, kept to herself. She worked long hours at the school, decorating the classroom for the evening program and working individually with the children on their pieces or paintings. She would have one child or another with her nearly every afternoon until dusk. She ignored the debate going on around her over Lloyd's resolution and appeared indifferent to its outcome. Jessica York, stopping by at the school to pick up Daphne late one afternoon, said, "Oh, Karen, I wish Jerry'd want to go so's you'd be sure to stay."

Karen replied, "I'm not worried about that, Jessica. The main thing now is that we have a good program."

But though she kept to herself, Karen did not consciously avoid the islanders. She went to the store every boat day for her mail and appeared not to mind if conversation among those who were there ceased abruptly as she came in. She would linger a few moments after her errands, as she always had, exchanging a remark about the weather or inquiring after some lobsterman's wife or child, then leave unobtrusively. If islanders she met on the high road chose to look away and not speak to her, Karen too lowered her head and pretended not to notice them. But she was ready enough to respond or to take the initiative if she thought they wished to be civil.

Karen's beauty took on a strange incandescence during those days. It was as though the emotional turmoil of the preceding weeks had stripped all the angularity from her features and laid bare the natural harmony of her face. She was thinner than usual, and pale, but she appeared absolutely calm. Rudolf York and I came upon her alone one mild afternoon, in a sudden burst of sunlight through gray overcast. She was taking a shortcut home through the meadow above Abigail's Spruces and had stopped to watch a bird. She didn't see us. We watched her in silence for some minutes, absorbed in her bird. She had loosened her hair and now absentmindedly pushed it from time to time out of her eyes. Then she moved slowly on, humming to herself.

"I do b'lieve," Rudolf said as we moved on ourselves, "she grows purtier every day. How's she do that . . . with all her troubles?"

Jerry and Karen saw less of each other than before his illness. He occasionally dropped in at the school to see his "kiddies," with whom he was still a favorite, but Karen paid little attention to him. Sometimes he met her after school and walked home with her, and they always had supper together with Lucy. But there was no display of warmth between them that I could see. And certainly no manifestation of passion.

These were difficult days for Jerry—more so, I think, than for the rest of us. He was by nature gregarious, accustomed to making friends easily in any society, especially male, and he was stung by the aloofness of the islanders. After Winifred had given him breakfast (usually late in the morning, for Jerry's full recovery from his illness was slow and he still slept a good deal), he would amble down the high road looking for company. Sometimes he'd stop in for a cup of coffee with Jessica or Marian York, with whom he kept up a sort of weary intimacy. He might spend half an hour at Caleb's, joining as well as he could in the conversation, grown desultory around the stove, then go down to the harbor. Often he joined Arthur on the car, waiting for the lobstermen to come in. He would shout to them noisily across the harbor as they picked up their mooring buoys, hoping for a response, craving some sign of friendship. But he rarely found it. . . .

He couldn't understand, he told me once, why islanders he knew to be sympathetic toward Karen seemed to snub him as much as those who were against her. What he failed to see was that the islanders weren't aloof out of disrespect for him, or Karen, but out of respect for each other. The debate over Lloyd's resolution had seized them all, and they knew instinctively they shouldn't aggravate one another by showing either favor or disfavor toward one of the principals in the case. Maine islanders don't easily dissemble; they simply grow uncommunicative.

As I had suggested to Karen—and the conviction grew with me as the days passed—left to himself, Jerry would undoubtedly have quit the island of his own free will before the plantation meeting, not because he thought this would help her, but out of sheer boredom.

"Man, this is a creepy dump!" he told me one dismal wet afternoon as we walked up from the harbor to pick up Karen. "I'd clear outa here in a flash if she didn't keep sayin' she wants me to stick around."

So Karen, out of stubbornness or perversity, blocked the one certain avenue of escape for her and our dilemma.

29

The evening before the plantation meeting I had supper at Lucy's with Karen and Jerry. Karen, in her somber way, was almost gay, telling us about the last-minute preparations for the concert and exhibition. She appeared totally unconcerned about the decision to be taken in the afternoon at the church.

"Karen," Lucy said, bringing more coffee from the stove after we'd finished eating, "I want to be sure you understand about tomorrow. . . ."

"I understand, Lucy," Karen said.

"I want Jerry to understand, too."

"He does. He really does."

"Well, let me just go through it once again—for my own peace of mind, if you like. The matter is now outside the school board itself and in the hands of the district meeting. That is, all the islanders over twenty-one. We have to vote on a resolution that makes your job . . . well, I guess you know what the resolution says."

"We know, Lucy."

"It's not a usual resolution. I don't remember another one quite like it, ever. But it's perfectly proper to vote on something like this. The plantation meeting can vote on just about anything it wants to. . . . Now, I have no idea which way the vote will go, but I do know it will be close."

"Oh, I think it will pass," Karen said calmly enough.

"I hope not, dear, but I don't know. . . . If it does, then Jerry will be expected to leave the island. Within a few days, I should say. If he doesn't, then you would be suspended from your position."

"Or fired," Karen said. "But it doesn't make any difference because I'd go anyway. That is, if Lloyd's what-do-you-call-it passes."

Lucy looked steadily from one to the other before she spoke again. "This is the way you both want it? Karen, you don't choose to ask Jerry to leave so you can continue your work at the school, which everyone thinks—"

"Lucy, I'd never think of asking Jerry to leave. It would violate his rights. . . . Why, I just couldn't do it."

"And, Jerry," Lucy went methodically on, "you don't choose to leave of your own free will to save Karen's job?"

"But my job's nothing compared to forcing Jerry to go," Karen said.

"I'm not talking now about forcing Jerry to do anything, Karen. I'm asking whether he wants to change his mind about leaving of his own volition. Let Jerry answer for himself."

"Well, I agree with Karen," Jerry said, scratching his head. "She's got it right. Can't you see, Lucy, if I pull out 'cause I'm told to, then I'm runnin' away. Same as it's always been. We never gonna better ourselves that way. . . . No, long's she needs me out here, I'm gonna stay. It's a question of Negro rights."

"There's no question of Negro rights, my dear boy," Lucy began, but she decided to pursue the matter no further with these two. "Anyway, you both understand what's involved. So we'll just wait and see what happens. . . . I wish I had been able to manage things differently."

"You mustn't worry about that, Lucy," Karen said with a sudden show of warmth. "I don't mind at all, really I don't."

Lucy said, "But I do."

Karen asked a few moments later, "It won't take effect immediately, will it, Lucy? Lloyd's resolution, or whatever it's called? I mean, it won't keep us from having the program tomorrow night? That would be really unfair after all the time the kids have put into it."

Lucy assured her that whatever happened at the plantation meeting in the afternoon would not affect the evening program, and soon thereafter Karen and Jerry went off to the schoolhouse in a light drizzle to complete the decorations.

Lucy poured us more coffee, and for a change we went to sit in the parlor. I lit a fire in the Franklin stove.

"I hardly ever come into this room," Lucy said as she sat in a rocker facing the stove. "We spent most of our time here early in the war listening to the wireless. Frank had it by his bed. . . . He spent his last years in this room, after he grew too crippled to get up and down stairs."

I'd never heard Lucy speak of her husband, and asked about his illness.

"A common arthritis," she said, "but it grew progressively worse. . . . Oh, he was gruff enough for ten cripples at the end."

"Was he in great pain?"

"He was in pain all right, but pain itself never bothered Frank. He tore off his little finger in the engine of the first boat he had and pulled the rest of his traps before he came in. It was inactivity he couldn't stand . . . after his active life."

She paused, and I sensed that she was purposely distracting herself because what she really wanted to talk about was Karen. "We had a curious relationship, Frank and I. I'd be hard put to call it love, even when we were first married. What little I know about love I've learned from books. But we understood each other. We could spend a whole day without speaking to each other, yet know what was in each other's mind. . . . And we had the children. Belle could bring him out of his blackest moods simply by coming and standing in the door. I don't believe he ever said an unkind word to Belle. . . . Yet it was Stanley in the end who broke his heart. Frank never got over the futility of that accident. He lived about three years after Stanley drowned, but he was never himself again."

She stopped talking, and after a moment went on in the same tone, as though she were pursuing the same topic.

"I've thought a good deal about Karen lately, and, you know, I've come to like her. I never thought I would. With that cold, immaculate beauty of hers . . . and so impersonal. . . . I think I've discovered what's so strange about her. I always used to think her coldness was due to her being so self-centered, so absorbed in herself she wouldn't let anyone near her. She was like a china doll, perfectly lovely to look at, but you couldn't touch her. I was thinking particularly of the men, of course. . . . Then she'd no sooner arrived out here this winter than Sam Clayton made up to her, and to my amazement, she encouraged him. Later Jerry Lincoln arrived, and she made herself available to him as well. Heaven knows what else happened along the way." I volunteered no additional evidence, and Lucy continued. "She has certainly proved herself touchable then. She is *physically* capable not only of attracting men but of responding to them as well. And yet *emotionally* she seems as cold as ever with her suitors. She showed no real warmth that I could see for poor Sam, and she shows scarcely more for Jerry."

I remarked that Jerry had seemed to me a pathetic figure in recent days.

"Ghostly, isn't he?" Lucy said. "Almost as though he weren't here. Karen's shadow . . . I've puzzled over her choice of Jerry, a perfectly pleasant but ordinary person. His being a Negro, of course, must have attracted her, with her ideas of equality and so forth. But then Sam isn't a Negro, and she seemed on her way to choosing him before Jerry arrived. And Sam's just as ordinary and pleasant as Jerry, when he isn't drunk. . . . What I mean to say is that Karen is so undiscriminating in her choice of lovers, with all she has to choose from, that she must be . . . well, contemptuous of men. She deliberately chooses lovers inferior to herself to show her contempt for the opposite sex."

I started to speak, but she waved me to silence and went on.

"Then I remembered something. When Karen came out at the end of last summer, Belle was still here, and I've never seen Karen more radiant. She positively shone, like a star, when she and Belle were together. And then this winter the only times I've seen her eyes light up and a smile spread spontaneously over that pretty face was when she first arrived, before Belle left. . . . You know, I think Karen's in love with Belle. Girls *do* fall in love with girls, don't they? I mean . . . I can't imagine she gets much response from Belle, but just to be near her would be satisfying, wouldn't it? Well, once I started thinking along these lines, I began to remember other things. Little things, like Karen holding Belle's hand when they were sitting together, or slipping her arm through Belle's when they went out. She used to love to comb Belle's hair. Then a week or so ago I gave Karen a batch of Belle's recent letters to read—she'd only received one or two herself from Belle—and she took them up to bed with her. When I came up a half hour or so later, I heard her still giggling to herself. She must have read those letters through a dozen times, poor dear. . . . Now you can tell me what you think of my amateur theories," Lucy wound up, settling back in her rocker and sipping her neglected coffee.

I told her she might have learned more about love from her books than most people did from experiencing it. There was nothing I could see in her analysis that wasn't plausible, and indeed probable.

"Well, thinking this way makes me feel more tenderly towards Karen," Lucy said. "But what a turmoil there must be in that poor child's head, with Kevin in love with Belle as well. . . . I wonder if Belle has any suspicion."

We were both silent for some moments, gazing into the fire and listening to the rain beat in spurts on the storm windows as the wind rose from the north.

"I do admire her courage in this present business," Lucy said at last. "I think it very brave of her to take a position she knows won't be understood out here and hold to it on principle. Don't you? Even if the principle's not quite clear?"

I said I'd settle in the present case for a little less principle and more common sense.

"You're too pragmatic," Lucy told me. "Is it better to do something that has a safe outcome but requires a compromise of principles, or to do what you believe in even though it brings you less advantage?"

But her question was rhetorical, and Lucy didn't expect me to answer. She went on presently: "I only hope Belle, if the time should ever come for her to do something odd or unconventional she believed in, would be as brave as Karen."

The day of the plantation meeting was blustery with squalls and strong northerlies. It was clearing weather at last, the lobstermen agreed. They came in early from hauling their traps and went straight home to eat before the meeting. There were never more than two or three islanders together at the store that morning, and conversation was subdued. Lloyd's resolution was on everyone's mind, but the islanders had talked about it so much the past week, in their homes and informally wherever they met, that as the hour approached to vote on it, no one cared to discuss the matter further.

We all gathered in the church at three o'clock. This was the first full meeting of the plantation I had attended—and the first, in any case, when I could vote as a legal resident. There was little talk as we took our places, waiting for Turk to call the meeting to order. He stood on the dais behind a podium that doubled as a pulpit when the *Sunbeam* was in or when Mr. Hargrave came over from Rockland. Marian York, who was plantation clerk, sat at a table beside him with her ledger. As the door swung open periodically to let in new arrivals, the children's voices rose in song from the schoolhouse, across the road. And there was irony, I thought, in this. Lucy had suggested that Karen might not wish to meet the students that day, but Karen wouldn't hear of it and held school as usual. She only asked Lucy not to tell her the outcome of the meeting until after the evening program.

The first part of the meeting was given over to annual island business. There were the plantation officers to elect, and all were continued for another year: Turk as moderator; Caleb Brewster, Arthur Dacey, and Rudolf York as assessors or selectmen; Marian York as clerk and treasurer; Clyde Grant as harbormaster; and so forth. Even the school board remained the same, Lucy and Lloyd Cutler, whose terms had expired, being elected for another three years. Caleb presented the budget, which came to just under $10,000, the lion's share of it for the school. It also covered road repairs, snow removal, replacement of a piling on the pier damaged during the recent storm, and modest salaries for the town officers—including $25 for Horatio Leadbetter as commissioner of graves. This caused a few sniggers when it was read out, but for the most part the islanders were subdued. The usual whimsical interventions that enlivened plantation meetings, as I understood, were conspicuously absent. Even Jenny Brewster, admonishing Walter York to speak up in his report on expenditures for church repairs over the past year "or we're gonna think you put it all in your pocket," drew only a ripple of laughter.

Lloyd Cutler's resolution was the last item on the warrant, and it was after four-thirty when he introduced it: "To see if the inhabitants will vote for a resolution to suspend the teaching contract of Karen Bannister for the remainder of the school year unless certain conditions are met—to wit, her making suitable apology for her recent behavior and providing concrete assurance it will not happen again." Lloyd had originally wanted to include specific reference to Jerry Lincoln's leaving the island, but Arthur had dissuaded him from this on the grounds that it would not be appropriate to single out by name a person who was neither a resident nor an official of the island; moreover, the plantation might someday be held in libel for doing so. However, it was generally understood that the "concrete assurance" sought from Karen was in effect her asking Jerry to leave; and this, it was agreed, would constitute a "suitable apology" as well.

We had heard the children leave the school half an hour earlier, after their last rehearsal; shortly after that, glancing over my shoulder through a window, I had seen Karen leave the school and walk slowly up the ridge alone, without a backward glance at the church. A hush fell over the room as Lloyd came forward to explain his resolution. He was brief and to the point.

"It's as simple as this," he said. "We got a schoolteacher who's misbehaved— the worst kind o' misbehavior, as I see it, for a woman in charge of children. And she don't apologize or promise she won't do it again. She don't even act like she's sorry. Then we ask her to send her boyfriend away so's we're sure it ain't gonna happen again, and she says she won't do that neither. . . . Now if anyone can tell me why we should keep on a schoolteacher like that, I'd like to hear it."

He returned to his seat, and there was silence again. Turk recognized Lucy. She stood at her chair and spoke in a low but clear voice.

"There's no doubt Karen misbehaved," she began, and several of the younger lobstermen snickered. "She doesn't try to deny it. I guess it's not the first time a young girl misbehaved like that . . . including some of us in this room." There were a few gasps at this from the older women. "Whether or not a girl is sorry afterwards depends on a lot of things, and you can't always tell whether she is or not. Karen Bannister may well feel some remorse—that is, feel sorry—for the way she's behaved but not want to show it publicly to all of us, whom she doesn't know as well as we know each other. . . . But I'm not trying to argue one way or the other about how Karen feels. I simply don't know, and I guess I know Karen now as well or better than any of us." Several heads nodded in agreement with this.

"What I do want to say concerns her attitude toward Jerry Lincoln's leaving, and this bears directly on Lloyd's resolution. To Karen it's a matter of principle whether Jerry goes or stays. She believes that for a Negro to be told to leave a place is not only humiliating but a violation of his human rights. She therefore sees what is proposed in Lloyd's resolution as biased and anti-Negro. . . . Now I don't happen to agree with Karen in this. I don't believe there is racial bias on this island, by Lloyd Cutler or anyone else. But I do believe that it is improper to ask someone who has committed no legal offense and who has not bothered us in any way to go away—simply because it is . . . well, more convenient for us. This is why I think we should vote against Lloyd's resolution, even though I know he offers it for our good."

Lucy sat down, and Jessica York spoke immediately, without waiting to be recognized.

"Lucy, I can see why Karen mightn't want to ask Jerry to leave, but supposin' it was the rest of us who asked him? And supposin' he left. Wouldn't Karen stay then?"

"I'm afraid there isn't a chance of it, Jessica," Lucy said. "She's made this very clear. If Jerry is asked to go, she'll leave too."

"Good riddance t' the both o' them," Ginny Clayton said.

Turk lowered his gavel sharply. "Keep to the subject, Ginny. . . . You got any more you want t' say?"

She didn't, and he recognized Leonard Ames, at the back of the room.

"I've a mind to ask Winnie how they've been behavin' lately at her house. They been doin' any cavortin' there, Winnie?"

"Not for the life of you," Winifred Dacey said tartly, reproving Leonard with a look for even suggesting such a thing. "They've sat a few times in the parlor, and when he was sick, Karen came every afternoon to sit with him for a spell upstairs. But either Sharon or I was always with them. . . . He's been a very well-mannered gentleman," she added, facing front again. "Although he's a little . . . well, lazy."

"Plumb wore out," Clyde Grant said, and there were guffaws from a number of the lobstermen. Turk tapped his gavel again but said nothing.

"How 'bout Cutler's Cove?" Leonard asked me. "I don't 'spect they been down there again, have they?"

"Except to visit with me," I said.

"What's the drift o' your question, Nardy?" Turk asked, using the name the lobstermen reserved for Leonard.

"Well, I been thinkin', Turk—Mr. Moderator—that if'n they been behavin' themselves as they'd oughta, maybe we don't need no resolution. Maybe this ain't gonna happen again."

Lloyd was on his feet. "Mr. Moderator!" he said, irritation in his voice. "We're gettin' off the subject. Maybe this ain't gonna happen again, and maybe it is. We ain't got no way o' knowin' for sure. What're we supposed to do—wait around till someone catches her at it again?"

"Harold'll spy 'er out," Clyde said, and there was laughter again from the lobstermen.

Turk said, "Let's take it easy, guys. We got a job to do. . . . Anyone else want to speak to Lloyd's resolution?"

Jesse Cutler did, and Turk recognized her.

"I just want to ask Lucy *why* in heaven's name Karen won't make a promise that she'll behave . . . since Lucy says she knows her so well."

"Jesse, she feels no one should be told how to behave in their private lives. Mind you, I don't believe Karen *will* misbehave like that again while she's out here, but she won't be forced into an oath or promise. . . . And, you know, that's quite reasonable. Public officials aren't obliged to take an oath that they'll behave themselves. In matters of private morals, that is. We don't require such an oath of Turk—"

There was general laughter at this, as Turk made a droll face at Sharon.

"What about Horatio?" someone shouted.

"We'd oughta!" Clyde said. "Be on the safe side."

When the laughter had subsided, Lucy went on, ignoring the interruption. "For you see, Jesse, again it's a question of principle with Karen. She feels—"

But Lloyd was on his feet again. "Principles and more principles, but none of 'em as does us a lick o' good. . . . Mr. Moderator, I move we vote on my resolution."

"I'll bring us 'round to the vote, Lloyd, don't you fret. . . . Now, is there anyone else wants to speak on this issue? . . . Lucy, you said all you want to?" Lucy nodded. Turk had Marian read the item on the warrant once again. "Well, you all know what you're votin' on, I guess. An 'aye' vote means you're for Lloyd's resolution, and that'll mean we'll lose our schoolteacher, probably pretty quick. A 'nay' vote means Karen stays, and Jerry Lincoln'll stay, too, so long 's he's a mind to. Everybody clear on it?"

A hush fell again over the room as a sharp gust of wind rubbed the branches of a pine tree in the cemetery against the eaves. Lucy turned to me and whispered, "There's no point prolonging it. I couldn't change any more votes if I talked another half hour. . . . We have to live with each other, with or without Karen."

Turk took the vote, by hand, and Marian counted the ayes and nays. There were twenty-eight of us at the meeting, all the adult islanders except Widow Barnaby; Claudia Jenkins, who was looking after Sharon's children; and old Clarissa Grant, who was with Clara's baby. Fourteen voted for Lloyd's resolution, twelve were opposed, and two abstained—Turk, as moderator, and Horatio Leadbetter, who didn't believe in voting. The voting was much as expected. The

Grants and Claytons joined the Cutlers in support of the resolution, along with Caleb and Jenny Brewster. The Yorks, however, were divided. Rudolf, Leonard, Jessica, and Marian were against the resolution, while Marian's husband, Walter, and Tucker's family were for it. Three family divisions, I noted to myself as Turk was tallying the vote. In addition to the Yorks, Sharon and her parents, and Clara Young and Jessica York, who were sisters, Harold Toothacher unexpectedly voted against the resolution—perhaps to atone for his gossiping, which brought on the crisis.

"Well, I guess the resolution's adopted," Turk said when he had announced the vote. "I'd 'a voted against it if there was a tie—but there ain't no tie. I hope we done right. . . . Lucy, will you break the news to Karen?"

Lucy said she would, and reminded everyone of the school program that evening. "It would be a shame if they didn't have a good turnout. They've all worked so . . ."

But before she'd finished, her words were drowned out by the scraping of chairs as the islanders rose to leave. Lucy sat on, gray and drawn, and I sat with her. Leonard and Jessica stopped to express their regret to her on the outcome of the vote, and she smiled bleakly at them. We were the last to leave, along with Turk and Sharon. Sharon's eyes were misty.

"I wisht I could've counted different, Lucy," Turk said.

"You ran the meeting very well, Turk," said Lucy, pressing his hand. "It was too much to expect a different outcome."

The school program was scheduled to begin at seven-thirty, but at a quarter to eight fewer than half the forty-odd islanders in residence at the time had gathered at the schoolhouse. The room was elaborately decorated with spruce boughs and greenery. The walls were hung on all sides with drawings and paintings done by the children during the winter. Most of them depicted typical island scenes, but a few ventured further afield. Chucky, for instance, had done a pencil drawing of the New York City skyline with a tugboat in the foreground that he managed to make look as large as the *Queen Mary*. Rudy York had done an alpine scene in color, with tiny figures skiing down sheer cliffs. Bubber had made a detailed map of the island, with every building shown, and Daphne had made a cardboard model of the church. Karen went about with the guests, explaining the exhibits with considerable animation. She showed no disappointment that the turnout was so meager. Nor did she express the slightest concern that her fate had been decided across the road that afternoon, and no one, of course, brought it up; Lucy cautioned the guests, as they came in, that Karen had expressly wished not to be told until after the program.

Karen wore a simple but spectacularly cut blue dress, flaring at the hem and shaped to her lean figure. Penny York and Judy Torrey gasped when they first saw her, then couldn't take their eyes off her, struggling for a free hand. Karen had applied makeup in moderation—I believe for the first time since she had arrived—and this gave her coloring and accentuated her handsome features. Her long blond hair, normally gathered together in a ponytail, fell freely over her shoulders. She was, in a word, more startlingly handsome that evening than I had ever seen her.

Jerry had on a clean shirt and one of Arthur's ties, and busied himself with the stoves, beaming when the guests complimented Karen on the decorations and exhibits. She asked him to do little chores with a faint smile and once stood holding his hand for several minutes while she talked to Janice Torrey. But Jerry was restless when he realized not all the islanders were there and several times went scowling to the door to see if more were coming along the ridge.

At eight Karen suggested we take seats so the program could begin. As we sat down, Jenny Brewster came in, puffing and red-faced, followed by a solemn Caleb; Sharon, who had come earlier with Turk and the children, was behind them. Lucy said under her breath, "I bet that was some hassle"—and later we learned that Sharon, not finding her parents there at a quarter to eight, had gone down to the store and told them bluntly if they didn't get up to the schoolhouse immediately, she would never set foot in their house again. Thus were the family divisions of the afternoon carried on into the evening.

Karen thanked us all graciously for coming, making no reference to those absent, and introduced the performers one by one with a brief explanation of what they were doing. Which, more often than not, was necessary. Each child had at least one piece on the piano, and she played duets with several. The older children recited poems as well, prompted sotto voce by Karen as required. All six sang in the chorus, rendering a dozen songs that ranged from "Three Blind Mice" to a short passage from a Bach cantata. The volume was low at the start, but it increased after our lusty applause following each song, so that by the time we all joined in "Auld Lang Syne" at the end, the chorus drowned out the audience. Jessica and Marian York had brought cookies and grape punch for refreshments after the performance.

Karen received the praises of the parents in silence, a shadow of a smile at the corners of her mouth. When it came time to say good-night, she embraced each of the children and told them how well they'd done.

"We havin' school tomorrow, Karen?" Bubber asked.

"Let's have a holiday tomorrow, shall we?"

Judy and Daphne protested simultaneously. "Oh, Karen! Please! . . . We gotta come clean up anyways."

"I think it looks nice just like this," Karen said, looking about her. "Let's leave it."

All the children, of course, knew of some controversy about Karen, and the three older ones already knew that a decision, which they didn't quite understand, had been taken at the plantation meeting that afternoon. But none of them could imagine life without her. At the same time they sensed the solemnity of the moment. Daphne, clinging to Karen's hand as her mother tried to put on her jacket, burst into tears. And this started off Chucky, who hardly ever cried. The parents of the other children, at Karen's urging, led them off as quickly as they could before there was a general collapse, and within five minutes the schoolhouse was empty.

We walked back along the high road under the stars, Karen beside Lucy with her hand in Jerry's. I walked just behind with Arthur and Winifred. The wind had fallen, and the night was clear and dry.

"Karen," Lucy said, "I just want to tell you what a wonderful thing you did this evening. Those children will never forget it."

Karen was silent a moment, then she said quietly, "Did it go as I expected this afternoon, Lucy?"

"The resolution passed. By two votes."

Jerry said, "Why, the crummy bastards," but Karen pressed his hand and silenced him.

"Well, that's that," Karen said presently, and changed the subject. "What a superb night! The weather really has changed, hasn't it, Arthur? I haven't seen stars like this in a month. . . . I suppose the lobstermen will be out at dawn, won't they?"

"If not before," Arthur mumbled.

Karen chattered on uncharacteristically about one thing or another until we reached the turnoff to Meadowlane, the rest of us disinclined to join in. She and Lucy left us there, disappearing arm in arm between the hedgerows.

30

That was the last I saw of Karen Bannister. She went straight to her room, Lucy said, but slipped out after midnight with only her duffel bag and went to Arthur's. She eventually persuaded him to take her and Jerry to Rockland that night in the *Sarah Lou,* the seas being so calm. Arthur, needless to say, was at first reluctant to be party to so wild a plan, not because the trip itself presented any hazards but because it seemed somehow Karen was running away from responsibilities. But when she convinced him she would be leaving on the morning ferry anyway, and for reasons which must be clear preferred not having to meet the islanders again, he agreed. They woke Jerry while Winifred made coffee, and the three of them set out, clearing the harbor long before the first lobstermen appeared at dawn. Arthur left them at the public landing in Rockland, and they went straight off to the station, he told us, to catch the early morning train to Boston. Lucy found a note on the kitchen table when she came down at seven. In it Karen thanked her for all she'd done, apologized for leaving so suddenly, and asked that her suitcase be sent on when convenient to Bucks County. There was neither a message nor a note for me.

Six weeks later Karen was dead. For some time we didn't know where she'd gone. I wrote George and Sally a detailed account of all that had happened— saying that despite the turn of affairs at the end, I thought Karen had conducted herself with a certain nobility—and Sally wired back immediately, "But where is she?" She didn't go home, as I had assumed she would, and Bennington College knew nothing of her whereabouts. Meanwhile, Jerry Lincoln's family, whom George contacted right away, didn't know where he was. His mother thought he was still "with one of his girlfriends somewhere in Maine." George initiated a search for Karen through the Missing Persons Bureaus in several eastern cities, but it was impossible, of course, to know where to begin looking for her. She had a hundred dollars or so in cash, he believed, including her school salary through February, but no activity was reported in her checking account.

Belle finally received a letter from Karen a month after she'd disappeared, postmarked in New York City but with no street address. It was a short letter, saying she was living with Jerry and they were "trying to work things out." When she was settled, Karen said, she would come to Northampton to see Belle; she wanted desperately, she said, to talk to her. Karen said nothing about the crisis on the island except that "things got pretty messed up, as you most likely have heard."

The search then narrowed to New York, but still without success. Kevin, taking time off from his studies at Columbia, spent his evenings roaming the bars in Greenwich Village, where he knew Jerry had friends, but he found no trace of either of them.

The third week in April, Karen showed up at Gloria Thatcher's in Wilkes-Barre. The two girls had stayed on good terms even after Gloria and Kevin had finally broken up, and Karen had been maid of honor at Gloria's wedding on the Cape the previous June. Gloria, who of course knew of Karen's disappearance, greeted her warmly, and after a "good frank talk" (as Gloria described it), let herself be persuaded to keep Karen's presence a secret for several days—until Karen was recovered enough to go home. She was emotionally exhausted, Gloria said, but otherwise totally rational and calm. Gloria didn't press her for details of the Ram Island episode, but she did learn that Jerry Lincoln, after several quarrels, had left Karen a few days before. Gloria had to go with her husband to a bar association dinner that evening, where he was speaking, and when they returned at ten they found Karen on the floor of their bedroom, shot through the head with a wartime Luger Gloria's husband kept loaded in his bureau drawer.

A few days later, after the family burial, I undertook on George and Sally's behalf to find out more about how Karen had spent her last weeks. I think George was afraid to ask Kevin to do this, for Kevin was bitter about Jerry Lincoln's role in the affair and said several times in George's hearing that if he ever came across Jerry, he'd tear him apart. We now had an address for Jerry, which his mother had given us, in East Harlem. He was out when I stopped by early one evening, but the landlady of the tenement said he would probably be at a bar off Third Avenue, which she named. I found him there with a mixed group of Negroes and whites, young people in their late teens and early twenties. He recognized me immediately and stood up to greet me, a broad smile on his face.

"You're a long way from home, man! How'd you-all find your way down here?"

I said his mother gave me his address and his landlady had told me where I'd find him.

"Say, that's some footwork!" Jerry said. "But if you're looking for Karen, she's gone. She's blown, man. I don't know where she's at."

He pressed me to join them at his table, but I said I wanted to talk to him alone, and we moved across to the bar. I would have preferred to walk outside. However, Jerry seemed uneasy when I proposed this, and I didn't press him.

"Well, how're them nigger-lovin' fishermen up in Maine?" Jerry asked as we sat on bar stools and ordered drinks. I ignored his question and told him briefly about Karen's suicide—he'd had no clue of it, of course, since there'd been only brief notices in a few of the New York papers. He was more startled than dismayed.

"Goddam! What d'ya know 'bout that! . . . Why, I was jus' around to her place, yesterday it was, to see how she was gettin' on . . . only they said she'd moved. She didn't leave no—"

"What happened to you two, Jerry? She gave up a hell of a lot for you."

Jerry was at first evasive, but at my prodding he eventually filled in some details of their month and a half together. There were few surprises. They'd come straight to New York and found a cold-water flat on 116th Street. Jerry found a few old friends and made new ones, mainly Negroes. Karen went out from time to time, but more often he went alone. When her money ran low, they both looked for jobs. He had one in a restaurant for a while, but lost it.

Karen found a good position as receptionist in a small midtown advertising agency.

I asked Jerry if she'd been happy. "Was she glad she'd run off with you?"

"Karen wasn't big on laughs, you know that."

Had they quarreled, I asked—knowing from Gloria's report that they had.

"Jesus, a few spats! Like anyone. . . . She had a tight fist on the money, you better know, considerin' all she's got."

"And what happened in the end, Jerry? Why did you leave her?"

"Hell, man, you know she was never the one for me. . . . I mean, like with all that college education. We'd never 'a made it. We was gettin' nowheres . . . just nowheres."

He looked back at his group across the room and winked at a pale Negro girl with short hair who was watching us.

"But Karen was a good kid," Jerry said, getting off his stool. "She was a real fighter, a real fighter for Negro rights. . . . Someday we gonna make a . . . a martyr of her."

We shook hands, and I left, sad and depressed. Poor Jerry Lincoln. I tried hard not to blame him, and of course he wasn't responsible in any specific way for Karen's suicide, but he seemed so pathetically unable to appreciate the sacrifices she'd made, so little deserving of them. . . . But then, Karen would in all likelihood have taken the course she did whether Jerry were deserving or not. She was driven by a force beyond Jerry Lincoln, beyond all of us, to her ultimate calamity.

Jingle had been urging me for some weeks to spend a few days with her in Portland, since the doctor had forbidden her to travel in the early stages of her newest pregnancy. I stopped over on my way home from New York after finding Jerry Lincoln. We dined out, with her husband, and went on to Otis's after dinner when Emil went back to his office to work. Otis had just come in from a hearing in Bangor and was sprawled out on his leather sofa listening to a Red Sox game. He looked gray with fatigue, but his spirits were as high as ever. He was an antidote to my depression in the aftermath of Karen's suicide.

"Stealing my girl again," he said, flicking off the radio as we came in. After we'd greeted each other, he studied me for some moments as I sat on another sofa with Jingle facing him. I'd noticed he often did this when he met an old friend he hadn't seen in some time—trying, I think, to take in visually any changes that might have occurred in his friends before exploring the changes in discourse.

"You know, pal, we're both nuts," he said. "Two middle-aged bachelors scrapping over a squiff barely out of her teens. And she's married at that. . . .

Lucky she keeps herself pregnant all the time."

Jingle said, "Typical locker-room jokes." But anyone could see she was pleased she had us in the palm of her hand.

"Begin at the beginning," she said to me, settling into her corner of the sofa to listen. And since we were not pressed for time, and they knew only bits and pieces of Karen's story, I recounted it to them in detail—not excluding even the episode when Karen bit me. Otis guffawed at this (the sadistic bastard). But on a more serious note, he said when I had finished, "How did I overlook this tragic beauty?"

I also told them Lucy's theory of Karen's curious attitude toward men and its relationship to her affection for Belle. Jingle listened attentively to this.

"You know, that's very perceptive of Lucy. I think she's right."

I said that committing suicide after being jilted by a man didn't exactly square with lesbian tendencies, however latent.

"But it does, don't you see? Karen couldn't do anything about her love for Belle in the kind of world we live in. With Belle, least of all . . . But if she could manage a normal—or normal-appearing—relationship with a man, then she'd be free to . . . well, free . . ."

"To bugger Belle?" Otis suggested. "Or whatever the ladies do?"

"Nothing like that, you clod," Jingle said, making a face. "But at least free to love Belle in her own way. . . . Anyway, she picks the most masculine thing she can find—and I guess her Negro was that all right—and she makes sure he's simple enough to manage. . . . But it doesn't pan out. The guy's too simple to appreciate her. Or he's too masculine for her to satisfy, and he runs off with another chick. Either way, her world falls apart."

I told Jingle that if I didn't know her so well I'd swear she'd been reading Freud.

Otis let out his belly laugh and said, "She wouldn't do it! I had to tell it to her piecemeal." But then, as he often did after he'd put in his wisecrack, he grew more serious. "Still, that's not bad, Jingle. . . . Only you don't believe it yourself, do you?"

"Why don't I believe it?" she said, ready to defend her view.

"You don't really believe these warmed-over theories in abnormal psychology actually explain Karen's behavior."

"Not all of it, perhaps. Her stubbornness about Jerry's leaving, for instance, or her refusing to promise anything about her personal affairs . . . these were conscious decisions. I mean, they came from her code of honor, or what-have-you. She reasoned these things out. But the parts of her behavior we can't understand so well—like her choosing obviously inferior males—can certainly be explained—"

I interrupted to remark that at one point she chose me, or appeared to be trying to. Was I so "inferior"?

But Jingle wouldn't be put off. "She chose you to bite, if I have the story straight, not to hide behind. . . . Moreover, even if she did choose you for yourself . . . as I would, dear"—this with a gentle pat on my arm—"it would only prove, don't you see, that she wasn't one hundred percent abnormal. Which nobody claims she was."

Otis said, shaking his head, "Jingle, you're either a fraud or a diplomat."

I said I wasn't aware there was a difference.

Jingle ignored both of us and went right on. "Karen didn't *know* why she chose men like Jerry Lincoln and Sam Clayton. She probably didn't even *know* she was in love with Belle. People don't necessarily *know* they are abnormal, or what we think of as abnormal—"

"Until wise old owls like us come along and tell 'em," Otis said.

"And I wonder whether we should," said Jingle in the same tone. She was silent a long moment. "I guess I'm beginning to feel a little uneasy talking about Karen this way. I never thought a great deal about her before . . . except, like everybody else, I loved to look at her. Somehow, poking into her secrets at this stage seems pointless and . . . well, unfair."

Otis and I looked solemnly at Jingle, ever attentive to her changing moods, ever responsive to her woman's wisdom. Otis flicked the radio on again, for the bottom of the ninth, and went off to his kitchen for ale.

Much of what remains in my story—and I say it with regret—unfolds away from Ram Island. It could not have been otherwise, given the cast of characters I have assembled. Belle, who becomes increasingly the centerpiece of my narrative, is off the island far more often than on it during these years. Jingle, adamant islander though she is and always will be, makes her home in Portland. Otis, who plays more than a passing role in my tale, had less reason to visit Ram Island after the lobster war, and his visits were infrequent. Kevin Bannister, the second principal in my story from this point on, returned only once to Ram Island—and very briefly— between his post-Christmas visit to Belle at the end of 1947 and the fall of 1951. Kevin's prolonged absence, unlike his mother's, was unrelated to Karen's tragedy; it was due to complexities in his life, which we will explore.

We may, in fact, begin with Kevin and Belle.

Book 4 Kevin

31

Belle was deeply affected by Karen Bannister's suicide. I'm sure, knowing Belle, she felt the personal loss (although she would be the first to acknowledge that her friendship with Karen was still in its infancy). But it was her own responsibility in the matter that troubled her most. It was a tragedy, she felt, that she might have averted. She blamed herself for not having kept in closer touch with Karen after too casually involving her in the treacherous shoals of island life. She rebuked herself for having been too eager, during their talks in January, to show off the islanders to best advantage and therefore having failed to warn Karen sufficiently about their prejudices. Then, of course, she was shattered that when things began to go awry she was not there. Why was she not summoned, Belle wrote her mother, when Lucy learned of the decision of the plantation meeting? Lucy, sensing reproof, conceded that Belle's being there might have changed matters, but pointed out—altogether reasonably— that the crisis came on so quickly and during a period when mails were erratic because of the stormy weather that there had not been time to communicate. This was small comfort to Belle.

In her next letter to Lucy she showed a bitterness toward her fellow islanders that shocked even an indulgent mother. "How can that leather-tongued Lloyd Cutler, who has never shown an ounce of charity to anyone in his entire thankless life, take on such a pious attitude?" And "What do Clyde and Clara Grant know about 'morals' after all that's gone on in that blasted family?" For Harold Toothacher, her venom had no limits. Lucy ruefully read me portions of this letter, then locked it away in the attic and said no more about it.

This was in March, immediately after Karen's departure from the island. Belle was not initially worried about Karen's disappearance. Under the circumstances, she wrote Lucy, it was altogether natural for Karen to avoid family and friends for a time. Belle did not trust herself, in her black mood toward the islanders, to come home—as she had originally planned—during her ten-day Easter vacation. She spent it instead with Kevin, part of it searching futilely for some trace of Karen and Jerry Lincoln in Harlem and Newark, part of it in Bucks County trying to reassure George and Sally; she and Kevin spent the last three days of her vacation by themselves in the Adirondacks.

As the weeks passed without news of Karen, Belle grew increasingly uneasy, the more so since it had been her optimism that had sustained George and Sally so long. When, therefore, she received the short note from Karen in mid-April, Belle was jubilant. Her confidence was vindicated; everything would come right in due course—with or without Jerry Lincoln. She dropped everything she was doing to telephone the news to George and Sally, Kevin, Lucy, and anyone else who might be interested, including Jerry's mother in Newark. This euphoric mood lasted until Kevin telephoned her with his grim message two weeks later. Belle was utterly crushed. She went immediately to Bucks County—in such a daze she forgot to tell even her house mother where she was going or why. Her idea, of course, had been to console Sally and George, but as Kevin told me later, describing the private family burial, it was a toss-up which of the three needed the most consoling.

Belle and Kevin having been drawn more closely to each other than ever during the emotional weeks before Karen's suicide, Belle naturally assumed, when she missed a period, that she was pregnant. She found, somewhat to her surprise, that she was not in the least troubled by the discovery. She was by this time so committed to Kevin that whether she married him sooner or later was of little consequence. The awkwardness of an early wedding was in its coming so soon after Karen's death. A wedding on the island, which in happier days she and Kevin used to contemplate with relish, was of course out of the question. Meanwhile, it seemed unfair to add to George and Sally's troubles a premature wedding because Belle was pregnant, although Bell and Kevin knew that neither George nor Sally would object to the marriage itself (I could have told them that George at least would have welcomed the marriage at any time). Since they persuaded themselves it would be inappropriate to discuss marriage with Kevin's parents at this time, Belle chose not to tell her mother either. They would, therefore, marry secretly and let their parents know in due course. They wanted me as witness. These were the decisions they reached when Kevin went up to Northampton a week or so after Karen's burial.

I received Kevin's letter a few days later, and since I had to return to New York for an editorial conference before the end of the month, I proposed a weekend late in May. Kevin met me in New Haven at seven-thirty on a bright Saturday morning, and after breakfast we drove to Northampton to pick up Belle. She came out of a late-morning class, somber yet radiant, a satchel of books over her shoulder.

"You look about as pregnant as my Great-aunt Agnes," I said.

"That's about the way I feel," she said, embracing first Kevin, then me. "I mean, like Great-aunt Agnes."

"Sign out, Agnes," Kevin reminded her.

"I did," Belle said. "And it struck me it was the last time I would use that name—legally, at least. I'd grown to like it. . . . Kevin, why don't we keep *both* our names?"

"I don't mind. Talbot-Bannister? Seems there should be a 'Lady' or something in front of it."

But they were not serious. Kevin and I went off for the makings of a picnic lunch while Belle changed and packed a small suitcase. We picked her up at French House twenty minutes later. I tried to persuade her to sit in front beside Kevin, but she wouldn't hear of it.

"It seems a girl going off to be married ought to have the seat of honor next to her intended," I said.

"It might," she answered, "in an ordinary wedding. But this isn't one. In fact, it's so *un*-ordinary I could be expelled for this. You're supposed to ask the dean."

"You can hardly ask the dean before you ask your mother," Kevin said as we drove off.

"They seem to think otherwise. Deans count for more than mothers here." She kissed me lightly behind the ear. "You see what a risky investment you've made."

We headed east into the Berkshires and stopped for lunch on a hillside pasture half an hour from Northampton. We were talkative but not animated. Karen still lay heavily on our minds, and inevitably we spoke of her—but not so searchingly as I had discussed her with Lucy or with Jingle and Otis. Kevin and Belle were Karen's intimates and contemporaries. They had to fix Karen in their minds in their own way. So I listened for the most part to what they had had to say, filling them in on a few details they had not learned.

When the Beaujolais was finished, I stretched out between two boulders and slept for an hour while Belle and Kevin climbed to higher ground. At three we drove on, and an hour later reached the small Berkshires village where Kevin had made an appointment with the local justice of the peace. The ceremony—if it can be called that—was starkness itself, and the gray old man who performed it did little to embellish the occasion. Belle's eyes grew misty, I noted, as he mumbled the vows for her to repeat, but it was from the solemnity of the moment, not from any mood the gray old man evoked. She drew closer to Kevin and pressed his arm. When the old man pronounced them man and wife, they stood staring blankly at him until he prompted them, looking over his rimless glasses, "Well, go ahead and kiss each other. That's what ye do next." They did this, paid the old man his fee, and we left.

In Kevin's car again, driving to the inn where we had reservations, Belle and Kevin looked at each other—I had succeeded at last in putting the bride in front—and burst out laughing.

"It's crazy, isn't it?" Belle said when they had laughed themselves out. "We'll remember that silly old man long after we've forgotten everything else that's happened today."

Kevin said, "Let's hope so. He married us."

We came to the inn, set back from the elm-lined village street. I tried again to leave them, and even asked about trains to New York from Stockbridge, but Belle wouldn't hear of it.

"We're in this together," she said. "You're not to run off because of old-fashioned notions of honeymoons."

So I joined their "honeymoon," or the parts of it when they were not together in their bedroom. They were neither gay nor sad, neither demonstratively affectionate nor studiously restrained, neither jubilant nor solemn. Belle returned to the subject of marriage that evening at dinner—after I had presented her with a jade necklace that I had ordered for her in Lagos the year before but that hadn't arrived in time for Christmas.

"I keep thinking back to that ridiculous ceremony this afternoon and what it's supposed to mean. I can't really believe it means anything, can you, Kevin? I mean, how can mumbo jumbo like that change our lives?"

"Having conned me into marrying you," Kevin said with good humor, "I hope you're not already thinking of running away."

"If I were, nothing that man said would stop me."

Kevin studied her indulgently as she fingered the stones around her neck. "What's eating you, baby? We're married. Isn't that enough?"

"What I'm trying to say, I guess, is that a wedding—leave aside that silly business this afternoon—doesn't make a marriage."

"But you can't have a marriage without one," Kevin said lightly.

"Don't quibble with me," Belle said; she would not be put off. "The decision to get married is a tiny little decision. It's just the beginning of the whole thing, don't you see?"

"Amen," I said.

"Maybe we made ours weeks ago, when I found out I was pregnant. Maybe we made it last fall, when we first went off alone together. Maybe we made it long before that, when we began to know each other on the island. All I can say is that it was a small decision compared to all the others we'll have to make."

"Anyway, it was the right decision," Kevin said, still bemused by her earnestness, but gentle. "We start off with one correct decision."

We walked about the village for half an hour after dinner, under the tall silent elms, and retired early to our rooms. I lay in bed some time before dropping off to sleep reviewing in my mind the curious assortment of circumstances that had brought Belle and Kevin together in this fashion. It was only then I remembered that since picking up Belle at noon, we had not once talked of politics.

32

I did one other thing during that short trip away from the island in late May. I spent a night with George and Sally Bannister in Bucks County. George had written to thank me for my report on Karen's last weeks in New York—though there was surely nothing edifying or heartening in that report—and urged me to visit them next time I was down (or was it up or back, from Maine?—he never could remember). Sally had asked me many times before. They met me in their chauffeur-driven limousine in New Hope late in the afternoon, and we twisted our way through the byways of Bucks County to their sprawling farm set in a lush valley between rolling hills. They were still drawn and haggard from their experience, but they seemed genuinely pleased that I had come. Sally compulsively began to flirt with me.

"Rogue!" she said, embracing me warmly as I stepped from the train. "You've never come to visit us."

I told her she was looking lovely, as always, and she said, "Come off it! If I'm alive at all, it's thanks to tranquilizers and George. . . . " She added under her breath, still clinging to me, "and booze."

She and George were getting along better than I expected they might be. George was solicitous of Sally's comfort and pleasures. He opened doors for her, brought pillows when she stretched out on the divan, and asked her respectfully if there was anything he could do for her. I could tell that these attentions were not simply for my benefit but were part of a new relationship they were forging. He also filled her ever-present Scotch glass when it was empty—but I soon suspected this was due less to gallantry per se than to a hope he could keep her drinking within bounds. Sally drank a good many Scotches while I was there, and if I had to give a layman's opinion, appeared to be headed into an advanced stage of alcoholism.

Sally, meanwhile, was tender toward George. She had put aside the sarcasm I remembered from two summers before, when she would say things in public that hurt him—"Unbend, George! Don't be a goddamned stuffed shirt!" or "George, if I hear that crummy story again, I'll scream!" Instead, she would sometimes say, "Kiss me, George." And George would come gravely across to where she was sitting or lying and stoop to peck her cheek or forehead. It was a ritual, like many others in their life. For instance, when we sat down to dinner at the candle-lit table in their paneled dining room, he took her chair from Grace, the second maid, and held it out for her. "Thank you, dear," Sally said, and he patted her fondly on the shoulder. Again, this was no act put on for me, but part of the new ritual of their life. Whether it was the ritual that held the relationship intact or the new relationship that had created the ritual, there was peace between them.

Sally showed once at dinner how deeply Karen's tragedy had affected her. George happened to mention in the course of our conversation a small alteration he meant to undertake at Ram's Horn when they were back. Sally took him up immediately.

"Well, you'll have to do it without me, dear. I won't be there."

George looked at her patiently before he replied. They had evidently been through this before.

"We'll see," he said quietly. "Maybe you'll change your mind."

"But I won't." She spoke without passion, as though she were renouncing bridge or canasta. But her words belied her bland tone. "They murdered my baby. I'll never go out to that island again."

I remembered Cecil Allen's resolution to the same effect the morning after his house was burned during the lobster war of 1946. Looking sidewise at Sally, I decided she was as likely as Cecil to hold true to her word. This was, in fact, the only mention Sally made of Ram Island or the islanders (other than Belle) while I was there.

After dinner Sally had a call from Lou Thatcher in Pittsburgh and was twenty minutes or so in the library talking with her. George and I sat over our coffee on the flagstone terrace, looking out across a man-made pond to a pasture where George kept his Black Angus. We could just make out the cattle in the gathering darkness.

George asked after Lucy Talbot and the Daceys, then asked if I had seen Belle. I saw nothing amiss in my saying I had, and told him I had just come from her in Northampton.

"Was K-Kevin there?"

I could see no risk in acknowledging this as well, and said we had driven up together from New York. George seemed surprised I hadn't mentioned this before, then said that must have been a nice weekend for the three of us.

"Our little plan is w-working well, isn't it?" he said, meaning the financial arrangements for Belle's education.

"Very well," I said. "It's made a world of difference in the way she's maturing. It was a noble idea of yours, George."

I sensed George's flush in the dark. "What will she d-do after college, I wonder," he said. It occurred to me Belle would be having her baby in the fall, and we would have to make alternate arrangements for her senior year. I suggested, to prepare George for contingency plans without going into the whys and wherefores at this stage, that Belle might take time off before her last year at Smith.

"That's a c-capital idea," George exclaimed enthusiastically. "What if she were to go to F-France for a year? Kevin says she speaks French very fluently."

I said I knew she did, and agreed that a year's study in France someday would be good for Belle.

"Talk to her about these p-possibilities, won't you? . . . We've had poor Karen so much on our minds these past weeks that I haven't thought enough about Belle. I want her to do whatever she cares to about her education, George."

Sally's laughter rose from the library, where her conversation with Lou Thatcher continued, and George reminded me again that he had not discussed with Sally our arrangements for Belle's education. I assured him that, so far as I was concerned, none but the two of us would ever know of them.

I asked George, on an impulse, what had drawn him so strongly to Belle to make him want to be her patron saint; if I wasn't mistaken, his interest in helping Belle with her education had preceded Kevin's falling in love with her two summers before. "I wonder if it was any single thing," George said thoughtfully, setting his demitasse on a low glass-topped table. "She was a lovely child, of course. Everyone enjoyed w-watching her."

I said the same was true of Karen, as I had heard.

"Yes, everyone admired Karen, too. But Karen was . . . well, more aloof, more brittle. Belle was warm. And so s-serene. She would climb up on Arthur Dacey's knee in Caleb's store, or on old Rudolf's, and sit for half an hour at a stretch, thumb in mouth, while they swapped yarns. If she walked up to the ridge road with you, she took your hand. Anyone's. I remember walking up one day with Wylie Thatcher, the first summer he was out, and she came up between us and without saying anything took a hand each. Wylie looked down in some surprise and said, 'George, it looks as though we're going to adopt another little girl.' Belle said, 'What's "adopt"?' and when Wylie told her, she thought a moment and said would we adopt Mummy and Daddy and Stanley, too."

George paused to light a cigarette and cocked his ear to judge whether the phone call from Pittsburgh was coming to an end. Then he continued. "Perhaps there *was* a moment, though, when doing something for Belle first came to my mind. It was before the war. She was still only ten or eleven. I think we were getting the children ready to go to camp. Anyway, there was a lot of confusion around the house. Kevin had broken something of mine, and I was giving him a tongue-lashing for it while he pretended to pay no attention. Sally had just criticized Mary Lou for something in the kitchen, and she had sassed back, so they were squabbling away. Karen was in tears about something else.

"Then Belle walked into the house with lobsters we'd ordered from Stanley. We were making so much noise, I guess we didn't hear Stanley drive into the yard with his old truck. He left Belle and went on to do another errand. Well, the sight of B-Belle brought us up short. Karen stopped crying. Sally broke off in the middle of a sentence. I quit shouting at Kevin, and Kevin came out of his sullen mood. Even Mary Lou's pouts turned to smiles. By the time Stanley came back for Belle ten minutes later, we had forgotten what we were all quarreling about, and I don't think there was another unpleasant word the rest of the day. . . . Well, I reasoned that a little girl who could bring that much s-sanity into a home was worth doing something for."

I nodded in agreement. We could hear Sally winding up her call from Lou. George went on in a more subdued tone, "Stanley Talbot's accident later that summer also had something to do with it, I suppose. Coming on top of Frank's arthritis, it put a strain on Lucy's resources. I didn't think Belle should suffer for those unkind turns of the wheel."

He flicked his cigarette out onto the grass, and a moment later he said reflectively—more to himself, I thought, than to me—"That was the summer Sally had a c-crush on Stanley Talbot. . . . I think she even fell in love with him, strange as it may . . ." His voice trailed off, and we were sitting in silence when Sally joined us a few minutes later.

"What are you two doing? Getting stoned on cold coffee? George, get the poor man a drink."

We stayed out on the terrace another hour or so, watching the fireflies and talking about one thing or another until George, after yawning several times, announced he was going to bed.

"I'll be along soon, dear," Sally said. "I'll chat a bit with my lover."

George kissed her on the forehead and shook my hand. "Don't keep each other up too late," he said.

"Let out the dogs," Sally said after him.

We sat in silence for a time, listening to the two Labradors barking into the night on the other side of the house, then George climbing the stairs, and finally just the frogs in the pond.

"Fill 'er up," Sally said, handing me her glass. "Not too heavy on the water."

When I returned, she motioned me onto the wicker sofa beside her and slipped her free arm through mine.

"Can't talk unless I'm in physical communication," she said. "Old habit." After a few more moments of silence, she said, "Nothing turns out right."

"Some things do," I said neutrally.

"Such as?"

"Kevin and Belle?" I suggested.

"The happy warriors . . . Don't talk about happy people, knucklehead. I want to talk about me."

"Let's," I said. "You begin."

"Don't be a clown. I'm serious."

I assured her I was, too, and she settled closer to me.

"Story of my life," she began. "Ten percent luck. Ninety percent failures . . . First, I met George. Irish working-class kid makes good. That used up all my luck. Well, I was going to be a great society hostess. Lace curtain Newark to Park Avenue in one step . . . Actually, I wouldn't have been bad at it. But George didn't buy the idea. Correction—he vetoed it with a vengeance. He wouldn't even live in New York. So I fell back on Plan Two: I would raise a huge happy family. *That* was surefire. Anyone built like me could have a bunch of kids. That idea burst when I was told after Karen I couldn't have any more."

"That's hardly a failure," I interposed.

"Don't interrupt. So then I made a really big decision. I was going to be just a good wife and mother. You know, devoted as hell, learn to cook and sew, family picnics, all that gas. That gets boring after a while. Even if you're good at it, which I wasn't. So my little libido began to suggest that maybe I could be a good wife and mother *and* have a little lovin' on the sly. You know—well, you probably don't know—this idea comes easier to a girl who knows she can't have children. You can be pretty sexy if you don't have to carry around a bagful of paraphernalia. . . . But finding a good lover, my friend, is like finding a needle in a haystack. When I was younger and didn't want 'em, I couldn't keep 'em away. Then when I wanted 'em, they were nowheres around. Fancy that!"

She paused to pour back half her drink. "Oh, I had a few," she said. "And don't try to guess which ones they were."

I said I wouldn't dare, since I had always been under the impression there were so many.

"You're a phony," she said. "You never thought any such thing. . . . But my lovers didn't give me much pleasure, beyond feeling wicked. Except for one; until he died . . ."

She drained the rest of her drink and handed me her glass. When I seemed dubious, she nudged me and said, "Go along, you prude. Or I'll have to go along myself . . . and not so much water. I'm serious. Should always have the biggest ones before you go off to sleep. Then if you're sloshed, no one minds. I'm always drunkest asleep. What d'you think 'bout that?"

I said I thought it a waste of money.

"Money's no object 'round here," she said, standing up unsteadily. "Run along and fill my glass. I'm goin' pee-pee."

She came back from the downstairs lavatory as I returned from the pantry, and we sat again on the wicker sofa, the Labradors curled at our feet. She went on as if there had been no interruption. "So I was happy that once. It helped me over a bad time. Then when I was ready again, you showed up. And for a while I had fancy ideas about you—as I 'spect you noticed. Only you wouldn't play."

I was startled by her phrase—the same one Karen had used that night in Cutler's Cove—and I must have shown it, because Sally looked up at me suddenly.

"What's eatin' you? You look as though you'd seen a ghost," she said. I said nothing, and after a few moments she went on. "You could have made the dif-f'rence, actually. I mean, you could have tided me over another bad spell, after the war. And I would have been in better shape for this last failure. . . . Oh, this one hurts," she wailed, and I could feel her quiver beside me. "My poor little baby! Maybe I wasn't the best mother to her, but how I miss her now. . . ."

I put an arm around her, and she wept soundlessly for several minutes, then blew her nose and said in her normal voice, though thickly, "Well, that's the story of my life."

I said it rang true enough, except she had the percentages mixed up: measured by any criteria that mattered, it was success, not failure, that tallied ninety percent. "Your only trouble, Sally, is you can't count."

Ten minutes later I said it was time for bed and pulled her to her feet. She made no resistance, but when I tried to guide her into the house she shook me off.

"I'm not that decrepit," she said. "Put the dogs in. Laundry."

I called them, and they followed me through the house. Sally stopped in the pantry to top up her drink. At the foot of the stairs, she put her finger on her lip and said, "Don't tell George I cried. Thinks it"—she hiccoughed—"unmanly." She wouldn't let me help her upstairs. At the top she kissed me on the cheek and weaved down the hall to her bedroom next to George's. I waited until she disappeared inside, then turned in myself.

Sally was still asleep the next morning when I left. George drove me to the station after breakfast and a brief tour of the farm. At New Hope, waiting for the train, George said, "What can we do to p-put order back into our lives?"

33

I did not see Kevin again until the Progressive Party convention in Philadelphia in July. Although an indifferent supporter of the Henry Wallace revolt, I was disgruntled enough with American foreign policy at this time to respond when my former college roommate, an aide in Wallace's entourage, asked me to help in drafting the platform. The platform committee met for three days before the convention, and we finished our work as the delegates were filling hotels in downtown Philadelphia. I have to say I was a disenchanted hanger-on after those three days, coping repeatedly with the heavy-handed pressure on the Wallace camp from the extreme Left: Which priorities? Flexible or inflexible wording of the planks? Was Russia to be criticized as well as the United States for the Cold War? And so forth. I very nearly left Philadelphia when the platform was completed, but decided to stay through the giant rally planned for Saturday evening in Shibe Park. The launching of a third party in American politics had, after all, a certain historic interest. Moreover, I hoped to catch a glimpse of Kevin, whom I hadn't seen since the Berkshires; I knew he would be in Philadelphia that weekend.

There had probably never been a political convention quite like this one. The externals were not very different from any political convention: the crowded hotel lobbies; the flustered volunteers at registration desks; the harassed hotel staffs; the wandering in and out of upstairs bedrooms; the display of lapel buttons (but no straw hats); and everywhere the vacuous, pretentious chatter of amateur politicians. What was different was the participants. The majority were under thirty, and many were not yet old enough to vote. The proportion of women was high—not the pretty, well-tailored sort that appear traditionally at major party conventions to boost the appeal of some uneasy candidate, but plain, serious girls wearing horn-rimmed glasses and dressed in slacks, or dynamic little ladies with short gray hair bustling to and from with bundles of petitions. There was also a high percentage of blacks—high for that era—as well as of stony-faced workers, dressed in inexpensive brown or blue suits and ill at ease with college students in open shirts and seersucker trousers. There were also aging intellectuals—professors, writers, artists—who gravitated to each other in small clusters.

The signs of Communist sympathies and influence were persistent. Near the elevator of my hotel a Party activist was explaining to an enrapt audience of

Midwest coeds the strategy to be followed in voting a certain amendment to the platform. Another activist, a copy of the *Daily Worker* poking ostentatiously from his pocket, was talking to a group of sullen coal workers on a carpeted landing about the "Indictment of the Twelve," which had been handed down earlier in the week—that is, the indictment of twelve Communist leaders for conspiracy. A Negro girl with a high hairdo and a tag on her blouse identifying her as a Communist delegate from San Francisco was puzzling over a two-week-old copy of *Pravda* with a blond male delegate from New York. At the hotel entry a flutter of excitement signaled the arrival of a high Communist official, escorted by a Wallace aide, on his way to a conference upstairs.

Correspondents and reporters for all major radio networks and newspapers, as well as for many lesser ones, milled aimlessly about, hardly knowing whom to buttonhole in this ragged assortment to gather material for their releases. A reporter whom I knew slightly spotted me and whisked me off to a bar across the street as though he had captured the only human being at the convention who spoke his language. He was incredulous when I told him I had been working on the platform, and quickly gathered half a dozen fellow correspondents who had come away from the milling throngs in the hotel lobbies in despair of finding anything but background stories.

"Get this!" my reporter friend said. "He wrote the goddam platform."

"G'wan," one of them said. "It was all made up in Moscow."

I told them they wouldn't need me if it were. I explained several of the foreign policy planks in the draft, which had already been released.

"Jesus, man, do you *believe* this crap?" one said.

Another asked if I were a Commie, and when I threw up my hands in protest, he asked why, in that case, I was for Henry Wallace.

"Wallace is no Communist," I said.

"Well, everyone around him sure as hell is . . . and these crazy kids!"

Conversations generally went like this with the outsiders. With those involved in the convention itself, communication tended to be saccharine.

"Isn't this wild?" a freckled girl not out of her teens said to me while we were going up in a crowded elevator. "I mean, everyone's so terrific. I don't think there's a phony anywhere in Philadelphia."

An ageless man in dark glasses standing in the rear of the elevator—probably an FBI agent—peered at her stonily over intervening heads.

I did not see Kevin until the rally in the baseball stadium Saturday evening. But first, a word about Belle. She had written ten days after their wedding that she hoped she hadn't involved me in a hoax, because she wasn't pregnant after all. She guessed things had simply "gotten a bit mixed up inside" during the emotional strain over Karen. Neither she nor Kevin minded, she wrote. They were glad they were married, but since there was now no need to tell anyone about the secret wedding, they had decided it keep it secret for the present, and would I agree to this. I wrote back that of course I would. I proposed to her—in line with my conversation with George Bannister in Bucks County—that if she thought a year, or even a summer, in France would profit her at this stage, and if this suited their plans, my "legacy" would easily cover it. In her next letter, written at the end of her examination period, she thanked me for the suggestion and said she very much counted on going to France someday, but not until after her senior year. Besides, she would not feel comfortable borrowing more from me until she had begun to pay some back. She had a job in Washington in one of the government agencies until the end of July and planned to go there directly without returning home. She would spend weekends with Kevin in New York. Kevin, she wrote, was "up to his neck in politics again, poor boy."

When I saw Kevin he was standing on a street corner a block from Shibe Stadium hawking a special convention edition of the *Sunday Worker*. He wore slacks and a turtleneck sweater and had on a white cap, like a milkman's, with "Daily Worker" stitched across the front. He had his ribbons—including, conspicuously, the Distinguished Flying Cross and his Purple Heart—pinned to his chest; he also had his cane looped over his arm, though it was two years since I had seen him use it. The crowds moved slowly past him, noisy and uninhibited.

"Get your *Worker* here! All the details on the convention. Step right up, folks. . . ." And people who had never read the *Daily Worker* in their lives bought copies as though they did it every day.

I detached myself from the group I was with and worked my way grimly toward Kevin. He wasn't surprised to see me since he knew I had been working on the platform. I came straight to the point.

"What's this all about, Kevin? Have you joined the Party?"

"Won't we all!" he said, infected by the euphoria that surrounded us.

"Where's Belle?"

"She's coming up tomorrow," Kevin said as he turned to sell more copies of the *Worker*.

"Does she know?" I asked him when he was free again.

"Know what? . . . Buy your special edition of the *Sunday Worker*!"

I felt like shaking the silly hat off his head. "Does Belle know you joined the Party, you dolt?"

"Sure . . . sure she knows."

"And what does she say about it?"

Kevin turned away to deal with a group of delegates from Chicago, and was busy for some minutes with them while I stood by.

"How's that again?" he said when this group had moved on. "Oh, Belle . . . We're working on her."

We're working on her! This was his wife he was speaking of. But before I could respond, we were interrupted again, this time by a red-haired boy in a dirty corduroy shirt, also wearing the milkman's cap.

"Say, Bannister, got any more *Workers*? These things are goin' like hotcakes!"

Kevin introduced me, and the redhead said, "Ain't this a ball, man? This is gonna be where it all began!"

"What?" I said rudely.

"I mean, can't you feel it all around you?"

He took a spare bundle of *Workers* from Kevin and snaked his way through the throng to the opposite corner. Kevin was busy with new customers. It was clear there would be no conversation with Kevin that evening, so at the next opportunity I attempted to bid him a hasty farewell before looking for my platform colleagues.

"Listen," Kevin said, "there's a party after the rally. Come along." He mentioned the name of a Swarthmore professor I knew by reputation who lived in Rose Valley. "It's a mixed group," he went on. "I mean, not just our people. You'll feel at home."

I said I'd be in bed by the time the party got started, and moved away. I remained depressed most of the evening. Throughout the elaborately staged rally—the deep-throated songs of Paul Robeson, doyen of American radicals; the lilting cowboy ditties of Wallace's running mate, an ex-radio performer from Idaho; and the thundering rhetoric of the ever-optimistic Progressive Party spokesmen, including Henry Wallace himself—I kept seeing Kevin Bannister standing on the street corner with his ridiculous milkman's hat and his ribbons.

As things turned out, I did see Kevin again that night. After the rally I went out to Media with several of my platform colleagues for a nightcap at the home of one of them. On our way back into town, my friends suggested we stop off in Rose Valley, where they too had been invited. It was after midnight when we arrived, and the party was in full swing. There were fifty or more guests standing or sitting in clusters on the broad terrace or in the downstairs rooms of the spacious, untidy house. It was a very heterogeneous gathering, more or less mirroring the convention itself. We found our hostess, a convivial but distraught woman in her forties, with some difficulty and greeted her; her husband, she said, was upstairs quieting the children. We moved about among the guests, a dozen or two of whom I recognized. Kevin was sitting on the floor of the library with a group of young people and waved when he saw me at the door. I signaled to him to stay where he was and after finding a drink attached myself to another group on the terrace.

They were talking about the survival of the family as an institution in the coming socialist era, and I plunged—perhaps too recklessly—into their discussion. The family had survived for some millennia, I pointed out; why shouldn't it continue to?

"Well, since the family was held together by despotic fathers or grandfathers," a willowy, dark-haired girl patiently pointed out, "that suggests—"

"Or despotic mothers and grandmothers," I interrupted.

She conceded the point. "I mean, whoever held the property and had control of the inheritance."

"There is no other reason, I suppose, for a family's holding together than the expectation of inheritance?"

"Well, what's to hold it together," the freckle-faced girl I had seen on the elevator asked, "if someday there isn't any private property? I mean, if there isn't even inheritance . . . or anything?"

I suggested blood ties, kinship, clannishness. "Some even used to say . . . love."

"O, well . . . love," she said.

I asked her—my tongue loosened by the Scotch I had drunk earlier—if she had ever been in love.

"Well, sure . . . Who hasn't been?" she said warily; I think she was afraid I was trying to proposition her.

"And didn't you enjoy it?" I pressed on.

"Of course. It was cool."

I restrained myself from saying I hoped not too "cool" and went ahead with my argument. Didn't she think that if the emotions unleashed by that love of hers were developed and reciprocated, they would be sufficient to keep her and her husband and their children in a special relationship to each other through a lifetime—even if no property was involved?

Several now started to talk at once, but the willowy brunette finally made herself heard above the others.

"The point is," she said, "that if there is property, the family is held together artificially. That's not at all the same thing you're talking about, where the family is held together by the husband and wife really being in love—"

"I mean, love doesn't last *forever*," the freckled girl broke in.

I asked why not.

"When you're seventy-five or eighty? Creepers!"

I said she confused love and sex. Sex was a small part of love.

The girl blushed, despite her brazen posture, and several of the boys sniggered.

"That's your trouble, Gladys," one of them said. "All sex and no love." And the boys laughed again, the more readily since Gladys had no conventional sex appeal.

"What's happening to the family in Russia?" another boy asked, evidently recognizing me from a lecture I had given some years before—I forget where—on social problems in the Soviet Union. I told him that if he was looking to Russia for a sign of a withering away of the family, he was in for a shock—the family in Russia was more idealized and propagandized today than it ever had been in the past; divorce was virtually impossible.

"Impossible?"

"It might as well be, the time it takes to get one."

"So what do they do, busted-up couples?"

I said they cohabited elsewhere, if either cared to. There was no stigma against common-law marriage in the Soviet Union.

"What about premarital sex?" the red-haired Communist, Kevin's co-hawker, whose name was Daryl, wanted to know.

I said there was little stigma against that either, though it was probably less prevalent than in the United States. Sex, in any case, was a private matter in the Soviet Union; it was never discussed in the media.

We talked a little longer about family relationships in Russia before Daryl abruptly asked me what I thought about premarital sex—as though anybody gave a hoot; I judged from the way he kept rubbing up against the brunette that he was trying to make points with her. I didn't enter much into the spirit of his inquiry but said I agreed with the Russians: Sex was a private matter. I stood up to get myself another drink, weary of playing anthropologist to these youngsters. But they wouldn't let me go and soon wormed from me an assertion that premarital sex was a serious matter.

"Why is it serious?" Daryl persisted. "Does it bust into the sanctity of the bourgeois marriage?"

"Even the proletarian, Comrade," I told him curtly. Then I decided to make my last stand. It used to be, I pontificated, that a girl's virginity had a certain cachet. It enhanced the value of the bride—and I was sure that they, as good Marxists, all understood the meaning of value. The girls struggled to keep their virginity with varying degrees of success. In some parts of the world, including most of America, it was still like this. But among the more liberated gentry—like themselves—sex had lately become another of the little goodies of life, like a T-bone steak or getting plastered. So, at least, they— But I didn't finish, because Daryl broke in.

"Life has passed you by, man. Like you're chained to the nineteenth century. . . . I mean, if I ball this chick here tonight"—he just *happened* to indicate the willowy one—"whom I met for the first time yesterday and may never see again, we don't do each other no harm. We do it because it pleases us, right? It's a mutual pleasure we have, me and her. Nobody else is involved. No one tells us, 'No, you gotta do it with *this* one an' you gotta go to the goddam church first.' See, man? We're doin' what we want to do. . . . You're makin' sex into some great phony thing you gotta do this way or that way, according to some fuckin' rules written by jerks two thousand years ago."

By this time I had had enough of the vapid discussion—certainly no less vapid because I had been at the center of it—so I simply said "Amen" and went off to find a drink or Kevin, or both.

I had not been able to see Kevin from where I was sitting on the terrace, but through the French windows I could see the black-haired girl beside him. She wore navy-blue slacks, a white blouse, and a large silver chain around her neck. I glanced at her several times as our discussion progressed, but not because she was particularly eye-catching—or even in my line of vision. She was leaning against his knees and occasionally turned to smile at him as they exchanged a remark. I was too far away and in my case too preoccupied with the conversation on the terrace to know what the group in the library was discussing.

As I came away from the makeshift bar in the dining room, where all but the last few quarts of beer had run out, she was waiting for me at the door.

"You're Kevin's friend," she said.

"That depends," I said. I gathered she was, in any case, and she asked how I gathered that.

"From certain portents," I said, the numerous beverages through the evening making me more elliptical than usual.

We moved to a settee in the hall, apart from the still-numerous guests who lingered on despite the low reserves at the bar. The grandfather clock facing us showed two o'clock, which was very nearly the correct time, although I realized a quarter of an hour later that the clock wasn't running.

I asked Kevin's friend what she did, and she gave me a précis of her life. Her name was Carmen de Silva. She came from Scarsdale. Her mother, a widow, was Orthodox Jewish, but she and her sister were agnostic. After graduating from high school in Scarsdale, she won a scholarship at Barnard, where she majored in economics. She had just graduated. Now she had a job in Congressman Marcantonio's office in East Harlem. She told me all this in a concise, clipped manner, but deferentially—as though she thought I was entitled to know this much about her, and indeed anything else within reason I might ask about. I gave her an A for precision. I also decided I had underrated her as I watched through the French doors into the library. She *was* eye-catching. But she was also cool and collected. She had an animal-like quality that made her physical appearance incidental—as the leopard's handsome coat is incidental to its instinct for survival.

I asked her for her verdict of the convention.

"I thought it was great," she said promptly. "Not every resolution or all the speeches, but the atmosphere. It had . . . well, purity. I didn't see anyone drunk tonight, did you? I'm sure you never say that of any other political rally."

My eye fell on a figure sprawled out on the floor of the living room, dead to the world.

"Oh, Peter." She laughed, following my gaze. "He always falls asleep after a couple of beers."

"So apart from Peter, it was all as pure as the driven snow. That's your idea?"

"That's my idea," she said equitably, not put out by Peter. "What's yours?"

I thought a moment. "Much enthusiasm. A nice ambiance—if you like things that way. And little of consequence."

"Boy! You *are* a spoilsport, aren't you?"

"I assume you don't expect Wallace to win?" I said.

"Well, victories in New York and California and perhaps Illinois would be quite an accomplishment, wouldn't they?"

I said they would indeed.

"And if we can do that, we can try again in '52."

" 'Wallace in '52,' " I said, quoting the slogan that had lately gained currency among the so-called realistic delegates at Philadelphia. I told her—more stuffily, I think, than I intended—that New York and California were pipe dreams; Illinois was a mirage—in '48, in '52, and forever.

She studied me quietly a moment, lit a cigarette, then said—still with no sign of hostility—"If you're so cockeyed sure we've no chance, why are you here?"

I said I'd asked myself the same question the last few days.

"Well, what else do you expect us to do? Would you like it better if we staged a revolution?" she asked.

I said I wouldn't necessarily *like* it better, assuming "they" could stage one, but I would find the posture more credible.

"You mean there's nothing between all-out revolt and accepting things as they are? The status quo!"

"That's not what I said. No one has to accept anything, but there are different ways of changing the world." I went on to explain what I thought they were—and I have to confess I enjoyed playing devil's advocate to this crisp young radical.

I had brought our discussion to an impasse, so I changed the subject abruptly and Carmen appeared not to mind. I asked how long she had known

Kevin. She said about two months, but she had heard of him through friends before that.

"How much do you know about him?" I asked.

"Know about him? Well . . . I know he's rich, if that's what you mean." She said it simply, as a fact of little consequence to her—but it was of consequence to him, she suggested. "I think he feels uncomfortable with all this money, and that's why he wants . . . to make up for it."

"By joining the Communist Party?"

She looked at me with her large gray eyes but said nothing. I asked if she were a Party member, too, and she said she was.

"Who recruited whom?"

"We joined together, as a matter of fact. About a month ago. But we're not supposed to talk about these things outside, you know."

I said I didn't know and asked if Kevin had told her about his sister.

Carmen nodded gravely. "That's another thing he wants to atone for. Her wasted life."

I said Kevin had found enough extraneous reasons for becoming a Communist. I hoped he had relevant arguments of his own as well. Carmen again said nothing, and I asked if she knew any of Kevin's friends.

"You mean Belle?" she asked with her usual directness, and of course that's precisely whom I did mean. "His girlfriend from the Maine island where his family goes summers . . . and where you live too." *His girlfriend!* "I haven't met her yet, but he's told me about her. She's supposed to come up from Washington tomorrow."

Carmen looked at me somberly, trying, I think, to see in my face whether Belle was a threat to her friendship with Kevin. But I was bound to secrecy where Belle was concerned and changed the subject. We talked for a few more minutes about other matters before my colleagues came to reclaim me for the drive back to Philadelphia.

I met Kevin on the way out. He was smiling faintly, without embarrassment, and seemed in good humor. His right ear protruded more comically than ever. I was glad he had put aside his silly cap.

"You sent your friend to entertain me," I said.

"Did she succeed?" Kevin asked.

I said I liked Carmen, but I didn't like what I saw of him through her. Kevin was silent, and the smile slowly faded until it was little more than a smirk. I resisted an idiotic temptation to slap him across the face. I started down the steps to the driveway, then turned back. It was better to unload what was on my mind.

"You've let me down on two counts tonight, Kevin. On one count, I simply think you're crazy. You may regret your Communist affiliations someday, or you may not. It's not of great consequence. But the other business bothers me considerably. You're trifling with disaster."

Kevin had stopped smiling now and tugged at his ear. "Things aren't as you may imagine them," he said softly.

"I imagine nothing—yet. I merely caution you. Remember what Belle said the day you were married—about that decision's being the easiest one of all. If you're not careful, you could lose her forever."

Kevin stood staring for some time at the steps as I turned to leave him. "I hear you," he said, "and most of what you're saying, I already know. . . . But thanks anyway. There's more to sort out than you know about. Meanwhile, with all the fuckups in the world, it seems almost . . . well, indecent to be fussing over one's personal problems."

We shook hands perfunctorily and I drove off with my friends. We reached our hotel as dawn was breaking over the city.

34

The end of that summer was, I believe, the most felicitous period I spent on Ram Island during those early years. The weather was warm and dry thanks to a prolonged high pressure system over New England. What fog there was invariably burned off each day before noon or gave way to light westerlies, leaving the island bathed in sunlight through the long afternoons. Even the sparkling northerlies were benign. Lobsters were plentiful that year, and since the prices they fetched rose ever higher, the islanders were in buoyant spirits. The new diesel-powered boats Turk Jenkins and Leonard York had ordered early in the spring were delivered in midsummer. They were named, respectively, *Sharon* and *Jessica,* and were objects of fascination to all. The new boats greatly extended the range of fishing for Turk and Leonard, and both took in most of their traps around the island and ledges and reset them south of Isle au Haut, fifteen miles seaward. They would leave at daybreak and often not return until late afternoon, having hauled up to three hundred traps each.

"Why'n'cha put out three hundred more, Turk?" young Tony Cutler asked the day he went out on the *Sharon.* "You could pull 'em every other day . . . Less'n you figure on stayin' up all night'n pullin' 'em all."

"Haulin' at night's illegal. You know that, Tony. . . . Three hundred's 'bout right, you place 'em good." And Turk was indeed experimenting constantly with his traps, placing as many as a dozen each day on a new submerged ledge he discovered with his fathometer. If he made a good catch on one, he would shift a string of fifty pots or more from another location where the take had fallen off.

I went out with Turk soon after the new boat arrived and could sense, in addition to the prospects of greater income for Turk, the exhilaration of deep-water lobstering. Living on the seaward side of the island, I was already accustomed to the slow swells rolling in from the open ocean and knew the fury of those waters in easterly gales, but I had not appreciated how much we were protected by the outer islands and popplestone ledges. Even on a mild day off Isle au Haut, the swells measured three or four feet in height and grew quickly steeper if the wind rose. After a storm at sea the great combers would lay bare a ledge marked on the chart as half a dozen feet under water at mean low tide. Yet Turk would calmly haul a trap within thirty feet of that lethal outcropping, occasionally glancing at it to measure his margin of safety. He and Leonard went out together in those first days and were in frequent communication over their shortwave radios, tuned to a channel used by lobstermen in the area.

"Turk?" Leonard called over his ship-to-shore as the two lobstermen felt their way toward each other in a sudden patch of fog off Western Ear. "I doubt my old man 'ud made it a lifetime fishin' out here."

And Turk, flicking his switch to broadcast, replied, "Rudolf's sure one for gettin' twisted up in fog, ain't he?"

But normally their exchanges were more perfunctory, since the Coast Guard monitors discouraged idle conversation over the shortwave radios. "This is *Jessica* callin' *Sharon*. Headin' for Saddleback. Over." "*Sharon* to *Jessica*. Okay. Be along 'bout ten minutes. Out."

The real Sharon and Jessica, meanwhile, waited by their own ship-to-shore units in their white-walled kitchens so their husbands could communicate with them if there was a need.

Memories of Karen Bannister, it is true, lingered in the minds of the islanders. I would not say they felt anything as precise as a sense of guilt or self-recrimination, for Karen, of course, had taken her life as the result of a complication beyond their control. Yet they knew that if she had stayed the tragedy would not have occurred. They had done penance during a stubborn and depressing spring marked by almost continuous wet weather and fog. By summer the islanders were ready to put the grim episode as far out of mind as possible. The schoolchildren still spoke of Karen from time to time, but I never heard her name mentioned that summer by an adult islander—other than Lucy Talbot and the Daceys. The only way one knew Karen was not forgotten was the deferential way the islanders spoke about the rest of the Bannisters if there was occasion to. Ram's Horn had not been opened that season; Sally had stuck to her word about not coming back to the island. George planned to come out for a few days with Kevin late in August, when the Thatchers would still be at

Northeast Cove. The islanders received this news in silence and their anxieties
returned.

What for me gave special pleasure during the August dog days that year was
not simply the fine weather and the islanders' prosperity and returning good
spirits, but the fact that Jingle, Otis, and Belle were on the island at the same
time. The four of us were together for the two weeks before Labor Day.

Belle was the first to arrive—in fact, less than two weeks after I returned
from Philadelphia. She arrived unexpectedly the day after her job ended in
Washington. I was surprised, since I understood she was to spend a week or ten
days in New York with Kevin, returning about the same time he was due to
come up with his father. Or was I really surprised? In any case, she didn't drop
down to see me the day she came, as she always had; nor did I see her the next
day. I knew she was avoiding me intentionally and charged her with this—in
good humor, of course—when we finally met at the crossroads the third afternoon following her arrival. She admitted it and said she'd wanted time to adjust.
"Things are in a proper muddle, aren't they?"

I proposed a swim at Southwest Beach. I rationed myself to one dip a season
in those days and said this seemed as good an occasion as any for the ordeal. We
went for our bathing suits and met ten minutes later on the high road. Walking
down past the Claytons' we talked idly of whatever came to mind, but I purposely made no mention of Kevin or of Philadelphia. I had not seen her there
since I left on a morning train before she arrived.

After changing into bathing trunks in the alder—Belle had her two-piece
suit on under her skirt and blouse—I followed her gingerly into the sea, frigid as
only Maine water can be. It was nearly high tide, so we had to walk a mile and a
half—it seemed that far—before we could plunge in. Belle was far ahead of me,
making sport of my misery.

"Don't . . . pretend you . . . enjoy this," I called to her, and she splashed me
with a spray of icicles in reply.

I said no wonder the lobstermen never learned how to swim: it would be
better to drown than try to keep afloat in these waters.

"And you a navy man!" She laughed. "For shame!"

I said frostily (yes, that's the word) that the object of the navy was to keep
men *on* the water, not *in* it. Eventually I did manage to submerge myself for thirty seconds, with appropriate squawks, before splashing back up to the beach to
my towel. Belle, laughing like some careless Ondine, lingered on another five
minutes doing rolls and somersaults. I shouted to her that I disclaimed all
responsibility; if she drowned, I left her to the fish.

She came out at last, and we lay on the warm sand, the light southwesterly drying our bodies quickly. Belle was propped on her elbow facing me.

"You're putting on weight." She giggled, pushing her fist lightly into my stomach.

I said it came and went according to its own laws, irrespective of my diet.

"Well, put on your glasses at least," she said. "It's all I can do to recognize you without clothes."

I fished my glasses out of my shoe and lit a cigarette, studying her in turn. Now that I could see again, I said, she didn't seem to have much on either. I gave her a detailed inspection. Her hips were full, as I knew, but not particularly rounded since both her waist and thighs were thick. Her buttocks were low and firm. Her calves were well shaped; they were covered with a light down. Her breasts were full and high on her chest. The skin across her stomach between the two pieces of her speckled bathing suit was milk-white. Her belly button was slightly distended.

Belle seemed not to mind my inspection—which, of course, did not take as long as it takes to report it.

"What did you expect to find? Venus?" she said, smiling at me.

I told her I had found what I had expected to find: a body that suited her face.

"Thank heaven for that," she said. "Suppose it hadn't?"

I opened the two cans of beer I had had the forethought to bring along, and for several minutes we idly watched two young gulls dropping mussels on the soft beach, then crying in perplexity that they hadn't broken open.

"Were you the hero of the convention in Philadelphia?" she asked finally.

"Hardly. I was called a spoilsport, a pessimist, and a nineteenth-century reactionary."

"You mean the Communists called you that?"

"I mean the young people. Not all of them were Communists."

Belle said, "I don't know how you stood it for three days. One was all I could take. . . . Of course I was out of it, I admit. They'd been together since Thursday or so and they had their own mood. No one could break into that. . . . Then they were *exhausted*. Nobody seems to have slept in days. Kevin just collapsed into bed and slept for twelve hours. I had to wake him to tell him I was off to catch the train back to Washington."

I said nothing, and Belle presently asked me if I had met Kevin's friend Carmen. I said I had.

"I liked her, actually. I guess I'm not supposed to in situations like this . . . but I found her to be very straightforward. No nonsense about her. I expect she's very good for Kevin," Belle said.

I mumbled that I couldn't agree with that at all . . . under the circumstances.

"But you mustn't imagine there are special circumstances," Belle said, sitting up and clasping her knees. "Our getting married was a fluke. It was my own stupid fault. Of course, we're married. There's no changing that . . . I mean, unless we get divorced. But we don't have to behave like husband and wife. In fact, we're *not* husband and wife in any real sense."

I said it was a bit early to talk of divorce when they'd been married only two months.

"Ten weeks tomorrow," Belle said.

"Things *are* in a muddle."

We watched the two gulls again, now moved on with greater success to a ledge at the end of the beach. "Why keep it a secret, Belle?" I asked after a moment.

"Why the dickens not?" she came back at me. "What earthly good is there in telling anybody now?"

I said they'd give their marriage a chance at least.

"That's just the point. There isn't a marriage to save."

"I'm not talking about saving as much as starting. I think Kevin would be ready to try."

"Well, I'm not," Belle said with spirit; it was clear she had somehow been hurt these past ten weeks. "If a marriage can't start off on its own, I can't see forcing it into existence. What's the use in that?"

I shrugged. " 'Use'?" I said. "Who knows what's useful?" Belle said nothing, and presently I asked her in a matter-of-fact way whether she loved Kevin.

"I love him and I hate him," Belle said without hesitation; she had obviously been thinking a good deal about this. "I love him when he's just Kevin. I . . . ." She appeared on the verge of making some further declaration, then thought better of it. "But I hate the things he does."

"Such as?"

"Well, I don't mean anything about Carmen particularly . . . in case you're wondering. Of course I shouldn't like to think of them sleeping together, but the way things are, I don't mind his seeing other girls. After all, I do . . . see you. I'm as close to you, I suppose—in our way—as Kevin is to Carmen." She looked at me archly, shaking damp hair out of her eyes. "Kev kids me about you," she confided. "He sneaks up behind me and throws his arms around my neck in a bear hug, nibbling at my ear. 'Beware of middle-aged men who put you through college,' he says in his Dracula voice. 'They'll eat you up!' "

I had no response to this little joke of theirs at my expense, so I changed the subject. If it wasn't the "other woman" syndrome that bothered her, I said, it must be Kevin's politics.

"His mother-lovin' politics," she said. "Marxism used to bring us together, I thought. Now it's the reverse."

I said Kevin was more activist than Marxist, but Belle was quick to defend him as a theoretician. "I've heard Kevin argue for hours with students at Columbia—law school students, political scientists, even young instructors. He's very persuasive, you know . . . not enough for Otis, I admit, but he's impressive." She paused and shook her hair out of her eyes. "No, it's his damned *Party* that gets me down. You'd think it was some oracle, it's so sacred. A Greek Adelphi. He stops thinking altogether . . . and the people he rates high because they're Party members. Well, some are clever, I admit. Like Carmen. But most are so imma- ture, so . . . so impressionable. I feel like somebody's maiden aunt with them. And they try so hard to shock you. Not only with political action . . . with sex, anything. They're so tasteless."

"Daryl, for instance?"

"There's one. You met Daryl? Well, Daryl will say, after I've spent the night with Kevin, 'How's the little fucker? She pretty good at it, Kev? She show you the *soixante-neuf?* All the tricks?' Really! I ask you! What kind of creep talks like that? But Kevin says he's 'authentic' because he comes from a small town in Vermont and his father's a plumber!"

I let her go on without interrupting. Eventually she came to a stop of her own accord. "Whew! Did I get a load off my mind," she said, lying facedown again in the sand. "I haven't unwound like that in years."

I said it did her good. We lay some time in silence, our fingers intertwined in the sand. She remembered seeing an old movie once, she said, the plot of which was built around a justice of the peace's marrying a couple who didn't want to be married anyway, then discovering his license had expired. "Suppose," Belle said, "the same thing happened to our funny little man in the Berkshires? Suppose we weren't married after all?"

Jingle came out with her husband and child in mid-August—her doctor finally agreeing, under pressure, that the danger period in her pregnancy had passed. Emil stayed a week before returning to Portland, leaving Jingle and Zbigniew another two weeks. This was the first time Emil had been on the island since the wedding, and he obviously enjoyed himself without ever losing his courtly manner. He turned out to be a dedicated fisherman and spent many hours by himself in Arthur's dory off Little Ram. He wore his street clothes, with tie and jacket, even out fishing. His only concessions to the garb of the sea were a ribbon under his Panama hat to keep it from scaling off and knee-high rubber boots, which he ingeniously rigged with pockets for his hooks and sinkers. The lobstermen would occasionally stop to suggest a different bait or another ledge where there were mackerel or flounder, and Emil would listen gravely to their advice. The islanders were amused by his perseverance but didn't appreciate his skill until the afternoon Clyde Grant pulled alongside his dory as they were coming in together around the Nose and asked whether the fish had been biting that day.

"There's been a few, Mr. Grant," Emil replied, and Clyde, looking into the dory, was astounded to see three buckets full of mackerel, skate, pollock, and other varieties.

"By golly!" Clyde exclaimed. "If I hadn't seen you around all day, I'd swear you'd been to the fish market in Rockland!"

"Could you take one home to Mrs. Grant?" Emil said, holding up a ten-pound flounder.

"Well, I guess I most certainly could," Clyde said, and took it with thanks.

Then, as Clyde later told the story, Emil set aside several good-sized fish for Jenny Brewster, Lucy Talbot, and of course his mother-in-law, and calmly dumped the rest back into the sea, where they quickly revived and swam out of sight. After this there were generally half a dozen islanders around the pier when Emil came in—to verify his catch as much as to receive any surplus.

When he was not fishing, Emil would sometimes walk slowly along the high road and down to the harbor, his son on his shoulders. He would stop to chat, politely and quietly, with any islanders he met. He addressed all of them formally, by their surnames, including Arthur and Winifred. He was a man who eschewed intimate friendships, though he was friendly to all. At Jingle's suggestion, he had consultations in Winifred's parlor with a dozen or so islanders about their teeth, managing to put in a few fillings with dental instruments he had sent over from a dentist in Rockland, and even extracting an abscessed tooth Horatio Leadbetter had been suffering from all summer. Emil, of course, refused payment for these services and promised to bring more equipment with him the next time he came.

By the time he left, then, Emil Zukin had won a good measure of respect from the islanders. The erect, somber figure who came briefly to them two years before to carry off their Jingle had now taken on substance. A fair number of islanders were at the harbor to bid him farewell the morning he left. He moved gravely among them, saying his good-byes—Zbigniew, in his usual perch on Emil's shoulders, as solemn as his father. When Horace Snow touched the whistle for boarding, Emil shifted his son to my shoulders, with some protesting from Zbigniew, and shook my hand.

"Take care of my Jingle," he said.

He kissed his wife on the forehead and boarded the *Laura Lee II*, black bag in hand and rubber boots over his arm. He waved his free hand several times with a brisk flutter as the mailboat moved out of the harbor.

I said something to Jingle about Emil's visit's being a huge success.

"Did you ever doubt it?" she asked.

"I wondered whether you did."

"Not in the least. I'm never nervous about anything Emil does."

Caleb Brewster voiced the prevailing judgment on Emil Zukin to a group gathered at the store later that day: "He ain't a great talker . . . but he's one mighty fine gentleman."

Rudolf York said, "I guess Zip ain't gonna be spreadin' tales 'bout how many fish he hand-lined yet awhile."

Harold Toothacher finished the alcove off my living room in Cutler's Cove in mid-August, and Otis insisted, as the originator of the idea, on his right of first occupancy. He arrived two days after Emil Zukin left and completed our foursome.

We were a foursome—Belle, Jingle, Otis, and I—more unconsciously than consciously. We surely barred no one from our society, and indeed we all had simultaneous ties and obligations outside the foursome. Jingle, for instance, had Zbigniew to care for—though, to be truthful, Winifred was grateful for any time she had her grandson to herself; Jingle developed closer ties to her mother that summer than I believe she ever had before. Belle, meanwhile, spent a considerable amount of time with *her* mother and renewed ties with other islanders she hadn't seen particularly often in several years; her irritation with the islanders after the plantation meeting had begun to subside. Otis spent a fair amount of time with Turk. He had finally looked up the smuggling conviction of Turk's father in the 1920s and discovered, as he had suspected, that far from being lenient, the sentence was severe for that era: judging from the record of the case, Otis surmised that the penalty was harsher precisely because Charles Jenkins had refused to collaborate with the investigators. Turk, it is true, had not been greatly troubled by this episode for many years, but it was clear he was grateful for Otis's findings.

"Mom'll be powerful glad to hear it," he said. "That's what she's always said." That was the Sunday we all went out on the *Sharon* to the other side of Isle au Haut, children and dogs included, and spent the afternoon roaming the sheep paths and bouncing stones on the popplestone beach.

We were thus in no sense exclusive, the four of us, yet strongly drawn to each other. We were most congenial when we were four, and only four. Lucy Talbot sensed this and was amused by it. Far from being put out, she actually encouraged our companionship. When occasionally we asked her to join us on some outing, she would decline.

"Run along, the four of you. You're impossible when you're together. No one can make the least sense of what you're saying."

Our friendship rested on no profound level of discourse, let it be said. We rarely talked about anything serious, least of all about anything that touched our personal lives. We did not discuss Karen Bannister, for instance, and hardly mentioned Kevin. Jingle and Otis, who of course had no suspicion of the secret marriage, assumed from Belle's failure to make even passing reference to Kevin that the affair was cooling off. Most of our conversation together was utterly trivial—Otis's rich fund of Jewish jokes, for instance, or episodes Jingle and Belle recalled about their legendary grandmother, or imaginary nonsense about nothing at all. One evening we read through, almost in its entirety, taking turns, the collected short stories of Saki. Sometimes we had no conversation. One afternoon, for instance, we lay on a grassy bank above Sheep Cove, after finishing a bottle of Anjou with our lunch, and one by one fell asleep until the south-west haze rolled in at four and woke us. Another day, the only day it rained, we mindlessly played canasta at Cutler's Cove in front of the fire from mid-afternoon until dinner and then reassembled in the evening to play again until midnight.

Belle, I think, was most affected by the intimacy of our companionship. Jingle and Otis saw each other regularly in Portland, and I had been with them on several occasions; we had thus experienced the exhilaration of an uninhibited relationship like ours and expected it whenever we were together. Belle, by contrast, inevitably had separate relations with Jingle and with me, and she hardly knew Otis at all at the beginning of that time. She was, moreover, many years younger than Otis and me and eight years younger than Jingle. She had never before known a group relationship like this, uncomplicated by jealousies and physical desire . . . although I won't say there was *no* desire. But sex was so far sublimated among us that it constituted a negligible force in our relationships.

Belle was reserved at the outset and even a little shocked by Otis's and Jingle's ostentatiously earthy manner of treating one another. But Belle grew accustomed to this sort of talk, recognizing it for what it was—their way of expressing affection for one another in the absence of physical intimacy. She wouldn't join in their ribaldry, but she learned to smile indulgently when it spewed forth, as inevitably it did. Gradually she relaxed. The difference in our ages became irrelevant. Our idiosyncrasies and mannerisms ceased to jangle as we became accustomed to each other.

If anyone had asked before that few weeks how we would probably pair off, if there was a need for it, I would have said Otis and Jingle, who were such boon companions in Portland, and Belle and me, who shared a secret. In fact, it was not this way. On the occasions when we did become twos—making partners at cards, walking down a lane too narrow for four, or simply obeying a natural instinct to be couples—it was invariably Otis and Belle, Jingle and me. But this was rare. On nearly all occasions we were a foursome, and it was Belle, I think, fresh from the skirmishes of her personal life, who profited most from the easy intimacy of our curious relationship. She would lie contented for hours, bare toes dug into the bear rug in front of my fire or into the moss of some spruce glade where we had paused, taking in Otis's artless fantasies.

"Suppose the fallout from an atomic blast killed everyone in the world except us," Otis interposed into the general silence one evening after I had finished reading the account of recent testing at Iwo Jima. "Where would we go?"

"Well, if we'd survived here, we'd better stay," Jingle said reasonably.

"Not practical," Otis said. "There'd be no wine after a couple of weeks and I'd run out of cigars in a week. To mention only the barest necessities of life."

"Then we'd go ashore."

"Rockland? Camden? There's no good cigar store in either."

"Why Rockland or Camden—or anywhere in particular? South in the winter, north again in the spring. Back here for the summer."

"How would we travel?" Belle asked.

"What about one of those yachts in Camden Harbor?" Otis suggested.

"Who'll deliver my baby?"

"Good point," Otis conceded, and looked at me. "That'll be your department, chum."

I asked on what conceivable logic I had drawn that assignment.

"Don't quibble," Belle said. "I'll manage."

"Dr. Talbot," said Otis. "Or are you a midwife?"

"I'll have to have Zbig, too, of course," Jingle interjected. "I won't go out without Zbig."

"Zbig, all right. But that's it. The point of the game is everyone's dead. You can't start off with your whole goddam family."

Belle said, "I insist on three days at the Museum of Modern Art in New York."

"I can't stand New York," Jingle said.

"We'll take the Presidential Suite at the top of the Waldorf," Otis proposed.

"With no elevator?"

"Correction. We'll move into a ground-floor flat I knew in Brooklyn Heights."

"What will we eat?" Belle wanted to know. "Are chickens and pigs and lambs all wiped out, too?"

"That wouldn't be realistic," said Otis.

"Realistic!" Jingle exclaimed.

"I'll allow two survivors from each of the species, like Noah, one of each gender. That ought to do it."

"Be a long lean winter to lambing time," I said.

Jingle said, "How come only two for all the other species and four of us?"

"Well, that's the way Noah did it. We can't improve on Noah."

"Apropos," Jingle asked abruptly, "how do we procreate?"

"The usual way, Cleo," said Otis. "You're a great one to—"

"No, you jughead! I mean, will we be . . . couples?"

"Oh, that," said Otis. "I'll take up that business in my constitution. Anyway, no couples. They're old-fashioned."

"Roger," I said. "No couples."

And Belle and Jingle, on reflection, agreed: "No couples."

The only other time the issue of couples came up, even frivolously, was when Otis reminded Belle of his advice to go slowly with Kevin—the day he told her he favored their romance.

"I remember," Belle said.

"Well, I was probably a bit disingenuous there: I wanted you to go slowly in case I sometime had an idea I wanted you for myself—in this never never land we're all building."

"Otis," she cried, "don't be goofy. You're old enough to be my father…and wise enough to be my grandfather."

"Look, baby," Otis came back quickly. "You know as well as I we're not talking about relative ages."

Belle was silent. Then she said: "But if you should need me at any time, Otis, in the never never land or elsewhere, I would come to you."

So we worked our way through the lazy afternoon as far south as the Yucatán and west to the Golden Gate, untroubled by the fate of our fellow man. We fashioned the rules of our society as fancy dictated. If any insights into human nature or into anything else were reflected in our meandering conversation, this was coincidental—for none were intended. We asked nothing more of words beyond their conveying whatever ephemeral fantasies came to mind. It was this, I think, what Belle most needed: to distract herself from the sudden harsh realities of her earthly life.

35

While the four of us gamboled our way through the last weeks of summer, an intermittent romance the islanders had watched with interest for several years came to its climax. Elmer Brewster came home for a month's vacation early in August, and Mary Lou Grant ten days later. Their vacations had overlapped the summer before and they had "kept company" then—a circumstance that prompted occasional ribald jests among the lobstermen—jests that, when he heard them, appeared to pass wholly over Elmer's head. There had been no reports that they had seen each other since the previous summer. Indeed, Elmer seemed oblivious of Mary Lou's whereabouts, burying himself as soon as he arrived in the mysteries of Turk's new diesel engine and, when Turk was out, in the caprices of any mechanical gadget on the island called to his attention.

The day before Mary Lou was due on the mailboat, Clara Grant reminded Elmer of her expected arrival with heavy innuendo.

"That'll be a pleasure for you, Clara," Elmer said politely. "Where's she been at?"

"Elmer Brewster! Don't set there with your bare face hangin' out 'n tell me you don't know Mary Lou's been in Rockland."

But if Elmer knew it, he didn't let on. "That so?" he said. Nor was he around the harbor when the *Laura Lee II* came in the next morning. Mary Lou, it was clear to see, was disappointed as she scanned the faces on the pier. She was dressed for conquest, in a bright red frock cut low at the neck. Her hair was a mass of ringlets, presumably just out of curlers. She was heavily made up, including eye shadow, but makeup never spoiled Mary Lou. She was, in short, as brazenly seductive as she always had been, with perhaps an increment added for the absent Elmer. The male islanders about the harbor gawked at her as though she were some outsider and not one of their own. Mary Lou's arrivals, before she changed into more serviceable island attire, always elevated the male pulse. She was everyman's secret passion. To behold Mary Lou on these occasions and not have fantasies of bearing her off forthwith to the quarries was to be unmanly. And this, of course, was precisely the effect Mary Lou wished to have.

"What a bird!" Belle said beside me as Horace Snow nudged the mailboat alongside the pier. "Isn't she something?"

Mary Lou lingered about the harbor and at the store for half an hour before walking home—more to catch a glimpse of Elmer, I assumed, than to be admired by her fellow islanders. But she was too proud, at that moment anyway, to ask after him. When Caleb, passing the time of day, said Elmer was back, she pretended not to hear and changed the subject. A glimpse was all she did catch of Elmer that day, as he rattled past the store in Harold Toothacher's pickup, too absorbed in a conversation with Harold to notice her—or to show it if he did.

Belle met Mary Lou the next afternoon on the high road and asked her, in the course of their casual conversation, whether she had seen Elmer yet.

"Nope," said Mary Lou, "and at this rate I guess I'm not gonna. If Elmo doesn't come after me, I'm gonna have to go after him."

And that's the way it was. Mary Lou, pursued so persistently since she was fourteen that she had come to take pursuit as a matter of course, now became the pursuer. But entrapping Elmer proved more difficult than she imagined. His preoccupation with machines and gadgets was not merely vocation and avocation; it was a love affair. There was no room for anything else in his life.

Mary Lou had no trouble making contact with him—that was simply a question of putting herself in his way so he couldn't ignore her—but arousing his passion was another matter. Elmer was working with Harold Toothacher at this time on the plumbing for a toilet I was putting in, along with the alcove, and Mary Lou often came down at lunchtime to pass the time of day. One afternoon, after Harold had left and they were alone, I heard their voices under the house when I returned and went quietly about my business in order not to disturb them. Ten minutes later their voices were still coming spasmodically up through the floor and it was clear that plumbing, not dalliance, preoccupied them. I went around to see what they were doing and found Elmer on his back connecting two lengths of pipe and Mary Lou crouched beside him holding his tools, her face smeared with dirt. Her skirt was hiked up over her knees about six inches from his face, and two buttons were undone on her blouse, exposing the better part of one well-shaped breast, but Elmer had no eyes for such irrelevancies. She looked out at me through two floor beams and smiled contentedly, shaking the hair out of her eyes.

"I'm his grease monkey. Isn't that a laugh?"

"Well, grease monkey, hand me up my goddam pliers . . . no, the small ones, you nitwit."

When they finished their work, I asked them to stop for a beer. We sat out on the grass behind the granite boulders, and Elmer tried to persuade me to install a generator; mine was the only home on the island, except Widow Barnaby's, without one. I said I was too old-fashioned to put up with the noise, or too lazy to start one up, but promised to wire into an island generator if there ever was one.

"We'll have one, couple of years," Elmer said, and launched into a detailed discussion of the merits of various models then on the market. Mary Lou had washed her face and, out of modesty in my presence, buttoned up her blouse, but she managed to keep her aura of seductiveness. She sat next to him, occasionally brushing gently against his shoulder. He seemed not to notice, absorbed in the details of his explanation. After they had finished their beer, she fidgeted, wanting to leave, but Elmer was not to be hurried and continued with his minute calculation of the cost of island-generated electricity to the customers. Mary Lou pretended to listen, but her mind was obviously on more important matters.

When finally he said, "Okay, let's shove off, Lou," she was on her feet in a flash.

Mary Lou nearly lost Elmer to Turk at one point—that is, lost the prospect of spending days with him as his grease monkey, which she had sensibly decided was a quicker way to his heart than any other. Turk had finally persuaded Elmer to go out lobstering with him on the *Sharon,* and on a nearly motionless sea one hot August day Elmer thought perhaps he liked being out on the bay better than he'd figured; he thought maybe he'd fish with Turk on shares. But a modest swell off Isle au Haut the next day was all it took to disabuse him of any illusions of seaworthiness, and he returned gratefully to land—and Mary Lou. She could again follow him around the island from one malfunctioning machine to the next, handing him tools and making herself useful while she patiently awaited his *coup de foudre.*

Jingle kept us informed—that is, the rest of the foursome—of the stately progress of the romance, for Mary Lou had always been uninhibited with Jingle and told her virtually everything that passed between them.

"Creepers, Jingle, the guy's made of granite! I could take off all my clothes and he'd say, 'Pass the number two wrench, pinhead.'"

"Try wearing *more* clothes," Jingle advised.

"I've tried that, too. I've tried everything."

Elmer, it must be said, was not indifferent to her company and indeed came to rely on his apprentice. If she failed to meet him at an appointed place, he would walk up the ridge to the Grants' and find her—perhaps still in bed at nine or ten in the morning; on those occasions he would go up to her room, whack her on the backsides, and tell her to get the "goddam lead" out of her pants. But Mary Lou might as well have been neuter for all the deference he paid her sex. One day, walking ahead of her through Abigail's Spruces and talking as usual of some mechanical mystery, he stopped suddenly and absentmindedly began to relieve himself at the side of the trail, still talking.

"Damn it, Elmer," Mary Lou said, "don't be waving your cock at me like that!"

"Christ, Lou, can't a feller take a leak? There's nothin' wrong with my cock."

"Only trouble with it is you keep it to yourself."

And Elmer, chastened, walked on in silence.

Jingle savored these episodes and others with us wantonly during our daily expeditions. We never discovered how Mary Lou finally broke through Elmer's reserve, for at a certain moment she ceased to discuss her affairs with Jingle with her usual candor. We lost sight of the frustrated romance for several days, until I happened one evening to be going over accounts with Caleb, as he periodically liked me to do. We sat at the table in the Brewsters' upstairs parlor. It was after

ten, and Jenny had been restlessly crossing to the window every five minutes or
so looking up the road for Elmer.

"Where's the boy at? This time o' night!"

He had gone off after supper, with Mary Lou, to call on Turk and Sharon—
but as we later discovered, they never reached the Peaks at all. The August moon
was full and the night was mild.

At ten-thirty, as I was preparing to leave, Elmer came in, tossed his cap on
the couch, and without preliminaries said, "Well, guess what! Me 'n Lou's gettin'
hitched."

There was a moment of suspended silence, then Jenny rasped, "Over my
dead body you are!"

And Caleb—somewhat to my surprise, I confess—immediately supported
her, going red in the face. "You ain't doin' no such thing, son. . . . That girl's a
trollop. She's been bedded by nearly every man on this island!"

Elmer was flustered, his Adam's apple working up and down. Perhaps he
hadn't expected praise, but it was clear he was unprepared for this outbreak of
hostility from his parents.

"Well . . . well, so what? Maybe I've screwed every bitch in Bangor. This—"

"Don't you talk that way, boy, in front o' your mother."

At this point I beat a hasty exit, not wanting to be party to what promised
to be a bitter family quarrel. I could hear Jenny's shrill voice through the open
windows of the parlor long after I had turned the corner on my way to the
ridge.

There was no reconciliation that night. The more Jenny and Caleb, Jenny
especially, reviled Mary Lou, the more Elmer defended her. In the end Caleb and
Jenny stubbornly refused to accept Mary Lou as their daughter-in-law, and
Elmer, just as stubbornly, determined to make her just that whether they accepted her or not. Sometime after midnight Elmer left the house and went to the
Peaks for the night. The next morning at daybreak he went to the Grants', before
Clyde had left, talked the whole matter over with Clyde and Clara, and carried
his bride-to-be off to a justice of the peace in Rockport later that day. Turk took
them over in the *Sharon* and stood as witness. They wanted no other islanders,
though it nearly broke Clara's heart not to be there.

"Funny the way a guy gits caught, ain't it, Turk?" Elmer said as they came
out into the bright sunshine from the dingy back room that served as the office
of the justice of the peace. "If t'hadn't been for the way things turned out, Lou 'n
me mighta been a couple years gittin' 'round to gittin' married."

Mary Lou said, "That's what you think, honey." And she winked broadly at
Turk.

The weeks following were a bad period for Caleb and Jenny. Nearly all the islanders were against them in the matter of Elmer and Mary Lou, the Grants so much that for some weeks they stopped coming to the store and shopped once a week in Rockland. Zip Clayton picked up their mail. Sharon was also cool toward her parents and several times walked out on Jenny when she was holding forth on Elmer's "ingratitude" or Mary Lou's "sly ways." Still, Jenny continued to complain to whoever would listen to her, though her complaints fell increasingly on deaf ears. Jingle, during a visit later in the fall, listened one afternoon to about all she could from Jenny on the subject of Mary Lou's morals and then spoke out—falling into the vernacular.

"I'm gonna tell you something, Jenny Brewster, 'fore you talk yourself out of any chance of ever seeing Elmo and Mary Lou again, let alone your own grandchildren. Maybe she chose him and maybe he chose her. It don't make a mite o' difference. That girl ain't never gonna lay eyes on another man in the way you're thinkin' as long as she lives. And I'll lay you generous odds on it."

Eventually, Jenny and Caleb ceased to talk about the marriage, though you could tell from their manner that they were deeply hurt. They made no move to restore relations with Elmer, and Elmer by this time was too independent to mind. He and Mary Lou settled in Bangor. Mary Lou easily found work as a seamstress and nearly matched Elmer's pay in his body shop. They were in touch with the Grants, of course, as well as with Turk and Sharon and periodically with Jingle, but there was no communication with Caleb and Jenny for nearly two years. However, I leave the denouement of the episode until later in my story.

36

George Bannister finally came out to the island alone after Labor Day. Sally would not change her mind, and Kevin held up his father's departure for more than two weeks, until he at last let George know he couldn't manage it; he absolutely had to finish a paper on Hobbes before classes started at the end of September. To Belle he gave a more candid reason: He didn't think it fair to force her to play out the role of a neglected wife (he first wrote "estranged" but crossed it out) under the curious eyes of parents who didn't even know they were married. He apologized for causing her discomfort in Philadelphia and wrote that, despite appearances, he still loved her. At the same time, he did believe in the correctness of what he was doing—that is, his political work—and felt this had to take precedence over personal convenience. He hoped she appreciated that this was not an easy time for him either and particularly hoped they could both keep their lives in perspective "until we see where we are." He felt badly about letting his father down, for he realized it was not easy for George to come out to Ram's Horn without him. But he had to make a decision between concern for his father and for his wife. "I don't forget you are my wife," he wrote.

Belle, quite properly, did not show me Kevin's letter, but she told me about it—with somewhat misty eyes—as we sat on pilings overlooking the harbor one soft September afternoon. This was three days after Jingle and Otis had left.

"It would be easier, wouldn't it," she said, "if he were a bastard?" But she would not discuss the letter further, or her feelings on having received it, and I did not press her. I was quite sure she did not answer Kevin's letter.

George had hoped to arrive while the Thatchers were still on the island, thinking their company would ease his loneliness in the big house at Ram's Horn, but by the time he made up his mind to come, even without Kevin, the Thatchers and their guests had left. George wired Jenny Brewster the date of his arrival, and the nervousness of the islanders grew as the date approached. None of them could imagine George as vindictive or spiteful, yet they dreaded his coming. They eased their consciences by offering to help Jenny open the house. She never had so many volunteers to remove shutters, fold up dust covers, sweep out the year's accumulation of dead flies and cobwebs, rake the driveway, and lay in supplies. Fresh flowers were placed in every room. A collapsed trellis was repaired. The shrubbery was trimmed. Ram's Horn, in short, had never been better groomed. But the islanders would not, if they could avoid it, meet George face-to-face.

The morning he arrived, a misty day that gave no promise of improving, the harbor was deserted—except for Belle and me, and Caleb, down to pick up the mail—when the *Laura Lee II* came in. George seemed not to notice, or if he did, he was too flustered by finding Belle there and then by her warm embrace to pay attention. We walked to the store, which was also deserted—a thing unheard of when the mailboat came in.

"S'funny. Where's everybody at?" Caleb said, putting down the mail pouch. He called down the stairs to the storeroom. "Jenny? You there? Come see who we got up here."

And Jenny came wheezing up the stairs, wisps of gray hair coming our from her faded bandana.

"Well, bless my soul! Things been so quiet 'round here, I didn't pay no notice to the time. Mailboat's come 'n gone, has it, Caleb?"

"Come 'n gone."

"I declare. . . . Seems like everybody's dug in for the winter, don't it? It gets pretty quiet out here after the summer folk leave. . . . Don't it, Caleb?"

"Well, I hope to tell ya. Like a graveyard." But he was immediately embarrassed at having mentioned a graveyard, thinking of Karen, and busied himself with the top of the pickle barrel. "Consarned thing don't fit."

"And how's . . . how's the missus?" Jenny asked George, coming to Caleb's rescue. "Fairly, I hope?"

I noticed then, and remembered later, that the islanders for some time never addressed George or referred to Sally by her given name, as they always had. They could hardly call George "Mr. Bannister" without insulting him, so they compromised by calling him nothing at all and referring to Sally, if they needed to, as "the missus" or "the wife." But their ingenuity in this was not sorely tested, for the islanders continued to avoid George during most of his stay. He would have welcomed their company and came several times to the harbor in the first days to greet the lobstermen as he often used to when they came ashore. But they turned back to sea if they saw him at the pier, or lingered on their boats fussing needlessly with their gear until he had left. It was the same at the store and on the high road. If the islanders could manage it—all but a few like Lucy Talbot, the Daceys, and the Jenkinses—they avoided George altogether. It was not his anger they feared, remembering the grief they had caused him by banishing Karen from the island, but the keener reproof of his quiet forbearance and forgiveness.

If George was stung by the remoteness of the islanders—and he was too intelligent to imagine that thirty-odd islanders could stay so permanently out of his way without design—he minded less because of the attention paid him by Belle. Belle attached herself to George from the moment of his arrival. After Caleb left us with his pickup that first day, she unpacked George's suitcase and made him lunch while he and I went over the house to see what repairs were needed before winter. The three of us ate in front of a roaring fire as the mist thickened into a steady drizzle. Belle did not go back again that day, but when she came around the next morning and found George in his pajamas at nine-thirty struggling over scrambled eggs and coffee, the blackened pots from his canned stew and vegetables the evening before still in the sink, she decided he needed round-the-clock attention. Thereafter she spent most of every day at Ram's Horn.

She would go down in the morning and make his breakfast, accusing him of meddling if she found he had done housework while she was away. Often she would bring breakfast to him in bed, since George had insomnia and usually read for two or three hours at dawn, before dropping off to sleep again. She would sit on the edge of the bed with her cup of tea and they would talk or listen to newscasts for a half hour before she went back to the kitchen to clean up. Occasionally she would walk down to the store with him for mail or groceries, but more often she would stay behind and tend to his laundry or make a casserole for lunch. George, of course, protested all these attentions and asked why they couldn't find someone else to do the housework.

"Because I want to," Belle said, and sent him to put another log on the fire.

George was especially embarrassed when he discovered that Belle would not accept anything for her work, and he asked me suspiciously one day whether I had told her about our arrangement for her education. I assured him Belle had no inkling of it.

"Then it must be for K-Kevin," he said. "Because I'm Kevin's father. . . . Do you think she's in love with Kevin?"

"She is and she isn't," I said, and changed the subject, refusing to be drawn into a discussion of that suspended romance.

George gradually accepted Belle's presence at Ram's Horn as his voluntary housekeeper and indeed came to depend on it so much that he would have been helpless without her. When she said one afternoon, after having made a shepherd's pie for dinner, that she would eat at home that evening—her mother was beginning to complain about her absence—George looked so startled that she nearly burst out laughing.

"But c-c-can't we invite her here? W-w-would she come?"

"Of course she'd come, you goose. Would you like her?"

So Lucy Talbot joined them for dinner at Ram's Horn that night, and from then on they were never without company. Arthur and Winifred dined at Ram's Horn the next night, then Turk and Sharon, and I ate with them more often than at home. This solved the problem of George's loneliness during the long evenings, for we would often sit talking in front of the fire in the library for an hour or two after dinner. George, whatever inhibitions he suffered in his personality, was a true dilettante, and there was hardly a subject on which he could not, in the right company and setting, converse for hours. If he himself was ignorant of the subject, he would ask searching questions, then make relevant observations. With Lucy, it was the early settlements on the islands. With Winifred, it was the last of the China Clippers she had seen. With Sharon, it was island medicine and the herbs she used. With Arthur and Turk, it was the fishing industry and the steps necessary to preserve it. But in one respect George also looked forward to the ends of those evenings, for it was then he received his parting kiss from Belle—that uninhibited island kiss, full on the lips, that startled and delighted him as much as it had me some years before.

"What is there about it?" he asked me when we discussed it one day when Belle was out. "It's not s-sexual, is it? It's so wholesome. Yet, by God, it's so personal."

George came down with a heavy chest cold just before he was to leave, and I think he was very pleased. He was always meticulous about his plans, rarely

changing them once they were set, and he had been beginning to regret his decision to spend a single week on the island, especially when he discovered Belle
still had another week before she had to return to college. He began hopefully to
identify certain symptoms even before they had become obvious, but the afternoon before his scheduled departure it was clear he was in considerable discomfort. Belle sent him to bed and went for Sharon, who took his temperature,
pulse, and blood pressure. It was no more than a bad cold, Sharon felt, but he
should stay in bed until his temperature went down and then recuperate for a
day or two before leaving. George was all attention and full of respect for her
judgment. Sharon asked if he wanted a doctor to come over from Rockland, and
he said absolutely not; he couldn't stand doctors' "p-pontificating." So Belle sent
Sally a telegram and added to her role as housekeeper that of nurse.

The pattern of their life now changed for several days. Belle moved into
Karen's room for the next few nights and administered Sharon's medications as
instructed. Before George went to sleep, she lathered his back with oil and gave
him long leisurely backrubs as they talked desultorily about one thing or another. She would have given him an enema when she discovered he had gone thirty-
six hours without a bowel movement, but this he absolutely refused.

"W-w-what do you take me for? A b-b-baby?" He never overcame his stammering in her presence.

The islanders now lost their uneasiness about George's being at Ram's Horn.
George sick was less awesome to them than George aggrieved. They showed
their concern not only by talking more freely among themselves about his recov-
ery, but also by dropping down to Ram's Horn to inquire of Belle or Lucy, who
spent most of the days with her daughter, how George was "comin' along." The
women brought pies and cookies, and Belle would escort them to the door of
George's room to call in their greetings. The men brought lobsters, remembering
George's strong liking for them—so many finally that Belle had to refuse them.
But she would show the lobstermen in nonetheless to exchange a word with
George, moving them on before they wore the sill down with their shuffling.

"Anyone would think I was about to d-d-die, the attention I've been receiving," George complained. But it was easy to see he was pleased by their concern.

Even Harold Toothacher dropped by—I happened to be at Ram's Horn at
the time—and tactlessly brought up the matter of the plantation meeting the
preceding March. It was ironic to hear Harold, of all people, trying to justify to
George his part in the episode.

"I voted for 'er, I'll say that. Ask anyone. She mighta been a bit headstrong,
but—"

"Well, never m-mind about that, Harold," George interrupted. "Come back
in a few days and we'll talk over a few things I want done to the p-p-porch."

Belle shooed Harold out through the kitchen without ceremony and slammed the back door on him in the middle of a sentence.

"He's abominable!" she said through clenched teeth, her face crimson with rage.

George was out of bed on the third day. He was pale and weak and seemed to have aged. His hair was thinner and grayer. The skin under his eyes sagged. I dined with the two of them that night. We ate in the library, which was cozier than the dining room, though farther from the kitchen, and built a huge fire against the driving rain of a building easterly. Belle served us lobsters with a casserole of local mushrooms as a side dish, since George liked mushrooms in any form and on any pretext. George sent me to his cave for a Chablis, which Belle chilled while we had cocktails.

This was the company George preferred. With Belle alone he was nervous, I gathered, afraid he would somehow offend her, and so was inhibited in his speech. With her mother, as with the other islanders, he was formal and gracious, but never quite at ease. He was always afraid of talking down to the islanders, or appearing to do so. But when the three of us were together he could talk through me to Belle, and that was what he wished.

I happened to remind George, over coffee, of our conversation in this room three years before, immediately after the war.

"I heard about that," Belle said, kicking off her sandals and stretching out on the floor.

"Did you?" said George. "What did you hear?"

"Well, let's see. Sally said she believed in security and privacy. Gloria wanted a family. Karen passed. Wylie Thatcher said he believed in free enterprise, the church, and so forth . . ."

"That's right. You remember it almost better than I do. Who t-told you?" He glanced at me, but I shook my head; I remembered mentioning the conversation once to Jingle, but never to Belle.

"Kevin," Belle said briefly, then went on. "I never heard what you said."

"I didn't," George said. "We never got to me."

I suggested we might correct this oversight now. Three years should have sharpened his perceptions.

"I don't know about that," George said. "You go first, B-Belle."

"I pass. Like Karen . . . Besides, I don't know what I believe in at this point."

George looked down at her and poked her gently in the ribs with his slipper. "All right . . . let's see, what are the rules?"

I said as nearly as I remembered we started off on war objectives but quickly shifted to the moral and ethical values that should guide one's behavior.

George thought a moment in silence, gazing over Belle's head into the fire.

"If I could shift the emphasis from one's own behavior to one's own perception of others' behavior, then I would say c-compassion ranks high in the book of virtues. I'm sure I didn't always think so. I used to be very intolerant when I was younger. I was really quite contemptuous of bad manners, poor taste, boorishness. Even inferior b-breeding—"

"In short, you didn't think much of islanders," Belle broke in.

"No," George said meditatively. "I don't think I ever thought islanders inferior in breeding. I was capable of it, I admit, but I never held that view. That was because of F-Father, I suppose. He had great respect for islanders. . . . But to get on, it's one thing to set up a standard of behavior for yourself, even if you don't live up to it, but it's an altogether different matter to judge others by that same standard. In a w-word, I substitute compassion for judgment . . . or, I should say, I try to. I guess none of us wholly succeeds in what we try. If a man tipples, this may run against my notions of self-restraint and good sense, but I would try not to condemn him for it. If a man and a woman live in sin, this may not be according to my moral code, but I would not hold them in contempt for it."

"Living in sin is not so unusual today," Belle gravely informed George.

"It never has been, my dear. Yet this has not prevented society from self-righteously—and often hypocritically—ostracizing people for it. Like Anna K-Karenina."

Adultery and drunkenness, I suggested, were social transgressions. Did George's compassion extend to serious crimes—for instance, murder?

"Much would depend on the circumstances: whether it is a murder of passion or revenge, of honor, of greed. Murderers are usually disordered, I should think—I've never actually known one. A psychopath needs psychiatric help more than he needs p-punishment. . . . But the main thing is, I'm not passing judgment on the act itself. Courts exist for that. I'm speaking of the attitude of one human toward another. A murderer needs understanding, consoling like anyone else. Indeed, more so. In a word, he needs compassion." George paused for several moments, then continued in a subdued but even voice. "Even self-murder. Suicide. I used to think this a cardinal sin. It seemed weak, selfish, melodramatic. But I don't condemn K-Karen. Indeed, I think now I even respect her for what she did. . . . But let's not talk about poor Karen."

Silence fell upon us, and suspecting Belle might be upset by the turn the conversation had taken—she lay motionless on the floor, her head buried in a pillow—I redirected the conversation. George, I gathered, opposed capital punishment for any reason.

"Absolutely," he said.

"What about the Nuremberg Trials?"

"Hmm . . . I must be consistent. The trials, I believe, were fair, and surely execution is a punishment meted out over the ages for certain crimes. . . . But I keep coming back to the same p-position. I do not pretend to sit in judgment, like M-Moses. There is some good in every man, and my compassion, I suppose, is directed to that ounce of dignity. . . . But you press my thesis very hard, I admit, with your Nuremberg Trials. If you compel me to answer, I would have to say I do not believe in an eye for an eye. I do not believe in retribution per se . . . but perhaps I hide behind the knowledge there will always be punishment for crime whether I b-believe in it or not."

Belle said after a pause, "What about a Communist? Does he deserve your compassion too?"

"A Communist," George repeated. "You mean if Kevin, say, were to become a Communist." Although Belle and I had not discussed it, I was reasonably sure George knew nothing yet of Kevin's having joined the Party. "I should be disappointed, of course, to see his t-talent wasted in that way. I would try to dissuade him . . . but, no, I would suffer it. I would be understanding. After all, it would be inconsistent of me to be less compassionate toward my own son as a Communist than toward those Nazis at Nuremberg. Isn't this what all men deserve?"

Belle said, "George, you sound like Jesus Christ . . . no, seriously."

George gave a small, wry smile. "I'm not trying to compete with Him," he said.

"I wonder if you could run the world on compassion," Belle said, her head back on the pillow.

"Well . . . I'm not trying to run the w-world," George said. "I'm not trying to run anything."

That, I think, was one of George Bannister's happiest evenings. He left two days later, fully recovered, and there was a fair-sized gathering at the landing to see him off.

37

Belle was ill that autumn. How seriously ill few of us knew at the time, and only Jingle knew why. She told me some weeks later, when the crisis had passed, and only then because she had refused to promise Belle she wouldn't. She argued with Belle that I had a right to know, since I was putting her through college (as both supposed) and the episode was going to cost me a term's tuition.

Belle had become inadvertently pregnant early in July—ironically, on a weekend with Kevin in New York when their affairs were beginning to go badly. Since she had made a mistake about her periods in the spring, she ignored the symptoms of pregnancy and assumed the two periods she missed during the summer were merely part of some continuing irregularity. By the time she returned to college she had doubts; a test with a local gynecologist in Northampton confirmed them. Belle did not want Kevin's child and had no intention of resuming marital relations with Kevin at this stage—if, indeed, ever. Her interlude with George on the island had not shaken her on this point. She accordingly decided on an abortion. A senior on her floor who was reputed to have had two abortions—though in reality she had had none—knew of a new doctor in Springfield who performed abortions for one hundred and fifty dollars, and Belle went off one afternoon to see him. He was young, she told Jingle later, and lecherous, fingering her on the inspection table far more than Belle was sure he needed to. Still, he seemed competent, and Belle made the necessary arrangements, drawing out most of her spending money set aside for the fall term. She was to come to his office the following Friday afternoon for the brief operation, then go to a nursing home on Saturday where he could keep her under observation over the weekend. She would be able to return to college Sunday evening.

The operation on Friday passed off on schedule and, so far as Belle was aware, satisfactorily, though it was more painful than she had been led to believe. The doctor told her as she left that if she had any difficulties she was to go directly to the nursing home, even before they were expecting her at noon the next day. Belle was in considerable discomfort that evening, but the major difficulties began only about one in the morning, when a segment of the fetus aborted, followed by massive hemorrhaging. Sheets and towels were drenched with blood, yet she could not staunch the relentless flow. She felt her strength ebbing and woke Dolores, the senior who had recommended the doctor in Springfield. Dolores called for a taxi, and the two girls had a harrowing drive through the darkened early-morning hours to the nursing home, Belle becoming unconscious from pain and loss of blood several times. It was some time before Dolores could rouse anyone at the nursing home and still more time before they could muster enough staff to carry Belle inside on a stretcher. The woman Belle was to have asked for at the nursing home was not on duty and could not be reached by telephone. The registration book merely indicated that a B. Talbot had reserved a room for noon Saturday—"for convalescence." The staff members present had no knowledge of abortion cases, which they immediately recognized this to be, and were reluctant to do more than make Belle as comfortable as they could—in a ward with four aged women suffering from rheumatoid arthritis. They tried to reach Belle's doctor, but he had no home telephone in the area and the answering service at his office merely advised to call back at nine in the morning.

The hemorrhaging mercifully stopped at last, but infection must have quickly set in, for Belle's temperature began to rise sharply before dawn. By eight o'clock, it was 103 degrees and Belle was periodically delirious. It was still impossible to find her doctor. At nine a secretary answered at his office and said he was not expected in that day; she didn't know where he could be reached. There was no record of a Belle Talbot among his patients. Dolores went over to the office to see whether in talking privately with the secretary she might locate the doctor, but she found the secretary had already left.

When the woman Belle was to have asked for at the nursing home came on duty in mid-morning, she said, "Jesus! Not that guy again!" and suggested they call the college to find out what to do. Dolores proposed Belle's family instead, and at a moment when Belle was lucid enough to talk, she gave them Jingle's telephone number in Portland. Jingle had just come in from shopping when the call came through and she started immediately for Springfield by car. A doctor attached to the nursing home staff looked in on Belle from time to time, prescribing drugs to stop the infection and bring down her fever, but he was an aged general practitioner attempting to eke out the lives of his similarly aged patients and was not at all equipped to deal with Belle's complex and serious ailment. When Jingle arrived at four in the afternoon, Belle's fever still stood at 103 degrees and she was intermittently delirious, but the infection seemed not to have spread.

Jingle took a quick look at Belle and called an ambulance. While it was coming, she called the college physician at Northampton and asked for the best hospital in the area to handle a case of acute uterine infection following induced miscarriage. He gave her the name of a hospital in Holyoke, and she told him to alert the emergency room there and the relevant surgeons. By six Belle was in surgery for the removal of the rest of the fetus and for whatever cleaning out could be accomplished at that time.

Belle's life was thus saved—for the surgeon in charge had left no doubt it had been as close as that—and she began the long, slow road back to robust health. Belle spent three weeks at the hospital in Holyoke before coming home. Jingle stayed with her for five days, until Lucy could arrive after a stubborn northeast storm eased its grip on the island long enough to allow her to get ashore. But Belle would not let her mother know the entire story, even then. It was not simply that she was ashamed of having had an abortion and of having done it so badly, still less of any implied reflection on her morals. What she could not bring herself to tell her mother was that she had murdered Kevin's child when Kevin was her lawful husband. She could tell Jingle this—and did— and agreed reluctantly to Jingle's telling me, but the tangle of emotions involved in telling her mother was more than she could stand in her weakened condition.

It was accordingly agreed, the doctor concurring, that for the present Lucy should merely know that Belle had suffered a severe but benign ovarian disorder; that indeed was all anyone was meant to know, and Dolores too was pledged to secrecy. Whether Lucy believed the story we never knew, but if she guessed the truth—or part of it—she respected Belle's privacy too much to press for further details.

Two consultations were held in Belle's hospital room the day before Lucy arrived. The first was in the morning with the gynecologist, following a second brief visit to the operating room the day before for removal of further dead tissue and an inspection of the damage that had been caused. The doctor told Belle she might not be able to bear children; it was not a certainty, but a strong probability. Belle listened stoically to his explanation, Jingle asking most of the questions, but when the doctor left, she wept soundlessly into her pillow and Jingle left her alone. Later in the morning, after Jingle had returned, Belle asked, "Would you have done the same thing? You wouldn't have, would you?"

"Well, don't take me as a model where babies are concerned. I'd have anyone's baby, you know that."

"Even if . . . if Emil didn't love you, or you didn't—"

"Don't bother to conjure up impossible situations, honey. I tell you, even if I was raped by a raging maniac, I'd have my baby. I'm a nut about babies." Belle was silent, and Jingle presently added, more gently, "But if I were *you*, dear, not me, I wouldn't want Kevin's baby . . . not just now."

The second consultation was with an assistant dean at Smith, whom Belle, at Jingle's suggestion, had asked to come down in the afternoon. Belle told her the entire story: how she had been married in May when she thought she was pregnant, and married secretly because her parents-in-law were in mourning; how the marriage had fallen on bad times during the summer, before she discovered she now was really pregnant; and finally her decision to terminate the pregnancy.

"To watch the old crow's eyebrows go up and down," Jingle told me later, "you'd have thought she was more bothered by the secret marriage than by that hideous abortion."

Disciplinary action was indicated, the dean said, and after a telephone call to her superior in Northampton, this was fixed as suspension for the rest of the semester, which Belle could not in any case have completed in her present health. Belle asked permission to tell her mother she was taking sick leave, rather than telling her of the suspension, and the dean said this was "most irregular." She grudgingly acquiesced, however, when Jingle described Belle's mother as an aged widow too frail to bear such evil tidings—a description that would hardly have held up had the dean dropped by after Lucy had arrived.

Jingle told me all this in Portland—one evening when Otis was out of town—a few weeks after she had returned.

"Aren't you the sly bastard?" she said, referring to my part in Kevin's and Belle's wedding. "Horning in on all the secrets and not telling me."

What good was a secret, I asked, if everyone knew it? But the secrets surrounding Belle's private life continued to multiply, in layers, until some years later I needed a diagram to remember who was supposed to know what. . . . But of that, more in due course.

Jingle, with her flair for juicy morsels, had a sequel on the abortionist. She took the trouble, when Belle was napping, to make inquiries in Springfield about him and discovered he had a double life of his own. "Would you believe," she told me, "the cockeyed guy had been having an affair with the one at the nursing home. That's how he set up his business. Then he ditched her and started an affair with his secretary, a previous patient. She was the one who got suspicious when the nursing home called that morning, and they both blew town. Neither's been heard from since."

Kevin was almost the last to learn of Belle's illness. Jingle had asked Belle several times in Holyoke whether she didn't want to let Kevin know, but Belle had been clearer on that point than on anything else: Kevin must absolutely not be told. She would tell him herself in time, but for the present she wanted neither his sympathy nor his affection—though Jingle was not convinced on the latter point. Toward the end of October, having heard nothing from Belle since she returned to Smith, or indeed, since midsummer, Kevin telephoned her and heard with astonishment that she had left college. About the same time he telephoned home, and it was George who told him, in morose terms, for now he had realized how far his son had drifted away from Belle, that she had almost died a month before of an acute internal infection. It was Kevin's turn to feel remorse at the gap that had grown between them. Did he suspect the truth any more than Lucy? If he did, he must have put his suspicions aside during the frenzied last ten days of the Progressive Party campaign, which at this time preoccupied him wholly. He wrote Belle in any case, but I was never certain she read his letter. I recognized Kevin's handwriting on a letter I brought up to Meadowlane one afternoon from Caleb's with the rest of Belle's and Lucy's mail; two days later the letter still lay unopened on the hall table and thereafter it disappeared.

38

The election that fall left a deep impact on Kevin. I saw him three weeks later in New York when I was down for another conference with my publishers. I hadn't planned to see him on this brief trip, but he learned of my coming from his parents, with whom I was lunching, and insisted that we get together. I was free in the evening before my train left, and we met at the Oyster Bar at Grand Central Station.

Kevin was pale and gaunt, and his eyes were somber. He had been working ten or twelve hours a day, he said, to catch up on the work he had missed during the last weeks of the campaign.

"And a fucking waste of time it was," he said moodily, picking at his oysters.

I assumed he meant time wasted because of the poor showing of the Wallace ticket nationally and said something to this effect.

"I don't give a shit how we did," he said. Kevin was rarely profane, so I knew something was on his mind and let him come to it in his own way. "As a matter of fact," he continued, "I was relieved the next day we hadn't bombed the election. I mean, if Dewey had carried New York because of us . . . Not that I've suddenly discovered I'm from Missouri. What I meant was a waste of time was going into the goddam mess in the first place. I'm through with politics."

"Or with one-shot stands in politics?" I asked.

"One-shot stands, ten-shot stands, the whole mother-friggin' business."

I wondered, as they announced the Chicago train, how long Kevin would take to come to some point. It would be a novelty, I said to fill a gap in our conversation, if a student of political science stayed permanently out of politics.

"Here's one who's going to try," Kevin said. "Oh, I know *your* view: work within the system if you want results; don't fritter away energy starting up one-shot movements that leave everyone worn out and that much less responsive the next time the call goes out. That's not bad advice if you plan to be a politician; that's sound Machiavellian doctrine. But you don't have to go *into* politics to be relevant *about* politics. Active politics in a know-nothing business, and I doubt if it's any better with Republicans and Democrats than it was with us—probably a damn sight worse. I've learned more about politics in three weeks reading for orals than in three months of mindless strategy sessions for Wallace and Marcantonio."

I said at least they had succeeded in reelecting Marcantonio.

Kevin said, "Oh, boy!"

I had listened attentively between gulps of the rich, scalding stew in front of us, and when Kevin paused to gulp a few mouthfuls himself, I remarked there was nothing he said with which I disagreed. Kevin, who seemed hardly to have heard me, warmed now to his subject. He went on to describe the sort of political scientist he wanted to become. He was interested in measurement, in quantification, in bringing precision into political analysis. He was contemptuous of normative theory and ridiculed the work of several well-known scholars—the deans of the discipline, in fact; he compared them mischievously to half a dozen contemporary empiricists, most of whom I hadn't heard of and said so.

"You will," he said. "I'll be one of them."

When he paused again to attack his oysters, I cautioned him against swinging too far to the opposite extreme; politics, after all, was not an exact science like mathematics.

"I'll worry about going too far when political science has started moving even a little. Know what most texts offer as an example of modern democracy? The Weimar Republic, extinguished fifteen years ago."

At an appropriate moment I asked him quietly whether his new attitude toward politics meant that he had decided to resign from the Party. Kevin shrugged.

"Why bother?" he said. "I'm tired of dramatics. It's not worth the trouble to quit . . . turn in your card and all that crap. I'm just drifting away."

I suggested it might be tidier all around to make a clean break, so there would be no ambiguity, but again Kevin seemed not to be listening.

"Besides, I have no particular quarrel with them. They're working for what they believe in. . . . If I'd turned from Marxism, that might be different. But I figure I have no quarrel with Marxism either. It's how you use it."

Kevin was slow coming around to talking about Belle, which I assumed was the real reason for his wanting to see me. It was not until we were waiting for coffee that he said suddenly, looking me squarely in the eye, "How is she? Is she better? . . . You know, I haven't heard from her since August."

"You know how sick she's been?"

"Dad said she almost died. What was it . . . really?"

"Ovarian cyst," I said, staring back at him.

"I thought it might be...well, a miscarriage after..."

"Ovarian cyst," I repeated. I said she was regaining her strength slowly. She was still weak but would be able to go back to college in February. Kevin wanted to know every detail about her I could give him—how she had arrived from the hospital, what she did with her days, what she was reading, whom she saw. I couldn't begin to satiate his appetite.

"Are we washed up?" he said finally, in a voice no more robust than Belle's had been in the last weeks.

Instead of answering, I asked him where Carmen was.

"Baltimore," Kevin said, eyeing me steadily. "We were more comrades than lovers, you know."

"Were?"

"As I say, she's in Baltimore."

I returned to his question. Why should he imagine he was "washed up" with Belle if they were still husband and wife?

"But I can't just go out and claim her."

"You can come out and see her," I said.

"Can I? Would she . . . I mean . . . She hasn't told her mother, has she?"

"One question at a time. No, she hasn't told Lucy. Yes, you can certainly see her. You can stay with me."

"I'm not going to force myself on her if she doesn't want me," Kevin said, still uneasy—but his eyes brightened at the prospect of seeing Belle again.

As to Belle's "wanting" him, I said, he shouldn't raise his hopes too high. She had been hurt, more than she admitted even to herself. Not because of any particular injury, like Carmen, but because of his having let her go. I said she was chagrined at having dragged him into a marriage he apparently didn't want, at least then. And she ended by not wanting it herself.

Kevin shook his head slowly back and forth as I offered this explanation of their affairs, not in disagreement but in self-reproach. I thought it better, while he was in this mood, to disabuse Kevin of any hope of a quick reconciliation. Belle was not an impulsive person, I said. It might be a long time, even years, before she could accept the relationship they had before they were married. But she was not capricious or vindictive. I said I was certain she would see him and I would in any case talk to her and let him know. I suggested he plan to come out after Christmas.

We finished our coffee, and Kevin walked me slowly out to my Pullman along the half-deserted platform. His limp was more pronounced than usual; the inflammation of his old war injury had returned in one of its mysterious cycles. He waited until the train pulled out ten minutes later and waved me off—a stooped and rather lugubrious figure grown old before his time. But I had a better feeling about Kevin that night than I'd had in many months, and I had higher hopes for his marriage than I'd dared let on to him.

Kevin didn't wait until Christmas. Four days after I returned, a power boat pulled into Cutler's Cove late one gray afternoon and nosed into the steep granite slabs on the south shore, where Kevin jumped off, nearly losing his footing on the slimy surface. The power boat sped back toward Rockland, and Kevin, carrying a briefcase, worked his way around the cove to the cabin. I met him halfway.

"This is wild, I know," he said when we were still some distance apart. "I was going nuts waiting. . . . What if you wrote that Belle didn't want to see me after all?"

When we reached the cabin, I gave him a stiff drink to calm him down after his exhilarating ride across the bay, and he told me of his decision to come out to see for himself how things stood. He hadn't been able to work since I left, he said; he could hardly sleep. So he figured he might as well waste his time this way as staring at the walls in the library. He had made up his mind the evening before and driven all night to catch the mailboat. But his fuel pump gave out in Portland at dawn, and he hadn't reached Rockland until mid-afternoon. By that time he had decided it was smarter in any case to arrive quietly, so he arranged the boat-taxi—leaving his car as surety since he didn't have enough cash with him. He would get word to the Rockland man if he needed a taxi back.

I said Belle had been down with a cold since I'd returned and I hadn't spoken to her about his coming, but I was sure she would see him—especially since he was now on the island. I proposed talking with her first thing in the morning, and he would see her at Meadowlane later.

We had a leisurely dinner, with a bottle of Gevrey-Chambertin, and were sitting around the fire talking about Kevin's reading schedule for his orals when we heard someone on the path from Meadowlane. I assumed it was Lucy and called out to watch for the loose rock by the birch tree. But it was Belle who came into the circle of light from the door.

"Kevin!" she exclaimed, catching sight of him behind me. "What on earth . . ."

Well, I went out as she came in, without troubling to find a pretext, and left them alone for more than an hour. When I cautiously approached the cabin again, I could see their heads close together over the back of the sofa as they talked. I knocked and Belle called out for me to come in.

"You don't have to knock to come into your own home, I hope," she said.

Kevin said, "I sort of wish he did," and I knew from that they had crossed the threshold of their reconciliation.

Kevin stayed two days before returning to Columbia. He saw a good deal of Belle during those days. They were not intimate, of course, since Belle was still not physically ready for that, and I doubt whether they were even amorous, either. But I left them alone as often as I could—Kevin was staying with me— and they had long and serious conversations together. I did not know for certain, since Belle never discussed her abortion with me, and Kevin would not have known how much Jingle told me, but I had the impression that Belle told him about it the night before he left. He came back to the cabin after walking her home and sat wordlessly on the edge of the sofa for some minutes staring into the fire.

"What the poor kid's been through," he said finally, and when I looked at him a moment later, I was astonished to see his head drop into his hands and great tears seep between his fingers onto the bear rug. I went quickly outside and wasted five minutes gathering an armful of logs for a woodbin that was already full.

"It's like a new romance, isn't it?" Lucy said to me after Kevin had left. "As though they were learning to know each other for the first time."

A new romance it was, but with the important difference—which Lucy still didn't know—that they started off as man and wife, at least in the eyes of the law, if not yet in their own eyes.

Book 5 *Belle*

39

I left at the end of 1948 for what was to have been a six-month assignment in Indonesia, but with numerous extensions and side trips, I was away for more than two and a half years, apart from one brief visit in the summer of 1950. Lucy, as usual, kept me posted on developments on the island. The first winter was mild and the lobster season following it was long and profitable. The prices went higher still, breaking all records. Turk and Leonard York fished all that winter for the first time, working the outer ledges off Vinalhaven. Hauling traps even twice a week, which was a good winter average, each of them came close to doubling his income. Clyde Grant and Zip Clayton went together into a forty-foot diesel the next summer. The second winter, however, came early and lasted long on the coast. There were fewer than a dozen days from Christmas to Easter when it was safe for even the diesel-driven lobstermen to fish outside. The loss in traps during back-to-back storms in February cut earnings for the winter season to virtually nothing. In March, after a severe ice storm, Caleb Brewster fell on the wharf carrying a box of supplies from the *Laura Lee II* and fractured his hip. Caleb's recovery was painful and slow.

Despite the severe second winter, however, and mishaps like Caleb's, the islanders on the whole fared well. There were no deaths, though everyone expected Widow Barnaby to go when she came down with pneumonia just before the ice storm. She was moved to Meadowlane, where the women kept a round-the-clock vigil over her, watching her fragile strength waste away. But then she suddenly and inexplicably rallied, and by mid-April she wanted to return to her jetty. They tried to dissuade her, but Lucy, realizing she would pine away sooner away from her shack, finally assented, and the men bore her back. They installed an all-weather window facing seaward so that in inclement weather she could remain inside and watch boats entering the harbor—and wait for John. No one left the island while I was away, and there was one addition to the community—Sharon's fourth child, Carol, born in February of the first winter. Carol, in fact, arrived only two weeks before Jingle's second child, Winni.

"The odds were against me all along," Jingle wrote. "It was supposed to be ten months' notice the competition had begun, eight that it was over. Sharon, the crumb, never gave me warning."

The Thorn Islanders did not make out so well, Lucy wrote. Clarence Darling died that first year—and with him the economic structure of the island. The store was closed and his lobster car rotted at its mooring. His widow, who had been postmistress, moved to Camden, and the farm was boarded up. Several other lobstermen, including the Hopewells, decided to move ashore for the winter, leaving only the Orcutts and Allens on the island. With the post office now closed, the *Laura Lee II,* to economize, dropped Thorn Island from its schedule.

Then, in January of the second winter, Rod Allen, Cecil's brother, lost his new boat on a reef off Brimstone, barely managing to scramble ashore himself through the breakers; another lobsterman picked him up later in the day. He too now joined the migration to the mainland, and was uncertain of his future plans. Cecil and Constance Allen moved to Matinicus in the spring. It would have been more logical, of course, and far less expensive simply to return to Ram Island, where Constance still had land and where they were welcome. But Cecil never forgave the Ram Islanders for the fire. He refused, for instance, to sell his lobsters to Arthur Dacey after Clarence Darling's death, although Arthur offered the Thorn Islanders the same terms for bait, fuel, and other supplies that he offered all his customers. Cecil preferred the long run twice a week into Camden or Rockland to opening any dealings whatsoever on Ram Island. So Thorn Island over two seasons shrank from a tangible community of two dozen or more to Sam and Bertha Orcutt, Barney and José, and Danny.

"That's the way the islands go," Lucy wrote. "A few people hold these communities together. Take away the critical ones and nothing is left. One day it will happen here." But she ended her letter on a more cheerful note, speaking of Lucille Cutler's pending marriage to Danny Orcutt in June. "Wouldn't it be a piece of justice if they decided to build on Constance Allen's site here?" she wrote.

Belle, meanwhile, returned to Northampton after her illness and spent her last semester there; she made up for credits lost the previous autumn by attending summer school at Cornell and was awarded her degree in September. She was in good health, she wrote, but "chastened." She saw Kevin quite frequently during the spring and summer of that first year—but "platonically," she wrote. She had decided to defer living with him as his wife until she had grown up more. "I'm still a little island girl when it comes to life. If I'm to take up this marriage we stumbled so thoughtlessly into, I want to be ready for it." She proposed, if my offer was still good, to spend the coming year in Paris studying the Postimpressionists. She had been working part-time since returning to college and had already repaid part of the loan. I wrote to George Bannister, who of course cabled his approval, and I in turn cabled Belle to go by all means to Paris.

I had fewer letters from Kevin, who was preoccupied through the spring of that first year with his orals, then with his thesis, and by the end of the summer with preparing courses for his first teaching post in Maryland in the fall. He was moving steadily forward in his professional life. An article of his on mathematics and politics appeared in a Western quarterly on politics in July, and he had written a chapter in a forthcoming volume on contemporary political behavior. A friend of mine at Columbia, who was on Kevin's orals committee and knew he was my protégé, added a footnote to a letter to me about another matter: "If I could be sure all our radicals here would turn out as well as Kevin Bannister, I'd start a School of Revolution to set them on their way."

But Kevin was clearly unhappy about the "platonic" relationship with Belle and unhappier still when he heard of her plan to go to Paris, which would prolong their separation even further. "I'm paying for my follies," he wrote in one of the few letters I had from him. But he made no move to oppose her going and, according to Belle's report, even put on a show of enthusiasm for the venture as her departure date approached. He saw her off on the *Mauritania* at the end of September.

The most disquieting news from my friends was from Otis—or rather about Otis, for he was not one to complain of ailments. Indeed, an early letter from him a few months after I left, bursting with irreverence and complaining of Jingle's preoccupation with her two children ("and the crazy bitch wants two more"), made no reference to his troubles. Jingle wrote in the summer, after she had finally persuaded him to consult an internist at the Maine Central Hospital, that the prognosis was "not good." The back pains he had had intermittently for several years, she wrote (I never even knew he had them), were associated with an obscure kidney infection that the doctors could not precisely identify. They did feel, however, that he was overworked—Jingle agreed that Otis drove himself at a frantic pace—and recommended that he take off several months to regain his strength.

He left for Europe in mid-August, and after wandering restlessly about for six weeks—"dodging the goddam ex-GIs come back to relive their conquests in the cafés of France"—he settled in a villa in Corsica for the last weeks of his holiday. Or what were to have been the last weeks. In fact, he engaged the villa through the winter. What he wrote was that he had always been a sucker for islands and thought he could find himself a nice, unattached Corsican girl ("or one attached but willing") with whom to while away the time. But Jingle, with her woman's intuition, suspected another reason: that his condition had worsened. She wrote me all this early in January of the second year I was away. The letter reached me only in March, on the eve of my departure, as it happened, for a round of conferences in Geneva. As soon as there was a break in my schedule, I went to Corsica.

I arrived on a sun-drenched Mediterranean day. Otis met me at the airport in response to my cable. I saw him standing against the white stucco wall of the terminal building as we taxied in, his great hulking figure unmistakable among a cluster of French and Corsicans. He was dressed as he always was: dark, baggy suit; collar unbuttoned under his tie; shoes creased and dust-covered. A Corsican boy of about eighteen in a crisp white shirt and dark shorts stood beside him. I left the plane with the other passengers and joined Otis and the boy.

At closer range I could see the ravages of his disease. He must have lost forty pounds since I had last seen him eighteen months before. His black eyes were set more deeply than ever in his tanned face. Still, out of ancient habit, I said he looked well.

"And you look crappy," he said. "A liar always looks crappy."

When I tried to protest, he cut me off. "Look, pal," he snapped, "let's mince no words. I'm dying. And that's the last I want to hear of it. . . . Let's go, Toro. Grab the man's bag."

And that, in fact, was all Otis said directly about his illness.

We walked behind the terminal to his prewar Citroën, and Toro drove us up the coast to Otis's villa on Cap Corse. The headlands were bold where the narrow coast road wound around them, but the deep valleys where streams flowed down from the mountains to the sea were verdant. Otis, who in his usual compulsive fashion had studied the habits and economy of the Corsicans, gave me a running commentary on the villages we passed. Once, during a pause, I found him looking at me thoughtfully from his corner, and asked why.

"I hope you're broad-minded, chum," was all the answer he gave me, and turned back to his commentary.

Otis's villa stood by itself on a shelf between two lush valleys. It faced northeast, overlooking breaking ledges three hundred feet below. No other dwelling was in sight. The vegetation around the villa was mainly juniper and pine, dwarfed by the Mediterranean breezes that flowed more or less constantly over this sector of the cape. A wide, rocky track winding down a few hundred yards from the coast road served as driveway, until it gave way to a narrow path. We walked on foot to the villa itself. And there, waiting to greet us, as at home as though she came with the villa, was Belle.

After recovering from my initial surprise—indeed, shock—at finding her there, I said this explained why I could never reach her in Paris.

"The Postimpressionists should have painted in Corsica," she said. She was entirely at her ease. "Did you really try to telephone me?"

I said I had put in a call just about daily for the last several weeks. "Finally, your landlady admitted she didn't know when you'd be back—from your *petit tour aux Pyrenees.*"

Otis guffawed. "That's what you get for trying to buy up college girls with your phony financial aid scheme."

I said I'd heard that one before, and winked at Belle. She flushed slightly but was composed. "At least I'm saving you the cost of my keep in Paris," she said.

"Damned skimpy stipend it must have been, too," Otis said. "Drove her straight to the wages of sin." He was in a buoyant mood, back again with Belle. She slapped him lightly on the backsides, and we walked through the book-lined living room onto a stone terrace where a table was set for lunch.

We stretched luncheon over an hour and a half, talking leisurely of whatever came to mind—common friends at home, my mission in Indonesia, affairs of the world. Toro filled our glasses with a Corsican rosé and brought in platters of food from the kitchen. Belle spoke to him in French, Otis in pidgin English. Toro seemed very attached to them. I asked Otis how he had found him.

"He found me," Otis explained. "He was in the driveway when I arrived, and when I couldn't find the key, he jimmied a window and climbed in to unlock the door. He's been here ever since."

I put off the more fundamental questions until I could ask them of Belle alone.

After lunch Otis sprawled out on a deck chair and took a nap. Belle and I drove up a narrow, winding cart track to a high promontory overlooking the cape. We scrambled up the last hundred yards to an ancient pirates' lookout (according to local legend).

"Well . . . how do you find him?" she asked when we had caught our breath and were admiring the spectacular view.

"Ravaged," I said. "And wiser than ever."

"If his poor body were as sound as his mind."

I asked what the outlook was.

"How long, you mean?" Belle asked. "They can't say for sure. Perhaps a year. Possibly even longer. But they've given up on the disease itself. They're only trying to slow its spread. . . . It's inoperable."

"At least he's seeing doctors."

"I told him he had to. I wouldn't stay if he didn't."

"That did it, I bet."

" 'Rank bribery of a raunchy old man,' he called it. But he does go to the clinic now. Every other week."

I asked if there were good doctors at the clinic, and she said there were—especially two French specialists in kidney diseases. "He hadn't seen a doctor since he came to Europe."

I asked Belle when she had arrived.

"In January," she said, "after Jingle wrote urging me to. She suspected he was sicker than he let on. And he was. I came down for a long weekend . . . and never left."

"Who knows you're here?"

"Jingle might suspect, though I haven't told her. I wrote Mme. Aristide, my landlady, explaining the situation and asking her help. She agreed, good Parisian that she is. She forwards my mail, posts mine in Paris, and wards off callers. Like you."

I whistled and told her she had missed her calling; the Secret Service needed her more than the Postimpressionists. "And what—"

"And what about Kevin?" she anticipated my question. "That's the sticky one, isn't it? . . . Are all girls' lives so complicated?"

I said not many girls were married secretly at nineteen, aborted at twenty, and living with another man at twenty-one. She meditated on this a moment. She had been holding my hand, and I could feel the pressure of hers as she thought things through.

"Well, yes, I'm living with Otis," she said slowly. "But not really like his wife. I mean, I'm taking care of him. I'm his nurse. . . . I'm his mistress, too, of course. But I'm also . . . Oh, heck, I don't know what I am."

It crossed my mind that Belle's nurse-and-mistress relationship was a fair equivalent of Kevin's "comrades and lovers," as he had once described his relationship with Carmen de Silva. I asked Belle if she had told Otis about Kevin. She looked at me in surprise. "I don't mean about the marriage," I said quickly. "But do you ever talk about Kevin?"

"What would there be to say? It would be . . . well, embarrassing to Otis. He never mentions Kevin." She went on presently: "As to our being married, yikes . . . If Otis knew that, he wouldn't let me stay."

I said I questioned that but didn't press the matter.

"Anyway, that's how it is, isn't it? He wants me and I want to be here."

I agreed and said I didn't mean to criticize.

"Besides, it's not forever. It can't be forever."

Belle was silent again. "As to Kevin," she said finally. "If he were to . . . to claim me right now, or whatever one does to runaway wives, well . . . I just wouldn't be able to go back to him. That's all." She mumbled, more to herself than to me, "But I must write to him. I haven't written since I came to Corsica."

I nodded without speaking, and presently we walked a short distance along the crest before circling back to the Citroën.

Otis, it was clear, had good days and bad days. The day after I arrived we drove around the tip of Cap Corse to lunch at a small fishing village wedged in an inlet between high cliffs on the western shore. We parked near the market, where Belle and Toro bought vegetables and fish while Otis and I strolled along the quay. We met half an hour later at the Café du Havre, overlooking the harbor. We sat at a table outside under a blue-and-white awning. Toto had an aperitif with us, then went off to visit cousins—he had them all over Corsica.

Most of the fishermen were still out, but there was activity along the quays. A cluster of women were stretching out a net to dry on the seawall in front of us. Children just out of school for lunch were playing a game between stacks of coiled rope farther along. A battered truck was unloading sardines from an equally battered fishing vessel just in. Three aged Corsicans were playing boules under the eucalyptus trees in front of a neighboring café.

Otis made typically trenchant comments on all this activity and I marvelled again how he could retain so much extraneous information. He had been in this village, he said, fewer than a dozen times, yet he knew the structure of the local government, the average income of the local fishermen, the volume of commerce they generated, and the grievances the community had against neighboring communities and against the French. He had attended a murder trial here a month before and discussed the case later with the magistrate. Otis even knew a fair number of the residents, and he nodded to several of them as they passed or greeted them in his atrocious French; but he understood their dialect better than I.

"This is Belle's side of the island," Otis said after we had ordered lunch. "Rugged cliffs, gales, and high seas. Good for the Puritan character. Trust a slovenly Jew to find the lush easterly shore."

"I don't think of Corsica as an island," Belle said.

"I do," said Otis. "I wouldn't be here if it wasn't."

Belle said, "I mean, Corsica's so large. It's like being on the main."

"Nice try, Mrs. Donne," Otis said. "It's a piece of it."

Belle went on presently. "I guess everyone's island is different. My idea of an island would be . . . say, Little Ram, where the sheep are."

"A place to escape to," Otis said, watching a fishing boat maneuver through the heaving seas into the narrow gap in the breakwater.

"A place, in any case, where you do something different from what you do every day," Belle said.

We ate our lunch and talked aimlessly into the afternoon, watching the desultory activity in the harbor and along the quays after the children went back to school. There was no sense of time, no sense of purpose. Our words conveyed no sense of urgency—like the two weeks two years before when we were together, with Jingle, on Ram Island. Toro came by in the Citroën at three to ask if it was time to go home for Otis's siesta.

"Life is a siesta," Otis said, and waved Toro on to another round of cousins. He ordered a third carafe of wine. I had never seen Otis more unwound.

The next day, by contrast, Otis was at odds with the universe. Chairs stood in his way. Ashtrays slid perversely off tables. A freshening breeze in the morning was the beginning of another three-day blow that would drive all of us inside—though the breeze died before noon. He snapped at Toro to take away the goddam garbage as he'd been told and bellowed at him when Toro didn't immediately understand. He greeted me lugubriously on the terrace when he shuffled out in his slippers and bathrobe at ten, looking haggard from a sleepless night. Belle and I had been chatting idly over a second cup of coffee, and Otis rudely turned up the radio so loud we couldn't continue.

Much of his behavior that day was too petulant to take offense at, but he could also hurt. When Belle asked him later in the morning whether he felt up to driving down to a farm where she had ordered cheeses, he said curtly, "You two go."

"No one needs to go," Belle said. "I'll send Toro."

"Go, for Christ's sake! Don't always be complicating plans."

"The fun's going with you, Otis."

"Fun, my ass! Go get your damned cheeses and let me be."

Belle said nothing further, but I could see her eyes well up as she went to the kitchen to bring his fresh coffee. Otis looked morosely out to sea, none too pleased with himself, I gathered.

Belle and I did in the end go for the cheeses. She said as we drove away, "You have to get used to him like this, too. It's not always like yesterday."

The next day, the day I left, Belle went in early to the village with Toro to pick up the mail. She was subdued when they returned. Otis, his spirits recovered, sat on the terrace with me discussing the recent insurrections in Southeast Asia. Belle gave him his mail, dropping into a beach chair beside him. Otis thumbed through his letters, extracting one from Jingle that he read aloud. Belle seemed hardly to listen, gazing distractedly down at the reef below. Before he finished reading, she went inside and puttered about the kitchen, though Toro had cleaned up earlier. Otis, absorbed in the rest of his mail, did not notice Belle's changed mood.

I was to leave on an early-afternoon flight to Marseilles, and the two of them had planned to come with me to the airport. Just before we were to leave, however, Otis thought he would not go—if I didn't mind. But he insisted that Belle go. We said our good-byes, warmly but briefly, each of us conscious we might not meet again. At that time I was still scheduled to return to Indonesia at the end of the month.

Belle's strangely subdued mood persisted as we drove down the coast, but when I tried to ask what was on her mind, she brushed my questions aside. It was only as we approached the airport outside Bastia that she opened her purse and handed me a letter forwarded from Paris. I saw immediately it was from Kevin.

"This came this morning," she said. "Read it."

Dear Belle,

We seem to have fallen on bad times again. It's over three months since I've heard from you and now I don't know where you are. I tried to find you in Paris last week (on my way home from Amsterdam, where I read a paper) but your land-lady was away for a few days and the only person around who seemed to know anything about you was sure you hadn't been in Paris for several months. I saw some letters in your box—including the cable I sent that I was coming—and gath-ered, since all of them had recent postmarks, that someone forwards your mail to wherever you are. I hope they forward this. Or do I?

Since everyone takes it for granted you are still in Paris, you obviously are hid-ing something—from me as from everyone else. There's no good reason why you shouldn't, of course, given the circumstances, but you'll agree it puts a strain on our relationship. I'm not going to pry into your life, Belle. Naturally I must suspect you are with another man—for why else all the secrecy?—but I don't feel I have a right to insist on knowing. I do feel, however, we should reconsider where we are and whether we wish to continue our marriage. It's two years next month that we were married in the Berkshires and in that time we've spent hardly a fortnight together as man and wife.

So that there are no further misunderstandings or ambiguities between us, let me tell you that Carmen is back in Baltimore and that we see each other fairly often. I suppose, if we were divorced, I might in due course marry Carmen (she, of course, knows nothing about our marriage)—but this is no certainty, either from her perspective or mine. In any case, I mention Carmen only to lay everything on the table, not because any decision you and I reach on our marriage should relate to her.

I still love you, Belle. I have no clearer idea than you whether we could really make a go of our marriage, but I am willing to try if you are. I only know that the present situation is impossible. The uncertainty is eating away at me and I suspect it must be doing the same to you.

Affectionately,

Kevin

I read the letter over twice, slowly, and started to speak, but Belle put a finger on her lips, nodding toward Toro. It was true: Toro understood enough English at this point to know what we were talking about even if he couldn't always piece together the sense of our words. We watched an incoming plane bank seaward off the airport and start its run in to land.

After checking in at the terminal, I stood with Belle apart from the other passengers waiting for the Marseilles flight. We still had a few minutes before boarding.

"Short happy marriage of Belle Talbot," she said.

I said, more severely than I intended, "Don't joke!"

"Believe me, I'm not joking."

"Kevin's in no hurry," I said. "Wait a bit."

"I can't keep Kevin waiting indefinitely."

"I don't suggest indefinitely."

"But it is indefinite," Belle insisted. "I won't leave Otis before . . . well, before it's over. And that's indefinite."

I suggested she might meet Kevin—in Nice or Marseilles—and explain the situation. He would come on a moment's notice.

Belle rejected this idea, and I asked why she didn't then *write* him the true facts. That would at least clear the air. She shook her head again. "I don't think you can write your husband and say, 'Look, sweetie pie, I've got this other man who's awful sick and needs me real bad. Bye-bye. Be home 'fore long.' It's too tough on the guy's ego."

My flight was announced over the loudspeaker. Passengers began to file through the exit onto the tarmac.

"No, I know what I've got to do," Belle said. "Give him a divorce. It's the only fair way."

I studied her a moment in silence, conscious of the cluster of passengers thinning at the boarding gate.

"Look, Belle," I said with more severity than I had ever used speaking to her, "you rushed into this marriage. I'm not going to stand by and watch you rush out of it. Do anything you please about this letter today, but give the thing six months."

She weighed this but seemed unconvinced.

"What if *I* wrote Kevin?" I said.

"Absolutely not!" she said with force. "Nor Jingle, nor anyone. I'm tired of people worrying over my problems."

"Fair exchange," I said. "Six months, then?"

She looked at me and slowly smiled—I thought with a sense of relief. The last call was given for my flight. "Crummy blackmailer," she said, embracing me. "Six months."

We embraced again moving toward the exit, and I passed through the gate at the end of the line.

40

I was unexpectedly held over in Geneva through the spring, then ordered to New York for further conferences at the United Nations before returning to my assignment in Indonesia. There was no time to go back to Corsica before I left Europe, but I was in regular communication with Otis and Belle— and with Belle separately. She had written Kevin she would not stand in the way of a divorce if that seemed the best course for them, but wanted to wait until fall to sort things out. She wished she could be less mysterious about what she was doing, she wrote him; however, there were reasons for it. She hoped he understood that she, too, had not given up on their marriage, but neither was she free to take it up at this time. Kevin answered promptly and in the same spirit—via the Paris address, of course—and seemed gratified that there was at last some communication again between them. He proposed meeting her anywhere in Europe, if only for a day or even a few hours, but Belle had to write him this was not possible for the present.

"I'm keeping to your six-month plan," Belle wrote me in Geneva, "but I'm not sure it isn't simply prolonging agonies." I was more sanguine. Otis, meanwhile, held his own through the spring and even seemed to improve slightly during the summer.

A few weeks after I reached New York I was able to take a four-day weekend in Maine. I called Jenny Brewster to ask if she could arrange to open up the bungalow for me, and it was exhilarating—if a bit deafening—to hear an island voice again. She was shouting so loudly into the mouthpiece and holding the receiver so far from her ear (I had seen her do this many times) that we had some difficulty communicating, but I finally got my message across. I asked after Caleb, and she said he was still lame from his fall in the winter.

"We got a s'prise for you here," she bellowed.

I asked if I had to wait until I arrived to find out what it was, but she didn't hear clearly.

"How's that? Speak up, young man. I can't hear a blessed word you're sayin.'" I heard chuckles in the background and knew the store must be full. It was the end of the afternoon and the lobstermen would be in. "Hold the wire. Turk's shoutin' at me 'cross the room." More indistinct babble in the background, then Jenny was back on the line. "Turk says buy yourself a one-way ticket. He'll run you back. D'you git that?"

After a few more confused exchanges, the line clicked dead—either because Jenny hung up or because the operator in Rockland cut the connection before her eardrums burst.

I arrived at the island on a cloudy morning when the overcast seemed not to have decided whether it would burn off to a hazy midsummer sun or thicken to drizzle. The weatherman whose broadcast I heard over the loudspeaker at the Rockland airport suffered a similar uncertainty. There were no Ram Islanders on the mailboat, and it was disconcerting to recognize so few of the other passengers. Horace Snow explained that they were from islands up the bay that had been added to the *Laura Lee II*'s schedule when Thorn Island was dropped. In any case, the Gut was unchanged as we churned up toward the harbor. The osprey rose, circling above the nest at the narrows. The sheep munched on indifferently on Little Ram, then scrambled up the hillside as we passed. Tucker York's fish shack tilted as precariously into the estuary by the quarries as it ever had. And Widow Barnaby came forth, in answer to Horace's whistle at the red nun, to keep vigil on the jetty.

There were a dozen islanders on the pier when we inched in, and Jenny's "s'prise" was prominent among them. Elmer was back. And from the way he took over the unloading of the mail and supplies, it was clear he had come to stay. Lucy gave me the details as we walked to the store. Caleb Brewster had not made a good recovery from his accident. He had been in discomfort all spring and was dispirited. He constantly had to rely on the other men to help him, and if none were about, supplies would sometimes sit several hours on the pier in all kinds of weather before being brought under cover. Jenny's rheumatism, meanwhile, was not improving with the passing years. They were not yet in their sixties, Lucy (who was seventy) remarked, but they were aging. On top of this, the store was busier than ever with the closing of the store on Thorn Island and the addition of three new summer families on Ram.

A month before I arrived, Caleb had put Sharon in charge of the store and gone off to Rockland with Jenny, allegedly to see the doctor.

"That in itself would have been a novelty," Lucy said, "since Caleb boasts he's never seen a doctor, except after his fall last winter. But of course they didn't go to the doctor at all that day. They went straight to Bangor and came back three days later with Elmer and Mary Lou."

Elmer was planning to open a boat shop in an unused shed below the store. There were more lobstermen in the bay that summer than ever before, and boat shops were scarce. If a lobsterman had troubles with his engine or gear he couldn't take care of himself, he might have to lay up for two or three days in Camden waiting for repairs. Sam Clayton had already spoken with Elmer about building a thirty-five-foot diesel together next winter. Elmer was also to serve as agent for the new generator the islanders, at his urging, had finally agreed to support.

Mary Lou helped Jenny in the store, and it was remarkable to see how famously they got along after the bitterness two years before.

"Will you kindly keep your fingers out'n the boy's hair?" Jenny called out through the grill as Elmer stooped behind the counter with a box of groceries and Mary Lou lightly ran her hand over his head. "Can't you see he's payin' you no mind?"

"Oh, he's mindin', Mama. He just ain't talkin'."

And there were guffaws from the men around the pickle barrels—a larger number of them than I would have expected to find on a July morning.

"Run 'long, you no-good lobstermen," Jenny called out as she sorted the mail. "Can't you see Mary Lou's got work to do?"

But if some went away, they invariably drifted back during the course of the day. They were drawn to the store like metal to a magnet—not only the Ram Island lobstermen but the lobstermen from other islands—as word spread that Mary Lou was back. Jenny discovered after Mary Lou had been back a week that sales had jumped thirty percent. When Bill York came in for the third time one day to buy cigarettes, Jenny bellowed at him across the store, "What'cha doin', Bill? Buyin' 'em one by one?"

Mary Lou, meanwhile, played out her role, and it was hardly surprising the men kept coming back. She wore a different outfit every day, generally something tight-fitting above the waist to show off her generous bust. She was not so far advanced in her first pregnancy (which she had announced joyously the day she arrived) to deny herself clothes that set off her still-fine figure. Jenny teased her about her wardrobe, making sure only that she kept herself properly buttoned up, but she drew the line at the curlers in which Mary Lou appeared the afternoon before the July social.

"Child, go take those things off. You look like you're gettin' ready to go to bed."

Caleb, in his rocker by the stove, was more tolerant. "Leave 'er be, Jenny. Ain't nothin' in the world wrong with a girl curlin' her hair before a sociable . . .

Jus' 'cause you had nat'rally curly hair all your life . . ."

Jenny made no reply, but Mary Lou disappeared soon thereafter and came back without the curlers.

"She certainly manages to keep herself . . . well, provocative," Lucy said as we walked away from the store two days later after coming down to greet Jingle, who had arrived on the mailboat.

"Provocative, my eye," said Jingle. "She's just plain sexy."

And Winifred, who was with us, said, "Jennifer! How you talk!"

But if Mary Lou provoked the men, that was all there was for them. When a lobsterman laid hands on her, she would say at first, "Now, that'll do right there." And if he tried again, she would be likely to swing at him, eyes blazing. This put several of them off at first, for there were few adult male islanders who hadn't at some juncture pawed Mary Lou, or more, as she grew up. But they soon learned she was serious and accepted her as she was. As for Elmer, he paid no more attention to her than he ever had. He would keep up a conversation with someone about the new island generator while Mary Lou draped an arm over his shoulder and swung her hip against his. If she grew too distracting, he would likely as not push her aside and say, "Hey, Lou, lemme be."

I naturally saw a good deal of Lucy and Jingle the few days I was on the island. Although Jingle had just been out for three weeks when I wrote her my plan from New York, she turned right around in Portland and came back; she left the children with Emil. I had rehearsed with myself before arriving how to handle the tangled affairs of Belle, Otis, and Kevin, for I knew Lucy and Jingle would be pressing me on points I could not discuss. Lucy, so far as I was aware, still knew nothing of Belle's marriage. Neither knew the romance was in jeopardy. As for Belle's living with Otis, they knew only of her visit in January, about which she had written each of them. I was not supposed even to have seen Belle in Europe, since she had written her mother she was "away" when I called her in Paris. This labyrinth of deceptions, each justified in itself, was simply too complex to cope with in intimate discussion with Lucy and Jingle, so I confined myself to my visit with Otis in April and omitted any reference to Belle. Jingle quite naturally wanted to know every detail about Otis: how he looked, what he did all day, what he ate, who took care of his villa . . . did he have "that Corsican peasant girl" he wanted? I said if he did he kept her out of sight while I was there. I made a good deal of Toro's services.

"Toro can't give the guy what he needs and you know it," Jingle said. She studied me intently as I described Otis's life, and once, when we were alone, she accused me of holding something back. She made the same accusation on another occasion when I refused to be drawn into speculation on Belle and

Kevin's future. Lucy was with us this time and, quick to sense I had my reasons for being uncommunicative, pressed me no further. Jingle yielded with less grace.

"You're about as candid as a clam," she grumbled.

My lack of candor, as Jingle put it, did not place any lasting constraint on relations with Lucy and Jingle. We were as open as always in exchanging experiences and views—most of the latter, not unexpectedly, concerning developments on the island. We had one such discussion walking up the ridge from the Peaks on a blustery afternoon, after sitting for an hour with Sharon on her new back porch overlooking the harbor. As we came to the crossroads, where the whine of the new island generator installed behind the church a fortnight before was most insistent, Lucy involuntarily quickened her pace and fell silent, lips pursed. After we had passed and the whine had receded somewhat, she muttered half under her breath—but meaning us to hear—"Damned contraption!" Expletives from Lucy Talbot were so rare that Jingle burst out laughing. But Lucy was grim. "No, I'm quite serious," she said. "I'm delighted Elmer's back. But must he bring this monster with him?"

"We mightn't have got him without it," Jingle said. And I knew this to be true: Elmer's return had been in no small part related to the installation of the generator, which he would maintain, at the same time acting as agent for the power company that installed it; in this way Elmer hoped to close the gap between his anticipated earnings on the island and his combined income with Mary Lou in Bangor.

But Lucy was less interested in particulars than in generalities—nothing less than the depredations of modernization itself. Gazing backward over her seventy years on the island, she found the "progress" of the last few years more disturbing than any she could remember.

"Oh, we've always had changes. It was a mighty change when they first used gasoline engines in the boats . . . the 'make and break' before the other war. We thought nothing could ever exceed that change. And they did catch more fish. But the cost of maintaining the boats also went up, so there wasn't as much profit as they expected. Above all, they still fished around the islands, not much farther away than they used to go by sail. . . . Now Turk and Leonard go fifteen or twenty miles to sea every day."

"Uncle Frank went that far during Prohibition," Jingle remarked.

"Yes, I know he did. . . . He felt some compulsion to go," Lucy said thoughtfully. "Lord knows, he didn't need the money. . . . Still, it was an occasional venture—not every day, like Turk and Leonard and Clyde." Lucy went on after a pause. "Then there was the wireless. Then the telephone. Then the shortwave radios, so that everyone knows what everyone else is doing every blessed moment of the day or night. And now this noisy generator to sweeten our lives, even though almost every house on the island has its own—"

"Come, Aunt Lucy!" Jingle interrupted. "Surely you're not against *all* progress. Sharon sits in her kitchen and talks to Turk off Isle au Haut whenever she wants."

"And Ginny Clayton will sit all afternoon in front of her television set when she should be cleaning house."

"She'd be gossiping at the store if she wasn't watching soap operas."

"Gossiping's better for her," Lucy said defensively. "I say nothing against Ginny. She's a good soul. It's the television that troubles me. . . . Maybe it's what troubles me most of all."

"You and Otis on television! You're a pair!" Jingle said. "What's the matter with willpower? Turn the damned thing off. Don't you turn off your radio when you don't want it?"

"It's a little the way it was with the first radios, yes . . . once we were sure the announcer wouldn't be offended. But radio, of course, commands only your ears, not your eyes as well."

"Tell it to the blind," Jingle cracked.

We slowed our pace after we passed the Cutlers' and approached the turnoff to Meadowlane. The generator was now a distant hum absorbed in the normal sounds from the harbor.

"I'm not opposed to everything modern," Lucy said, relenting. "Your language, for instance, Jingle. It's jarring sometimes, but it becomes you. It comes naturally. Young people's clothes too. They often appear . . . well, slovenly to older folks, but they seem to suit the young. They express something. Even your uninhibited relations with each other . . . your morals, I suppose they are . . . come naturally."

"Our morals are no worse than Granny Belle's," Jingle said.

"Oh, I think they're a great deal better, dear. I never thought highly of my mother's morals when she was a young woman, as I heard tell of them." Lucy was silent several moments before continuing. "I suppose you think me very old-fashioned, and I suppose I am. . . . You ask about progress, Jingle. Yes, I *would* halt progress for a spell out here if I could. I believe there is a pace to life on an island and it won't be speeded up without risk to the life itself. It's not the same on the main, where there are many ways to adjust to new situations. Resources are more varied. . . . We adjust too, mind you, when we must. When secondary education, for instance, became general, we made arrangements with the school boards in Rockland and Camden rather than lose half the island families to shore communities where there were high schools. We did lose some families, of course, but that was inevitable. . . . Education is a necessity. One

doesn't trifle with education. But island electricity and individual telephones—
the next items on Elmer's agenda, I understand—are *not* necessities. Television is
a step backward. It meets no conceivable need I can think of. It's an utterly useless invention. And now they've invented it, they have to think of tasteless programs to put on it."

"Aunt Lucy," Jingle said, "have you ever *seen* television?"

"Oh, I've seen it. I won't admit to being a specialist, but I've been exposed.
Last week Winnie and I had luncheon at the Thorndike Grill in Rockland with a
television set inconsiderately placed right in front of us. We could hardly converse with each other, let alone enjoy our Blue Plate Special. It insists so."

Jingle said, "As between TV and the Blue Plate Special, I'd take TV."

We had come to the turnoff to Meadowlane and paused there a few
moments before Jingle and I continued up the ridge. When we came to her
house, we decided to go on out to the Head since neither of us was pressed.
Jingle was uncharacteristically silent for some minutes, evidently brooding over
Lucy's gloomy forebodings.

"Lucy's more depressed by the evacuation of Thorn Island than she lets on,"
Jingle said finally. "And she's probably also depressed by another matter she
doesn't discuss: Ram's Horn being boarded up for the second season. If that end
of the island should go to developers—"

I interrupted to say I doubted George Bannister would sell Ram's Horn, let
alone to developers. Jingle shrugged, neither agreeing nor disagreeing with this
opinion.

"Lucy's quite right," she went on, "about the precarious survival of these
islands. A handful of people—sometimes one or two—keep them alive. . . . I
used to feel after Stanley died that what has happened on Thorn Island would
inevitably happen here. Elmer had gone, and it didn't seem Turk and Sharon
could swing it alone. But they did, as you've seen. Now Elmer and Mary Lou are
back. And everyone's having babies all over the place. . . . What I mean, I guess,
is that there's more than one combination of personalities to make things work.
Oh, I agree with Lucy there's been a big change in the pace of life in the last few
years. A change in values, too. Maybe these are the greatest changes ever, as she
suggests. But changes aren't necessarily for the worst. This is what I want to say. .
. . One style goes out, another comes in. Elmer *is* important to us, and if the
price for Elmer is Lucy's 'monster,' I'll buy it. I'll buy a lot more, too . . . So we're
at a watershed, so to speak. Why not a watershed for better times?"

The question was rhetorical and I merely nodded, weighing Jingle's bright
optimism against Lucy's grave pessimism. Jingle was in a sentimental mood that
afternoon and presently she changed the subject to Otis. I had by this time given
her the full negative prognosis on his disease. "There's no upward watershed for

that colossus, is there?" And she added presently, "Somehow I've *got* to see him."

We walked on to the abandoned lighthouse, which Harold Toothacher had been renovating since early spring. The light had long since been extinguished and now the automated fog whistle was silenced in favor of a powerful diaphone farther down the bay. The new owner of the lighthouse—a "comely deevorsay," as Harold called her, with three small children—had been out earlier in the summer, without her children, to see how work was progressing but did not plan to move into the lighthouse until the following season. Harold had left for the day; the door was unlocked. We wandered through the bare, empty house, admiring how the renovation plan had kept the pristine character of the building while making it livable for a modern family; Jingle, who had met the new owner briefly when she was out earlier, said she had drawn the plan herself. As we walked away, and before we gave our attention to other matters, Jingle said, "Maybe this will be the one, my friend. You never fetched one of your own. She's coming to you."

Jingle left on the *Laura Lee II* the next morning, the day before Turk was to run me across to Rockland in the *Sharon.*

Another islander I saw something of during that brief July visit was Sharon Jenkins. It was easy to take Sharon for granted. She was pivotal to life on the island, of course, but she was self-effacing. Her even, uncomplaining character, in a predominantly extroverted community, tended to make you forget her . . . not precisely forget her—for "Sharon will see to it" was a byword on the island whenever some tiresome detail had to be tended to—but forget that she might have a personality of her own. Meanwhile, married to Turk, she naturally fell in the shadow of that towering personality and her individuality was further obscured. Her marriage to Turk when she was five months pregnant with Stanley Talbot's child had been the one great drama in her life, a drama only a handful on the island knew of; it seemed unlikely, on balance, she would experience another of such intensity.

This, in any case, was the way I perceived Sharon. So it was a little unsettling, one afternoon while we sat on her back porch, to hear her tell me she hadn't been at Cutler's Cove since my dinner party for the Daceys, Talbots, and Jenkinses four and a half years before. My discomfort was not eased by recalling that I had sat in her kitchen at the Peaks dozens of times over the years. I said, to cover my embarrassment, that it must have been because she was always having babies.

"Well, I'm not now," she said without reproach, and I said in that case she should come calling before I left.

I was not surprised, therefore, to see her coming down childless through the spruce trees the next afternoon. I greeted her at the door and she gave the house the minute inspection most islanders did who hadn't been to Cutler's Cove since the improvements two years before. She distinguished Elmer's work from Harold Toothacher's, and she immediately recognized Otis's design of the alcove.

"He did my porch, too," she said, and I remembered Otis working on a sketch for it two years before. I also remembered Otis speaking affectionately of Sharon as a "rare beach orchid who had to be sought out to be appreciated."

"Elmo'll have you in electric lights, I suppose," Sharon said. I replied that I had committed myself to the undertaking but not to turning them on.

"That's right. Keep the old gas lamps for flavor."

As I gave her sherry and stirred the fire against a thickening fog from the east, I told her about the conversation I'd had with Lucy and Jingle the day before concerning electricity and the survival of islands. She nodded in agreement several times, appearing to share both Lucy's appraisal and Jingle's instincts, but I could see her mind wandered from the subject. I had her attention again when I gave her something of my laundered version of Otis's life on Corsica, and she asked several intelligent questions about his disease from the perspective of a nurse. I lost her when I started to describe the work I had been doing in Indonesia.

"Do you dream?" she asked abruptly, stopping me in the middle of a sentence.

I said I supposed I dreamed like most people, but I never remembered my dreams for very long.

"Are dreams supposed to mean anything?"

That depended on whom one asked, I told her. Freudian psychologists took them very seriously—then I wondered whether "Freudian psychologists" might silence her. But Sharon was undeterred, and after repeating the words went on.

"Do they say why people dream?"

I disclaimed any special knowledge of the field but said I understood people were supposed to dream—or at least remember their dreams—only as they were waking. Dreams, in a way I never fully grasped, came out backwards: that is, the last of the dream was remembered most distinctly, the beginning buried deep in the subconscious before one began to awaken.

"Then there's not supposed to be a way to fix . . . I mean, to determine what you dream?"

I said I didn't think so; dreams might relate to what one had been doing recently, but usually reflected subconscious thoughts one was not even aware of having.

"I must be some freak," Sharon said.

"I challenge that."

"Well, I have this crazy dream that goes on like a story, like a novel. I mean, it's not all connected up like a real story, but a lot of the people are the same . . . and the places."

"Do you have the dream every night?"

"Not every night. But I can sort of have it when I want it . . . usually. It happened a long time ago—I mean, what happens in the dream was a long time ago. I think it started after I'd been reading Chucky's history book about the Revolutionary War . . . George Washington and everybody. Anyway, it's all about that period."

I asked whether she played herself in the dream.

"That's another dumb thing," she said. "I always seem to be somebody different. Once I was . . . what's her name? . . . Betsy Ross, the one who sewed the first flag. Other times I'm a young girl, all dressed in long skirts and petticoats. Another time . . . no, I won't tell you."

She covered her face with her hands, but she couldn't cover her giggle, and I wondered what amorous adventure had prompted this sudden display of modesty. I said, having started, she'd better give me the whole thing.

"Once I was a soldier," she said, peeking at me through her fingers. "I know it because I was in love with somebody who looked just like me. I mean the real me."

"More and more interesting," I said. "We'd better not tell Turk. He'd be jealous."

"*Don't* tell Turk!" she said, giggling as she drank her sherry. "He'd skin me . . . . But seriously, have you any idea why I have these batty dreams?"

I said I hadn't a clue, but we nonetheless spent a relaxed half hour exploring several fanciful hypotheses: she was unaccountably weary of her woman's life and wanted to pull traps off Isle au Haut, leaving Turk at home at the other end of the ship-to-shore; she was secretly in love with herself and could indulge her passion only by becoming a transvestite in her dreams (I explained the meaning of the word, which predictably she didn't know); it was really George Washington she was in love with, but because of his reputation as a lady's man she thought she stood a better chance catching him as Betsy Ross than as Martha Washington. And so on.

"And the best part of it is," Sharon said as she stood to go, "I can go back there almost any night I want."

At the door she turned abruptly and kissed me—the old island smacker. I must have looked startled because this was not our customary salutation. Sharon flushed.

"Well, that's what Jingle and Belle do. And what they do, I do," she said, and started up the trail.

So gentle Sharon—pillar of the plantation, the island Nightingale, Otis's "beach orchid"—had her own private fantasies in dreams. I resolved never to take her for granted again.

41

Late in August, while I was still in New York, Kevin telephoned to tell me George had had a heart attack ten days earlier. He was about to leave the hospital and Kevin wondered whether I might not come down to Bucks County for the weekend. It would do George a lot of good, he said.

"It would do both of them a lot of good," Kevin added.

After protesting that he should have let me know sooner, I asked how Sally was making out.

"Mother? She'll pull through. Don't worry about her."

I was able to get away for only twenty-four hours, as matters turned out. I drove down Friday evening after a dinner meeting at the Indonesian mission. I arrived about ten-thirty in the evening. George had already gone to bed—or rather to sleep, since he still spent most of the day in bed—but Sally was waiting for me. She greeted me at the door, glass in hand.

"Couldn't wait," she said, waving the glass. "But you should see me. I'm practically on the wagon."

She fixed a Scotch for me, started to top up her own but thought better of it, and we went out onto the south porch. We sat together in the hammock. The Labradors—there seemed to be more of them than before—circled around us, then settled at our feet.

"Two years last May, you mutton. That's too long to stay away from friends. And lovers."

I reminded her I'd been away.

"Away, my eye. You've been two hours away since July eleventh."

"Who told you that?"

"Immigration. Don't press me."

I asked about George and she grew more somber. "George won't live forever. I mean, there was more damage than they thought at first. He'll be on his feet again in a few days, but he'll have more attacks. . . . Damned doctors. They're so cold-blooded. Insisted on telling him the truth just because he asked. Would you want to be told you're going to die?"

"It depends," I said. "I might."

"One last lousy article."

I said nothing. "No, that's unkind," Sally said, leaning against me on the hammock. "That would be a perfectly worthwhile thing to do . . . so long as you didn't make me read it."

I pressed Sally for details of George's attack and she supplied them willingly. "Well, it was at night, as luck would have it," she began. "He hadn't felt well after dinner and went upstairs earlier. I got sloshed, as usual. Watched some zany whodunit until I couldn't stand it any longer, then poured myself my standard nightcap and toddled off to bed. Lucky for all of us I didn't have time to drink it." I had seen those mahogany bedtime toddies and knew what she meant. "Purely by chance—or was it intuition?—I happened to stop outside George's door before going down the hall and heard his breathing. You know, short rasping breaths. I tell you, sport, I must have sobered up in thirty seconds flat. The old boy was awake, but really in pain. I asked why in the world he hadn't called me and he just looked at me sheepishly with those baby-blue eyes. . . . Well, there was Simon and his wife in the garage apartment and Elsie in the ell, probably with her boyfriend again, but I suddenly decided, goddam it, I'm going to do this by myself. I called the doctor after taking George's temperature and pulse, and we agreed he should go to the hospital immediately. The hospital's only fifteen minutes away. I asked the doc if we needed an ambulance and he said he didn't see why if I thought I could cope. Well, by this time I was so sober that even if he knew, the old geezer, that I have a so-called drinking problem after dark, he wouldn't have believed it."

Sally finished her drink slowly and set the glass down on the table in front of us.

"So I dressed George and eased him downstairs into the back of the station wagon, where I had dragged an old mattress. Drinking coffee like mad the whole time. And inhaling breath mints. We arrived at Emergency without incident. And they said it was a damned good thing we did. He was a sick little baby that night. I hung around until they got him to bed, then they shooed me away. It was about two in the morning. . . . Ever leave anyone at a hospital at two in the morning? It's the loneliest feeling going away. You feel so useless, superfluous. I debated between an all-night bar and a diner and decided on the diner. A truckers' place. I drank scalding black coffee for an hour listening to the conversation, everyone giving me the eye. One guy even propositioned me. And, boy, that's good for the ego. . . . You ought to try it."

"Each to his own style," I said, but I put an arm around her. She wiggled closer to me, and I could feel she really did want to be kissed. It wasn't just an act. . . . But then what? I let myself go inert and pretty soon she stopped wiggling. We sat quietly for a time listening to a whippoorwill behind the barns.

"It's a lousy deal," she said, thinking of George again. "He's not even sixty. Quiet, sedentary life. He should be living till he's eighty. He was just beginning to enjoy himself, too. And we were getting along better. I think he began to love me again after Karen. . . . And that Belle! What did she do to him out there that September? He came back walking six feet in the air. He'd bring her name into every conversation—sheep, horses, food, clothes, weather, name it. Really, the guy was obsessed. Finally I had to tell him, Jesus, I like Belle, too, but it wasn't good for me to be compared to her every bleeding minute of the day. And that hurt. He was so contrite. Then he stopped mentioning her altogether so that it was me had to bring her name up now and then, George trying to look indifferent, even when she was sick. . . .

"After she got well again and went back to college, he would write her these long letters. They would take him days. He'd close himself in his study and surround himself with books. Christ, he'd go to the library in Philadelphia for *more* books. It was like you writing some scholarly article. He never told me what he was doing, but I sneaked into his study one day when he was out to have a peek. Know what he was writing the poor girl? The whole damned philosophy of art, as near as I could tell. I couldn't get the half of it. . . . Some love letters!"

"You didn't really expect to find love letters, Sally?"

"Well, no. George wouldn't steal his son's girl."

I asked, since Belle had never mentioned it in her letters to me, whether she had come down to visit them in Bucks County the year before—that is, after she was sick.

"Once. Kevin brought her down . . . when was it? . . . A year ago last June, after she left Smith. Nothing special happened. Kevin was gloomy. He'd just had his orals."

"Kevin did very well on his orals, you know."

"Well, maybe he should have done worse. He was gloomy as a thundercloud anyway. They walked lugubriously around the countryside, about as gay as two octogenarians with the gout. I was on my best behavior, of course, and turned on all my charm. But it needed a bonfire to heat up those two."

I said I doubted the visit was as grim as she described it.

"It was so far as I was concerned," Sally said. "George enjoyed himself, of course. He made up his mind he was going to enjoy their visit and goddam it, he did."

I asked if they had seen much of Kevin during the current year, since he had started teaching.

"Kevin's been very good," she said. "He comes out at least once a month. Lately, since George has been sick, he's been out often. He'll be here for lunch tomorrow. . . . He's . . . he's got another girl, you know. What's her name? Carmen something or other. Well, I can't blame him, with Belle gallivanting all over Europe the way she is—on your money."

I let this pass and asked if Kevin ever brought Carmen to Bucks County.

"God, no! George would have kittens! He doesn't even know she exists. . . . I met her in Philadelphia once. They took me to lunch." I said nothing, and after a moment Sally went on. "She's all right, that girl. I'm not big on the Jewish thing, you know. But she's a tough little number. I liked her."

I still said nothing, and after sitting in silence for some moments we stood up to go to bed. The ship's clock in George's study rang seven bells—eleven-thirty.

"I will have that drink now," Sally said, handing me her glass. "Not too heavy. I mean it."

When I had made her a mild nightcap and one for myself, we walked slowly upstairs, arm in arm.

"Get into bed," she said. "I'm coming to kiss you good-night whether you like it or not."

I heard her go down the hall to check on George, then into her dressing room next to his. I was reading when she slipped into my room a quarter of an hour later. She had on only a transparent silk nightgown, the curve of her breasts and brown nipples showing clearly through. She sat on the side of the bed, took off my glasses, and slowly bent over to kiss me, playing cat and mouse with my tongue. I put my arm lightly around her shoulders.

"I should rape you, you fat slob," she said after a time. "But I won't."

She kissed me again quickly and left.

I had breakfast in my pajamas in George's room the next morning, the strong September sunlight streaming through the easterly windows. Sally had already had her coffee and gone out. George was still in bed reading the morning mail when I came in, followed by Elsie with my tray. He was pale and had lost weight, but he was cheerful. He joshed me for not coming down sooner, when I could have found him in more robust health. I said robust types put me off; I liked serenity and was glad I'd waited.

I fell to my heaping tray, which included kippered herring and scrambled eggs along with grapefruit, coffee, and a few other options. George eyed me enviously.

"You wouldn't believe what heart p-patients are allowed to eat. Or not allowed to." But that was all he said about his illness. Like Otis, he had an extreme aversion to talking about his health. Sally had cautioned me about this, and I skirted the subject.

George pressed me for details about my work in Indonesia, and I was astounded, once again, by the breadth of his interests. The two or three letters I had written them from Southeast Asia were hardly enough to have given him more than the sketchiest outline of our operation, let alone the complex political situation in Batavia, yet he knew a great deal about both. He had obviously read up on Indonesia after my letters arrived. This was George's style, I reflected, watching and listening to him that morning. Stripped of a compelling initiative of his own by the circumstances of his birth and wealth, as well as by certain inhibitions in his personality, he derived his intellectual pleasure in large part by following in considerable detail the pursuits of his friends. When I first knew George, I heard him talk so knowledgeably with Wylie Thatcher about the ball bearing industry I assumed he must have some connection with it; later I discovered this was not so. It was the same with Belle. Those long letters he wrote her, I assumed, were part of a process of familiarizing himself with the things that interested her. His recent absorption with Kevin's work was also part of this pattern of vicarious intellectual preoccupation. He had grown very proud of Kevin after reading an article by him in one of the professional journals. The article was also attracting some attention in scholarly circles.

"Did you read it?" he asked. I said I hadn't, and he went right on. "You know, it's a capital piece. I was really very much impressed. He gave it to me as he left on Sunday, saying it was a thing he had been working on that might interest me. Well, interest me it did." George went on to describe the article in some detail, and I recognized the arguments as deriving from Kevin's train of thought the night we had met at the Oyster Bar in Grand Central Station after the 1948 election. "His ideas seem very fresh, original. They're trying to bring politics at last down to something you can test. No more *pronunciamentos* about how things *ought* to be."

I suggested a normative politics was probably more in George's style than the empirical studies that attracted Kevin, but George would not agree.

"You of all p-people!" he said. "Out there calculating the electric power they need in a village in Borneo. You ought to see the value of measurement."

I said measuring electric power in Kalimantan was hardly the same exercise as measuring political power in Batavia. But I went no further, not wishing to dampen George's enthusiasm for Kevin's work. "Kevin is a pioneer in his field," I said.

George took this in. "That's a pleasant thought, isn't it? After so long a detour through Marxism . . . Is he still a M-Marxist, do you think?"

I said I didn't know but doubted the influence was strong today. "Was it really so long a detour, George?"

"It seemed so while it was going on," George said. "It seemed an eternity."

George had been holding a letter in his hand as we talked, occasionally striking it gently on the blue bedcover to make a point. He looked at it now.

"This is from B-B-Belle T-Talbot," he said, his stammer increasing. "Shall I read it to you?"

I nodded, and he read the letter slowly. It described a walk into some mountains, a sudden rain squall in a high sloping valley where she took shelter in an abandoned shepherd's hut; later she came down into a small village that wasn't on her map but where there were two dozen farms and even a small Moorish chapel. She commented on the chapel in some detail—detail that made sense to George but none to me.

When he finished reading, I asked guardedly where this mountain village was.

"Oh, I don't know," George said. "Somewhere in the P-Pyrenees, I suppose. She's very hazy about geography. . . . This is postmarked Paris. She writes all her letters after she gets back to Paris."

"Does she write often?" I asked.

"She answers every letter of mine. They usually c-cross."

I didn't ask if he had written Belle about his illness since I knew in advance he hadn't and wouldn't.

He was preoccupied for a few moments rereading part of the letter—the part about the Moorish chapel, I could see. He seemed to forget I was there. In time he folded the letter and put it away, looking at me a little sheepishly.

"I don't show these l-l-letters to Sally," he said. "She gets upset."

Before I left him to dress, George asked about the fund for Belle's education. I assured him that no one knew of his part in it and that there was an ample balance; I did not, of course, mention that nothing had been drawn since the first of the year.

"There must be no question about her having all she n-needs for as long as she wants it."

He was looking past me at the fields across the pond where the men were taking in a second crop of hay.

"I'm so sorry both you and Kevin missed her in Paris. I so want someone to see her in the f-f-flesh. . . . I don't suppose you have any idea, do you, from her mother or her friends on the island, how soon she'll be coming b-back?"

I shook my head, and George said, "Well, let's hope it's b-b-before . . . before too long."

Kevin arrived toward the end of the morning, and the four of us lunched together on the north terrace out of the midday sun. It was an airless but sparkling day, more like July than September. Kevin was somber, but this apparently was his usual demeanor now. "Professorial," Sally called it, mimicking his long face. The only comic relief in his appearance was his right ear, projecting more winglike than ever from the side of his head.

"Just think," Sally confided to me as Kevin went in for the sherry, "if he hadn't had that mastoid operation when he was six, he could fly."

During lunch I pressed Kevin about his research that summer and eventually drew from him that his book, the first chapter of which was the article George and I had discussed over breakfast, was to be published by Columbia later in the fall. George, who had not heard this news, beamed.

"But . . . but how long have you known this, Kevin?"

Kevin said he had signed the contract three days before.

"And he waits until dessert to tell us!" said Sally. "How's that for grandstanding?"

After coffee George went back upstairs to rest and Sally went off with Simon to an auction of old glass. Kevin and I strolled through the farm buildings, immaculate as always, and up onto the hill behind the pasture. We walked slowly since Kevin's war injury was bothering him again. I had taken it for granted Kevin would want to talk about Belle and waited for him to open the subject. No one had mentioned her at lunch: George, I assumed, out of deference to Sally (although Sally had brought him his mail and knew he had a letter from Belle); I because it seemed inappropriate—even deceitful—knowing what I did of her affairs yet bound to secrecy; and Kevin, I suppose, because he had nothing to say. Yet alone with me, I thought he would open up. And, of course, I wanted him to, for I was particularly interested in his reaction to the current state of their relationship. But Kevin kept any reactions to himself, and finally I brought up Belle, asking him if he had heard from her.

"We're in touch," he said briefly. I waited for him to say more, but he merely remarked, tonelessly, that he hoped I hadn't been witness to an abortive marriage.

"I hope so indeed," I said.

Kevin said, "We'll see."

There were, to be sure, other matters on Kevin's mind that day. It was during this walk that I learned for the first time of the gravity of his difficulties in Maryland over past political ties. I had expected Kevin to have trouble with his initial appointment, given the ugly mood in the country respecting alleged Communist subversion on the campuses, but when he was appointed in Maryland, I had assumed the matter was settled. The Maryland legislature, however, had in the interim passed a tough law on loyalty, and it was this law that brought on Kevin's current troubles. I knew, from my friend at Columbia who had been on Kevin's orals committee, only that his contract was under review. I asked Kevin how matters stood.

"It's an open-and-shut case," he said. "They want to fire me."

"Who's 'they'?"

"The dean, the administration—egged on by some alumni, local veterans' groups, and half-assed politicians fired up by the war in Korea."

"For having been a Communist?"

"For not saying bluntly enough I'm not one now."

I looked back at Kevin, limping along on the wagon track behind me. "But surely you're not still in the Party, Kevin."

"Not as far as I'm concerned. I haven't paid dues or been to a meeting since the 'forty-eight election. . . . That doesn't mean I'm off their mailing lists."

"But isn't there supposed to be a Party card or something?"

"I haven't a clue where mine is. It's probably lost."

I asked why he didn't simply write to Party Headquarters or his cell leader or wherever he was supposed to, with a copy to his dean, saying he had given up his membership.

"That's what they want, of course, a denunciation of the Communist Party by a former member. . . . It's very fashionable these days to be an ex-Communist turned Red-baiter."

"Why denounce anything? Just quit."

"Whatever I wrote would be twisted into a denunciation."

We came to the top of the hill and stretched out under an oak tree, watching a chicken hawk through the branches high above us.

"That's only the half of it, my friend," Kevin went on. "The pressure I'm getting from the other side to hold on is just as rough. From the Travelers, the Comrades, Party Headquarters itself . . . They're running a profile of me in the *Worker* next week: PORTRAIT OF A FREEDOM FIGHTER."

"Can't you stop it?"

"Ever tried to stop a piece in the *Daily Worker*?"

I said I hoped the pressure from the Left was not at least coming via Carmen. Kevin flushed but looked at me evenly. "Not via Carmen," he said. After a moment he added, "But Carmen does come into the picture in a different way. . . . The dean called me in last week and asked what was this rumor of my living with a woman out of wedlock. I said I assumed my private life was my own affair—as his was. . . . I doubt if that helped matters."

I was silent, and Kevin, answering my unasked question, continued, "Well, we're *not* living together, in case you're interested. She has her apartment in Baltimore and I have mine. . . . We did consider living together last spring, but we decided against it. I decided against it." Kevin did not elaborate, nor did he need to; I was pretty sure I knew why he had come to this decision.

Kevin then went on to explain how matters stood with respect to his contract in Maryland. Under the new loyalty statute, institutions receiving public funds, like his college, had to satisfy the state authorities that they had no subversive persons on the payroll. The law did not specify how the colleges and universities were to determine this, and in his case a faculty committee had been set up to hold hearings. There was still confusion over the authority of the faculty committee. Faculty spokesmen naturally wanted the committee to have the final word on any contract. But the trustees refused. Kevin paraphrased one of them as having said, in effect, "If you suspect a crook, you don't go to a bunch of other suspected crooks for a verdict." In any case, the committee was going ahead with the hearings, which were scheduled in about two weeks, just after the start of the fall term. They were to be closed to the press and outsiders. Kevin was allowed to call in any witnesses he cared to, and the committee could ask whatever questions it wished.

I asked Kevin what witnesses he was calling. "I thought your friend at Columbia who was on my orals committee. A few colleagues here. Several students—conservative. And you, I hope, if you haven't left."

I told him I thought his list sensible and assured him I could put off my departure if necessary. We were silent as I reviewed in my mind the details of his case. I said finally that when all was taken into consideration, I couldn't see what damage there was—to his pride or honor—in simply announcing as unambiguously as he could that he was no longer a Communist and hadn't been in nearly two years. It was, after all, a movement from which he was now disaffected and had no intention of rejoining. It seemed only prudent to protect himself from unjust accusations during an era of rising anti-Communist hysteria.

Kevin shook his head. "It's exactly the rising hysteria that makes me take a different course. . . . Look, if I join some group, and the group, over my protests, takes a position that offends me, I leave that organization and I make some statement as to why. But if I simply lose interest in my organization, I just drift away. Well, it's the same here. There are positions the Party takes, of course, with which I disagree, but then I always disagreed with these positions. They seemed insignificant beside the ultimate objective. The Communist Party, take it or leave it, is an instrument for total change. It's not for isolated issues. I've lost interest in total change during the last two years. In short, *I've* changed. Not the Party. So to make a big thing of quitting the Party is tantamount to saying *I* was a jerk—and everyone who still belongs is a jerk. . . . I don't believe this. I have no quarrel with a good many Party members: grimy coal workers, the flea-bitten old ladies with good intentions, the starry-eyed students hoping to change the world. I'm not embarrassed at having worked with them any more than you're embarrassed at having a long-standing interest in Marxist theory. I'd be a damned sight more embarrassed, God knows, if I'd worked the same length of time with Bucks County Republicans. . . . No, I've simply drifted away from my organization. I bear it no grudge. I've no reason to deny it publicly because people for whom I have less respect than I have for many of my former comrades ask me to. If the price to pay is my job, tough. I'll find something else to do."

He glanced at me after this lengthy justification of his position and must have found me looking rather bleak, for he said presently, "Don't think I'm unappreciative of your advice, old friend. . . . I pretty much anticipated what it would be." And then he smiled slowly—for the first time, I believe, since he had arrived that morning.

As we walked down the far side of the hill to find the abandoned town road leading back to the farm, Kevin told me he had not yet explained the situation to his parents; he was waiting for George to recover his strength. But he would have to talk to them about it before he left the next afternoon, for there would be news items on the case within a few days.

Driving back to New York after dinner that evening, I reached a decision, and after returning to my temporary apartment spent some time over the wording of a cable that I sent next morning to Belle in Corsica: "George Bannister convalescing after heart attack. More attacks expected. If Otis agreeable suggest you return for two weeks. Funds available."

Belle called on Wednesday and said that she would arrive in New York on Sunday.

42

When I met Belle at LaGuardia Airport, stories about Kevin's loyalty hearing in Maryland had been in the newspapers for several days. The more-radical press had already made a cause célèbre of the case, running impassioned editorials on academic freedom. Maryland papers kept the story alive with patriotic releases from aspiring politicians and, if no politicians were immediately available, with rank speculation: TRUSTEE VOWS TO PURGE FACULTY OF COMMIES; LEGION COMMANDER PLANS GIANT RALLY AT FACULTY HEARING; WAR HERO WEIGHS RED DENUNCIATION. I had gathered an envelope of clippings that I gave to Belle to read as we struggled through the Sunday traffic on our way to Bucks County.

"Kevin's grown famous," Belle said, sifting through the clippings.

"Notorious, anyway."

"How will it turn out?"

I said Kevin might be fired, but he'd be a hero in some circles whatever happened. Belle read on.

"What's this? What's this?" she said, coming on an item I hadn't noticed on the back side of a clipping from a Baltimore tabloid. " 'RED PROFESSOR FACES MORALS CHARGE. It now appears certain that members of the faculty committee will question young Bannister on his private life. A bachelor, he is known to have been living openly with another ex-Red . . . ' "

"It isn't true," I said.

"True or not, is it relevant? Can they really question Kevin about his private life?"

I said in these times it was impossible to say what would be dredged up.

When she had finished going through the clippings, Belle said, "I came back for the father but it's the son who seems in greatest trouble. If I didn't know you so well, it would almost seem . . ."

"It would at that, wouldn't it?" I said, and we both laughed.

Belle's plane had come in too late for us to reach Bucks County in time for dinner, so we ate along the way and arrived around nine. I had telephoned Sally to tell her Belle was coming from Europe for a couple of weeks at my suggestion, and I would bring her down en route to Washington for a Monday morning meeting. "You sly devil," she said when she had taken in the plan, but she welcomed Belle's coming—"especially after this terrible last week in Maryland." Kevin had warned his parents the previous Sunday of the coming storm over his contract, but neither of them had expected such an outpouring of publicity about the case. Kevin had been up again for the weekend but had had to leave a few hours before Belle and I arrived.

George was still downstairs when we drove into the courtyard. He greeted Belle at the door in his red smoking jacket, leaning lightly on his cane. Belle embraced him and scolded him gently for waiting up.

"'Ten horses couldn't have dragged him to bed, dear, before you came," Sally said.

George was tongue-tied. I'm sure he had rehearsed things to say, but he stammered so helplessly each time he opened his mouth that he finally gave up trying to speak and simply stared at Belle. Sally soon sent him up to bed.

"You play nurse tonight," she said to Belle. "His pills are by his bed. A red one and a white one."

So Belle took George off to bed, and I drank a highball with Sally in the library before driving on to Washington, where I had an early meeting the next day. I asked how George was taking Kevin's case.

"He's extraordinary," Sally said as I lit her cigarette. "At first he was . . . well, humiliated by Kevin's difficulties. I think he felt it was a matter of bad breeding. But by the middle of the week he had absorbed himself in the whole debate on academic freedom. Read everything he could lay his hands on. Sent Simon into Philadelphia for the latest journals. You'd think he was personally leading the campaign against loyalty oaths. . . . What a Red he's become! I'm expecting the FBI at the door any day. . . . So, when Kevin came up yesterday, George was able to discuss every aspect of the case with him. George really sympathizes with Kevin's stand, you know. At one point when Kevin was ready to throw in the towel, all the pressure he's under, it was George who said he had to stand firm. 'It's the p-p-principle of it, Kevin. Not your own gratifications.' "

I asked whether George had seen reports of Kevin's alleged romance with Carmen de Silva.

"You know, that's the damndest thing. He's bound to have seen those stories since he reads everything, but he's never mentioned them. I guess he thinks this is a gentleman's . . . well, prerogative. Poor form to discuss it in public."

Upstairs we heard the ripple of Belle's laughter as George called something to her from the bathroom.

"Aren't they cute?" Sally said. "He thinks he's twenty-one again."

Belle had not come down when I left for Washington a quarter of an hour later.

The next weekend, the one before Kevin's hearing, we were all gathered in Bucks County. I arrived late Saturday morning from Washington. Kevin had been there off and on all week, although the term had begun. He had come up Monday night to greet Belle, planning to return on Friday, but he was back on Wednesday and again on Thursday. In fact, he was commuting between Maryland and Bucks County though it was a two-and-a-half-hour drive each way. He and Belle were just returning from a long walk as I arrived, and I could see at a glance that they were at ease with each other—even before Sally drew me aside to give me certain particulars.

"I don't know what sort of an establishment I'm running here," Sally confided. "The guy hasn't slept in his own bed all week. He hasn't even the decency to rumple the sheets."

"Let them be, Sally. They know what they're doing."

"Oh, I don't doubt that," Sally said. "But doesn't he already have morals problems enough?"

I could see, however, that Sally was not in the least troubled by her discovery. Indeed, she doubtless took satisfaction in knowing that George's paragon was not, after all, above reproach. I let the matter drop.

After a spirited luncheon, during which George seemed more relaxed than I had seen him since his illness, Kevin drove off with Sally to shop and George went up for his nap. Belle and I stretched out on the lawn overlooking the pond. I had sensed during lunch that she wanted to speak to me.

"Well, the cat's out of the bag," she said as the sound of the tires died down the gravel driveway. "Half out, anyway."

I looked at her blankly, not understanding.

"I told George we're married."

I must have looked incredulous, for she laughed and said, "Don't ask me why. It just came out. He was being a bit sentimental, you know, the way he is. He said his fondest hope had always b-b-been that Kev and I would get m-m-married. I thought a moment and I said, 'George, we did.'"

"Just like that?"

"Just like that. He didn't understand at first, of course, but I explained it all. I told him we kept it a secret because it was so soon after Karen died. Then things didn't go so well between us so that we didn't feel we wanted to tell anyone. I told George we still weren't a hundred percent sure where we were and that, anyway, I had to go back to Europe. I absolutely had to, for as much as a year. He didn't press me why. He only asked for a promise: that I would eventually return to Kevin. And do you know what I did? . . . I promised."

I whistled lightly and said the two of them had solved a great many outstanding problems in those few minutes. I asked if she'd told Sally.

"Tomorrow, or the next day. I wanted my letter to get to Mummy first."

"And Kevin? You told him what you told George?"

"Of course I told Kevin, dummy. We're all right, you know, me and Kevin."

I said that was obvious—even without Sally's citing to me circumstantial evidence.

"Oh, that," Belle said, laughing. "We didn't try too hard to keep it from her."

"Did you tell Kevin about Otis too?"

"Not specifically about Otis; simply that I had to go back to Europe and I didn't want him to ask why. He put on a long face and said couldn't we at least meet sometime. So we have a tentative plan to get together for a few days at the end of the year. In Nice, most likely."

I was silent for some moments, taking in the dimension of this new turn in their affairs. Belle must have thought I didn't wholly approve, for she said presently, "You do understand about Otis, don't you? Things wouldn't have worked out if I couldn't go back to Otis . . . to the end, whenever that comes."

I assured her I understood completely and marveled only at her ingenuity.

43

Kevin's hearing was held on Monday and Tuesday of the following week. I missed the first afternoon since I had to be in Washington again for a final conference before my long-delayed departure for Indonesia. I telephoned Bucks County in the evening to ask how the first session had gone and got Belle. She and Kevin had returned from Maryland a half hour before. Kevin was upstairs with George and Sally.

"It seems fair enough, I suppose," Belle said. "Kevin brings in anyone he wants to testify and the committee asks questions. They don't have strict rules. . . . Kevin had your friend from Columbia, the sociologist. He was very good, very professional. Then there were several of Kevin's students. Most of them got dumb questions like 'Does he teach you any Communism?' One of the students got a laugh when he said he wished he did; that would at least be simpler than the stuff Kevin *does* teach. . . . But it was mostly depressing."

I asked if the members of the committee seemed impartial.

"Impartial, I doubt. Fair, maybe—except for one economics professor who's a curmudgeon."

"Was it crowded?"

"Not very. Apart from the six committee members and witnesses, there were never more than a dozen or so. You have to have a pass. . . . Carmen was there. But she left before the end, so I didn't have a chance to speak to her."

"Just what did you plan to say?" I said lightly.

"Oh, I hadn't *planned* anything. Certainly not what a jealous wife is supposed to say to her husband's former lover—if I knew what that was. . . . Anyway, I'll feel better when Kevin has a chance to tell her how things are."

Belle said they were taking Sally with them the next day. George had wanted to go, too, but the doctor, not unexpectedly, vetoed the idea in no uncertain terms. Before I hung up, we made a plan to meet for an early lunch before the hearing.

Rain was falling in a slow, relentless drizzle as we walked across campus the next day after luncheon at the inn. About two dozen picketers moved slowly back and forth in front of the administration building where the hearing was held. Several of them carried limp placards: STRIKE A BLOW FOR ACADEMIC FREEDOM!; KEEP KEVIN BANNISTER ON THE . . .—the rest was too streaked to decipher. Two state troopers in a police car down the street kept the marchers under watch. Some thirty onlookers had gathered, among them two or three in trench coats standing unobtrusively at the side, caps pulled low over expressionless faces. A solitary photographer, huddled under the eaves of the building trying to keep his camera dry, missed Kevin's arrival. A man of indeterminate age in a broad-brimmed hat stood conspicuously at the top of the granite steps gesticulating to a companion.

"That's the curmudgeon," Belle told me.

Kevin was recognized as we approached, and a few shouts went up from the picketers: "Give 'em hell, Professor!"; "Keep America free!" From the onlookers came at least one countervailing cry: "Go back to Russia where you come from, ya lousy Red!"

Kevin paid no attention to the shouts. He walked slowly past the demonstrators, staring stonily into the faces of several and giving no answer to their greetings.

"*Say* something to them, Kevin," Belle whispered to him.

"Why should I? Not one in three's a student here."

Inside, we walked up the broad circular stairs to a faculty committee room on the second floor. Sally and Belle showed their passes at the door and an attendant checked off my name. The committee members were assembling at one side of a long oak conference table. A single chair was opposite them, for witnesses, and behind this were several rows of fixed seats. Kevin sat in the front row and we sat behind him, Belle in the center. She identified the committee members in a low voice. The chairman, with long, flowing white hair, was Professor Hughes of the English Department; he was near retirement. The economist, Professor Hawkins, had steel-gray hair and a thin moustache; he sat at the chairman's left. To Hawkins's left were two professors who looked to be in their forties, one in mathematics, the other in physics. On the chairman's right was a bearded professor of Romance languages, reading a dog-eared copy of *Candide* and paying little attention to what was going on around him. The youngest member of the committee, an assistant professor of sociology, was at the chairman's extreme right. The make-up of the committee, it was clear, was along normal divisional lines.

The chairman rapped for silence and asked Kevin if he had further witnesses. Kevin said he had one, and he introduced me. I took the chair facing the committee. The object of the hearing, the chairman explained to me, was to consider Kevin Bannister's fitness to continue teaching at the college; the committee was charged with making a recommendation in this matter to the board of trustees prior to its October meeting. I nodded and said I was familiar with faculty procedures in such matters. Professor Hughes explained that the committee's rules were intentionally informal and asked if I cared to make a general statement before the committee put a few questions to me. I said I did and took eight or ten minutes to develop what I understood to be Kevin's intellectual development since the end of the war, as long as I had known him. Understandably, I felt a bit ponderous describing Kevin's intellectual growth to these strangers while Kevin, who knew it far better than I, sat silently a few feet behind me.

I argued essentially that Kevin's interest in Marxism was in no way abnormal for a concerned person of his background and experience. During the war, before he was shot down over Germany at the end of 1944, he had been repelled by the cynicism of his fellow pilots in officers' clubs in England and France where the talk was loosely of pushing the Russians eastward to the Vistula and beyond. Accordingly, when he was in prison camp near the Polish border, he looked with greater rather than less favor on Soviet pretensions in Eastern Europe. There was even a certain intellectual toughness in his doing so, I said, for I knew of no American casually won over to a pro-Soviet perspective through observation of the Russians' behavior in their zone of advance into Germany. When he returned after the war, the bankruptcy of our bipartisan containment policy, as Kevin perceived it, as well as the failure of Republicans and Democrats alike to show any significant initiative in resolving domestic social problems, led him to identify with forces in the United States seeking to launch a third major party. Historically, such efforts showed a bleak record yet were a legitimate part of our political process. I said I, too, had been attracted to the Wallace movement for a time and had taken part in drafting the Progressive Party platform.

Why it was that some third-party enthusiasts, like Kevin, were drawn to the Communists was a matter, I confessed, I did not fully understand. I suspected it was a matter of chance as much as anything else—the chance of associations, the chance of proximity to sources of Communist appeal. Communism in the United States was always strongest in New York, where Kevin was studying during this period, and it was perhaps natural that he should encounter Communists among those dissatisfied with the course of our policies at home and abroad. There might have been an additional consideration in Kevin's case, I added: his personal uneasiness at being born into a financially privileged family and wishing to compensate for this by working toward a more equitable distribution of the nation's wealth.

"You mean," Professor Hawkins interrupted, "the Bannisters could bail him out if he got himself into trouble?"

I said that was not at all what I meant and hoped his question in turn did not mean that he, as an economist, believed the function of wealth was to bail young scions out of their troubles. It was not very deep logic but it was enough to silence him—for the moment. I continued. The 1948 election had been a turning point for Kevin, as for many others interested in the third-party route. The poor showing of the Wallace movement at the polls, measured against expectations, had a sobering effect on political activists. They either transferred their attention to other avenues of political expression, normally within the two major parties, or, like Kevin, they abandoned politics altogether and turned to other pursuits. I added a personal observation: While I respected the contributions Kevin had made and would continue to make to the *study* of politics, I hoped the disappointments of his political involvement two years earlier would not discourage him from becoming active again. The vigor of a democratic system, I felt (and this was the end of my pontificating), depended upon the persistent efforts of those who were both concerned and knowledgeable.

"Even if they're Reds?" the economist broke in again.

"Kevin Bannister is no Communist today," I said, "if that's what you mean to imply. But if you ask whether I think Communists should be allowed to pursue political activity, I answer yes, I do believe this. Though I doubt that my view is germane to this committee's inquiry."

"No, I should not think it was germane," the chairman said mildly.

"Well, it's germane to me," the economist grumbled.

"Fine," I said. "Let's pursue it—the committee willing." I waited for him to speak.

"You say that Reds, Marxists, Commies—call 'em what you want—ought to have the right to take part in our elections and hold office, knowing full well that—"

"I don't say they should hold public office," I interrupted him in turn, "at least without swearing an oath of loyalty to the appropriate constitution." I pointed out that most of the states had laws to this effect, as Maryland did, and I said this seemed proper in any political system. Participation in elections, however, was a different matter. If Communists were denied this right, they would inevitably be driven to more desperate measures. If their philosophy was distasteful to most voters, wasn't it better that they be defeated in the open? Did he seriously imagine, I asked, that any significant number of Communists could be elected to office in the United States?

"I shouldn't want to take the responsibility of giving 'em a chance," he said, "knowing they'd overturn our system in a flash."

I conceded that the republic would indeed be in danger if voters so disabused my faith in them as to vote Communist in large numbers.

Our exchange prompted questions from other members of the committee, three of whom now began to speak at once. I asked the chairman if I might make one further observation, then I would be glad to answer any questions I could. Professor Hawkins intervened again before I could proceed.

"I want it a matter of record, Mr. Chairman, that I mean to come back to the question of whether Mr. Bannister is still a member of the Communist Party, a question that was neatly slid over a moment ago."

"Well, we have no official record, John," the chairman said. "But I'll keep what you say in mind." He motioned for me to go ahead.

I said I did not presume to lecture members of any faculty on the distinction between Marxism and Communism, but I wanted to be sure, in Kevin Bannister's interest, that the distinction was properly made by this committee. Marxism, as I understood it, was a system of inquiry, an aid to investigation—

and therefore comparable to many other systems and ideologies, such as the
Malthusian, the Keynsian, the Ricardian, and so forth. It had more currency in
some eras than in others. It was very much part of my own intellectual background in a midwestern college in the early 1930s, for instance—not Stalin's
brand of Marxism, but the earlier versions of Karl Kautsky, Rosa Luxemburg,
even Leon Trotsky. After the war there was another surge of interest in Marxism,
especially in Europe but also in the United States. I suggested Kevin's interest in
Marxism might have been stimulated in part by my own.

"I call attention to these matters," I continued, "because I feel in all fairness
no one should be charged with being a Communist merely because he expresses
an interest in Marxism. Quite frankly, I don't know whether Kevin Bannister
considers himself a Marxist today or not. I haven't questioned him closely
enough on this in the last year or so to be sure. What I do know is that he is not
a Communist, nor has he been one in any real meaning of the term since
November 1948. . . . This, I gather, is precisely the point on which you wish to
question me further. I am ready for your questions, Mr. Chairman."

"Well, yes," Professor Hughes said, running his fingers through his silvery
hair. "We're very grateful for your remarks and I guess—"

"Grateful, hell, Pendleton!" Professor Hawkins put in. "I'm not in the least
grateful for anything he's said. I've got a dozen questions here and—"

"Oh, I'm sure you have, John. And we'll come to them. Only I think we
should have a little order, don't you? We'll start around the committee, shall
we?"

"Start any way you want. Put me at the end if it pleases you. Only let's not
start by being grateful for a bunch of arrant hogwash."

"Well, good, I'll put you last. . . . Let's see . . . Aristide," he said to the bearded
professor on his left, "have you a question?"

The professor of Romance languages looked at the ceiling a moment, deep
in thought, then said, with the trace of a Gallic accent, "One little question, yes.
Is it true, as you say, that Rosa Luxemburg was so much thought of here in the
1930s?"

Before I could formulate a reply, the economist had banged his fist on the
table. "Mr. Chairman," he said, "are we having a seminar on Marxism? Or are we
here to find out whether this young man is fit to teach at this institution? Where
the deuce is Aristide's question supposed to get us?"

"It does seem a rather far-fetched question for our purposes," the chairman
said. "Don't you think so, Aristide?"

"Well, I want to know the answer," Aristide said rather plaintively. "I once
met her."

"Ah, in that case . . ." said the chairman, and Professor Hawkins slouched in his chair in disgust.

To move things on I explained briefly that while Rosa Luxemburg never had the reputation in the United States she had in Europe, she had a devoted band of partisans among older Marxists—none of them particularly sympathetic, needless to say, with Russian Leninists or Stalinists.

The chairman, sensing that Aristide might pursue the matter further, spoke quickly past him to the sociologist at the end of the table.

"Mr. . . . Mr. . . ."

"Roberts," the sociologist prompted him.

"Yes, of course, Roberts. Have you a question?"

Mr. Roberts leaned forward on the table and squinted at me through his thick tortoiseshell glasses. It was difficult to say whether he was assuming the pose of a young professor giving his class the first quiz of the term or that of a district prosecutor manqué.

"When actually would you say Mr. Bannister joined the Communist Party of the United States?" he asked in precise, clipped words.

I said Kevin could give him more accurate information on this than I, but I assumed it was in the late spring of 1948. Probably June.

"When did you learn of this decision?"

"Not before meeting him in Philadelphia at the Progressive Party convention in August."

"You were actually there?"

"I actually was," I said. "As I stated earlier."

"Did you try to persuade him at this time to quit the Party?"

"He was well aware of my disapproval."

"And he thought so little of your friendship he ignored your advice?"

I made no reply to this, simply staring at him. And my staring must have disconcerted him, for he appeared to lose the thread of whatever argument he had and began thumbing through a stack of papers in front of him.

"Any more questions, Mr. . . . Roberts?" the chairman asked.

"One or two more, Mr. Chairman," the sociologist said, struggling to regain his composure. I felt a little sorry for him.

"Did you meet him again while he was an active Communist?"

I thought a moment and said I believed I had not.

"And when did he actually leave the Communist Party of the United States?"

"You'll have to ask Mr. Bannister that question, Mr. Roberts," I said. "So far as I am aware, he had no further dealings with the Party after the—"

"But this is just the question," Professor Hawkins interrupted. "When did he leave the Party? Did he *ever* leave the Party? That's what we want to know."

"Now be patient, John," the chairman said. "We'll come to your questions in due course. . . . Have you any more questions, Mr. Roberts?"

"None at present, Mr. Chairman."

"Then we'll move to the other end of the table. Mr. Lansdale?"

Mr. Lansdale, the mathematician, was wiping his glasses and continued to do so for a moment before putting them back on and addressing himself to the gathering at large.

"I'm trying to discover where our responsibility lies and what we need to know in this case. The state laws require the college to certify that its employees, including its teachers, are not subversive. If the state administrators are not satisfied we have made a reasonable investigation, they could cut off funds—indeed, they *would* cut off funds—and given our present financing, as I understand it, that could well mean the closing down of this institution. Now the faculty has taken upon itself the task of deciding whether Mr. Bannister is subversive or not. We have no clear mandate from the trustees to do this. We don't even know whether they will accept whatever recommendations we reach. But we go through the motions anyway. . . . The simplest thing for us, of course, would be for Mr. Bannister to state clearly that he is not a member of the Communist Party and hasn't been since such-and-such a date, and doesn't plan to rejoin the Communist Party. But he hasn't said this so far. And it's not easy for us, as professional teachers, to force him to say so. Either that, or get out."

The chairman had nodded at several points during this discourse.

"You state the matter very well, Mr. Lansdale," he said. "You put your finger on our dilemma."

"I believe I have no questions of the witness, Mr. Chairman. Any questions I have must be put to Mr. Bannister himself."

"Very well. And Mr. Durkin?"

Mr. Durkin identified himself with Mr. Lansdale's argument and also had no questions. The chairman passed on to Professor Hawkins.

"You see, John?" he said good-naturedly. "It all worked out very nicely. No one has any more questions, so you can ask all you want."

"And I've got a heap of 'em. But just to keep from shilly-shallying around all week on this business, I'm going to cut my questions to six. You can answer them in any order you want. And you'll have to do some pretty slick talking to worm your way around them."

I said "slick talk" was the last thing I would try before this committee, but if I could answer his questions, I would. Nice and cool.

"Brace yourself," he said. "Here they are. Number one, were you yourself ever a member of the Communist Party? Number two, would you hire a known Communist if you were dean of a liberal arts college? Number three, would you hire a so-called Fascist? Number four, do you believe in loyalty oaths for public employees, including teachers? Number five, what's your view of a college teacher living with a woman he's not wed to? And number six, what would you do in this case if you were the president of this college?"

The chairman had been frowning through these questions, his left hand flowing repeatedly through his white locks so that they now stood on end. "John," he said, "I don't think those are all proper questions to ask a witness."

"Dammit, Pendleton. These are just the questions I want answers to. I can't make up my mind without the answers."

"Well, I doubt that," the chairman said.

"You'll see; he'll answer 'em—or he'll try to. Won't you?" he said, turning to me.

I said most of the questions were clearly intended to establish my credibility as a witness and that not being under investigation myself, I felt no obligation to answer them—but would attempt to do so in the hope it would help the committee reach a fair appraisal of Kevin Bannister. I said to Professor Hawkins I doubted whether my answers would go very far in satisfying *him*.

"I expect you're right," he said.

"Well, just answer the ones you want to," the chairman said. "The committee places you under no compulsion to do more than that."

I took up the questions at random, as I remembered them. The last one— what would I do were I president of this college?—coming first to mind, I started off there and said I would heed the recommendation of the faculty committee.

"You mean you'd have no mind of your own?"

"I might have a mind, but if an appropriate faculty committee is in charge of investigating a member of the faculty, I'm certainly not going to destroy its work by going against its recommendation. And I'd press the trustees to do the same."

I went on to the question of whether, as a dean, I would hire a known Communist or Fascist. The problem, I said, was not in the label but in the approach. There was a presumption of bias in any partisan of a strong and militant ideology. I would want to question with the utmost care any prospective candidate holding extreme views, and this would apply for a religious zealot as much as for the better-known political fanatics. I drew a laugh from most of the committee when I suggested that there were so few Communists left today in the academic world it might be a good investment to have one or two on every faculty to keep things stirred up.

"You propose we do this here?" Professor Hawkins said, the first trace of a smile on his face.

I said that, as dean, I naturally left that tender decision to the wisdom of my faculty. I went on to the question of loyalty oaths, reiterating my acceptance of affirmative oaths as normal in the case of elected officials—though I could not count myself a champion of the practice even there—but firmly rejecting their validity in the case of college teachers, public or private. I advanced a few of the well-known arguments for this position and said I doubted whether I needed to elaborate further before this committee. Most appeared to agree, but not the economist.

"Yet what can be the harm in it?" he said mildly enough—for him. "We need only a simple declaration that would dispel all the uneasiness a nervous public feels toward college teachers. As a self-proclaimed democrat, I should think you'd leap at this easy opportunity to appease the people."

Not, I said, when the declaration was at variance with so sound a principle as academic freedom. Professor Hawkins shrugged his shoulders but did not pursue the matter further.

As to the question of my having ever been a Communist, I said this was a question I would normally not answer, since it violated my constitutional rights of free association and privacy, but I had no objection to answering under the present circumstances, so there would be no ambiguity in the matter. I had never been in the least tempted to join the Communist Party and indeed had never known, except abroad, more than half a dozen active Party members—none of them as well as I knew Kevin Bannister. Professor Hawkins had no additional questions on this matter, and I asked him, since I had forgotten, what his sixth question was.

"I thought that'd be the one you'd slip over," he said grimly. "Mr. Bannister's morals."

I said there was nothing I knew about Kevin Bannister's private life that had any bearing whatsoever on his competence as a teacher.

"That's no answer," he said.

"It's all I'm able to give you," I said. "And I'm sure your chairman will back me up in this."

"Oh, yes, assuredly. You're under no compulsion to answer any of our questions. You've been very obliging. . . . Well, John, are you satisfied?"

"I'm not satisfied, but let him go. I want to hear from young Bannister."

I resumed my seat next to Belle, and Kevin took my place at the conference table. A hush fell over the high-ceilinged chamber.

Kevin began by recounting, since he assumed the committee was interested, his experiences in the Party in 1948. He spoke from notes he had made. His voice was clear but subdued. He described his work in East Harlem, chiefly with Puerto Ricans and Italians. It was social work more than political at the outset, and one of his responsibilities was to transmit grievances to the office of

Congressman Marcantonio: wage disputes, evictions, Social Security problems, and so forth. Most of the families he dealt with were Communists, in which case all adult members would usually be Party members. Among other things, he organized a few Communist picnics in the early fall, one at Bear Mountain, another at Jones Beach. As the election approached there was more political work, Kevin explained: rallies, neighborhood get-togethers to meet candidates, most of them representing the Progressive Party. He spoke on several occasions, but was not judged very good at it. His group leader told him he didn't have the "common touch." ("I bet it was his Ivy League accent they couldn't take," Belle whispered to me.) Kevin summarized by stating that there was little he could call "subversive" in his work. The most subversive action he remembered was joining a dozen other Party members to heckle a Democratic candidate speaking at a rally in the Silk Stocking District.

"Did you silence him?" the chairman asked.

"We did that night. But the next night we were chased off by his people."

"Did you know any Party leaders?" the chairman asked. "I don't mean to pry."

"Our group, our cell, occasionally had up a minor member of the Central Committee. But I never saw any of the top brass . . . except to say hello to at a Party rally."

There was a pause, after which Professor Hawkins said, "Now that we're through with this interesting bit of proletarian folklore, I trust we can get down to some boring specifics . . . like, when did you decide you'd had enough, for instance?"

"I ceased being active after the election," Kevin said. "Right after, in fact."

"And to whom did you communicate this marvelous news?" asked the economist, his voice dripping with irony.

"I just quit going to meetings. . . . Some people in my group contacted me to see what the problem was, and I told them I was busy reading for orals."

"Reading for orals. And that, I assume, constituted your alleged break with the Communist Party."

Kevin, looking stonily at the table in front of him, did not reply.

"Why, if it is not impertinent of me to ask, did you not let your comrades know of your momentous decision to quit the Communist Party?"

"Er . . . just put the questions naturally, John," the chairman said. "Don't lather them all up."

"Leave out the lather, then," John said to Kevin. "But answer me why."

"There was no reason to make a second-class melodrama of it," Kevin said, still cool. "I had no personal quarrel with them. I simply grew bored. I drifted away."

"Yet, if I understand you, you went to no more meetings?"

"That's right."

"Then you didn't drift away, according to your own testimony. You *broke* with the Reds. And I can't for the life of me figure out how you could have over-looked so obvious a step as telling someone—*anyone*—you had done so."

"Mr. Bannister," the chairman broke in—and it was a relief to hear his kind-ly voice after Professor Hawkins's—"er . . . when you were hired here, did you . . . er . . . mention to the dean your past membership in the Communist Party?"

"I did," Kevin said.

"And did you tell him you had resigned your membership?"

Kevin thought a moment before he answered. "The issue didn't come up directly. I told the dean I *had* been a member but that I had not been active since 1948. I don't recall the exact phrasing we used. Perhaps he does."

"He does indeed," Professor Hawkins said, back to the attack. "He says you told him flatly you were *not* a Party member."

"And that was true. I wasn't. In my own eyes I was no longer—"

"In your own eyes! What are we to infer from that? That reality exists only as you see it through your own eyes?"

Belle was fidgeting beside me. "Kev doesn't defend himself," she whispered. "He leaves himself vulnerable."

The mathematician intervened at this point. "Mr. Bannister, I am perplexed on one point. I think I can understand your feeling it unnecessary to make an explicit statement of quitting the Communist Party after the 1948 election, or even the following spring when you received your appointment here. But during the last year or so, the question of loyalty and possible subversion in the univer-sities has been widely discussed on all campuses and in the press. Has it not occurred to you that a simple statement of your withdrawal from the Party would clear the air in your case?"

"It did occur to me, of course," Kevin said slowly. "But I decided against it."

"But *why*, in God's name?" Professor Hawkins broke in, bringing his fist down sharply on the table.

Kevin glanced briefly at Professor Hawkins but gave his attention to the mathematician, explaining to him—as he had earlier to me—the distinction he made between drifting away from an organization and explicitly denying it.

"Doesn't it come to the same thing?" the mathematician pursued. "You're out of it whichever way. Only in one case people *know* you're out. In the other they don't."

Kevin conceded it might be convenient for others to know how matters stood, but he would not yield his principle. He drew a parallel to a friendship that had cooled: It was kinder to drift apart than to force a confrontation in order to sever relations.

"Are you still such a friend of the Communists, Mr. Bannister?" the sociologist asked.

"Neither friend nor foe. We were friends once. We didn't abuse each other. I'm not ashamed of the relationship."

Kevin went on to make his further point—his least convincing, I thought—that in the present climate of opinion in the country, an explicit disavowal of Party membership would be interpreted as a denunciation. The mathematician pressed him on this point, as I had several weeks before, but Kevin seized on this principle and wouldn't let it go: The simplest statement he might make would be construed as a denunciation of the Communist Party, and it was this which in present circumstances he wished above all to avoid.

"Even if your career depends on it?" the chairman asked.

Kevin shrugged. "That's as may be, Professor Hughes. We live in an imperfect world. I won't improve matters if I behave irresponsibly—according to my lights—simply to satisfy some passing standard of public taste."

There was silence after this remark, broken finally by the chairman's announcing a five-minute recess. Kevin remained in his seat but glanced briefly around at us. Belle smiled and he smiled wanly back. He seemed drawn and defeated. Belle spoke for a moment with Sally and a faculty guest sitting next to her, then turned back to me.

"Kevin's wrong, isn't he?" Belle said, speaking in a low voice. "I mean, about a simple statement of nonmembership necessarily being taken as a denunciation?"

I said he probably exaggerated the risk, but there was no denying he believed it.

"It seems such a . . . such a narrow point of honor to stand or fall on," Belle said, and after a moment she went on, lowering her voice still further. "It reminds me of Karen. Standing against the islanders on a principle of her personal privacy . . . when a simple promise of good behavior could have saved her. Now Kevin risks his career on an obscure principle of not denying publicly what he's already denied to himself. They both seem to lack an elementary sense of survival, don't they? . . . I hope Kevin's proves . . ."

She didn't finish her sentence, and I reminded her, pretty sternly, that there was a vast difference between Karen two years before and Kevin now: Karen had been deeply disturbed, though we might not have known it at the time; Kevin was wholly rational—not to mention, I added, blissfully happy in his personal life.

"I hope so," Belle said, gazing at the back of his head as he leaned over the table. I had assumed he was consulting his notes, but when I looked more closely I saw he had put these aside and was reading the latest issue of the *American Political Science Review.*

Professor Hughes gaveled the hearing to order and asked whether the committee members had further questions. Professor Hawkins, to no one's surprise, did. First of all, he wanted to know Kevin's position on loyalty oaths. Kevin answered that in principle he was opposed to all loyalty oaths.

"For everyone? Or just teachers?"

"Let's put it this way: I would oppose legislation requiring loyalty oaths for anyone, and I would support legislation for a constitutional amendment outlawing any such requirement."

"Suppose legislation contrary to your views got passed anyhow? What would you do then?"

"You mean as a teacher? . . . Well, I would have to study the wording of the oath. If it was a positive oath—say, to uphold the Constitution, defend public order—I expect I would sign it, though without much enthusiasm. If it was a negative oath—like 'I am not a member of this or that organization'—I probably would not sign."

" 'Probably.' Don't you know?"

"As I say, I would have to study the language of the oath. I don't know how I would act."

"Come on, Mr. Bannister," Professor Hawkins said, needling him with another of his grim little smiles. "A good Communist ought to know whether he'd sign a loyalty oath or not."

"My uncertainty, then, must be proof I'm not one," Kevin said.

"Or only a poor one."

But that was the end of any banter between them. Professor Hawkins pursued his questioning for some minutes more in an increasingly insinuating manner, and Kevin's answers grew shorter and more careless. His patience, it was clear, was wearing thin. Once or twice he asked Professor Hawkins rather rudely to repeat his question; he hadn't realized, he said, a question was being asked.

"What's this about your living out of wedlock, Bannister?" Professor Hawkins asked abruptly.

A hush fell over the already tense conference room. All eyes turned on Kevin. Before he could answer, however, the chairman intervened.

"John, I don't see what Mr. Bannister's . . . er . . . private life has to do with us."

"You don't see it, Pendleton, but I do. We've set ourselves easy rules for this hearing. Young Bannister's been able to bring in anyone he wants to testify what a fine young man he is and how great a scholar he's supposed to be. And we've been obliged to listen to all this. Now it's our turn to ask *him* a few questions, and I mean to do it. What a man believes shows up in the way he lives, I say. If a man is given to Communist thinking, he probably doesn't make much of having a new woman whenever he's a mind to. And, Pendleton, you can't tell me that's a healthy situation for our students."

"But, John, you're jumping to conclusions," the chairman said. "Nothing's been said here about—"

"Nothing's been *said* here—and that's the trouble," Professor Hawkins broke in. "Now yesterday, Pendleton, you must have noticed a young, dark-haired woman in the back of the room. Well, I know that woman. Bannister himself introduced her to me last spring in the Commons. I've heard it said they live together and, true or not, I want to ask him whether he thinks this is proper behavior for a college teacher." He turned to Sally and said in a deferential tone, "I assume you're Mr. Bannister's mother. I hope you won't take personal offense at what I'm saying, but . . ."

"Don't mind me," Sally reassured him in a singsong voice. I had noticed, glancing sidewise at her several times during the proceedings, that she was indeed wholly absorbed in their progress and not in the least embarrassed.

"Meanwhile," Professor Hawkins went on, "there is this other young woman who I do not know"—he looked at Belle—"but with whom young Bannister came into the hearing today, holding hands. She even gives him a little kiss when she thinks no one's looking."

"Oh, God!" Belle murmured under her breath.

"What are we supposed to think about all this, Pendleton? If you strike out any discussion of Bannister's behavior, the trustees and everyone else will be asking about it and we won't have done what we're supposed to do. Nobody's got to attach weight to the answers he gives us—we can't force him to answer at all if he won't do it—but let me put my questions to him. What's the point in having no rules if you rule out my questions?"

The chairman thought a moment, his hand again combing through his white locks. "Well, put your questions, John. And Mr. Bannister, you answer whichever of them you choose to. Ignore the rest."

Silence fell again over the conference room as Professor Hawkins leaned forward on the green-topped table. In front of us, Kevin slowly raised a hand to scratch the side of his neck.

"Oh, oh," Belle whispered to me. "I know that motion."

"Look, young man," Professor Hawkins said quietly in a reasonable tone, "all I ask you to try to explain to us is how it is you have these different women in your life and how you reconcile this with your responsibilities as a college teacher. Now that's not much to ask, is it?"

Kevin stared at him motionless for a good thirty seconds before he said, in a flat and no less reasonable tone, "You're a hypocrite and a bastard, and my personal life's none of your goddam—"

The chairman's gavel came down sharply before Kevin finished his sentence. "Now, Mr. Bannister, that's no way to speak to a senior member of the faculty. You know that, don't you?"

Kevin said nothing.

"Mr. Chairman," Professor Hawkins said, "I see no object in continuing this hearing. This young man refuses to answer our questions. He insults members of the committee. I move we go into executive session."

Belle, who had had her hands over her face since Kevin spoke, suddenly took an envelope from her purse and scribbled on the back of it. I watched her. She wrote: "Can I say something—as your wife?" She gave it to me to give to Kevin. Kevin read the message slowly, then turned to her and shrugged his shoulders. Several of the committee members had meanwhile started to speak simultaneously to the chairman and he was busy exchanging remarks with them. When there was a pause, Kevin said quietly to the chairman, "Sir, I have one more witness."

"Ah? I understood . . . I understood you had called them all."

"I thought I had, but there's one more."

"Pendleton, I object to more witnesses," Professor Hawkins put in. "What can more witnesses tell us at this late hour?"

"Who is your . . . er . . . witness, Mr. Bannister?"

"The young lady behind me."

"Look, Pendleton, I must object—"

"Hold your peace, John," the chairman said. "You yourself brought up the question of this young woman. I guess she has a right to say what she wants. . . . Miss . . . er . . . Just take this chair."

Kevin returned to his seat, and Belle sat at the table facing the committee members.

"Now, please tell us first your name," Professor Hughes said.

"Belle Talbot Bannister," she said in an even voice. The members of the committee, it was clear from their faces, were confused.

"Bannister?" the chairman queried.

Belle said in the same even voice, "I'm Kevin's wife."

"Why . . . er . . . I don't think we knew that Kevin, I mean Mr. Bannister, was married."

"I'm not surprised," Belle said. "We only told our families a few days ago."

"Well, how extraordinary! And . . . er . . . when was this marriage contracted?"

"May twenty-third, nineteen forty-eight," Belle said.

"Nearly two and half years ago! Why . . . why, that means before . . . er . . . Mr. Bannister became a Communist."

"About six weeks before."

"My, I hardly know where to begin. . . . Perhaps you'd better help us by telling why the marriage was kept secret for so long."

"If indeed there even was one," Professor Hawkins muttered half under his breath but loud enough for Belle to hear.

"Oh, we were married, Professor Hawkins," she said with no note of resentment in her voice. "Have no fear of that. We kept it secret at the time because Kevin's family was in mourning for his younger sister, who had just died. In fact, it was her death—she was also a good friend of mine—that brought Kevin and me so close together during those months. . . . Well, in the normal course of things we would have told our parents about the marriage after a year or so, perhaps when I finished college. Because at Smith, you're not allowed to stay in college if they know you're married. But then I had a chance to study art in Paris for a year. And Kevin agreed that I should go. . . . You'll see it wasn't the normal sort of marriage. I was in Europe and Kevin was here. It wasn't the best arrangement for us, I'll admit, but it was what we'd worked out. It was what we wanted."

Belle recounted all this so artlessly that she immediately won the sympathy of the members of the committee, including even her "curmudgeon," Professor Hawkins. One could tell this from the expressions on their faces, heads tilted forward and nodding as she told her story. I reflected too that, while there were obvious omissions from her account, there was nothing she had said so far that was untrue. I could feel her choosing her words with care, from time to time biting her lip before revealing a new episode in their strange marriage. It was clear there had been no rehearsal of her testimony.

"If I may put a question, Mr. Chairman," the young sociologist said. The chairman nodded, and he asked whether Belle had been aware of her husband's political activities during the 1948 election.

"Oh, yes. I knew about them. At least as much as I could stand his telling me."

"Did you yourself become a Communist?"

"Heavens, no! I'm from Maine."

That brought a laugh from the committee members, and when it subsided the mathematician asked whether she shared his political sympathies.

"Well, a good many of them, yes. We used to talk about Karl Marx before we were married. I was studying the Marxists during one term at the University of Maine before I transferred to Smith. It seems a crazy way to start a romance, doesn't it, talking about Marxism? But it wasn't really. It made us very . . . well, congenial to each other. . . . But I was never interested in politics."

"Did you ever try to dissuade Kevin from his political activities?"

"He knew how I felt about them . . . but, remember, Kevin is much brighter than I am. When he was a Communist, he knew what he was doing. I couldn't out-argue Kevin when it came to politics."

"Did his politics—that is, his being a Communist—complicate your marriage?" This was still the mathematician questioning her in his precise, systematic way.

Belle thought a moment. "Well, yes, it did. For a short time, that is. He wasn't active for very long. But, yes, it did complicate things for a while."

"Let me ask you about another complication," Professor Hawkins said. "Did you notice yesterday in the back of the room—"

"Carmen de Silva, you mean? Yes, I know Carmen."

"And you were aware . . ."

"Yes, I know all about that, Professor Hawkins. You've got it a little mixed up, if you don't mind my saying so. Of course no wife likes to think of her husband with another woman. But you've got to remember that it was my decision to go off to Europe the way I did. You can't expect to do that and have everything exactly the way you want it when you come back. . . . I think Carmen is a very fine person, and I'm glad Kevin had her friendship while I was away."

Professor Hawkins was shaking his head back and forth.

"I see you don't approve of our generation's behavior," Belle said. "Well, you know, sometimes we don't approve of yours, Professor Hawkins. The best we can do, I guess, is try to understand each other."

Several of the committee members smiled guardedly at this, but Professor Hawkins continued to look dour. Then he too allowed himself a smile, looking under his eyebrows at Belle. "You're a very independent-minded young lady, Mrs. Bannister."

The chairman said into this beatitude, "So now you've come home to . . . er . . . rejoin your husband."

"Well, yes and no," Belle said. "That's what I want to tell you next. I don't want to leave you with a false impression. I came home especially to see my father-in-law, who's had a heart attack. While I've been here, Kevin and I have decided that we've lived too long apart—I mean, we've hardly lived together at all, really. But I have to go back to Europe again. I don't know just how to tell you why. In fact, I *can't* tell you. Kevin doesn't even know. I suppose you'd call it . . . well, an obligation I contracted in Europe. Anyway, it's something I have to see through. It'll be about a year."

The committee members were drawn together by her candor and began to speculate humorously on what Belle's "obligation" could be.

"She'll be on some secret mission, don't you think, Jeff?" the mathematician said to the physicist.

"But for whose *side*?" Hawkins put in.

"Oh, no question about that," Jeff said. "Central Intelligence. That's why she can't tell her husband."

"There'll be a . . . er . . . man in the picture somewhere, mark my words," the chairman said.

"Well, of course," the mathematician said. "That's the Red chief of espionage for Western Europe, the one with the bomb plans."

"Under his mattress," said Professor Hawkins.

Belle said, "I can't wait to get back to see how it all turns out."

They talked on for some minutes in this fashion, the committee members reluctant to let Belle go—although the business of the hearing was to all intents and purposes over. I happened, as they talked, to look behind me and recognized Carmen de Silva sitting near the door. She had on dark glasses and was slouched low in her seat, her face a mask. I had no idea how long she'd been there, but assumed it was after Professor Hawkins had made reference to her; otherwise, he would have called attention to her presence. The committee members, facing the entrance at the rear of the chamber, were the only ones who could have seen her without turning—but I doubted any of them noted her entry, absorbed as they were in Belle. It must have been a rude shock to Carmen, I reflected, to discover in this way—as she must have discovered by now—that Kevin was married. I knew from conversation at lunch that Kevin hadn't been able to reach Carmen by phone that morning and planned to contact her after the hearing. But, of course, none of us knew beforehand the strange course the hearing would take. I debated calling Kevin's attention to Carmen but decided against it.

The chairman in due course asked the committee members if they had further questions. They did not, and Belle was dismissed. Professor Hawkins said, as she returned to her seat, "Mr. Chairman, I think we all owe a debt of gratitude to Mrs. Bannister for bringing some pleasure into what was turning into a grim afternoon."

"Hear, hear!" said the mathematician.

Kevin was asked if he had any final statement to make. He said he did not, but he thanked the chairman for conducting a fair hearing and the committee members for their patience.

"I would like to apologize to Professor Hawkins," he added in a low, even voice, "for using language that obviously has no place in a setting of this sort." Professor Hawkins nodded but made no reply.

Professor Hughes told Kevin he would be notified of the action of the board of trustees after its October meeting, and adjourned the hearing. The committee members and spectators mingled for a few minutes before leaving the conference room. Carmen, I noted, had already left.

I was to stop at Bucks County on my way back to New York but had an errand outside Philadelphia on the way, so I left the others outside the administration building. A few picketers still lingered and raised a wan cry as Kevin limped down the granite steps. The photographer under the eaves came forward and tried to arrange a picture of Kevin between Sally and Belle, but Kevin vetoed this; he let himself be photographed on the steps alone. He gave a brief statement to a small cluster of correspondents about the fairness of the hearing but declined to predict the outcome of the case.

The rain was falling steadily as I drove away, early leaves slithering down from the maples and lying flat on the pavement. At a stoplight several blocks from the campus I recognized Carmen crossing the street in front of me, jumping over puddles. I hailed her and she climbed in beside me while I maneuvered the car out of the traffic. We parked and went into a neighborhood café. We were alone except for two elderly men watching television at the bar. I ordered draft beer for us and we sat in a booth near the window.

"I wouldn't have recognized you if I hadn't seen you at that goddam hearing," she said, taking off a wet bandana and shaking it on the floor.

I asked how much of the hearing she had taken in.

"Too much. I wish I'd never gone."

The bartender brought us our beer and I paid him.

"He should have told me they were married, the lousy son of a bitch," she said.

"He meant to. As soon as he could find you after the hearing."

"Fine time! He won't find me now."

I was silent, and after a moment Carmen went on. "How long has this been going on? It sounded like years the way she talked."

"It is years," I said. "About two and a half."

She shook her head bitterly. "That means almost from the time I first knew him. No! That's really too goddam much! . . . Did you know?"

I explained that I was a witness at their marriage but no one else knew until a few days before, when Belle told Kevin's father.

"Why the secrecy? What were they hiding, for Christ's sake?"

I said I guessed they were hiding the fact the marriage hadn't amounted to much. "Thanks to you, in part."

"Now *I'm* to blame! That's a bunch of crap and you know it."

I assured her it wasn't a question of blame, but it was a fact that she was one force that came between them before the marriage was many weeks old; the other was the Party.

Carmen took this in, then said more gently, "Belle must think I'm a bitch."

"On the contrary. She told the committee she was glad Kevin had your companionship."

"Yeah, I heard that hogwash. . . . That was quite an act Belle put on, wasn't it? A real ingenue. I had her read all wrong. Kev never talked much about her and I only met her once. So I had her figured as this decent little island girl, sweet and all that jazz, but with about as much kick as a lame mule. . . . What made her take the chair anyway? Kevin hadn't planned that, had he?"

I told Carmen how Kevin had blown his cool and nearly broken up the hearing, calling Professor Hawkins a "bastard" and a "hypocrite." When Belle asked Kevin if she could testify—as his wife—he had agreed.

" 'Bastard' and 'hypocrite'! That's famous! That must have taken courage . . . even though he's a bastard and a hypocrite himself."

"I doubt if Belle would have testified if she'd known you were there or were coming."

"Well, I wouldn't have thought less of her if she did," Carmen said. "I'm not big on decency and that crap. I liked Belle the way she was . . . shrewd and tough."

Carmen snuffed out her cigarette and lit another before going on. I ordered two more beers.

"No, I won't try to steal him back. I'm mad as hell at Kevin for not telling me. You should never put someone as close as I've been to him in my position, no matter what the circumstances. . . . There was a time when I would have fought for the guy. Last spring I thought we'd probably marry someday. We talked occasionally about it. . . . That was when we were thinking of living together. Then Kevin suddenly quit talking about it, and we were back where we were."

So Carmen talked on, unwinding. Her moods fluctuated among frustration, anger, bitterness, and gloom—not necessarily in that order. She was hurt by this episode, and for one not used to being hurt, or believing herself tough enough not to show it if she was, the experience was unnerving. She said several times in her gloomy moods, "If only I could get the hell away . . . Mexico, for instance." At one point I said lightly, a scheme taking shape in my mind, "If funds are a problem . . ."

"If funds are a problem! When are they not? What the hell are you suggesting? Kevin's hush money?"

"Neither Kevin's nor certainly hush," I said, flushing despite myself. "After all, I finance Belle's education, as Kevin has probably told you. I'm proposing to help out on part of yours."

George's special fund was indeed so swollen, as he continued to make deposits while Belle refused to draw from it, that it needed invasion. It required little reflection on my part to know that George, if he knew the circumstances, would approve entirely of financing Carmen's trip to Mexico. Carmen was looking at me cautiously.

"People don't go around throwing away money," she said. "You hardly know me."

"I know you, Carmen," I contradicted her. She still looked dubious, and I told her I wasn't trying to proposition her. I was simply offering her funds for a short visit to Mexico. After all, it hardly involved a fortune.

"Well, I wouldn't take it as a gift," she said.

"A loan, then. You can pay me back when you want to, without interest—as Belle plans to."

A quarter of an hour later, after another round of beer, we had arranged the details and Carmen had brightened considerably. From the way she talked it seemed likely she would leave before the end of the week. As we stood on the sidewalk outside the café saying our farewells, she bound me to silence about our meeting.

"I don't want my feelings pored over in some Bucks County postmortem," she said.

"What about my seeing you at the hearing?" I asked.

"His mother recognized me, I think. And if I know her, she'll mention it. But don't you be the first to bring it up if she doesn't."

She walked off to the bus station in the rain, and I drove on to my errand outside Philadelphia.

There was champagne that night in Bucks County. I arrived late for dinner, having telephoned them not to wait, and George ordered the champagne soon after I joined them. They had talked of little but the hearing from the time Kevin, Sally, and Belle returned. George, restless all day, had wanted to know every detail of the proceedings, and they had given him an almost complete précis. Even Kevin, taciturn for days on the subject of his hearing, was positively communicative.

"I drink to a four-to-two decision," George said, raising his glass after Elsie had poured the champagne.

"Which way, love?" Sally asked.

"Why, ours, of c-c-course."

"I'll buy that," Belle said. "Which are the two?"

"Your c-curmudgeon and the sociologist," Sally said. "It's your bearded friend who is the unknown quantity." George, who had admired a recent article on Diderot by the professor of Romance languages, was chagrined that he had played such an insignificant part in the hearing.

"What if it's a tie?" Belle asked Kevin.

"Don't forget the committee recommendation isn't binding on the trustees," Kevin said.

"You're awfully glum, chum," Sally said to me. "What's your forecast?"

I said I agreed with Kevin: There was no scoring until the trustees met.

Before we left the dining room, George said, "Well, wh-whatever way it turns out, I'm p-p-proud of both of you, Kevin and B-B-Belle. I couldn't ask more of you than the way you both behaved."

George went upstairs after dinner, and the four of us sat in the library over our coffee, amusing ourselves with minor episodes and exchanges at the hearing.

Belle remarked during a pause at one juncture that she was a little surprised Carmen hadn't been at the hearing that afternoon.

"But she was, dear," Sally said.

Belle and Kevin both looked at her quickly.

"Oh, Sally!" Belle said. "Surely you're wrong. We would have seen her."

"She was very much there," Sally insisted.

Kevin said, his face gray, "When was it, Mother?"

"Well, close to the end. Belle was speaking, I know."

"Oh, Kevin!" Belle said, her voice choked with remorse. She turned to me. "Did you see her too?"

I nodded slowly. "She was there. Very briefly."

"Why did neither of you mention it to us?"

I said nothing, and Sally said, "But, darling, I thought you must have noticed her. I thought you said nothing about it out of . . . well, delicacy."

"Delicacy! Kevin, go try to call her again. I'm really altogether crushed."

She indeed looked it. Kevin went out to the telephone off the pantry. Sally, hurt by Belle's tone and understandably perplexed by what role she was supposed to play, said, "Well, goddam, you'll have to write out instructions for us. How do you expect us to know what to say when you young people get your lives all screwed up the way you do? When I was a girl, if you had an affair you didn't go broadcasting it everywhere. You kept it to yourself."

But Belle was quick to sense injured feelings, especially where she herself had caused them. "Sally, you're altogether right. I shouldn't have criticized you at all. I didn't mean to. . . . I just felt so badly about Carmen, learning for the first time about Kevin's being married—not from him but from *me,* and in a public hearing."

It was difficult to stay out of temper with Belle for long, and when Sally went up to George a few minutes later, she was mollified. Belle's forgiveness included me, too, for she made no further reference to my also having failed to mention Carmen's presence—either immediately after the hearing or since I had arrived. And I, of course, invited no further discussion of Carmen. I showed Belle a brief account of the hearing in an evening paper I had picked up in Philadelphia on my way to Bucks County. The last paragraph in the story read: "The possibility of a morals charge against Professor Bannister was to all intents and purposes eliminated, according to sources close to the case, when it was revealed at the hearing that he had been secretly married for two and a half years. Mrs. Bannister, who was present at the hearing, is the former Belle Talbot, who has been studying in Europe."

Belle said, after she read the item, "Better that Carmen learned this at the hearing than through the newspapers. . . . But you're thinking of Otis, aren't you? So have I. I didn't have much time to think while I was talking at the hearing, but I've thought some since. I don't think there's much risk of Otis's hearing of this. It's not the major part of the story . . . as this item shows. Besides, Otis reads the *London Times* and the *Paris Herald-Tribune.* He hardly sees American newspapers anymore. . . . But even if he should hear, it won't make the difference now it would have five or six months ago—for instance, when you visited us. He relies on me now. He would want me back whatever I do or have done."

I nodded but said nothing.

"I'm a bit tired of playing percentages, trying to figure out the safe course. If Otis finds out I'm married, we'll cross that bridge when we get to it. For the present, everything cried out for my squaring with George, Sally, Mother . . . and, as it suddenly happened today, this loony committee."

"And do you square with Kevin about Otis?" I asked, listening to be sure he was still at the telephone.

"It would seem consistent, wouldn't it? And I believe I could . . . but I'm not going to. I have a lifetime to live with Kevin. I can't believe his knowing about Otis will be of any help to his living with me in the future. He trusts me, that's the main thing. He knows I'm coming back to him. . . . Truth is relative, don't you think? It has no value of itself. One person dying of cancer will want to know the truth. Another will not. Yet the truth is the same in each case. I think if Kevin *asked* me, I *would* tell him. But he knows I'd rather he didn't."

Belle fell silent, and I knew before she spoke that she had Carmen more on her mind at that moment than Otis.

"I feel so badly we didn't reach her sooner," Belle said, shaking her head.

I was on the point of making some facetious remark about the irony of a wife feeling so chagrined she had reclaimed her husband from a lover—but forbore. It was no joking matter with Belle. Moreover, I recollected, I knew—as

Belle did not—that the condition of the victim was not critical.

Kevin returned, saying he couldn't reach Carmen and none of her friends knew where she was. "So they say anyway."

"I expected as much," Belle said. "Go write her, Kevin. That's all there's left to do."

Kevin went off to another room, and I went upstairs with Belle to say my farewells to George. I was leaving early in the morning for New York.

44

The last phase of my Indonesian assignment lasted about eight months. During the first three I was in a remote section of Borneo and received no mail at all. It was not until after the first of the year, when I returned to Djakarta for a few days, that I caught up on the activities of my far-flung friends. I lay on my bed in underwear most of one afternoon, a ceiling fan lazily revolving stale air, and read two dozen or more accumulated letters.

On the island, Lucy wrote, all was well. The school had eight children that fall, the largest number since the war, and another eight were at high school on the main. Arthur Dacey had at last retired, selling his car and boat to Clyde Grant: "And that was a good deed all around. For Clyde was talking again about leaving us." Arthur and Winifred had driven to Florida at the end of October, planning to spend the winter, but they were so homesick by Thanksgiving they drove back. Caleb stayed about the same; Lucy thought he and Jenny probably *would* go to Florida after Mary Lou's baby was born—or babies, for "she's as big as a mountain . . . and, if you'll believe it, as provocative as ever." Elmer had met installments regularly on the loan for his boat shop and it seemed an established thing now. "Whoever's not around the cracker barrel with Mary Lou is down in the shop with Elmer." Lucy didn't mention it, but I learned in a Christmas letter from Sharon (the first I ever received from her) that Elmer had signed up most of the households on the island as customers for the generator and was busy wiring them in. Turk, meanwhile, had been off in Vermont on a hunting trip in late fall, his first visit west of Camden (he claimed), and was so enthusiastic about the Green Mountains that he planned to take Sharon and Chucky on a ski holiday to Stowe in February.

Lucy wrote that Danny and Lucille Orcutt had been over once or twice to talk with Horace about fixing up the cottage opposite the old Cutler place; they had given up for the present the idea of building on the burned-out site because of high costs, but they did plan to use the barn. Danny was still lobstering with his father and brother on Thorn Island, but the community there, Lucy wrote, was a thing of the past. Three quarters of the island had been sold to a real estate developer in Massachusetts.

Lucy wrote warmly, needless to say, of her brief reunion with Belle in Boston before Belle flew back to Corsica after Kevin's hearing. It was during this reunion, I later discovered, that Belle unraveled to her mother the mysteries of her double life. I believe the only reason Lucy did not make explicit reference to this in her letters to me was that she treated a confidence as just that—not a subject to be discussed even with the only other person who shared it.

Jingle's letters, of which there were half a dozen dating from early fall, constituted a running commentary on whatever came into that restless mind. Unlike Lucy, who wrote methodically and in a majestic, flowing style, Jingle wrote effusively and impulsively. A passing meter reader with whom she discussed the problem of teenage abortions in the Portland high school received as much attention as the first long-awaited visit from Arthur and Winifred en route to Florida. In a letter written in mid-November she became so absorbed in miscellany that she neglected to mention she had just come back from the hospital with her third child, a girl named Carol; she wrote the next day to cover the omission—"Lest you think I've abandoned my game plan." The main event in Jingle's life was her decision, with Emil's approval, to visit Otis in Corsica after her baby was weaned in the spring; she had just written Otis with this happy news. Since she didn't mention Belle in connection with the projected visit, I took it for granted she didn't yet know Belle was there. I was confident that by the time she arrived, she would not embarrass them or be embarrassed by existing arrangements.

Belle's letters, and at least one from Otis, miscarried, as did mine to them, for I had only one brief note from Belle written early in December. Otis was better, she said, evidently referring to some relapse he had had earlier in the fall, but she did not elaborate. She now felt certain he was strong enough so she could leave him for a few days after Christmas to meet Kevin in Nice. "Otis still knows nothing," she wrote. "He did call my attention to an item in the Paris papers about the final decision on Kevin, but the item made no reference to me. So we live on with our secrets."

I learned the "final decision" on Kevin from Sally Bannister, as always one of my most faithful correspondents. Announced by the board of trustees in mid-October, it amounted to suspension for the remainder of the year and a review of his case in the spring with respect to another contract. This had not been the recommendation of the faculty committee, which voted four to two—as George had predicted—to clear Kevin of any suspicion of improper behavior and to reinstate him fully; the two dissenters, Sally discovered (and I never knew how), were Professor Hawkins and the young sociologist.

In the interval between the hearing and the trustees' meeting, pressures for firm handling of the case had apparently built both on and off campus. Legislators running for reelection were noisy in their demands for dismissal and threatened to cut state funds to the college unless it tightened its procedures for clearing faculty members "beyond all reasonable doubt." Kevin, chilled by the prospect of becoming a perennial cause célèbre in the struggle for academic freedom in the onrushing McCarthy era, quietly wrote the dean two weeks after the trustees' decision that he had no wish to be considered for reappointment and formally resigned from the faculty. He moved back to Bucks County, and when he had sent off final proof and the index of his book went into the Veterans Hospital in Philadelphia to have an abscess from his war injury tended to. He had been home from the hospital for about two weeks when George had his second coronary, milder than the first but still a sober reminder that George would probably not regain his health. Sally converted the library into a bedroom so George wouldn't need to use the stairs.

Finally, there was a letter from Carmen in Guadalajara, absorbed in the details of her new life. She was making pottery and she had friends (plural). "I may have to team up with one of them eventually to share room and board," she wrote. "I can't live off Daddy Warbucks forever—worst luck."

I dressed, walked for three hours around the port section of old Batavia, and came back to the hotel bathed in sweat to shower, lie on my bed again in underwear, and reread most of my letters.

George Bannister's third and final heart attack, as I learned some weeks later, came early in February. He died in his sleep. Kevin was back from Europe, where he had stayed on for several weeks after his five days with Belle at the end of the year. Belle did not return—Kevin had called her at the Paris address (which she still used) that it was unnecessary—but Lucy went down for the funeral. Kevin had immediately notified her of George's death through Mary Lou at the store, and Lucy telephoned back an hour later that she would arrive in Philadelphia by plane the next afternoon. "She was unbelievable!" Sally wrote. "She walked into the house two days before the funeral and simply took over. She stayed until the last Bannister had left. 'Sally!' they would say, '*Who* is that aristocrat you have in the kitchen?' I absolutely couldn't have managed without her."

Sally's letter, written a week or so after the funeral when she had sent out her last note thanking friends for their flowers and condolences, went on: "The big surprise for all of us was George's will. What a foxy old guy he was! He left the house here and the bulk of his estate to me, as he had told me. Then he left a big chunk to Kevin (I won't embarrass you with figures). But he left Ram's Horn to *Belle*! He attached a note to Kevin explaining the bequest—maybe he thought

Kevin would be angry, but Kevin, I can assure you, was ecstatic. George explained that since I wanted no part of Ram's Horn (for reasons you understand), it would in the natural order of things pass directly to Kevin. *But* should anything ever come between Kevin and Belle, Kevin would hardly wish to have a home so near hers, and the house would in all likelihood pass to strangers. So he left Ram's Horn to Belle so that, whatever happened, it would revert to the island. Now wasn't that cute of him? He worked the whole thing out on his own after she went back to Paris."

George died too soon to know of a happy turn in Kevin's academic fortunes. His book came out in mid-February and was immediately identified by most reviewers as a major contribution to the field of political analysis. In April he was appointed to the Department of Public Law and Government at Columbia.

My mission in Borneo ended early in May, and I returned home via Europe, stopping in Corsica as I had promised Belle I would. Their letters to me had continued to miscarry, and when I cabled my arrival date, I had been without direct news from either of them for several months. Jingle's visit to Corsica, she wrote from Portland, had been put off to June—and, she added cryptically, she assumed I knew why. I didn't.

The plane from Marseilles circled in over the coast below Bastia on a day nearly identical to the one when I had arrived the year before. The white-walled terminal stood gleaming in the cluster of runways. Corsicans worked in orchards up to the edges of the airfield. Donkey carts inched along the network of dirt roads in the nearby countryside. Here at least was a corner of the universe that made its concessions to progress reluctantly. Lucy Talbot, I reflected, would approve.

As we taxied in I picked out Belle against the terminal building, her blond hair nearly white in the Mediterranean sun and her fair skin burned bronze. She seemed curiously stout from a distance—until I realized with a jolt she was pregnant. Indeed, from my limited knowledge of these matters, I judged her time was near.

After we had greeted one another and drawn away from a group of Europeans with whom she was standing, I remarked that I hadn't realized babies grew so quickly; it must be the Mediterranean climate.

"Then you never got my letters?"

I said none had reached me since the first of the year, just after she returned from her five days with Kevin in Nice.

"No wonder you looked so stunned as you came off the plane! That's why I wrote you, of course . . . so you wouldn't drop dead when you saw me."

"I've survived the initial impact," I said. "Dare I ask—"

"Oh, Kevin's. Absolutely no doubt of it. It wasn't part of the plan, of course."

"You and your plans."

"I agree. No more plans, no more secrets . . . except one last little one," she added archly.

"Don't tell me. Otis thinks it's his."

"How did you guess?"

"And Kevin thinks it's his."

"No, there you're wrong. Kevin doesn't know."

I asked how Kevin could *not* know since they had been together for five days after Christmas.

"Because I wasn't sure myself until after I got back. My insides are so mixed up from that other business . . . you know. The doctors were so sure I'd have to have an operation to have a child that I took it for granted I couldn't possibly get pregnant without one. With Otis I'd never paid attention to—"

"Okay, okay," I interrupted. "Spare me the details. . . . So finally you realized you were pregnant and the timing suggested it was Kevin."

"Not *suggested*, you prune! I *knew*. What I didn't know was whether the baby would be born healthy. I still don't, though the doctors think so. . . . Anyway, after all the mix-up in the past over pregnancies, I didn't want to get Kevin's hopes up only to have them dashed. I mean, if the baby were stillborn or deformed or something awful . . ."

"I assume you'd still tell him about it."

"Eventually, no doubt. But he's spared the worry now, don't you see?"

I said, "Meanwhile, what about the risk to Kevin's wife?"

Belle bit her lip. "You sound hostile," she said sullenly.

I assured her, as we got into the Peugeot with my baggage, that I wasn't; I was merely playing devil's advocate. To change the subject, I asked where Toro was. Belle explained she had left him in Bastia to do errands.

"Lucky thing, too. If I'd sent him to meet you and done the errands myself, you'd have asked how I was and he'd have drawn his picture of me bursting at the seams and said, 'Me and Missy making bambino.' It's his way of flattering me. . . . Then you *would* have dropped dead."

As we drove away from the airport, I asked when the baby was due, and Belle said in three weeks; by cesarean section.

"Jingle's coming," she said. "She'll take care of Otis while I'm in the hospital."

"Aha," I said, now understanding Jingle's cryptic message about the delay in her visit.

Otis was, of course, the central figure in our minds. Belle told me about his deteriorating health as we drove up the coastal road to Bastia past the vineyards. He was slipping away, Belle said, almost perceptibly. The skin hung slack on his great hulking frame. She realized how much he had wasted when a suit she had bought him six weeks before, three sizes smaller than his last one—he would never wear anything but dark poplin, even here in Corsica—was now so loose on him he could hardly keep it on. The medical prognosis was still the same: a steady deterioration of the abdominal tissues with no significant pain until the very end. But the orneriness was gone, Belle said.

"He's so gentle at times you wouldn't believe it. He'll lie for hours rubbing my belly with oil. It's . . ."

"Okay, okay," I said again.

Belle glanced at me—as though I were some sort of freak, I suppose—and we drove in silence into Bastia. We picked up Toro at the market, and he drove us up the coast to their village.

As Belle had suggested, living with Otis at this stage in his disease was calming. Belle usually read to him a good deal, but at no fixed times, and I read to him while I was there. One afternoon, as he lay on the side terrace out of the sun, I read him an entire Maigret; Belle, preparing a bouillabaisse in the kitchen, called out translations to us when both of us were stymied. There was general conversation if Otis wanted it; there was silence if he didn't. What talk we had was artless and normally inconsequential, not without a measure of wit.

After dinner the first evening, Otis dozed for half an hour on the sofa while Belle and I had our coffee outside, watching a rare display of lightning along the distant Italian Riviera. When we came back into the living room, Otis lay with his eyes open. He was staring at the ceiling.

"Women are superior to men," he said tonelessly.

"Well, don't sound so unhappy about it," Belle said. "Rejoice."

"It has nothing to do with their brains, their powers of reason. It's because of their intuition."

"Still, women *can* reason," said Belle.

"But men can't intuit. There's the difference."

"And to what," Belle went on in her mildly bantering way, "do we owe this extraordinary gift of intuition? The apple?"

"Closeness to the cycle of life," Otis promptly said. "Birth and rebirth. What does a man ever do that resembles the spontaneous contracting of a woman's belly when a child is born?"

"I'm having a cesarean," Belle said. "I must be neuter."

"About as neuter as Mae West," Otis remarked.

"Let's concede," Belle went on after a moment, "that a woman has the edge over a man in childbirth. What then? . . . Does this more than compensate for our supposedly small minds in other respects?"

Otis was undisturbed by her sarcasm and went on with his theory. "What happens is that a woman tempers reason with intuition. She thinks a problem through, like anyone else, then she gives it that last little something. She vitalizes the solution."

"Does that make the solution better?"

"Better in what sense?"

"More relevant, more . . . appropriate to the circumstances."

"Then, no. Not better in that sense. Rather, more earthy, more fundamental."

"My feeble brain," Belle said, "prevents me from discovering why something that's relevant isn't also fundamental."

"Then use your intuition, baby. That's what it's there for. To supplement reason."

"But, Otis, if *my* intuition tells me what your *brain* has figured out is bullshit, where are we? If, as you insist, women are so superior, then it would seem—"

"My God!" Otis exclaimed, sitting up. "She has me by the short hairs! I'll have to change the thesis. Women *aren't* superior to men. . . . I always thought there was something screwy in that logic." And he lay back on the sofa.

Another conversation we had later the same evening, long after Otis's normal bedtime, could have bordered on the macabre but didn't. It concerned life after death, and Otis himself brought up the subject, quite casually, after Belle had read aloud a review of a new production of Noel Coward's play *Blythe Spirit,* recently opened in London.

"For laughs, life after death is good theater," Otis said. "Philosophically, it's rubbish."

"Why rubbish?" Belle said. "You mean nothing survives?"

"Nothing corporeal."

"A ghost is hardly corporeal."

"That's the point. It tries to be. It's meant to emphasize there is a hereafter. . . . The only things that survive death are, on one side, a man's bank account or property, and, on the other, his creations. In a word, his art. Nothing particular to man himself survives."

"Or *herself,*" Belle added lightly.

"That's right, nothing particular to man herself."

"What about memories?" I asked.

"Memories are in the minds of the living," Otis said. "Moreover, each person's memories—or hallucination—are different from another's."

"So a spirit might appear to one person," Belle said, still fixing the parameters of his idea, "but not to another?"

"You've got it. The reality of man goes with him to the grave. He exists only in memory . . . or in his recorded works."

Belle thought about this. "I don't like it," she said.

Otis said, "Tough. That's the way it is. . . . Paint something if you want a hereafter."

"I study paintings," Belle said. "I don't make them."

"Then you're doomed to oblivion."

"It's not fair," Belle went on, ignoring him. "A person struggles through life, not just scraping together enough to eat but trying to improve things, trying to make things work better. And what's the reward for all this? Nothing . . . an inscription on a tombstone. I don't like it."

"Okay. Tell us what happens."

"Let me think, let me think."

"All the poker players go play poker somewhere on velvet-covered card tables? All the boozers booze? Wenchers wench?"

I said afterlife sounded a bit monotonous.

"Speak for yourself, chum," Otis said. He turned back to Belle, who was biting her lip in thought. "I hope you're not going to fall back on religion. Religions were invented to keep the living in line. Heaven or Nirvana for the righteous. Hell or endless transmigration for the fallen."

"Or is religion a reflection of man's vanity?" I said. "He couldn't bring himself to acknowledge there was no hereafter."

"All that time wasted," Otis said. "Then they added Heaven for the virtuous and Hell for the damned as an afterthought. . . . Come on, baby. Stop thinking and straighten us out. We're adrift."

"Well-l-l," Belle said, stroking an imaginary beard. "You chaps have a problem. Will this straighten it out?" She took a sip of her brandy. "Seriously, if you insist everything is rational, you wind up with as many questions as answers. There's man's vanity for you: imagining human reason can unravel all problems."

"Name some it can't," Otis said.

"Well . . . time and space, for starters. Reason can't explain the mysteries of time and space."

Otis said, "What about the theory of relativity?"

"I doubt that relativity would help *me* understand," Belle said.

"Intuition's no help?" I suggested.

"None at all. Worse than none. My intuition tells me to give time and space a wide berth . . . the hereafter, too." She pondered, her chin pressed onto her fist. "I might bring myself to believe in some theory of rebirth . . . as in Hinduism. If I ever understood enough about Hinduism."

"Genetically it's unsound," Otis said. "There's too little linkage between the higher and lower species."

"Oh, it's not scientific," Belle conceded. "But aren't you right back where you started? Anchored to reason. I'm looking for a way out."

Otis said, "There's no escape from reason." He passed the Armagnac around again, and we sat silently for some moments, each of us contemplating in his or her own way the ancient riddles of life and death.

"I've got it!" Belle said suddenly, sitting up straight as a ramrod, her belly thrust forward. "The only life after death is through our children. We're perpetuated through our offspring."

"Suppose my child turns into a smasher," Otis objected.

"That's not your problem. You don't determine the personality or character of your child . . . any more than *your* parents, God help them, determined yours. Parents exist in their offspring passively, benignly."

"Hmm . . ." Otis murmured.

It was my turn to object: "And bachelors, I suppose, are scratched out straightaway?"

"Why so?" Otis said. "He can count all those bastards he left behind in Borneo, can't he, Belle?"

Belle appeared not to hear this exchange and went right on. "The point is the link is not from one individual to another but throughout mankind. When you live your life, you have your own individuality, your own identity. But when you die, you lose this identity and become part of the human species. Humankind bequeaths to the newborn its accumulated experience—its soul, if you will. But the bequeathing is not by families, or races, or nationalities. All mankind is involved."

Otis and I stared at her solemnly as we sipped the last of our brandy.

"Now, you guys," she intoned, "if you have no more questions, I'm putting Otis to bed."

The next morning I sat with Otis on the terrace overlooking the blue ocean. He had a blanket over him in the deck chair, against a steady though warm breeze blowing off the water. Belle had gone on an errand with Toro. We had been listening to a mid-morning newscast from London when he switched off the wireless.

"Take care of her," he said.

I looked at him but said nothing.

"I don't mean financially. She'll have enough to live on for a while. She can even pay you back what she owes you. I'm leaving her what I have, of course. . . . I mean, take care she grows."

I nodded, still silent.

"She'll go back to her Kevin. I wish it were you, chum. But it'll be Kevin. He'll be the man in her life from now on. . . . I'm not supposed to know about this. Not good for my morale."

I was surprised he knew, or guessed, this much about Kevin, but I held my peace.

"There was a time when I favored this idea, then as I became smitten myself the idea drove me nuts, giving Belle up to that arrogant Marxist. But I've grown used to it. I don't mind now. . . . Tell this to Kevin sometime, if he remembers who the hell I was."

"He remembers," I said. "And for Christ's sake, stop talking in the past tense, will you?"

That was all he ever said about the future while I was there, and so far as I could learn from Belle, it was more than he ever said to her.

I left the following day. Otis was not up when Toro and I had to leave for the airport, so I went to his room to say my farewells. We both knew, of course, it would be the last.

"Otis—I'm off."

"*Adios*, old sport. Hoist one for me along the way."

"I'll do that, pal."

Belle, from the door, said, "You two sound like second-rate Scott Fitzgeralds."

We shook hands, and I was surprised that his skin already had the soft dry quality of a much older person nearing death; I remembered sitting at my father's bed when I was ten—for what seemed to me at the time days on end— his dry hand clasped lightly over mine. Walking up to the car with Belle, I reviewed once again with her the plans for the weeks ahead. Jingle would be there for two and a half weeks, about a week each side of Belle's stay at the hospital; the date of the Cesarean section was already fixed. After Jingle left, Belle and Toro would make out with no trouble. There was Toro's mother to help if they needed her. Later in the summer Belle would work out another plan to meet Kevin and—if all went well—to show him their child. Meanwhile, when the end came, Belle planned to bury Otis in the cemetery above their Corsican village. She had the address of Otis's only relative, a half sister in Brooklyn whom Otis had not seen in ten years. When all had been tended to, she would return home.

"And where's home?" I asked.

"Home," she said, "will be wherever Kevin is."

45

All went according to plan on Corsica. Jingle arrived five days before Belle went into the hospital and in her usual fashion had taken over complete management of the household before Belle left. Otis, Belle wrote, had been uneasy about Jingle's coming, wondering whether she would be "restful" enough for him: "He's grown used to my lazy ways and he shrinks from anything that seems energetic." But Otis needn't have worried, Belle went on; Jingle immediately paced her life to his. She would sit whole afternoons knitting beside him on the terrace, spectacles on the end of her nose, making typically shrewd observations about the Corsicans or describing some strange bird she had seen near the shore. She even found time to put in an herb garden outside the kitchen. It was as though she had lived in Corsica all her life.

Belle's operation was long and complex but successful. The baby, a girl named Eliza after Belle's great-grandmother, was healthy and normal. Belle, despite her excellent physical condition before the delivery, was greatly weakened and stayed a few extra days in the hospital to regain her strength. By the time Jingle left, she was quite recovered, and with Toro's help was able to manage as before.

I was in New York when Jingle flew home, and I met her at LaGuardia between planes. She was exuberant about her trip, although she said it was a crazy way to see Europe for the first time—"from the coast of Corsica." Belle had persuaded her to stop over in Paris for a few days, but after twenty-four hours of walking the streets and coping with French waiters, she was so homesick for her children that she changed her reservations and flew home early; she cabled me in flight to meet her. Jingle hardly stopped talking during the half hour we had together after she cleared customs. She had to fill me in on every detail of life at the villa: the weather, the flowers that came into bloom, the height of the sea in a rare storm off the Italian coast, the villagers coming up to see the new baby, and so forth.

"And that Toro! What a card! He says that now he and Missy have had their bambino, he and I should make one too. . . . To hear him talk, he's compromised all the marriageable girls on the peninsula."

Otis was going . . . going, she said. He was less interested in the baby than Belle's coming home to him.

"I'm not as sure as Belle he thinks Eliza's his," Jingle said. "I don't think he cares. I put the cradle right beside him several times so he could watch her sleeping, but he'd look over the cradle and talk about something else."

I asked Jingle what anyone was supposed to know about Belle's life at this stage.

"We need a diagram for that, don't we?" She laughed. "Well, everyone but Otis now knows Belle and Kevin were married several years ago, and they'll know soon about Eliza—assuming it's Kevin's, of course. No one, including Kevin, knows about Otis. I mean, about Belle's living with him. Only Lucy, you, and I are supposed to know everything—at least, I *think* we know everything. And Otis, that wise old owl, I think he suspects everything, too, but he ain't talkin'."

Otis died sooner than we expected, six weeks after Eliza was born. Belle had written that he was beginning to feel occasional spasms of pain in his groin, but at the same time was more venturesome than he had been in several months. They had driven around the cape one afternoon as far as Ile Rousse. Another day they lunched in Bastia and walked around the old port for a half hour before leaving. He was taking more interest in the baby. But then he died one afternoon during his nap, Eliza asleep in the cradle beside him, Belle and Toro outside in the garden.

Belle didn't cable. She wrote me the day after the funeral and asked me to notify Jingle and put a notice in the papers for any of his friends to see; she had already written her mother and Otis's half sister. Belle said she would be leaving by boat from Genoa at the end of August. She was fully recovered, she wrote, and in good spirits; she simply needed time to find her bearings.

Belle had already written to Kevin about the baby, of course, and sent him almost daily reports about Eliza's progress; she still used the Paris address. As plans took shape for her return, she wrote Kevin that if he agreed she would go home with Eliza ahead of him—home, that is, to Ram's Horn—and would let him know as soon as she arrived so he could join her there a day or two later. That was the way they left things.

I doubt if Kevin ever knew for certain—at least for some years—about Belle's year and a half with Otis. He certainly never made inquiries of me. I happened to be lunching with Kevin at the Columbia Faculty Club a few days after the notice of Otis's death appeared in the *New York Times*. He hadn't seen the notice, but a common acquaintance of Otis's and mine stopped by our table and asked if I had.

"In Corsica, of all places. What the hell was the poor guy doing in Corsica?"

After he had left us, Kevin was silent, looking out over Morningside Heights. He had just that morning received Belle's letter telling him she was returning home in two or three weeks.

"Otis Lieberman," he said. But that was all he said. So far as I know, he never brought up the matter again.

Sally Bannister's style changed extraordinarily in the six months following

George's death. She sold the farm in Bucks County—after making certain Kevin would never settle there—and moved into a penthouse apartment in Newark. It seemed, when I first heard of it from Kevin, the worst possible course for her to take. But all is not as it seems.

"Go see her," Kevin said, smiling.

Sally invited me for a late dinner after work, and I arrived at dusk. A doorman looking like an admiral intercepted me in the lobby and called on the house phone to announce me. Another attendant took me up to the twentieth floor in a red plush elevator. The door to Sally's apartment was ajar and Sally, when she heard the elevator door open, called out to me to come in. As I did, a teenage girl in panties and bra scampered out of sight. Another, in bra and a knee-length skirt Sally was fitting onto her, stood in the center of a spacious living room; she looked at me uneasily, arms folded over her chest.

"Don't be a goose," Sally said to the girl, feeling her stiffen. "He's old enough to be your old man."

"But I don't like to be looked at, Aunt Sal."

"I bet! Just hold still. He won't look. Will you? Let me get these pins out of my kisser and greet you properly. . . . Now, you go look the joint over while I finish up with these fillies. . . . Isn't that a gorgeous pattern?"

I did as I was bade, inspecting the duplex apartment from flagstone terrace, with its spectacular view of the New York skyline, to Sally's marble-floored bathroom and her sumptuous bedroom. The decor, which Sally had designed herself, was all new; she had finished it a week or so before.

"Some sex box, isn't it?" she said after her nieces had left.

I told her it was overwhelming and she beamed.

"This is more my style. I couldn't stay on in Bucks County without George. . . . But don't get any ideas. I'm a reformed woman. On the wagon. Thoughts as pure as the driven snow . . . why, you couldn't have me if you wanted me. . . ."

"I want," I said.

"Yeah? Fine time. . . . Go mix yourself a nice genteel martini. Apricot juice for me, chum. . . . Elsie!" she called through the dining alcove. "How things goin'?"

Elsie, whom I recognized from Bucks County, put her face through the swinging door from the kitchen. "Good, Mrs. B., great. You gonna come make that gravy?"

"Sauce, honey, not gravy. I'll be right there."

We walked out on the terrace to watch the lights flickering over Manhattan and a cluster of tugs nursing an outgoing liner away from its pier. Sally told me about her enterprise, just under way in a street-level shop in the same building: a dress shop in two sections—an elite salon for a middle-class clientele and a large bargain boutique, with focus on style and novelty, for low-income clients.

"They're starved, these kids. No taste, no flair. How can they enjoy life if they can't dress? So that's what I'm doing. Bringing them pretty things to wear at prices they can afford. . . . Of course, I'm losing money hand over fist, but who cares? Who is there to care?"

This, then, was the new Sally, back to within three blocks of where she had been born, stripped of all need to play a role for which she had never had much inclination. George, meanwhile, was present everywhere in the penthouse apartment. The library was paneled like the Bucks County library, and Sally had kept the same furniture there and all his books. There were pictures of him everywhere, including an enlarged photograph of him by the cow pond in Bucks County. It was hung in a niche off the dining room—and he looked so dramatically alive that it made me catch my breath. Nearly every third sentence Sally spoke included some reference to George.

"I didn't exactly set him on fire, did I?" she said at one point during dinner in her usual blunt way. "But we had a good life on balance. I satisfied him. . . . Even in those terrible last years for us, I gave him pleasure."

I said I never doubted it.

"I bet you doubted I'd come out of it though, you old square. Admit it. What would I be without George? Well . . . it takes a lot to kill off an Irish working girl. Especially one who's lost half her forebears through booze."

After coffee she shooed me off because she was expecting three models to try on new dresses she'd just received. "These aren't the fillies," she said. "This is the real McCoy, and I don't want you hanging around getting any ideas . . . the way George once did."

Indeed, the house phone rang as I was saying my good-byes, and as I emerged from the elevator, three animated beauties were coming through the lobby.

I suppose an experienced novelist would have ended this story by now. The tangled relationships have unraveled. Those who were to experience a significant shift in their personalities or in their attitudes or in their fortunes have been shown to have done so. Those scheduled to die have died. It would seem to be trifling with the plot to carry the story further. Yet nothing living ceases to stir. If there is any reality to the characters in my story, it cannot be imagined that they cease to exist or to carry on for the convenience of publishers. They rise and go through the daily business of living—as you and I on our most humdrum days.

But before I belabor this thought out of all relevance, let me use it to explain that I mean to deal with one last episode that has no bearing on character development or plot but merely gratifies my sense of rounding out. This is Belle's return to

Ram Island, six years almost to the day from the time she left it to go to Orono. It was not a permanent return, of course, since she would soon leave with Kevin to establish their new home on Morningside Heights near Columbia, but it was a symbolic returning nonetheless, and was seen as such by her fellow islanders.

46

I finished my report on the Indonesian mission before Labor Day and returned immediately to Ram Island for a long stay. The island was never more bewitching than during those soft September days before Belle's return. The weather held steady day after day, glassy seas in the morning, mild southerlies in the afternoon, temperatures reaching the high seventies by three in the afternoon before cooling to the low fifties at night. The tides worked their way around the clock from neap to spring, when the flood left long rows of seaweed high on beaches and strange objects were unloosed from the shore to float on the currents until the next flood deposited them on another shore. During the spring lows, at dawn and dusk, half the islanders dug razorback clams in beds normally under water. I was reminded again and again during that period of the September immediately after the war.

"There do seem to be cycles," Lucy said when I mentioned it to her. "I suppose everyone remembers differently, but a dozen times or more I've known a combination of weather and tide to bring back vividly a mood of thirty or more years past. . . . The surprising thing, I guess, is that with only so many tide patterns and so many changes of weather, it doesn't happen more often."

Belle was due to arrive on a Saturday. She had written Mary Lou in August to open Ram's Horn, leaving all decisions to her: "After all, you know the house so much better than I. Do what you think is necessary." You could feel the mood of anticipation build as Saturday approached. The schoolchildren, the youngest of whom hardly remembered Belle, painted WELCOME HOME, BELLE! on a large piece of plywood that Harold Toothacher rigged over the pier. The high school students, seeing the sign when they returned on the ferry Friday afternoon, shouted out anxiously from the *Laura Lee II* even before it docked, "It's tomorrow, i'n it? She didn't come yet, did she?" And breathed a sigh of relief when they were reassured.

Jingle arrived unexpectedly on the same ferry, with Zbig and Winni, and seemed surprised anyone had for a moment doubted she would be there for Belle's homecoming.

"I wouldn't miss this for . . . well, half a dozen of your pies, Jesse."

"You can have those, too, dear," Jesse Cutler said. "The ways you've come."

" 'Tain't the ways Belle's come," Rudolf York said judiciously. "Totin' that ten-week-old baby . . . How's she called again?"

"Eliza," Jessica York said. "Eliza Talbot Bannister."

"Where's Kevin at? He'd oughta be comin' with her." This from Harold Toothacher as he came into the store.

"You hard o' hearin'?" Jenny Brewster bellowed at him. "You been told twenty times he's comin' next week. . . . She wants to see her own people first. Ain't that right, Lucy?"

"That's about it, Jenny," Lucy said—but when we were walking up to the ridge she said, "I hope they're not making all this fuss over Belle because she's the new mistress of Ram's Horn."

"Never fear, Aunt Lucy," Jingle said. "Belle's Belle on this island, wherever she sleeps."

Saturday broke like the preceding days, soft and still. An hour before the *Laura Lee II* was due, the islanders had begun on one pretext or another to gather at the harbor. The children had reconnoitered the best vantage point to catch first glimpse of the mailboat and still get back in time to give fair warning at the pier. Most of the lobstermen had gone out early in order to be back before eleven, and several, including Turk, planned to meet the *Laura Lee II* off Seal Ledge and escort her in.

Rudy York, red-faced and panting, was the first to bring the news that the *Laura Lee II* had been sighted coming into the Gut, but this was loudly disputed two minutes later by Chucky Jenkins, who argued that Rudy couldn't possibly have seen the mailboat from where he was watching. The debate ran on for some minutes with good-natured partisanship on both sides. I found Sharon placidly standing beside me in the midst of this.

"How's the dreamer?" I asked.

"The other night I dreamed I was you," she said conspiratorially.

"Good God! You're in more trouble than I thought."

"I didn't really. I just wanted to see what you'd say." She poked me lightly in the ribs and went on.

The argument between Chucky and Rudy was finally extinguished by a blast from the *Laura Lee II* behind the Nose, with answering blasts from the escort boats and others at mooring. The mailboat made its turn around the red nun and eased into harbor. Belle was immediately visible to us on the foredeck, Eliza wrapped in a blanket in her arms. Widow Barnaby came out from her shack and teetered slowly out onto the jetty. Belle waved to her with a free hand, and the old woman slowly, tentatively waved a thin arm in reply.

"The Apocalypse!" Lucy murmured beside me. "I've never seen the Widow wave to anyone before."

I said I'd seen it once; she'd waved to Belle, in fact, the day she left for Orono.

"Did she really? What do you suppose makes her? She must think Belle is the embodiment of something, don't you think?"

But Lucy expected no answer, and we turned our attention to the approaching landing. Turk Jenkins, recalling his fireboat act of six years before, had rerigged the pumps and hoses, with Elmer's help, and was able to send jets of water twenty feet into the air—until the system broke down. Then Turk substituted a full-throttled slalom through the lobster fleet to howls of approval from the teenagers while the adults watched nervously. For a time, Turk's antics attracted more attention than Belle herself. I could see Sharon shaking her head in resignation.

Then the *Laura Lee II* was at the pier and Belle was ashore, amid a crowd of curious islanders jostling with each other to stare into her face, looking for any changes time had accomplished. After Belle had greeted Lucy and given her Eliza, she turned to embrace her fellow islanders one by one, deliberately, young and old, male and female—even Harold Toothacher. Horace Snow, absorbed by the scene from his bridge, had to be reminded by other passengers after twenty minutes that there was the rest of the schedule to run.

Elmer had the pickup at the pier to take Belle and her luggage out to Ram's Horn. But Belle wouldn't ride.

"Elmo, you know I never trusted you behind that wheel. I'll walk." Then, on a sudden impulse, she said, "I know what! Let's all go have a look."

So Elmer drove off with the luggage while the rest of us walked to Ram's Horn, taking turns carrying Eliza. Mary Lou had a time keeping the advance guard of children from going into the house before Belle arrived to lead the way. Inside, the islanders pored over the house from attic to cellar, each finding some feature of the famous structure to marvel at. It was the most complete inspection of Ram's Horn by the islanders, Lucy said, since it was built nearly thirty years before.

This, then, was how Belle came home to Ram Island. Two days later Kevin arrived to take up life with his wife and daughter.

Postscript

My editor, David, suggested I do a postscript, an *après-mot*, to clear away any residual ambiguities. I agreed to try, but warned him that such an exercise might help an author but could hardly edify a hardened reader. He said go ahead anyway.

Well, why should a person—let's say more or less satisfied with his or her professional life—attempt, at the end of it, to wrap it up with fiction? Good question. I lived happily (relatively so) for several years in the Soviet Union without diddling with fiction. That might have been because my job there was functional: buying books for the Library of Congress, tens of thousands of them, the titles of many of which I could not instantly translate, and when I did found I was no wiser. I was party, in short, to the acquisition of a significant quantity of Soviet wisdom (or intelligence) spanning several decades, without the opportunity to analyze it. After World War II, I confess, I did turn briefly to fiction, but with too meager rewards to continue.

There is a particular dilemma between history and fiction, a point where truth leaves off and imagination takes over. Having written half a dozen volumes of Maine island *history*, I found turning to island *fiction* a bewildering enterprise. One could say with some truth that in history nothing is invented (or should be), while in fiction everything is (or should be). I was once scolded by a reader of my histories for retelling some old and factually dubious legends about islands because they were amusing and, I thought, helpful. If I could not distinguish fact from fiction, my reader warned me, I better lay down my pencils.

But this is too narrow a view. Fiction is in no sense less valuable than history as a tool of analysis because it is invented rather than perceived. Take Belle Talbot, for instance. She would stand out in any cast of Maine islanders—Haskells, Barters, Bunkers, Greenlaws—whenever she appeared. Indeed, it is precisely her appearance that prompts fiction. The British mountaineer George

Mallory explained in a deservedly famous entry in his journal that to his satisfaction it was enough for Mount Everest to be "there" for him to want to climb it, "for [he went on] there's no dream that mustn't be dared." So it is enough for Belle Talbot to exist for a nameless wanderer to want to capture her in prose.

Finally, I should confess that while such literary productivity as I can claim lies clearly in nonfiction, I have always been more comfortable with myself writing, or attempting to write, fiction (even when the plot line had stalled). Carol, my wife, understood this. She would call after me, as I headed for my spruce dell by the sea to write for yet another day, that she would send down soup and sandwich with one of the children—*if* I was really working. If, on the other hand, I was simply amusing myself with fiction, I could fend for myself.

— *Charles B. McLane*
April 2004